Cover Image: Painting of Hades and Persephone from an Attic kylix.
Copyright The Trustees of the British Museum.

The Greek Dialogues

The Greek Dialogues

Explorations in Myth

Betty Mallett Smith

Edited by Deborah A. Wesley

To order additional copies of this book, contact:
Xlibris Corporation
1-888-795-4274
www.Xlibris.com
Orders@Xlibris.com
37306

Contents

In loving memory of my husband, Myron Smith, and our daughter, Shelley Schubert.

Acknowledgments

I am deeply grateful to my good friend and editor, Deborah Wesley, for her tireless work and skill in preparing this book. For the fact that the mythological dialogues, presented orally in my seminars over three decades, are now in book form, I am indebted to the guidance of her generous and perceptive mind.

My appreciation is ongoing as well to fellow explorers in myth who have lent their imaginative hearing to the dialogues in the course of many seminars.

Editor's Preface

Some twenty-five centuries have come and gone since the great mythic tales of gods and heroes were told in ancient Greece, yet they still appear on the stages of our theaters, in stories told to our schoolchildren, as themes in our movies, and as images in our poems. In all this time, scholars have given many explanations of the origins of myths and of their lasting power over the imagination. Once, they were seen simply as history—as the imaginative retellings of real events. In our time, psychological understanding, especially that of C. G. Jung, sees them as expressing inborn patterns of human life, which recur again and again. The gods and heroes can now be understood as living energies within the individual human soul. This book of dialogues arises from such a perspective.

Opening the book, the reader will not find yet another systematic scholarly survey of every Greek god and goddess. This is a selection from the Greek pantheon. And not even every adventure of that select company is included. There is little attempt to assign labels or simple meanings to them. Rather, we find clusters of imaginative dialogues, each cluster centering around a particular mythic being—a god, a hero, a goddess—and illuminating its nature in an intimate and telling way (e.g., When Aphrodite visits Hephaestus's working quarters, a forge, she is appalled to find that there is no ease or comfort there, not even a single couch!) This method of exploration, the author calls *poiesis*. The reader or listener participates imaginatively in the dialogue, and this leads to a kind of inner distillation of the material into an individual experience of meaning.

These dialogues arise from a deep imaginative source in the author, informed by her trained philosophical mind and by her love and long study of Greek literature and myth. The charm and liveliness of the material is enhanced by her extensive travel on the Greek mainland and islands, which have left their mark on the dialogues in rich details of the Greek landscape. In addition, long-term experience with the psychology of C. G. Jung underlies the author's deep understanding of human psychology and provides the link between the world of ancient Greece and our own. The mythic beings of the dialogues are as fresh and immediate as our contemporaries; it is easy to find their experiences and emotions reflected in our lives.

The material of this book has been collected from mythology seminars given over the last thirty-five years and from twelve mythology seminar tours to Greece, which Mrs. Smith led between 1973 and 2007. These dialogues are noteworthy for their concern with the feminine elements of the myths, something often underemphasized in mythological analysis. There is a unique essay on the often-demonized goddess Hera. One might notice, also, that the first dialogues of the book deal with the princess of Crete, Ariadne, while Zeus and the masculine heroes bring up the rear. The book has been long in coming and is invaluable for preserving that portion of Mrs. Smith's work which was formerly available primarily to seminar members. The compilation is the product of an original ear, heart, and mind brought to bear on the Greek gods and goddesses and, through them, on ourselves.

Deborah Wesley

An Essay on Dialogue

Among the enduring refuges of the human spirit, none was more earnestly sought out than Delphi in ancient Greece. Here the traveler revealed his predicament, whether personal or that of his city state, within a single question brought before the oracle of Apollo. Catalogs survive of the god's historic replies as well as legendary ones. So crucial was the voice of Apollo to Greek life that even in time of war, Greeks were provided with a truce that allowed safe passage to Delphi. But the voice of the oracle has long been silent. In our times, the oracular seat, once occupied by the priestess Pythia seated on the tripod, appears to be given to the scientific outlook. In spite of our culture's debt to the sciences, this proves to be not wholly satisfying. The human thirst for a sacred refuge and for a voice of life wisdom appears to go unsatisfied.

There still exists a refuge accessible to all, however, one that is long familiar in human experience. It is dialogue. Admittedly, it is far more modest and less monumental than the ancient oracle. As dialogue is explored in this work, it is less a conversation between two persons than an effort to capture a sustained encounter between two voices that embody opposite realities seeking resolution in the human soul. In an extraordinary way, myth, in its keen account of human struggle, contains such dialogue. Its movement is a narrative that shapes a journey, pressing forward toward the place of hospitable arrival. Making its way through the clashing rocks that make up existence, the process of dialogue provides a safe, yet temporary, abode. At the door of this abode, one's everyday awareness greets the stranger, often an unfamiliar level of consciousness, and together they enter the sheltered space. Of all human actions, dialogue excels in providing a safe passage through the encounter with reality, evoking as it does the best consciousness available at the time.

Without question, dialogue was a central mode of Greek existence. The ancient marketplace of Athens witnessed the earnest exchange of philosophers as they strolled among the columns of the Stoa of Zeus and the Painted Stoa, where even today the ghosts of philosophers such as Socrates and Zeno haunt the ruins. Carved upon the pediments of Athenian temples were the predicaments of existence, each full of the implicit dialogue found in myth: individuals assaulted by centaurs, warriors pitted against Amazons, the hero faced by an overwhelming ordeal, and the gods themselves doing battle against earth's gigantic sons. Here action and gesture represented the conflict and raised before the awed viewer the substance of dialogue. When a festival was in progress, the gods were addressed in yet another upsurge of dialogue—in the form of poetry, ritual, drama, and the singing of odes.

What makes up this human experience manifesting in such myriad forms? It is first a being summoned. In response, there is a turning toward a largely unknown presence that is acknowledged. What follows is a slow metamorphosis of familiar consciousness as the two polarities are altered, losing their extreme opposition.

Like a few columns left standing of an ancient temple, myth is a luminous survival. At the same time, it is a living dwelling place of psyche in present time. An undertaking in myth cannot succeed, surely, without a certain dependence upon the imagination. In ancient Greece, it was the Muses who carried forward the many-faceted life of the imagination. Mind and spirit are thought to move through many rooms, but the imagination alone moves through the room that is *windowed*. Through the apertures, compelling presences are glimpsed, bearing the enduring images active in human longing, fear, dream, fantasy, and vision. Myths emerge through what Coleridge called the primary imagination and what Yeats described as the process by which the soul sees in many mirrors. The sense of imagination as expressed here is not a mental capacity to manipulate things as they are in favor of what is clever or novel. Instead, the greater imagination at work, like a quiet lake in nature, reveals itself as a profoundly receptive faculty, mirroring the images that arise out of a source that goes beyond personal memory and is penetrated by the richly layered unconscious.

A person's life is shaped by myth; the enigma often lies in deciding which one. Within an individual's life, personal protests and unfulfilled longings seem to echo a timeless narrative. An unacknowledged fact presents itself: it is an interior theater, which provides the invisible stage on which the many episodes of life are played out. Then, the intellectual distance of the mere observer is put aside while the interior drama holds reality as the flesh of experience. Such unedited experience takes on mythological contours. Although it is interior, this theater is less personal in nature than one might have supposed. Fundamental opposing realities meet here, address each other significantly as they engage the struggle, and move toward a resolution that can be lived. Here are decided the crucial issues of adult life. As for dialogue, it functions as a container for these significant encounters as it carries the angst of the struggle.

A person does not "make up" his myth, which arises from a larger source than personal history. As for this greater source or reservoir, the ancient Greeks saw it as the goddess Mnemosyne, Memory, who became wife of Zeus and mother of the nine Muses. In our time, C. G. Jung has described this vast objective source, layered with age-old accumulated experience (the enduring archetypes and myth), as the collective unconscious.

Lived and unlived aspects of a person move on the stage of the interior theater. One is faced by the archetypes, the masked presences—that is to say, gods, heroes, demonic forces, the unsuspecting brides of the gods, and the many human voices. Under this impact, the intellect forsakes its protective distancing. Unaccountably one is summoned and finds himself engaged. There occurs a lingering within each condition, each episode of the tale, as one undergoes the timeless life that the myth delineates. A sensuous texture of response emerges as a soft wind of nostalgia from a misty early time embodies the present. Paralleling this experience, the dialogue seeks to enter the myth in its shining or terrifying immediacy, shortly to engage its alternate mode, which is reflection.

As for reflection, it must follow at its own pace the vivid moment of the inner experience, which can seem fleeting, even careless. Only when reflection is allowed to ripen in its own time does the illuminating moment appear, which we ordinarily call meaning. Not the province of experience alone, meaning contains evidence of the brush with the luminous enduring images.

On the interior stage, the myth becomes embodied, and a palpable sense of destiny moves. As the figure of myth makes his way through the severely narrowed passage of his action, a certain illusion of freedom falls away, the illusion that one possesses an impressive range of choices. Nevertheless, as the dialogue proceeds in the intangible theater, a hopefulness emerges in a growing realization that through the myth, one is being reshaped. This is not simply a fateful happening, for it rests in part on the individual's own discerning choices. What then can serve as a reliable bridge between the place of myth, archetypes, and the gods, on the one hand, and the everyday life of the individual? The mind replies, "Knowledge." Yet it is unarguable that, of all our dwelling places, it is psyche or soul that actually embodies us. It is psyche gazing full into the face of myth that has the capacity for the new beginning as it processes longing, fear, angst, thought, and hope in the Herculean ordeal of bringing about a new level of being. At best, dialogue seeks to capture some of the essential text of this undertaking. And what comes to be *known* is beneath and before conceptualizing.

PART I

The Ariadne—Theseus—Dionysos Cycle

The Myth of Theseus and Ariadne

An Introduction

There is a lively interior phenomenon when one moves into an encounter with a great myth. This is the awakening of the imagination. Myth reveals the imagination as *receptive presence*, much like a mountain lake that reflects the surrounding landscape in serene containment. Entering the myth of Theseus and Ariadne in its 1500 BC Minoan setting on Crete, one may find one's experience marked by two characteristics. One is recognition of both hero and maiden as archetypal memory is stirred, for indeed one is persuaded that one knows Theseus and Ariadne. The second characteristic happening lies in manifesting a spontaneous hospitality as one greets this ancient human story in present time. Such a reception, involuntary as it is in the life of the imagination, engages the forgotten voices that echo in the labyrinth of old memory. Mnemosyne, goddess of memory, is at hand, nor are her daughters, the Muses, distant from the scene.

Leading the company of the fourteen Athenian youths and maidens destined to be fed to the Minotaur is Theseus, most of whose life has been that of the long lost prince of Athens. In the prow of the ship that brought him to the shore of Knossos on Crete, the sacred image of Aphrodite was carried in the place of singular honor. Considering how desire and longing for the golden bond of connection haunt the human adventure, it was wise to seek Aphrodite's protection. A well-known aspect of her bountiful nature lay in providing the fair wind so needed on the sea journey.

Two images especially haunt the myth: the Labyrinth and the thread of Ariadne, images that invite contemplation as each yields its inherent tale. When one considers the thread, so central to the story, nothing at first glance could appear less promising. The thread has no backbone, no stature, no head on splendid shoulders, not even strong appendages for laying hold of things. Serpentlike it lies, bending and winding as though without purpose. How disconcerting it must be to Theseus, in whose hand the thread comes to be held, to find it soft, lean, endlessly winding. What the thread does know about is continuity and unbrokenness. This knowledge is far from insignificant, for it is vital to meaningful existence. Twentieth-century philosopher Karl Jaspers asserted that the malady of our era is *brokenness*. With brokenness, the essential thread of vital connection is lost, surely. Ariadne's counsel for Theseus as he enters the Labyrinth of Knossos is, "Do not drop the thread!"

Theseus makes his way into the dark and solitary depths of the Labyrinth that penetrates the underground of Crete. As he goes, he keeps firm hold of Ariadne's thread, itself a path marker. One wonders if he thinks of those everlasting weavers of the thread: Clotho, Lachesis, and Atropos—the Fates, holding human destiny in their hands. When he finally reaches Naxos, there will be a powerful encounter with his destiny and that of Ariadne. Lying yet in wait for him in the depth of the Labyrinth is the Minotaur, much like the bull that is shackled in the obscurity of the human soul.

Theseus on Crete

Down the long echoing corridors, through courtyards forested with ample wooden columns and filled with cool, filtered light, Theseus, prince of Athens, strode. Gazing from side to side, he was aware of a feeling of awe in response to the beauty of the Minoan Palace of Knossos where he, a stranger from an alien shore, now made his way. After all, was he not the leader of the fourteen youths and maidens who had just arrived as Athens' required payment to the voracious appetite of the Minotaur? He shuddered at the fateful thought that he had managed to keep suppressed during the sea voyage. The oracle of Apollo had counseled him to make this heroic journey. "Bear that in mind," he said to himself, setting his jaw. He found himself at the foot of a broad stone stairway and climbing it toward the royal chamber. Before the handsome tall doors, he encountered two young Cretans armed with spears, their fine bronzed skin exposed down to the waist of their slender torsos. Observing the fair young Greek, their eyes widened for a long moment before they lowered their spears and nodded for Theseus to enter the chamber. At the far end of the chamber seated on a high-backed throne, the King of Crete waited for the Athenian to approach. It was King Minos who spoke.

— Young man of Athens, I've been observing you since you came from your tall ship. You move as one who quietly commands, I notice. Who are you?
— King Minos, I am Theseus, son of Aethra, my mother.
   Momentarily, Minos was astonished.
— Does an Athenian mark his lineage through his mother then?
— In my case, it is the truer tale. My mother, you see, is wise and walks in the strength of woman. As for my father, he is Aegeus, king of Athens.
   With these terse words, he ended.
— If you are son of Athens' king, why did you not say so forthrightly? After all, what could be a more distinguished ancestry for a Greek?
— The truth, O King, is sometimes an unsorted thing, baffling the usual account. It is said that the god Poseidon is my true sire.
   Now the king was incredulous as he pressed his questions.
— Earth Shaker? Do you claim to be son of Poseidon who at will shakes cities and mountains alike?
   Theseus was unflinching.
— Yes, I do.
— An extravagant claim that is, young man. I find it difficult enough to understand why Athens' king would send his own son as blood tribute to the Minotaur.
   Theseus sighed as he let his breath out slowly.
— King Minos, I speak the truth, nevertheless.

The king fell silent pondering what he had learned before instructing Theseus to wait in the chamber on the stone bench while he went aside to consult his counselors. For some time, he was closeted with the counselors, at last returning to where Theseus awaited him. A man of singular authority, he spoke now.
— Man of Athens, you have answered me boldly with a strange account of yourself. Here on Crete, it is an unheard-of thing to claim two fathers since only one is ever required in the natural way of things. Do you have anything to add?
— Again I say that I have only told you the truth. Truth is the first priority of my people.

Minos smiled a small skeptical smile and shook his head slightly.

— What is unquestionable is that you are hostage of the kingdom of Knossos. As for telling the truth, what passes as truth may be the path of expediency for one in your position.

Theseus, frowning, shook his head, and his body grew visibly taut at the slur on his character. The king continued.

— In any case, I must say that I am strangely drawn to you. You have spirit, young man. Nor do I doubt for a moment that you are a foreign prince. As you must perceive, what is troubling is your claim to being son of Poseidon. There is nothing for it. I am obliged to put you to the test.

— A test, O King?

— Exactly. Come with me at once. We'll go down to the sea where already my counselors have outfitted a ship with Cretan sailors.

Utterly taken by surprise, Theseus stared at King Minos and was unable to find a response for a sustained moment. Meantime, the king relished his advantage. When Theseus spoke, he attempted to recover his authority.

— King Minos, tell me what lies in store, I beg you, for I might prefer to bypass this sudden voyage in favor of meeting the Minotaur!

— Come, Theseus, I give you no cause to dread our brief sea excursion, provided, of course, you truly are who you say you are. Your father, after all, is god of the sea . . . . Here we are at the ship lying at anchor. We Cretans do know how to build seaworthy vessels. Is this not a handsome one?

— A fine ship indeed. I cannot deny it.

He was surprised to see Minos climb on board the small ship now. Still puzzled, Theseus leaped in after him with a grace the sailors observed. At once, the anchor was raised, and when they were well out to sea although yet in view of the shore, the men rested on their oars. King Minos rose to his feet slowly in the midst of the silent crew, and all eyes settled upon him. With a gesture, he indicated that Theseus should join him in the bow. All attention was upon Minos as with a slow significant movement, he removed the royal ring from his finger and held it aloft, a dazzling treasure.

— See this ring, man of Athens? It has a long and fabled past. Is it not beautiful? It is my treasure, and I am exceedingly attached to it. Yet I am about to cast it into the depth of the sea!

Not only Theseus caught his breath, but all the men joined him in astonishment. King Minos had reached his instructions.

— What I command you to do is to dive overboard at once in the path of the royal ring and recover it from the sea, returning it safely to me.

It is a fact that I am not willing to lose such a treasure. It is well that you know this.

The ominous, authoritative words rang out over the shining waters, and inwardly Theseus trembled.

— King Minos, what you ask of me is not humanly possible!

— I have thought of that, naturally. We shall see whether or not Poseidon assists you. This is the test, as I've pointed out.

— And if I do succeed?

— Then you may ask of me a favor for yourself, and I shall grant it. You have my word.

The king placed one foot on the rim of the boat now, steadying himself before hurling the golden, gemmed ring in a great outward arch over the sea. At once, Theseus, his face drawn yet attentive to the pull of some inexplicable far goal, dived swiftly into the sea.

In the Sea Grotto

His eyes burned as he stared through the dense water of the Aegean Sea, hoping to discern some trace of the path of the fallen royal ring. Skillfully he circled the extensive area into which King Minos had hurled his ring, assigning him the impossible task of fetching the treasure. However, not a single glimpse of the gold band was to be had. Briefly he surfaced for air before plunging in one powerful movement toward the ocean floor. A small satisfaction came to him momentarily as his feet found the sea's cold ancient floor. At once he was surprised to find himself at the entrance of a sea grotto where he caught a brief glimpse of a white garment slipping into the dark depths of the cavern. Although he would only acknowledge the odd fact later on in retrospect, he breathed normally here. He managed to make his way, now striding within the grotto along a narrow passage that ended in a high-vaulted chamber. Stopping on the threshold of the chamber, he looked about him in awe, for seated on a majestic throne of coral sat a very beautiful feminine figure, a sight that rendered him speechless. She was the first to speak.

— Greetings, Theseus, welcome to our grotto in the Below!

He bowed to the goddess, having figured out who she must be.

— I am grateful indeed for any welcome at all in this dim abyss of sea. What good fortune is mine to come into the presence of Goddess Amphitrite!

— I suspect that our undersea abode seems strange to you, you being born to the light of day and exposed ever to the merciless Greek sky. Ah, but there is much to be said for our deep abode. It is an intimate, private place with no public paths to access it, for one thing. And, of course, it has its own emerging satisfactions.

Theseus regarded this description ruefully and with a small smile of acknowledgment.

— The truth is that I am vastly out of my element here, Lady Amphitrite.

— Sooner or later you had to come.

— What is this you say?

— Well, are you not Poseidon's son, and do I not share this realm of the sea with Poseidon himself?

— There is one who is testing this connection you speak of, I must tell you. That is to say, he questions that I am son of great Poseidon. What value, I ask you, is a great heritage that no one believes in?

Even Theseus was startled at the hopelessness that surfaced in his question.

— It is an invisible heritage that you speak of. Surely it is of value to the one who possesses it.

— Within this crisis where I find myself, my belief in this heritage is badly shaken, I confess.

The goddess was visibly disturbed by Theseus's admission.

— Do you no longer acknowledge Poseidon as your father?

— I . . . I don't know . . . An invisible parent can be hard to deal with for a mere human being. At the same time, the fact is that only by settling this issue can it be determined whether I live and whether the Athenian youths and maidens who accompanied me to Crete will survive.

— The situation is indeed in crisis. Ah, look who comes!

A tall broad-shouldered figure with a powerful build and a lordly face framed by an abundance of windblown locks and a short beard entered the chamber now. Poseidon gazed from Amphitrite to Theseus. Now he smiled at the young Athenian with pleasure and affection.

— Well, Theseus, you have sought us out in the Below at long last! I wondered when you would come. Some desperate hour has overtaken you, has it?

— It has, yes, Father Poseidon. I am faced with having to retrieve the royal ring of Minos, which he tossed into the sea, entrusting the impossible task to me.

— Entrusting you say.

— He is testing me, I meant to say.

— Ah, but inadvertently you said "entrusted." Some glimpse, a grotto truth, likely, suggests that King Minos trusts you, Theseus. Surely he would not dare to throw away his royal treasure unless he did.

— Oh, he is skeptical of my being sired by you, to be sure. The notion of his placing some trust in me strikes me as absurd, to be honest.

— Many a truth begins with the absurd, as Apollo would say, I believe.

Theseus looked down at the grotto floor, gazing at it for some time as he pondered what Poseidon said.

— True, it is a thing not to be believed that he would gamble on throwing away the treasured ring . . . Alas, time grows short for what seems an impossible retrieving. I must not delay!

A tender look of concern was on Amphitrite's face as she spoke now.

— Ah, Theseus, do not worry so much. Hurry will not accomplish such a feat in any case. What you do not realize is that the abode of Poseidon and myself is a realm without haste.

— Is there help for me here, I wonder?

— There is. My gift awaits you, actually. It is the altering of time. You shall see presently that the time of your sojourn on Crete will become spacious. It will accommodate the expansive happenings in which you shall engage life paths not previously known. Soon time itself shall reveal itself beyond the limited accounting of the water clock.

Puzzled, Theseus shook his head from side to side slowly before smiling.

— Thank you, Goddess.

Amphitrite arose from her chair and stepped toward Theseus, regarding him intently.

— Poseidon and I are not indifferent to the task at hand entrusted to you. In this very moment, that task is addressed, I assure you.

She extended her left hand slowly toward Theseus, whose eyes never left her as she made the enigmatic gesture. Now she turned her hand palm upward, and to his utter astonishment, he saw that within her hand lay King Minos's ring! He gasped, staring at the golden gem.

— You found it! Or, Lady Amphitrite, do my eyes deceive me?

— It is the gem of Knossos, I assure you. You see, when Minos tossed into the sea his ancestral bond, I was watching and wondering about it. I could not think of the loss of such a treasure and salvaged it as it fell into the depths. Am I not like Aphrodite in that I value the bonds that bind the human heart? Still, you look pale and worried. You need not be. I shall not keep the ring. It is for you to take, Theseus, to do as you will with it.

Smiling, she laid the ring into his hand, and nodding to him as if in dismissal, she turned and departed the rock chamber. Theseus remained staring at the gem in his hand in amazement. At the same time, the sense of his good fortune was rapidly returning, and his cheeks were no longer bloodless. Poseidon observed him quietly throughout the exchange and the change in Theseus that followed. He spoke now.

— Well, son of Aethra and Poseidon, what shall you do with this recovery of the great ring that the grotto has given you?

— You speak as if I have a choice, Father.

— O yes, you do as a matter of fact. I observed you admiring the Cretan treasure in your hand. Are you not tempted to keep it for yourself—not a booty from the journey to far Crete? Only consider the kingly power that lies in it.

A flash of anger passed Theseus's face and was gone.

— O Father, why do you tempt me in this way? Would you test me severely as Minos has done? True, I am not without ambition toward kingship. I admit as much. What sort of prince would I be if I were indifferent to the leading of the kingdom?

— Hear me. I know much about excess. Indeed, I've been accused of it on more than one occasion. What I've witnessed in the human world is the shadow play of ambition, for one thing. Ambition, you see, is able to seal fast the unopened wine jar, with the result that the real wine is never touched. Satisfaction is not savored. The amphora containing the wine remains yet lodged in the dark of earth. It is right that you are drawn toward it, for it holds the passions that will yet bring you concourse with life and the gods. Ambition, on the other hand, is a way of excess that perceives its goal through dry, repetitious modes of accounting. Although it may arrive at forms of power, it is permanently alienated from earth's harvest. Hence, what it possesses is tasteless, its triumph empty.

— Father, tell me what you advise in my situation. What am I to do?

— Be earnest to open the wine jar that is still buried in the earth. In no case must you settle for the goading gadfly that can drive a man mad and immune to true satisfaction—ambition, I mean. If you are to be Athens' king and a true son of Poseidon, listen well!

— I treasure your counsel and vow not to feed some fantasy of wielding power at will. Nevertheless, I face peril if I fail to return the gem to the king's hand with all speed, you understand. Much depends on securing the king's favor.

— As an Athenian hostage, my son, what is this favor you hope for?

An energy arose in Theseus as he pondered the question, and his eyes flashed with an inscrutable excitement.

— I am fairly certain that King Minos expects that I'll simply beg for my life, escaping the encounter with the Minotaur in his den altogether. Ah, but this is not what I'll ask for. Instead, the royal favor I seek is that I be allowed to go alone to meet the Minotaur in the Labyrinth!

Astounded, Poseidon raised his hoary eyebrows as he regarded Theseus closely for a long moment. His smile now was one of admiration.

— Ah, you are brave indeed. It is well. Had you asked him, Minos might well have granted you this desire to meet the Minotaur and saved himself from the risky plan of throwing the royal ring into the sea and you with it!

— But it was coming to the sea grotto that stirred and shaped the desire, you see. Strangely, since coming to the Below, I am not the same man I was. Ah, but the hour urges me. I must go at once to where the king awaits me on the ship. To Lady Amphitrite I shall ever be in debt for the recovery of the ring. And will you, Father, grant me a blessing for the moment when I hand over the ring to King Minos?

— So be it, Theseus. Go well through what is yet to come!

Theseus smiled and made the sacred gesture. Now, making a fond farewell, he departed.

The Threshold of the Labyrinth

Darkness cloaked the palace of Knossos on Crete when at the hour of midnight, a figure moved soundlessly through the courtyard, careful to keep in the shadow of the walls. Strikingly fair the Athenian was, unlike the men of Crete. He could be one of those *kouros* figures come to life among the splendid statues bordering the approach to Athens' Acropolis. An observer, had there been one, would notice that he moved like a young god in any case. The path descended now into the depths of the palace and brought him to the narrow entrance to Crete's Labyrinth where he discerned a slight movement. Now he was relieved to see a woman, her dark-cloaked arm extended toward him. Stepping forward, he gazed into the maiden's eager face and nodded before giving her a brief but ardent embrace.

— Ariadne! You kept your word! I was afraid our meeting would pose grave problems.

He regarded her with shameless admiration, bordering upon wonder. She smiled, shaking her head.

— Do you forget that I am priestess of our goddess Potnia? I am faithful to my promise. O Theseus, worry has hounded me for your plight here! Still, I've some good news: the night itself presents the good omen for what you must accomplish within the Labyrinth.

He spoke with faint amusement.

— The night is dark as pitch. By what hidden torch did you observe this omen?

She laughed softly.

— Light—why, that is all you Greeks ever think of! Everywhere you must have blazing light. Is it only hearsay that your gods live on a bald, sun-soaked mountain peak?

— Olympus, dear, is not hearsay, no. Look, I believe you are trying to prepare me for the dreaded Labyrinth. True?

He searched her face and saw the sheen of sudden tears in the great dark eyes.

— Ah well, then tell me what this omen is. I'll welcome any help I can get.

— Theseus, it is the new moon! Do you not see that the new moon has risen—a slender radiance emerging out of darkness? It is the time when goddesses are born.

Theseus was momentarily awed by her words.

— What you are telling me is that there is some hope in this venture . . .

— Yes. The time is auspicious.

He shivered involuntarily as he gazed toward the darkness he was about to enter.

— Only feel the darkness that envelops us, and yet I must now enter a greater darkness, dense and oppressive, one that the kingdom of Knossos has nurtured. Alas, it could be a part of Hades' realm!

She was quick to reassure him out of her own knowledge, it seemed.

— Remember this: the Labyrinth is sacred for it holds within it the shrine of Potnia. I myself know the way as far as the goddess's shrine. Beyond it, the passages appear to be as black as night, and they wind about without plan, it is said. You have no choice but to follow the strange path. O Theseus, your familiar heroic way will surely be of no use to you!

— I don't like the sound of this, frankly. Remember, you did promise to meet me here to encourage me and even to supply me with some tips on locating the Minotaur. I do believe that you have some knowledge of the Labyrinth. Tell me, is your goddess the Lady of the holy double axe?

The question about her goddess startled her. Perhaps he took in the fact of her priestess's experience after all.

— Yes, this is our goddess. Does it seem strange to you that she dwells within the Labyrinth as one who is at home? You will not have gone a great distance when you'll come upon her shrine. There the axes glow with their golden light. By all means, do pause and make the sacred gesture before you pass, man of Athens. The lair of the Minotaur lies far beyond the shrine.

With this final information, Theseus groaned.

— Could you possibly supply me a torch that I'll light when I've gone beyond the shrine of your goddess?

— Alas, I'm sorry but no. There is no way but to enter the unmitigated dark. Theseus, hear me. The darkness is no evil thing. Instead, it is earth's own dense and fertile body. Besides, it is the goddess's dwelling place that shelters her. In her presence, one comes upon treasure . . .

Ariadne's voice trailed off as if she were touching upon a secret with some risk.

— So this is what lies before me. I must engage what the Fates have allotted me . . . . What is it you hold in your left hand, Ariadne? Why, it's round like a ball.

— It is the thread. I hold the ball of the essential thread, you see.

— Inexplicably, it causes me to shudder. The thread you say. As you unravel it, it's like the serpent that weaves about your goddess's image.

— Look closely, Theseus. The thread is the way into the Labyrinth and the way of return as well, that is, if you live.

Her words were sobering, and he regarded her solemnly for a long moment. Now something of his confidence appeared to return with a little humor.

— A solemn thing indeed is this thread, yet such a soft, light, bending nature it has, reminding me of yourself. A woman's thing, surely. Well, I've nothing else to aid me in this extraordinary situation, and I welcome any help available.

Ariadne looked anxious as she took in his words.

— O Theseus, take the thread and remember this: *it is life, the only life that's worth it!*

— A magic thing it is, then. Something tells me that the Labyrinth is not the place to experiment. Dear Ariadne, believe me, I am grateful. I shall indeed hold fast to the thread!

Reassured, she sighed audibly. Theseus, studying her closely, questioned her.

— Tell me, why do you risk helping me in this way? Won't your father, King Minos, regard such assistance as a betrayal of Crete's interest? After all, the Minotaur is a powerful force belonging to him.

She did not hesitate in her reply.

— There is no doubt that I shall appear as a traitor to Crete's interests. I must warn you that as soon as you emerge from the Labyrinth, you must depart at once with your company of youths and maidens under cover of night. Do not delay. As we have agreed, I'll go with you in the Athenian ship! I shall risk all. Oh, it is not for lack of love for Crete, you must understand. It is for love of you, Theseus!

For a long moment, Theseus seemed stunned and stared off into the distance. When he found his voice, his words were spoken so softly that she could hardly catch them.

— Here's a gift of incredible proportion. Oh, how can a man reciprocate when the measure is beyond him, I ask!

— Go into the Labyrinth without further delay. Hold the ball of thread close and unwind it slowly as you go, trailing it behind you. You will see that it makes a luminous path. I'll remain here at the door of the Labyrinth holding one end of the thread, as you see.

In this manner, Ariadne prepared the Athenian prince for the hidden depths of the Labyrinth and its dark passages. He weighed the enigmatic ball in his hand and smiled, entering the low door. Now he turned to face her question, "What of Minotaur? What shall you do?" Instead, he quickly asked his own.

— He isn't a god, is he?

— I am almost certain that his father was the bull god!

— O ye gods on Olympus, hear this! What about his mother then?

— Here there is no doubt. Minotaur's mother is my own—Queen Pasiphaë.

A wind arose in this moment and howled about the walls so that Theseus had to raise his voice in order to be heard.

— *O that secret love that haunts the hidden grotto and the far pasture of the heart!* There gods mingle with human folk.

— O Theseus, you've still not answered my question. Quickly, man of Athens, answer me and then go.

— How can I predict what words, what actions Minotaur will call forth from me? I have yet to discover. After all, a man must engage his destiny. Bull Man is mine. So I go! Dear Ariadne, if I return alive, together we shall sail away from Crete! First we'll free the youths and maidens of Athens held hostage and hustle them aboard ship with us. And now, farewell, dear one!

— Farewell, Theseus. Only hold the thread!

At once, the Labyrinth received him into the maze of narrow passages that wound about within the vast darkness as the path descended. His hand remained firmly cradling the ball of soft, luminous woolen thread. As for Ariadne, she remained at the entrance holding the fragile end of the thread, and the night became bone-chilling in its heavy silence. At times in her long vigil, the sense of one abandoned assailed her, and she sought to push it aside. An indeterminate time passed, and the thread lost its slack, becoming taut. It seemed to become a lifeline, communicating and strong between courageous Theseus and herself. Surely he had arrived at the center of the Labyrinth where the Minotaur awaited him. A certain peace brushed her thoughts now. She smiled with lively hope.

In the Labyrinth

Through a maze of black corridors narrow and twisting like some enormous serpent, he descended and muttered to himself, "I dare not drop the thread." The descent grew steeper, and the ceiling of the passage was so low that he had to bend double to proceed toward the far lair of fabled Minotaur. The thought of meeting the celebrated killer face-to-face stirred up a sense of dread. The passageway had become extremely narrow and full of twisting turns so that he made his way at a painfully slow pace. He reflected grimly, *It seems that I am bold first, while I think only afterward!* At that moment, almost as if confirming the fact, something roared, which was yet at a distance. He surmised that the sound had come from the core of the place. Slowly an awareness registered that he was no longer alone. At the same time, something shone like a bright coin in the middle of the passage.

The image of his own goddess began to take shape as a sudden cry was wrenched from his throat.

— Goddess Athena! You are in this hole of a place? What a welcoming sight to my eyes!

The illuminated figure before him spoke.

— Greetings, Theseus, son of Athens. I would not abandon you in your task, you see.

— What good fortune! Always you are known to come to the help of a hero, of course.

The pause was palpable before she replied. She was asking a question.

— Is the hero a label freely applied to a man? The hero, after all, is some fruit that ripens only with time, when the path to the meaning has narrowed. Then he finds himself bound to the path as he begins to engage acts of his whole being.

— I blush at your words, Lady Athena. I expect I shouldn't refer to myself as a hero . . . Tell me, do I have far to go? I am in something of a hurry, you see.

— Really? Well yes, you do have far to go.

Theseus groaned audibly before it occurred to him that he must confess.

— May I tell you a secret?

— No one else shall hear it, I assure you.

— It is this: I am not as brave as I look!

She nodded soberly.

— I understand.

— You already knew it, I see. I might have known that it was not hidden from your eyes. The truth is that here in this Hades place, I realize that I cannot handle Minotaur alone.

The goddess took account of this soberly and nodded.

— Wait, Theseus. It is enough that you entered the holy-unholy Labyrinth alone. And are you not carrying the thread of Ariadne toward the core?

— You don't understand. It is absolutely necessary that I vanquish the beast! If I fail, Athens will pay the blood tribute to Crete of fourteen youths and maidens. Then we shall die, every one of us!

She looked thoughtful in the way Olympians do when they suspect the reliability of human logic. She murmured aloud,

— Yes, but it is not so straightforward a task as killing a beast, I think.

Utterly startled by this information from Athena, he stared at her, rendered speechless until he managed a frantic question.

— What do you mean?

— I speak as goddess of work. Do not make haste to achieve your goal as you have been envisioning it, son of Athens. What I can tell you is that there is a work here in the Labyrinth that is more valuable than time. Indeed, it changes the character of time.

Theseus shook his head slowly from side to side in an effort to clear the fog.

— Please will you give me your counsel, Goddess?

— Listen carefully then and remember my words. Understanding is a tardy thing at best with individuals, I have noticed. As for the monster of Crete, Minotaur is not what you thought him to be.

The beast is a man, and the man is a beast.

Do not be simple in what you do, for if you kill the one, you slay the other!

Athena's voice echoed down the narrow passageway of the Labyrinth. Incredulity cloaked Theseus's voice, yet there was a fresh element present now, not unlike determination.

— If Minotaur is human, as you say that he is, then I'll speak with him.

— Ah, it is the only way!

— But I'll give him no quarter.

— Remember that he is powerful and very ancient, ancient as great Bull, who serves Crete's goddess.

— What shall I do then?

— When you reach the core of the Labyrinth, Minotaur will be there in the depths. His voice when he weeps is that of a woman in affliction. First, endure the grief, for it is age-old and will penetrate your heart as it echoes down the corridors of human memory. Next, tell him who you are and what your mission is. Only speak freely with him, your sword at your side. O how hungry Minotaur is to hear human speech! His isolation has been bitter.

— Now I trust you will tell me what action to take, what blows to strike and where?

Athena shook her head.

— Only when you have made the hidden covenant with Bull Man—a covenant for your life ahead—will you perceive what must be done.

— Strange, but you speak as if we were brothers, Bull Man and I.

— Perhaps the most difficult companion the soul knows is one who is
both enemy and brother.

Suddenly the desire for action rose in him, and he was impatient
for the encounter ahead.

— We are making our way down the path at a snail's pace! Hear that
mighty roar? It can't be far to go.

— Wait, Theseus. Can you see me?

— Not distinctly, but yes. You are shining and silvery, much as you appear
in the oldest temple on the Acropolis of Athens.

— What do I have in my right hand?

— The spear. Ah, it is raised as if ready for action!

He waited. As he stared at the spear, a hopefulness leaped up within
himself.

She replied simply.

— Now you know.

A joyous look on Theseus's face replaced grave concern.

— O incredible Athena, you are planning to slay Minotaur for me!

She laughed briefly. Again her voice was sober, and she spoke,
emphasizing her words.

— No, Theseus. No. That is not possible. The single act called for is
an act of human awareness, not a god's deed. Do you recall hearing
about the Battle of the Giants when I had cornered the immense giant
Alcyoneus? Heracles had to be called to deliver the deathblow. One of
the gods will not act for you while you are the appreciative spectator.
Always the human stroke is required.

Overexercised in patience, he groaned aloud, his anger rising.

— Then why, Goddess, have you tempted me to hope in your lifted spear,
which every Athenian knows is both powerful and victorious?

— Gently, Theseus. I do not tempt you. You see, the raised spear is the signal
that now is the time for the encounter in the Labyrinth, not sooner and
not later. And yet, the spear indicates something more. It evokes the thrust
of your will to approach Bull Man directly. Only be faithful to it!

— That purpose burns even now in my passion . . . Wait, do not depart
until you show me what is in your left hand, for I have only observed
the right one.

Athena turned back and extended her left hand toward Theseus, and
he recalled the left hand of the goddess in her most sacred wooden image.

— Why, you hold the spindle and the distaff with the owl on it, woman's things!

— Indispensable to you, nevertheless. You are mortal, but the great thread is not. Nor are these instruments of mine perishable. Look more closely. See how the distaff holds the thread aloft in its cleft? Through the narrow passage, life itself—*zoe*—is threaded into human existence. What a slender luminous thread it is, but it is everything!

Briefly a memory illuminated Theseus's face.

— Ariadne knows about the great thread, I think . . . What does it mean, Goddess?

— *Zoe* does not mean something other than itself. It is the meaning.

— Wait. What of the owl with the large eyes that sits on the distaff?

— Through the darkness she guards the thread that enters human life.

— Lady Athena, the owl must be your own nocturnal self! As I watch, the spindle spins in your hand, winding the thread over and over again in this grim place. The meaning is here, I perceive. It is in the Labyrinth!

Athena stayed behind now while Theseus went forward into the center of the Labyrinth alone. Before him appeared a massive shadowy form. He knew in that moment that all postponement had ended. In a loud voice, he proclaimed,

— Minotaur, I have come! O man who makes his way through the beast, O beast who roars on the human threshold, Theseus greets you!

The Lair of the Minotaur

The lair of Minotaur, dark circle that it was, seemed to Theseus not unlike the bottom of a well gone dry. The place caused him to shudder as he stood on its boundary silently regarding it. From the shadowy shape within the lair, a voice called out, emerging out of the heavy silence. Full of anguish it seemed, aged in some grief and yet surprisingly childlike.

— They were nameless, all of them, the ones they sent to me! Nobodies they were who just stared at me and wouldn't come close. So why should you have a name, stranger?

Theseus listened in amazement. Minotaur went on.

— A name is a thing you can't pass over. Keeps you looking, looking hard and wondering at a person. Is he a somebody? Are there any somebodies anywhere? Who are you anyway coming here and calling yourself Theseus?

The voice was petulant. Astonished and deeply penetrated by Minotaur's words, Theseus replied. Even so, he kept his distance.

— Truly my name is Theseus. What I can tell you is that I am a man with a task. Minotaur, I come from afar.

Minotaur took a small gleeful leap into the air, laughing as he did so.

— Then you come from the same place I do! I am from *afar*. My mother said so. When I was born, she looked at me and cried out, "Alas, this one comes from afar!" Still, she didn't give me a name. Oh, if only I had a name!

— Aren't you called the Minotaur?

— That's no name. It's a corral! A corral is a place that keeps you penned up without a name, where you can't be a person.

With these mournful words, Minotaur sank into grief and began to cry with huge sobs.

— Oh, please don't cry. I can't stand it, you see . . . You know, I can give you a name if that's what you want. You are nodding toward me. It's a fact that people say that you're the divided one. That's it. I shall call you Bull Man!

Minotaur tried out pronouncing the name twice, and his question that followed sounded doubtful.

— Will it work—this Bull Man? Will it really call me like it knows me and likes me? I am smart. I know that your name has to like you.

— It can do even more. It stitches together into one person your two parts.

Hearing this, a mournful cry issued from Minotaur.

— I am broken in two! You know it too. Ow, I'm broken!

Being alone in the depths of the Labyrinth with Minotaur's grim fate assailed him with a sadness that gripped him against his will. The creature's mournful chanting was heavy on the air as Theseus spoke.

— O for a bridge that can unite bull and man! Disconnected, things don't work. Wait, Bull Man, I am beginning to see a way through. Listen to me and consider this: are you willing to give up the uncorralled beast in yourself? After all, his enormous appetite is unworkable. You must answer the question.

Like a spear, the question struck Minotaur, and an unearthly scream came from him.

— No! Never, Theseus! You just want me to give up the place from afar that's inside me, don't you? Why haven't you given me a close look? Then you'd know for sure that I am bull. I can't be corralled!

— I have been afraid to come close. That's the truth of the matter. For a long time, I have seen you in my mind's eye, though, and I am certain that you are fierce and threatening to human existence.

Bull Man's voice in commentary could not have been more scornful.

— Nobody sees the great bull! A man of Crete just might, but an Athenian is too stupid.

Under other circumstances, Theseus might have smiled at this summary of Crete versus Athens, but the stakes being high, he replied earnestly.

— Wait. The great bull is a god on Crete. He is like the descending thunder, powerful and unmeasured. Thunder always gets its way. The thought of your bull power makes me tremble. What power have I against such a beast?

The last statement was a mere whisper. Bull Man took this in like a saving drink from a spring, and his voice was tender now.

— Theseus, I am not *all* power. Look again.

— Yes, there is more to the bull that I perceive. Now I see him as a gentle beast following the green pastures with nose close to moist, fertile earth herself.

These words caused Minotaur to weep again.

— Oh, oh, oh! I have lost the green world! Where did it go? It's all because of the *man* in me. He leads me astray!

Theseus perceived now that the second remedy must be offered as the only hope.

— Look, Bull Man, since you refuse to part with the bull that you are, you must give up your human mind and voice. Just think. If you quit being a man—for look at what a miserable specimen you are—then the people of Crete can put you out once more in their pastures. You can find the satisfying green world again. But this is only possible if you give up the man inside you.

Bull Man scowled at the Athenian but was silent. It seemed he was attempting to use his mind, long rusty from disuse. At last he emitted a great groan and spoke.

— You are not a good Cretan. You're a dreamer. I won't give up being a man. I'll bet you wouldn't either, if given a chance. The bull and the man are mine! I want both!

— Minotaur, divided one, it won't work. The two are at war in you. You can't deny it.

Sweat poured down the cheeks of the hero, and the look of dread in his eyes was that of a man who had glimpsed a deep and yawning chasm. Both figures fell silent. Occasionally a groan arose from Bull Man and was sustained like the voice of doom. Theseus spoke at last.

— There is only one solution then: it is the bridge! The bridge must be found between beast and man. Otherwise, the work in the Labyrinth fails. Face your condition, will you, Bull Man? You will see that it is unworkable in life or in the world of Crete.

Their words ceased, but Theseus did not depart. Minotaur paced back and forth, making a narrow path as though in a cage. Abysmal sighs and groans escaped him from time to time. Once, a word full of unearthly passion was hurled by him into the dim hollowness of the Labyrinth to find its echo: *bridgeless!* Theseus remained at a little distance, waiting, attentive. After some time had passed in the ghostly dark, Bull Man came to a stop. Now he turned his great horned bull head toward Theseus and spoke.

— I am way down. It's all because of *it*.

— Down where? Where are you?

— I'm way down inside the terrible crack!

He seemed annoyed with Theseus's lack of understanding, having expected better of what came from far Athens. Theseus questioned him.

— Tell me about this crack.

— It's the crack between bull and man. It's what we've been worrying about. Have you forgotten? Man of Athens, I cannot go on. Look at me. I have no future!

The plea of Bull Man to be seen lodged an arrow in the heart of Theseus now, and within the fateful Labyrinth, a feeling of slender hope began to arise, putting forth fragile tendrils. A smile came to his eyes as he spoke, as one who muses over his incredible journey.

— Companion of this dark hole, I am a man bound to a single task on which my life and that of the Athenian youths depend. The task brought me to Crete in order to free both Athens and Crete from being any longer done in by Minotaur—yourself.

Bull Man's eyes had gleamed with surprise and satisfaction at being addressed for the first time as companion! A profound alteration had come about between the two, who no longer were antagonists. He spoke eagerly like a child.

— What will you do? Do with me what you must. I'll be made famous by what you do to me. Besides, there could be a little fame left over for you too, Theseus!

Theseus shook his head from side to side in amazement at what seemed Bull Man's cheerful refrain and strode forward to face him at close range. Laying a hand on each of the great shoulders, he cried out in a powerful yet anguished voice,

— O bull that dwells in the human depths,

O man that makes his way through the bull to world,

Theseus must act!

Unwinding the ball of thread from Ariadne, he encircled Bull Man's great waist with the strong thread, drawing it firm and leaving a fair length as a lead, which he held in his left hand. He nodded silently to his mighty companion and spoke.

— Come, Bull Man, together we shall leave the Labyrinth, for the world awaits us both!

Theseus's voice was older and steeped in some solemn authority he had not known before. Now he began the return to Crete's breaking day. Bull Man followed close behind, and his steps seemed both strange and newborn.

Ariadne Journeys

The Second Gateway

On the headland of the island of Naxos, windswept and washed by an intensely blue sea, arose the Doric-columned temple of the fifth century BC. Even today, the stately gateway of white marble remains, offering its solitary threshold. History claims the temple as Apollo's, while for one who savors Naxos' mythological past, the associations with the god Dionysos are suggestive.

It is Dionysos, hailed in ritual as *Dithyrambos*, god of the double gateway, who stands at the second gateway of Ariadne's life story. Her growing up in Crete in the royal house of Knossos, falling in love and fleeing Crete aboard the ship with her lover Theseus, and her subsequent abandonment on Naxos constituted her movement through the first gateway of her existence. When the radiant stranger of Naxos appears, Ariadne comes upon the second gateway. Like the vintage of Dionysos on the island, she moves toward the satisfying harvest and a luminous existence.

The Ship to Naxos

Theseus sat in the prow of the Greek ship, gazing always forward into the distance, and not once had he taken a backward look at Knossos. Beside him sat Ariadne, who pulled her cloak of sheep's wool more tightly about her against the chilling wind. She spoke.
— Without you, dear Theseus, Crete would still be under the fierce demands of my brother, Minotaur. And what's more, you have removed

forever from Athens the bloody tribute. Both Crete and Athens are blessed as a result.

— True. But without your bold help, bordering on treason actually, the outcome might have been tragic.

Theseus turned an appraising look upon the Cretan maiden, his face somewhat troubled.

— Are you consoling yourself for choosing me and the escape to Athens, I wonder? Know that I love you, Ariadne. The gift of Aphrodite lies richly between us, surely.

— Oh, it does! It's that a person must gaze solemnly on what she has done. That's all.

— The truth is that I treasure your lightheartedness more than your solemnity. Besides, is there not high excitement in our sea adventure and in moving to a bright, new land unknown before?

— Oh yes . . . there is a certain fear too, you see. I have never known life apart from my parents and my home. Alas, there is a poignant absence that fills my heart!

— Come, Ariadne. I thought that you were the adventurer, the altogether brave one who could defy habit and custom! *This melancholy is more than I bargained for!*

His last statement was said to himself.

— Grant me, dear hero, my due measure of homesickness and misgivings. These are but spasms of reflection, not regret. Without these, I should not be Ariadne, daughter of Minos and Pasiphaë . . . How I shall miss lighting the lamps at Potnia's Shrine of the Double Ax . . . But rest assured, there are rash deeds that the heart would not think of withdrawing!

She leaned against him now, smiling, and his arm drew her close. At the same moment, the boat lurched wildly, nearly unseating them.

It was far into the darkness of the third night at sea that they put in at the island of Naxos, bone-tired and chilled. Nor were the island's lush vineyards and green groves visible in the deep night. Theseus led the way on foot, climbing the steep path of the hill beyond the beach, and Ariadne and the Athenian youths and maidens, exhausted, followed. Twice Ariadne stopped and turned to gaze upon the temple, radiant and sovereign upon the headland. Theseus turned back to her and inquired, "You are coming, aren't you? Not much farther to go." Numbly, she nodded. High above the beach, they came upon a densely foliaged fig tree that grew out of a great boulder at the entrance of a cave. Separating from their Athenian companions, Theseus led Ariadne gently into the depths of the cave out of the fierce wind. A quiet not unlike serenity itself greeted them, and they set about making a bed with gathered branches, a bed that presently claimed them. The night was moonless and the two of them bone-weary on what was to be their wedding night. Although he turned to her with tender gestures, they were brief before their passions brought them together, sealing their union. And Ariadne loved Theseus greatly. Such knowledge was as clear to her as the night's first star at Knossos, yet muffled thoughts trailed her descent into an uneasy sleep.

Ariadne's Dream

The night flight from Crete aboard the Athenian ship captained by her beloved Theseus was accomplished, and they had put in at the isle of Naxos where she and Theseus had taken shelter in a grotto high above the windy beach. It was just before dawn on this night of love that Ariadne had a dream in which in their ship she again rode the waves of a turbulent Aegean Sea. Theseus stood at the helm while she sat upon the deck in the stern. Who was the third figure, the woman standing erect in mid ship, her head helmeted, a shield resting under her left hand? Slowly the figure turned, thoughtful gray eyes upon the Cretan maiden, and addressed her.

— So you have fled from your homeland and your royal parents, Ariadne?

— You are mistaken. I do not flee from anything. Instead, I go toward something fair and wonderful!

— Ah, so speaks the voice of desire when under Aphrodite's hand. I do perceive her hand in this.

Gazing at her extraordinary companion, she grew excited and, at the same time, uneasy. Slowly she voiced her question.

— Could you possibly be the goddess of the Athenians? The one who came to him in the Labyrinth?

— Yes, I am Athena. Do you love Theseus? Is this what causes you to sail with him toward far Athens?

Ariadne nodded silently as the words "far Athens" smote her with a cold hand. Perhaps she should have realized how much she would miss home at Knossos and especially her mother, Pasiphaë, when, clinging to her hero's side, she boarded his ship for distant Athens. The wind tore fiercely at the sails now as the goddess spoke.

— Abandonment, you shall find, is so much easier to deal out than it is to receive. You will do well to remember my words in the days to come.

— Lady Athena, why do you accuse me of abandonment and lay its guilt upon me? Am I not moving forward in my life? Surely with your woman's heart you can understand being in love.

— Indeed I perceive that love has claimed your heart, and I do not judge you harshly. Yet it is in the interest of truth to acknowledge what it is you do. This is my counsel. Behind on the shores of Crete, you leave those who love you. It happens with great pain and loss, sharp as the sword's thrust. It would be blind to refer to this movement as progress.

— O Goddess, the love that Theseus and I have is worth it!

— Know that such love has my blessing. I only spoke of its cost. You have in your bosom a strong and passionate soul, Ariadne. May the Graces come to your assistance when you meet what the Fates allot you. One question more, does Theseus return this exuberant, all-sacrificing love?

The question lay heavy upon her as the fierce gale rocked the ship. Her heart beat loudly in the long pause in which Athena's thoughtful gaze held her own. Was it compassion she saw in the look? When she replied, her voice was low.

— Theseus is truly grateful to me, for he says that I saved his life and that of his Athenian companions. He speaks many times of the thread and very little of the Labyrinth where he took Minotaur captive.

— Theseus is an exceptional young man, and gratitude comes naturally, I expect. But does he love you as a man loves the woman he desires to spend the remainder of his life with?

Ariadne sighed an abysmal sigh.

— I do not know. Alas, I do not know! . . . . O Goddess, look. We approach the shore of a green island!

Her eyes returning to mid ship, she saw that Goddess Athena turned to depart, first having raised her shield above Ariadne's head in a benevolent gesture. Did it also bestow protection? She wondered.

Abandonment

Ragged fragments of a harrowing dream scurried across her mind as she awakened. The sun was well above the eastern horizon as she stepped out of the deep shadow of the old fig tree, ending the first night on Naxos. It was their wedding night, one that would forever echo in fond memory. Ah, where could Theseus be? All seemed strangely quiet. No one was about evidently, strange as that seemed. At once she climbed the steep path to the top of the overhanging rock, there to gain a view of the life of the harbor below. *Where is our ship?* Frantically her eyes swept over the harbor where no ship was at anchor, none at all. The beach that extended from the port was serene, forsaken. Lifting her eyes to the far horizon, briefly she glimpsed the familiar Greek ship flying its black sail, and now it was swallowed up into the distance. Even as she took this in, Ariadne seemed to grow old, her face pale as the sea foam. Her voice rang out now on the chaste morning air.

— Theseus! O my beloved hero, where have you gone?

Her legs gave way, and she sank down on the rock weeping, as a dark cloud of sorrow seemed to envelop her, a sorrow alien to hope. Shrouding her spirit was the vivid image of the departing Athenian ship, its prow toward Athens, surely. Stretching out her arms to embrace the boulder, she laid her face against the silent stone and cried aloud,

— O my dear mother in Crete, why did I leave you? O Aphrodite, Goddess, with many you are known to be generous. Why have you loved me so little?

Hours passed, and still Ariadne remained beside the stone. At last she arose to gaze solemnly out to sea once more as she spoke her sobering thoughts.

— Can it be that Poseidon has taken golden Theseus in order to deliver him back to his father's house, obedient son to become king of far Athens? O Poseidon, why must you take him from me? Only see how desolate I am, refugee that I am on a strange island! For me there is no return to parents and homeland. No return! What death tolls in those words. Like a pearl, my mind holds love's brief voyage. Even now I see his admiring eyes and hear the wonder in his voice when he spoke,

I stole away from Crete the lovely maiden of Knossos, and did she not come all willingly at my side? A brilliant conquest some will say . . . but what's this before me? A solitary woman is in our ship's company with the look upon her of the Nike who rides the prow of our ship! Ariadne, dear, are you indeed this woman who blooms here aboard? Lily one with eyes that are shining black dolphins washed by strange depths, depths unknown to me, answer me this: what is it that you bring me?

How I treasured those words as those of deepest love, a love long thirsted for by the sleeping woman within me. Nor did I reply but took this moment as a treasure to be always guarded. Again he spoke,

Ariadne, you do not answer me. Perhaps those eyes are peering into some vaster labyrinth you now make ready for me. Dear girl, strange one, it was not easy to hold on to the thread, I want you to know.

O Theseus, surely you do not regret taking the thread from my hand!

There and at that hour, certainly not.

Ah, how those words pierce my heart as even now I repeat them! At that time aboard ship, I supposed them to express my lover's idle fantasy meant merely to tease me, but no more. He abandons me! Theseus abandons me! This is no idle fantasy. Alas, my grief swells the tide of Naxos, yet it does not bring him back!

O Theseus! Hear me even now on your ship bound for Athens! The girl of Crete is no more! A woman gazes toward you everlastingly from this Naxian shore, a woman newborn and abloom in the labyrinth of her sorrow! She grew upon the root and stem of your brief love, and although she comes to be only in the presence of love, she is left in solitude. O gods of Naxos, take pity on me!

The Voice of the Stone

Climbing the steep slope above the sheltering cave that was now her refuge, Ariadne reached a spot affording a clear view of the harbor of Naxos far below and sank down on a low rock next to a tall vertical stone. The grief of her abandonment on this alien shore lay heavy on her spirit. Exhausted, she leaned against the standing stone, which brought her some comfort, oddly. Not a person was in sight as she murmured her thoughts aloud.

— Just look at the vast stretch of wild sea that washes this remote shore. It separates me forever from my homeland, Crete! There is no return, alas! When I stepped aboard the Greek ship at Theseus's side, how happy my maiden heart was. At the same time, there was that awesome moment when the realization washed over me that the royal child Ariadne was forever left behind. Soon I am sure that the people of Knossos will forget all about me. Alone here on this remote island, left here by Theseus whom I loved, what is to become of me?

Her anguished question hung upon the air, and tears streamed down her cheeks. Did she hear a voice? Quickly she wiped away the evidence of her tears as best she could. She saw no one, yet a voice was speaking close at hand, speaking as one who might be in the middle of a long conversation. She listened now.

— So does the keeper of the thread know where it will yet penetrate, through what unknown passages, before coming to rest?

Ariadne, hospitable by nature, replied to the unseen visitor,

— No, I suppose not, but who can this thread keeper be that you speak of?

— Yourself, who else? Wasn't it you who stood in the night at the Labyrinth's entrance holding the end of the thread? I am told that you handed the ball of it to Theseus, that Greek prince.

The reminder of this event caused her to gasp. Still she replied.

— Yes, I did. I dared not drop the thread. Between both hands I clasped it for dear life when it became taut from Theseus's unwinding of it as he penetrated the Labyrinth. Why, without the thread, I am certain that he would never have located the spot where Minotaur dwelled. Nor could he have found his way out of the maze.

The voice fell silent, as if taking in her account. After a long moment, it began again.

— So do you happen to know the Labyrinth well, maiden of Crete?

— Only so far into the dark maze as the Shrine of the Double Ax. The shrine holds the holy image of Potnia, our Lady, on its altar . . . How odd it is to be speaking to an upright stone!

— Hm, perhaps so. Tell me, are you a priestess of the goddess then?

— Oh yes. I am daughter, you see, of King Minos and Queen Pasiphaë.

Now the voice seemed somewhat annoyed.

— Actually, it is not your royal credentials that interest me. It is the thread itself that is in question. It has a call that is like a cry in the labyrinthine night.

If the tall stone was slightly annoyed, she herself was growing impatient with the conversation and now asserted herself with strong feeling.

— I am a practical person, I must tell you. It seems to me that you make rather a great deal out of a ball of woolen thread! Every woman has to deal with thread, surely.

The Stone was single-minded, however.

— Do you have it with you? Did you bring the thread to Naxos?

— As a matter of fact, I did. I just remembered. I have it here in the pocket of my garment.

Now she drew the luminous thread out a little so that it became visible.

— Ah, so you do value it, after all.

Did he imagine her to be indifferent to the companionable and useful thread? His absorption with it, nonetheless, caused her to contemplate the thread anew.

— I should not like being without it, so I keep it close, you see. How I do like to feel its softness, its mute, flowing life, its roundness too. Besides, there is comfort in knowing that there is so much of it that I'm not likely to run out.

The Stone heaved a great sigh of satisfaction now before responding.

— It may yet make a great deal of cloth!

This announcement had the ring of an oracle. However, Ariadne's attention was not to be diverted for long from her problem, and the expression of it tumbled out of her now.

— Alas, all of my life has come unraveled!

— You're not saying that the thread has lost its strength, are you?

— O why do you insist on the thread as so important? The fact is that the weaver herself has lost heart!

The time he took in receiving her cry of woe convinced her that the Stone was not without heart. Now he was again speaking.

— I notice that you, Ariadne, have taken care of the ball of thread. I think you dare not lose it. As yet you have not discovered its full power, however. What else did you bring away from Crete on love's rash voyage?

His last words caused her to gasp. Who did this stone think he was? Still she was intent on answering his question.

— Well, I brought the woolen cloak I'm wearing.

— That is all?

— Two things more, actually. They are holy things which I took from the shrine of our goddess.

    His curiosity grew even keener, she sensed.

— And what would these two things be?

    The Stone's interest sharpened. It indicated more than curiosity. In any case, she felt it would be a relief to confess at last to the two things stolen.

— I have the small wooden image of our Lady. It's very old. Already it was ancient when my grandmother's mother was a child.

— Ah, so you have the goddess's image. And what else?

— One thing more. It is an image wrought in gold of Bull God himself!

— Indeed! Well, it is truly good news to know that you didn't leave that behind. I should lose hope if you failed to adore Bull God, you see.

— What are you saying, voice of the Stone? Do you mean to say that you don't condemn me for stealing a holy treasure?

— I? Certainly not. Tattling to King Minos would hardly be in my best interest, I assure you.

    The voice of the Stone, although seeming to rise from a hard, even implacable floor, had now taken on a current of excitement that puzzled her. Had he actually laughed? As for herself, her confession had the effect of lightening her spirit somewhat, while at the same time, the deep-voiced Stone distracted her grief. An interval of silence followed before she raised the question haunting her mind.

— Surely there is no sweeter launching than love's own voyage. And yet, you called it rash. Why?

— For one thing it surely is rash when one loses one's connection to one's history, what has actually been your life to date. Even more rash, however, is a thing that takes place with lovers, for falling under Eros's arrow, each falls into another person's place of dire need.

— Oh, Stone, you must be mistaken! Aphrodite rode in the prow of the Athenians' ship in order to guide their voyage and brought them the fair wind. Naturally they paid her honor. Surely it was Aphrodite herself who bestowed on me love's radiant vision, which is her gift. Look at me and you see the proof in my love of Theseus.

    It took some time for Stone to sort out Ariadne's logic, it seemed, but now he made reply.

— Well, I see that love's vision is one thing for you, Ariadne, but it is a different matter for Theseus. Just consider, will you, can the hero in the midst of his great task risk succumbing to Aphrodite's magic? Probably not. As for you, you are a priestess besides—

Ariadne's eyes widened as she hastened to educate Stone.

— Why, a priestess can certainly fall in love!
— Yes, but what is a priestess? She is one who makes the faithful and rhythmic return to the sacred place, tending its needs. So what can she have to do with the hero, I ask? Why, he is full of departure, of journey, and the lust for deeds in the far place! That's the hero.

His voice had held scorn.

— Would you cast doubt on love's sweet vision, which is my greatest treasure?
— It is not love's vision that I doubt, Ariadne, although I must say that you've been inclined to spend it blindly on this hero. Ah, how sudden is the vision's arrival, one is unprepared. So what does a person do? Squanders it at once!

He paused, regarding Ariadne with an odd mixture of impatience and compassion before continuing. His voice grew gentle now.

— Know this, Ariadne. I do not chastise you in my heart.

The words caused her to murmur to herself, "Does the stone on which I lean have so great a heart then? Strangely, the voice of Stone is reminiscent of a god's voice." Now she spoke aloud with a firm declaration of spirit.

— You find me here in this spot in deep sorrow, Stone, because I loved a man!

The confession momentarily unburdened her, and now she arose and turned to leave. The Stone protested.

— Don't turn away from me, daughter of Minos and Pasiphaë! Sit down here beside me. Will you?

She responded to his urgent entreaty by entering again the deep shade of the tree and sitting down next to the great stone. Within the now deeply shadowed place, she glimpsed for a moment the figure of a man, his looks comely while his head of thick black hair was garlanded with green leaves. The shadowed figure gazed at her, and his gaze was penetrating, sensuous, and yet tender. A wave of sheer pleasure passed through her. When the voice was heard again, it was like the voice of an old friend.

— I have something to say to you. Will you hear me, woman of Crete? You see, my words are not far from who I am, so that not to be heard is a wounding.

— Oh, I see. It is that I've been so absorbed in my own sorrow. Something begins to turn now, however. Please say what you have to say.

— It is that you are in danger of being swallowed up in the Cretan princess. You cannot afford to have your whole life claimed by her.

  Shocked by his words, Ariadne gasped.

— What is this you are saying?

— It is that you must not be arrogant in your grief, for if you persist, all can be lost.

  Ariadne leaped to her feet, and her eyes flashed with anger.

— I gave all my heart's love and devotion to a man, and Theseus took them briefly before abandoning me! Have you no feeling for my plight?

— Believe me, Ariadne, I too have known all the anguish of rejection. The fact is that the Fates have beckoned to Theseus, urging him toward Athens to take the throne awaiting him. A man cannot oppose the Fates. I am convinced of it.

— Oh, what am I to do!

— Let him go, Ariadne. O yes, as woman of Naxos, you'll find the grief that belongs, I think, without defying the gods. And know that I shall companion you. We shall walk together, you and I!

  The words of Stone hung upon the air, and as they echoed in her consciousness, they lost their original heaviness and the harshness of their truth. She was alone, and yet she spoke, her voice now emptied of all agitation.

— O Stone of Naxos, you are a mystery to me. Even so, your companionship brings me a kind of goldenness. It is a radiance I've not known before. Please do not be hard-hearted with me as slowly I gather together your unusual words. Do deal gently with me. Ah so . . . how astonishing . . . I begin to perceive that something of the god of Naxos has visited me!

  Returning in the dusk to the high rock cave, Ariadne entered her earth dwelling and, having made her bed, lay down and slept the night. Under the fine Cretan cloak slept the woman of Naxos, for the princess of Crete had departed.

The Radiant Stranger

Meeting the Man of Naxos

For a long time, her eyes anxiously scanned the harbor below the high, overhanging rock where she, the maiden from Crete, kept her vigil. Anguish swept over her as the hounding thought returned that here on the far island of Naxos she was entirely alone. No sign of the Athenian ship, none at all. The certainty grew that she was abandoned, and sorrow seized her in its rough tide. Surely Theseus had loved her. Of this she had no doubt. How could he board his ship secretly with his young comrades and depart, captaining his ship toward far Athens leaving her behind? Heavy with his absence, a day and a night had passed. A strong gale assailed both sea and island coast, the sky fiercely blue and unsmiling on this early morning. As she continued to gaze out to sea, a subtle change caught her attention. It was as if she were no longer alone, although she saw no one near her windswept shelter. Now, turning back toward the island itself, she drew in her breath sharply as she found herself facing a man. His demeanor was extraordinary, combined as it was with an engaging grace and subtle authority.

He was regarding her with his great dark eyes, smiling a private sort of smile as he did so. It was he who spoke.

— *Kalimera*, maiden! You are a stranger on Naxos, I see.

— *Kalimera*, man of Naxos. Yes, a stranger indeed. I come from the city of Knossos on Crete. Did the sea bring you? Your arrival has startled me.

— Many a journey has claimed me, but for you I have just arrived.

At this reply, her eyes widened. She studied his dark, garlanded head.

— Why do you wear a green crown of leaves, for there is a shining about your dark locks?

— It seems that the vine is ever with me. It entwines more or less the whole
of Naxos.

He sensed the tension in her and noticed her eyes roving in their
search.

— You are waiting for someone, I observe.

— Yes, yes, I am.

— Let me tell you, maiden, that the one you are waiting for will not be
coming, so it is well that you take your anxious eyes away from the far
horizon. The Athenian is gone, refusing the wine cup of Naxos. An
uneven yoke is shed, I'm afraid.

At these words, for he spoke as one who knows, hope seemed to
collapse within her, and Ariadne bowed her head in sorrow. His words
continued with growing concern.

— I tell you, unrelenting expectation is a hard master, surely one not wise
to follow. Do I sense some deep sorrow? Are you an unwilling traveler
to our island?

— Oh, never would I have chosen to come ashore at Naxos! It was Theseus
who captained the ship and brought us into port here. Alas, this is
journey's end!

— Indeed? How do you know this?

She shook her head numbly.

— When anger invests sorrow, it can call a beginning an end.

She raised her head, listening.

— What strange words you speak.

— Rather, I speak plainly. You see, woman of Knossos, I know Naxos to
be a place of *beginning*.

She shook her head with something close to disbelief in her face.
He gave her a gentle look of encouragement.

— What if you were to withdraw your anxious scanning of the sea toward
Athens?

She smiled wanly and replied.

— It is very little you ask of me in courtesy to this place.

Now he flashed her an incredible smile, his face radiant.

— Ah, that's better. Shall we walk the island path out of the wind, the
path that winds up around the next outcropping of coastal rocks?

Together they set out upon the path of the rugged island, the sea
at their backs.

— Tell me, why did you leave Crete, since it is your home? Nor do you
need to describe all the circumstances, private as they must be. Already

I have gained knowledge of the dramatic event of the vanquishing of the Minotaur, you see. Besides, I must tell you that I observed the Athenian hero sail away from this shore.

She gasped, stopping to face him.

— You actually saw Theseus departing in his ship, leaving without me?

— I did, yes. I am sorry, Ariadne.

— Why, you know my name!

— I learned that too. Again I ask you, why did you leave Crete?

— It is that I loved a man . . .

— Others love without leaving homeland and all they have known. Why did you flee?

— Flee? Yes, I expect I fled, didn't I? It was a decision in the dark, and we fled in the night. Strangely, in you, man of Naxos, I find a gentle comfort. Can we sit down while I tell my story?

He nodded and gestured toward two large facing boulders with the air of one who offers his rich hospitality. Once seated, she smiled tentatively and began with some misgivings reflected in her hushed voice.

— Always I have known a longing, and sometimes it would fairly overpower me.

— Ah, longing is no stranger to me, maiden.

— All my life, ever since I was a mere child, I've longed to be free, you see. O man of Naxos, you with the great dark eyes that burrow into my unknown core, how can I make clear such longing?

— There is a far place—it is interior—where longing shelters. It is a holy place, a temenos. Actually, it is the dwelling place of what has not yet stepped up to the threshold, for it is not fully shaped, certainly not ready to enter life. Yet human longing beckons to me in a way that can't be refused.

His words perplexed her even as, oddly, they brought comfort. She confessed,

— Outside of this longing, I am nothing, nothing at all!

Momentarily he appeared astonished. After a long moment, he nodded and spoke.

— You have spoken your truth, a truth that draws us inexorably close. I have seen how longing makes deep grooves in a person. When were you first aware of it?

— It arose when I would be with my mother, Queen Pasiphaë. How could I ever match her—such a high and accomplished lady? The thought would plague me as a child, especially when citizens of Crete would make fanciful predictions concerning me.

— Such a burden for one so small. But tell me, for now time is different, for you are on Naxos, do you continue to regard yourself as daughter of a royal house?

Suddenly his voice grew solemn in authority as he continued.

— Hear me, Ariadne. One who remains altogether daughter is never free!

At these words, her color paled and her eyes stared sightlessly. Getting to his feet, he extended his hand and drew her toward the path again without words. For some time he did not release her hand, and as they walked, she found the dense and moist silence not only comforting but pleasant indeed. When they had continued on the winding, sheltered path for some time, they reached a very old fig tree, its branches low spreading. The smile he now gave her was a slow, lazy one as he gestured for them to sit down in the shade. Reaching overhead, he plucked a large fig, which he held to her lips. She smiled, accepting the lush fruit.

— What you called "this forsaken isle" has ripened her fruit for you, you observe. Consider what it is you will do. Ariadne, will you forsake Naxos as you yourself have been forsaken?

She shook her head from side to side, puzzled.

— How strange you are, man of Naxos. Am I not the one who suffers being forsaken? What can the island feel after all? Ah, the fig is sweet. Oddly, I find it rich, a bountiful thing from earth in the time of my misery.

After a time, he spoke.

— I have something to say to you. Will you hear me?

— No one has ever asked for my hearing before. Does it matter?

He was shocked by the callousness of her question.

— Does it matter? Of course it matters absolutely. My words are not far from my very being. They arise out of me. If I am not heard, then am I wounded.

— Alas, I am afraid I spoke automatically as one enclosed in her own misery. Something has turned, though. Yes, I shall hear you.

— I want to warn you about the daughter, that one you appear to have known intimately as yourself. It is she who loses for you your freedom. The daughter believes she is to be looked after always. She is not truly accountable. It is the parents or someone else who must respond directly to life and arrange it for her.

Anger came to her eyes briefly, but reflection was not far behind.

— Can this be true? Ah, but when Theseus came, all was different. I loved him, and yet he abandoned me. O cruel, cruel man!

— Did love owe you a future to fit the maiden's wish and expectation?

Hearing these hard words, Ariadne felt a wave of resentment as he went on relentlessly.

— Wait, Ariadne. My heart is not cold. I know your anguish. It is that there is a reality to be reckoned with. It lies with destiny. The Fates beckoned to Theseus to return to Athens and assume the kingship, and he has gone with them. O give him your womanly grief instead of the daughter's bitter anger! Ariadne, know this. I shall wait for your sorrow to heal, but I shall not father you, not ever!

Tears of anguish flowed now as Ariadne felt even more profoundly abandoned. With passion, she cried aloud,

— O hard-hearted man of Naxos!

Ariadne and Dionysos's Toys

Overlooking the Aegean Sea where roaring waves fiercely assaulted the beach at Naxos was a deep cave, her new dwelling place. As she sat on a stone within the sheltering dimness of the rocky cavern, the maiden Ariadne pondered.

— Alas, I'm at the end of the road! Did we not have between us a golden treasure, Theseus and I . . . the gift of Lady Aphrodite? Oh, oh, we're finished! O world, O life, I am young to suffer such a fate! The text of my heart is rich and full. How can he think of discarding it? Yet it has happened. One night only the Greek ship anchored at Naxos, and now it has sailed without me. O Theseus, how could you wound me with fearsome abandonment?

As she cried aloud into the empty cave, the nearby spring continued its incessant fall over the face of stone with a voice that was seemingly indifferent to her despair. But presently another sound reached her. It was a whirring sound like a small wind and was followed, surprisingly, by the light laughter of a child. Ariadne turned about to peer into the dark depths of the cave as she listened intently, but she saw nothing. Once again the high, musical laughter emerged from some far interior chamber of the cave. A different sound was heard now as light running footsteps approached. She caught her breath before calling out,

— Who comes? Who comes from far inside the cave's core?

As she waited for a reply, an owl outside the cave seemed to repeat her question—*who, who, who?* The voice in reply, however, was near at hand now. It was the voice of a young boy although she saw nobody at all. Instinctively, she bent down to catch what he was saying.

— You saw it, didn't you? You liked my toy, and you took it!

She was plainly astonished at the accusation and replied at once.

— What toy?

— My top, of course.

His voice was impatient as if some interruption had occurred in his play and he considered it a grave matter.

— Little fellow, I haven't seen your top. Believe me. You have mixed me up with somebody else.

He took this in and seemed puzzled in his reply.

— I thought you were the Cretan person.

— I am the Cretan person.

— Then it was you who caused the happening.

Clearly this was something he had figured out, and he was certainly not a child to let one of his conclusions get away from him. Some strong emotion crept into his small voice now.

— You captured my top! No one has a top like mine, Cretan person.

She shook her head slowly from side to side, for she was the one puzzled now. As she stared toward a dark nook of the cave, she managed to make out, although only faintly, a small boy with abundant dark curls and large shining eyes that were steadily regarding her. Clearly there was no way to divert his attention from his toy. She sighed and addressed him.

— There seems to be some mix-up. Now if you were to describe your missing toy, perhaps I could be of some help. Will you do this?

Receiving her suggestion, the boy began to sway back and forth gracefully while at the same time keeping step to some imagined music. Now he was humming pleasantly as well. When he finally spoke, his voice sounded a little dreamy, she thought.

— My top is solid, not at all flimsy, you see. It is much of the time silent and still and looks rather unimportant. The truth is that it is very important indeed. My top knows how to stand on one foot while it begins to spin. Cretan person, *spinning* is its secret!

Ariadne was wide-eyed with amazement. She interrupted with a question.

— You say that your top has a secret? Why, everyone knows that a top is for spinning.

— Oh? But who knows what spinning really is? It's a secret. Only the spinner truly knows what spinning is. Say, do you know why you happen to be so sad, Cretan person?

She shook her head slowly as tears fell on her cheeks. When he spoke again, his voice seemed a little tender.

— I know what happened. In fact, I'm certain of it. My top was spinning in its fine way, and suddenly it fell over. That's when it lost its humming, whirring voice that makes one so happy. That's when you lost the wonderful circle dance!

Ariadne nodded now, and a sharp perception filled her consciousness.

— Oh yes, that's true! I've lost what you described, boy. Look at me and you can tell that the life has gone out of me. Alas, I am the spent top!

The boy reacted as if struck by an arrow.

— Not you! No, Cretan person, you are not my top. My top is the gift of the gods. It is everlasting. By that, I mean that it never runs out. Still, it can fall over and become silent as if it were dead. But it lives on. My top lives on.

— Then why has it gone missing? Why did you think I stole it?

— You wanted to own it. I saw it in your face, in the way you looked at that Greek prince. My top cannot be owned, I tell you. But listen, Cretan person, don't look so sad. It's not the end. You've only just begun.

— Oh, the life has gone out of me! There's no hope.

The boy began to hum again. Then he stopped as if he just remembered something.

— Do you know what? I have a message for you. It is from my top. Here it is,

Ariadne! Ariadne! We shall again do our circle dance, never fear—whirring and humming and spinning with delight . . . only not quite yet.

For the first time on this fateful day, Ariadne smiled. But when she bent down to thank the extraordinary boy, he was gone.

The Bull Roarer

Ariadne stood within the morning chill of the cave, clasping her arms within her woolen cloak, and shivered. The silence of the cave seemed hollowed out of earth's very core, so dense and unbroken she found it. Besides, her heart ached for Theseus and for the happy bride she had so briefly been. Now a smooth draft of warm air like a soft summer breeze came from the unexplored depth of the cave, drawing her attention. She dropped her arms to her side as a sense of expectancy came over her. There it was, the voice of that child! Still, no visible sign of him was to be found as her eyes searched the cave's darker recess. And then came the greeting, astonishingly close at hand.

— *Kalimera*, Cretan person!

— *Kalimera*, boy, and I must tell you that my name is Ariadne.

    He thought a moment before seeming to discard the information.

— It doesn't matter. A name doesn't really tell.

— What do you mean? My name matters to me a great deal. And, boy, it does tell, as you put it. Why, it tells you that I am daughter of King Minos and Queen Pasiphaë of Knossos.

— Oh yes, it tells *that*.

    Obviously he found such a fact immaterial in his world. He went on.

— Your name doesn't tell things the way the bull roarer does. But I expect you don't know about my toy, do you?

— No. Do tell me about your toy.

    He considered, not knowing how he might go about it. He began.

— He can't find it all at once. It takes a little time for the bull to find his true roar. At first he circles about the center, eyeing it, and he begins to grunt a great deal and to paw the ground. He only has so much patience, after all. Always he wants to get going. He wants to get at the thing that's facing him. The world can't really matter unless he does, you see. Next there comes a zinging and a whirring sound on the air as I make the bull roarer circle about over my head on its cord.

    She shook her head in perplexity.

— It sounds intimidating and not at all like an amusing toy.

— Of course it's scary, but it's wonderful. Can't you see that? Besides, a good toy shows a person what's real and true before it has a chance to get trampled about in the world.

— You called your toy "bull roarer." Well, where is the roar?

    Her question startled him.

— Do you mean to say that you come from Crete, from bull country, and you don't know?

    Ariadne drew herself up with dignity as she replied.

— Have I not spent many an hour on the dancing floor built by Daedalus, watching the most skilled bull dancers as they engage the great bull? O yes, little friend, I am not a stranger to the bull and his ways.

He gazed at her, and the ecstasy of the bull dance filled his imagination for a long moment.

— Then why do you ask me about the roar?

Now Ariadne wanted to get on with things. She bent forward, and her voice was earnest.

— What I should like to know is how can your toy contain the bull's great roar?

No sooner had she voiced the question than she saw the child before her in the dimness. His large shining eyes were gazing at her, and she saw that he was grinning as he replied.

— It's magic, my toy is, for how can anything store up the bull's roar and then release it to the air when it's ready? Well, my bull roarer does that. And do you know what? I can't be without my great toy!

The last words, confessed like an afterthought, held some poignant acknowledgment that was like a tangible presence in the cave. Silence fell between them. It was Ariadne who spoke then.

— Such a fierce thing is the bull's roar.

— Fierce? Yes, it is fierce. For a thing to be true, it has to be fiercely what it is. For a Greek, pride is fierce, and courage too. And, maiden, hear me. Love is fierce! Didn't you hear the bull's roar when you left Crete forever with your Greek lover?

These unchildlike words astonished her, and she turned to gaze more closely at her companion. She caught her breath in amazement as she beheld a man of singular comeliness, although he was only faintly discernible. And then he was gone as the voice of the boy was heard, lyrical upon the air.

— Around and around my toy goes, circling the air while the bull eyes what's in the center, watching it and making a drumming beat with his breath as he paws the ground. It does take time for him to get ready for his great roar.

Ariadne shook her head, frowning, before she asked abruptly,

— What is in the roar besides being fierce, I mean, that attracts you so greatly, boy?

— The roar is the special happening. It's when the bull tells. He tells what he knows, see? When all that he knows fills up his mind, and his body as well, then he opens his mouth and bellows. Best to remember this, Cretan person.

    Strangely, the conversation with the extraordinary boy had captured her attention altogether, her grief presently forgotten. She pressed him further.

— Tell me what it is that the bull knows.
— He knows the beating of earth's heart. When he cocks his head to the side, I know he is hearing it.
— That is interesting, but what good does that do?

    A look of alarm came to his face.

— Cretan person, do you mean that you don't know? If a person doesn't hear earth's heart beat, why, everything gets out of rhythm and fails to work right.
— Ah, so. Thank you, my little friend. I hope that you will return many times to see me.

    He bowed and, bidding her good-bye, left the cave.

The Mirror of Dionysos

    High on the hill overlooking the coast of Naxos, Ariadne in her abandonment took refuge within the cave. As she sat upon a large boulder and stared into the unexplored depth of the cave, she was astonished by the appearance of the small boy, faint though his image was within the dimness.

— Why, little friend, you have found your way here again! Welcome.

    He gazed at her with his large dark eyes as if searching for something in particular. Then he nodded, clutching something to his chest.

— What have you brought with you this time?
— Why should she be startled that the voice that was replying was that of so young a child?
— I've got my mirror!

    She encouraged him, while his eyes, old yet young in their gaze, were rendering her somewhat uncomfortable.

— I am glad that you brought something along. A mirror can be useful.

    Clearly her words disturbed him, for he replied with disdain.

— Useful? Anything can be useful. This is my true toy. It knows better than to be useful. Why, it knows about *play!*

    His reply was disconcerting.

— All right. If you should like to play with your toy, please do.

He smiled now and, setting his mirror upon a rock, began to gaze into its shining face as he leaned forward on his elbows. Now he began to hum a little tune as well. Had he forgotten that he had a companion? After a long pause, she cleared her throat audibly. He looked up at her and spoke.

— Do you know what? I'll tell you something. My mirror is a real pirate!

— A pirate? How can a small mirror be a pirate, boy?

— Why, it manages to capture whatever pleases it, so it must travel under a secret sail, see?

— Boy, if it were a pirate, it would be after treasure. Stealing treasure is what pirates are known to do.

— That's right. My mirror gets the treasure and then guards the hoard.

— Why, it's a bandit and a thief then!

Moral indignation quite overwhelmed her now. Who were the parents of this child? Surely his moral training showed neglect, and for the moment, she couldn't avoid feeling superior in the situation at hand.

— Sure it knows how to collect the treasure!

The boy clearly felt confident, if not exuberant, in the logic of his own mind. She persisted.

— But your toy mirror is a thief, I say.

She wiped her brow with her handkerchief.

— Maybe that's the way it looks to you, but my mirror is under different laws, Cretan person. Something gives it the right to find the thing that counts. This becomes my mirror's hoard.

Following this boy's thought was exasperating.

— And what does your mirror do with its . . . its hoard?

— What it has captured becomes the treasure, naturally. Do you realize what the mirror's secret amounts to? It's in knowing what is truly the treasure and then, having captured it, to hide it.

— Wait. All the mirror can possibly capture are images. It can't take hold of the real thing or of an actual person. Anyone can see this. As for images, why, they are like illusions—they've got no substance, none whatsoever.

She had leaned earnestly toward her companion in the misty dark as she spoke, and now she was startled to observe that the figure held a grave look and appeared older than a child as he shook his head slowly at her words. There was a silence that cloaked them so that it was a while before he again spoke. Even so, he held his mirror tenderly against himself.

— Maiden of Crete, hear me. What my mirror holds is not about illusion. Do you happen to know about vision, I wonder? You see, my mirror possesses the extraordinary vision. Without it, what a person sees and understands is what is observed by everybody.

Ariadne's pulse quickened now as she became aware of some new excitement she could not have described. Her voice was almost dreamlike as she spoke.

— You are holding up your mirror toward me. Tell me, dear friend, what is it that you see now?

Slowly at first, the boy began to speak. Instead of the short childlike pronouncements, which her ear had grown accustomed to, the voice began to take on a depth. It ambled through a meadow, she thought, with a sense of spaciousness and ease that she found unusually pleasing. Now the voice took on a steady pace filled with expectancy as of a Cretan procession making its way to the mountain shrine of the goddess. She bent her ear toward her unusual companion to catch his words.

— Where is the Cretan person who was here? There is a burst of birdsong from the top branches of the old fig tree, filling the air. Whom do I look upon? Why, she is the maiden herself. How like a new flower she is that has not been plucked! She might be Artemis herself. How desirable she is. Unfettered and at ease, she is held by my mirror. Ah, it will not lose her!

The words sang in the air, and Ariadne felt gladdened in her heart. Was she found to be beautiful? Her companion had not mentioned it, if so.

As she looked toward him anticipating more of his extraordinary report of his mirror's finding, she saw that he made his way into the greater depths of the cave and was gone.

The Boy Dionysos Returns

Solitude had severely changed. Once, it had been her magical companion, leading her into reverie and fresh delight on her ramblings away from the palace of Knossos, which was her home. Abandoned as she was here on Naxos, had not solitude deteriorated into harsh isolation? Oh how lonely she was! Her spirits were low as she stood far into the cave's interior, facing the unexplored chambers. As she gazed at the stone floor, she was startled to see a small shining circle of light. As she stared, the light shimmered as though it possessed a life of its own. Indeed, it crossed her mind how like a tiny fallen moon it was, although surely less intense. It seemed magical as it held her attention. And then she heard small footsteps approaching. At once she lifted her eyes to face the small boy companion. Thick dark locks framed his lively face dominated by the great deep eyes, which were examining her closely. Inadvertently she gasped before finding her voice.

— Good evening, lad. I do not know your name, you realize.

— Greetings, lady. It's just as well, I tell you. What does a name do but fill folks with expectations? The name clamps a lid down on what a person is allowed to be. Leaves a fellow all bunched up, it does, so he can't stretch out for the life of himself. You know, maiden, I do quite like it when my name goes missing.

— Indeed? How strange. Well, how can we become friends without our names?

— You've got the problem backward. How can two persons become true friends with the name of each one busy marking out its territory?

She shook her head slowly in some perplexity, and then she spoke with sudden impatience.

— I am weary and I am lonely, little friend. Don't confuse me, please.

He regarded her at some length, and a tender look came into his face as he asked a question quietly.

— I wonder, maiden of Crete, do you like your name?

— Not really, now that you ask.

His face took on a sadness as he gazed at her, and he nodded. She went on.

— Still, the fact is that I am Ariadne, daughter of King Minos and Pasiphaë. There is a long ancestry that is alive within me. That's the way it is. Who I am cannot be altered!

Her voice was heavy as if under a great burden. Where he sat on a boulder now, the boy leaned a cheek on his fist and pondered. His question startled her.

— So you think that you're all finished, do you? You speak as if you were the last line of a story.

— Finished, yes! That describes me, I fear.

What she saw in his eyes now was not tender feeling but a smoldering fire.

— You're on Naxos, you know. What about the temple gateway then?

Genuinely puzzled at this shift in the conversation, she responded.

— Oh yes, of course you are a Naxian. Almost I forgot. Why, the gateway is a splendid stone structure standing below us far out on the headland of the island. It is beautiful, and often I stand and admire it, if you want to know.

The boy groaned aloud.

— Admire, admire—admiration is a withdrawal. I know about it. What it amounts to is a postponement!

He was thoroughly annoyed now, looking for all the world like the person on whom postponement had been mercilessly inflicted. She was aware of small stones kicked into the air by his feet as he paced back and forth. Whether he was consumed by exasperation or some darker emotion, she did not know. Now he stopped before her and gazed into her face. In that moment, she beheld in the dimness not a small boy but a man of radiant beauty. As she gazed in astonishment, his face suggested that of a shepherd coming upon his fallen sheep, tender and concerned for the predicament at hand. The figure spoke quietly and to the point.

— Ariadne, for such is your special name, *a gate is for entering!* It always was and it always shall be.

Temple of Naxos

Below her lay the deep blue sea, its waves heaving and crashing on the windswept shore. Finding her footing on the steep, narrow path, she descended toward the shore while the wind tore at her hair and her loose garment. Soon she was heading purposefully along the shore toward the dramatic headland that extended its sturdy arm into the Aegean Sea. Rising from the headland in solitary splendor stood the flesh-hued temple of marble, its great gateway looking toward the sacred island of Delos. Although she looked to the temple for shelter, the assault of the wind became even fiercer as she made her way among the columns of the *pronaos*. At the same time, like a sudden tempestuous wave, her sorrow swept over her as one abandoned. Seeking support, she leaned against one of the great columns when a voice broke in upon what seemed the silence of human desolation.

— Sister of Bull Man, you have come, I see!

Startled because she had seen no one at all, she gazed about thoroughly only to confirm that she was indeed alone. Still, she was inclined to reply aloud.

— Who calls me by this title, I ask? Alas, I am utterly alone, a Cretan woman on a strange island!

The deep male voice spoke again.

— Ah, is solitude such a monster, woman of Crete?

— Well, at one time I was in the habit of regularly longing for a bit of solitude. That was in my home at Knossos. That was before the Greek prince came on the Athenian ship bearing the image of Aphrodite on its prow . . . Ah, little did I dream how prophetic it all was or how my life would be swept up in radiant joy for a little space of time. Then I found myself on Naxos. Oh, solitude is a monster worse than the Minotaur of Crete, I say!

Now she saw the owner of the voice—a man of astonishing beauty with great dark eyes, which were softened now in their steady regard. He looked familiar. Indeed, he was not unlike the man of Naxos. On his head he wore a wreath of ivy as if adorned for some festival. What caught her like a mere butterfly in a net, however, was the slow smile that was directed on her, a smile that brought an inestimable balm to her distress. He was speaking.

— Solitude, Ariadne, is but the pause of beginning! It is your jewel. One must guard her jewel, surely.

Now Ariadne's hands covered her ears, and her distress consumed her.

— No, no! I want Theseus to return to Naxos—return and take me with him to Athens. The anguish of waiting again overtakes me!

No sooner had the old confession returned, bursting from her, than a thought found its way through the turbulence: how can I speak so candidly to the stranger? Already he is shaking his head, solemn in his demeanor, and will speak.

— That one you wait for is gone and will not return. Ariadne, do not let your grief render you helpless. I have come to the temple for the purpose of meeting you. However, I must tell you, it is not for the maiden of Crete that I have come but for the new woman of Naxos!

Her eyes were large with perplexity, and speech failed her now. The two figures regarded each other silently. Presently he invited her to join him in finding a place out of the wind, and side by side they left the temple and the headland behind to seek shelter under an ancient fig tree, its broad branches laden with still-ripening fruit. Well out of the howling wind, they sat down under the roof of branches. When he reached up to pluck a fig for her, she perceived the radiance in his face beneath the ivy garland. It was in that glimpse that recognition came, causing her to cry aloud.

— Oh, you could be Lord Dionysos himself!

    He smiled at this outburst, handing her a fig in silence. She received the fig wonderingly, recalling at the same time that the sacred image of the god was carved from the wood of the fig tree. When she had feasted on the sweet fruit, a boldness arose in her so that she spoke at last.

— My lord, will you hear me? Abandoned here on the island, Naxos has become my prison, its shores my bondage. How I desire freedom, for it is the fruit of great price! Will you set me free?

    Her plea hovered on the air between them, and the great dark eyes blinked as if a series of gateways to possibilities opened and closed, one after the other. Still she waited. When he spoke, his voice seemed to come from some considerable distance.

— Freedom is what you ask of me? What is freedom? Were you set free when Theseus took you from your native land, stealing you away from your parents, snatching you from your royal heritage? Ah, well, you came to know a new bondage, did you not—that which Aphrodite brings, she who binds us with the delights of love. Yet departing from that love, you find yourself in a new bondage, this time the bondage of painful memory of love gone astray. How is it that you say that your present bonds are those Naxos imposes upon you? The island is innocent. Still, would you have found me as companion had you not been left here?

    Ariadne tried hard to hear him out, but what he said perplexed and overburdened her weary mind. In desperation, she raised her voice.

— Oh, do listen to me! I only long to be free of all bondage whatsoever!

— From what would you be free? From the new woman of the Labyrinth's depths? Would you be free from her as Theseus is now freed? And being thus freed, would you desire to be freed also of the mysterious cup of Dionysos? I think you have not tasted that yet.

    He bent toward her, meeting her intense plea with grave concern.

— Beloved Ariadne, hear me. There is something more to consider. I tell you that *all true freedom is bondage!*

— It is a riddle. What does it mean?

— Those who are free know the close bonds of meaning. Listen to me. There is a small dwelling place that belongs to you alone. It has a doorway shaped in such a way as to admit you alone. Within this place, you enjoy a fellowship both with the past and with future possibility, and yet all this comes about in a lively present time. Destiny is received in this dwelling place that is yours alone, destiny that sketches the new way for you on the ground of earth while it never neglects its age-old knowledge.

She shook her head slowly, frowning.

— I know no such dwelling place that belongs to me!

— Never mind. That dwelling is being shaped by what you truly know and have received over the living threshold. Where else can you actually abide? Some call it meaning, although it always comes unlabeled. Nor can one depend on the things commonly said to make up meaning . . .

— It is a ghostly thing you speak of—*meaning*. My lord, but what of love?

Ariadne's response caused her temple companion to throw back his head and laugh a great rippling, carefree laughter. It brought a tentative, wondering smile to her face. Now he took both of her hands into his own and spoke earnestly.

— Ah yes, love. I have not forgotten love. Meaning cannot claim one without love, nor can human love endure long without heaven's arc of the luminous and sustained sight. Together they make up the dance of existence! Ariadne, will you join me in this dance? I must tell you now how it is. It is that my heart chooses you!

Conversation with the Man of Naxos

Two days passed before once again the man of Naxos appeared at the entrance to Ariadne's sheltering cave on the cliffs above the sea. Seeing him, she felt a rising anticipation not at all unpleasant. Indeed, her response reminded her of one who gives her hand to the other in a joyous circle dance. Nevertheless, as she moved toward the entrance, she repressed this unaccountable feeling.

— Well, man of Naxos, you have come.

He regarded her thoughtfully before uttering his enigmatic statement.

— Where there is great longing, there is a long tale that wants telling.

— Ah, if only my life were of my own making, why then I should be free. Come in to the cave, out of the wind.

He entered the high chambered room of the cave before replying.

— What is freedom but a seductress who ignores the nature of things? As for your finding freedom, it will be an arduous journey through one captivity after another, I expect, each one having a face that looks like freedom.

— Oh, I hope not. How dreadful you make it sound.

— Well, freedom is not dreadful. Hear me, Ariadne. Instead, freedom is the new wine which has been mellowed in the dark, ripened through the seasons. Nor can one demand to know its actual taste before it is poured out. Tell me, woman of Crete, of the captivities you have known. Or tell me of your life as priestess of Potnia, goddess of Crete.

— How did you know that I was her priestess, I wonder? Actually, I was yet a child when I was prepared for this office. My thoughts, my very sinews, were tamed to serve my lady. O man of Naxos, believe me when I say that I love her dearly and could not exist without her love of me.

— I believe you. Is there something that troubles you though?

— I don't know. I fear to say.

— With me you may speak freely and it won't be held against you.

— Well, what happened was that in time, even Potnia became my duty, something on which my good marks depended. Daily I must arise early and perform the rites required. These I would perform within the Labyrinth before the Shrine of the Double Ax. Never could I be relieved of these responsibilities. All I desired was a little freedom, not really very much, you understand.

    Tears were in her eyes. With his shining look, he took her measure and spoke gently as if drawing his words out of a far place.

— Dear Ariadne, listen. You really should ask for more! Why ask for such a small measure?

    The response had burst from him with passion. Having steeled herself for an unsympathetic response, she was visibly amazed and stared at him.

— Why, you have taken up my cause after all . . . You have changed! Are you suggesting that I ask for a full measure of the freedom I so desire after all? My heart fairly leaps at the thought.

— Yes, of course. The heart longs only for devotion, not for duty, which could dry you up like last year's fig. Perhaps Potnia asks far too much.

— Oh, do take care what you say of our goddess! I both love and honor her.

— Then be simple in what you do. Why not give her that love instead of so much duty? Potnia is not unknown to me. I do not think that she desires to dry a woman up. What's more, I seriously doubt that she gets much joy out of routine ministrations at her altar performed by a dried-up priestess.

Ariadne stared at the man of Naxos for some time, alternately puzzled and annoyed by what he said. Musing now, he spoke.

— Being daughter to the goddess is fitting for you—that daughter who becomes earth's fruit like grapes lush on the vine in late summer. Duty will never produce these grapes, however. Be warned.

— Things begin to appear different than I imagined them to be. What am I to do?

She spoke slowly as the shape of combat between them dissolved into thin air. With his dark eyes, labyrinthal in their depth, he regarded her quietly for some time. Drawing a deep breath, he spoke at last.

— *The season of the woman of Naxos is upon you*, the woman to whom I am inexorably drawn, for again I say that I am not drawn to the maiden of Crete. And now I must go. Farewell, Ariadne!

She watched him leave the cave, her eyes following his graceful form as he descended toward the sea. Solitary once more, she murmured to herself,

— Oh, what is to become of me!

There was a change nevertheless, she noted. No longer did her eyes search the sea for a returning Theseus. Already the Athenian hero was losing the overwhelming vividness in her heart and mind. Some subtle alteration was under way that she could not explain. How extraordinary was the man of Naxos. With this thought, her pulse quickened. Was not each look he gave her like a luminous path unknown to her? One moment she received a bounty of delight while the next he would be speaking of an arduous path. In his presence, however, she was no longer empty. This was the unaccountable fact. And how he rebuked her despair as she hugged the text of a dismal future to her breast!

Many hours had passed. Already it was evening now. Standing there in the cave, she must have lost track of time. A sound at the threshold caused her to look up, and a small cry of surprise escaped her as she saw him at the entrance, a ghostly presence. He spoke, and his voice seemed to come from a greater distance.

— Good evening, Ariadne. Do I detect a light in your eyes at last? Is hope returned?

— Man of Naxos, it is not hope for Theseus's return, for something has
  altered. Look. The moon rises behind you. For the first time on Naxos,
  my heart is lifted!
— Ah, can it be that you yet will find gratitude toward my island? Observe
  that it shelters you well, and, Ariadne, I have come to tell you that love
  is closer than you can imagine!

With these final enigmatic words, he smiled his dazzling smile,
which filled her with an elaborate forgetfulness. Now he turned and
departed. Stepping to the entrance, she watched his departing figure once
more until the narrow rosy line of the far horizon swallowed him up while
the hope that he would return lingered with her.

At the Temple Gate

Towering behind her was the steep rock face that contained
the grotto, her present dwelling place, as she wandered alone onto the
headland of Naxos that juts out into the Aegean Sea, deep blue and rough.
Viewing the majestic white gateway of the temple from the high grotto,
she had each time felt strangely provided for. Now at the gate itself, she
encountered the wind of the headland as it swept back her garment and
blew her dark hair across her face. Although the sorrow of abandonment
still possessed her, she was aware of some new measure of satisfaction.
It might even partake of joy. Her thoughts lingered on the extraordinary
man of Naxos. Thus engaged, her eyes upon the stone walkway, she was
aware of being addressed. The familiar voice held no surprise. Could it
be that she was expected?
— Greetings, Ariadne! I see that you have returned to our temple gateway.
  I never tire of its beauty and its grandeur—immortal things they are.
    She spoke lamely in reply.
— I thought I must have another look at it.
— But will a look satisfy you? I doubt it.
    He shook his head, smiling as he spoke in a hospitable manner.
— It has great power, you see—a power that has to do with receiving,
  welcoming, and also the gate possesses the power to exclude.
— Oh, I do know about gateways, for it happens that the Labyrinth of
  Crete possesses an awesome narrow entrance. It was I who showed
  Theseus how to cross the threshold of our mysterious passage. I gave

him the thread to mark his way, besides. The requirements of entering such a gateway were familiar to me, you see. Being priestess of the Labyrinth's shrine, I dared not forget these.

All eagerness faded from the voice and memory of the maiden suddenly. A voice that could have been old spoke now.

— Still, for Theseus and myself, there were no further gateways.

Her shoulders sagged as, forlorn, she stared into the distance. The voice of her companion penetrated that distance, it seemed.

— Ariadne, only look. Naxos presents its great gateway in this moment. What shall you do? Will you receive the life of my island in its fertile greenness? Or will you flee from it? The gateway poses the question, you see, the question of whether one will cross the threshold or not.

Tossing her long hair back, she turned her dark eyes upon him, and for a moment, he knew that he was faced with the heir to Knossos' throne.

— It really doesn't do for a woman to have to make up her mind so often!

The man of Naxos regarded her fondly before bursting into a peal of laughter. Now he spoke eagerly.

— Come, let us climb the path to the great fig tree. I have something to tell you.

Leaving the temple behind, they began to climb the steep slope side by side. She turned and asked with growing interest,

— It's about the god of this place—Dionysos—isn't it?

He nodded and replied as one who begins to share puzzling thoughts.

— Dionysos, god of Naxos, is god of the double gateway. Does this seem strange to you? He bears this title: *Dithyrambos.* This is due to the fact that two gateways belong to him. Ah, it is hardly possible for the human individual to choose one and skip the other.

— What are these two gates? Does each one open to a different territory? I hope that you are going to make the matter plain.

— I have no choice.

His sudden smile, as always, was like a mantle of delight. Indeed, it brought a cloak of forgetfulness that fell upon her shoulders. Nor was it without comfort. He continued.

— Often we must shepherd the voice of the god if we are to come to hear it fully. It is the voice of Dionysos that I hear. It says,

The first gate that I knew in my earthly existence was the Gate of the Child and Play. It opened upon the floor of my birth cave on Crete where I was adored by my mother and played with remarkable toys. And then I came to a tragic end, for I, son of Zeus that I am, was dismembered by the old gods, the Titans.

Ariadne had turned pale, her hands to her cheeks, unprepared for such an outcome.

— Oh no, no! It wasn't fair!

— Fairness is not in the mind of the Fates, I think.

As he continued, she wondered whether these too were the words of the god. Unaccountably, the man of Naxos spoke as one who had suffered the text he was supplying.

— Do not despair since there is the second gate. It happens that one is stricken with loss of hope and filled with bitter complaints when the way of the first gate comes to an end. Until one finds the second gateway, one is doomed to flounder and to experiment. Mostly one spends his time demanding the return of the Gate of Play, I fear.

These last words shook Ariadne, causing a cry to escape her.

— After my first night ashore on Naxos in the sea grotto, I awakened to find the child Ariadne dead indeed, I tell you! Alas, destiny is a cold and unfeeling mother! O how I long for the pulsating heart of life—love's fire, I mean. If only the pleasurable days in their seasons would come once more!

— Do not despair. Always we want the pleasure we knew to return. Not pleasure but the joy that is Dionysos's shall come, joy that is enduring while pleasure is not. Dear Ariadne. I am wondering . . . when we stood before the gate of Naxos' temple, did you hear the summons?

— The summons? No. I only know that I was inexorably drawn to the gate. Its beauty was lyrical. It drew me like a song on Apollo's lyre.

— It is true that you have wanted to flee from Naxos, yet the second gateway summons you. It is the gate of Naxos!

— The first gate belonged to the child and the maiden that I was. It has closed, you are saying. It closed with Theseus's departure, didn't it? O how difficult is the change one never dreamed of!

— Yes. But both gateways must be lived, both honored. There is no other way. It is not simple to be devoted to Dionysos, I am afraid.

— O man of Naxos, I do believe that for a moment I glimpsed my true dwelling place.

For the first time on Naxos, laughter returned to Ariadne. A deep joy filled her, and she felt the welcoming of a luminous gate that was opening. Her wise companion was speaking.

— Ah yes, the second gateway is Naxos. Indeed, it is the gate of the second way. Here on Naxos, Dionysos himself will companion you. Shall we go together and I shall show you where already the grapes begin to ripen on the vine? A labor awaits that cannot be postponed. It is the gathering, you see.

I should have thought there was nothing for me to gather, for my basket has been empty!

— The vine must be tended. Come and abide with me, Ariadne my love. You will see where the fabled wine cup is to be found!

The look that held between them was a text full and overflowing much like the wine cup itself. Together, hand in hand, they set off for the green hills covered by the vineyard.

Aphrodite Comes

Ariadne slept peacefully, untroubled by dreams of sudden abandonment, and she awakened refreshed. The sun was well over the treetops when she stepped out of the cave and descended to the rock grotto at the water's edge. Just inside the grotto, she came upon a basket heaped with clusters of purple grapes, a loaf of bread, and tangy goat cheese. What a lovely find, she thought, considering her sharp hunger, and at once she sat upon the rock floor and partook generously of the basket's contents. Only as she ate did she notice the message pinned to the basket, which read, "For Aphrodite Ariagne!" Alarmed, she exclaimed,

— Alas, this is a holy offering, and I've taken of it for myself! I wonder if this could be a sacred grotto then?

Staring into the dim depths of the grotto, she invoked the goddess.

— O Goddess, most lovely, Aphrodite, hear me! I am a Cretan woman only recently exiled here on Naxos. Why, I really don't know the island at all, it seems. Could this be your sacred grotto, I wonder? You see, I came upon this basket of food, and it never occurred to me that it could be an offering to a god. I was very hungry and astonished besides to come upon such bounty in such a desolate place. Why, I am afraid I couldn't resist helping myself. I do apologize!

Tears appeared, and she looked pale and frightened now so that she did not notice at once the approach of a radiant woman. What first alerted her senses was the enchanting fragrance on the air. Standing a few feet from her now within the grotto, the woman addressed her.

— Many an offering meant for Aphrodite goes astray, losing its way. This is hardly the first time.

She uttered a sigh. Now Ariadne, being herself a priestess, was keen in her awareness of a goddess. Gazing full on the figure, she now dropped her eyes, made the sacred gesture, and spoke in a subdued voice.

— Lady Aphrodite, all hail!

The goddess nodded, acknowledging her.

— You have something further to say to me, woman?

— Yes. It was more than need, you see. Temptation overtook me so that I partook of your offering.

Aphrodite smiled ruefully considering this and replied.

— Under certain circumstances, Temptation can be a faithful companion to a woman, for sometimes Temptation is Persuasion herself in disguise. Always Persuasion has been my friend, of course. Ariadne, you have captured my keen attention.

— Why, you know my name! I expect that those in guilt and sorrow attract the notice of the gods—as if they make huge muddy footprints everywhere.

Aphrodite smiled at this briefly. Her voice was dry as she spoke, shaking her head.

— Such persons do cease to interest me when they begin to feel *outstanding* because of these footprints. Be forewarned, woman of Crete. Did you know that Theseus carried my image and mine alone in the prow of his ship? I have been his guiding goddess, you see.

— Yes, I know. I too was carried on board Theseus's ship with the Athenian youths and maidens. He honored you greatly, my lady. I must know, what did you mean when you praised Temptation to me? Such a strange thing it was to my ears.

— Ah, must you still look deathly pale with fear? Hear me. You have tasted unknowingly of my offering. It is only human to be hungry. Now I suggest that you accept my generosity, Ariadne, and eat freely of the basket's offering. Here, I shall join you. Let us divide the grapes of Naxos! Dionysos is, after all, never far from his vineyard.

With these words, she laughed happily, and the brown crust of sorrow that still sheathed Ariadne began to fall away. The goddess looked to an approaching figure.

— Look who comes, your companion of Naxos.

Ariadne gazed wonderingly at yet another surprising arrival of the man of Naxos, who addressed the goddess.

— May I join this special company?

Smiling with grace, she answered in a way that convinced Ariadne that they were not strangers to each other.

— Of course, you must join us, and we shall be honored, for is not the whole of Naxos yours?

Ariadne gasped audibly at this statement and yet found words of invitation.

— O yes, do feast with us on these wonderful grapes, man of Naxos. Surely they were brought from some far shore by ship, perhaps even from Crete.

He smiled his slow smile and replied.

— Wrong, Ariadne. Tell me, when will you accept Naxos? Why, these grapes before us are the finest Naxos produces. As for the vineyard, I know it to be very old, its roots penetrating the far, hidden passages of earth's musings.

— Ah, a gratitude rises in me, one that has lain afflicted, I am afraid.

— Gratitude, it turns out, can hardly be rushed. More often than not, it hobbles along lamely in human experience.

Ariadne's attention was more and more claimed by a train of thought, ghostly in its contours and yet luminous, so that she fell silent for a time.

The question of the man of Naxos startled her.

— How is it, Ariadne, that your name resembles Aphrodite's own title of *Ariagne*?

— I cannot say. *Ariagne* means "most holy." No human person can bear such a name, of course. This I know.

Now he spoke idly, his voice low and musical.

— Does your heart not long to enter the realm that is Aphrodite's? Ah, the god of Naxos nurtures the great vine from which the ecstasy—the true vintage—comes.

Now he turned facing Aphrodite.

— But it is you, Aphrodite Ariagne, who alone brings love in its sweet bounty!

The goddess smiled fully into his face and then, turning, she gave Ariadne a long look of regard that reminded her of grapes grown plump and ripe.

The Cup of Dionysos

Already the sunlight streaming from the sky of intense blue cloaked the island in serenity, for the winds had grown quiet as the two of them, man of Naxos and the woman of Crete, made their way slowly down the path that threaded the old vineyard. His eyes rested on her with their own indefinable source of light as he asked an idle question.

— Were you lonely when I departed at dusk yesterday?

— I was lonely, yes. How did you know?

— Was it for Theseus you were longing?

Her pulse began to pound as his question echoed in her mind. This was the significant question, and she must answer. Only the truth was acceptable, she realized.

— At first I believed that it was the painful longing for Theseus that again assaulted me, but shortly I was astonished to find that I was mistaken. How easy it is to cloak the new, shapeless time with old dogmas of complaint! No, it was no longer Theseus's absence that made me lonely, it was yours, man of Naxos!

She smiled at him shyly as she admitted to it. At once he threw back his head, shaking the curly black locks, and laughed a great joyous laugh that seemed to go on and on, covering the silent vineyard with the music of it. At the same time, he encircled her slender waist with his arm and drew her close. In amazement, she gazed at his face. Nor had the innocence of the maiden gone missing in her. His voice was low and solemn now.

— Ariadne, my dear, what joy you bring me! Your loneliness is at an end.

— How can a heart that has been in deep sorrow remember the way to joy? I ask myself. And yet, my heart is happy. Still, when I gaze toward the future, I am troubled. What is to become of me? A woman alone, an exile?

Even as the anguished question hung on the air, his attention was diverted to a great cluster of fully ripened grapes, black as night and yet shining. It was a cluster the harvesters had missed. He stopped and gave the fruit his full admiring regard, and the pressure on her arm drew her to pause as well. He spoke, his hand cupping the grapes.

— These grapes are unmatchable. They will satisfy since it is on the solitary path that you have come upon them.

— The solitary path . . . the words chill me.

In her eyes, he saw dread and withdrawal and sought to comfort her.

— Have you not desired what is yours alone? Behold the grapes. You perceive them in solitude, in the place where all general descriptions, common expectations, and comparisons cease to possess you. Oh no, you cannot stand in the presence of these grapes of mine so long as you belong to the busy, chattering throng. I tell you the solitary place is simple and at hand, Ariadne. It is indispensable territory, so do not give it away. May it be bountiful and hospitable to you at the core. That is enough to ask.

She was silent as the solitary way took on a reality not known to her before, and her dread faded away. What she said now startled and even amused him.

— Too much solitude is oppressive, even so. I do so want to be with folks, to be in good company with friends, you understand.

He smiled and, after a long moment, nodded.

— Why not? A friend will not deprive you of the solitary way, I think. It is the path crossed by the gods, remember, and their gifts to life. Indeed, it knows the Labyrinth. One dare not lose one's access.

— Often your words comfort me, and sometimes they please and delight me, but words such as these cause me to tremble.

His response was murmured in a low voice.

— It is not easy to be human . . .

Now he arose to his feet, and his generous smile returned as he held out his hands to Ariadne. Laughing, she put her hands into his as he spoke.

— Shed the old mask called freedom, I say. It is the green world of the vine, of bloom, and the fruit that will bring you the dance and joy of living. Ariadne, are you listening? Dionysos offers you the full cup here on Naxos! Half measures won't serve.

— I would be with you alone, man of Naxos, for a freedom never known before washes over me like waves that wash the shore below us! An extraordinary thing it is. Almost I imagine the presence of an invisible spouse! It defies reason. Dimly I perceive that you, man of Naxos, have made the invisible visible to me at long last!

— Listen. Do you hear the voice of the flute mounting the air? There follows the cymbals' clashing in their age-old summons. All is invitation as the celebration of the rites of the god are under way. It is the call that echoes down the soul's long corridor. Soon its dense evocation will cause the shining world to descend over our countryside. O joy, for all captivity ends bestowing the graceful order, the steady earth pace, the eternal song, and the exuberant step! Come with me, Ariadne, for we go to the procession and shall soon dance in the vineyard of fair Naxos!

PART II

Dionysos

Dionysos—an Introduction

A strange truth haunts the god of joy Dionysos as his myths bear witness: *he is difficult to bring to birth and has difficulty in surviving on earth.* Because of this fact, he requires two births. With his first birth play enters in the sheltered world of the cave, bringing with it a participation in the flow of life and imagination in present time. Within play and its inherent satisfaction, life's tale of the moment emerges and assumes its winning shape as it summons one to a full engagement. A forgotten child is called forth, a recovery that is hardly trivial, for play comes laden with pleasure and the bounty of two realms, earth and underworld. Invading the birth cave on Crete, jealous of this son of Zeus, the Titans descend upon the babe Dionysos at play and slay and dismember him. Mother of the gods, Rhea, mourning this great loss, gathers up the severed parts of the god to restore him to life according to an early myth. Nevertheless, the god's second conception results when Zeus loves Semele of Thebes. Her tragic death results in Zeus's carrying the unborn god and bringing him to birth from his thigh. While he is still a young lad, Dionysos's life is again threatened, this time by the madness that has overtaken the kingdom of Orchomenos, where he lives with his aunt Ino. It is the god Hermes who successfully rescues Dionysos from a similar fate.

Of all the Greek gods, Dionysos is most present at festival and its joyous procession. The ecstatic women who escort the enthroned god with their faces lifted to the sky, the goat-tailed men, the cavorting satyrs, lead the procession to the piercing voice of the flute and the cries of the celebrants. Some of the satyrs and sileni are staggering, apparently overcome by the wine of the god, for held in the hand of Dionysos is the two-handled kantharos from which the mysterious wine is poured. The name of Silenos, Dionysos's old teacher, means "that which bubbles as it flows." The full draught of life is being poured out as routine consciousness is overcome, and the celebrants are swept by the eternal flow of being itself in all its renewing force. This is not an ordinary drunkenness, which in pursuit of play fails to overtake it. The erratic path these figures make portrays to the observer the immense flow of life beyond the rational mind, a path steeped in a rich-textured, nonrational kind of knowing. Play enters the scene as well, as the celebrants become participants in the luminous tide of play, which has the earmarks of ecstasy and unconsciousness.

Play at its core is a ritual participation in the strong flow and movement of life that claims one in present time. One who plays is without reflection. The cares and problems of familiar life are forgotten as a concentrated pleasure intrinsic to play emerges. For one who plays, his participation is a tale that takes shape as he assumes the role that the imagination creates. Often there is the awakening of the forgotten child in himself. Such a recovery is hardly trivial and comes laden with the meaning of two realms, consciousness and unconsciousness, earth and underworld.

What of the play that Dionysos brings? It finds its scene in the god's festival where procession and ritual give it form. The psyche of the celebrant is renewed. Instead of a repetition of one's familiar childhood, there is the movement toward ripening. A new delight in life appears following the shattering of the natural child's first relationship to pleasure. In the presence of Dionysos, play itself becomes second-born. As a more ripened manifestation, its text is rich, denser with meaning.

With his second birth, Dionysos came to participate in two realms, the human as well as the divine. He is hailed by the title of honor, Dithyrambos, which means god of the double gateway. The god himself bridges two births. It is not adequate, I think, to say he is lord of the outer realm and the inner realm, for these terms may lead to a more trivial interpretation of him as lord of external reality, on the one hand, and lord of what is felt or subjective, on the other hand. We must look to his myths as well as to his rites if we are to find a fuller explanation of the two realms.

While play brings a freeing, satisfying pleasure, it is not joy, for joy is the fruit of a certain consciousness. One must be young to play but old in order to know sustaining joy. In order to play, one needs to find freshness and youthfulness; while in order to shelter joy, one must be ripened. The central gift of Dionysos appears to be joy, and the rites of the god indicate that joy belongs to the time of harvest. On the Greek calendar, this is early autumn, when the grapes have ripened, are gathered in the baskets, and are pressed. The joy of Dionysos is a vintage gift, being the fruit of a long, arduous, and patient process that spans all the seasons. While the image of the Mysteries of Demeter at Eleusis was the ripened grain, that of Dionysian rites is the wine cup. In the rites of both deities, there is the celebration of the faithful abundance of earth itself, for earth is not merely the ground for crops. It cradles human flowering and well-being also.

What is it for the follower in the rites of Dionysos to experience the gift of the god's joy? In the course of the rites, one becomes aware that there occurs a heightened awareness in which existence itself reveals its manifold richness, bringing satisfaction and delight to the celebrant. Even so, joy appears to be bounded by human limitations of time, energy, and finite capacity. Within the experience, one becomes aware that this epiphany of joy is a fragile event. It is best expressed in mythological image. Joy is the kantharos, the wine pitcher filled with wine in the hand of Dionysos. It is the wine within the measure of the pitcher, for it is both flow and containment, the serene union of the flow and the nonflow. Such opposites are embraced in a lively and poignant awareness that serves to quench the soul's thirst. By contrast, in play, the opposites are not discriminated in one's awareness but appear to be joined in the flow of all things. The sense of individual measure is ever crucial in the rites, for the wine of the god is no general commodity to be doled out. Within the festival of Dionysos, play and joyousness alike are experienced, and both are healing states of soul.

In the Anthesteria, the early spring festival of the Athenians honoring Dionysos, a curious and dramatic course of ritual marked the three days' celebration. Day 1 was Day of the Wine Casks. The sanctuary of Dionysos in the marshes was opened for this single day only within the entire year for the opening of the large wine casks so that the tasting of the new wine could take place. Libations were poured out to the gods, for it was the Greek custom that the first drink of wine be that of the gods. On day 2, the Day of Choes, or the Wine Cups, each family received its measure of wine, and the day was one of festivity, enjoying the wine, and even comedy had its role. Although there was high celebration, the second day of Anthesteria in Athens stopped short of drunkenness, apparently, as some readiness for the third day of the rites would have made its demands on the consciousness of the celebrant. With the presence of Dionysos, it is not surprising that the dead are stirred up as well as the living, for the god is known for his connection to the underworld. As a result, on day 3, the Day of the Pots, the *keres* or ghosts come out of the graves, for the gates of the Lower Realm are opened briefly. Nameless souls, long forgotten, walk the earth for a day, and fear and dread are stirred in the celebrant. It is hardly a reunion with familiar or beloved departed ones. Not only does new wine flow with the coming of Dionysos, but the graves of past experience, darker things held in a rigid housing, perhaps, are opened with the energy flowing once again. How somber is the contrast between the Day of the Cups and the Day of the Pots! Assiduously the celebrant chews buckthorn in order to ward off ill effects, the miasma.

When we come into a fuller relationship with Dionysos, the depths of reality are stirred and a territory is penetrated beyond the familiar context of conscious life, it seems. Not only is this unconscious realm stirred, it takes on life and demands to be fed. The ancient Greek responds by retiring into his own house and gathering together seeds of various kinds that he then boils. He produces a meal in a pot. Nor does he taste it. Instead, he carries his pot out of his house and out of the city to a great rock having a cleft. Within the cleft, he leaves his pot so that the wandering spirits of the dead might be fed. One recalls that an offering of seeds to a god was not unusual in a sanctuary, the offering being referred to as the panspermia, but the seeds were not boiled.

Reflecting on the Day of the Pots, the final day of the Athenian rites, one's first reaction may be a sense of a severe setback in discovering the joy of Dionysos. Just when the long winter of waiting has passed and the casks of new wine are opened, ready to pour out their abundance, when the springs of play, of laughter and celebration, and even ecstasy once more flow, when once again one's embrace of the natural world as well as the bond to the community are present, just when this event of beauty and enormous satisfaction is taking place, the dreaded dark aspect makes its presence felt.

The Greek recognizes in the margins of his experience that this unwelcome aspect belongs somehow, and he must carry enough awareness to prepare to turn toward it, honoring it. He must use the safeguard of ritual to protect himself as he does so—the preparing of the pot of boiled seeds. Here is the darker pole of Dionysos's joy, the source of which penetrates the unknown. From the Lower Realm comes forth a vital need, a hunger to be fed by the joyous living folk, it seems. Thus the celebrant is aware of the *keres*. Some of the ghosts are identified as coming from the great flood of past time. At such a time and in the presence of Dionysos, there is a kind of marriage of life on earth and the hidden realm, which in its life has integrated our deaths. As a result, the joy of Dionysos is ripened in the ground of the great opposites.

Rhea Restores Broken Dionysos

Shortly after the slaying of the child Dionysos by the old Titan gods, the Titans, Rhea, mother of the Olympian gods, enters the deep cave and comes upon the bloody, dismembered fragments of Dionysos. Seized with horror and grief, she cries aloud.

— O ill-fated day! Who could have done this terrible deed? O Dionysos, Dionysos, so brief a time you played here before a dreadful death snatched you from us! . . . . You lurking there in the shadows, who are you? Speak, I say, for I am Goddess Rhea, who once gave birth to Zeus himself in this very cave!

Among the shadowy figures in the dim cave, one spoke and then another, measuring out the words boldly.

— We are many, Rhea, and we are as one! Like a great wind, we fell upon the miraculous cave where the new god played.

A mournful sound came from Rhea.

— He plays no more! You did this unspeakable act, then! Why, oh why, would you destroy the god of earth's joy?

— Because our strength is great. That's why. We've got the right to the power that belongs to us and was vanquished. Oh, true, we only meant to seize him and shake his gifts from him in order to get them for ourselves . . . but we felt the soft round flesh and saw his shining eyes brimful of laughter. Then it seized us, an appetite big as Dikti's cave. He must be our *feast*!

— What monstrous thing is this?

— It's that we looked close, and we saw the little fellow's main gift, and we had to have it, the dance of life! There was never before anything like it. Why, it made a golden circle about him that was a thick radiance, and as it moved, there was a whirring sound, I tell you.

— Ah, so you saw it. You glimpsed the secret of the little god. What else
did you see?

— The wool lay in his hand unwinding, on and on like the snake in the
hand of Crete's goddess. Again we looked, and he held a golden apple
wonderingly. And how could we miss what sang and whirled about the
child's head like his bull roarer toy that lay on the cave floor? It was
joy, joy that we had never known before! It spun like a top making us
dizzy with ecstasy.

　　　Rhea spoke with wonder.

— Every delight is known to Dionysos. And tell me, were you close enough
that you could perceive what it is he does with time and destiny, how
they fall from his hands like a pair of dice?

— So he had that power too, did he? That's what we want. We Titans
deserve to control our destiny once more!

— Brothers, what can you know of Dionysos's power? It is from earth that
it comes. I know. Nothing that bursts from seed can tunnel its way to
the light without Dionysos. Without him, the fruit does not ripen and
deliver its sweetness to gods and the human world. O yes, time and
possibility lie in his hands!

— Not now, Rhea. Those gifts used to be in his hands. He is dead, our
rival!

　　　Rhea summoned all the force of earth's vital, generative memory
as she cried out in reply.

— Hear me. Dionysos's death is but a knot in the great thread!

　　　Derisive laughter rose from the Titans and filled the chambers of the
great cave, echoing from the walls. In the chilling clamor, Rhea trembled.

— Do you doubt my power? Brothers, for you are my brothers, you have
been in the darkness too long. You seemed to have forgotten possibility,
which is life's sweet pulse. Go now. Leave me alone here, here with
broken and dismembered Dionysos.

— Now don't fret yourself, Rhea. We'll just stick around. No one is closer
than a brother, and in us, you've got six of them. Ha-ha!

— Go! In your presence, my power forsakes me. How your hellish grins
poison every future, it is mine to perceive. Leave, I say!

— We'll leave when we are ready, and not sooner. Besides, we are planning
to roast these limbs of Zeus's son and have ourselves the feast we've
counted on.

　　　Her eyes came to rest on the fire where the spits already were
roasting the members of the child. One small member of his body lay on

the ground outside of the flames. Quickly she snatched it up and tucked it into the folds of her garment, unobserved by the Titans. The phallus of the god was yet warm with life and unharmed.

— Tell me, brothers, which do you most desire, power or divinely begotten joy? It is a choice you must make.

— Power comes first. Next we'll devour the boy and get the great joy.

— No.

— What do you mean no?

— It won't work. It is the wrong order.

— You can't fool us, sister. We know all about power, having had it, lost it, and now gained a lot of it back.

— You may know about elemental power, but you know nothing of the god's dance of life.

— Oh, but we know all right. The thing is like child's play—all fun for a while, and then it bursts like a bubble in the spring.

— Dionysos's gift to existence is of another order. It is new, a tender thing at that. I believe that this is what you truly must long for. It bubbles and bursts, yes, but it returns and bubbles again like an eternal spring!

— That's it! That's what we want! We aren't leaving this place until we have staked out our claim to this, by Uranus, god of the heavens!

— Do hear me. You chose power first, so you will never have Dionysos's gift to life!

Glaring with rage, the Titans now took one giant step toward Rhea. Their menacing looks fell upon her like stone. Savage with frustrated desire, they reached their hands to the fire and lay hold of the now-roasted members of Dionysos. As each drew his sizzling portion to himself, there was a sound at the cave's entrance, and Rhea heard decisive footsteps approaching the scene. The moment was long and cavernous. In the high-vaulted chamber of birth and night, Zeus appeared. Tall and majestic, he stood very still as he surveyed the tragic scene. In a low voice, filled with disbelief, he spoke,

— Titans, my own kindred! Lay down the sacred flesh! You shall not touch it again!

Rhea spoke.

— Zeus, my son, I thought you would never come!

— Be calm, Mother, I am here.

Pale and wide-eyed with fear, the Titans dropped the spits of their feast and swiftly drew swords, turning as one against Zeus, their vanquisher in the past.

— Olympian, you are no more than a flea before us! See, we are six! Besides, our power is older and vaster than yours, and it has the menace of Tartarus in it—Tartarus where you thought you had banished us forever, we might remind you.

Zeus gazed at their fury and their drawn swords, shifting uneasily. The words when they came were those of the lord of the gods.

— Optimism could be a god's undoing, I grant you. What is at issue in this crisis is my son Dionysos, born to Persephone. He is the hope for life's enduring greenness, gravely needed by the human world. Without Dionysos, there is no surging pulse, no keen delight! Hear me, Titans, he shall not be banished by you!

White-faced and ghostly, their eyes large with hate, the Titans made a single thrust toward Zeus with their swords, but he leaped aside nimbly. At the same moment, Zeus stretched his arm high behind his head, took aim, and let fly the thunderbolt. A flash of lightning illuminated the cave before falling upon the old gods, burning all about them and driving them backward out of the birth cave. A trail of ashes and soot remained. Nor did the thunderbolt quit its pursuit until they were once again housed in underworld Tartarus.

Zeus knelt down and touched the burnt members of Dionysos's body tenderly.

— The murderers are gone, Mother. Never again will they touch Dionysos. Even so, it is late in the scheme of things. O broken vessel of Zeus's light!

Rhea replied.

— It is only a knot in the great thread.

— O sweet body of life's hope broken!

— Although hope is dismembered, it will rise again.

— What's this you say, Mother?

— These members that you are retrieving and holding, they are waiting.

— Waiting for what, Goddess? You speak in riddles.

— I shall have to see. I cannot yet say. Truly I perceive in these broken members the condition of waiting, however muted an expectancy!

— Shall I leave the dead Dionysos in your care and under your protection, then?

— That is my wish.

Zeus embraced Rhea and departed the Cave of Dikti. For a long time, Rhea sat before the charred remains, and sorrow returned in full force and veiled her. At last, night had fallen outside the cave, doubling the cave's own gloom. At this moment, Rhea perceived that she was no longer alone. Demeter stood near her.

— Have you come, daughter, to lift with me the yoke of this loss?

— I have come from one of the back chambers, never having left the cave where Persephone gave birth.

— In our presence, hope begins to revive, I think.

— The dead child is in your care, Mother. What will you do?

— What step would you take, I wonder?

— Ah, I should look to the human world for Dionysos's care. I would nurse a human child, oh, some offspring of human purpose, dream, and labor, who in time will assume the little god's shape and speak his thoughts. O Rhea, something human is needed to house this god, or all shall surely be lost!

— Hmm. I do remember how you in your grief for your lost daughter went searching and entered the house of the king of Eleusis to become nurse of the small prince, Demophoon. Nor was he charred when you laid him on the fire in order to make him immortal. As for Dionysos, he first must be restored to life. Otherwise, the human world shall never know him.

— I bow to you, Mother Rhea, for only you have the power to restore Dionysos to life. As for the human household, most of the knowledge available there is hindsight. It is your knowledge of earth's secrets that is sorely needed. It is a rare knowledge that, as it perceives what is to come, readies oneself for it.

— Ah yes. A future that is natural and true must be drawn out of earth's substance.

— Rhea, you possess *pronoia*, the wisdom of seeing ahead. Have you not carried our Olympian births? You are the generative one, and I am persuaded that you will be able to restore Dionysos to life. Now I leave you.

Alone now in the vast dimness, Rhea knelt on the stone floor and gazed at the charred parts of the child god. Picking them up one at a time as she transferred each one from the right hand to the left, she sang and wept and cradled the fragments against her bosom. In this way, she labored within the opaque walls of life's mystery. In time, she bent forward and set down the tender burden, and oh astonishment, there lay before her a body whole and shining in its beauty! At once she took from her garment the hidden fragment, and with the original phallus, the child was completed. In that moment, a peal of laughter tumbled forth from Dionysos, who is delight itself. In this manner did the second birth of the god come about. From this day forward, the Greeks hail him in his festivals as god of the double gateway: *Dithyrambos!*

Hermes Rescues the Boy Dionysos

Shining Orchomenos, once the dwelling place of the deep-girdled Graces, lay in deep shadow. A heaviness had descended on the spirit of its people, and the voices of poets and lyre players alike were silenced. Rising and falling upon the air as the citizens made their way in slow procession was a mournful lament as on their shoulders they bore the funeral pyres of their queen and the two young princes. Had not an unaccountable horror fallen upon them? Madness, no less, had seized the royal house. King Athamas had slain his son thinking him a deer while Queen Ino had leaped into the sea taking her other son to die. *Oh, who can withstand the royal madness?* The question hung like a black cloud over the city of Orchomenos, forsaken indeed by the Graces, goddesses of the favorable outcome.

Mercifully, dusk moved over the landscape bringing with it a faint sense of hope, as low on the hillside, a shepherd wearing a voluminous cloak, a traveler's three-cornered hat, and carrying a staff led a small boy through the deeper dusk of a small wood. Putting a finger to his lips, the shepherd spoke quietly.

— In a few minutes, we shall reach the city gates. See this goatskin in my hand?

— It is very black.

— Right, black as the oncoming night. As we come in view of the gates, I shall signal you to hunch down on the ground on all fours like a live goat. Then I shall cover you completely with the goatskin. No one must be allowed to recognize you as nephew of Queen Ino. And do not speak or whisper until the gates are well behind us, do you understand?

The child Dionysos nodded as he admired the goatskin with delight.

— Say, I think I'll like being tricky. Can I keep the goatskin afterward then?

— With your knack for getting into trouble, son of Zeus, you may have to . . . . Now, down on all fours. Here goes!

    The dark hide transformed the lad so that in the faded light, he easily passed the sentry of the gate. Not until they had left Orchomenos far behind, however, did the shepherd god Hermes remove the goatskin and permit him to go upright. Dionysos gazed back at the now distant dark hulk of the city.

— I never want to go back there, not ever. How did you happen to come and rescue me, Hermes?

— Zeus summoned me. He recognized the madness that afflicts the core of a person. Time was short, and we had to get you out.

— Is madness catching, then?

— Oh it is. It happens like this. One person, or else a handful of people, forsakes the workable ways of earth. They are regarded by others as odd, that's all. Ah, but add more people with the same distortion of mind and nature, and the madness becomes acceptable, even becoming the model for everybody. How relieved I am that I reached you in time, boy.

    The lad turned to Hermes wide-eyed, intense.

— Are you very sure that I am not mad?

— I am certain that you did not succumb to the royal madness. One more day with the mad queen or your caretakers, and it might have been tragic for you.

— It's a funny thing, Hermes, but I heard that an oracle has said that I shall be lord of the vine and of madness.

— Already you have learned this?

— Yes. Now the "lord of the vine" part I like, for I shall like trampling grapes with my bare feet and seeing the river of purple juice flowing out and then pouring it into the big clay jars to set into the ground up to their necks.

— Hmm, so that's how you see it all.

— The part of the oracle that frightens me, though, is the madness part. Oh, I don't want to go mad!

— Look, Dionysos, it won't be like the royal madness. Rather, it will be a gift that you alone bring to life. It is a possession of mind and senses by earth joy and by that luminous abundance in present time that will be recognized as the ecstasy of Dionysos! The city's madness put you in grave danger, you see. That is why Zeus said to me, "Do what you must but extricate Dionysos from the royal house of Orchomenos and take him to a safe place!"

The lad was one to catch on quickly. Hermes perceived this at once.

— What you say is that there are two kinds of madness, the bad sort and the good one that people want.

— There are several kinds of madness, actually, but yours, yes, is the kind that people have great need of. It is good like the sap of the tree, the juice of the vine. You shall measure out your gift to life with the kantharos.

— What is that?

— The small pitcher you shall hold in your right hand.

— Will it be big enough? It sounds too small to hold what I've got.

— Yes, it will be the right measure. The important question is, will the hand that holds the pitcher be steady? This depends on you, naturally.

Now a faraway, rather dreamy, look came over the child's face.

— Say, what will it be like if I pour wine out of my pitcher all over Olympus, the home of the gods!

The notion quite delighted his fantasy. Hermes, though amused, spoke with authority, much like a skilled charioteer taking the reins out of the hands of a beginner as the horses begin to rear up.

— What a child you are yet. Look here, boy, you shall not rain wine down on Olympus! Besides, Olympus doesn't need it. Your pouring forth is toward the human world. Do not forget that your mother, Semele, was mortal, for you shall forever be connected to the human world.

The mention of his dead mother made Dionysos sad.

— I miss my mother . . . Does being part human mean that they might not let me on Olympus, though? After all, like you, I'm a son of Zeus.

— True. You know, I shouldn't worry if I were you. The divinity of a son of Zeus doesn't require having a particular, prestigious address.

— But Hermes, you forget that I don't have any address at all!

It was with a sob that the last words fell out. The god of the road turned and knelt beside the lad, comforting small Dionysos before he spoke again.

— I realize this and that it is wretched for you, lad. Be comforted, though, knowing that I won't leave your side until we find you a new home. I promise! I am taking you to Mt. Nysa where the lovely nymphs of the high mountain glen will give you a home.

— Will it be nice? I mean, will they want me?

— Yes, yes, to both questions. There are no better nurse companions to small gods growing up than these gentle nymphs. They are as extraordinary as the nymphs of Mt. Ida, who raised Father Zeus.

A slow smile spread over the face of young Dionysos that was soon followed by a joyous peal of laughter in which Hermes himself joined.

Dionysos and His Toys

Two figures walked along the steep slope of the mountain in the solitary wilderness. Nor would the identity of the two gods have suggested itself. Had there been an observer, that one would have observed a shepherd wearing a voluminous cloak and a broad hat moving with consummate skill among the rough stones with a young black goat at his side. But there was no observer in sight. The escape out of the madness that overtook the city of Athamas and Ino was accomplished. Hermes the shepherd regarded his young companion thoughtfully and murmured, "Yet another escape for the lad!" He bent to young Dionysos.

— This rocky cavern has turned up conveniently, I'd say. Shall we stop here for a little rest and nourishment? There are no pursuers in sight, but it's advisable to nip into the cave quickly . . . . Ah, it's cool and dark here, and notice the echo of the voice off the ancient stone walls. Best keep our voices low, lad.

— *Your* voice, Hermes. I wasn't talking.

Hermes hugged his little brother.

— Well said. Are you feeling a little better now that we've put distance between you and the royal house of Athamas?

Dionysos shivered involuntarily.

— Madness took over that place, Hermes.

Hermes nodded as a look of sober concern spread over his face.

— The madness that strikes at the core of the kingdom can soon reach everyone, I fear. We got you out in the nick of time, lad.

— The madness didn't just strike. It started a long time ago. Didn't you know?

— What do you mean?

— You see, what happened is that my toys began to lose their *play*. That's when I knew that something was wrong in the kingdom.

The boy's information startled him.

— Tell me, how was it when the play went out of things?

— You know about my nice bright wool thread that was in a soft ball, don't you? I liked it because it was soft and light as a feather, and yet you couldn't break it because of its being so strong. It would unroll, gradually making a luminous path sort of the way a good story does. When it would begin to unroll, I knew that it was beckoning to me, and I would laugh and jump up and follow it. We were a pair, Hermes.

— What you describe reminds me of the thread of Ariadne, the maiden of Crete. She gave the ball of her thread to Theseus so that he could find his way into the Labyrinth and out again.

— Say, maybe my thread is the same one. Come to think of it, it did look *used*.

Disconcerted, Dionysos frowned while Hermes smiled at this reflection.

— What is evident is that your thread possesses a history that stirs within it. Does it still make a path in the dark like a thin stream of moonlight?

— Of course. See, it's the color of wheat when the late summer sun is on the field. That's why it gleams in the dark. Do you know what I like best about my thread?

— I hope you are going to tell me.

— Well, it does what it does by *bending*, see? That way it creates all sorts of shapes and new paths as it goes along.

The description caused the shepherd god to grow pensive as if gazing into the future.

— You know I believe that you will be depending on this thread of yours in the dances and processions yet to come.

— No, Hermes.

He looked sad.

— No? Why not?

— Because something has happened to my thread. One day when I tossed it gently, it failed to unroll or to make any path. Instead, it fell all in a tangle!

— Alas, one feels abandoned when the beckoning path is lost!

Dionysos nodded solemnly, as if childhood had this moment slipped from him.

— I had always trusted it, and it had always been there for me. We would unroll by the hour, and still there was a supply left in the ball of thread. Hermes, it was a grim day when my thread only made tangles!

Compassion made the god of the road silent as he gazed at the extraordinary boy.

— Yes, I know about that, actually. So what did you do?

— I put the thread aside and turned to another favorite toy of mine, the golden ball. Always its brightness would comfort me in the dark when I would be all alone.

— And the ball's shape, does it please you?

Remembering, Dionysos became excited.

— Nothing was as round and smooth as my golden ball! I took it to bed with me every evening. Under the covers, my hands would move over it slowly, and I never once found a bump or a flaw. Then the question would always come . . .

— A question you say. What question?

— It was in the chant I made up and sang softly: "O ball of mine, where do you begin, and where do you end?"

The question was the last thing Hermes expected. There was surprise in his expression.

— And would you get an answer?

A flash of disappointment passed the boy's face.

— No, no answer at all. My ball just kept on in its circle path, on and on and on. But do you know what? I just realized something. I'm glad it turned out like that because I don't much like beginnings and endings!

Hermes gasped audibly at this last statement as Dionysos's own beginnings and endings came vividly to his mind. As Hermes is wont to do, he moved to rescue what he could out of the situation.

— Look, Dionysos, lad. The ball has neither beginning nor ending, being perfectly round. So this makes it complete and strong as well. It is just possible that the golden ball knows about what is *forever*.

— Maybe so. I loved to hug it in the night and did this a lot when the royal house became frightening. Yes, my golden ball is strong.

— So where is it now?

— That is what I have been going to tell you. I can't find it. I looked everywhere for it just before I hid from my mad aunt in the bushes.

His shoulders drooped now, and the light that had shone in his eyes clouded over. Hermes slipped an arm about his shoulders.

— Never mind. The ball will find you again, I believe. After all, the two of you seem to belong to each other. In fact, I am certain of it. Still, the separation is something to be borne a while longer.

— Hermes, listen. This is the second time that all my toys forsook me!

The horror of that earlier cave on Crete overtook them. Hermes spoke.

— O the horror of that first time! Do you mean to say that you can remember what happened? You were only an infant.

— I remember. I was playing on the floor of the great cave with all my toys around me. How splendid and magical they were too. Suddenly the old gods rushed into the cave with their faces whitened with ash and shouted, "He's ours! Grab him quick and don't let him go!"

Grief momentarily seemed to bow Hermes down in the long silent pause. At last, he spoke.

— When the Titans seized you, an enormous loss was suffered by the gods and the human world as well!

It was the lad's turn to comfort his elder Olympian brother, and he did.

— Don't grieve anymore, Hermes. I'm back on earth again and grown into a lad already.

Do you remember when you brought me as a baby to the house of Athamas and Ino?

Well, the first thing I did when I got there was to gather all my toys around me.

Hermes smiled now.

— Your faithful companions, right? Here, have a chunk of goat cheese and some bread. You need energy for our journey ahead. When you've eaten, I hope you'll tell me about the other toys.

Still wearing his black goat disguise, Dionysos accepted the ripe goat cheese, the pungent odor of which filled the cave, and a hunk of dark bread to go with it, realizing that he was very hungry indeed. Once satisfied, he resumed his account of his fabled toys.

— This particular toy is altogether different from the thread. It's the bull roarer. I love to swing it above my head faster and faster in a circle until the bull wakes up, see? You know when he is awake because he begins to roar deep in his throat, but not too loud.

— Are you telling me that this toy actually opens the gate to the voice of the bull himself? That's quite incredible. The bull's voice, like the golden thread, comes from Crete and is steeped in ancient memory.

— I only know that it would be very scary if you should meet him face-to-face on the path and you got his look instead of his voice!

Hermes gazed into the distance as if trying to perceive some force that was lost.

— Ah, the Bull is the fierce natural king. He is uncompromising, being a powerful god of earth. The folks of Crete saw in his eye the mysterious dark corridor of the fertile knowing.

— About my bull roarer, I began to feel the bull circling about me. And do you know what? It turns out that he wants to play.

— So you have the bull for a playmate, it seems. Well, that may be the circle of your protection. Strangely, it is widely said that you possess a bull foot.

Hermes, still incredulous, shook his head from side to side while Dionysos at once gazed down at his feet looking for the evidence. Hermes suggested that the bull foot might be an invisible one, which, in any case, bestowed an essential connection on him.

— Where is the bull roarer toy now, Dionysos?

— It was there with me in the royal house until it stopped working and things changed. I would begin the fast spinning circle in the air, swinging it with all my might, but the voice of the bull had fallen silent. O Hermes, he was my only playmate that had a *voice!*

A loneliness cloaked the lad, and his own voice trembled.

— Look, when this journey of ours has delivered you safe from the general madness, you'll see that the bull and his voice will return. Up now, lad. We must be on our way while it is yet light. Besides, this cave could be known to the king's pursuers.

Again the handsome shepherd of the great cloak and his shining black goat were on their way, moving in step, ascending the narrow path of the mountain, and the two fell silent as they climbed.

As night descended over the hills and a cold wind had risen, the two sons of Zeus took shelter for the night within a rock grotto high above a mountain stream. Hermes saw to it that the weary lad was supplied with food and drink and a blanket. Under the god's tending, Dionysos was beginning to lose the look of shock and desolation he had when Hermes had located him in the bushes near the house of King Athamas. He was looking comfortable indeed stretched upon the stone bed the grotto offered, and he called to Hermes, who made his bed in a yet darker nook in the hollow grotto.

— Hermes, are you awake?

— Naturally. Didn't you know that I am god of the gateway between sleep and awakening, as well as between entering and going forth? So why do you ask, boy?

— Because I'm wide-awake, and I want to tell you about my other two toys.

— Well, I hoped that you would get around to it.

Certain that his companion was listening, Dionysos plunged once again into the realm of his magical companions—the toys he received in infancy.

— There's the top, you see. From the first time I watched it spinning, it was wonderful.

You know what it looks like to me? A funny round fellow without a waist. Although I never located its head, I found its mind right away. That was no problem.

— The top has a mind, you say?

— It does. All it thinks about is that there is nothing finer to do than to spin! I am sure of it because of the way it at once begins to whirl about in a sort of dance, see? At first I thought that spinning must be a sky thing to do.

— How so?

— Well, if you hold a little wheel up into the wind, it begins spinning. That's a fact.

Still, I found out in time that my top is not a sky thing, not at all.

— And how did you figure this out, lad?

— Through the evidence. All the time, the top keeps its single foot on the ground. It never quits being a ground thing. What I've got is an earth spinner, Hermes, and it makes me laugh every time I watch it. And something else, it doesn't ever want to go anyplace else because, unlike most folks, it so loves the spot it's in! Haven't you noticed this?

— Actually, I am beginning, thanks to you, to perceive the top's nature. I also notice how like your own nature the top is. Before long, you will be honored as *the god of the dance of present time,* I expect.

Dionysos overlooked what sounded to him like a digression, continuing his enthusiastic description of his top.

— There is something a person can't explain. When I bend my ear toward the whirling top, I hear it humming to itself. It must be so happy. Don't you think so?

— Curious about humming. It opens to a different kind of time for some of us, a time that is brimful and sustaining. One takes care, not wanting to disturb it.

Now Dionysos, sitting up in bed, looked at his brother in amazement.

— Hermes, I didn't realize that you already knew about my top!

— Oh, but I've seen it, and I've heard the humming. After all, you and I have journeyed together before, little brother.

The boy's pleasure slowly drained from his eager face, and a sadness, even desolation, was returning. He shook his head numbly before he could speak.

— About my top, it doesn't dance, not anymore. And worse, the humming is gone. When it tries to begin spinning, it plops over instead.

Silently he drew the top from his pocket and extended it a little so that Hermes might see it. His words held despair.

— It's gone dead, see? It is just an object!

For the first time during their long trek out of the house of madness, Hermes showed a concern bordering on alarm.

— Ye gods of Olympus! I had no idea that the affliction of the house of Athamas and Ino might assault the toys of Dionysos. It seems that this crisis is large, even engulfing. Alas, it is deadly. Ah, lad, your joy can have no feet, no hands, no voice without your very own intimate toys. This is clear to me. It is late. Get some sleep now and be thankful that for the present, we have the hospitality of this excellent rock grotto.

With these words of the god of the road, both fell silent, and presently sleep overtook them.

The day was cold and overcast while a strong wind howled through the low trees on the steep slope. Like a wild charioteer, the meltemi was driving the waters of the Aegean Sea before it in a fury. Hermes regarded his young companion anxiously. He saw that he was not only travel-worn but also forlorn, like one who is unclaimed. Hermes spoke quietly at his shoulder.

— Today this great cloak of mine is going to have to shelter both of us, for we have no choice but to be on our way. Look at it this way. The journey that will restore the true play and the joy once more to gods and the human world can afford no postponement, none whatsoever. Let us be going, lad.

Together they made their way on the rough path of the hill, lowering their heads against the fierce wind. Dionysos had to raise his voice to be heard.

— Where does our journey end? I hope you know, Hermes.

For the first time, his voice registered a doubt.

— I know. It ends at Mt. Nysa. There on a high plateau hidden from all observers dwell the Nysian nymphs. They are splendid ladies. You are going to like them, and they shall care for you with affection. They'll be your nurses. You'll see.

Dionysos was silent taking in this new information about his future. After a pause, he asked the question that haunted him.

— But what if the madness strikes them, what then?

— You need have no worry, none at all. The nymphs are well protected against human madness. The nymphs will shelter you. They are going to keep you safe in a place where always you are recognized and honored as yourself, son of Zeus.

Dionysos smiled now, altogether reassured. This portion of the path now gave some protection against the wind, and Dionysos returned to thinking about his toys.

— There is one more toy that I am missing, Hermes. It is my best treasure of all.

— The fourth, yes. I wondered when you would speak of its fate as well.

— It is my mirror. It's odd, but I don't even call it a toy. That's because it doesn't fit any group or any labeled drawer. Back in my birth cave on Crete, it was the first treasure I picked up and made my own. Holding it in my hand, I remember gazing into the mirror the very first time. Why, I was astonished!

— How so? Explain yourself.

— I'll bet you can imagine how it was. I looked into the little mirror, and I saw that I was so beautiful that I could hardly stand it!

Hermes laughed heartily. When he started to speak, laughter again overtook him.

— Well, there was nothing amiss in your perception of things even at that early time, I must say.

— Almost at once came the terrible happenings, though.

The silence was solemn and taut that held him now as he recalled his death by dismemberment and later the death of his new mother-to-be Semele followed by his birth from Zeus's thigh, and a few years later, the madness that overtook the house of his childhood. Like a goat on which a flood of water is poured, he trembled and shook greatly. Hermes laid an arm around his shoulders, and what he said pierced the gloom.

— You've had more than your share, boy, but I look at you and see that Dionysos is well and the joy of life is close by. Now, what happened to your first and last toy, the mirror?

— The mirror was the first of my treasures I tried to find among my things when I moved into the house of Athamas and Ino.

— And did you find it?

— No, not ever.

A look of loss and displacement was there. Piercing Hermes' heart was the realization that the mirror must be restored at all cost.

— When you were a baby on the floor of the Cretan cave, you beheld your god face in the mirror when you looked the first time. I am convinced of it. When that extraordinary vision is lost, it can take a long seeking before one can restore it. Did you see anything else in the period that the mirror was with you?

How swiftly the small son of Zeus passed from sorrow to delight, it seemed.

— I did, Hermes. Once I saw the faces of mountain nymphs, smiling and tender, bending over a child's bed. Another time I saw a circle of women bending and swaying in the dance, and I thought I could hear cries of ecstasy. Oh, and, Hermes, once I saw you in my mirror. You were wearing your big woolen cloak and your broad traveler's hat. Come to think of it, you looked exactly as you look right now!

— My traveling attire, no less. It serves me on all legs of the journey, as a matter of record. That includes the present one, of course.

Connecting his mirror to the present moment was not a path the boy was ready to pursue, however.

— There is something hard to describe about things in my mirror. They seem to come from afar, for one thing, and they are edged with a kind of light that always makes me content.

— Your mirror must be the luminous window to a world where dance and play flourish, and joy, vulnerable though it be, comes.

— One day in Aunt Ino's house, I found an old mirror—not mine, you understand—and I was terribly excited. I carried it off to my room so I could gaze into it, hoping to see those wonderful folks again.

— And did they come to that mirror?

Dionysos shook his head numbly.

— No. Only darkness was there.

— Ah then, here was the sign that the human madness was approaching, I imagine.

The eternal images must be caught in their radiant stillness in order to be present to your very own mirror. It is when the luminous stillness goes missing that the context of the radiant gods also goes missing. In the house of Athamas and Ino, this stillness had departed, you see. That was the beginning of affliction, of madness . . . That place is now far behind you, and we need not speak of it again. Pick up your feet now, lad! Remember the gift of the joyous step because it is yours. Why, we are going to reach Mt. Nysa before this day is gone.

— And, Hermes, when we get there and I make my new home with these nice ladies—the ones with the smiling, tender faces—will I find my wonderful mirror once more?

Time seemed to stand still within the delicate question, sustained on the crisp mountain air. Hermes turned his look full upon him and smiled before replying.

— Ah, Dionysos, I do not hold the oracle of Delphi, you know. That is Apollo, of course. Still, I fully expect that your extraordinary mirror will return to you. After all, in it lies one of your splendid gifts to life!

Dionysos laughed, and Hermes saw that the shining light had returned to his eyes.

Dionysos and the Nymphs

Having finished their long journey from Orchomenos to Mt. Nysa in far Thrace, the god Hermes and the child Dionysos gazed about themselves at the high green plateau they had reached. It was encircled by a woods where the nymphs of Nysa surely must dwell. As they sat resting on a boulder, they were surrounded by the immortal ladies, their voices filled with pleasure as their attention fell upon the handsome child, whose large black eyes regarded them with curiosity. At once, the nymphs set about to make their two extraordinary guests comfortable. They prepared a simple feast from the wilds. They made a bed for the child in a sheltered spot and began at once to introduce him to the life of the far pasture. After a brief lingering in which he shared a meal with their fair hostesses, Hermes took leave of his small brother fondly, giving him into the hands of the nymphs who were delighted to be nurses of young Dionysos. Now they comforted him in his tears at Hermes' departure. In a short while he was telling them about his former life with Athamas and Ino in the royal house of Orchomenos. They inquired of him eagerly,

— Oh, what was it like for you, a young god, living in a house with human persons?

He thought about it before answering.

— Well, nymphs, it was a little odd, you see, for it was all about *tomorrow*.

— What do you mean by that, lad?

— The human persons were full of their plans. Aren't plans mostly *tomorrow*?

— Now that you mention it, yes. So what was it like in this household?

— They would speak always of what they were doing at the moment in order to make the next thing they had in mind happen. It was like this. Learchus, the one to be the next king, would call at certain houses at the beginning of the year. When he mentioned the fact to me, he did look bored, so I asked him why he did this. He said,

— Why, it's all a part of the plan, boy. Soon I'm going to be king, and that's what I live for.

I pointed out that that could be a long way off and asked him a question.

— So what about today, Learchus?

— What about it, son of Semele?

How come he couldn't see the sense of my question? I cried out then,

— Today is the best time of all! I don't ever want to lose today, Learchus!

My notion caused him to slap his knee and laugh heartily. He patted me on the back, like a dog, before sizing me up.

— I'm thinking that today is best for you because it's clearly all you've got, Dionysos, you being an orphan. Poor little fellow! But look at me, lad, and you're looking at the future of Orchomenos.

Now I'm not without a stubborn streak, I expect. At least I was determined that he see what's true. My voice was excited as I spoke then.

— Look, Learchus, don't you see that the future is a ghost? It doesn't matter if it's a royal ghost. How can you put all your hope on a ghost? What I know about today is that it has a body. You know it's there. You can feel it.

Learchus smiled at me indulgently and began to hum a little tune, idly. He began to back up what he believed with evidence, it seemed.

— Just consider the queen, my mother. Queen Ino lives for her plans. We make the future with our plans and preparations, she and I. Why, tomorrow is not ghost: it is the confident path we have taken! At your tender age and with your tragic background, I don't expect you to understand this. I'm aware that you've had the floor drop from beneath you when you were a mere baby.

O nymphs, his words set me to trembling!

The seasons passed, each in its leisurely stride on Mt. Nysa, and Dionysos was no longer a child. He had grown slender and tall, his youth pressing the threshold into maturity. One day, Nymph Melissa found him gazing afar off, and she took a seat at his side before speaking quietly.

— I believe that your sight is beginning to draw away from our mountain abode, Dionysos. Already I see you a great kouros, that youth of irrepressible spirit who strides forth into life, his eyes luminous and adream.

— Ah yes, Melissa, it is true that these days my eyes are always trying to pierce the distance.

— Soon you will leave us, I believe.

— Alas, the thought saddens me! You see, there is a summons I am aware of. Could it have originated on Olympus? I must respond, and yet I long to take this meadow and all you nymphs with me. I do not wish to part with you.

    She considered for a long moment.

— Ah, but already you have the secret that we implanted in you, and it will be your companion.

— The secret, Melissa?

— Yes. We nymphs tend the floor of life, as earth herself decrees that we must. What we have invested in you is confidence in the true and natural ground of things.

— So this is the rich bounty I have from you nymphs—confidence in earth . . . Yes, the gift is incomparable. Until Hermes brought me here to Mt. Nysa, all I had known were the perils of being ever on the edge of existence. Confidence is a modest name you give it, however. Why, it brings me joy as well! As a small child, I despaired at times of ever possessing joy.

— Dark roots have been your beginnings, for strange is the path to great joy. Do you feel rich now?

    The question caused him to grin happily.

— I am indeed. Come, let us walk along the border of the woods.

    Melissa joined him, and they walked in silence for some time, musing. Now he spoke with some excitement.

— What is joy anyway? Although it feels at first like strong pleasure, it is not the same, I think. Pleasure soon subsides, expires, for it is a fragile mortal thing. Whether it will return is always a question. But joy is of a different origin. I believe that it must be held hidden in Mnemosyne, Memory. Oh, I do strain to perceive it better. It appears to be a full, fragrant bloom whose roots, long and dark, penetrate the core of existence! People wait for joy as they might wait for a beloved familiar face. Yet when joy does come, the expected face does not appear. Instead, the face of joy astonishes us like a face seen for the first time. What appears is an illuminated face full of life, and yet it appears against a dark background. Ah, how long have I been musing alone with my thoughts? Melissa, are you there?

— Here at your side but soon to take leave of you.

— Before you go, tell me this: what shall Dionysos become when he leaves Mt. Nysa and his beloved nurses?

— O Dionysos, you shall be the god of earth's joy!

Companion of the Maenads

The journey had been long that brought the god Dionysos and his devoted women companions, the maenads, to the boundary of the Edonians' kingdom in Thrace. The dusk that was settling thickly over the wooded hillside was a comfort to their weariness as they sat down to rest within a small clearing. A question haunted them: will these people of the far northern region welcome us in our joyous street procession carried by the music of the flute, the clashing cymbal, and the cries of the celebrants? And how will they regard our holy rites of summoning Dionysos? Ah, memory is painful, for in some places, these rites were scorned. Among the maenads, Lysippe leaned forward and spoke, addressing the god.

— I for one should be happy to remain here in this secluded wood, my lord. Here we are able to make our devoted dance and the rite that calls Dionysos to earth again.

Dionysos, holding the pine branch thyrsus now upon his knee, smiled at Lysippe.

— Avoiding all observers—is this your desire then?

— Oh yes. For safety's sake, I mean.

He bent his ivy-wreathed head considering this before replying.

— There is that in our rite that was never meant to have observers. The outpouring of the heart must be sheltered from all appraisal, whether harsh or mild.

— So, should we not keep away from the city of the Edonians? It is certain to be filled with observers.

His gaze was toward the city now as he spoke.

— What is the observer of which we speak? He is an outsider, one who is walled off from this deep life that I bring, one who has never known the satisfying stream that flows from my wine cup, I believe. Ah yes,

Lysippe, as you say, it is not easy to encounter the observer. Yet he too thirsts for life, you see.

In the small circle that surrounded the god was the maenad Arsinoe, who shook her abundant dark hair in protest.

— Surely the procession of Dionysos is for all eyes to enjoy! It is not a hidden thing, Lord Dionysos.

— What you say is true, Arsinoe, for the rite possesses two faces. One is its tangible human face which is ecstatic in celebration while the other is its hidden face. It is this one which remains luminous and unfathomable.

The third maenad, Theoclyia, was a person of practical mind who attended well to the details of the reality that was at hand. That she now passed a hand in front of her face as if to shoo a fly away appeared to express her approach to the problem. She spoke simply.

— Frankly, I truly fear the Edonians. Their king, Lycurgus, is known to be far from a gentle, reasonable man. I doubt that he offers a friendly gateway to the gods.

Her look remained troubled while Lysippe returned to her original suggestion.

— You're right, Theoclyia. So why don't we perform the rite here, well outside the city?

Dionysos smiled ruefully at Lysippe and Theoclyia. As he spoke now, a loneliness having a pervasive chill cloaked him.

— Am I not known as the *god who arrives*? Always I desire that the human community greet me. How can I deny the Edonians this opportunity of giving me hospitality? After all, Zeus himself is lord of hospitality, *Xenios*. The heart's passion to receive and to welcome resides happily in hospitality. Unless hospitality is given, how can my gifts be bestowed, I ask you?

Lysippe persisted, her face anxious.

— God of the arrival, what if they refuse you? What then? I have a dark premonition . . .

— Alas, Lysippe, we take that risk, don't we? If one requires a guarantee of safety, then one would not have come on this journey, surely.

The three maenads drew together in one movement as if banding together for what was to come, and their faces seemed held by a solemn quiet as the branches of the trees over their heads swayed in a sudden gust of wind. The god's look was tender as he watched them. As if the wind had carried the energy of some shift in things, Dionysos's voice took on a change now so that when he spoke, one felt the lilting spirit of the flute.

— Come now, I would reenter those morning hours when you arose and began your circle dance! For a time, your voices were silent as your nimble feet moved in barefooted steps on the mossy ground. The rhythmic movements of your upraised arms and swaying bodies were like speech too delicate to be uttered. O what satisfaction lies in that dance! The observer went missing, fortunately, and so no judgment was made, no comparisons. From my seat, at its very core I perceive this dance, for is it not an essential dwelling place of the heart's history, of its poignant longing?

The god gazed into the far distance before continuing.

— What do you know? The rite becomes an open scroll to me! Suddenly in my reverie, the maenads' voices cry aloud, "*Liknite*, come to your cradle! O Dionysos, come and be born again!" I look, and I see you lift the sacred winnowing basket cradle above your heads, as though offering it to the sky with your repeated cry.

Dionysos fell silent as if in sustained reverie, and the women pondered his words and sighed in some secret satisfaction. It was practical Theoclyia who spoke.

— Each time it is the same: we cannot know whether you will actually come to your cradle and to our tender care again, or not. How intense is the waiting!

Arsinoe mused still on the circle dance.

— Again and again we return to the circle dance, seeking your presence. How strong and unbroken it is. Why, it claims a person, and she becomes a necessary link in that circle where none holds a winner's place. How strange it is to realize that held within the circle dance, I am myself, yet enjoy a bond as one who is ever at home!

He nodded almost imperceptibly.

What you describe, my companions, is a true hospitality to Dionysos in present time. Nothing, no gift of mine, is real until it enters present time. Neither is your desire for me real until it happens. And remember, I cannot be the god of riches unless I arrive somehow! Within the circle dance, this deep knowing comes upon you.

He regarded Lysippe thoughtfully, his sensuous face in repose as a question took shape.

— Lysippe, didn't I see you standing alone with a small rabbit held against your bosom? On your face was a look of intimate satisfaction, I think.

Lysippe dropped her eyes. Her voice was low when she spoke.

— The circle dance finished, we dropped our arms, smiling, and turned to walk in the woods. That was when it happened. I fell behind my companions, the vision of Dionysos still upon me, when I came upon the rabbit.

— Ah, then you perceived the rabbit that is beyond the rabbit, it seems. This is the one you have come to know, I believe.

Her eyes brightened as she responded excitedly.

— Yes, yes! Ah, that wild creature that must hide away, that fears the whole world—she who would rather die than be seen or hear others' assessments of herself! Always she must look for the lower, denser bush that can hide herself. Only by being in her company, though, have I discovered that her appetite for shoots growing out of the earth is so great that she will take enormous risks in order to get a small supply from that wondrous green world!

Now Lysippe blushed as a maiden who has revealed more than she meant to. The god realized that her account was not complete, however.

— There is yet another fact to be told. You caught the rabbit. You interrupted her narrow existence and brought her human feeling, didn't you?

— Yes, my lord.

— The creature will never be the same!

He smiled at the look of wonder on the maenad's face. Now he turned to Arsinoe, who had listened to Lysippe's account in amazement.

— Arsinoe, I saw you while hunting on the mountain slope take a lion cub captive. You gave the club your breast, I believe.

— Yes, lord of the double gateway, I admit it. It happened when, strangely, I was exhausted with my tasks.

— That's it, you see. The lion cub is ever at play, and what engages us more than play? How sad it is when we lose the gateway to it. Too many tasks cause a person to be tense and anxious, distant from play, I fear.

Momentarily, Arsinoe appeared to be claimed by the chasm that gaped between work and play until the slow, dazzling smile appeared on the face of Dionysos. His words were especially for her ears.

— Remember that you have nursed the lion cub, who has the secret of play. Most important, Arsinoe, you must never forget the deep laughter that belongs alone to my cup!

Dusk had settled over the wooded hillside now while a deeper moist darkness cloaked them under the wide-branched trees. Dionysos spoke to his small company now.

— The time has come to take our rest, for tomorrow we enter the city of King Lycurgus.

Encounter with Thetis

Under cover of night, Dionysos descended the stony slope below the fortified city wall toward the rough sea below. Now he entered the heaving waters and made his way swiftly to the sea's floor as all manner of creatures of the depths observed him with curiosity. His face troubled, he pursued the watery path, black as the underworld itself, until he reached the high arched entrance of a vaulted sea cave. Stepping upon the threshold, he called softly into the dim interior.

— Thetis, are you here? O Thetis, I have come!

He waited, calling upon his own rhythmic patience, for was he not accustomed to the long and demanding season of the grapes' ripening? Light footsteps were now heard, and the lovely nymph appeared within the cave's entrance, her face registering astonishment.

— Why, can it be you, Dionysos? Welcome to my house! Tell me, to what do I owe this extraordinary visit? Surely my place is not on the route to any of your festivals.

Her question served to puncture his somber condition, and once again, his slow, dazzling smile returned like a forgotten sun.

— You have always been en route to the significant happening, dear Thetis. Were you not on the way, I should not have come, not now given the urgency of things. What turns out to be on one's way only reveals itself as life proceeds, wouldn't you say? It never gives advance notice. Ah well, so be it. I am happy to be in the presence of the nymph so dear to the gods.

Thetis lowered her eyes with acknowledgment, leading him into the dim corridor of the grotto.

— Perhaps you will explain how it is that your path leads you here. When the great gods have called upon me here at the bottom of things, they were usually in jeopardy of some sort.

— Alas, jeopardy describes my predicament well enough. You see, I thought that you might help me, Thetis.

Thetis pondered his words solemnly before replying.

— If I can, I'll gladly help you, Dionysos. What has happened?

They had reached a cool inner chamber, and now she threw a soft purple cloak over a large boulder, offering it as a seat for him while she sat down on a stone ledge facing him.

— Lycurgus, the powerful king of the Edonians, has rejected me and my maenad companions in his city. He managed to capture three of the devoted women and cast them into a dungeon, for he was infuriated at the sight of our procession and festivity. The maenads all cried out to me to flee, which I did, knowing that, had I been taken prisoner as well, their hope for the cup of joy would be lost.

— What a shameful deed is Lycurgus's! Isn't the music and dance in which your followers invoke you a thing surely made of delicate soul fabric? But then the Edonians did not get a chance to observe the dance, I imagine.

— Oh yes, they did.

— So they have a sense of what the king has stolen from them. Had I been one of your devoted women, I would have trusted the sacred thyrsus in your hand to bring me protection, I believe.

Thetis's face was thoughtful while a dark foreboding shone in his eyes.

— But, my friend, I tell you that the thyrsus and I were helpless before the Edonians! It was as if some vast hostility arose up against us.

— Ah, I see a glimmer of truth.

— What do you see?

— I see that what Dionysos brings about—that summoning of the soul to be free, to be possessed of life's dance, and to partake of the festive peace—why, that requires *hiding*.

Dionysos was on his feet, a shining look returned to his eyes as he took in what the sea nymph told him. He nodded, speaking.

— Sometimes the rites do take place in the shelter of a woods, you realize. Yet there are times when we must hear the deep summons of a city's heart as well. Hearing such a human summons has taken us to different cities with my festive procession. Thetis, how can this ecstasy of mine be hidden, I ask you, and yet brought to the core of a city's life?

The god spoke with passion, but Thetis was not to be defeated by the question.

— You must find the way to hide it, to hide this extraordinary happening. It is you, Dionysos, who in the last analysis must look after the eternal vine and its vintage! Again and again your gift suffers from being easily trampled, dismembered, or banished! Hiding is the art you must find, I am convinced.

Dionysos let his breath out in a long sigh, winding as a labyrinth. He was shaking his head as he gazed at her in wonder.

— I realize that you speak as the dweller of the great sea cave. All that is spacious and deep and hidden would seem to be your domain, Thetis.

She replied with a tone of rebuke.

— You have no time for the luxury of wonder and perplexity. O yes, I love my dwelling place in these sea-given chambers. If I did not, I should not be Thetis. Come now, my chambers themselves may instruct you.

— Is that an invitation? If so, I accept with gratitude.

He was smiling, his brilliant glance holding her. She nodded that he should follow her at once, and they continued through the narrow passage to the next room of the cave. At once, he commented on it.

— I must say that this chamber is low-ceilinged and rather constricting compared to the one where we sat, which was vaulted and grand.

— You can feel the change, can't you? This room is a narrow and exacting place because it holds a person exactly in place, not free to move here and there and to pursue the many things. A task takes on significance only by one's spending time here. Close attention it requires.

Dionysos groaned audibly before giving his own view.

— Were I to spend any time here, I would be like the ox that is yoked to the plow! Thetis, freedom is very dear to me indeed.

She smiled indulgently, it seemed.

— But surely the task presents first the yoke of the undertaking. After all, Athena created the yoke herself, the Greeks say. Without the yoke, one gets nothing done, nothing at all.

— So this is the place of work. When is the time of Dionysos, I ask you?

— Afterward.

— Afterward?

Thetis smiled at him, idly wondering who was the teacher and finding her present role odd indeed. Now she spoke eagerly.

— Oh, I see that the freedom that is yours is a thing of generous strides, loud summons, rhythmic feet invoking the earth to the flute's song, and the great delight. Still, it is the narrow room that comes first, or the place of the yoke. This is the way that I perceive.

Slowly they were making their way again in the cave's corridor.

— Nymph, you speak the truth. Ah, and now we enter another chamber. What's this? I see that it is very long, very narrow, and it winds about. I do believe that it reminds me of the writhing of a serpent. Can this be the Labyrinth? Are we on Crete?

Thetis laughed.

— A labyrinth, yes. Crete, no. Not only does earth create the great Labyrinth but the sea has its own. In the realm of the shining waters, all is path.

— Ariadne herself would be at home here in this chamber, I am certain, for she knows the path that has the continuing movement.

— I too bear witness to its turnings and its inexorable pull forward on the way!

They reached yet another chamber, one with a very low entrance, making it necessary to bend low in order to enter. Standing within the chamber, Dionysos gazed about himself, looking astonished as he did.

— What an awesome place is this with its exquisite throne! Here you are queen, are you not, Thetis?

— Yes. However, standing here with you before my throne, which has never been challenged, I somehow feel an abysmal sadness!

As he observed her, he saw the change in her face.

— What is this grave sadness? Is the burden I have brought so heavy then?

— The dungeon which holds fast the maenads in the kingdom of the Edonians haunts me. The darkness that women suffer is especially acute for me here in the Queen's Room. Here what I sense is magnified, it seems. If only the three maenads could join me here in my dwelling place, their sorrow would be greatly lightened!

The two immortal companions fell silent, and the sorrow that hung over the chamber was palpable. It was Dionysos who broke the silence.

— I have come to your ancient place of refuge in their stead, Thetis. I seek a refuge for all that is mine, that it might not suffer either demeaning or rejection. Do you understand? How exposed the maenads are to every encounter, every hostile word or act! But your chambers have revealed a way of protection. I see it now. How I desire that the devoted women come to know the wisdom of your chambers, Thetis. Here they will find the deep and abiding shelter that you know well.

— Hear me well. The realm of the sea holds a mirror to the soul's life in the many rooms where knowledge is unspoken. Hiddenness is its key.
    Dionysos mused aloud now.

— As I experienced the life of these chambers, have I not been sheltered and comforted? Almost I would say *feasted*. An essence never to be seen with the eye is the hiddenness of Thetis!
    She questioned him as they now stood at the arched way between her cave and the sea.

— Will you return to the imprisoned maenads soon and take them my gift?

— It is a rare gift indeed that I have received from you. Will it set them free?

— You shall see that it will bestow upon them a new freedom and delight that possesses its own enigmatic shelter!

PART III

Athena

Athena—an Introduction

Athena is a more richly layered presence in Greek consciousness than has been realized in our times. Manifesting many levels of thought and action, she startles and puzzles the modern mind. Familiar contemporary categories for feminine being do not accommodate her. What proves especially disconcerting is Athena's extraordinary prominence in the Greek vision of the divine. Although her fellow Olympian gods acknowledged her authority and wisdom, on the human scene she most frequently enjoyed the audience of a single individual sought out in a time of crucial need. The fact that in myth we encounter her most often as guide of the hero illustrates this characteristic action. Worshipped as Promachos, goddess of war; and as Nike, victory; as Ergane, the worker; and as Pronoia, she who sees ahead, owl-eyed Athena was highly honored throughout Greece. Wise Solon hailed her in Athens as "Mother of our city."

Unquestionably, however, Athena's primary aspect was Parthenos, for it was the eternal maiden who for centuries evoked from the Greek soul a radiant response. It is not surprising that her great temple on the Acropolis of Athens is the Parthenon. As Parthenos, she is unable to be duplicated. She brings with her the context of the fresh threshold to be engaged, for the maiden archetype is a carrier of *the first time* as it emerges from the earthly nature of things. What possessed the ghostly reality of possibility moves across the threshold of happening when Athena is present. The immediate critical situation is illuminated, and there enters the human condition a measure of joyous expectancy. As she manifests her attributes, she might well be called *goddess of the next step*, and a lively step it was.

Certain images of Athena haunt the imagination. Her zestful stride has been captured well in ancient sculpture. The presence of the shield of Athena evokes the assurance of an invisible protection. The spear in her hand may introduce its own familiar narrative of Athena's decisiveness as she strikes the facts that matter in a situation, holding these in focus until the human individual is able to undergo the requirements of resolution. In her great festival, the Panathenaia, she was robed anew with the saffron peplos, finely woven with significant scenes of the encounters of the gods and the Greeks. In this manner, Athena presented the enduring text of Greek life as penetrated by the forces of heaven and earth.

Throughout the mythological and historical accounting of this great goddess, two aspects of Athena's essential nature are distinctive. One is her central *passion of caring.* The other is her capacity for *intimate participation.* Although the latter in particular defies description, both these aspects suggest a depth of feminine being that is an important source for the human soul. Athena, in short, proves to be indispensable.

Zeus's Headache

The gods of Olympus were known not only for their beauty, their grace of movement, and their powers; a serenity of countenance distinguished them as well. For this reason, it was a grim and alarming time when the countenance of Zeus was altered by wracking pain. Alas, he was stricken by a headache of great intensity. The first long day of his suffering led to yet another day of hammering pain. Through light and darkness, Zeus supported his head in his hands while the gods trembled with each of his deep groanings. In those fateful days, there was no peace to be had, not in any godly bosom.

There were those among the gods who remembered an earlier time when Zeus's action shook Olympus. Then Zeus was married to Metis, goddess of wisdom, and one day she disappeared. All Olympus waited anxiously, but she failed to return. Certain of the gods approached Zeus and questioned him, "What has become of lovely Metis, your queen and spouse?" Zeus gasped at his companions for some time in silence before his reply came with an abysmal sigh, "Great Uranus and Gaia warned me that an offspring of Metis would surpass me, who am lord of Olympus." Saying this, he turned aside while Poseidon and Demeter stared at each other with growing concern as memory of an earlier age haunted them. Vivid was the image of their father, Kronos, watching the approach of their mother, Rhea, with her newborn child in her arms, only to observe Kronos's swift taking up of the child, opening his great mouth, and swallowing his offspring! Only young Zeus, with the aid of Rhea's deception, had managed to escape the fate of his siblings, and indeed he survived to put down the Swallower while at the same time freeing his siblings back into life. Such was the grim memory that burned in the questioning look that Demeter and Poseidon now turned upon Zeus. Meeting their gaze with candor,

Zeus replied simply, "Yes, it is true. *I swallowed my pregnant wife, Metis!*" At once, there descended over the Olympian circle a pall, as though banished Kronos, the Swallower, had returned among them.

The cooling waters of the river Triton drew him to Crete, and Zeus sat down now on the shaded green bank. Hermes, sure-footed, his stride rhythmic and assured, had followed him at a little distance, for he sensed that Zeus did not welcome a companion. Some time passed on the secluded river bank before a thundering blast of pain rocked Zeus's head, blinding him momentarily and causing him to cry aloud. Immediately Hermes reached his side.

— Alas, Zeus, Father! What can I do? It grieves me to see you so afflicted.

A look of grateful relief passed over his face before he gasped his reply.

— Go and find Hephaestus and bring him here. Quick! And, Hermes, thank you.

— I go at once. Hold only, I say.

With these words, he was gone. Swiftly he traveled to the far isle of Lemnos in the northern Aegean Sea. The god of the forge was emerging from his work in the cavern when Hermes appeared at the entrance calling his name urgently.

Hephaestus was astonished to see his brother.

— Hermes, is it you? Strange, but I heard my name called out of great distress while I was still working over the fire of the forge, but it was not your voice, surely. What's up?

— Zeus summons you to come at once to Crete to the bank of the river Triton. It is not a bad idea to bring along your ax, I'd say. I'll lead you to the spot.

— My ax, you say? Are there trees to be felled, or something worse?

Hephaestus seized both cloak and ax as he spoke and fitted his round cap firmly on his head.

— Not trees, craftsman. What I fear is the felling of a deathless god. Make haste!

Their faces set in grave concern, they set forth southward over the now rough waters of the Aegean for far Crete. When they had gone in silence for some distance, Hephaestus turned to his companion.

— Tell me what this is all about, Hermes. You appear to have been a witness to some dire predicament. After all, a craftsman like myself needs to know what he is supposed to be crafting. Surely you see this.

Hermes smiled and nodded.

— Here you have it in brief: Zeus is gravely afflicted. You see, he has a torturing headache with blasts of pain not to be described. He simply sits on the bank of the Triton in anguish, waiting.

— This is beyond belief! Great Zeus afflicted! What am I to do? I am no healer!

Hermes shook his head from side to side.

— In a recognizable crisis, one can have his strategy ready. Ah, but in the great crisis, familiar strategies do not work and one is without instructions, I think!

Hephaestus groaned.

— You're no help.

A flash of an idea marked Hermes' face briefly.

— You know, it is just possible that when you enter the strange temenos, you will know what to do.

— What temenos will this be?

— The temenos of Zeus's ordeal. It is a temenos that is just ahead, and it summons us both . . . . Look at the bank just beneath the plane tree there.

Hephaestus trained his gaze on the spot to which Hermes pointed.

— There he is! That's Zeus! He is rocking back and forth holding his head between his two hands and moaning, I'd say.

Swiftly the two gods descended to the plane tree on the river bank, and Hermes led the way.

— Father, we are here!

— Ah . . . h, at last you have come . . . This pain is all too human, I tell you. Still, it recounts creation when day is wrested out of the abyss of night.

His voice faded now, and he closed his eyes. Hermes, clinging to a plank of hope, commented.

— Then the whole world awaits the creation to emerge out of Zeus's pain!

Zeus signaled to Hephaestus to draw close, and the craftsman stepped to his side. Zeus's words, unmistakable in their urgency, were gasped now.

— Hephaestus, all rests upon you now.

— O Father, my father, I'm at a loss! I'm no surgeon, and what can a craftsman do for such affliction?

— Be calm. Forget my anguish and perform the deed. Now is the moment. *Give my head the skillful stroke of your ax!*

Exhausted, Zeus fell silent, closing his eyes. The ax hung limply in Hephaestus's left hand while his face showed a pallor of horror and disbelief.

— Zeus, such an act is too great for me to perform. Surely you see this.

An impatience threaded through a new intensity of energy that arose in Zeus.

— Are you not my son . . . you who work arduously in your Lemnian forge? Olympus honors you as our great craftsman. Look, I am your metal. Do with me what you must!

His face grave and attentive, Hephaestus gazed upon Zeus as in a reflective voice he continued.

— I wonder, must you hammer me out on the anvil to reshape me, who am lord of the human realm? Must you hold me over the blazing fire? Oh, by your wise hand I shall be changed!

Hermes cleared his throat, drawing their attention.

— Zeus, well are we familiar with Hephaestus's credentials, but let me remind you that time grows short, judging from your hard panting. Hephaestus, the urgent question is not one of skill or instrument but whether you can bring yourself to do the act. Can you? I ask. Rather, will you set about it?

The silence was taut in which the craftsman regarded Hermes, and an enormous weight was upon him. Zeus addressed him quietly.

— From birth, your mother, Hera, found you imperfect while you with your irregular feet bestow perfection and unsurpassed beauty upon what you create at your forge. Such a strange contradiction . . . As Hermes points out, time is running out. Birth consults neither god nor man when it lays its claim upon time.

Hermes shook his head, frowning.

— Best cut short the words and save your breath, Zeus. I fear that at best you will prove less skilled than a woman at this. Hephaestus, this may be your finest hour even though you cannot foresee your handiwork. Alas, all is postponement!

With Hermes' words, Zeus gasped in pain.

— Hephaestus, why do you hesitate? As for dread, no Olympian can afford the luxury of it. You have the courage . . . Spare no pains to accomplish your work. *Only create me who am your father!* My son, raise the ax!

His shoulders sank, and his head was bowed, but his quiet voice was defiant.

— How can I take the ax to Father Zeus's head? Never can I do it!

It was the comforting voice of his father he heard now.

— I tell you that the stroke of the ax began in me well before this hour. It began with knowing that my head alone must be struck. My son, finish quickly what is under way!

Hermes stepped toward his brother, laying his hand on his arm to reassure him.

— Your aim is flawless and your arm is strong. Hephaestus, raise the ax! O Olympus, what awaits the world with this keen stroke we do not yet dream of!

Now Hephaestus shifted the ax to his right hand and slowly began to raise it high over the head of Zeus where he held it suspended for a long moment. His forehead was beaded with sweat, his eyes shadowed with grief. In a particularly intense spasm of pain, Zeus cried aloud, "O make haste!" In that fateful moment, Hephaestus let the ax fall precisely on target. When the two gods witnessed that the skull of Zeus sustained a deep and unfathomable crevice, they cried aloud in anguish. As they gazed, there emerged now out of the crack a maiden. Full grown, robed, and armed as well, she ran zestfully down the crest of her father's head, setting foot on the Cretan earth with a cry of great joy. In her right hand, she bore a golden spear. Calm at last, his wound healed, Zeus was no less astonished than were his sons as a hearty fine laughter came from him and was joined in by Hermes and Hephaestus. Heaven and earth shuddered at this extraordinary birth while the sea heaved up its waters exuberantly. So it was in this strange manner that the inimitable Athena came to birth.

Athena and Hephaestus

The days of the Panathenaia festival were under way, splendid with procession and music, the races of ephebes, and the drama of the torch runners while, most glorious of all, the sacred ship on wheels had borne as its sail the exquisite new robe of Goddess Athena. Her very ancient wooden image within the temple now wore the new robe, a peplos that hung in thick folds, its many scenes of Greek life woven in fine detail by the women of Athens. The admiring observer would have sighed in sheer pleasure to behold the peplos' fiery hue of the saffron crocus.

The moon was dark on this August evening, the temples all but indistinguishable upon the hill of the Acropolis. Across the Agora below the sacred hill, a stillness hung over the marketplace, a stillness that swept up the small rise where the temple of Hephaestus stood, a veil of withdrawal cloaking its stately columns. Within the depth of the deserted temple, the god himself looked down from his tall cult statue, taking note of the palpable emptiness, his eyes falling upon the altar fire lit by the torch runner's low but steady flame. As the god gazed, the fire leaped up as though fanned by a gust of wind, although no breeze stirred.

The temple was no longer empty, for a dark figure now walked back and forth, turning his head to acknowledge the altar's lively fire. He himself appeared to be illuminated by some unaccountable light, and as he walked, he limped. He was a swarthy figure with a torso that was muscular and powerful. The heavy brows were knitted, and the altar flame was mirrored in his intense dark eyes. At once the moonlit silence was shattered by his voice, although he spoke in a quiet enough manner.

— Well, I've waited until waiting may have become my highest skill,
  patiently observing her descent from one of those three great temples
  that bedazzle my view of heaven every day! I thought repeatedly, "Surely

she will come. Athena will pass this way and stop to pay honor here to the god who, after all, was midwife at her birth." But has she come? No. No indeed. Can she really be ignorant of my feeling for her? Or is this something she scrupulously avoids? I've had this discussion with myself time and again, and it wearies me.

He fell silent for a time until once again the fire crackled and the flame leaped up. It reflected in the god's eyes like a blaze of gold. He nodded, smiling slightly.

— That settles it. All this waiting is at an end. I am going to her!

Swiftly he removed his triangular helmet and laid his hammer and tongs safely aside before setting out upon the Sacred Way that had borne the day's procession to the oldest temple on the rock of the Acropolis. Nearby an owl hooted and was answered by another a small distance away. Reaching the high temple plateau after a steep climb, he leaned against a large stone to contemplate the old temple, its stately form ghostly in the darkness. It pleased him to envision within the temple the goddess's wooden likeness adorned with her new robe, the peplos. As his eyes penetrated the darkness, he observed a movement outside the temple entrance, a flutter of dazzling yellow, rather like a tide of crocuses glimpsed at winter's end. He waited motionless while the graceful movement rounded the Porch of the Maidens and was moving directly toward the rock against which he leaned. It was Athena herself! As she approached, he discerned on the exquisite new peplos the scenes of the loves of the gods. The garment shone like moonlight. Out of the waiting dark came his own voice now, speaking in a gentle manner.

— Greetings, Athena!

— Why, Hephaestus, it is you!

She was astonished. Whether it was the nocturnal hour she took into account or his turning up at her place was not clear. There was a smile in his voice when he spoke.

— It is flattering that you recognize me even in the pitch dark.

The two figures stood facing each other a yard apart. She did not drop her eyes once to his crippled foot as Aphrodite had done, embarrassing him for his lasting affliction. Instead, chin lifted, she met now his fiery gaze for a moment before lowering her eyes modestly. Were they not long friends? She spoke remembering this.

— How could I not recognize you, Hephaestus? It was you who, after all, made the bold and skillful assault upon the head of Zeus so that I was born!

Is this the way she imagined it happened? he wondered. He was uncomfortable with her summary of the momentous event, whose memory caused him to tremble.

— Assault on Zeus, you say? I assure you that Zeus had implored me to relieve his bursting head pains with a stroke of my ax. It was an act of pity, I'd say.

— Still, an ax is an ax . . .

In this moment, Athena's words caused an enormous guilt to engage him.

— My very own father . . . why, I cleaved his skull in two! It was an unthinkable act, and I was truly in anguish, Athena.

— Things had already gone too far, was this not so? There was no way out but to take them a bit further. I see this, Hephaestus.

The old scene continued to haunt him.

— When I entered, answering Zeus's summons, I found him bowed down with his painful head held by his two hands. All was in the hands of the Fates. There was no way to alter what must happen, you see.

— Wait, Hephaestus. What is this you say? Would you have stopped my coming to birth if you could have done so? Athena aborted . . . was this your keen wish in that hour?

He was smiling at her now as he took his time in examining her every look and gesture with pleasure. Now his voice was tinged with amusement as he asked his question.

— Does it matter so much to you what feelings I entertained toward your coming into the world? To tell you the truth, neither Zeus nor I had the foggiest notion of what would be the consequence of the dreaded ax stroke.

— Not the foggiest notion, you say? Ah, but was there not an oracle that prophesied my coming?

— Well, yes, you are right. There was. Still, an oracle is easily forgotten in the hour of extreme crisis. Besides, of what use is distant wisdom when the problem at hand requires some immediate hammering out and the skillful stroke, I ask you?

Athena shook her head slowly but not without some private amusement, it seemed.

— Hephaestus, the forge is ever with you, I can see. Is it that you would set about handling the highest work of the gods with your tools or else not at all?

He regarded this as a simple question and spoke not without dignity.

— Naturally. How else? My handiwork is sought out constantly, as a matter of record.

Athena's right hand flew to her mouth, and she appeared startled.

— I will never make light of your work, smith god, for it is handsome indeed and greatly admired by all, gods and human individuals alike. Still, I implore you to consider that the crisis of Zeus we are talking about was my birth. Am I a thing of metal to you to be violently wrenched from the ground of Zeus, then to be hammered and shaped over the fire of your forge?

Her large gray eyes held a fire now as they fell on Hephaestus, who was taken aback and could not answer at once. When he spoke, it was as if, after traveling side by side, they had reached a far lookout place.

— Of course not, Athena. You know me better, I think. There are many who see in you the bright shield of Zeus carried by the heroes of Greece. There is an important recognition there. As for me, from the moment I laid eyes on you, I beheld Parthenos, the eternal maiden of singular beauty and dense soul! Nor were your stride and strength inferior to that beauty. You were like a shining waterfall. Oh no. I saw nothing of metal in you . . . only everlasting woman, real as flesh. In that moment, I knew that neither hammer nor anvil could ever touch you, you who are neither man's nor gods' handiwork. In that first moment, I loved you! As for your unusual birth, you are worthy indeed of Zeus's great wounding, I tell you!

Athena's face was soft with wonder, and she smiled, relaxing her former wariness. A silent pause fell between them. Hephaestus, feeling a pleasant fire rising in his veins, spoke.

— Come, walk with me on the sacred hill in the dark of the moon, will you? Athena plus her new peplos—what a treasure to explore!

He fingered a fold of the beautiful garment, holding it out to study one of the intricately woven scenes. She watched with delight the absorption of the great craftsman in the women's handiwork as he surveyed it with an uncompromising eye. At last he nodded.

— I believe that this is the finest handiwork the women of Athens have yet wrought for their queen goddess!

She smiled with satisfaction.

— I feel an enduring gratitude to the women, you know.

  She and Hephaestus were now walking side by side on the path at a leisurely pace that claimed the two of them while even his limp was integral to its pleasant rhythm. Athena continued.

— I have taught the weaving women, you know.

  He shook his head with some disbelief, it seemed.

— Always I think of you as you appear in the temple of the Maiden, wearing a helmet and holding your spear erect. You a goddess of the loom and needlework? Impossible!

  She smiled as if indulging a child his fantasy.

— The sculptor of that cult statue was a man, I remind you. A man would hardly pay attention to the thread in my hand if he knew that I could lead the city into battle, would he? He would regard shield and spear as the equipment more necessary to the city.

— Being male, I must persist, I'm afraid. I cannot comprehend how and when your work with the cloth comes about, Athena. Explain, will you, as one craftsman to another?

  They had stopped to rest, and now the goddess rose to her feet and began to pace in the shaded spot, quietly collecting her thoughts.

— True explanation is a circuitous thing, surely, for it involves life's unfolding. Let me tell you how it is when a woman approaches me. Whether she is yet young or more mature in years, I perceive in her glance that it is the maiden who rises and dances there. Attentive to this happening in her, I wait, for surely no woman knows me except through the everlasting maiden! If she is not summoned like a spring singing out of the rock, then the woman can have nothing to do with me. And although she may spin, weave, and embroider, it is not my work.

— You amaze me with this account. But yes, I expect that it would have to happen in this way since you, Athena, are the everlasting maiden Parthenos. Not to walk in the vision of this maiden is not to perceive you. This explains the many exquisite *kore* statues dedicated to you, those maiden figures left as gifts among the columns of your temple. Tell me more about this handiwork.

— When the *kore*—the maiden—rises within the woman, a certain radiance falls upon her that was not there previously. It is the beginning of a tenuous time, for in this state, the woman is tender and is easy game for what would exhaust her radiance. She may be naive toward this bounty that falls to her, you see.

— Although these are not happenings in my realm, I can guess what follows. You insist on making these women your priestesses, keeping them here on the sacred hill and away from the marketplace below. In this situation, are you not like a mother with the safety of her daughters uppermost on her mind, keeping them safe from a man's touch?

— No, no, Hephaestus, never. Naturally I expect my priestesses to attend to details in the temple, but I've no desire to separate a woman from the marketplace or from that life that presses in upon her! Actually, this is one of the temptations of the woman in this tender state—a longing for a cocoonlike existence. This she must not embrace, for it is not my way of life.

Hephaestus was observing the mobile feeling on her face, which, like a magical text, moved out of dim corners onto a somewhat luminous trail before him.

— Are you not called Promachos? She who is in the forefront of battle? Certainly you lead the way into life and the world fearlessly. Makes me wonder even more how the women you speak of can image you as a spinner and weaver. Why, I've seen you move before the Athenian warriors like the bright point of your spear, and you know well where to set the wound. Tell me, Athena, do you truly relish a good fight?

— How can you ask such a question? Don't you know me? No, I don't relish battle. I am not like Ares in this respect. True, I draw close to Nike, Victory, who companions me. She draws me forward so that I will undergo the battle and all that it exacts for the sake of the brave and needed resolution of things. O yes, it is the resolution and the tranquil condition it brings about that draw me.

With his powerful and expressive arm about her waist, the creative god drew the goddess closer as he pondered her account of herself, and they walked in the silence broken only by the stirrings of nocturnal creatures. He regarded her as she mused and saw that she was contented. At last he spoke.

— As we descend the path, tell me about your beautiful peplos, this one that was the recent gift of the people during your festival. The peplos draws us once again to weaving and the cloth. See this scene on the side fold that I have drawn out? By Zeus, here's a whole tale boldly told in threads of many colors! Look. Here is a woman at a loom holding a large finished piece, and she looks pensive. Ah, could this be Penelope?

There was surely no greater compliment to her robe than to have so great an artist examine it with delight, Athena thought. She smiled warmly.

— The same. One can tell that Penelope's radiant beauty has drawn many suitors. But we know that it's the loom that saves her. It was her weaving that came to provide her very own tapestry of time and love—a protection against hearing the pleas of her suitors.

— Hmm. I'll bet that your hand was in on this. Homer thought as much.

Athena gave a shy laugh.

— Let us say that I was always close to Penelope, who faithfully held down the home place while the journey of Odysseus consumed a large portion of their life.

— Penelope's look is pensive. Yet there is something else, I believe.

— Now that you mention it, yes. There is a tentativeness manifested in the weaving, isn't there?

The two friends gazed at each other as if observing time in those fragile moments that disturb trust and cause uncertainty. Hephaestus pointed it out plainly now.

— So you see it too. Penelope has woven death into her piece, the death to come of Odysseus's aged father, Laertes. See how the cloth accommodates it within the work of the rhythmic loom. Here is the passing of a great force, the progenitor. It is no mere closing of a man's single deed or a single lifetime. Within Penelope's cloth, Laertes is loved and explored in a way that evokes some greater script, while vivid colors flow like the dance of his life. In yet another part, the weaver moves upon the somber path of his passing, a path that begins to accommodate the loss and sorrow.

— And yet, Penelope's tentativeness persists. It looks like she has completed the funeral robe. Why wouldn't she show satisfaction in this, as an expert weaver would in finishing the project?

Athena pondered her own question before offering her insight.

— It is the turning point, the moment of crisis, I think. She has accomplished the resignation of what was long needed and loved, and she has paid the wages of grief. Penelope is at the dangerous moment, I believe.

Her summary of things startled him. His question was blunt.

— What is this moment then?

— She may triumph in a way that won't work for her, that is, if she drinks in the power that Laertes leaves behind, the masculine heritage. If she should seize this lordly power as her own, thinking it to be her new freedom, all is lost, I fear. Truly this power cannot hold her freedom.

Hephaestus breathed a deep sigh, relieved that Athena would not ask that Penelope be paid back for what she had endured in her life.

— Athena, I believe that we see this crisis alike. Only if Penelope takes care of this lordly power by seeing to it that it is (1) in good condition and unspent and (2) held waiting, in reserve, is Odysseus's return possible. Well do I know that there exists no spacious, golden place for a man to come to, be he god or mortal, unless a woman hollows out the way to it.

Athena showed astonishment at Hephaestus's statement, and then she smiled as she echoed his words.

— Woman hollows out the way to a golden place? What you say is wise, and I value your unusual perception. Look again at the handiwork of the peplos. See how Penelope appears to ignore her rightful triumph achieved through her art? See how in this scene she is now unraveling the whole of it! Ah, and there is another scene. Here she sets about the task at the loom as if she were just beginning!

— Come now. I'm not easily fooled by a woman's tricks. She is but playing for time, Athena, playing against her suitors who await her in the main hall of the house.

— O Hephaestus, hear me! A woman always has suitors taking many forms in her life and bidding to take her over, body and soul. What she does for protection is not a trick, however. It is the only way. When a woman is hard-pressed so that life appears unbearable, I would say, "Have you a woven piece of your own handiwork which you treasure? Take it up and now consider that it is unfinished after all. What you must do is to set yourself to unraveling the whole of it. Only then can the new beginning get under way."

Hephaestus shook his head as he took in what Athena was saying.

— Difficult counsel at best, Goddess.

— Wait, Hephaestus. Do not turn aside. The thread must undergo once more its rhythmic dance in present time under the woman's hand. Then the cosmos again will hum as it is enlivened. Ah, but Penelope understood, as a woman must, that she could only weave using her very own thread. As for that thread, it is given but once.

Hephaestus took in this account of Penelope's weaving with raised eyebrows. Superb craftsman that he was, he dealt in the bronze of hard fact with the result that any feminine fantasy having to do with thread left him behind.

— My dear Athena, how extraordinary you are and how pleasing to my mind and senses! But I tell you that I for one should not be able to endure beginning after beginning. Truly, I am no Penelope.

   Athena showed some alarm at this admission.

— Oh, but don't you see how it is? The new beginning is not the same as its predecessors. It is as new as your next artistic act when the shield you have been making is finished.

— How can it be the same, I ask you? I acknowledge the finished shield. I do not destroy it. Surely it were ruthless to counsel the destruction of good work! As craftsman god, I should not countenance it.

   Both hands enclosed her cheeks now as she replied in a gentle voice.

— Hear me, my friend. I too abhor destruction and have high regard for excellent work. Think about how high upon Hymettos in winter the water freezes in the small stream so that crystals form designs in the ice. All is still, beautiful, complete. But spring comes, and the stream flows again, and the crystals are no longer to be seen. Is this destruction?

— Of course that is not destruction. Yet when the handiwork representing long and devoted labor is undone, this is another matter.

— It is with passion that I love the handiwork of the women. This is why I shall keep it ever in process. First in order, the woman at the loom sets about to make a distinct design, using her highest skill devotedly. As she proceeds, the work claims her which she loves without reservation. Then the crucial moment comes, a summoning time, I should say. It is the moment of giving her cloth to the gods in order to form the new beginning for which she does not have yet a blueprint. You see, the woman has only to be ever present to the thread, the particular thread that is given her. Nor is this the thread of the Fates, which measures out the life span with its patterns. Ah, the thread which is woman's own measure of interior life, is it not this that creates the singing path in human existence?

— Ah so. And the excellent work, doesn't it thread the singing path in the cosmos as well? Dear Athena, Zeus was wise when following your birth, he smiled upon you and said that you would be great in his eyes!

The time of the new moon cloaked the city with heavy darkness as Hephaestus emerged from between the Doric columns of his temple and descended the path into the silent marketplace below, for he was drawn to a solitary stroll when all the bustle and cries of merchants and bargainers were silenced along with the mournful braying of the donkeys relieved of their burdens. He proceeded now through the deserted marketplace when rounding a curve of the path under a group of trees, he came face-to-face with another walker.

— Why, Athena, can it be you? What brings you to the deserted Agora in the night?

— Greetings, Hephaestus! Much stirs in me when the moon cloaks herself in darkness. Actually, I was born in such a time, as you may remember.

— How could I ever forget that night? Besides, every Athenian feels in his bones the birth of his goddess when at high summer in the dark of the moon, your little girl priestesses descend to the Acropolis cave carrying the sacred basket of the hidden things never to be uncovered. I can imagine the girls would like nothing better than to steal a single look!

He smiled at the notion.

— Ah yes. The rite is very old. Each time it is a question whether the sacred basket will make its return journey safely to the temple with its contents secret. Do you know, Hephaestus, when I walk in this dark face of the moon, once again I realize that uncertainty and dread haunt the human world.

She appeared to tremble a little, and this caused Hephaestus spontaneously to step nearer, laying a hand on her arm as he smiled down on her.

— Come with me, saffron-robed Athena. Let us walk in the slumbering marketplace, its silence like the meadow of the night. There are things I have to say to comfort you.

He spoke in gentle passion, pausing to gaze silently back at his beautiful temple on the rocky rise, and Athena's eyes followed his. How erect and majestic it stood, its sovereignty luminous as a moon yet to come.

Curiously, she had been wholly unaware of his limp as they approached this place on the path. His gaze returned to her now, and he smiled as one who is carried by pleasing reflection until she spoke with eagerness in her voice.

— When you drew near me on the path where I waited this evening, I saw them all, each one!

— Who?

His question was somewhat curt, for he was disconcerted knowing that her eyes had not been for him alone.

— The heroes, I mean. Each one moved upon my mind's keen slate. There was lithe, quick Perseus, so fearless, his feet winged as he moved toward mad Medusa. Again I glimpsed Bellerophon moving forward in stealth with my silver bridle held high as he made ready to harness divine Pegasus. But no, it was Heracles that my eyes sought for reassurance, that strong and bold man striding swiftly into the dark of Hades' deep realm to pluck lovely Alkestis out of death and oblivion!

Athena continued as though she invisibly greeted one hero after another, all of whom had had her assistance one way or another. Actually, Hephaestus found himself idly marveling at her, for she was much like a hen clucking to all her chicks. The thought, in any case, caused him to grin. Now he interrupted her reverie.

— Well, Athena, since you never permit yourself to forget a hero but continue to offer him your companionship whatever his quest, I am vastly reassured.

— Reassured? What do you mean?

— Simply that you also are not likely to reject me!

Her eyes grew large, astonished and a little wary as he continued to smile at her.

— Why, Hephaestus, I have never rejected you. Your torch has often warmed me with its intense earth fire.

— Wait, my dear. Only consider, will you, that it is the fire that is myself that is in question.

A color suffused her cheeks, and she dropped her eyes, speaking in a low voice.

— I believe that I always knew, even from the first quick side glimpse toward you standing there all bloodied at the moment of my birth. On your face there was amazement and yet something else difficult to decipher. Could it have been delight? Or was it your sense of claim upon me, Hephaestus? Here in the nocturnal darkness one can speak of the hidden things, surely.

An impetuous force seized Hephaestus, sweeping over him like a spring torrent. His long accustomed patience was no longer in evidence nor his meditative shaping of a thing. He held both of Athena's hands in his own as he spoke with passion.

— You are mine, and yes, I claim you! Since the moment of your birth, I have known this. Was it not I alone who dared to free you from the head of Zeus lest you be forever housed in a corner of the mind of everlasting Father? Athena, only think. It was my stroke that set you free upon the earth!

Athena's face took on a tender look tinged with inexplicable delight at this confession, and she was wordless for a time. Nearby, an owl called in an olive tree and was answered by a more distant winged companion. Now Athena spoke.

— What a lonely deed was yours, my friend, striking the head of great Father with an ax! Always I have sensed in you the weight of that loneliness. Please know that in my heart it is no thankless action, for sweet gratitude ever flows toward you, dear Hephaestus!

— Your words are nectar to my ears. Only think how things might have been had this act not fallen to me to handle. Athena, of the owl vision, would not have come to earth. You would have been no more than a dark mood, an excruciating headache, the feared but ever unborn progeny of the gods! At least now I am vindicated. Only one thing remains, lovely Athena. I believe you know this.

As if stopping midsentence, Hephaestus drew her to himself within his fiery embrace. His voice was low as he spoke.

— Be my own beloved, Athena, eternal maiden!

A long sigh escaped Athena's lips affirming her contentment, it seemed, as she murmured

— O Hephaestus, dearly beloved Hephaestus! None other has your measure.

A silence descended upon the two gods as they were held within an indescribable bond. The time seemed to grow like the crocus, sturdy and green, rising toward the moment when it will pierce the earth and emerge into the light. An owl hooted again in the heavy darkness. It was Athena who stirred out of the sweet silence.

— Such time is our time. It is the feast of the gods. But now, Hephaestus, it must be allowed to pass as though it were a mortal thing.

Hephaestus cried out in protest.

— No, no, Athena! Let our time endure!

— No. Some things are forever as they are, unchanging. So I am Athena Parthenos, the Virgin. Nor may I ever be bride of god or man.

Hephaestus, if you love me, you love this unalterable one that I am.
Only consider, you desire me because I am thus.

Now the creative god cried out in a voice of anguish.

— O Athena, Athena! What everlasting seduction is this that the gods
have brought about among themselves that Athena walks the earth and
holds the sacred rock while she remains untouchable, belonging to no
one, yet ever desirable in beauty and wisdom?

Athena's face had paled with these words, and her shoulders sank.
Almost she was conflicted. Hephaestus continued.

— You are known for your mercy and your care. Have pity on me, I beg
you, for my love for you exceeds all the wealth of my work!

— O my friend, pity is not worthy of your great love. Know that your
love brings me joy and deep honor. I can say no more, oh, no more! I
must go at once!

Turning about swiftly so that her garments whirled about her, she
set out running lightly over the path in the direction of her own ancient
temple on the Acropolis. Distraught and determined yet, Hephaestus
followed in pursuit. They ascended the hill of the Acropolis when, drawing
close behind her, Hephaestus called to her softly,

— O Athena, do not run from me!

— It is from myself I flee, dear Hephaestus, for I am sorely tempted!

— What is to become of our love then? Even now my seed rises within
me!

Gazing toward her oldest temple, Athena cried out,

— O holy hill, hear Athena! Receive Hephaestus's seed even now in your
earth! Shelter it well and give it the body that great love deserves! When
the time has passed and the seed has ripened, let it emerge full-fleshed,
the shining offspring of our love to walk here among us. So be it!

Thus did Athena reach her temple where instead of the familiar
columns, she thought she glimpsed stately maidens in procession, lifting
the roof of the temple above their heads. Hephaestus stood below the
temple watching the retreating figure while her shining peplos, yellow as a
full moon rising, sent shafts of light into the night.

The Mystic Child

Energetic in her stride, the young woman walked alone on the steep north slope of the Acropolis of Athens, stopping to gaze upward toward the oldest temple of Goddess Athena. Aglauros, daughter of Athens' king, was a priestess of the goddess and knew well all the rituals within the temple required of her and her sisters, keeping the lamps supplied with oil so as to burn brightly before the holy image. Returning to the familiar olive tree's shade, she sat down beside the finely woven oval basket with its domed lid, letting her arm rest protectively upon it. For some time she kept company with her thoughts although, if the truth were known, she found solitude rather troublesome on the whole. Continuing to gaze at the closed basket, she mused.

— Being the eldest of us sisters, I like to think that I am her favorite priestess, the one she depends on. What an odd task is this one she has brought me, I must say. Certainly it's one I'd never have chosen, had she asked my opinion, but she didn't. I'll never forget the day I looked up and saw her in that strong, graceful stride coming toward me. She looked radiant, she did, and on her arm she carried a covered basket, I noticed. Naturally, my curiosity was aroused. Was she going to bestow on me some special bounty of late summer, perhaps, as a token of affection for me? Well, I couldn't take my eyes off the basket, not even when she stood directly facing me. Receiving her greeting, I waited for her to speak further. What an exchange followed!

— Aglauros, my good priestess. As you see, I have brought the basket. It is the basket that holds my treasure, and it requires a caretaker.

— Greetings, Goddess. You've brought your treasure for me to look after?

It was impossible for Aglauros to keep the excitement out of her voice, even if she tried.

— Is it gold then?

— Better than gold, for there is that of the gods, their progeny, that grows only in the dark!

— And you have chosen me, Goddess, to be the caretaker?

— I have indeed. Even so, there is the danger of the lifelong onlooker, I fear.

— Who?

— She resides within the human individual, this onlooker does, and her main fire is curiosity, I think. What she is skilled at is looking on life and experience from a safe distance.

— But just supposing a person is close at hand, you know, like the caretaker. Why, she's involved. She needn't be one of those onlookers, but still she had best know what she is taking care of, surely.

— Of course. I do plan to tell you what the basket contains. Otherwise, how can you know its immense value? Within this basket is my child, child of the hidden love that only the gods witnessed. From this time forward, you are to be his nurse, and remember, he is very dear to my heart!

Although normally not at a loss for words, Aglauros was speechless as she gazed wide-eyed at her goddess, not without fear.

Athena continued.

— My son has no world shape, you see, and must wait on his shaping within the dark of the basket. I can reveal an important fact to you, however. His father is the great *shaper* among the gods since from his hands come things of great beauty and usefulness as well. My own guardian serpent, so often at home behind my shield, shall protect the babe's well-being. Always remind yourself that within the dark of the basket is the beginning of Athens' future, and it must under no circumstances be aborted.

Aglauros's eyes returned to the closed basket and remained staring upon it for some time. At last she lifted her gaze to Athena, and her voice was subdued as she asked the question.

— What, then, are your instructions for me, the nurse, Goddess?

— Care for this child with your full attention and devotion, tending to his every need. However, under no circumstance are you to raise the basket cover and look upon him! Remember this grave precaution even though you are tempted to observe him. As yet he possesses no world shape. Therefore he remains the vulnerable one.

With these uncanny instructions, Athena had smiled and departed.

The sun was setting in the west toward Salamis when Herse, her sister, approached Aglauros and the basket under the olive tree.

— Well, Herse, what dreamy, idle life have you been up to while I've been minding the goddess's basket?

— I never find you in your old haunts, Aglauros.

— Lady Athena cares little for a person's old haunts, I'm beginning to think. You know, do you, that I am under her instructions now that I am nurse of her hidden child?

Herse nodded. Apparently the situation had already been discussed at length between Aglauros's two sisters. Herse questioned her.

— Does Lady Athena come often to visit the mystic child?

— Well, she only comes evenings when the room is well darkened. Even so, she never forgets to send me away for a time while she lingers beside the babe. I imagine that she picks him up out of the basket for a change, poor little codger. After a while, she calls me back into the room and repeats the instructions. Does she suppose I could forget them? Maybe she reads a kind of sullen disappointment in my face. Do you think so?

— It is possible. Look, Aglauros, it is an immense honor that the goddess has given you in making you nurse of her only progeny! Hasn't that occurred to you?

— That may be true, but look, Herse, it is awful not being able to see what you are doing! She knows, of course, that I am sorely tempted to have a look. Just a peek is all I ask! After all, I can keep a secret. I wouldn't tell a soul what this babe looks like. Herse, it is only sensible and normal to look at a baby you're responsible for!

— O Aglauros, you dare not disobey Athena!

— I do wonder why she chose me instead of you to be the nurse. On the other hand, she could have passed the job around among the three of us, her priestesses.

Herse was beginning to register alarm.

— Each of us has longed to be the goddess's chosen one, but Athena has chosen you and you alone. Think, being the nurse of the child of virgin goddess Athena. What a position you hold!

— Yes, it sounds awesome, I know. Still, the responsibility does get tiring. Tell me, Herse, wouldn't you be curious to have a look at the child you care for all the time, sitting by his basket?

Herse leaped to her feet now, her head striking a branch laden with olives that now swayed back and forth as if it too were seized by the emotion of the situation.

— O Aglauros, listen to me. Resist that temptation of yours! Do not let your mind be hounded by such a notion, one that is against Athena's counsel.

— Well, it isn't simple to get my mind off the issue, I tell you. By the way, I've learned the name of the child. It is Erechthonios.

— Why, that means he is breaker of earth! I wonder if he is to be like the spear of the goddess, piercing the ground of the Acropolis . . .

— Well, we are never going to know what he is really like unless I am bold enough to look him over, I think. Herse, you've always been the sweet and gentle one while, look at me, I've got spirit!

Herse sighed rather mournfully.

— Yes, you do have that. When I think of you among us sisters, I think of you as having something like the lamp's fire.

Aglauros laughed now at Herse's regretful tone.

— Well, if I've got the fire, why am I pinned down to these strict instructions and rather dull routine? I mean, they don't match my nature.

— Perhaps you can't know why as yet. It does frighten me that you dare to raise the question. Still, I'm convinced in my heart that Athena favors you and is showing you the highest privilege.

— It is not as high an honor as she reserves for the baby, you have to admit.

— Oh, Aglauros! Your mind and your mouth operating together in this way shall surely do you in!

This commentary caused Aglauros to grin.

— Come, Herse. Isn't this what you look to me for—my mouth and my mind, both being bolder than your own?

— You know, I do believe that your strong, independent spirit has drawn Athena to you with her affection. Yet you must do this one thing she has laid upon you, and forget the other things you dream of doing for now.

Aglauros's face took on a gravity now as she spoke.

— I am grateful that you care so much about me, Herse, believe me. The honest truth, I realize, is that I am feeling, well, afflicted by Athena. She has made me like her ox yoked to the plowshare. It's that I can't bear the limitation!

Tears overwhelmed her now, and Herse sought to comfort her as she herself remained pale with worry.

Athena Meets Hermes

Dusk was settling over the hill of the Acropolis where the gleaming white temples withdrew into solitude as Hermes, god of the gate, walked beside Athena on the dusty path. Hermes regarded his companion thoughtfully.

— This is quite a story, you know. Tell it to me, Athena, for I want to hear your version of it. In the first place, how did this mysterious child come to you, since clearly you did not bear it the way a woman does her pregnancy?

— It is best that you have the account from me and not from hearsay. Well, it was actually at this time of day, in the margin between light and dark, that Earth Goddess herself emerged out of the ground before me in a most startling manner. That is to say, she emerged halfway, from the waist up. I was too astonished to speak at once.

— Athena at a loss? I must say this was an extraordinary happening. Nor would I have expected Gaia to be capable of such drama.

— Nor did I, but she faced me addressing me as one does who has urgent news to report. In her arms she held a tiny robust child.

— Ah so, and her report?

— She wasted no words such as women are wont to do, inquiring after each other. What she said was

Athena, did you think that I would remain absent when you and Hephaestus walked on Athens' hallowed ground as love's great passion was upon him? And I heard your sighs as well.

Hermes stood stark still, and his face held amazement. His voice was altered.

— Indeed, Athena? What defense did you make to Earth Goddess?

— For shame, Hermes! Well do you know that no one of us dare defend herself against great Gaia. I simply bowed my head, and she continued to speak.

Always you have known that you will remain the Maiden, one never spent, never owned, the everlasting threshold for human individuals. Is this not true?

I could only nod in assent to Gaia's words. Was she about to rebuke me, I wondered, for arousing desire in Hephaestus? She continued speaking although the babe had begun to squirm in her arms.

In the craftsman god's passion for you, his seed spilled forth upon the earth. I took it up, and in my womb have I carried and brought to birth the child of Athena and Hephaestus's love! Receive this wondrous child!

— Never before has such astonishment overtaken me, Hermes. For a long moment, I could not speak. Then gratitude to Gaia flooded my heart, and I cried out,

"O mysterious womb of the gods' joyous life! O inscrutable labor of earth!"

Then I fell silent, taking the child into my arms.

The God of the road nodded as he took in the extraordinary account. Now he smiled as he put the question.

— So is the child beautiful?

— Yes, indeed. Always I see to it that he is kept covered in his basket, for here on the Acropolis, my eyes alone have looked upon him. My priestess, Aglauros, is caring for him and knows that she must under no circumstance attempt to look at him.

— Oh? And why did you choose Aglauros as nurse of this special child? She's a good sort, but surely no one is less inclined to keep something hidden than Aglauros! Athena, only think, if secrecy is essential to this task with the newborn—

— Oh, it is essential. To hide the child, this is the true task. You see, Hermes, it is the woman task required of the human soul. I've long observed Aglauros, and I came to realize that it was the time to summon her to this great task. So I have placed my very own treasure into her hands, instructing her to guard it well in the dark.

Hermes frowned in concern and was shaking his head as he spoke.

— But dare you risk placing the mystic child in her sole care? This is the practical question. Why, this girl has never hidden anything—that is my guess!

— Ah, and that is why the task must fall to her. You see, in the great task for the human individual, there is something that opposes one's nature, that does battle with it, I think. It is difficult and leaves one no choice but to concentrate all passion and energy upon it and then to beseech a god for help.

Hermes had not lost his worried look, in spite of Athena's reasoning.

— All I can say is that she has not asked me for help. Alas, I sense that a certain desire for independence from your counsel tempts the maiden. She appears absorbed with the question, "What can this child give me?"

— Perhaps this is true with Aglauros. I value your perception, Hermes. Still, my priestess must play out her nature, much as one lets out the rope that releases the ship to the sea. We must be patient.

— And yet, there is the welfare of the babe, Athena.

— Oh, Hermes, Aglauros may be a difficult road for me to travel, but she belongs intimately to the journey. I cannot replace her, you see. It can't be easy to nurse the offspring of the gods . . . I am aware of a certain darkness settling about Aglauros, and it causes me anguish. Yes, she is greatly tempted to do the forbidden thing! At the same time, there is the excellent path that can only take shape in the course of her struggle.

— As god of the road, it is not easy for me to stand by idly.

— Dear, dear Hermes, I do believe that you shall be needed sooner than I wish to acknowledge!

Aglauros Acts

Aglauros, daughter of King Cecrops of Athens, mused at the close of day.

— I must remember that I am Goddess Athena's choice of a nurse for the hidden baby in the basket. It's a full-time job, and I have come to miss sorely my former duties of trimming the lamps of the temple before the holy image. All these duties and privileges now fall to my two sisters. There was ever a lovely freedom in making one's way over the path of the Acropolis to the temple at early dusk, and at sunrise, being alone and breathing in the moist air and dense quiet of those hours. How I miss it, confined here to my chamber, minding the basket and its child. Still, I must not complain.

As the days slowly went by, more and more there arose in Aglauros a sullen anger, the anger of a person who is punished by too stern a duty. A familiar litany came to her at these times, which she was in the habit of repeating under her breath:

Baby Erechthonios, you must hold the holy fire of the gods.
I Aglauros want to uncover it!
I Aglauros want to be the first mortal witness!
I Aglauros want some of that fire for myself!

After such a confession, she would remonstrate with herself to such an extent that for the entire day, she became an even more devoted nurse. Time passed, and a determination began to take shape within Aglauros. She ignored it until it became like hard ice on a mountain lake in winter. One early morning, she moved toward the loosely woven basket with its dome-shaped lid and stood gazing down upon it for some time. Finally she spoke aloud in a voice in which all tentativeness had been purged.

— I have waited long enough. I deserve to look!

With her left hand, she drew back the domed cover. Wide-awake and kicking, the babe gazed up at her with large dark eyes. In that moment, she beheld a boy of incredible beauty of face and torso while, observing his legs, she let out an unearthly cry of fear, hastily replacing the cover on the basket. The child had begun to wail lustily while people outside on the path, alarmed by her cry, came running into the chamber to see what was the matter. They questioned her anxiously.

— What has alarmed you, Aglauros?

It was the question asked her repeatedly. What she replied was that she had seen a large coiled snake, which could not have been the sacred snake of the temple, surely. Aglauros had spoken the truth, for coiled about the child's lower body had been a great shining snake. Even so, she did not reveal that she had looked upon the long-hidden mystic child of Athena with her own eyes. Only Athena knew the entire truth of what took place, and she bided her time.

Transgression

The two women searched for their sister Aglauros, but could not find her. Nor were they aware that she had rebelled against the instructions of the goddess. Ever since the fateful evening when she dared to lift the cover from the sacred basket in order to have her first look at the child of Athena, Aglauros had become one who was set apart, the solitary one, having lost her desire for human companionship. Sitting alone in the dusk near the cave that she had long known through the sacred basket ritual of the little girl priestesses, she took account of things.

— It is a cold, hard fact that I'm no longer fit to be Athena's priestess, let alone her favorite, for haven't I flagrantly transgressed her will in the matter?

When words such as these came to her, she wept in misery. Still there were times when something would swiftly surface in herself, coming to her stout defense as surely as one of those smart speakers at the court of the Areopagus. The words came clearly.

— A practical mind preserves good sense and checks each thing out in order to determine whether it actually is what it proposes to be. Thus did Aglauros act when she uncovered the babe!

These words spoken by an unknown person held a formidable strength. They echoed in Aglauros's mind and managed to revive her spirits for a time. At times she would say to herself forlornly,

— But Goddess Athena doesn't serve common sense. No. She's got the wisdom that comes like her owl in the night. I too want some of that wisdom. Oh, why was I forbidden to look?

The last words trailed a deep wailing. Her weeping was shortly interrupted by a voice at hand.

— You were forbidden because *the human look can imperil the mystery child.*

Aglauros raised her head from her arms and gazed about, and she saw that she was indeed alone. Still, she must answer that voice.

— What? How can a mere look do such a thing?

The voice replied at once.

— The look is the human access to experience, of course. Often it proves useful. Still, it does tend to package up neatly, and at once, what it has seen and ends up drawing a hard conclusion.

— Well, what can a person expect? I am sure that if Athena were here, she would say something wise that explains things.

There was a sudden intake of breath on the part of the owner of the voice, who now replied.

— I am Athena, Aglauros. I have come to you in your misery, dear priestess. I had hoped, you see, for the ongoing protection of the hidden child.

— Oh my goddess, surely one look could not hurt him. Why, always I have expected that your child would be strong.

Her conclusion startled the goddess.

— Oh but, Aglauros, this child is fragile, I tell you. His strength is yet to become firm. He is as fragile, I think, as was the infant Dionysos, who played with his toys on the floor of the Cretan cave until the Titans broke in and slew him!

Aglauros's voice rang out in new anguish.

— Alas, what have I done!

Athena's voice was filled with tender concern.

— You have indulged yourself with the look. That's all. What you must remember is that the child lives. Erechthonios will yet enjoy a great future on Athens' hill, I assure you. Aglauros, you must not lose hope.

These words of Athena brought comfort to the maiden's heart now. Yet even so, remorse followed her with its weighty presence. When she looked up, she saw that she was alone. Nevertheless, she was grateful to Athena for seeking her out.

A new day dawned on the Acropolis when, coming to the temple of Athena to perform their tasks, the two sister priestesses approached the table of the sacred offerings. At once they saw a single offering in the middle of the table: a sizeable winnowing basket, which they recognized at once as a cradle. The two priestesses, their eyes large with dread, turned to face each other. It was Herse whose voice gasped the words,

— Oh! It is the covered basket!

Both maidens bent to the sacred basket and saw that attached was a note written in a familiar hand that said, "With all your heart and mind, care for Athena's child but never look upon him."

Later the news came that caused grave sorrow, for Aglauros had fallen to her death from the cliff of the Acropolis. In grief, the two sisters took the basket of the goddess and undertook the care of the child so that in due time, Erechthonios would reach his natural strength and beauty. Darkness finally descended upon the sad day. It was in the far reaches of that moonless night when all slept that the owl's voice, rhythmic and tranquil, broke the vast silence, causing the leaves of the sacred olive tree to tremble. Afterward, a speaking voice was borne on the moist air:

O Aglauros, chosen by Athena, hear me, departed one!
Nurse of the hidden child of the gods you are, of that babe
born from earth's cavernous womb
    into the ordinary basket of human life.
How great was your desire to feel his flesh,
    to behold his delicate form and hold him in your arms!
Lovely is desire, yet perilous is a path close lying.
On this path, the wayfarer comes to possess the pulsing life,
sizing it up and assigning it to a choking category
A corpse uncoffined it becomes.
O Aglauros, you who pathed the way with devotion and
transgression, bequeath to us Athena's child!
Even now the heart greets you with love and gratitude.
Behold the smile of Athena!

The Contest for the Acropolis

Between dawn and the rising of the sun over the Attic plain, the ten gods of Olympus made their way in informal procession upon the hill of the Acropolis of Athens. Awaiting them on the summit were Athena and Poseidon. Although they were prepared to see Athena, the presence of the sea god caused eyebrows to be raised in curiosity. When Zeus had expressed the greetings of the Olympians, it was Athena who responded.

— Welcome, fellow Olympians! Your presence honors this sacred hill of Athens, to be sure. Poseidon, do not be gloomy.

The latter was a whispered aside met by a thunderous look. Zeus faced Poseidon, frowning in some perplexity.

— Brother, I did not expect to find you here, actually looking quite at home. As savior of ships, how do you find time to enjoy the ambience of Athens' summit?

Poseidon searched his brother's face for reassurance that his sense of justice was in good order. Now he replied.

— Zeus, let me explain. There is the issue of supremacy over this Acropolis, and Athena and I are contending for that sole position in a contest that the rest of you are to judge.

— Ah, the contest which the ten of us shall judge, for we have been instructed in justice by Themis herself. What is decided here will be crucial to the whole Greek world, brother. Of this I've no doubt.

— As you know me well, I never am known to take any issue lightly, not even the loss of Aegina in my struggle with you for the power there, for that matter.

Apollo, who had been standing close by, interrupted with his usual grace.

— Father? Uncle? Shall we get on with it? Tell us, Athena and Poseidon, what is to be this test of your powers? I find it difficult to imagine how we can even witness your extraordinary acts, let alone judge them. Nor am I known to be short on imagination. Poseidon, one possibility haunts my mind. You wouldn't have in mind causing a flood of water to swallow up this hill, would you?

Worry settled on the god's brow as he asked the question. Poseidon shook his head, and Apollo turned to Athena.

— Athena, as for you, you are observed to have unlimited power of persuasion with a potential hero. Still, demonstrating this power calls for some ripened situation on the human scene, one you do not invent. Besides, I see no human candidate at hand.

Aphrodite, who rested nearby on a boulder, sighed and spoke quietly.

— You speak of persuasion, Apollo. Peitho, Persuasion, is usually in my company, you see.

Apollo answered her, smiling as he spoke.

— Your accomplishments of persuasion are of a somewhat different order than those of Athena, I would point out, Aphrodite.

The goddess of love responded to the god of the oracle at once.

— How quickly you seem to forget Troy and how the Greeks, fighting before her walls, called out for Helen who is my reflection, of course.

Apollo assured Aphrodite that he had not forgotten. Zeus was studying Athena as he spoke.

— Athena, you are given to the bright, darting vision that finds the true and exacting shape of a human event. No sooner does this vision arise than a plan forms, keen and still invisible. It is at this point, I have concluded, that the path of the hero is perceived and embraced by a person you persuade.

Apollo added to this description of the making of the hero.

— I'd say it has to be a person with a full measure of energy and one who is paying close attention.

Hermes had been engaging in a lazy smile throughout this discussion and now added a word.

— Ah, it is the heart and head of Athena that shape the hero, and victory in the task as well. In any case, it is pretty ground. Still, it could be tricky to get a footing on.

He added the last with a glint in the eye. Zeus took the lead now.

— Come, it is only just to regard Poseidon's gifts now.

And they did. As for Demeter, she spoke of the time in a far meadow when she was companioned by Poseidon and walked with him. She recalled his words describing his nature.

— He said to me, "Demeter, I am the tide behind thought, the untamed abandon behind all order, tradition, and law. Do you realize that my memory is older than the Olympian age while within it thoughts and events of the past still have their power?" Those were his words. Indeed, I speak truly when I say that Poseidon brought me the touch of the ever-flowing, windswept waters. In springtime when the Ilissus River begins to heave and swell its banks, it seems that I hear Poseidon's voice once more calling to life the grain in earth's furrow!

The gods fell silent, considering the power of Poseidon. Now they formed a half circle, positioning themselves to witness the contest. Zeus made a decisive gesture indicating that the contest should proceed. Stepping forward as actors to the stage, Athena and Poseidon faced each other solemnly, unflinching in purpose as each appeared to make a sober withdrawal from the place of friendship. First to move was Poseidon. Holding his trident aloft, he strode forward and cried out in a thundering voice.

— Behold the power of my trident upon Athens' rock!

There was a silvery flash as the trident struck the rock of the temenos, causing it to crack loudly. As it split open, a great spring emerged casting its waters swiftly over the dry ground. The gods bent forward, eyes wide, marveling at the miracle.

Without delay, however, Athena now stepped forward, her peplos, of the hue of the crocus in springtime, flowing about her. She raised her long spear and sank it into the ground near the flowing spring. As the gods watched expectantly, their eyes upon the spot where the spear pierced the earth, there emerged a green shoot that began to grow rapidly until a fine olive tree, its branches swaying in the breeze, stood before them. Awe filled the gods as a silence cloaked them in a sustained pause. Now they spoke among themselves quietly. The waiting that held them in thrall was tense. Turning in time to the two contesting gods, it was Apollo who moved forward as spokesman of the ten Olympian gods. Before speaking, he touched the crown of laurel he wore.

— On Olympus, each of us has his sovereign place and none competes for another's. Such is our covenant among ourselves. But today we stand in the human world at its political and moral center, that is to say, Athens.

It is a pity that this world is rarely able to accommodate more than one
god at a time in any given situation. This accounts for the sadness that
necessarily falls on us with the knowledge that one god's power will fail
here.

He paused and turned his face to Poseidon.

— Poseidon, you have lost out. Athena, you are supreme here on Athens'
hill! The responsibility for the well-being of the Athenians falls upon
you.

Athena turned her eyes upon Poseidon, and in her sensitive face
appeared some vast complexity.

— Poseidon, do not give way to a heavy spirit. It is clear to the gods that
what Athens needs is the fertile, growing earth, heavy with olive harvest,
more than it needs the salty spring that you have called forth here. We
have so much sea surely! I perceive the reality of soul and body that
is Athens and shall defend it against those who would overwhelm her.
That is my vow.

Refusing to bow either his authority or his dignity, Poseidon
spoke.

— However true your words, the fact is that I have been dishonored!

— Not dishonored. On the contrary. You rule in many places in sandy
Pylos's strong kingdom, while the people of Troizen bring you the
first fruits. Ah yes, and at the sacred marriage rite, do they not provide
you a local Troizen for your bride? The races and games in your honor
at the Isthmian festival vie with Olympia in fame. Surely, you have no
need of Athens' ancient Acropolis.

— Neither do you go begging on Greek soil in other places, Athena, let
me point out.

He paused and looked thoughtful before adding,

— Nevertheless, I bow to the judgment of my fellow Olympians.

Athena nodded in appreciation while Zeus and Apollo breathed
sighs of relief. Athena turned now to face the Olympians, assuming her
new position of supremacy and spoke, the words seeming to be drawn from
some older source, a source radiant with the memory of the gods.

— There is another who is greatly honored by the Athenians and who
shares this holy ground with me and receives sacrifices.

Poseidon looked startled, even confused by these words. He
questioned her.

— Is it a god or a hero you speak of?

— Well, he is both. He is Erechthonios, breaker of the soil. Now he is no ordinary plowman, I hasten to add. He is my son, although not born of me.

— Alas, you speak in riddles. Explain yourself.

— As you know, I am Parthenos, the everlasting maiden. Hephaestus, long attracted to me, pursued me in his passion, and I fled from him here on the Acropolis. The result was that his seed fell upon this ground, and earth took it into her womb. When her time was accomplished, the great goddess held up Erechthonios so that he broke the crust of earth to be received into my arms here on the Acropolis.

Poseidon stroked his beard wonderingly as he spoke.

— A curious tale at best. How does it concern us here?

— It is to announce that henceforth you shall receive honor and offerings here as Poseidon-Erechthonios, for you, Poseidon, shall be united with our ancient ancestral god!

Poseidon's cheerfulness was restored now, and he smiled. He reflected upon this before nodding his acceptance with dignity. In this manner, the gathering of the gods had reached amicable agreement in the disposition of the Acropolis. Now each god departed, leaving Athens' hill.

Creusa in the Birth Cave

Drawing the wool cloak about her slim body as the cold wind buffeted her, she turned to descend the narrow stairway that was cut into the northern face of the Acropolis. The Long Rocks, the haunt of Pan . . . memories were vivid and fragrant, echoing the voices of earlier times. Had she not made this trek annually from the time she was seven until age eleven, accompanied by other small priestesses of Goddess Athena? Oh yes, they had carried the sacred basket of "the unspoken things." Watching her step on the steep and rugged footpath, she reached the small plateau in the dusk and stood once again within the sanctuary of goddess Aphrodite. Such blossoms not to be found anywhere else! That is the way it is with Aphrodite. She knew this. The garden's fragrance covered her with a veil of inexhaustible sweetness, and she sighed in sheer delight. This spot that had witnessed the crucial happening of her life had not changed. Only she was altered, alas! The thought summoned an inexplicable sorrow, one to be borne in utter aloneness. Not even he—her radiant, splendid lover—shared the sorrow, for had he not failed to return to her? Creusa murmured aloud, "I am the abandoned one! Love itself has left me behind. Oh, how can this sanctuary of Aphrodite remain unchanged when she has treated me so badly? The holy cave was visible just ahead, but it took courage to approach it. At its entrance she bent to enter its deep darkness and stood motionless within the vaulted chamber. Unlike the night of the holy rite in her childhood, neither torch nor lamp burned here. It was more recent history, her very own, that cloaked her in gloom as, staring at the tablelike surface of the standing stone, she saw that her child no longer lay cradled there. Sinking to the floor of the cave, she wept. Despair has no timepiece. A mere hour can beget its gaping century. Stirred by a nearby sound, she looked up and was amazed to see a woman stranger standing before her, her form illuminated as if by candles. The stranger spoke, and her voice was like a path of fine stones.

— Why have you returned here, daughter of the House of Erechtheus?

Creusa had difficulty finding her voice, and when she spoke feebly, it was not to answer the stranger but to question her.

— You are not one of them—not one of the priestesses of Athena. I know each of them. Who are you, stranger?

The woman shook her head slightly and pressed her question with a note of urgency.

— The question remains, why have you come back here?

Grief choked her voice as she answered.

— My heart brings me back here. Oh, it cannot be helped!

— Ah yes, the heart. It is favorable for a woman when life pours from the spring of the heart. Ah, the heart is not like the mind. For when the mind becomes weak and blunders, it still remains determined to see through its plan at all cost!

— Alas, lady, I've got no plan, none whatsoever. I've only come here to visit the sacred cave where as a little girl I took part in the holy basket rite of Athena.

— Maiden, I am aware that this cave has witnessed more than the Arrephoria rite you speak of. Have you not returned because it is the cave of a great love?

Creusa gasped, and her cheeks paled visibly.

— You know about it? You know my secret? Alas, somebody knows!

If the stranger knows, she thought, *it is only a matter of time until my love affair will be known by Father. What grim punishment lies in store for me for forbidden love?* Wide-eyed, her face drawn in worry, she stared at her companion who regarded her quietly with thoughtful gray eyes. Claiming the two figures now in the cave's dimness was a silence. Strangely, it was not accusatory but comforting, and the intense worry seemed to leak away slowly. As Creusa gazed on her companion, her eyes observed now the rich overgarment that she wore. On the woven peplos there were scenes that were finely worked. One by one she observed the scenes with lively curiosity. *Surely that is Perseus holding the shield of Athena, staring into it as he slays the Gorgon. And that must be powerful Heracles wrestling with nine-headed Hydra of Lerna's spring. Ah, a suspicious fellow is overtaken by a young hero . . . why, that is Theseus laying hold of the robber on the road to Epidauros!* A sense of awe settled over her as she again raised her eyes to the face of the stranger and, trembling now, uttered the words.

— O great Goddess Athena, this is the sacred peplos you are wearing! I didn't recognize you, you see. All hail!

She made the sacred gesture before plunging into what she hoped would explain things.

— Apparently you know about the trysts I had in the cave with my lover.

— Ah, who is your lover?

— He comes from Mt. Parnassus, and he calls himself Apollo. I know so little about him, you see.

— What you have just told me is a great deal indeed! Still, there is the knowledge that only Aphrodite brings, I think. What of this?

Creusa grew pensive for a time. When she spoke, her voice had a deep resonance as though the cave added its timeless echo.

— Why, I came to know what love knows . . . I mean its meandering, golden song, which I'd rather be dead than cease to hear. Ah, what a pain is in my breast!

The goddess leaned toward her and nodded her understanding as she spoke quietly.

— I am here to help you, Creusa, daughter of Athens.

Not recognizing the lifeline offered her, Creusa went on to give a full account of her misery.

— There is something else about my beloved, and it distresses me greatly. The fact is that he isn't *dependable!* Oh, again and again it is this about him that makes me miserable.

— Come, woman, would you judge great Apollo like a man? Wait a moment. I do believe that you think your lover is a man. Is this true?

Now the question stunned Creusa, and incredulity showed in her face.

— How could he not be a man? Though a gift of heaven, our love is an earthly thing, I tell you. When I remember his touch and its delight, there is a song not only in my heart but it courses all my veins!

Silently the two figures regarded each other as a chasm opened between them. It was Athena who ended the tense pause.

— Will you describe your lover to me?

Now every lover enjoys nothing more than to describe the beloved. Creusa smiled for the first time, a wistful smile that lingered over some image that pleased her as the anguish of the hour drained away. When she began to speak, it was no longer the strident voice of the maiden victim. Almost it was the ripened voice of woman.

— Oh, his beauty is astonishing! He is the *kouros* of dreams, and yet he is the marvelous youth become man, if you know what I mean. Such grace and authority are in his stride that I could gaze on him for a lifetime. Yet for my Apollo, this was only the beginning, for on his left arm he carried the tortoise lyre, which he would play, singing tale upon tale. Oh, his language was a music I had not known. It swept over me, lifting me at once into its deep and speaking current. And his golden hair, so abundant, was crowned always with a garland of laurel. Sometimes he would gaze at me and smile, and always it filled me with delight when in his resonant voice he spoke my name. Still, his gaze was never long, for regularly he would lift his face to contemplate some unseen, distant place, his lyre falling silent. In such moments, he would listen as one who is never distracted, hearing what others surely cannot.

The goddess received Creusa's long hidden account tenderly, recognizing that it was the heart of the hidden place that was speaking. Athena spoke now.

— Ah, indeed he is the *hearer*, and that is why his word when he speaks is so highly valued. Creusa, *your lover is no man*. He is the god Apollo, Far Shooter himself! The word of Apollo is not born from the union of the mouth and the swift-galloping intellect. No. He hears the voices of all things in their rejoicings and their lamentations before shepherding them into the fold of his music. Out of the ecstasy of his priestess, he summons afresh his word from his fold. Yes, Apollo's word emerges out of the knowledge of the many essential voices to become the vision that is measured out. Such is Apollo's word.

— What you say is strange to my ears, Lady Athena. The thought that my lover is a god makes me very lonely.

— Come, did not Apollo choose you as his beloved? What is even of greater import, did you not bear his child, Creusa, the child you kept hidden?

The tenderness of Athena's concern was palpable as her questions hung on the air between them. Creusa's face was flushed with color, her eyes bright with tears as she replied in a low voice.

— I did. In this very cave I brought little Ion to birth. Afterward I came to dress him in fine garments I had secretly made for him, wrapping him in the cover I wove of wool . . .

She could say no more, for deep sorrow overtook her. Athena waited.

— I adorned the baby with my most precious ornament, you see. Many times each day and night, I would slip to the cave to feed and care for him, and I told no one of my secret. O my lady, can you fathom how great was my need to save him—the one who can never be explained—and save myself as well?

The anguish in Creusa's cry lodged like an arrow in Athena's breast, it appeared. At the same time, the goddess was eminently practical in a crisis. She pressed Creusa.

— What was the danger that threatened you?

— If my secret love and bearing a child became known, it would bring scandal upon the royal house of Athens, the House of Erechtheus. Surely you are aware of this possibility.

— Oh yes.

The raised face of the goddess became inscrutable as she gazed toward Olympus. Creusa meanwhile held the curt reply like a mere crumb thrown to the hungry. At last Athena was speaking.

— The way of the gods is not established by rulings of the court of the Areopagus here on Athens' hill, however noble that body. Nor are custom and public opinion the source for decisions made by Apollo. You see, Creusa, the love of a great god is a movement between heaven and earth as important as an act of creation. You must forget this irrelevant charge of scandal.

In that long moment that followed, Creusa felt a profound bond to the goddess, shaking her head with the incongruity of it. Some revengeful, shadowy presence was no longer present to threaten her. Athena spoke again.

— Exceeding all other concerns, I must tell you, is my concern for the child—the birth from yourself and Apollo. There is something I must know. Did you come in time to abandon this child?

Creusa's reply was so faint that her companion leaned forward to catch her words.

— I did!

— Alas! What a fate for heaven's child!

Her sense of solace had been brief as the horror of what she had done descended on her once more.

— O Lady Athena, a fate worse than abandonment has taken him, for surely he is dead, dragged away from the cave and devoured by some wild beast! One evening when I came down to the cave for my usual visit, the babe was missing—nowhere to be found! A shadow of guilt haunts me everlastingly and a sorrow too great to describe. Help me, dear Athena. Otherwise, I shall go mad.

Athena laid her hand on Creusa's arm. Her words challenged the dark cloud.

— Come, Creusa, do not despair. After all, you are only human. The demands laid upon you by the house of your father, the king, already have been enormous. Now you are feeling the demands of Apollo's child, which you have borne. I am here to bring you comfort, and it is comfort due you, I must say.

— How grateful I am for your caring words, my lady. Still, what comfort is possible so long as Ion is lost or else dead?

Athena picked up her spear as if preparing to depart. Holding the spear in her hand, she looked thoughtful and spoke these final words,

— My temple is the gateway to Apollo's sanctuary of the oracle at Delphi, I know Apollo well, well enough to know that he would never allow his child to be seized by a wild beast. There is a report now circulating among the Olympians, the report that Hermes was seen carrying an infant within his cloak and striding toward Parnassus. Having learned from you of the disappearance of your baby, I believe that little Ion may well have been carried inside Hermes' cloak in a scheme of rescue. Only hold this good hope, Creusa, and never forsake your divine love and its excellent progeny! Farewell!

The goddess turned and left the cave while Creusa remained in utter amazement at her encounter as she observed the departing goddess, who was trailed by a thin path of golden light. Or was this trail of light threading its way in her own mind at last?

Creusa in the Garden of Aphrodite

Creusa of the royal house of Athens had added age and experience during the years of her marriage to Xuthus, now king of Athens. Still, she was ever haunted by the extraordinary love of her maiden days, a love that was inexplicable, for was it not a golden time? Ah, and the child that was born in the cave! Since that secret birth, she was barren. The harsh, cold fact fell like a heavy stone upon the marriage, wounding it. It was the hour before dusk as she descended the slope of the Acropolis to the garden of Aphrodite near the awesome cave of Pan. Stepping within the garden, she was greeted by a single white flower of a sweet, lingering fragrance that caused her to sigh in sheer pleasure.

— How can such a flower survive on this austere north slope, I wonder? Alas, I was once such a flower! "My sweet flower!" my beloved called me. That flower is long gone.

Her voice was heavy with the absence of hope or delight. At the same time, she reassured herself that her life as queen of Athens was not without its reward. From nearby, a voice addressed her.

— Oh, but the solitary flower lives, you see.

Creusa was startled, and protested.

— Such a thing is impossible. Only when I was a young maiden was I like the flower. It is illusion for a person to think that she can turn back the clock.

— Oh yes, that is so, but who is trying to find the return to youth? Certainly I am not.

Where was the source of this voice? Creusa shook her head in response to the serene confidence of the speaker and replied.

— Given the chance, anybody would return to her youth.

The unknown companion made no response, but fell silent as what had been a gentle breeze playing over the leaves of the fig tree growing out of the rock had become a sudden gust of wind that bent the branches sharply. When the voice spoke, it was musing.

— Look at the fig tree, which is heavy with fruit. Fruit requires its time to ripen. It possesses an undeclared order, one that has a distinct rhythm. Surely you must have noticed how a fig cannot be *hurried*.

Again Creusa shook her head.

— You don't understand, I am afraid. It is the *flower* that I am missing more than the fruit. Yet both are absent from me, alas!

— Ah, the flower. The flower is the maiden who is so dear to your heart. Indeed, it is she who calls forth the lover.

Creusa's face registered now a stirring of hope. Almost she smiled.

— Oh, I believe, my lady, that you do understand! . . . I wonder if it is Aphrodite who speaks to me. See the cave that lies just beyond the goddess's own garden? It is the place of my great love, and nothing is dearer to my heart. Mysterious it was and, like the lovely child whom I bore, it contains what is hidden forever.

— Hidden, you say?

— I could never show this love nor speak of it to anyone.

— Still, a flower is perceived with delight. True it has no voice for speaking. Yet, the flower is authentic and never to be doubted.

The dull look which is the mask of despair no longer was Creusa's, for a certain brightness appeared in its place s she exclaimed with passion,

— My child, the child of the great love in the cave, he is the flower! I see it now.

The voice that companioned her was like a woman working at the loom as she picked up the threads of different hues to work into the whole piece.

— Your son Ion is the flower, yes, but he is also the fruit that is coming. The fig tree bears you this knowledge. Remember that the tree is before the cave of your great love with Apollo.

— What, my lady, am I to do?

— Well, surely it is best to tend the tree that bears this ancient knowledge. Do take into account one thing in particular about the tree, however.

— And what is that?

— Its virtue.

The word brought momentary laughter from Creusa.

— How can a tree have a virtue?

— Oh, do not laugh, woman. Take account of the lively memory that sustains the unfolding of life, for one thing. Most of all, the virtue I speak of is the tree's wise and mysterious patience.

— Alas, has my life not been a chronicle of patiently waiting? Waiting for the return of my wonderful beloved came first. But, to my sorrow, no return happened. And now for many a year Xuthus and I have waited for a child as our progeny, but again there has been severe disappointment.

    The voice spoke quietly.

— Not all patience, however demanding, has the wisdom, though. The tree is full of an expectancy, the expectancy of the rhythmic unfolding of what is alive and well. And now I must leave you. Go well, Creusa!

The Sirens and Athena's Owl

In the faithful, sea-worn ship, Odysseus and his men approached the solitary island. Could this be the home of the Sirens that Circe had so solemnly warned them about? Such irresistible voices, she had said, describing the winged bird women. Circe ought to know, being of an irresistible sort herself. Now the sound of distant voices given to pleasurable song drifted toward the ship, and as they grew closer, the voices advanced toward them. Gazing toward the shadowy isle, Odysseus frowned and sighed like a harassed man. Idly he worked the beeswax within his hands into a soft, malleable ball and moved toward his comrade at the helm.

— Well, Philo, I've got the wax here. Tilt your head to the side so I can fortify you against the Sirens.

Philo looked a little regretful but complied as his captain placed the soft wax deep into his ear canal, blocking out all sound. Quickly Odysseus was explaining, speaking to Philo's one open ear.

— It's temporary, you understand. Looking back on this episode, you'll be grateful that two deaf ears shielded you from the Sirens.

— Wait, Odysseus. The Sirens themselves look to me like a temporary problem. I think of them as the show of the day, actually.

— Temporary? The Sirens? Don't fool yourself, man. Unless you resist them, you're permanently in trouble. They hold a fateful power over heroes. They can lead us to be forever captives of whatever is the greatest pleasure. Fall under their power, and we've lost our freedom.

— I'm a fellow never given to extremes. Besides, I have been pretty crafty in resisting women in the past.

Odysseus suddenly looked tired.

— Look, Philo, the Sirens are not women. They are not like mortal women. You underestimate their strange power.

— Maybe. But we are heroes of no small reputation, Odysseus. With this silly strategy of Circe's, won't we look ridiculous to any passing seamen? We'll be the laughing stock of the day.

— Being laughed at is the least of our worries. Best take the wax in your other ear now. Circe has a crucial knowledge that we have no access to, and she makes it clear that there are only two ways to withstand the Sirens' seduction. The first way is to go deaf. Why else am I using the beeswax? The second way is to submit to being tied to the mast.

— I know, I know. You already told all of us when we gathered around you. I expect you noticed that no one chose to be tied to the mast.

— That did not escape me.

Odysseus groaned audibly. Now he spoke quickly.

— When I'm satisfied that every man of our crew has his ears deafened, then you can rope me to the mast. One of us has to undergo this way of survival, and it has to be me.

Philo nodded, and now he turned his other ear to receive the wax. Slowly Odysseus moved to each man, stopping both ears with the wax. Some of them grumbled that they were being deprived of what was going on, for Greek men are ever lovers of song. Their ears deafened, the men bent to their oars, rowing hard in an effort to move beyond the island of the Sirens. Such a goal was not to be accomplished in haste, they saw, contemplating how the island's shoreline stretched far ahead toward the horizon. The air they breathed, they knew to be saturated all the while with luring calls and tempting song.

Roped to the mast high above the heads of the men, Odysseus was furiously buffeted by the wind, yet the wind as foe could not be compared to the assault of the irresistible voices in their unending songs, their intimate calls to him. He must find some way to keep his wits in this terrible predicament. The truth was that he alone had to undergo this vast inhuman temptation! While he was finding himself worthy of pity, feeling overwhelmed by this dark trial, a small trickle of light made its way into his thought and glowed there like a small flame. Of course, that was what he would do. He would call upon Goddess Athena!

— O fair Athena of Athens' sovereign rock! Lady Athena, hear me!

The only answer seemed to be the groaning of the wind and the crashing of the waves as they met the Sirens' rocky shore. Now Odysseus was not a man to repeat himself, nor was he given to pleading his case. Instead, he was one who recognized the stone of truth, measuring out his words with frugality. The Sirens' voices, carried on a gale, assailed him once more, making him tremble. This wave of ecstatic sighing and singing seemed to hold a new element, however. What was it? A different voice, faint and low in tone, undergirded the sweet madness of the Sirens. Acknowledging this new voice, he muttered to himself.

— I have heard it somewhere before. I'm sure of it—that slow, sustained voice with its rhythmic beat. Ah, yes, it is the voice in the night, peaceful, persisting. Why, it's the voice of an owl! But the owl is a land bird. What can he be doing at sea? I must have forgotten what an owl sounds like. Listen!

Again into the moist darkness came the solitary voice, low and echoing as if spoken down a long corridor,

Who . . . who . . . who!

— Greetings, Owl. Your voice is very close to me now. Still I see nothing.

A silence followed. Now a voice that was quite human indeed was speaking. Incredibly, it was the voice of a woman.

— Odysseus, son of Laertes of Ithaca, father of Telemachos, I have come!

— Athena! Goddess, all hail! Curiously, what I heard approaching was an owl, the land bird, but not you. You have caught me by surprise, a grateful one, I must admit.

As he gazed at his shining companion of the night, he saw that she shook her head slightly in what might have been a mild rebuke.

— You called me, and yet can it be that you never expected to meet the owl, my companion?

— I wasn't thinking, I am afraid. One doesn't think too clearly when tied to a mast.

He spoke pointedly to his predicament as if she might have overlooked it. But Athena was not to be diverted.

— Without the owl, I should be diminished.

These words astonished Odysseus, whose watchful eyes recorded that the shoreline of the Sirens' isle still stretched before them.

— Lady Athena, any other time, I would show a hearty welcome of the owl, but at present, I am a man in crisis. Tell me, is the owl able to give me a hand?

There was an underlying skepticism in his voice, but Athena chose to ignore it.

— Indeed. Why else do we arrive together, Owl and I?

Now a glint of hope showed in his face as she continued.

— Owl brings the rhythm that is lost when life is seized by severe crisis. Ah, yes, she—Owl—comes with the steady voice, you see.

— The steady voice? How can such a thing save me?

— Owl's voice is tied to the pulse of what is true, her voice announcing each beat. Removed from its natural pulse, the human individual's life falls apart. Surely you see this.

— What you say makes me grateful to Owl, yes. Still, it is you, not the owl, that a Greek looks to for help in the anguishing hour of his crisis, Goddess, I must point out.

Athena fell silent through a long pause in which the gale battered at the mast, rocking the Greek pinned there. Her voice was low now as she spoke, and Odysseus inclined his head as much as he could to catch it.

— I, Athena, come with the steadying voice attuned to earth's true rhythm. Is not my ear laid to the pulse of what is true, of what can work in life for you? Listen again. Do you not sense the arrival of a peacefulness in Owl's voice? How am I the sustaining one for the Greeks without these qualities, I ask you?

— True, Lady Athena. I begin to understand. The capacity to understand is vastly narrowed for me at the moment, even so. You continue to speak only of a peaceful natural order of things while we Greeks when we think of the owl think of some wisdom.

— Ah, but what is wisdom? Always the Greeks are traveling to the oracle or to a seer to find the true answers. Owl does not make answers. I suppose you noticed that. And yet, she is wise. It is there in the voice. Almost it is fragrant within the peaceful order she restores.

Odysseus shook his head in his perplexity. Now he asked a question.

— So the wisdom of your owl is, tie the human individual to the mast of his vessel! Is this right?

The goddess did not reply but began to walk back and forth on the swaying ship, her eyes looking out to some invisible terrain. Now she raised her face toward Odysseus on the mast.

— Time is not bountiful when the wisdom is at hand. Do you realize this, son of Greece? Instead, there occurs a narrow opening in which one must neither vacillate nor argue, for one must act. Only keep your attention upon the sustaining voice of fertile Night!

— What then?

— Tend the voice of wise Owl, and dawn will come. All shall be well then, Odysseus!

Some time passed, and upon the now motionless ship, the oarsmen slept while the black hills of the land of the Sirens loomed yet near. A sudden gust of wind blew out to sea from the island, bringing a renewed assault of the seductive song with its sweet calls to the heroes. Odysseus alone remained in anguish and did not sleep. Once again he made a soft call,

— Athena, Lady Athena, where are you?

His eye caught the swift movement of a full overgarment as the figure strode into a view, and she leaned upon her shield. Odysseus thought he must address the question that had been smoldering within him for some hours.

— Goddess Athena, why must my men and I be subjected to such punishing precautions against the Sirens? For two decades, we have been warriors of the war against Troy and have a history of tough survival. We are even called heroes by the Greeks, as you know.

The goddess pondered his words.

— True what you say. It would be a straightforward matter if the Sirens were a human foe, but they are not human. Their seduction is ongoing, defying time. What is hardest to reckon with is this, Odysseus: their seduction can put to sleep your greatest gift.

— And what would that be?

— Human consciousness. Your consciousness must be guarded at all cost. Otherwise, you become one who merely repeats the familiar, following what others say, imitating their actions.

Odysseus sighed aloud, his body aching from its long awkward suspension.

— At the moment, I would gladly settle for the solution that brings the gentle peacefulness you said your owl brings.

— Owl is wise, yes. In keeping earth's rhythmic order lies his wisdom. Ah, but I must warn you. Be sure that the peacefulness you settle for is not the drugging of your consciousness, for such a peace is unnatural. Without essential awareness, one loses his freedom as well.

Odysseus fell silent as he pondered the words of Athena. It was the goddess who interrupted his musing.

— Well, Odysseus?

— I'm beginning to see that Circe's counsel of going along tied to the mast as one passes the Sirens is not such a bad plan after all!

He grinned now at Athena, and she smiled at him in return.

The Priestess of Athena at Tegea

The sun was setting as the young woman of Tegea made her way up the steep path toward the temple of Athena Alea. A strong wind whipped her garments about her slender body and tore at the tiny supply of calm she still managed to carry. Here in the south of Greece, war had descended upon them. Had not all the men of the city already left to join splendid Heracles before the walls of Lacedaemonia, battling for that city? Sterope's face showed her anxiety. Stripped of its able men, Tegea was not only abandoned but lay exposed and fragile in spite of its sturdy walls. Only women remained to stand watch on the walls now, along with some of the elderly men. It was her interval of rest from her post on the southern wall, and she had decided to make her way to the temple to seek Goddess Athena's help and protection. As she rounded the hill on the narrow path, the temple came into view. To her eyes, it was as radiant as moonlight and a source of startling beauty and peacefulness. She approached the stately columns as a final assault of the wind forced her to grab hold of the nearest column to keep from being thrown to the ground. Cautiously she made her way on the temple porch where the columns, like erect priestesses in a row, steadied her passage inward to the goddess's presence.

Once within the walls of the temple, she observed that the wind could only moan its defeat beneath the roof beams. Dusk made its way heavily in the dimness of the interior where she paused to catch her breath. Quite suddenly a small flame flared up, illuminating the sacred wooden image of Athena. Sterope saw that a woman hovered over the flame of the lamp, and she nodded in recognition, stepping forward and addressing the priestess.
— Is it you, Auge?

The woman was older than Sterope by several years and carried herself with a grace and a modest beauty, which everyone appeared to notice, but no one spoke of. Clearly she was startled to see her niece.

— Why, Sterope, I had not expected to see you here. In fact I've been concerned, knowing that you have been standing guard on the wall in the midst of this gale we're having.

— I needed a little break, you see. Isn't it early to be renewing the lamps with oil?

Continuing the task of replenishing the sacred lamps, Sterope replied idly,

— A little perhaps.

Any stranger observing the two young women would have guessed them to be kinswomen, if not sisters, so strong was the resemblance between them. Watching Auge, Sterope's face registered worry.

— Tell me, are you unwell? No one reports seeing you about the city these days. It is months since you visited the grandparents at their house. Do you realize this? My father spoke of the fact only last evening.

— Do tell my brother Cepheus he need not worry, will you? It is that the temple has required my ongoing presence, you see. Actually, it is my strong desire to remain here, even though I suppose I must appear secluded in the eyes of the family. Give each my fond greetings, will you, Sterope?

— How can I explain, then?

— Always it is best to speak the truth, even though one may not be able to disclose the whole of it, since truth has its pregnancy in time. Tell my kinsfolk that Auge must serve Athena's agenda rather than her own.

Sterope shook her head slowly as she was wont to do when Auge spoke obscurely. Her skeptical look caused Auge to smile ruefully at her niece, who continued.

— Besides, Grandfather, the king, has clearly expressed his desire to see you. No one refuses Grandfather. You have not been to the royal house since the time that they entertained the Theban hero, you know.

— Heracles!

The name had burst forth from Auge as some inscrutable passion passed through her. Sterope spoke quickly.

— Right. The Theban was certainly a magnificent man, wasn't he, although I admit his decisive movements, that powerful voice, and his thunderous laugh as he strode about the royal courtyard could be fairly frightening. Do you know what I've heard? That Heracles is a son of Zeus himself! How about that?

While Sterope seemed to be enjoying her lively gossip, Auge looked increasingly grave, and this fact did not escape Sterope.

— Oh, speak no more of him, Sterope.

— Well, I want to keep you informed. Otherwise, you'd have no idea what goes on in Tegea. You live such a protected life.

— Protected?!

Now Auge sighed, a sigh that appeared to travel through some deep, hidden corridor. She spoke quietly.

— You see, Heracles did come to the temple. After all, he deeply honors Athena. He came to present an offering and to sing an ode.

— He did? What happened? You were standing by, were you, maybe in the dim background?

Auge smiled slowly, remembering.

— Well, not really. I mean . . . the background became the foreground, one might say. There are momentous moments, and this was the most momentous of my life, Sterope.

— Wait a minute. It was festival time. It is strange that such a hero would be seeking out the temple when clearly he had come for the sole purpose of persuading Tegea to back his war against Lacedaemonia. His crisis was definitely urgent.

Sterope's candid questioning hung upon the fragrant air. Now Auge nodded slowly as some sense of resignation came over her. She watched the flame flare brightly before the wooden image of Athena as she moved to add oil to the lamp before Asklepios, god of healing. Next she replenished the lamp before Goddess Hygeia, noting again with gratitude that the three gods stood together here in Tegea. The snake that wreathed the arm of Hygeia seemed alive in the fitful pale light. Sterope moved forward and laid a small offering on the altar table as she softly intoned a prayer to Athena Light-bearer. When this was completed, Auge took her gently by the arm and led her to a small nook where they sat down together. Sterope spoke.

— You sent a message that I come to you. Is it then news from the battlefield?

— No.

Auge regarded her beloved niece silently before adding a thought.

— I do believe that you already may have guessed it.

A momentary wave of anxiety passed over Sterope's face before she managed to smile her knowledge. Auge pronounced the fact before them.

— Yes, I am pregnant! This is my message.

— Oh, it is true then! I couldn't be certain, you see. But you have been looking ill and off your food. Who is your lover, Auge? You must tell me.

— When we were in the midst of offering the Theban hero our best hospitality, Heracles visited the temple to honor Athena. Oh, one does not easily forget Heracles!

Sterope's hand flew to her mouth, and she was wide-eyed with astonishment.

— Heracles is your lover! Can it be? You speak of the one who even now commands the men of Tegea as they battle before the walls of Lacedaemonia?

— The same. None is braver and none is stronger except for the gods themselves. Sterope, the fact is that Heracles *was* my lover, but he is no longer. After all, he has gone from us.

— Well, he was certainly bold. I can say that. Had he no shaking knees at the very thought of making love to Athena's beloved virgin priestess, I ask you?

Sterope was not inclined to allow the famous hero of Thebes all the privileges he apparently saw fit to take for himself. After all, this was her aunt. Their closeness in age accounted for the valued friendship. Sterope observed that Auge's face took on a dreamy quality, and she groaned. Auge replied in any case.

— Ah, bold, yes. He was not intimidated in the least to find that I was a priestess of Athena, it seemed. Indeed, he said to me, "So you are Auge, daughter of Tegea's king. What torchlight I see in your eyes, yet something more. I do believe that the wise sight of Athena's owl is in your face. What a great guardian goddess Athena has been to me!"

Sterope responded warmly to this account.

— He only spoke the truth about you, of course. Attending her image here all your days, you do seem to grow more like the goddess herself. Others have noticed this as well.

As for Auge's mind, it was held fast in happy recollection.

— What he said after that astonished me even more. He said, "I too am close to Athena, for it seems that I am a hero dear to her heart. Auge, my dear, can you question for a moment that the goddess desires that the two of us should be together in love?" I can reveal no more, Sterope, for the rest must remain hidden.

— Hidden you say, except for the obvious fact that you shall bear the child of this love. At least I see that this love was hardly one-sided.

Auge blushed at this.

— I fear that things won't be easy for you. Just remember, my dear Auge, that I am truly your friend, will you?

Tears shone in the priestess's eyes, and she nodded, and both women were deeply moved.

Days passed, and Sterope again made her way to the temple, seeking Auge. The winds that had assaulted her so fiercely on her former visit were no longer present, and all was calm. Auge met her as she entered the columns of the pronaos, noting a deep frown on the face of the younger woman.

— O Auge, how can you look so calm when we are all on pins and needles to know whether Heracles and our men and allies have succeeded against the Lacedaemonians and restored Tyndareus to his throne?

— Be patient. We shall know soon enough, I think.

— Only think what happens if the Lacedaemonians have won the battle. Why, at once they shall set out for Tegea to invade our city! Whatever can we do?

Her last words were already overcome with grief. Auge placed her arm about Sterope's shoulders as she comforted her.

— But surely we know what we must do, Sterope.

— How can you say that? We are without arms or men on hand to defend ourselves.

Auge was gazing at her niece in grave perplexity.

— Ah, but Heracles told me when he was here that he had left with you a gift from Athena, a gift that would bring Tegea protection. Do you not have this gift in safe keeping?

Sterope answered without enthusiasm, much as one might answer a backward child.

— Yes, I have it. To keep it safe, I always wear this tiny bronze urn on a chain about my neck. See?

She took it out from beneath the fold of her garment to make it visible now. Sterope was puzzled.

— That's odd—what you say about its being a gift from the goddess—since it was the hero who gave it to me. I recall his words. He said, "Never open this small urn unless the darkest hour has come. Never, I say. And take care not to mislay it, for it is Athena's own aid for Tegea." You see, he knew what the urn contained. Auge, I expect that you haven't the foggiest notion what's inside the urn, have you?

— Yes, I know. Heracles told me. Because I am Athena's priestess, he thought that I needed to know that she had not forgotten us. Inside the small urn lies a lock of Medusa's hair!

— How awesome that is! And it is truly gruesome I'd say.

Sterope began to walk back and forth on the temple porch in an agitated manner.

— Time may be short, Sterope. Only think. Did Heracles not instruct you in the use of the small lock?

— O, yes, he gave some very odd instructions.

— Like what? Please do not delay, for we may soon be in crisis.

— Let me think. He said, "Watch well from the walls. Should the enemy appear over the brow of the hill, then open the urn at once and take out the small object. Whatever you are tempted to do, *don't look at it*. Instead, turn your face aside while you hold high the small object before the enemy host. At that moment, you must cry in a loud voice, 'Behold Medusa's lock!'" "What then?" I asked him. "Wait and call upon Athena, for it is the goddess who is entrusting you with the power of the Aegis over evil!" Strange, but I had not remembered those words until now.

Auge's eyes, sober in their intensity, remained on Sterope's face.

— You must do exactly as Heracles has instructed you, Sterope.

The young woman shrugged her shoulders briefly.

— Such a small thing is this lock of Medusa's, you know. This fact puzzles and troubles me. How foolish I should feel holding this tiny limp thing up before hundreds of armed men galloping toward me on horseback! Now a great shield or even an archer's bow would make more sense, surely.

— My dear friend, you must not doubt its power. So very much depends upon this tiny gift from the great Aegis!

Sterope shook her head stubbornly, frowning again.

— What have we got but a mere curly lock of hair and no more? How can it possibly stop an entire army, an accomplished one at that, from capturing Tegea and enslaving us?

— I know that the Lacedaemonians are legendary for their valor and skill in war.

— So, Auge, do be practical, even though you are a priestess who knows the power of the sacred images as another woman knows her pots and pans. Isn't this whole thing fanciful?

— From the way we are in the habit of looking at things, yes. Consider, however, what proves to be evil to one's welfare may contain a great deal of fantasy. While the facts of our undertaking appear lean, even frail, we must rely on what is given us and not be critical of it, I think.

Sterope was shaking her head as though she might be at wit's end.

— Listen, Auge. We don't have Athena's Aegis itself, the sacred goatskin of our goddess which we know wards off evil of all sorts. All we've actually got is a small lock from the Gorgon's head which hangs at the center of the Aegis. No more than that!

Auge's tranquility had descended upon her once more and was in evidence as she replied.

— The lock is tiny to be sure, yet it partakes of Medusa on the ground of the Aegis itself. It is like a mere phrase fallen from the mouth of madness and affliction, and yet the whole power of Medusa is contained in it.

Oh, I do not doubt that the lock has in it the needed power to protect us. Sterope, Athena has left us this small lock of hair for our defense, and we must make good use of it.

The sun had set, and the sky was bronze with the approaching dusk when a woman walked alone on the wall encircling Tegea. A cold wind gathered force, whipping the garments tightly about this watcher of the city. Sterope stopped in her stride as her gaze fell upon the temple of Athena Alea where Auge would be setting about the task of filling the lamps with oil, renewing the flames before the treasured image of Athena and before the gods Asklepios and Hygeia as well. After all, the three gods formed a trinity here in Tegea, it seemed, yet always Tegea would be Athena's city. There was some reassurance in the thought that here the goddess was Alea, bringer of light. But one must not pause too long when on watch on the great wall, she reminded herself. Her eyes scanned the southern approach to the city with some anxiety, making sure that no invader approached. Her right hand fell to her bosom where beneath her chiton lay the small bronze urn on its chain, and she clasped it with more desperation than confidence. She wished it were not such a small thing. What was it that Auge had said? "What is small is not negligible, remember." *Well, the day is safely past*, she told herself, *and not a single Lacedaemonian has been sighted coming to scout us out.*

Now a small cloud of dust caught her eye on the second hill. As she watched with growing alarm, the cloud grew. Probably some chariot is approaching, hastening to reach the city before dark, she thought. Even so, her pulse quickened as she monitored the nearer hill where several figures now emerged, black against the bronze sky. At the same time, a cry of battle rang out in the distance, and with sinking heart, she saw that a host of warriors plunged now toward the battlement on which she stood. Sterope gasped and cried out.

— Invaders! The Lacedaemonians have come! If only Cepheus, my father, my brothers, and all our men had not been persuaded to go off to fight before the walls of Lacedaemonia, leaving us defenseless! Now the enemy approaches our gates. And where is Heracles now when we so desperately need him?

The small bronze urn scratched her bare skin, pricking her memory at the very moment that the thought nearly possessed her: Flee for your life! Touching the urn seemed to bring her to full consciousness. At once she lifted the urn from its intimate nesting place, holding it before her.

Removing its seal, she now was able to feel inside the small vessel. Yes, it was there! The furry object was here indeed. Ah, she must remember not to look at it. In a low voice, she voiced her urgent thoughts.

— Remember, it is from the Aegis that has always stopped Athens' invaders. Can this small lock of hair save my beloved Tegea? Heracles thought it could. This I am certain of. Oh, oh, Athena's gift lies in my hand alone!

The invading warriors had spied her on the wall, and now they drew back their spears, taking aim. The words assaulted her mind, "Quickly or all is lost!" Turning her gaze away from the enemy host and from the urn's treasure as well, she stretched forth her hand high into the air holding the dreaded lock before the eyes of the Lacedaemonians. In that moment, she found her voice and cried aloud,

— *Behold the lock of the Gorgon's hair!*

As if they had been struck by many spears, confusion broke over the host. Excited cries broke out. Breaking into erratic movements in their fear, the men began turning back. The voices that had been close at hand were growing faint, although still edged with terror as the invaders retreated. When at last Sterope lowered her aching arm, she watched the last of the enemy host disappear over the far hill. Beyond a doubt, Tegea was saved! Turning about toward the temple below now, she murmured her gratitude and smiled.

The months passed, and Auge in her solitary abode brought to birth a son. Of necessity, his birth remained a secret guarded by the walls of Athena's temple. Each day when night cloaked the city of Tegea, life unfolded within the temple.

The priestess Auge would enter the inner sanctuary bearing a white bundle in her arms. Approaching the sacred image of Athena, she would lay down the bundle, kneeling as she did so and pulling aside the concealing wool to reveal the face of her lovely child. The bright-eyed, observing infant would follow her movements with his eyes. Speaking into the baby's ear, she laid a finger to her lips, and the baby smiled and cooed. Auge laughed happily.

— Only look, little one. Standing beside you are great gods Athena, Asklepios, and Hygeia, your protectors, you see.

With a sacred gesture, Auge's hand swept outward toward the holy images, each now illuminated by the golden light of its lamp. Then Auge would make a prayer to the gods that the child might find a safe and blessed childhood, in spite of the fact that she could not begin to imagine how that was possible. Tegea would not take well to a mysterious birth from their priestess. Of this she was certain and was not tempted to self-deception.

The son of Auge and Heracles grew splendidly and would happily crawl about over the smooth stone floor of the temple. He especially liked to lie on his back and watch the lively and noisy exchange of the birds that lived under the eaves of the high roof. One day when dusk had settled over the city, Auge saw with worry that someone approached the temple. She recognized at once the strong, echoing steps as the figure crossed the courtyard, and her face grew pale. There was no time to flee. Auge reached protectively toward her child as she raised her face to the figure who stood within the doorway now. It was the king, her father, Aleus.

— Ah, Father, you have come!

She pronounced the words simply and not without warmth, although they fell fatefully on the air. He came forward staring at the child, his face taut as quietly he asked the question.

— So what is this about, my daughter? Whose child is this?

There was a long tense pause. Auge seemed to be gazing down some long distant corridor as she spoke at last.

— This is my own son, Father.

Fury swept over the king, and he trembled. When he spoke, his voice shook, so great was his emotion.

— And who was it that dared defile my daughter the priestess? Who, I ask?

She met her father's furious gaze steadily.

— Father, I cannot say!

— What you mean is that you will not say. Tell me truthfully, are you keeping trysts with a secret lover?

— No. There are no such meetings. Indeed, there is for me no secret lover. It is a fact that I never invited a man across the temple threshold.

— Then he entered unbidden, I take it. Although I believe you, Auge, I
cannot save you. Always you had been dear to my heart . . .

He spoke regretfully, and grief was in his face until he could find
again the voice in which he was accustomed to give orders.

— Make yourself and the child ready to depart at dawn tomorrow. Do
you understand? I shall send a faithful, old servant along with you.

— Father, only one thing I ask of you: save the boy! His name—

The king interrupted her abruptly.

— I don't want to hear his name. Let him remain a nameless mistake. But
I shall honor your request. The child shall live, even though it is my
prerogative to destroy him. The time has come, Auge. Farewell to you.
The truth is that I shall never see you again.

Tenderness, pain, and loss crossed his face in succession before he
turned and left the sanctuary. And Auge wept in her sorrow and despair.

The shepherd counted the last three sheep to cross the cold brook
and scramble up the steep slope, there to join the flock on Mt. Parthenius'
high green ledge. Now to milk the nanny goat—but where had she gone?
Leaving the sheep grazing, he searched the scrub growth and the rockier
area as well, making use of his staff to poke into the thickets. Why should
she leave the flock, and where was she? A soft bleating from some distance
was heard now. It must come from the yet higher ledge of rock, he figured.
How had the goat managed to make her way through so much thicket,
climbing onto slippery, mostly vertical rock? He set out swiftly toward the
high ledge. Reaching the ledge drenched in the morning sunlight, he was
astonished at what he found, as the large nanny turned to greet him with
a gentle calling sound. The goat stood over a robust baby, who sat up with
a firm hold of the udder at which he nursed contentedly. The shepherd
grinned in spite of himself.

— Now, just who would you be, little fellow, I ask? Someone mighty
important is my guess, to be worth so much trouble. Just look at your
fine garments and the layers of delicately woven woolen covers about you!
I've never seen anything like it. And what's this pin you're wearing?

The shepherd fingered the pin, scrutinizing it closely. As for the
baby, he laughed at the question.

— It's gold all right. No question about it. Why, it's the Gorgon's head,
looking like the one on Athena's own Aegis, mind you.

Unconsciously he made the sacred gesture as a realization struck
him forcibly.

— Now we know for a fact that you're under the goddess's protection.

    The baby himself was hardly into explanations. Instead, he let go of the goat and extended both his arms upward toward the shepherd.

— All right, young fellow. That decides it. I'll just take you home with me. After all, you've already got yourself a wet nurse. Come along, Amalthea. Say, little prince, lucky for you that Amalthea found you before you fell off this ledge. I've got a name for you. It's Telephos, the finisher. It's going to fit you because I've this hunch that some day you'll have the last word.

    He laughed, delighted at the thought, and added,

— Of course, *they* don't know that, do they?

    The baby laughed as well.

    Meanwhile, Auge herself was taken by Nauplius, son of Poseidon, across the Aegean Sea to Mysia where King Teuthras of Teuthrania received her graciously. In time Teuthras made the lovely, sad Auge his wife in this far kingdom. Always she carried, nevertheless, an abiding sorrow for the loss of her little son, whose fate she did not know.

    Many years went by, and the day arrived when kind Teuthras, her husband, came to her chamber where she sat at the window gazing thoughtfully toward the temple on the hill. How often he had found her here looking at the temple with wistfulness. Now she turned to greet him.

— What is it, Teuthras? I sense an excitement in you. Have you opened some secret?

— Curious that you should put it that way, my dear.

— Well, do tell me.

— My excitement is due entirely to the fact that I just came from looking at you in a mirror, I do believe. Incredible, it is.

— You speak in riddles.

    Although she responded reasonably, something was alerted within her.

— Well, if you think so, you had best come with me. A visitor has just arrived who comes from afar, it seems. Most recently he started out from Delphi. This means that he is one to whom the oracle has recently spoken, of course.

    Auge was on her feet, and now she gasped eagerly with her question.

— Does he come with some message for us from the oracle, do you think?

Teuthras took her arm and led her from her chamber toward the hall where their visitor waited. As they went, he continued.

— Most likely the young man asked the oracle of Apollo for himself . . . . Ah, here we are. Before you enter, I must tell you that he has asked to see the queen of Teuthrania alone. So you must go in alone. I do trust the young man.

Auge, her dark eyes large in her slender face, nodded mutely, hesitating a long moment before she went forward into the room. Where the young man waited beside the window, his torso was bathed in light while his eyes were lifted to her face in an inquiry that almost seemed anguished. What caused Auge to murmur aloud was what her first look revealed. Here was a face so very much like her own, with the exception of a bolder set of the jaw. Oh, and those shoulders! They caused her an immediate, delighted recognition. How could she ever forget those shoulders of Heracles? And these were so like them, broad and powerful. He remained silent, his gaze never leaving her face, waiting modestly for her to speak. Only one word spilled from her now.

— *Alive?*

He nodded. Her voice had become a whisper. So much depended on this moment, surely.

— Is it truly you? How can it be?

Nor could he avail himself of his own voice, but instead he held something toward her in the open palm of his hand. Staring at the object, she alternately felt joy and a faint heart as she cried out,

— It is the gold Aegis! It was I who pinned this on the baby's garment, entrusting him to the sole protection of Athena at our sorrowful parting! Are you then . . . ?

— I am Telephos, your son who was banished. The oracle has found you for me at last. O my mother!

— Telephos, son of mine, found!

Telephos laughed happily as if he had just shed some enormous burden, and the two of them moved together to embrace. They wept for the joy of finding each other now, and the reunion was wondrous. Auge spoke now.

— You must wait here while I go to find my husband, King Teuthras. He is a kind man, but I must ask him if he will give you hospitality.

A small shadow of worry crossed her face, and he saw it. At once he spoke.

— Mother, do not trouble yourself. Things are already decided, you see.

    At this point, Teuthras entered, and he was smiling.

— What's this, my dear? At our age, we have at last produced a child and heir to the kingdom, I say!

    Auge looked astounded while Telephos smiled in gratitude, bowing to each in turn.

— My father, my mother, you shall not regret this day, I promise you!

    The king called to the servant at the door as he addressed the company.

— A feast is in order. Let us issue invitations far and wide for a great feast. The homecoming of our son, the future king of Teuthrania, deserves high celebration.

    It was Auge who spoke quietly now.

— First, let us go together, the three of us, to the temple and offer a sacrifice to Athena, for it is she who has protected Telephos from infancy to manhood!

    Telephos laid his hand upon his mother's arm now.

— I must tell you the crucial facts. There is a shepherd, but for his benevolence in rescuing me and giving me a home, I should not have lived.

    Gratitude again flooded Auge's heart, and Teuthras replied,

— By all means, we must bring this shepherd to the celebration and honor him, for he shall ever be welcome in this house.

    Later, before the public sacrifice to the goddess and prior to the feast of celebration, Auge made her way alone to the temple. In the dim interior she stood for a long time before the sacred image of Athena, perceiving within the deep silence some mystery at work that restores the fair order of reality. At last she took the gold pin of the Aegis, gazing upon it with wonder before pinning it to the goddess's own bosom.

Athena and the Plowman

His plow and ox beside him, the farmer stood looking out over the long stretch of rough field in the early morning light. It was the pause he had to have before beginning the huge task of preparing the field for the sowing. As he continued standing there enveloped in the vast moist quiet, which was broken only by bird calls, a figure appeared over the rise at the far end of the field walking toward him. Astonished as he stared at the figure, he observed that it was a woman—tall, slender, moving with a lively stride—who approached over the rough ground. Was it an illusion? What stranger would be arriving on the open field and at such an hour? As she reached the spot where he waited, a slow recognition was beginning in himself. She was radiant. It was the goddess Athena! Before he could speak and even as he made the sacred gesture, she was speaking.

— The ground has no furrows, I see. Only your brow, plowman, is deeply furrowed. Why are you anxious? Your plow appears to be a sturdy one and your ox is young and strong enough, I should say.

Were her words encouraging or meant to shake him up? He couldn't be sure. He would tell it as it is. No pussyfooting about for him.

— What you say is a fact, Goddess. You ask what worries me. Why, it's the same every time when the ground which ought to be soft for turning presents a thick, very tough crust that's hard to penetrate. I'm at the worst time, the time before the labor begins. Every year at this time, I wonder how I can possibly begin all over again.

As she regarded him thoughtfully, there was a softened look in her shining eyes.

— Ah, it's the beginning that shows its dark face. This I know about. Where is the spark that ignites the beginning, for it is needed? The winter has been long and has held you motionless.

He nodded vigorously, and his face was drawn.

— So you do know how it is for a plowman like me. Look at this big field. Why, it's too much. I'm only one fellow with one plow and one ox!

She nodded briefly as to a man who had looked into his purse and added up the correct sum.

— Actually, that is all that is needed. What is essential at this time is that you begin in earnest, bringing the fire of your energy to the task. Tell me, how shall you go about it?

— Why, I'll dig in with the plow, once I've harnessed my ox, penetrate the ground, tear it up and turn it over. I'm the one who has to do all this, and it isn't easy.

Athena gazed into the distance now and was quiet for some time. When she spoke, her voice was somehow changed, as if pursuing a different path.

— Ah, plowman, that is the old way, I believe. My way is different for I am goddess of plowmen, you must know.

— You know a better way of getting this cultivation job done, do you?

— Yes. Listen well. First you must see to it that it is not *you* who penetrates and turns the ground. It is not you, for it is the work of beast and plow.

He could not repress a small groan in reaction to the goddess's strange logic.

— Well, of course. Still, all the responsibility is on me. The fact is that there's no way I can back out, Goddess Athena.

She swept her hand in front of her lovely face as if to discourage a fly.

— Much to learn, much to learn. Already you are heavy with concern for what you want to see happen and what you propose to do with your land.

— What's this? Everybody knows that you're the goddess of work and the goddess of what heroes undertake as well. Would you talk a man out of his purpose, his plan? This is hard to believe. My goal has bent me, and it shapes me. It feeds me and pulls me inexorably forward in the project. Why, this is what a human being is all about. Goddess, it's a funny thing. I thought that I must be like you in this respect being altogether into the work.

She smiled now and hastened to reply.

— Ah, yes, plowman, we are akin indeed. After all, we both are workers. Still, observe a difference, if you will: I am neither bent by my purpose nor burdened by it!

— Really? Now that's odd. Is it possible? I am confused. At the same time, something is altering. Why, the purpose just went out of me like air out of a balloon. Funny but I feel a whole lot lighter somehow.

— That is good news. Here is how you must proceed. Listen closely, for each step is crucial. You must begin by setting about your specific purpose, namely the plowing of the fallow field. As you undertake this, your heart must be in it. Next, you must prepare to meet the ox.

— What do you mean? You make it sound like Ox is the king!

She nodded and appeared to be slowly pondering.

— Hm, yes. Yes indeed. Ox is a very, very old king, as a matter of fact.

Plowman slapped his knee soundly and laughed heartily at this.

— Ha-ha. That's a good one. You've got a sense of humor, Goddess. Here's the way I operate. I say, "See this stick in my hand, Ox? You're going to know who's boss."

He finished, smiling broadly, and again slapped his knee for emphasis. But Athena had not seen the joke, apparently. Were all Olympians like this, he wondered?

— No. No, plowman. You best never forget that such an old king still possesses great power.

Several emotions crossed his face—perplexity, fear, and then something more luminous.

— I just caught a kind of shining glimpse of something, and then it faded. Say, maybe there's a forgotten truth in what you're saying.

— Listen closely then. Ox, the old king, is alive with an old knowing that has been brewed through eons of time. He is your mighty storehouse that you dare not betray. What you must do is care for him. But whatever you do, you must not make a *pet* of him. Treat him well. Listen to his movements, for he knows what folks have long forgotten.

— This ox of mine knows more than we humans know?

— Oh, much more. What he knows is not honed down to ideas or to some subtle forms. Instead, it is massive like the face of the deep. This beast knowing and Ox's strength are one.

— So what am I to do, things being the way you say they are?

— Pluck from Ox's thought and strength the substance that supports your own strength in meeting the whole of existence. He's your earthly storehouse. If what you undertake fails to make its way through the Ox, then not even the gods can help you!

— Ah, Lady Athena, my faithful goddess, little did I know. It seems that I must make a friend of Ox, the ancient king. Best scrap the usual plan . . . Yes, Ox and I are going to go along together now.

Athena's face held a thoughtful smile and some grace difficult to describe, he thought. She left him some final words.

— The beginning has begun, I'd say. Ox will become your companion, I believe. He shall be closer to you than a spouse.

Several months passed before the plowman, returning to the spot where first Athena had visited him, sat down to wait, scanning the far line of the hills with hope. He was still staring at the far horizon when a familiar voice addressed him close at hand.

— Greetings, plowman.

— Lady Athena, you have returned!

— Ah, and how is it with your ox, I wonder?

He moved uneasily, frowning.

— Well, that's the thing I decided I must see you about. Actually, what has happened is that Ox is growing fat and quite independent while I am becoming more and more tired and, well, tense. As a matter of fact, we argue a good deal.

The goddess shook her head slowly and looked pensive.

— So you are at odds? I am sad to hear it. Tell me, how is the olive grove doing?

— The grove? Strange that you should ask. It has gone dry, and it's overgrown. Ox doesn't want to do the work in it, see?

Athena's eyes widened.

— Alas, I fear that you may have made a pet of him. Can this be the case?

— Look. You advised me to listen to Ox and to make close friends with him, treat him as very important. That's what I've been doing.

She leaned forward, and her voice held concern.

— A friend is an equal, not a pet to be served or indulged. Having made a pet of your beast, he has conquered you, it seems.

— Well, I can hardly believe it of myself! Make a pet of my ox? Let me tell you how it went.

He grimaced, shaking his head.

— Every day I was attentive to him, the way you said to be, and every day he would want more than was being offered to him. Why, I became like his faithful servant, you see, yet we were companions. I'd ask him each morning, "Do you want to go out in that juicy meadow over the hill and graze, or do you want to work the olive grove?" Sometimes I added, "The olive grove really needs us, old boy." Next I would follow Ox, and invariably he would head for the meadow. Now what am I to do, Goddess? My farm is going to ruin.

Athena had sat down on the boulder in the shade of the old olive tree, removing her helmet as she did so. She continued to study the plowman, her expression so full of thought as to remind him of the look of an owl. Finally she spoke.

— Cheer up, for it is not too late, I believe. You took the needed step with Ox, honoring him. It is that you overdid it. Still, certain things have been accomplished, I perceive. For one thing, you have altogether lost the arrogant sense of responsibility that was ruling your work. When I was here before, your purpose and its rational plan became the ruling monarch. Such a monarchy overburdened you, making you tense and dutiful while Ox functioned simply as your servant under the stick. This situation has changed.

— That's true. You know, I do feel better, and I laugh a lot more. It is just here lately that we've been quarreling, Ox and I.

— And there is another change. The natural realm in which Ox is king has become a place where you walk freely. You have come alive, plowman, for you have touched the energy and the deep knowing in earth's realm.

— Do you think so? Well, that's good news. What has landed me into the fix I'm in is this king bit, though, making Ox the king.

— So now you are ready for the next step. There is not a single Greek hero that has sought me out that I've not led him one step at a time. Even so, it can be slow going.

This hardly sounded like encouraging news to him, but he waited politely.

— Further delay would be a mistake. I should say that this new step is a difficult one and will involve you in paradox.

Paradox? The word fell on his ears as something alien.

— Goddess, I've never grown anything but olives . . .

— And you shall grow them again shortly—flourishing olive trees with shining black fruit that yields the virgin oil!

— What's this step you're talking about then? Something else has got to change is my guess.

Athena took something from beneath her peplos, extending it toward him in her hand.

— Look at what I hold, plowman.

— Why, it's a wooden yoke.

Of all things he was prepared for, not once did he imagine her bringing him a yoke.

— Now do you know?

Suddenly he felt a wave of resentment. Irrational though it was, it overwhelmed him.

— But Ox has had his freedom. He's been so—so happy! Why would I put him under the yoke?

— He is not really happy any longer, I'd say. Otherwise, he would not be so restless and argumentative, always wanting something different.

— It's true that Ox gets bored a lot.

— The ox yoke is the answer.

He ran his hands slowly over the yoke, taking in each of its smooth, sturdy features.

— It is rather heavy. It's going to keep him on track.

— Look well, plowman. Is your purpose sturdy enough to bear the yoke?

Momentarily his astonishment caused him to stare at her wordlessly. Now he spoke in a low voice.

— Do you mean to say that I am the one to be yoked?

— Had you imagined that you would remain outside the ox yoke?

— Well, yes, most certainly. This piece of equipment is designed for controlling my ox!

— If you have learned anything since last we met, it is this, plowman: you and the ox are one!

— But my freedom, Goddess! What of my delicious freedom? And what about his freedom? The yoke is harsh. How can I put it on him, on us, for that matter? How can I explain to him? It's important that he know that I still love him and consider him a great king, you see.

Athena had risen to her feet and began to stride back and forth, still within the shade of the tree, her eyes studying the ground during a long pause. The plowman observed her and waited. Now she turned to him.

— Faithful plowman, all I can console you with is a piece of knowledge. It is this: going under the yoke of Athena will bring the new satisfaction, and it will spread over the face of life!

— So that's how it works? Don't we call you Athena Nike, the Wingless Victory? I'm beginning to see what that implies—an achievement that happens right down on the ground. Well, Goddess, the ground is what I am going to work!

— Your very own ground is the source of your treasure. In time you will know that the ox yoke is the answer. Come, if you are ready, let us go together, you and I, side by side, carrying the yoke. I shall yoke your ox and bestow my blessing.

She smiled fully upon the plowman now.

— I am grateful to you, Goddess. Still, I have a lingering worry.
— What worry?
— Will we ever be free again, Ox and I—the workers?
— Yes. You won't see it at once, you see. It is a new and better freedom that grows under my ox yoke. What may appear strange is that this freedom will not be freedom from work or from a purposeful path. No. It is a freedom that will come to bloom under the yoke. On your land you will observe how the olive trees will grow abundant and beautiful when you and Ox have worked them. Only when the human individual and his working beast are yoked together by my hand do two worlds come to blossom.

PART IV

Hephaestus

Hephaestus and the Path of Work

It is a regrettable fact that in ordinary experience, love and work appear as opposing horizons with a distance yawning between them. While love is known to bring a variety of personal satisfactions, work tends to pose hard necessities. The worker is compelled to leave familiar affections or the unencumbered satisfaction that Aphrodite may indeed provide. Facing what lies before him, he must summon courage to enter the workplace where by the sweat of his brow, or else by particular skills, the worker earns his bread. In any case, this extreme opposition of love and work haunts the long corridor of the unconscious, at times emerging in a compelling need to defeat work by trickery of some sort. Such a shadow emerges when work becomes a glutton that feeds on human energy obsessively. Even the Olympian gods, on two separate occasions, were moved to take drastic action against the god of work, throwing him from Olympus' peak to the world below. No matter that creative, mild-natured Hephaestus had made the splendid houses of the gods. The craftsman god was looked upon as the odd one among them, the one who limped as he walked.

Among the Greeks, Hephaestus and Athena were the two great gods of work, and both were highly honored in their exceptionally fine temples in Athens as well as in their festivals. Locally, Athenian metal craftsmen were devoted to Hephaestus while the weavers held an unquestionable dedication to Athena. As it happened, love and work did manage to overcome their opposition, for it was on the Acropolis of Athens that, seized by love's vision and passion, Hephaestus pursued Athena as his beloved. Sworn to everlasting virginity, Athena fled from her lover, escaping capture, yet his seed spilled upon the ground. In her affection for the two gods, and possibly manifesting her genius for recycling, Earth Goddess herself took on the pregnancy and, in time, brought to birth the child Erechthonios. When she delivered the newborn babe into Athena's arms, Athena proclaimed the child to be her own mystic offspring destined to be founder-king of Athens. Curiously, the myth suggests that, when two gods love, what is brought to birth is more significant than the progeny of physical birthing.

Within the myths of the creative god Hephaestus, two extraordinary ideas confront us. One is the idea that the creative spirit produces enormous discomfort on its home ground, so much so as to be rejected as odd and unbearable. Certainly this is supported by the god's being hurled off Mt. Olympus on two different occasions, a fate that fell to no other Olympian god. This rejection is further affirmed in the fact of his settling for an earthly home on the remote volcanic isle of Lemnos, where in a cave he set up his forge. The myths suggest a second idea, namely, that the creative spirit, which in Hephaestus's case informs the whole of his work, is claimed by extreme solitariness. He must reside outside the society of which he is an integral part—the Olympians. That the solitary one requires appropriate sheltering and even seeks companioning is also a fact of the myths. It is in the realm of the sea that Hephaestus seeks this sheltering, where in the sea grotto he is companioned by sea goddesses Thetis and Eurynome. Here he remains for nine years while the goddesses provide him their warm hospitality and are recipients of his exquisite creations.

In spite of the familiar and ongoing opposition of love and work in human experience, the Greeks managed to find a reconciliation of a more lasting kind. This lay in the marriage of Hephaestus to Aphrodite herself.

On Olympus, the long absence of Hephaestus had become an unfathomable loss. Hermes was therefore dispatched to the deep sea grotto to negotiate his return, bringing to an end a nine-year idyllic life isolated from the world. However, Hephaestus would not consider the proposition of a return to Olympus until his terms were agreed to: *Aphrodite must become his wife!* Hermes negotiated this contract, and Hephaestus returned to Olympus where indeed Aphrodite became his bride. Out of such a profound resolution of love and work, it may be assumed that creative work was no longer a matter of skill, cleverness, and artistry alone. Now it was companioned by desire, persuasion, the fire of Eros, and Aphrodite's inimitable gifts to life.

The dialogues that follow have emerged out of work with the myths of Hephaestus's distinctive journey between heaven and earth. Gradually the path of the creative spirit and work is shaped in the far hidden realm of the sea nymphs while it is fully espoused within the luminous feeling realm of Aphrodite.

In the Grotto with the Sea Nymphs

In the *Hymn to Pythian Apollo*, it is told how the goddess Hera, examining her newborn baby Hephaestus, is overwhelmed with disappointment to discover that he has misshapen feet, and gives voice to a sense of shame and disgrace. At once, she seizes her child and hurls him off Mt. Olympus with the result that he falls into the realm of the sea, where Thetis and the sea nymph Eurynome offer him hospitality for nine years.

The fall from Olympus had left him bruised and mute on the floor of the sea. He was cold at the core, a condition beyond the weather of the sea, for it was the penetrating chill of one who has been scorned and rejected. How long he lay there, it was not possible to say, but in time he struggled to his feet and managed to find a path that brought him to a high-vaulted grotto. As he stood before the entrance peering into the dimness, low, musical voices drifted toward him. He wondered, does one knock at such a place? A decision was not required for presently the sea nymph Thetis herself stood within the dimness of the entrance—she who had won the hearts of both Zeus and Poseidon without meaning to. Astonished to see the god, she greeted him warmly.

— Hephaestus, can it really be you? Welcome to the grotto of Eurynome and myself! You will not regret our hospitality.

Already she took his arm gently and led him into the grotto's deep interior before he was able to find his lost voice. With a tender look, she saw that the luminous supply of energy that characterized the great worker god had been somehow exhausted. Leading him at once to an inviting couch, she returned to her own couch and resumed her weaving of dried seaweed. After some time, she spoke to him as if in the middle of an already long exchange, although there had been none.

— What a formidable happening it was to fall from the place of the gods!
Surely it was an event to shake a person to his foundation. And was such
your fate, Hephaestus? Nor do I ask for the details, for I abhor curiosity,
which merely serves itself and gives nothing in return. Still, you must
not continue to bear the fall alone, surely. Such an experience might be
reduced in its enormity if you shared it. Gives us your tale, Hephaestus!
After all, we sea nymphs have proved to be good listeners.

    Moved by Thetis's fair words, the god sat up on the couch now
and gazed earnestly at Thetis. As he did so, his face began to lose some of
its pallor, and it softened. In order to speak, he felt compelled to reclaim
his voice out of the abyss in which it had plunged.

— In the abyss, dear Thetis, all things tend to lose their substance. To tell
the truth, the abyss has been my most recent address!

— But no, your Olympian self cannot have been devoured by the abyss
of which you speak!

    The lovely nymph had leaped to her feet in protest.

— Strangely, I am beginning to feel a summons of a sort, one intrinsic to
yourself, reviving me somewhat.

— Speak of the fall, if you will, for it is an extraordinary thing that
happened.

— Alas, it was a sudden, mighty plunge downward out of the light and all
I had depended on, a plunge into vast and hostile depths of space and
time. I fell over and over again through the dizzying expanse between
sky and earth before I met the great raging sea! How could I dream
of the good fortune of coming upon the sea grotto of the nymphs? A
realization seized me instead with terror: *I am not a sea god!* What a fall
it was.

    Thetis was shaken by these words.

— But no god has ever simply fallen from Olympus!

— Am I not the living proof? Nor did I simply stumble at the cliff's edge
on the summit. I was pushed by my mother, Goddess Hera.

    For the hundredth time, confusion strongly mixed with sorrow,
and anger overtook him.

— No, no. It is beyond belief, for surely a mother cherishes her own son!
What had you done to prove this action?

— No action or gesture on my part affected her. What was impossible for
her to accept was the fact that my feet were crippled. In me she beheld
the flawed son of Zeus, a fact too incredible for her to live with, it
seemed. Look at me, Thetis, and behold *the god of the reluctant feet*!

Thetis arose, looked down for a long moment at the god's twisted feet and gave a cry of anguish. Next she pulled the veil over her face and withdrew into silence. The sympathy of a nymph could be short-lived, he thought grimly. Nevertheless, after a while, he engaged in a slow smile as hope stirred again within himself.

— There is no sweeter solace I can imagine than your good company, Thetis. You must not think me ungrateful. It is that I have been a wanderer in the dark like some soul in the underworld, without benefit of Hermes as guide!

— Oh! I wonder if you shall always be separated from the home of the gods. Surely such an exile is unthinkable for you.

— Well, there is no doubt about the fact that I am regarded as the outcast. Only look at me more closely, gracious nymph, and what do you see but the outsider!

The blue eyes of the nymph regarded him closely, before she threw back her head in objection.

— No! You are an Olympian god! No Olympian can remain an outsider to Olympus, surely!

— Am I not the living proof? Besides, my mother, Goddess Hera, threw me outward, hurling me into the abyss of sky and sea. The truth is that I do not fit . . . well, expectations, you see. I am too unlike the graceful gods.

Like all women, Thetis was practical.

— You are lame. I see that, but it is your only flaw to the eye. I fail to see how this condition fails the gods.

— If you watch my walk, you will observe that my feet never follow the footsteps of the others. This creates suspicion in others, my gait is simply awkward and unacceptable in their eyes. I tell you, Thetis, I must be reconciled to being the god of the unpredictable steps!

Thetis pondered this, her weaving dropped at her feet.

— Were you not such a one, how could you be the great creative one among the gods? What else happened in the fall?

— All choice fell away from me. I wasn't in charge. Also removed to a far distance was the delight in my Olympian house of bronze and the joy of work at the forge. All the familiar boundaries faded. Like a leaf borne on the wind, I breathed distance and alienation and the unutterable anguish of abandonment!

The voice that Thetis heard now was a voice out of the abyss, it seemed. He continued.

— Downward I fell through a passage without doors, without possibilities. Yes, Thetis, all that had been open in my life was closed, and I was compelled, like an ox under the rod, toward some unseen destination. Some inscrutable change was upon me, causing the thought to arise: I cease to be!

For a time, both figures fell silent. Now the nymph shook her head.

— Ah, but you did not cease to be. That passage was too terrible to fathom, but now the fall is completed. It no longer rules, Hephaestus. Do you understand? You shall make a sojourn with us here below, one that will be a joy to you. There is a certain sight, one that ripens here in our sea place . . .

— I believe that it is legendary. What does your sight reveal about the fall then?

— A mystery. A mystery of the god world.

— You forget that I have nothing to do with mysteries. I am not like Demeter. Always I must have the feel of the substance!

— And you shall have it again, never fear. I perceive Goddess Hera in a new light, I believe. She initiated the fall because she is taskmistress, and in this role, she is awesome. Oh, I know that the Greeks never called her this. Still, it lies in the mystery of her context.

— Great gods of Olympus! What you are implying is that the fall becomes a path of sorts, the path of a task!

— I don't believe that you arrived here at the grotto by mere accident, craftsman. Ah, here is Eurynome. Eurynome, do join our guest Hephaestus and me.

Hephaestus greeted the mother of the Graces warmly, and the three of them sat down. Thetis spoke to Eurynome.

— As mother of the Graces, I believe that you are likely to know how things are with Hera. Such knowledge could be of use to Hephaestus, who is more or less out of communication with her.

He smiled wryly at the understatement and added.

— I do remember that in my mother's oldest temple at Argos, the sacred image of her reveals her surrounded by the Graces as her familiar companions. Ah, always the Graces are known to create the desirable context for an undertaking, assuring human folk of the favorable outcome. Surely that is a puzzling fact considering that, according to Thetis, Hera is setting me upon a journey of the difficult task.

Eurynome became thoughtful, and her words were enigmatic.

— Ah yes, the deep favoring of the son can seem unlucky as life works out the text.

— Are you sealing my fate, Eurynome?

— That is not in my power, and besides, I feel only pity for your circumstance, Hephaestus. Ah, one moves from early truths to later ones that set the fruit. Thetis, what do you mean when you say that Hera sets Hephaestus to the task? I do understand how Athena is known to set the task before the hero, but Athena is not involved here.

— True, but what would you call the fall and what lies within its trail for Hephaestus? Surely with the gods, there is no accident and no stroke of mere chance. Something more momentous, more shaping of a long future is surely involved.

The lovely nymph who is mother of the Graces took this in slowly, honoring Thetis's insight.

— What I know best I should call the *undertaking*—that purposeful, consistent path that, given the presence of the Graces, is able to become radiant. It is my fervent hope that it is the undertaking that Hephaestus embraces now. A *task* has a way of overtaking one from behind, you see, which is most unfortunate and unpleasing, while the *undertaking* is met face-to-face and one smiles and nods, pledging oneself like a lover!

This animated speech of quiet Eurynome made its impact on Thetis and the craftsman. The latter spoke, smiling.

— So may I, the worker god, be the generous lover! What is yet assailing me, however, is this grim destiny that shrouds everything that is happening to me and appears to be dealt out by the Fates, for it is a fact that not even Zeus determines one's destiny. You nymphs appear to have an incredibly positive outlook on this newly unfolded destiny of mine, I must say. Quite frankly, I am aware that this destiny may turn out to be as gloomy as the perilous fall has been!

Thetis refused to allow Hephaestus to slip back into his initial crippling gloom. She spoke with animation.

— Wait a minute, Hephaestus. Without the awesome fall, you would not be the liberated son of your parents, freed from your past reputation among the gods. Do not let your new freedom go unclaimed and dishonored, a present tossed into the depths of the closet, yet to be unwrapped!

— You speak eloquently, Thetis. If only you could suggest a way that I can make a satisfactory impression on those august ladies, the Fates.

She continued as if he had not spoken.

— And do not forget the sacred festivals. Think of the runners, the chariot drivers, the poets and singers, those performing in the games. Remember how they pour libations to the Graces, seeking their blessing!

— Indeed. Let me assure you that I am in awe of the Graces and should welcome their aid, which appeals to me more than what the Fates may be inclined to deal out. But the question remains, have I a choice?

    Eurynome replied.

— Yes, the choice is before you. When you embrace the undertaking that belongs to you, your essence will be cast into many tangible forms, forms of great beauty that you shape, even useful objects. Instead of treacherous descents and laborious ascents, you will arrive at an ease in what you create. I speak of an ease generated out of the intimate context of green valleys, high pastures, and deep vales. Ah, and the mountain's high vision will be yours, I think, as well. These gifts that you will bring us, why, they will be the lighted glimpses!

— Eurynome, how can I bring the lighted glimpses unless . . . unless there is the presence of your daughter Aglaia, the radiant one?

— You bargain hard, O creative Olympian! My lovely daughter Aglaia you shall have, but let me tell you how she is likely to come, for she is mysterious. She will be present when the vision of your work to come undergoes its dawning. Indeed, she cannot be plucked away from her firm attachment to the dawn. When she comes again, you shall know her by the trail of golden light that appears late in the shaping of your work of art.

— And the time in between? Will she be my companion, my beloved?

— Only within the mystery of the work itself will you find her, I think. There. I have told my secret!

    Hephaestus fell silent, pondering Eurynome's words. At last he gave a dazzling smile of satisfaction, the heavy gloom of the fall dispelled. His strength returned as he spoke simply now.

— I go to undertake the work, shaping the substance out of the formless depths. Of course, nothing can be done without the fire of the forge!

    The cloak of darkness, no longer diminishing his spirit, fell limply aside. Visibly altered, he bore his godly stature once again. As his decision laid a light but definite hand upon him, his eyes held their own inner court in which invisible and luminous shapes moved before him. He turned to the sea nymph.

— Thetis, it is your sea grotto that is going to be the luminous place of my work. Show me, if you will be so kind, where I can set up the forge and kindle the fire! And, Eurynome, do let the Graces know that I require their ineffable veil cast over my labors!

Smiling happily now, the two sea goddesses led the way into the vaulted interior of the rock grotto, Hephaestus following. Only when they reached the cavern's dim core was the god filled with longing for sight of the fire of the forge—fierce, hot, and contained. The nymphs left him now, and he stood a long time staring into the cavernous and silent space. Slowly a dream, lyrical in its ample movement, presented the ghostly contours of a great work requiring nine years in the making.

Afflicted Feet

On the following day, Hephaestus found himself again sitting with the sea nymphs in the front chamber. There was a palpable ease that had not been there in the time of their earlier meeting, even a gentle expectancy was felt to be in the air. Thetis spoke, laying down her weaving, although it occurred to the god that she spoke as one who weaves threads skillfully.

— I do believe that Goddess Hera, your lovely mother and queen of Olympus, no less, must have had a dream she nourished about you.

— Oh? What sort of dream is it you imagine?

— A dream of great and noble deeds performed handsomely, in the manner of a celebrated Greek hero, by her son and Zeus's. And then she was presented with her son—yourself—the god of the reluctant feet, as you have called yourself mercilessly.

— Disaster, right, especially since this lameness is my destiny.

Hephaestus smiled grimly, for the image still brought him pain.

— Has it occurred to you, Hephaestus, that your feet, I mean in their reluctance, might have been responding to your mother's fair dream, a dream that did not resonate with your nature and destiny?

The god sat up abruptly, finding this an astonishing notion at best.

— Come, Thetis. Although you are dealing with facts in a candid and appealing manner, this does not mean that they behave as you would have them. Perhaps it is simpler to believe that I am a product of the caprice of the Fates . . . Still, I can't say.

Eurynome intervened thoughtfully.

— Ah, the fact of a Fate is more often an enigma, not a truth easily grasped. Still, even with those awesome ladies, I remind you that they are known to act in such a way as to protect a person from some unobserved foe. Their action would be based, of course, on the long and hidden sight they manifest.

Hephaestus nodded to the mother of the Graces and replied.

— Coming from you, Eurynome, such an observation carries weight. Although I long to embrace it, it may require some time. Let me understand you, are you suggesting that by the grace of the Fates, I am given these reluctant feet, which, like wandering children, compel me to give assiduous attention to every step?

His question hung upon the air for a long moment.

— Yes, that is so.

— One thing that really perplexes me is how this condition I must endure happens to be a *grace*. I realize that I am speaking to the best informed on the subject of grace.

— How can I explain? Although I am close to my daughters, the Charites, their very substance and life qualities are mysteriously compounded.

At this point, a beam of sunlight found its way through a crack in the vaulted ceiling of stone, observed by the three of them. Thetis commented.

— A light emerges. Now that is the best of omens. Your feet, Hephaestus, are those that refuse to serve mere habit and convention. I am beginning to sense how it is. Why, your feet think independently. Only observe how they create a unique way, a shining new form of movement, slow and thoughtful in its living pulse! You alone among the twelve Olympians are the creative god, and this were not possible, surely, without your reluctant feet!

The two sea nymphs arose and clapped their hands as if in celebration before going to the god and kissing his cheeks. At once they took up the garland they had woven of sea anemones and crowned his head with it. A sense of joyous relief settled over the grotto scene. And Hephaestus laughed heartily.

Hephaestus before the Fire

Hephaestus made his way slowly on the narrow path that descended into what seemed to be the stone core of the mountain, the high-vaulted chambers of the sea grotto left behind for the present. Gratitude to the nymphs swept over him. Where would he be, in what solitary abyss, were it not for the hospitality and good company of Thetis and Eurynome? Now the tunneling descent burrowing into darkness beckoned him strongly. By bending to the waist, he managed to make it through a low passage. Presently the tunnel opened into a chamber that was circular in shape, its ceiling of ample height so that again he stood erect, observing as he did so that a small but steady stream of muted light entered from some unseen opening above him. "At last!" he cried aloud, satisfied that he had found what he was looking for. He set down the heavy bag filled with wood that he had been carrying on his shoulders, and his tools as well, heaving a sigh of satisfaction. When he had surveyed the chamber and found it suitable, he set about making the place for the fire in the center, arranging the wood, and then striking the flint stones repeatedly to generate the necessary flame. Still the flame was at each effort feeble, and although he fanned it with his faithful breath, the powerful chest heaving, each time, it flickered out. The god hovered over the unborn fire, and an ardor that was primordial rose like a tide within him yearning for the fire. Again he repeated each skillful step of the age-old process, striking the flint more vigorously so that the spark was sturdier. Now the fire began to spread delicately along the log, not yet finding a steady support and yet full of promise. Hephaestus sat back on his heels and smiled. He spoke quietly.

— It has returned. The fire has returned to my summons! How fierce and utterly its own is its light, its bone-soothing warmth . . . Its golden dance is tireless, for surely no reluctant feet are found here! How oddly comforting that is to my own condition . . . Ah, the fire is mine, and I belong to the fire. This I know. It is the fire, not a woman, that is my everlasting spouse! Who would have guessed that it would be here in the water realm of the sea grotto that the fire would be restored to me without which I cannot create?

— Still, it was because the longing came over me, assailing me like a tempest of Poseidon's making, that the fire has been reawakened. Oh yes, desire arose in me. I saw the beautiful face of she who companions Aphrodite—Himeros, Desire. Desire burned in my flesh, and I ached for my lost work, the work that belongs to me alone! Nor is desire known for patience. But do not forget, Hephaestus old boy, that you remain the fallen Olympian god, and like an ox, destiny leads you by the nose! O joy, the fire burns steadily. I am not alone. It is my partner. I would address the fire.

— O fire, my faithful partner, you have returned! I welcome you with a full heart. You and I—have we not known the ardor that is primordial and that does not die? The cold, indifferent metals await us. It is you who melts them, causing life to flow again in them. And they await my ardent gaze to summon the hidden and beautiful forms from them. Still, I am the fallen god—a harvest fruit, even so, landing on ground that is alien to it. An inscrutable distance separates me from Mother, Father, and the other gods. Yet what is this desire, newborn, that sings even now in my heart? It longs for the covenant with you, O fire. When I lift my eyes into the far distance, I perceive works that gleam with your deathless golden light, for the metal has been shaped over the fire, endowed with beauty and grace of form, things completed and set down into life and world!

Hephaestus knelt on the ground and tended the fire, which crackled merrily and climbed the air of the chamber, removing the cloak of darkness. Now he moved back out of the great heat, continuing to regard the fire in its intense, yet contained, dance.

— In the presence of the newly emerged fire, something plays at the edges of mind and dream, it seems. Mined out of the earth, the raw metal is being carried toward the fire where—only look!—it yields itself up to the sweet reverie of the shaping! . . . . O feet of mine, once deplored and rejected, feet long reluctant in the world, you have led me on the path that kindles once more the essential fire! Well done, faithful ones!

The Gods Reflect on the Fall

The lonely seashore washed by the northern Aegean Sea was dotted with small caves and rocks opening into grottoes. Two male figures, each extraordinary in his bearing, made their way along the beach, deep in conversation. The taller and more majestic of the figures was speaking.

— There is trouble, you know. The forge has long gone cold and silent, and the fire is out. How many years is it now—nine?—since Hephaestus left us? The vision went with him, and what a delicate and luminous thing it was which no one on Olympus has been able to replace. It's gone, Hermes.

Zeus's lively companion stared at him

— The vision you say. I should have said rather that the god had this genius for creating beautiful and workable things in life. What do you mean by the vision?

— Certainly he is the most excellent creator and craftsman. No one would argue that. As for the vision, one only catches it by the hem as it walks well ahead of oneself with dawn on its face. Gazing upon the familiar things full of tangible matter, it receives the beautiful forms that hover with desire to enter earth's realm. The eyes of Hephaestus—have you never seen how they engage the vision, Hermes?

— Well, yes, now that you mention it, I have. And do you think that the time may be pregnant for his return, Zeus?

— I wonder. For all practical purposes he is long overdue. One hears rumors of his woundings—more than one, I'd say.

For a long moment, he looked as if Memory herself had laid a grim hand upon his shoulder. Sighing, Zeus continued.

— Hephaestus has taken up life in some sea grotto with sympathetic sea nymphs as his caretakers. That is the rumor. But nine years—how long does it take for a sensitive creator to be placated, even restored, I ask you?

— Ah, but my brother Hephaestus bears his wounds deeply, I think. Besides, that suffering arising from rejection may maintain its own ruthless calendar. Let's see, how was it that day on Olympus at the gathering of the gods so long ago? Hephaestus had decided to put the question that had been hounding him quite openly, and so he turned to Hera. All our eyes were upon him, I recall, for he moved forward with a decisive step, drew himself up, and spoke with the most authoritative voice I had ever heard out of him. He asked, "Mother, can you tell me this? Who is my father?" Disbelief was on the faces of all of us. As might have been expected, the Furies broke loose in Hera's reaction. Before anyone could tell what was happening, Hephaestus was falling from Olympus. I saw him in the air, headfirst, tumbling helplessly as he was carried toward the sea far below.

— His question insulted Hera, naturally, but it wounded me deeply as well. Were you aware of this? It implied that he, my mature son, failed to find anything of Zeus in himself. Nothing of me, I tell you. My son was lost to me in that moment! The creator of the beautiful and enduring things that charmed our life on Olympus rejected *me!*

— Zeus, I do see that he rejected you in that moment more than perhaps you lost him. Hephaestus cannot be lost, I think. Only consider.

— Rejection puts one in despair. Even a god has no armor against its thrust. O how dark and bitter the image of oneself becomes!

The beach had run out, and the two gods leaned against the large fallen boulder that blocked farther passage. Both were silent for a time, the only sound being the rhythmic wash of the low waves against the stone. Suddenly Hermes turned to his companion, a light firing up in his eyes, his lean body shining with energy.

— At last, I see it! I see what this is all about with Hephaestus. And to think that it has taken nine years.

— What is it?

— One has only to remember the scene on Olympus and what must have preceded it. This is what I believe must have happened. Gradually Hephaestus had become *unfathered!* Wait, don't be upset with me. What we witnessed was the fate of the creator, for the creator is not one who is continuing what went before. No. Nor is it a matter of his quarreling with his father or entering any observable conflict whatsoever. Rather, it is about the severing of the invisible umbilical cord of spirit. He had to be cut away from Father, as he also had to be cut away from Mother. *Hephaestus had to be orphaned!* Of all the Olympians, he is supremely the orphan! And he is the rejected one, I should add, not having been found flawless and beautiful to look at in the first place.

— You speak of being unfathered and orphaned as though this condition were an asset.

Clearly Zeus's voice, still gloomy with pain, was skeptical.

— Not an asset but a necessity, as I see it. By his fall he was freed, and yet he remains terribly alone, I imagine.

— Hmm, I believe you may be on to something, Hermes, . . . the unfathering of Hephaestus. It may be that such unfathering and unmothering can open the way for the vision. What a small and frail truth! Yet it is the vision that must father Hephaestus, isn't it? How else can he be the creative one?

Ah me, it is a fact that the vision requires *room!* There was hardly room enough on Olympus, strange as it sounds to our ears.

Hermes was nodding slowly as this new and strange thought occupied the minds of both gods. Shortly, they arose and turned back upon the narrow beach path, making their way in silence except for the pounding of the waves. The sun was slow on the western horizon as they came upon a sea grotto. The gods paused, turned a searching gaze upon a dark entrance, and sighed.

Hera and Hermes Meet

The scene was the plain of Argos looking to the deeply indented sea from the hill of Hera's sanctuary. In the cool of the morning, the goddess herself walked the unshaded path. Her companion was a man, a traveler wearing a light cloak and a broad-brimmed hat. He was indeed extraordinary in the energy and grace of his movements, his face ever alive in a subtle commentary of thought and response. She spoke.

— Hermes, what a welcome guest you are! Are you going to tell me what extraordinary circumstance brings you here? I can see that you are dressed for a journey.
— Oh, let's say that Memory, splendid in her own way—although never given to the salutary practice of forgetting—brings me to seek you out.
— Memory, you say. What an obscure answer! Have you in mind some past happening of significance, then?
— Indeed. You were always quick-minded, Hera.
— I shall never forget the look on your face at that moment when, seized in a fateful passion, I gave my son Hephaestus the . . . the push . . . oh dear yes, the push that caused him to fall from Olympus!

Her voice had ended in a whisper while at once a veil of extreme isolation fell over her leaving her speechless. Hermes took note and reached out to steady the goddess as she swayed. After a long pause, Hermes turned to her.

— It is an awesome act surely. My brother Hephaestus is especially dear to me. He has always possessed that rare art of casting himself aside as he strides toward his creative action. Now he is fallen to the sea realm. I've come at once to let you know, Hera.

The god of the road regarded her closely as she spoke.

— The fall . . . how it has haunted me! Always it has involved me. Yet I did not design or plot it, I want you to know.

— The implacable ladies, the Fates—was it their design for Hephaestus?
It is not possible for you or for me to answer that, I think. Destiny
is hardly ever a clear text handed out, and certainly never in advance.
Still, I am convinced that the fall had to do with my creative brother's
destiny. If it is any comfort, this is what I have been wanting to express
to you.

As Hermes spoke, Hera's mind journeyed from serene Olympus
to a dark abyss, and her face was mute with sorrow. After some time, she
spoke.

— These words coming from you comfort me, Hermes. What can we do?
He is so lost to me and to the gods, not to mention his absence to the
human realm where he once enjoyed an everyday presence.

The face of the soul's guide to the underworld was extremely
earnest.

— There is one thing we can and must do, you and I. We must companion
Hephaestus in his predicament!

— Impossible, surely! What can you possibly mean?

— I mean that the fall belongs to Hephaestus, and yet it causes us to
lose him. How is he to be found? He must be greeted within the fall
somehow. A remedy must ever depend on a specific action, the action
that is most relevant. The action that is called for, I believe, is our
presence to the fall.

Where the two gods stood beneath the old olive tree, Hera examined
the face of Hermes with grave scrutiny.

— How is such a thing possible, I repeat?

— It can happen without a single physical move. Indeed, it happens most
truly when only oneself can observe it. And so, I am departing, Hera.
In this very moment, I am on the way! I cross the threshold, exiting the
world, leaving behind all that calls me by name and makes way for me. I
am utterly solitary now and wholly removed from the familiar dwelling
place and the sunny corridors of my life with my companions!

As the god's form grew hazy in her vision and his voice more distant,
Hera felt only alarm. She cried aloud to Hermes,

— Come back! O don't leave us!

Hermes' reply came from a distance now.

— Those are words I must cry aloud to Hephaestus, who falls. As he falls
through empty space, the familiar lies forever behind, abandoned, cut
away. Ahead is the unknown. I must take in distance as food for the
soul and wish that I were an eagle, whose wing and eye engage distance

nobly. Still I descended, and level after level is palpably sensed. Ah yes, the distance which is new to me is now the gift of the gods that carries me onward!

The goddess raised her voice, calling to Hermes.

— Because you are the god who journeys, you know these things, things which are alien to me. Am I not Hera who loves her house?

— Yes. Only observe, Hera, as I fall, I perceive how it is to be unhoused and at the same time to be unmothered and unfathered! From this day forward, one who falls becomes the *originator* of who he is and what he will do!

— Oh, it is awesome indeed. It is too heroic for me, a goddess, to undertake. O *Hodios*, It is against my nature!

— Hera, you need only send your love in all its fragrant and cradling power to your son who falls. Surely he will then possess the best of earth's dwelling place.

— Do answer my question. When will he get to where he is falling?

— Already he arrives there. Be sure of this. He penetrates the ancient and primordial realm of the great waters and finds a hospitable grotto at last. He is in a far hidden realm, Hera. Know this: he is well!

— O what will become of him in such an ungodly and inhuman place!

— Come now. It is hardly ungodly. Besides, in time he may thrive again. You shall see. For there in the watery depths, Goddess Mnemosyne herself will surely bring him the wondrous voices and images from the forgotten past. We shall see, won't we?

Hermes Comes to Hephaestus in the Sea Grotto

Time passed. Dispatched by the gods, Hermes made his way swiftly to the far isle of Lemnos in the northern Aegean Sea, where earth periodically heaved volcanic bellows and spat out hot lava like a spring torrent coursing down Mt. Moschylus. Within the shadow of the great rock entrance to a sea grotto, Hermes glimpsed a movement accompanied by the graceful swirling of a white garment at the same moment that he called out "Hephaestus!" and waited on the threshold. It was Thetis, the sea nymph herself who appeared now and greeted him with dignity, inviting him within. Hermes smiled his cordial greeting and followed her down a narrow cave of a passage into what appeared to be core of the primordial rock.

Rising from the couch where he reposed, Hephaestus was astonished.

— So you have come, Hermes. You finally found the way here. I wondered how long it would take. Well, welcome to the magnificent grotto! The sight of you makes my heart glad, brother.

Led by Hephaestus, the brothers entered a somewhat circular high-vaulted chamber.

— This is your residence then, am I to understand—your spacious home away from home?

— It is the home of the lovely Nereids, who share it generously with me. Still, why should I regard it as "a home away from home" considering that I possess no other home?

There was a sadness underlying his reasonable reply.

— You are content to be at home with the nymphs then, are you? Excellent company, I should imagine.

— Excellent beyond description, actually.

— You should know, having savored this extraordinary companionship for nine years.

Hephaestus raised his eyes to Hermes' intense regard, and the gaze held them in some lonely corridor of dim memory. Hephaestus broke the silence with a lighter tone.

— Ah so? Does this mean that you have been counting the time of my absence, Hermes? I am moved by that. Tell me, have the rest of the gods been counting the years of my absence as faithfully as yourself?

— Absolutely. How can you entertain any doubt? My visit is expressly for the purpose of informing you that you are sorely missed, craftsman. Believe me. I'd have come sooner had it been left up to me, but the decision among the Olympians was that we should not interfere with what those awesome ladies—the Fates—had doled out to you. As for myself, I found your fall a true catastrophe that struck pain to the heart!

— Your words are a true solace to me, Hermes, and I am grateful. So as I understand, the gods are stumped at how to regard my having gone missing for nine years and the resulting lack of communication. Alas, they do miss me, you say. There is something unusually pleasant about that thought.

His face took on the tender look of a child as nostalgia swept over him. The alteration did not escape the observation of the god of the road.

— Tell me, what has this sojourn in the sea world been like? It must be different to abide in a place hidden by the watery depths and unpenetrated by the sun.

— Well, I had to forget Olympus. It isn't easy to learn forgetfulness. It's an art, as you must know. It is especially trying when one keeps remembering that his parents are in the lineup of the great gods!

— Anger and resentment can work against forgetting too. In fact, under their whip, one ends up *over*-remembering and possibly even feeling virtuous for staying at it.

— You do have a way of opening the cellar to things, brother, for what you say is true. You don't cast the light of your torch on the path to the underworld for nothing, I'd say. O yes, for a long time, over-remembering invaded all my solitude, and I could create nothing. Actually, the fire of the forge had gone out. Even worse, my hands lost all desire to shape things. All of this happened before the day Thetis found me and took me home to her grotto of the many chambers, which she shares with Eurynome.

— Mother of the Graces. Two incredible sea nymphs to host you, no less. Not at all a situation to complain about, I'd say.

— My gratitude to them is profound, Hermes.

Settling back comfortably now, Hermes' keen glance took reconnaissance of the inviting chamber of the rock grotto.

— Ah, so. I should say that the moist silence here in the grotto indicates a fertile realm.

— You feel it already, do you? This place is not only legendary with the life of the sea nymphs, but it is perhaps the most hidden of all dwelling places. There's the clear advance of being protected from intruders from without.

Hermes walked about and spoke an occasional word toward a far rock wall, only to hear it echoed; for he was heartened by the great sheltering silence. Surely a more select hearing resided in this place. Then he asked the question.

— And did forgetting the past become easier when you came to dwell with the nymphs?

— Those painful events at home on Olympus began to fade to some extent.

— Ah, and I expect your days came to be filled with the particular delights that the sea nymphs might well provide.

— You are poking fun at me now, Argophontes. Look. Life here in this hidden sea realm is a treasure I can't begin to describe. It surpasses what I earlier had created—the shaping of crowns, scepters, and shields with gold, silver, and gems passing through my hands.

— You have many great works on record, Hephaestus.

— Yet what happens here is not on record. What else can I say?

— Forgive me if humor tempted me briefly, for I am truly astonished and awed by this realm of the hidden treasure. At the same time, I must ask, how is it with the god of work? Has the work indeed resumed?

— Well, I have created pieces of jewelry for Thetis and Eurynome, but no more than this. I do have to admit that the fire of the forge has not been tended for some time.

— Zeus has sensed this, I am certain. He told me as much, saying that he felt the pang of the dead fire.

Hephaestus looked as if he had been struck. His dark eyes held the keen eyes of the messenger. The voice that formed the question was hoarse with emotion.

— What else did Father Zeus say, Hermes?

— That he was feeling the terrible cold and echoing silence of the forge. He said that it was no ordinary silence. How did he describe it? He likened it to the yawning emptiness of lost form!

These words struck to the core.

— Alas, what have I forsaken! Was there anything else?

— He said that he was assaulted by the languishing of matter that has never known the passionate care of the lifting, shaping hand.

— Ah, yes, I know that articulation that languishing matter cries out for—it is indeed the cry that summons my work! When I have shaped the things down here below, they have taken on a radiance, and although excellent in conception, they have lacked something. *Substance* is what they lack. Because substance is missing, they fall aside from the world much as dreams do.

Hermes inclined his ear to the direction in which the pounding of the sea was heard and thought of the great watery expanse.

— How can you dwell with the sea and expect to take hold of substance, Hephaestus? Surely substance belongs to earth!

— Earth, you say. Yes, I have missed earth. There is no question about it. Is life on earth much the same?

— There is trouble. The work has darkened greatly for human individuals. The shining glimpse has gone out of the work. To locate the small window which might let in the light is not easy. Alas, something of great value has gone missing. How is it to be described? It is that sudden transparency within a true work that for a moment unveils a hidden world in which meaning endures! How is work to find this resonance with the luminous undergirding reality? Everything seems to be, well, old hat.

— Alas, how did such a state come about?

— I can only say that during your absence, it has happened.

— You have sought me out to ask something of me, is this not so?

Hermes nodded briefly.

— Well, I best hear it.

— Return to earth, Hephaestus!

— And if I do? It seems such a solitary thing to do.

— By that, I take it you are thinking how you would hate to leave the company of the sea nymphs.

— Yes, and more. A return to human history and taking a role within it that looms before me as solitary and a little terrifying!

— It is difficult for you, creator, exceedingly so.

   The two Olympians fell silent in each other's presence.

Return to Olympus

An authoritative knock at the stone entry to the sea grotto, echoing through the cavernous space, startled the nymph Thetis where in the spacious chamber she worked at weaving of dried seaweed. Rising to her feet, she smoothed the folds of her chiton before proceeding slowly toward the dim threshold.

— Why, it is you, Dionysos! So you have come to us. Do come in.

A secretive smile played at his lips, the luminous eyes regarding the nymph as though perusing a pleasant narrative of the sea's mysterious depths.

— Greetings, Thetis!

He followed her into the high-walled chamber, after signaling his satyr companion to wait for him.

— You were expecting me, Thetis, were you?

— I thought that you would come in time.

He gazed about the spacious stone room, marveling at the vaulted ceiling, old in earth's sculpturing.

— This dwelling place of yours is a veritable stone palace, I'd say. I never guessed so much lay hidden here!

Thetis nodded, smiling, but did not break her pace in passing through chamber after chamber before, after a low tunnel, they entered the circular room where the hot fire burned in the center of the stone floor. Standing over the fire, tongs in hand, was Hephaestus himself, his attention held by the work in silver that lay upon the fire of the forge. Removing the beautiful cup, he set down his implements and looked up finally. Seeing who the visitor was, he smiled ruefully.

— Well, can it be you, Dionysos? To what do we owe this auspicious visit? Surely the vine penetrates all kinds of soil—but the sea realm?

Dionysos laughed, ignoring the prickly acknowledgment.

— Greetings, lost brother! Indeed I am out of my element, as you point out, but are you not out of yours as well? You have not been easy to locate, and I am not at home searching the realm of the sea. However that may be, you seem to have made yourself quite at home here these nine years with the sea nymphs.

With this frank observation, the god of the vine gazed at the work of the forge with some admiration.

— You mention the nine years' period of my stay. Does this mean that the Olympians have been keeping track of me more or less?

The very notion was oddly pleasing to him. Dionysos nodded briefly before turning the conversation.

— This chamber of your forge exudes, well, usefulness, to be sure. I myself should find so much *usefulness* wearisome.

Frowning, Dionysos continued to gaze upon the forge in its stark and dim setting as though viewing an alien realm. He spoke in a rambling manner now, as if to himself.

— What is usefulness anyway but an unending cord that binds human beings fast in their solemn necessities? An Olympian god surely is not bound by such necessities but is free to go about everlastingly much as he pleases!

This last speculation brought from Hephaestus a smile of amusement, tinged surely with a skepticism that passed briefly. Dionysos returned to his reflection, and his passion had grown in the meantime.

— The human realm lays a hand on your shoulder and demands the useful implements it needs, further demanding that they be of exquisite workmanship and fully beautiful. What hubris, I say! "Give me my armor, my wondrous shield, the queen's necklace, the scepter"—why lend an ear to these human cries? Were I not the god who exults in the subtle, green, ever ongoing life of the vine, knowing it like a musical instrument that plays the ode of my interior life, do you think I would be moved to create the vineyard in order to accommodate the human demand for wine? I would not!

The small smile on Hephaestus's face, as if partaking of the rambling vineyard under discussion, was ongoing. A note of brotherly indulgence might have been there. In any case, he was beginning to enjoy himself. Thus assured of hospitality, Dionysos sat down on a boulder and continued, his eyes flashing with their extraordinary light.

— Usefulness—what a dragon it is, swishing its deadly tails too numerous to count! Did we suppose that Zeus is the most honored god among human folk? Alas, it is not the case. Usefulness is the human god, I tell you!

Hephaestus raised his hand with the palm erect now, and Dionysos nodded and turned an attentive look upon the artisan god.

— Do you forget that the Greeks have a long and passionate marriage to the beautiful? If anything is to compete with what is useful, it is that which holds ineffable beauty. In my work, beauty goes ahead of me on a dim path, out of reach yet ever beckoning to me. Still, it is of usefulness that I wish to speak. What is usefulness for the human world, Dionysos? Is it not the bridge between life that works and life's failure? It has been my destiny to perceive that bridge with keen, unwavering attention and to create from that awareness the things useful in the world.

The two gods fell into silence now, with only popping sounds from the fire to be heard. Thetis, who sat at a little distance from the exchange, studied the two great gods silently. Dionysos turned to Hephaestus with his question.

— Have you ever considered engaging in something what was *not* useful?

Hephaestus sat back on his heels, studying Dionysos thoughtfully. A silence held with the question suspended on the air. Only Thetis had gasped audibly. Now the craftsman began to smile. Dionysos waited but not without a sense of foreboding.

— Have I thought of engaging something not useful? Well, yes, I definitely have. *I have decided that I shall marry Aphrodite!*

Thetis looked a little faint with shock while Dionysos threw back his head and gave way to a slow, musical sort of laughter that appeared to accompany some languid reverie. When he spoke again, questions tumbled forth eagerly.

— Well, well, you will marry Aphrodite you say? Hephaestus, isn't it an unlikely match at best? But were it to happen, are you saying that marrying the beautiful goddess would not be *useful?*

— That is correct. Delightful, most certainly. Useful, no.

Dionysos's words followed the descent of his sigh.

— Hmm, what do you know? You could be closer to my view of things than I realized . . . in spite of being occupied with creating works. Tell me, more explicitly, I beg, what is life in the sea grotto like? Does it leave you, well, in a state of desire?

The group of three was joined now by the old dwarf helper of the worker god, Cedalion. Hephaestus turned toward him, even as he replied.

— The sea grotto suits me in an excellent way. Cedalion, do you agree?

Cedalion was quick to respond, addressing awesome Dionysos.

— My lord Dionysos, I can tell you that living down below, that is, here in the grotto, suits Hephaestus fine, it does—just as it suits me, being brought up as I was in a cave on Naxos. There's a reason that explains it all, see? Folks who live altogether up above, in plain view, I mean, are mostly the talkers and not the workers.

Dionysos looked puzzled. He responded to Cedalion.

— Still, Cedalion, life in the sun and with one's fellows is surely to be desired. What would the vineyard be without sun, I ask you? It were impossible to grow grapes in the grotto! Something else, have you thought of what would become of my festivals were they to depend on you and Hephaestus?

The mention of the festivals of Dionysos caused an excitement to lay hold of the dwarf.

— Have you come here thinking to invite us to a festival then?

— I am afraid not. You see it happens not to be festival time. Much ripening of the grapes lies ahead. That requires sun, as I already pointed out. This causes me to conclude that everybody needs one prolonged season in the sun. Otherwise, the grapes lose their juice, or in the case of a person, he dries up. Life—*zoe*—without juice is hardly life!

The pointedness of this advice did not escape Hephaestus.

— Well said, Dionysos. Actually I am less of a recluse, under ordinary circumstances, than you make me out to be. I am known to frequent Athens' Agora where I am found very much among the craftsmen. Work, you see, really is my true passion. Brother, it is my wine!

— So it is. However, I should not want to engage anything for long that possessed no promise of music, of celebration, of dance. Does work ever possess these?

Hephaestus did not reply, for in that moment, a chasm was felt lying between work and festival. Dionysos moved to the harder issue.

— For nine years, you have clearly preferred the company of Thetis and Eurynome in the sea grotto to the company of your fellow gods on Olympus.

Before Hephaestus could respond, Cedalion did.

— What do you mean, Lord Dionysos? You can plainly tell that the sea ladies are nicer than the Olympian folk! Besides, they are less complicated.

Dionysos welcomed the element of humor to the difficult situation and smiled as he responded.

— You put me in an embarrassing position, Cedalion, although an amusing one, I admit. Coming here, I observe that Hephaestus is comfortable and settled in and much involved in his work of creating clasps, buckles, necklaces, and other objects of exquisite beauty. Certainly the great fall has not diminished the creative fire. Nor has it robbed him of graceful and pleasurable living, I should add. But you see, I am here for one high purpose, which I must delay no longer in voicing: it is to declare the fact that Olympus and the gods are missing Hephaestus sorely. Life is not the same in his absence.

Cedalion nodded as if to say he knew this all along. Hephaestus looked alternately sad, wistful, and remote. Dionysos addressed him alone now.

— Hephaestus, this is no idle call I am making.

— I never thought it was.

Saying this, he lifted a silver vase from the fire, wiped his hands, and turned to give his full attention to the god of the vine. Dionysos took from his cloak the kantharos, his wine pitcher.

— May I pour you some of my wine?

Cedalion eagerly seized three cups and set them before the god, who began pouring the fragrant red juice of the vine. Relaxed now, the three of them drank the wine, and a solemnity that had grown painful between the two gods dissolved. As is the nature of Dionysos's reverie, time lost its stern accountability. When they set down their cups, Dionysos spoke to his mission.

— I come with the proclamation of the gods. It is this:

It is the time of your return, Hephaestus!

If only you will agree to it and make ready your departure from the sea grotto and the nymphs, I am prepared to furnish you comfortable transport back to Olympus.

Hephaestus stood facing the god of the vine now, the dignity of a great Olympian upon him as his awesome autonomy was manifested.

— The time of the return—yes, I have felt its approach! Like the room of the forge, the descent and the return present a circle, this one yet to be completed. Cedalion, can you make things ready?

All was put in order at once for the departure. Donning his short cloak and setting two tools of the forge on his shoulder, Hephaestus sought out Thetis and Eurynome to make his fond, sad farewell. It was a farewell steeped in gratitude for the hospitality of nine years in this extraordinary realm of the sea. As he stood ready to exit the doorway of the grotto, Hephaestus paused to speak with his beloved dwarf companion.

— Cedalion, there is little use in asking you to come with me to Olympus. We have been over this ground before, and I know your scorn of Olympus as a place to reside. I make only one request of you, dear companion of the work. It is that, wherever I set to work at my forge, you shall come to me and again companion the work.

When Cedalion answered, his voice was rough with emotion.

— Come on, Hephaestus, you know I'll be there. Now don't dillydally any longer or else you'll have the sea goddesses crying into their handkerchiefs. Good-bye! And take my advice: don't take anything off those gods up there!

— I'll cherish your words, Cedalion!

Without looking back, Hephaestus departed the sea grotto. At some distance from the entrance, he saw the small group that awaited him in the shade of a tree, and he nodded as the thought occurred that here was neither fanfare nor elegance. Without a word, the satyr helped him onto the warm back of the quiet mule. Smiling, Dionysos led the small company on foot, the strong scent of the mule perfuming the slow, rhythmic return to Olympus.

The Forge on Lemnos

Although life on Olympus was never thought to be precarious, it proved so for Hephaestus. While his first fall was attributed to the hand of his mother, Hera, overwhelmed by her disappointment at her son's marked lameness, the second fall from Olympus was caused by the hand of his father, Zeus. A severe quarrel between Zeus and his wife, Hera, was the occasion of his harsh rejection. Hera was undergoing punishment meted out by her husband when son Hephaestus, being of a nature that was gentle and sensitive, rescued his mother. At once his action incurred the wrath of Zeus, who flung him from Mt. Olympus into what must have seemed the abyss. The first fall of the god had delivered him to the sea grotto and its gentle nymphs for a nine-year, not unpleasant, sojourn while the second fall delivered him to the harsh face of the Greek earth on the volcanic isle of Lemnos. In the episode that follows, Hephaestus's arrival on Lemnos with his faithful dwarf companion is explored.

It was on the island of Lemnos in the northern Aegean Sea that they came ashore, bearing their metal-working implements on their backs and assailed by a fierce gale. As they walked side by side, they constituted a strange pair to the eyes of an observer, had there been any observers on hand. The larger male figure was strikingly muscular and handsome in the upper torso but appeared to possess feet that were crippled, so that he limped as he walked. Of half his height was his companion, a sturdy little man bearded with age, who kept a sharp look out as they made their way along the strange shore. Finding the path that climbed the rugged mountain, they began the ascent. No sooner did they reach a low ridge than a grumbling, roaring sound shook them, and the ground beneath them seemed to rise. Cedalion, the dwarf, leaped into the air as if shot by an arrow before diving behind Hephaestus, peeking out between his legs. The god smiled grimly.

— So what has happened to your bold sense of adventure, my friend?

— What's the awful roaring? Maybe it's a great beast from Crete!

— Come now. Heracles slew the Bull of Crete, and Theseus conquered the Minotaur, didn't you know?

— Hephaestus, you can't trust something from Crete to die properly. Things are known to come alive again there—you know, the way they say in the old tales.

Even as he spoke, his confidence was returning, and he again took his place on the path. Hephaestus paused, gazing toward the summit still well above them, and spoke thoughtfully.

— It is the mountain itself that has roared, to be sure. Mt. Moschylus is known to have a core of fire and to spew out flames and lava. You realize, don't you, that I must find the earth place I can claim for my own, for clearly Olympus belongs to the past?

— They threw you out, the gods did. That's a fact. Say, how will you be able to tell when we come upon your kind of place?

— It must be a place that is able to contain my fire—the fire of the working forge—contain and withstand it as well. Do you understand, Cedalion?

— Well, when it comes to your kind of fire, you can depend on my not chickening-out on you. Didn't Goddess Hera commit you to my care on Naxos when you were a little bit of a fellow?

The memory caused Hephaestus to relax with a smile.

— No god child, I must tell you, ever had a better tutor than yourself. What would I do without your faithful company on our present trek, I ask myself.

They had made their way tediously for hours, Cedalion attempting to match the god's halting gait as best he could. At one point he cried out in exasperation.

— You are slower than a turtle!

— Have I a choice with these lame feet of mine?

— I am sorry I got impatient, craftsman of the gods' splendid houses.

At the mention of the Olympian gods, Hephaestus gave a deep sigh as an inscrutable comment before speaking.

— Where I come from—Olympus, no less—I am used to the wounding laughs. It's not easy to be the odd ball. About my walking, I am compelled to pay attention to every step I take. It is rather like cutting a gem, you see. I cannot skip a single step without falling on my face. These are the facts.

Cedalion's eyes widened, considering this.

— You know what? The fact that you can't move about easily is a whole lot better for the forge, I'd say.

— Ah so? It keeps me in place, you mean.

— Of course it does. Now supposing that you were one of those fancy charioteers, like, say Apollo or Helios. Why, you could go galloping through the sky any time you pleased. What would become of the work of the forge then? As I see it, the great ladies have fixed it so that you've got to pay close attention as you take one step at a time. Say, I just realized something. Why, everything you create has got these *careful steps* in it!

Hephaestus laughed heartily at the dwarf's droll and outlandish comparison. The exchange had rested them both, and Cedalion felt so contented that he began to sing a merry little song that matched their steps as they resumed the trek.

Dusk had thrown a dense cloak over the steep slope when, weary and hungry, they reached the entrance of a rock cave that penetrated the mountain. At once Cedalion peered inside the dark vaulted entrance and called back.

— A black hole into a black night it is! Let's get out of here.

— You were never an optimist, my friend. At the same time, you've been used to living in the belly of earth.

A deep rumbling came to them out of the cavernous place. Cedalion pulled the god back.

— Why choose such an awful place for your forge? I say let's get away from here before the mountain devours us!

— This is no ordinary mountain. Moschylus has the fire at her center. I am sure of it now. She spews out flame and lava from her volcanic core. An excitement rises in me like a tide returning to its shore. I have found the earth place of the source of my creations, Cedalion!

— Besides fire, what's the mountain got besides a lot of wind? One thing's for sure. You aren't going to have any competition for claiming this place for yourself!

Hephaestus regarded his practical friend with affection and shook his head.

— Listen to me. I believe that we have found what I've been searching for. This is my place at last! I recognize it, you see, like one who sees a ghostly longing become solid reality before his eyes.

The eyes of the dwarf widened as the two figures studied each other, a crucial pause upon them. Standing like two parched trees in the rain, slowly they sensed the passing of weariness and dread. Now the two friends embraced, and peals of laughter burst forth as if coming from a chamber of glad work.

PART V

Apollo

Apollo—an Introduction

Contemplating the Greek gods in an effort to arrive at the distinctive nature of each one presents a challenge. This is in large part due to the fact that the nature of a major Olympian appears to unfold in a narrative mode through the god's myths, his praise sung by bards, and in the festive rites in his honor. From March through October, Apollo was celebrated with honor in the festivals of the ancient Athenians while at Olympia a pediment of the temple of Zeus represents Apollo as the one who restores balance in the midst of deadly conflict.

Apollo is supremely god of the oracular answers to the urgent human question. Indeed, the oracle of Apollo at Delphi (ancient Pytho) became the revered tribunal of the human spirit for the Greeks. As often depicted in his sculptured images, Apollo is kouros, the youthful spirit of great beauty and grace who strides across the threshold when the human predicament summons him. He often carries his silver bow and quiver with the result that nature, whether animal or human, is significantly targeted and claimed into the god's realm. Apollo is as much the source of music and poetry as he is of the life of the mind. Fully gowned and carrying his lyre, he appears almost genderless when, striking the chords of the stately dance, he leads the Muses down Parnassus' green slope. Rooted in the earth and in the life of the greater imagination as well, the oracular god, much like the Doric columns of his temple, stands erect in the enduring spirit.

For the Greeks, Apollo is the *spirit that knows*, his knowledge possessing order, measure, and beauty of form. It appears independent of the will to power. As modern individuals, we do not err in seeing Apollo as god of *logos*, the word. At the same time, something of the god's extraordinary context of being and action is peeled away and left behind in such a classification. A vision is needed that embodies his entire essence. He is god of song, authentic song being a container of a golden measure of human meaning with its enduring satisfaction. Is it conceivable that Apollo pursues thought itself within song's luminous frame, shaping it for the encounter with the world at hand? It seems possible that such a vision unfolded nightly beside the Castalian Spring at Delphi when, taking up his lyre, Apollo in the company of Artemis led the nine Muses in stately song and dance.

Ever fresh and youthful and poised at the narrow gateway of the human situation, Apollo is Far Shooter as well, for he is cloaked in distance. Distance is the hallmark of transcendence. At the same time, this characteristic may account for the god's misfortunes in the pursuit of his beloved since it is the nature of eros to demand nearness and intimacy. It is with eloquent consistency that the myths speak to this fact. In the winter months absent from his oracular sanctuary, Apollo sought out the distant Vale of Tempe. There on the banks of the Peneus River, he came to love lovely Daphne, wooing her as best he could. Sadly, Daphne rejected him and was turned into the laurel tree for all time. The Thessalian maiden Koronis accepted Apollo, on the other hand, becoming his bride, and Asklepios was conceived as their son. While yet pregnant, however, she abandoned her god spouse for a mortal lover. Alas, her tragic death followed, and Apollo delivered Asklepios on the funeral pyre of Koronis.

An abiding loneliness appears to haunt the god as he walks among the laurel trees of his sanctuary at Delphi while his tangible presence receives his priests, the priestess Pythia, and the many who journey far with a pressing question. There on the sacred way, an extraordinary radiance comes to shelter the human spirit.

Daphne and Apollo

The glen lay in deep shadow when after his long journey, Apollo descended the verdant slope to the river at dusk. The fragrance of the flowering bank assailed all his senses at once, and the god breathed a sigh of pleasure. Already, wearying as the long trek was from far Pytho, he felt refreshed. Keenly aware of the voice of the river god, low and constant on the air of the glen, he was not yet inclined to approach the shining waters of Peneus. Instead, he kept a thoughtful distance. It was enough that he had left the high rocky plateau of the sanctuary at Pytho where his temple stood tall and majestic under the stern brow of the mighty cliffs of the Phaedriades. Yes, it had been necessary to wait on a certain boldness before, striding forth alone into territory not his own, he journeyed to the Vale of Tempe once again. Here, instead of the austere heights that exposed him to world and sky, he found a hidden and intimate shelter. That very thought of entrusting himself to the moist and shadowy river glen with its speaking waters and fragrant air brought from the god a radiant smile. In this moment, he stood on the threshold of another realm. Soon night, like Mother Gaia herself, cloaked him, and he took his rest like a weary human traveler.

The morning sun was on the shoulder of the glen when the lovely daughter of Peneus walked on the riverbank. Her light, quick step was interrupted repeatedly as she gazed upward on the wooded slope as though to penetrate its depth and to take account of its subtler life. Now she listened intently as she was aware of a new presence. Could it be a stranger, a traveler, perhaps, attracted to the river's water? Although she stood quietly gazing, she saw no one. And then, quite suddenly, she caught the gleam of sunlight on metal and was amazed to see leaning against the trunk of an old plane tree a great bow of silver that appeared to be finely worked. She saw that a quiver of arrows lay on the ground as well. In her excitement, she clapped her hands in delight. At once, out of the dense thicket, a young man stepped forth. Her startled glance took in the lithe, well-formed physique, the long golden hair, and most astonishing of all, the look he turned toward her, piercing and contemplative beneath a fine brow. Inexorably, she was drawn to the foot of the plane tree, its thick branches excluding the sun. Nor was the stranger less wondrous to her eyes when she faced him. He was first to speak, smiling slowly.

— Greetings, maiden of Tempe's fair glen! I am a traveler from afar, as you might guess.

— You are a stranger, and strangers are rare in our glen.

— My, what a safe and well-guarded realm you live in, maiden. Tell me, do you never venture outside?

— Outside of Tempe's vale? I know no outside. My realm has only the inside.

He was startled by these words.

— Can it be? Do tell me your name, if you will.

— I am daughter of the river god Peneus, and I am called Daphne. Surely you have noticed how constant is Peneus's voice here in the glen?

— Yes, indeed. What a realm this is, floored by the voice of the shining waters! Tell me, is this the only voice that you attend to?

Such an odd conversation the stranger made, she thought as she replied.

— Oh no, not the only voice. You see, I do like to listen to the voice of Artemis, my goddess. Still, it is hardly the same with her voice, its being not constant but coming when summoned.

— What is it like when Artemis is summoned?

— Well, it is hard to describe, especially since you aren't a maiden yourself. It has to do with the path of the maidens when we receive the goddess's sure, light steps. The path is never an experiment, you see.

His face registered some amusement as he nodded, and she continued eagerly.

— When I am on Artemis's path, I go serenely and am never driven. Her green moist, enclosed world is shared with her maidens. Why, it is like this glen!

— A world apart then, but can you manage to see far in such a world?

— I shun the cold, distant vistas. Only what is intimate and at hand is worth engaging. The goddess's way winds through the uncut wild places, and it joins the animals' path. And it has knowledge, stranger.

— Knowledge you say?

— Why, yes, for it knows where the hidden springs emerge from the earth. Sometimes I walk the steep slope, but mostly I am on the path in this deep vale. Ah, there is something else.

Apollo spoke languidly.

— Where Artemis is to be found, there is always something else.

— It is that her way is hidden. It has no map.

Apollo shook his head slowly.

— Alas, she was never one for maps or official instructions! So it is Artemis's own voice that guides you? How striking it is that I find you much like her. As for your realm—this wild green shaded glen so foreign to me—it beckons to me strangely.

Daphne bent down to examine the extraordinary bow that leaned against the tree. Gazing from the stranger to the bow, she thought the match unlikely.

— To whom does this great bow belong, I wonder? It is a bow such as gods carry.

He was silent for a moment as he struggled with a reluctance to impart what he must.

— The bow is mine. It serves me well.

— Traveler, it must be able to shoot from afar.

— Distance, Daphne, is my bread and butter, as a matter of fact. My arrow can travel from the far place to the place at hand. It is known to penetrate deeply.

She shook her head firmly in protest.

— No, stranger. Only a god's arrow can do that! The handiwork on this bow is wonderful, isn't it? I can hardly take my eyes from it.

She fingered it respectfully, lifting it a little in her hands. He saw her desire.

— Do you want to hold it? Here, let me help you.

He set the bow into her arms, and she sighed with pleasure, finding it surprisingly light. After a long moment, she thrust the bow away, shivering visibly.

Solemnly he asked her why she pushed the bow aside.

— Because there is something uncanny here. In the moment that I held the bow to my bosom, I sensed that a piercing arrow had arrived there as well!

— That is not an unfavorable omen, you know. Come, Daphne, let's walk the path on the riverbank together.

She arose, and side by side, they walked slowly down the path.

For some time they walked in silence and unaccountably, the god observed to himself, their steps fell together in the same rhythm as if some latent attunement now manifested itself without their decision. How could they enjoy the same text of the feet, an Olympian god and a young woman? He turned to her, and his voice was full as the river in springtime.

— You are like the shining river itself in its ever-changing, delightful path, Daphne! You are the maiden of the unexposed vale, and what good fortune for me that I've found this vale! There are human individuals who search a lifetime for this . . . Here I've come upon the living greenness of earth.

She dropped her eyes, shy with his words and unable to receive the dazzling light of his eyes. He pressed her.

— By the way, you have not asked my name.

And why had she not?

— I fear to ask it, you see. You are a stranger, a traveler on roads I have never known. It is enough to show hospitality to the stranger. Zeus requires it of us.

And Apollo thought to himself, *And many has been the time that Zeus did not settle for mere hospitality, nor do I desire hospitality alone.* He turned and took her hand.

— Am I not a person, a person never to be repeated? A person must have a name, surely.

When she answered, her voice was low as if she might be speaking to herself.

— How can I make room for a *person*? He will insist on a name that is his alone. He will want to be recognized and a place made for him, for a person asks for his own ground. I fear that a person could change my world. When I am with the maidens, we are never persons, yet we are happy. Stranger, surely you see how it is.

The pain of disappointment manifested in Apollo's whole demeanor now.

— Then, you do not care who I am, is that true? Do you assign every man you meet to a category, as though to drop him into a package, to become a dry label from which the living mind and senses have retreated, believing that you have understood him? O Daphne, no, no. Only see me! There is none other like me. Do not reject me, making of me forever the stranger!

Her companion had aged visibly as he spoke, she observed, and the anguish that underlay his words was tangible. She spoke simply.

— Man of the great bow, you are the best of all strangers who have ever come here to the Vale of Tempe. My heart tells me so. What is it? You bring something from very far away that I never knew before, and it delights me greatly.

Apollo felt some comfort, even a glimmer of hope in her reply. He spoke earnestly.

— And know this. You are one alone to me, for no one can possibly take your place. You, Daphne, are the treasure of this hidden vale which has become my secret dwelling place. Pytho is rocky and so exposed, you see.

— Pytho? Do you mean to say that Pytho is your home? It is said to lie many mountains to the west of us, being at the end of a long and ancient road.

— True. Pytho is my home.

She considered this.

— Ah, I should not like it much at Pytho, I am sure, if it is what people say it is.

He was astonished, gazing at her as if to find some hidden access to her refreshing mind.

— What is it people say?

— Well, that it's the place of the oracle. Only think what a distressing thing it would be to dwell where there are only *answers everywhere!*

His face registered incredulity, which gave way to an amused smile.

— Actually, it's not like that at all. Tell me, dear Daphne, do you hold some suspicion of answers?

— Oh indeed. I really don't care for them much. An answer looks so *finished*, like a path that abruptly comes to an end. For a moment, an answer may seem pleasing, but soon it is like a path that has lost its inviting aspect. With an answer, there is simply nowhere to go. It is plain to see. I suppose that Pytho's answers would be of this sort.

Some passion had arisen in him and overflowed as he spoke.

— By the gods of Olympus, I say that Apollo's answer is not a path that has come to an end! It dwells in an enduring form, rather like sculptured stone. At the same time, the answer causes the questioner to partake of its source, the living, knowing spirit.

Daphne shook her head as she sorted things out.

— Still, I shall not come to Pytho or seek its answers. Only notice that answers are made of words. Where I live, the river's shining waters are ever flowing and are never exhausted. Words may be handsome, but they are soon spent and their light exhausted.

    Apollo had stood still regarding her as she spoke. Now a slow smile swept before it all, the former distress, seeming to dissolve it.

— Ah, Daphne, dear Daphne! There is a boulder of truth here. Why else have I journeyed all this distance in search of you, unrepeatable maiden?

    Although she felt the surge of some hope, she remained perplexed and tried to pin him down.

— You will give up Pytho then?

— Alas, no. Attached as I am to this sacred place, I cannot be detached at will. Let me tell you how it is. In my dwelling place, the essential question arises, and it hovers on the air of the high temple plateau. When the question has been released upon the air, Apollo cannot turn aside.

    For a moment, she looked very sympathetic.

— Poor Apollo that he should be so caught by mortals and their questions!

    The god laughed heartily.

— Your compassion is something I value, daughter of Peneus.

    She shivered as if a cool wind had blown over her, and she studied him now with something of awe as the realization took possession.

— Could you be Apollo himself?

— I am. Daphne, everything I have confessed to you is true. Do not withdraw your companionship, I beg you.

    She regarded him in silence, her dark eyes wide. Gently he continued.

— There is something that you do not know. While I am in your company, the oracle is deeply affected. Without this hidden vale, the Pythian answer can have no warmth of heart. I think. I sense that within these shining waters below us, there where the current runs to greatest depth, understanding and life are bound together. The reply at Pytho must be dipped in these original, unspoiled waters, I am certain. Daphne, it is you who leads me to this wordless place of beginning anew! Never shall I permit my answers to go stiff, dry, or generalized, I tell you. Instead, I see that they shall be like the swaying branches of the laurel tree—ever green, fragrant, and pliant!

    Now she smiled at him, and her eyes shone for the first time with delight. Hand in hand, the two figures continued their walk on the shaded riverbank in silence.

    The days passed during which Apollo sought out Daphne on the fragrant paths of the river glen, and they walked for hours, their conversation spaced with thick-textured silences. On this late afternoon, the sun had shifted from the river's singing waters to the far reaches of the woods as they walked and spoke, hand in hand, in the deep green realm far from rocky Pytho on Mt. Parnassus. At times, their steps took on the confident liveliness of the young while other times they slowed as if overtaken in the pause of reflection. Surely two more-beautiful figures had not been seen together on the Greek earth. Apollo, turning to Daphne, spoke.

— You ask whether it is glorious at Pytho. Glorious? Yes, there is ample glory and splendor of gifts in my sanctuary, and there is the glory of winners in the games. Yet it is not as happy for me as you may think.

— Ah, I can guess why that is true. Is it not because your sanctuary is upon a high rocky floor of the mountain's chasm—a severe and exposed place? Why, it can possess none of the pleasures of my softer green and gentle country!

Apollo smiled at her words, amusing himself with imagining how it would be if she were to be in charge of promoting Pytho's image. They both were silent for a time, taking in the commentary of several crows, shining in their fierce black feathers. When Apollo spoke, it was to express something not mentioned before.

— In my life at Pytho, the hardest thing to bear is the loneliness.

She was plainly startled by the confession.

— Can a god be lonely?

— Am I not the enduring proof?

— What sadness, O Lord Apollo! Do tell me, what is such loneliness like?

— When I am lonely, the evidence shows up in human experience, actually, for I am intimately connected to life. When my songs grow full to bursting and not one singer comes forward to shape and to sing them into the world, then am I lonely. My thoughts enter the luminous ideas. Perhaps you have noticed. Well, when these ideas lose the winged quality of their divine origin, they become juiceless as dried grape stems. And I am left exceedingly lonely. Surely the worst time of all for me comes about when my oracle is sought out solely to deliver people out of the crisis at hand while they remain blind to the fine print!

— The fine print?

She was altogether puzzled.

— Yes, my dear. Most of my wisdom is found in the fine print.

He gazed into the distance as he spoke. That this was not an explanation for her hardly mattered. A stream of sadness engulfed her.

— My heart aches for you, Apollo. To think that so few know of your godly malady—loneliness!

— From a human point of view, I suppose it does appear as a malady. Are not loneliness and longing closely tied, like brother and sister? Without longing, which is the soul's voice speaking, existence is pale indeed. Ah, how different from obvious human need is that voice. It defines a person, you see, drawing sharp the contours of who she is. No single action, no words, no emotion present one's essential nature the way that longing does. Ah, and here is the rub, as a man will say, "No one approaches his longing except on the path of loneliness!"

Daphne's hands flew to her cheeks. It was all too much for her to take in. A sense of protest overtook her.

— I know neither loneliness nor longing, I must tell you. Both are strangers to my experience, Lord Apollo. As daughter of the river god, I have many sisters and am rarely alone. How full my life is, ebbing and flowing with shining life! Whatever should I long for, I ask you?

Listening to her, he perceived the voice of earth's own abundance. Was it possible to answer this? Gazing into her uplifted face, his smile was radiant.

— Listen to me, Daphne. I am not presently lonely. If you will stay with me, every wounding loneliness I know shall surely be cured!

— Is it true that we Greeks honor you also as god of healing? Surely you are able to cure yourself . . . Ah, something astonishing is happening to me at this very moment. In the happy chambers of my heart and mind, there comes a cry: *Go with Apollo!* Ah, but I fear to act!

— What holds you back, Daphne? Mine is the realm of beautiful singing form, yet form becomes sterile without substance! You are my substance, beloved maiden. There is an exquisite amplitude of mind shaped in logos, but words are dry leaves without the flowing stream of earth's happening. You, my river nymph, bring me the shining waters! Yes, the music of the lyre is mine, but you are the soul of song!

Daphne bowed her head, staring at the ground, for she was overwhelmed. How could a woman reply to such things? She must answer. The words that came stopped the god short.

— How is a woman to reply to such an outpouring? You are known for the wisdom called *sophrosyne*, yet you have flung it aside, it seems.

Apollo looked thoughtful and nodded somewhat admiringly to her rebuke.

— The wise measure in all things, you mean. O how is one to come to the
right measure who has not known the full tide of existence? Until I have
plumbed the boundless delight, my passion shall not know measure.
Come with me, Daphne. Join me without fear!

Daphne's legs felt unsteady beneath her at the same time that her
face was a narrative of delight, though mixed with fear. Her voice seemed
to come from some distance, now causing him to think of Earth Goddess
herself.

— Oh, Apollo of the high sunlit place, I cannot go with you! I am sorry . . .
Tomorrow I go to join the company of your sister, Artemis herself, in
the woodland by the stream.

Alas, she who goes with Artemis must guard the gift the maiden
alone knows! The words fell like deadly arrows, and Apollo was stricken
with sorrow.

— O grim news! My sister is everlastingly virgin. Must she therefore capture
the loveliest maidens for her companions, depriving gods and men? It
is too much!

For a long moment, it seemed that every vestige of Olympian calm
abandoned him. Only his majesty remained, and it was undiminished. Filled
with longing, his appeal came forth afresh.

— Look at me, Daphne. Do not look aside like the wary doe of my
sister. There. That's better. Yes, I see in the bloom of your cheeks the
knowledge that proclaims our love. Do not shake your head, for it is
true. My dear one, shining one, it is too late for retreat. You see that I
am under your spell as surely as if the nymphs bound me in their circle
dance. Strange, but when I gaze into your green eyes, long and quiet,
I behold two leaves of the laurel tree! Almost I am consumed in their
unfathomable silence! Daphne, you are mine! I shall yield you up to
neither god nor mortal!

Swiftly but not without gentleness, the god took Daphne into his
embrace, and the bliss of love claimed them both in a timeless moment.
Suddenly with a small cry, Daphne broke free, turned, and fled down the
river path. Now the maiden was a fleet runner accustomed to the rough
paths of the glen where often she paced herself with the deer for sport.
Presently within the densely wooded terrain, Apollo lost her to view as,
no laggard himself, he followed in swift pursuit. She succeeded in staying
ahead of her pursuer as she took the wide circle of the path she knew well.
It was under a great plane tree that she paused in deep shade to recover her
breath, and Apollo reached her side. He spoke quietly now.

— Why do you run away from me, dear Daphne? Is my love so fearful a thing?

    She shook her head repeatedly before the words came.

— I remembered the maiden Semele, and I knew that I must flee.

— What of Semele?

— Why, she was naive. She drew too close to Zeus in all his attributes, and his thunderbolt destroyed her!

    Apollo's voice was reassuring.

— Wait, my beloved. You don't understand. The thunderbolt is in the hand of Zeus, who wields it on occasion. As for me, I have no thunderbolt to bring you harm.

    Reservation held her, even so, and she uttered a deep sigh.

— But what lies in Apollo's hand is yet to be determined, I tell myself.

    As the god stared into the distance as though attempting to discern some solemn truth that at the moment would cast light upon understanding, Daphne slipped away and plunged again into the dense thicket that bordered the river. She had not gone far, however, when slackening her pace, she heard Apollo's voice coming nearer.

— Daphne! Where have you gone? I would not lose you for all the treasure of Pytho!

    Moved by his tribute, she replied.

— I am here in the woods I know well, in the hidden place. Oh, Apollo, let it be!

    He cried aloud in protest,

— Never before have I despised distance as I do now!

— Far Shooter, are you not the god of distance? No woman can draw close to what is by nature full of the afar!

— Ah, hear me, dear nymph. With all my heart I desire to destroy the distance between us!

— Then you would be no longer Apollo. The truth is that it is Apollo my heart loves!

    Always when you draw close to me, my world is cloaked with a presence that is luminous, singing, and wise. Although you guard a certain distance from me, the earth in between is made shining and sweet!

    Daphne's words declaring her love of Apollo faded into some grave distance of their own as she spoke, and Apollo strained to catch them.

— Your voice so precious to me is fading . . . Daphne? Daphne?

    At once, the god followed the path of the faint voice until it ended under a great laurel tree that stood at the river's edge. In that moment, he came upon her, their eyes meeting as they stood in what seemed a great cave, and he discerned her breath from the rise and fall of her bosom. Gently Apollo took hold of the corner of her flowing garment. A soft cry arose from Daphne, a prayer, "O Goddess, help!" As he gazed at her, time altered, and she also was changed. Instead of Daphne the woman, a young laurel tree, tall and graceful in its abundant branches, stood before him. Great grief seized Apollo, who cried out.

— Daphne, Daphne, no, no! Do not abandon me! How could you depart into the laurel tree everlastingly!

He stared for a long time at the laurel bough he held in his hand, and Apollo wept.

Some time passed, and embracing the laurel tree, he spoke his final words.

— When first I stood by an ancient laurel tree in the vale, you came to me, and we walked side by side on the paths, our love growing in this green world. Ah, but now, that sweet time has ended, and the green world claims you back to its bosom, Daphne! O Earth, great goddess, this is your work! Daughter of Peneus, hear me. Would you have me return to the severe rock of my sanctuary alone to spend everlasting days exposed to Zeus's fierce sky? Is this my fate? You who are all departure, Daphne, receive me even now under your green and fragrant boughs. There would I dwell for all time! Ah, the unplucked laurel bough rests in my hand, and I shall pluck it and carry it with me for my everlasting companion. Beloved Daphne, you shall crown Apollo's golden head from now on, for closer than a wife you shall be to me and dearest of all!

The Voice of the Laurel

Many pronouncements of the oracle were given by Pythia at Pytho on Parnassus' majestic slope where in his solitary depths, Apollo had his dwelling place. But winter came again to Thessaly, and Apollo returned to the Vale of Tempe. There within the river glen, he came again to the young laurel tree and saw that already it grew sturdy while its branches reached upward toward the sky, much like the arms of maidens in the dance. For a long time he remained beside the tree, for there was that in its presence that brought him peace, deep-textured and enduring. What he came to hear was the voice speaking from the tree, addressing him,

I am the stillness, O Apollo, that cups your voice! Without me, your voice goes unhoused and is fated to grate against the walls of the human predicament, depositing credentialed words, however brittle and gone dry. Yet held within the stillness of Tempe, my home, your spoken words will hold the living pulse, beating out the uncountable time span of wisdom. Listen! Do you hear the rhythmic, echoing steps of yourself and the Muses in Pytho's nocturnal dance beside the spring Castalia? Ah, but when my stillness is missing, even the music of your lyre falls on wearied ears, ears schooled in tedious repetition. Yet when the lyre finds its voice emerging out of primordial beginning, I am present. For I am the stillness that sways even now in the laurel tree below your temple where the wind and the tree join in the ongoing dialogue of Apollo and Daphne's love. And so we dance at Pytho, you and I, sketching in the gestures of our measured steps the beautiful greenness that's called existence O mortal bride! And radiant, everlasting Apollo!

Apollo Meets the Centaur

The Vale of Tempe, through which the river Peneus made its way below Mt. Olympus and Mt. Ossa to define his winter haunt, was a region he knew well, for surely it held his heart's history. Leaving the vale behind, Apollo began the ascent of Mt. Pelion, for he desired to visit the centaurs upon their verdant land. High country it was, its green wildness spilling over the slope and into lush ravines where springs poured out their waters in abundance. It was horse country, unquestionably. Unlike the god's own Mt. Parnassus where his sanctuary is found below the great gorge, Pelion showed no sign of familiar human habitation. Remote and yet greatly inviting it seemed to him. He was contentedly occupied with his reflections when someone approached him on the path. It was a being unlike any he had ever before encountered. The god assumed the initiative, as gods are wont to do.

— Would this be the land of the centaurs, can you tell me?

The being was not unfriendly and replied at once.

— It's ours, yes. I'm a centaur myself. As for you, you might be one of those unusual folk who live on high Olympus.

Clearly the words emerged more out of suspicion than any sense of respect. Apollo bowed slightly as he remained intent in his regard of the centaur.

— I must say that I marvel to observe that from ground to waist you are all horse. What strange existence is this? In this realm, does being human begin in a middle place from which it inches slowly upward? Is this the case?

— No one has named it before. The middle place, you say. I expect a person can't really tell where it begins and where it ends. What I can tell you is that it is where beast and man meet up. There's a lot of rearing, snorting, beating of hooves, thrashing of arms, and a hurling of spears! That pretty well sizes up us centaurs.

Apollo's eyes widened at this information before he gave a small nod of understanding.

— Actually, the human individual experiences this difficult place where beast and human consciousness meet, I believe. I myself have witnessed an especially difficult battle between Greeks and centaurs.

The centaur coolly observed Apollo and apparently reached the conclusion that he was not qualified to pass on centaurs in any way. He spoke with authority now.

— Only the centaur really knows such a thing. We centaurs are the first to take hold of life, lifting it out of chaos and depositing it into the horses' pounding energy. It's a huge leap, I tell you, out of brooding darkness. We centaurs are the primordial stem, and that's a fact. The human fellow has to wait until he can flower higher up on our torso, see?

— This leap you speak of, you imply that the human realm is greatly indebted to it, then?

The centaur bent now toward the god, severely appraising him before replying.

— Our leap isn't done once and for all, of course. It has to happen again and again. The leap of centaurs is urgent and all fired with passion. It is like a powerful horse.

— Such energy as you describe I've observed in the horses that draw my chariot.

Now this was an important piece of information indeed.

— You mean that you are one of those high-up folk who've got themselves a chariot?

Apollo smiled and affirmed it with a nod. Lest this traveler not give credit to where it was due, the centaur continued in his confident, hoarse voice, pounding his chest with both arms.

— Below the waist, I carry the foundation from which the human world arises. Do you understand?

— I shall never underestimate you centaurs. Tell me, do no men ever come here to the centaur realm on Pelion's fine slope?

— A few have come. The problem is that they don't know how to accept our hospitality.

— What do you mean?

— Why, they've got their eyes pinned on another mountain! It's insulting.

— What mountain might this be, centaur?

— Olympus, of course. That's where the gods live. Folks set their eyes on that misty, distant place while they end up trampling our virgin wilderness!

To this centaur, it appeared that neither gods nor men came off respectably. Even so, the god felt a rush of pity for his companion.

— It would be a shame if I came to Pelion and missed the delights of centaur land! I shall seek out your exuberant springs and the great cave as I prepare to meet the centaurs residing in these parts. I wonder, will you be my guide? At present I assure you that I've no eyes for Olympus with its chilly heights and its familiar bliss like wine in old bottles. There is a god-longing that consumes me. It is for the centaurs' earth here where Pelion's flank plunges joyously to the maiden plain below us. Run, my friend, and I shall follow!

The two figures took off, running swiftly down the steep narrow path, and they did not stop until they reached the shore of the shining lake. Now Apollo, standing apart, gazed up at lofty Pelion and murmured to himself,

— The land of the centaurs . . . why, this is the crucial place. It is here that the human spirit is endlessly peeling away its animal husk!

Apollo and Chiron

Winter winds blew cold as the god of the oracle at Pytho left the Vale of Tempe in far Thessaly and turned his face toward Mt. Pelion, which ceaselessly regarded the eastern sea beneath its brow. Fierce gales assailed the traveler, and yet he made his way with sturdy resolution. The rugged green land of Pelion that thrust into the Aegean was a formidable sentinel. How wrapped in its own solitude it appeared. He began to climb the steep path to the home of the centaurs. That Apollo was comely, slender and everlastingly youthful with an inscrutable lordliness, was evident to any observer. He drew his woolen cloak about himself more closely now. At an intersection of ways, he had no trouble choosing the path that narrowed abruptly and swung steeply upward among large boulders where in sudden recognition he found himself at the entrance to a high rock cavern. At once, a large burly centaur stood blocking the way. Apollo nodded and spoke.

— Greetings, Phocus!

The centaur peered down intently at the traveler, and his voice was like the clumping of hooves.

— Would you be one of those Olympians? It's hard to tell, you being wrapped up the way you are.

His tone was far from welcoming.

— The cloak is due to your weather, Phocus. To answer your question, yes, I am. Will you let Chiron know that Apollo has come to see him?

Phocus took his time with another long suspicious look and, with a begrudging nod, left his visitor standing within the cave's dark entrance. He had not long to wait before Chiron emerged out of the dark vaulted cavern. His torso bare, he presented a fine physique. What was most arresting, undoubtedly, was the centaur's face, for it held the distilled memory of one who keenly observed human history at close range. His lower body remained in shadow, but Apollo recognized the kingly centaur immediately.

— Greetings from far Pytho, Chiron! Our wind does not blow so cold and fierce as yours does, I must say.

Chiron smiled, receiving this as a tribute to Pelion.

— Welcome, Apollo! You only come to our region in winter, so what do you expect? We do nothing by halves here on Pelion. Found the Vale of Tempe sufficiently sheltered on the other hand, did you?

It was a well-known fact that the god of the oracle made Tempe his place of winter retreat.

— Indeed. How I love my secluded haunt . . .

The centaur noticed that he grew somber and pensive as he spoke, and he understood the god's loss.

— Tempe's vale is Daphne's place, of course. So it shall always be. What brings you to us, braving our winds?

— As you know, many have sought me out for their rescue in a time of pestilence. I believe that I have not failed them. But I come to you, Chiron, seeking your more hidden knowledge of healing.

Chiron raised his face to another memory.

— Is there not on the hill above a valley called Epidauros, an ancient altar to yourself as healer? I seem to remember this.

— Yes.

Chiron waited for Apollo to elaborate, but he did not.

— Well, you come asking for what you call my "hidden knowledge of healing." Exactly what have you in mind? Pelion has many restorative herbs, and I am something of a guide to these. However, they are not what one calls hidden . . .

Apollo allowed the cloak to fall from his shoulders, and a haunted look filled his face as he spoke.

— It comes to this, great healer. I desperately need your kind of medicine to cure my aching loneliness!

Apollo looked away, and compassion was in Chiron's face now.

— So like others, god of the oracle, you come to be cured. Well, I cannot cure you of your love of Daphne since it is an immortal thing.

An abysmal sigh escaped Apollo. Chiron nodded as if having assessed the condition, and continued.

— But wait. There exists a medicine for you. Yes, I am fairly certain of it, and it belongs to the realm of Pelion. When the sun has risen tomorrow, you must return here to the cave. Will you come?

The wise centaur's voice held a note of hopefulness that Apollo trusted, and he smiled in response.

— You can count on my being here!

— Allow me to remind you of what you know here and now: healing is not a fixing or the assigning of a single remedy so much as it is life embraced again for the first time!

As Apollo received the words, time seemed to expand and become like a fine dwelling place of many rooms. When he looked up, he murmured his thanks and departed. When he had pulled the cloak around himself, he faced the wind and descended the mountain.

Koronis and the Centaurs

Reaching the high rocky ledge where a great cavern opened, the young woman turned to gaze down on the forested slope of the mountain beyond which lay a tranquil sea. She sighed, contented in the sweet dusk that followed the dawn before the sun's rays penetrated the mountain slope. It was a time that veiled the cedars and pine trees in fertile silence, causing her to feel once again the indescribable shelter that Pelion provided. The maiden, daughter of Thessalian king Phlegyas, was dark-eyed with heavy, silken black hair that fell to her shoulders, and she was wont to climb the mountain paths like a wood nymph. She called from the entrance to the great cavern.

— O Chiron, it is Koronis. I've come to see you!

The king of the centaurs appeared immediately and welcomed her into his place. She responded, explaining what she had been about.

— How refreshing are the waters of Pelion's cold spring! I've just come from bathing there, you see.

— Found your own secluded spot, did you?

He was acquainted with her nature, it seemed.

— Yes. It is a spot where the young plane trees overhang the rippling water and the centaurs do not come.

— Ah, so you have found your own access to Pelion's spring. Will you claim it, I wonder? Be forewarned, though, who bathes in our spring will be altered!

She gave a startled small laugh when he failed to elaborate.

— Is it that you wish to frighten me away?

— Heaven forbid. No.

— Still, what you say is strange. Actually, as I swam under a small waterfall and as the bubbling waters poured over me, a woman appeared on the bank. I had no idea where she came from.

— Indeed? And who was this person?

— You will find it hard to believe, for so it was for me. The woman was Pythia!

— Apollo's priestess of the oracle at his sanctuary on Parnassus? She whose life moves between two sacred springs below the brooding cliffs?

— Yes. That one.

Koronis fell silent as if staring at some invisible scene, and some perplexity was in her face.

— You spoke together, did you, you and Pythia?

— No. That was what was strange. She seemed there and yet not there.

What about the springs at Pytho, Chiron?

— A great deal of mystery and some inexplicable power lies with each of them, I believe.

Pythia, like others who travel to the sanctuary, bathes in the spring Kastalia to prepare herself for the encounter with the god. Yet within the oracle chamber, she sits upon the tripod alone and drinks water from the spring Kassotis, which is the hidden spring. You see, neither spring is for general bathing or amusement.

— Oh, the image you describe causes me to tremble. It is said that when she sits upon the tripod drinking from the mysterious waters that pour forth out of dark earth, then it is that the god comes to her with his response to the question.

Chiron regarded her steadily, his expression thoughtful, but he did not reply. There was a considerable commotion at the door of the cavern, and the voice of two centaurs rose excitedly on the morning air. The king of the centaurs called out.

— Come in, Canopis and Eurytus!

As the two sleek and handsome centaurs entered, their voices were raised in some argument. Eurytus insisted that he was the fastest runner while Canopis protested, declaring himself the swiftest of the centaurs. Chiron addressed them.

— The two of you have been no doubt racing again on the northern slope. Is this right?

Eurytus spoke first.

— Yes, Chiron, and the race proved me the fastest.

Canopis was not about to let this interpretation stand.

— Chiron, hear what I have to say. Because Eurytus got to the top first, he says he is the fastest runner. I say I am the swifter runner because while he took the short straight route, I followed the winding paths to get to the goal. I traveled a much greater distance and yet arrived only a few minutes later.

Eurytus was angry now.

— A whole lot later. Don't be ridiculous. So I did slice off the winding parts. I arrived first, and that makes me the winner. Tell him so, Chiron.

Chiron studied both young centaurs quietly before replying.

— Coming in first seems to be the passion of a race. There is that. However, I must point out that there is a running that is not racing.

Eurytus raised his eyebrows.

— What's the point of such a thing?

— Well, think of the race, lad. It sets a specific goal, which is the point where the score is taken. Now the runner must head for this goal as directly as the track allows. The runner finds himself ignoring all that lies to either side of the track since the object is to reach one set goal.

Eurytus nodded impatiently while Canopis was wide-eyed and silent.

— There is yet a different kind of running that engages the path in all its meanderings and winding.

Eurytus groaned audibly.

— That's going to slow a fellow down for sure!

Chiron nodded, and Canopis spoke up.

— Eurytus, you and I used to have a lot of fun, but now all you think of is where you are getting to, and you're panting and shoving on me as well.

— You're my pal, aren't you? I'm trying to make you amount to something. A fellow has to push toward the highest goal.

Canopis looked confused. Chiron, never one to be caught up in the scuffle of the moment, was thoughtful as he spoke.

— At the start, you set a goal you want to reach; but in time, that goal can deceive you. It does possess a small glimpse of well-being in the future, but that's all. Just consider, lads. How can the goal know what you need to know when you have run half the way there?

Eurytus found it simpler to count the fouls of Canopis.

— And another thing, Canopis stops along the way to smell the wild roses! No decent runner does a thing like that.

— Canopis' way is not the answer for yourself, true, but neither is your plan the answer for Canopis, I'd say. The way that works best lies somewhere between the two of you, I imagine.

— Chiron, why do you speak in riddles?

— Keep your goal if you must, but don't give it the seat of a god, do you understand?

— So what should Canopis and I put in the highest place if we're to be the best runners around?

— The seat of the god is for the god and none other. It holds the unbiased wisdom for life. Now get along and make your peace, you two!

Again friends, the two centaurs grinned at each other, bowed politely to Koronis and, saying good-bye to Chiron, took their leave. Surprisingly, Canopis raced straight down the steep slope and was first to arrive at the foot while Eurytus, laughing, stopped to smell the outcropping of flowers. Shaking his head from side to side and smiling, Chiron turned to Koronis who sat in the shadow of the chamber.

— Those boys warm my heart. They burst in here quite often spilling over with life much like Pelion's spring.

Koronis was recovering from the impact of their great energy.

— How different are the centaurs from Pythia, who haunts me today!

— Ah, Pythia is neither centaur nor even male, but woman like yourself.

The comparison astonished her.

— Like me? How can this be? Or in your eyes, is it that all women are alike? Sometimes I am dimly aware that there exists a catchall for life outside men's life, and it is called woman.

It was Chiron's turn to be startled as he studied the maiden's face. He spoke solemnly.

— Heaven forbid that a woman should be catchall, as you put it. Already I sense a movement in the dim corridors of what is yet to be, which I believe to be your destiny and yours alone. I tell you it is a thing not only of magnitude, but it possesses grandeur. Still, it will not be easy, Koronis.

He fell silent, and the silence troubled the daughter of Phlegyas.

— So what am I, great teacher?

— Who can answer that? I can only speak of how I perceive you. I see fertile earth overlaid with a quiet concentrated presence. As I gaze at you, what comes to mind is the fragrant plowed ground, just upturned, and, well, waiting. Pythia also seems to possess this nature.

Her hands flew to her cheeks, which were flushed with her reaction.

— Plowed ground? Surely I am more human than that, and besides, I am myself—unduplicated! As for Pythia, she is more clearly distinguished than I am. When I think of her, I want to drop back lazily into being like all women, who are freer than Pythia is.

Such a role she has in Apollo's sanctuary . . . It can never be reversed!

— I was only reporting how your nature affects me. There is something else in you, a power to enchant, but it is a sacred condition like that of Pythia.

— Oh, I know of no such thing.

— In time, you shall be aware of it. This sacred condition I speak of is feminine, and it contains an impenetrable mystery. It is not explained by physical attraction.

— Does this condition produce a god's coming, as it appears to do with Pythia? She can only deliver the oracle in the chamber when Apollo's response fills her completely, it is said.

— The sacred condition I refer to is not a cause. It does not produce Apollo's coming. At the same time, he cannot come unless this feminine condition is in place. Always Apollo acts on his own, uncompelled. Never misunderstand your power, Koronis. It is human and therefore limited. But tell me, why is Pythia's image haunting you so much?

She relaxed visibly with the question, glad to leave the perplexing words of the centaur. Now she spoke as maiden recounting her day with some animation.

— There I sat solitary after my plunge into Pelion's spring, lingering on the green bank and listening to the musical current of the water. I could not have been happier, I think. Shortly, thoughts of Pythia, the priestess, at the spring of Pytho were lively in my mind. Did she go all alone to bathe in Kastalia, I wondered? And did she, like myself, dream of some enchanting encounter on the bank?

Almost imperceptibly, Chiron shook his head as though all maidens perplexed him and it was not to be helped. His response did not address her questions, it seemed.

— Pythia knows deep within herself that earth is our treasure and must shape the bounty of experience into a kind of manageable vessel, a vessel light enough to carry.

Koronis moved uncomfortably, rearranging her peplos, before responding.

— Still, there is something that disturbs me about Pythia. Indeed, it stops me. You see, Pythia doesn't own anything. Nothing belongs to her alone, not even the oracle of the god that comes to herself when she is seated on the holy tripod. Isn't this odd, Chiron? Everybody needs to call something her own, and when something is of special value, one wants to say, "I have some claim to this." Oh, I don't believe that Pythia has a fair deal!

Chiron's brow drew together with concern as he regarded Koronis and her words.

— And yet when the god comes to the oracle chamber, it is to Pythia alone he comes.

Surely this happening is her treasure that no one can take from her.

The maiden did not protest, but a slow smile began on her face. She murmured aloud.

— Ah, how I should like to know what that is like—Apollo's coming to myself alone!

— Perhaps you shall yet know, Koronis.

— What did you say, Chiron? What else draws the god, I wonder . . .

— A summons that comes out of the center of oneself, never merely an invitation at the margins. This call awakens the god. He refuses to be a decorative border or a companion to fill one's leisure, you see.

Pythia's fate, nevertheless, continued to haunt her.

— Still, the fact remains that Pythia is left short. She has neither husband nor lover nor companion, and she has no guarantees, I think . . .

Chiron regarded Koronis for a long while in silence now, and he was troubled.

Apollo Returns

Standing at the entrance of the rocky cavern, Chiron observed the figure who approached, his stride lively as he took the steep path up Pelion. He would know that radiant face anywhere: the fair, flowing hair, the gentle authority of his look, the eyes with their lyrical narrative, the small archaic smile. He called to him as the figure grew close.

— Apollo, welcome! So you have returned to our discussion here in Pelion's cave?

Apollo smiled as he greeted his respected friend and ally.

— That's true.

— Far Shooter responding to the lure of the far place then?

— There is that. When one is at home in the familiar setting, there is a passion that sleeps, it seems. That passion stirs in me now. Mt. Pelion has awakened it, and that is a fact.

— You know, Apollo, love is known to seek the mountain and the caverns of the far place, let me point out. Don't overlook this fact.

The god laughed, merry for the moment.

— Great teacher of Pelion, are you warning me?

— Well, you could call it a warning. I am more inclined to call it *anticipation*. Recently a lovely maiden visited me, and we spoke at length of your priestess Pythia.

Apollo was startled to find Delphi's trail somehow intertwined with his journey from Parnassus here to distant Thessaly.

— About your maiden caller, had she recently visited my oracle at Delphi, bringing a question? And what would be her name?

— She is daughter of Phlegyas, a local king, and she has visited me before. Koronis she is called. No, she has never traveled to Parnassus, it seems. What took place was that she visited Pelion's spring, and unaccountably Pythia presented herself there.

    Apollo shook his head, perplexed, and his interest sharpened.

— So what of Pythia?

— It seems that the maiden was bathing alone in the fount when Pythia appeared to her and remained for some time speaking with her.

— A remarkable thing. Tell me of the maiden Koronis. Is she one of those rare persons for whom the veil is thin between her mind and communication with gods?

    The centaur considered this.

— No, I believe not. She walks earth firmly and confidently and prizes her own world and its people. The drama of events claims her, it seem. This is my impression. Certainly she is a modern woman of lively intelligence. Koronis is a woman, I'd say, who takes pains not to miss anything significant . . . Nor will she miss her destiny!

    Apollo shook his head as if he might be having difficulty imagining such a woman.

— How different she is from Pythia then. Pythia is solitary, her life bounded by the stones of my sanctuary, her mind and soul quiet and steadied for the oracle. It is odd, isn't it, that the Thessalian woman should be visited by Pythia?

— The explanation may be simple. Certain women are found with a strange, rather prophetic, sense. It is possible that she sensed the approach to Pelion of Apollo from distant Delphi. It may be as simple as that.

— Are you saying that my approach is simple, Chiron?

    There was a dryness in his tone.

— Come. That is not what I meant, as you well know.

    Apollo looked thoughtful.

— I wonder if Pythia appeared in order to warn her of my coming. After all, Pythia has her art of making way for my coming. Indeed, I am indebted to this knowledge of hers. A god cannot come unless the way is opened somehow. You understand. Does some meeting lie ahead with a woman different from any I've known—this Koronis, perhaps?

— Possibly. Clearly she is no priestess. Now Pythia has neither been blessed or impoverished by Aphrodite, I'd say, which may be an aspect you find attractive in her.

— Ah, but, Chiron, few women can hold a candle to Pythia. She tends the dwelling place of the sacred with faithfulness, and she prepares the essential encounter.

— No one doubts the extraordinary qualities of Pythia. It is that I perceive in you, Apollo, the stirring of a different passion. Besides, a new purpose seems to be slowly shaping itself, if I'm not mistaken. Have you not made the far journey here to Mt. Pelion where you find earth to be unusually bountiful, fragrant, and shall we say, pleasant in her ways? How else is this mountain possessor of hidden ways of healing? On second thought, I hope you haven't come to centaur land to establish another oracle. Already we are abundant with answers that work!

Chiron smiled broadly at Apollo, and the god returned the smile.

— And I do value the answers that you, Chiron, are generous with. You know, I believe I should like to meet the Thessalian woman Koronis!

The two figures regarded each other in deep friendship, but they did not speak further.

Apollo Meets Koronis

On the following day, Apollo arose early in the morning noting the absence of the sun, for heavy clouds threatening snow hung low over Mt. Pelion. Making his way through the gray light, he climbed the steep path to the great cave of his centaur friend. Chiron was on hand and greeted him warmly, not surprised at the early call.

— Come in, come in! A friend of Pelion awaits you, Apollo.

As he spoke, he turned to a second figure who waited in shadow. The lovely young woman was dark with an abundance of shining black hair, her form graceful as that of a wood nymph. Her dark eyes lifted in curiosity toward the stranger before widening with something akin to fright, for truly he was a god come to earth. Smiling, Apollo took a slow step forward.

— Greetings, friend of Pelion! I am called Apollo. Would you be mortal? It is difficult to tell a lovely woman from a goddess, you see.

Wide-eyed, she gazed at Apollo in silence. She smiled a small perplexed smile and replied at last.

— The answer is not the answer . . . Are the feathers the bird itself, or is the bird the flesh and bones beneath?

Apollo laughed at her answer.

— Were you trained by the Sphinx herself on the road to Thebes, your riddle could not be better! Well, I suppose I must answer. I am in fact known not to be short on answers.

I should say that the feathers offer the senses the first touch of the bird itself. Yet when one meets the bird—round in flesh, shining like the dew, and giving voice to her world, then one has the good fortune to be in the presence of the whole bird. Will you tell me your name?

Her hesitation lengthened, for one's name is an intimate possession. At last, she spoke.

— I am Koronis, daughter of King Phlegyas.

— King of the Lapiths, he is. So you are Koronis—crow maiden indeed.

He said it as if he found it surprising but not unpleasant. As was usual with the god, he spoke his mind easily.

— The crow is the bird I hold in special regard, even gratitude. You see, the crow is my very own messenger.

Koronis somehow found this knowledge about the god uncomfortable and was eager to establish her credentials. She drew herself up to her full height.

— I am descended from the ancient line of Thessalian kings.

— Horsemen they were, is this not true? Doesn't your father have a brother who also rules a kingdom?

She frowned as if pondering something unpleasant.

— Uncle Ixion you mean, yes. Ambition is a force not tender with him.

He set her at ease, however.

— Tell me of yourself. What pleases you, Koronis? Are you often present when your father entertains strangers, and do you like their exchange?

She shook her head vigorously.

— Oh no. I like to explore the wooded bank of a stream with my maiden friends, and sometimes I ramble alone on the shore of the lake below. Best of all, I love coming here to visit Chiron on Pelion, listening to his lore. He's a rich storehouse of so much that I long to know. Perhaps you know this about him too.

At that moment, both looked toward the place where their host had stood, quietly looking on, but he had departed. Apollo understood this as a gesture of generosity not to be overlooked, and he invited Koronis to sit next to him in the cave's front chamber. His shining gaze fell on her admiringly, and he saw the blush on her cheeks.

— Always I've wondered why it is that the most desirable maidens seek their delight on the bank of a stream, often enough in some secluded place. Perhaps you will explain this to me.

Her laughter rippled merrily, and she gave him a tolerant smile.

— The stream in the hidden vale is so inviting, you see. It has a murmuring, shining life all its own that is always fresh to me. How different from talk in my father's chambers where I watch and am expectant, but am a stranger to such talk. When I find the spring, there is nothing to wait for. It welcomes me and my friends happily. Shall I tell you a secret? *What is worth happening is near the waters!* Lord Apollo, do you understand?

— That's an amazing thing you just said. The springs are very old in human
memory nor do the gods overlook the springs. Certain things about
maidens on the spring bank I have learned from my sister Artemis.
What unfolds at the spring has to do with earth's order and bounty,
I'd say. Never does it deceive us. Where the maidens' steps lead is to
the living boundary. Do you know, Koronis, there are springs that flow
abundantly at Pytho, which is my sanctuary. Only come with me and
I'll take you to them on Mt. Parnassus!

Just when she was happily thinking about the wooded bank of
a spring and he seemed to share her delight, there came this astonishing
invitation. She gasped audibly and turned a little pale.

— Alas, how could I leave Thessaly's shore? Oh, I cannot!

Even as she refused, she was aware that the stranger from Pytho
who called himself Apollo drew her powerfully, and she could not bear
thinking of leaving his company.

He was speaking gently.

— Ah, do not distress yourself. Come, tell me more about yourself. I should
like that. What are your virtues? Your passions? O lovely Koronis, who
are you truly?

Now she shook her head from side to side, her eyes not leaving his
handsome face.

— Oh, I do not know. Only in another's mirror do I see myself at all. Such
is the fate of maidens.

Apollo's brow drew together in protest.

— Come, you are so much more than a reflected image, I am certain. You
are of earth, earth dense in her winding passages. Why, another's look
can't dissolve you. What is of earth endures, steady and sure.

— How can you know, being a god who is a man besides?

No one had ever pointed out this limitation to him before. It caused
him to smile.

— Through my sister Artemis, I have come to observe the maiden, you
see. She is forever maiden as you must know. Still, there is that in the
maiden that goes unobserved and can never be seen at all.

Momentarily his kingly confidence slipped visibly, but he
continued.

— Koronis, you are like a cavern that is serene and far in a place that begets
the future not dreamed of before!

— How can it be that you see what can never be seen, I ask?

Apollo smiled his reassurance.

— I find you without winsome words and without plotting looks, a fact
   that pleases me. And yet, how powerfully you beckon to me, O bird of
   night's own hue!

Ardor, altogether unmasked now, radiated in the god's face. She
saw it, and she could not deny its reality. At the same time, she reminded
herself—with poor results—not to be deceived by fair words. One
consequence was favorable, however, for a confidence arose within her.

— Surely you, great Apollo, must require a woman of splendid attributes,
   the sort that people are wont to praise. She must be like fine sculptured
   columns for all to admire.

— Alas, no, dear Koronis. I do not desire a highly visible or an acclaimed
   woman! Let my beloved be unstudied in her being, and yet may she be
   complete in herself much like the laurel tree itself. Never do I long for
   a woman who is like an erect structure of stone! She must bend and
   take the pleasure of the wind, not as one who compromises herself but
   as one who moves in resonance with the greater way of things.

A pause fell upon them. When she spoke, it was the genial host
inquiring of the traveler.

— Why have you come to Pelion in winter instead of summer? In
   summertime, our doors stand open, and we call happily to all who
   pass.

— In summer in Greece, all is more exposed, I fear. You see, dear, the
   medicine I require in Chiron's territory is hidden. It lies in shadow. It
   is to be found in the intimate, unobserved place behind doors. Hear
   me, Koronis. Apollo does not seek hospitality as you know it. What I
   must tell you is that I come seeking your love and none other!

This revelation hung on the air. It took on fragrance. It was like
grapes that had ripened in the dark of the vine's heavy foliage. The revelation
of Apollo's love was a thing of immense beauty as she contemplated it.
Now she smiled slowly as though remembering a secret she had known in
the beginning but had discreetly laid aside. Her voice when she spoke at
last was that of a woman more queen than maiden.

— That love is at hand, Apollo!

His joy was radiant as he drew her to himself. A soft laughter
tumbled from her, and she commented.

— Ah, love is a winter thing after all!

Gazing at her, he became reflective.

— Always love seeks the enclosed space where the soul is indoors, safe
   from every trampling footstep, from every chilling indifference!

Practical always, Koronis turned her mind to the housing of their love.

— I know just the place. Deep within this cavern of Chiron's is an inmost private chamber. I shall take you there, dear Apollo.

Arm in arm, their steps eager, they began to penetrate the passage that led into the dark interior of the vaulted rock cave. The last words were the god's.

— Since this chamber you are leading me to is the wise and faithful centaur's very own, I wonder if the hidden medicine shall indeed be created there?

Visited by Aphrodite

Pelion's spring, swollen with winter snows, thundered down the steep slope, and Koronis, the Thessalian maiden, sat on the bank gazing upon it wonderingly. Speaking to herself, her mind and heart combined to overflow the words.

— I have met the traveler from far Parnassus who says his name is Apollo, a god's name. How my limbs trembled when I first looked into his face . . . This was not like me. Later at his side I walked, and, well, we rambled on the path I know not where. Ah, those wonderful hours in which we spoke and gazed upon each other mutely as well! Why, I was altered. Some part of myself reminded me that the traveler was not father's well-chosen guest in whose company I was permitted. No. This one does not move like one of those men in the royal house. That is a singular fact. He is the stranger, surely. Oh, but how beautiful he is to my eyes: youthful, yes, but not limited by youth; he has a wise brow above which a laurel wreath crowns his noble head. Surely he moves like a king without setting his mind to it. There's a grace that belongs to him and a natural authority that I've never witnessed before, no, not even in dear Chiron. Above all, I cherish the look that he gives to me alone, a look that is satisfied with what he sees!

She was surprised, being alone on the creek bank, when a voice spoke as if joining an ongoing conversation.

— There is none other like him, Koronis. And did you notice how radiant the traveler's smile is? Come, maiden. He is summoning you!

She cried out with sudden joy.

— Oh yes! You saw that, did you? Ah, I have a witness then. O voice, what is such a summons like?

The companioning voice seemed somewhat taken back by the question.

271

— What indeed? Above everything, do not try to reduce the extraordinary summons to some familiar category of things and events to be placed neatly in one's file!

Looking up from the waters, Koronis saw that a woman approached, one of indescribable grace, and she was alone. Recognition came over her.

— Can it be? Why, greetings, Goddess Aphrodite!

Aphrodite smiled her small inward smile. A lovelier woman the maiden had never seen. On her abundant hair she wore a garland of violets. She addressed Koronis.

— When the summons comes of which we spoke, I am present. Ah, that summons is golden.

— It causes me to tremble as you mention it.

— And rightly so. You ask what the summons is. It appears to have two parts. When the first part comes, there is a good deal of visible and immediate happening, nearly all satisfying. At once one seizes upon the happening as the wonderful whole prize. It is simply called *love*. Not only is there a quantity of delight, but an attachment, a bond, grows toward the other as well. Ah, who can describe it, I ask?

— And you, Lady Aphrodite, are goddess of this golden bond that is love!

Surely the goddess appeared somewhat downcast as she continued.

— People give me credit only for the golden summons, it appears. As for the second part, it also is present from the beginning of the love happening. How can I speak of it? It hovers over the delight and can be neither captured nor possessed!

— It is only human to want to seize the love and possess it for one's very own!

— So does it sound like misfortune to your ears, the fact that this invisible part cannot be possessed? Think of it in this way. This hidden second part of love is like an amphora of fermenting wine still sealed and in its deep, earth-ripening place. Naturally this vessel has not been opened. Remember this when you love, Koronis, for in time you will sense the unopened vessel. It is ill-advised to rail against the sealed jar, for it shelters the most important aspect of the summons of the god. True, one's thought and feeling can become swollen and heavy with restless emotion that circles about this condition.

— Tell me, though, Lady Aphrodite, can I count on this hidden, sealed-up part to support the golden love that has come to me?

Aphrodite did not reply at once. When she did, her voice took on a tender note.

— No, you cannot count on it, as you put it, for it will not be support as one has framed it in one's mind. Love, tangible and at hand, is the gateway that opens to a different dwelling place, one that is greatly desired. Accept the love by all means. And afterward, you must make way for the coming of the invisible part. Koronis, do you realize how honored you are that Apollo comes to you with his love?

Koronis smiled slowly, her sense of deep joy returning. Looking up, she saw that the goddess was about to depart. Her final words would be ever remembered.

— When the difficult time is at hand, know that I am close by, for I am companion of love's dark night as well. Ah, *you need not fear the way!*

When she looked up again, Koronis saw that she was alone on the bank while the litany of the plunging waters comforted her. Even so, the words of Aphrodite troubled her.

Apollo Loves Koronis

Beneath the old chestnut trees on Mt. Pelion, the god and the young woman walked side by side without words, for many were the ways of their communication. Each was content in the presence of the other as those are whom Aphrodite has abundantly favored. After some time, it was Koronis who broke the silence, her face brightened by some inner narrative.

— Oh, I see now how it is. Love turns out to be a deep cave. True, we first knew our golden love in the far chamber of Chiron's cave, which we approached hand in hand that day. Only now do I realize that our love is itself the cave, creating hidden rooms and corridors never dreamed of.

The god was pensive as he regarded her. He nodded.

— Ah, we must give thanks to earth herself for shaping the vessel.

— Why, I saw no vessel. What vessel?

Apollo smiled as if considering some truth that had more than one face.

— The vessel lay with you, Koronis, too close for you to observe, I expect. My dear, I feel an urgent need to warn you. This love of ours must remain a hidden thing. It must reside in the cave to which only the two of us know the path. Clearly, it must not be exposed in the house of your father, the king. Chiron's cave shelters it best, of course.

— Must we always come here to Pelion's far cave then?

— No. It is the beginning place, the place where it all happened, delivering us into delight and mystery . . . How difficult it was for me to surrender to the dark chamber! I am so accustomed to the light—the physical light and singing air of the high plateau of my sanctuary. Did you realize how intimidated I was?

He spoke earnestly, and she shook her head numbly.

— It was you, maiden, who led me into earth's deep chamber without fear where Apollo took root in earth, in the realm of centaurs, and am I not deposited in the human world as well? Koronis, do not look alarmed, for I am and shall always be enduringly grateful to you.

Her perplexity lingered yet.

— You say that the centaur's cave is the beginning place of our love. What comes after this, I ask?

— Love is the property of the soul, and the soul keeps its own counsel, not being given to announcing its plans. Even its greatest struggle is usually hidden from view . . . or else the language that might describe it is inaccessible. As to what is love's second part, I only know that it will impact the human world when it brings earth's gift to life.

Now Koronis, pragmatic that she was, took from her beloved's words the substance that gave her reassurance.

— Oh, what a future I shall have as bride of great Apollo! Is there much ahead of us?

— There is.

His tone was quiet, and he grew introspective.

— Will it bring us the happiness my heart yearns for?

— Human standards of joy and delight can be deceiving, you see.

— Apollo, what if I bear a child to you?

Her voice was a mere whisper, shrouded as it was with both fear and awe.

— Earth has taken the seed of the gods, and in earth, there is no illusion. Koronis, you shall bear this child. Does this fact frighten you so greatly? Yours will be the divinely human progeny, dear one.

She shook her head from side to side, the maiden now laden with woman's ancient knowledge, which does not change, a knowledge of body, time, and birth.

— Our love could remain hidden, but a living child? A child cannot be hidden! I am frightened, Apollo. Although our love is a thing of joy to me now . . . I perceive the shape of a grim predicament! Don't you see what I face in my parents' house as all of Thessaly looks on? "Koronis is pregnant with the undeclared stranger's child!" they will say.

— Listen, my dear. What is crucial is that you know differently from your parents and all the people. It is the truth that matters, not speculation and conventional expectation. That it will be lonely for you to bear this truth is something I cannot alter. Alas, it will be lonely for you! Trust me, Koronis, and trust Apollo's love.

Koronis turned her back now to the god and spoke with herself.

— I am suspended between two opposite forces, for two worlds have begotten me, each exacting its devotion. There is the deep cave of love with Apollo, and there is my life in the house of King Phlegyas, and between these two is a gaping chasm!

Apollo led her to his side again, and for some time, he sought to comfort her.

— Hear me. This is how it is. The son of Koronis and Apollo will be born in Thessaly on the shores of Lethe, and he will grow up to become the great healer among all the Greeks. O yes, he will bring joy and honor to us both, I am certain. It will not be easy. You must believe me.

A note of profound concern was in his voice as he gazed at her. She responded as one who strains to reach a ripened fruit just out of reach.

— Oh, my beloved, I want to believe you! I do!

That passion, bowed to devotion, was now evident in her demeanor, and the luminous autonomy of the god was heightened as he spoke.

— There exists an invisible and fragile place which shall come to be the dwelling place of our love, Koronis. It is the human soul!

When they had embraced tenderly, Apollo turned and descended Mt. Pelion. When he reached the intersection of ways at the edge of the woods, he turned and raised his hand to her, a stately figure standing still, and now he smiled. In that moment, Koronis knew that the strength Apollo left with her was enough.

Koronis Meets Pythia

    Hours had passed since she and Apollo parted at Chiron's deep cavern. It was late afternoon when she sought out the bank of the spring she had grown attached to. She reflected on the earlier time, the time of the golden summons in the god's presence when love had its way with her. How like a broad and flowering meadow it had been, and yet timeless! Above all moments, she treasured the one where, standing back from her, his eyes fully engaging her own, he had said simply, "Koronis, my beloved, I am Apollo!"

    In this moment of recall, a familiar voice, that of a woman not seen, spoke aloud.

— What a revelation to a mere woman! Surely it was the greatest moment of your life, Koronis.

    The comment, companioning indeed the train of her thought, drew her immediate response.

— Oddly, it was not as if something new and startling had been added to our friendship to crown other meetings, other ramblings. When he spoke his name, it was a treasured time to be sure, yet it partook of all the times of my life that revealed the god's presence. O voice, does this make sense? A satisfaction spread over me, filling all the dry crevices, and I was held within a radiant stream impossible to describe.

— I perceive that you are a modern woman.

    Somehow the tone of her invisible companion was disconcerting.

— Oh? What do you mean?

— For every modern woman, her experience is her treasure. It is the land she takes title to. Ah yes, that experience is not all happenings, for it also includes your thoughts and many feelings. There is a way you have of owning your experience, and perhaps taking charge of it, that reveals to me the modern woman with her agenda.

Now Koronis felt misunderstood somehow, and she drew in her breath sharply. Her question was terse.

— Who are you?

— I am Pythia. Remember how you summoned me when you bathed here in the spring of Pelion? In some ways we are alike, maiden, for both of us are chosen by Apollo. Each of us holds a unique place with him.

— Of course, I should have known. Greetings, Pythia. How do you find it in Apollo's presence, dare I ask?

— There is a deep satisfaction. Ah yes, and there is the sense of the radiant stream that accompanies a great god. Still, it is different from being *loved* by the god. Of this I am certain. When I sit upon Pytho's tripod in the oracle chamber, words fail me to describe his coming.

— Do not let your words fail you. A woman has her own words, surely. Won't you tell me what it is like abiding in Apollo's own dwelling place on Parnassus?

Suddenly Pythia laughed at her companion.

— I do like your strong spirit, woman. It lifts me somehow. Let me try to find the words. Be patient, if you can.

She fell silent while the sound of the breeze played through the branches of the plane tree above their heads. At last Pythia began speaking.

— There is a corridor that exists in woman. It is rather like a long hollow throat with a certain bend in it. It's flexible. Yes, that is how it is. Well, I'm attentive to this corridor, for tending it mostly amounts to keeping it empty, you see.

— What? No, I don't see at all. This corridor that belongs to a woman, where does it lead to? This surely must be determined before one goes walking there . . .

— Oh, one does not walk there. That is, I don't walk there at all. What I am doing is guarding the hollow space. Nor does my experience fill the corridor, which is reserved for the coming of the god.

With the impact of the final words, Koronis grew pale.

— Oh! You mean that the god himself comes by this corridor that belongs to a woman?

— He comes this way, yes. It is a narrow unobtrusive pathway, but it makes ready for the god and for his speaking as well. A god needs human protection and, well, assistance, Koronis. Didn't you know? There are many passageways that the world presents, but the gods regularly pass these up, I do believe. It doesn't seem to matter that some of these have grandeur and others may be dazzling.

— It sounds very sad indeed. Do you know any other woman besides yourself who keeps this corridor in shape?

— No. That is, I don't know.

Her eyes wide with astonishment, Koronis regarded Pythia in silence during a long pause. At last she pursued a different path of thought.

— Pythia, you have made a long journey from Pytho to Mt. Pelion here on the eastern sea. Tell me, why have you come?

— It is that when a woman is summoned by Apollo, I am not far away.

— For this companionship, I'm grateful. You, after all, are the one who knows Apollo best.

Pythia did not respond to this. Instead, she spoke of the present situation.

— I am aware, Koronis, that Apollo has come here seeking your love. Although you are an attractive and lively woman, it is not chiefly for the physical attraction that he has come.

— So is it that there is something Apollo asks of every woman that you are about to tell me?

Pythia sighed as if wearied.

— By Olympus, no! Apollo does not love in general. There is generality neither in the god's choice nor in his love. Mark this well. You are chosen, Koronis! What you offer him in response must arise out of your very nature and belong to yourself alone. No recognizable commodity of response is worthy, I tell you. Your love must be newborn and unrepeatable in each encounter with great Apollo. This counsel comes out of a long and devoted relationship to the god, you understand.

Koronis fell silent as she pondered the words of Pythia, priestess of the oracle of Apollo. At last she spoke simply, her voice low.

— I am thankful for your coming, Pythia, and I'll remember your words. That you chose to come to me moves me deeply. Ah, you are leaving. Farewell, my friend!

In Her Father's House

Koronis, beloved of Apollo and pregnant with his child, went home. As she walked once again in the rooms of the royal house of her father the king, her loveliness was marked by all who saw her. With her raven hair and eyes and her skin like warm milk, she resembled the lustrous moon. As for the maiden herself, she was troubled and refused food, growing pale and listless. Her father, Phlegyas, voiced his concern.

— What is it, my dear?

She shook her head and replied not a word. Days passed, and again he questioned her.

— Can it be that without my knowledge some young Greek youth, such as those who win the games at Pytho or sing the odes in the theater, has managed to capture your love? Speak to me, my daughter.

Koronis sighed audibly.

— No mortal youth anywhere has won my love, Father.

— Good. I certainly hope not, for I have myself chosen a fine one for you. You'll meet him today, and I believe you'll be pleased with the choice.

Hearing these words, she turned pale, and there was an unmistakable dread in her eyes as she gazed at her father.

— Oh no, Father! I cannot!

— Certainly you cannot question my authority in the matter of your marriage, Koronis. Is it my judgment that worries you?

— Alas, authority does not always walk with true love, if ever at all!

Phlegyas held a deep affection for his daughter so that her response troubled him. He sought to persuade her.

— Come, come, my dear girl. You are sure to be delighted with Ischys.

There was an alteration in her sad indifference, and a flame of interest shone in her eyes.

— It is Ischys the Strong, you say?

An eagerness was unmistakable, for was not Ischys known for his valiant conquests?

— That's right. He's a real winner and good material for ruling our kingdom when I am dead. Would I have chosen less than a real winner for you—a hero, and a prince?

Very soon, Ischys came to the royal house of the Lapiths where, after receiving fitting hospitality, he was brought into the chamber where Koronis waited. The prince looked on the maiden with admiration and growing desire. Thereafter he returned many times to be with her. Increasingly, however, Koronis kept her silence in the presence of the handsome prince. In the course of time, their marriage, expected throughout the kingdom, was discussed with the king, but Koronis drew closed the shutters of her mind and heart. Ah, how could she possibly forget the love she had with Apollo? Unspeakable it was, and yet was it not this love that nurtured the god child within her womb? Nor had she revealed the fact of her pregnancy throughout the royal negotiations. Time passed, and nature itself declared her visibly pregnant. In amazement, King Phlegyas came to her, bristling with anger.

— Only now is the true cause of your long silence and withdrawal obvious to me! Tell me, Koronis, who is this lover you are protecting?

Her face was ashen as she started down some dark and inscrutable road of the Fates. She replied quietly, her voice no longer the young maiden's but that of woman.

— O Father, I cannot speak of this love! No one would believe me.

Phlegyas stared at her for a long agonizing moment before turning and leaving.

Many times in the days that followed, he returned to ask her the question, "Who is this man, Koronis? Why are you protecting him?" And each time, Koronis shook her head gravely, for she would not reveal the identity of her lover. Day by day she watched from her high window hoping that he would appear, striding toward the royal house with lordly presence. But the god did not appear. Her loneliness grew as the child in the womb grew, and the anger of her father became bitter. No longer was she the beloved daughter. Ending a self-imposed isolation of many days, she sought out her father.

— Father, harass me no more, I beg you. Indecision is a diet of madness. I have come to tell you that I bow to you!

Amazement was on the king's face as for a long moment they regarded each other in heavy silence. Tears were in her eyes now as she drew herself up with great dignity and spoke.

— I shall marry Ischys!

The king took his daughter into his arms, and when he thought to congratulate her, he saw that instead she required comfort.

— It is a wise thing that you have decided, my dear. You'll not regret it. Ischys is a splendid fellow and worthy of praise. Now I go at once to make wedding preparations. There now, why do you look so sad? No more weeping, I say!

The day of the wedding had arrived. Wearing her wedding gown, Koronis walked with her husband-to-be on the bank of the nearby lake where water fowl swam. And Ischys' love for her flourished so that he praised her eloquently, his hard-won prize. Turning to face her, he asked.

— Tell me, my dear, what do you think of me?

Her smile was gentle but wan.

— How can I say? The marriage is so, well, swift to claim us, is it not? Truly I go with you to do your bidding and that of my dear father. Certainly you are a pleasing man to a woman's eyes . . . yet dearest to me, I admit, is the fact that you bear a startling resemblance to Pytho's great god, Apollo!

This pleased him enormously, no woman ever having compared him to an Olympian god before.

— My dear, how about calling me Apollo as your secret name for me, if your heart so desires? I give my permission.

Her hand flew to her mouth, and her eyes widened with alarm.

— Ah, Ischys, the god forbids that I mix two worlds! It is that what is divine can have no human equivalent!

— It is you who quibbles, my dear. Let it be. I am content, after all, in being Ischys the Strong. It is a name difficult enough to support, I should say. The two smiled at each other, having reached some agreement, it seemed.

The music of the flutes now filled the air, lyrical with the expectation of the wedding rite, and the maidens, moving to surround their friend the bride, moved with rhythmic step in procession. Carried along as she was in the exuberant public approval of her marriage, Koronis remained solemn-eyed, her cheeks pale.

The Crow Informs Apollo

The great white crow, messenger of the god, his wings spread wide, hovered for some time over the temple of Apollo on Pytho's high plateau beneath the awesome cliffs of the Phaedriades. Descending, he perched on the corner of the temple beneath the roof, indifferent at the moment to the splendid pediments. Vigilantly the crow's eyes swept the scene below, prepared to wait, wings flapping to mark the time. The sun had not yet risen when a solitary figure, luminous and with a stride that reflected his unquestionable authority, appeared before the temple. The bird dipped his bill and called to him hoarsely. The god acknowledged his familiar messenger.

— Greetings, Crow. Something is urgent, it appears. You have been watching over Koronis, true? Is she well? Does the maiden bear happily the divine seed in the hiddenness of her sweet being? Hold it! Stop that nervous fluttering of your wings and speak.

Crow stopped the fluttering but instead walked back and forth on the narrow lip of the column's capitol before replying.

— News! Bad news!
— Koronis has fallen ill?
— Worse.
— Worse than illness? She lives, does she not? Tell me that she does, she who sheds such radiance within my heart.
— She's alive. Useful girl too.
— Useful? Useful to whom? Speak up, Crow.
— Useful to the kingdom. Useful to father-king. Lapiths say the kingdom comes first.

Apollo's countenance took on a look of profound regret, its gray corridor too long and tortuous to see the end of it. His question echoed in a vast loneliness.

— Tell me, what has Koronis done?

— Attracted Ischys the Strong. He'll defend the kingdom.

— But Phlegyas is not at war. Wait. The king is not thinking of marrying Koronis to the Strong One, is he?

— Phlegyas doesn't think, Phlegyas acts.

— Alas, what dire news! And yet I believe that Koronis will be faithful to our love. How is she? I must know.

— Helpless.

  With this admission, Crow let forth a hoarse cry that shook the nearby laurel trees like a rough wind before continuing to speak.

— A god ought to choose better.

— This is tardy counsel at best, Crow.

  Apollo had replied grimly, shaking his head. Crow's assessment went on.

— Good daughter. Loyal to father. Poor wife to Apollo.

— Enough, Crow, of your moral summaries! The question is, what will Koronis do in regard to Ischys?

— Marry him, of course. Good father, she thinks, for the baby. Probably true.

— Alas, your dreaded words, how they pierce my heart with anguish! How you manage to stand apart from the fount of the heart's very life, I cannot fathom. In a way, your attachment to hard fact douses this fainting god with cold water . . . Strange it is.

  Apollo dropped his head and fell silent. Crow remained gazing down upon him.

  The sun's rays broke over the dark shadow of the cliffs, and Apollo spoke.

— In choosing this mortal marriage, what does Koronis's heart say to her, I wonder?

— She thinks her life is what's at hand, up close. Apollo is always off somewhere . . . Smart girl.

— Am I not Far Shooter, lord of what is distant? Still, I tell you I am as close as the human breath and as alive and faithful, mind you, as the woman's own pulse! You are my faithful messenger, Crow. Would you betray my side of it?

  Crow's only answer was in a lively readjustment of his wings. Now he added a thought, however.

— Turn Ischys away and the king loses. What's good is the kingdom.

  The god of the oracle stared off into the far purple distance, and his voice held a palpable sadness when he spoke.

— Ah, we come to the bare bones of the conflict: the vision and paradise of the gods on the one hand and everyday life in the human world on the other!

Apollo sank down upon the ground, supporting his bowed head with his right hand as anguish filled his heart. Crow showed some sign of worry for the first time. The sounds of his speaking grew gentler now.

— Koronis thinks of the child. Child's mother needs husband. Not a handy husband is Apollo!

Taking this in, a small smile came to Apollo's face. He stood once again, his stature again lordly, as he turned to what now appeared as business at hand.

— When is the wedding to take place in far Thessaly?

— Wedding begins. Make no delay. Come!

Even as Apollo and crow turned toward the road leading eastward, two things took place. Crow's plumage was no longer snow-white but had turned black as night. A third companion had joined them, for Artemis, having picked up her bow and quiver, fell into step beside her brother. Thus the trio made their way to the wedding of Koronis to a mortal spouse.

Apollo Comes to Ischys' Bride

He was said not only to be of royal heritage but he was also very pleasing to the eyes of all the maidens, and his many feats had earned him the title of Ischys the Strong. Her heart missed two beats in a row when she mused on these facts. Certainly he had to be both exceptionally powerful and handsome to look upon if he were to stand up to her secret lover in the cave on Mt. Pelion. King Phlegyas's daughter sighed as she ran her hand down her side, pausing briefly at the waist where her eyes widened briefly. Yes, her normally slim body had a fullness it had never before known. Whatever was going to happen must surely happen soon. *Father has invited Ischys several times now to be a guest in our house, and the two of them do get along famously,* she thought as she reviewed recent events. And now the strolls of herself and the prince together in the olive grove had grown more leisurely and more frequent. It was a fact that brought a gleam to her eye, causing her to laugh gaily. She recalled the words now of the king, her father: "Ischys, as son of Elatos, comes from the oldest Thessalian lineage, my dear—that of Mt. Pelion. Impressive I'd say. You could do far worse. According to old tales, his lineage is mixed with that of the centaurs. What do you think of him, Koronis?" She had smiled and kissed her father on the cheek before turning about and running toward the house. His question went unanswered.

It was dusk as Koronis walked in the olive grove alone to escape the heat of the summer day. Although the warmth of earth still rose up to meet her, increasingly she felt an inner chill and an anxiousness, diffuse and unaccountable. Where the path divided, she took, as was not her custom, the left fork that became a steep descent into a ravine with large boulders and where night would soon obscure the contours of things. Momentarily she felt free and distanced from hard choices. And then, to her astonishment, a familiar voice called to her as from the end of a long corridor. Each syllable of her name was lyrical and shining and somehow undressed by the caller.

— Koronis! Koronis! Have you forgotten my voice so soon?

— Oh, I am here. You have come, Lord Apollo! Not in my remotest fantasy did I expect to come upon you when I took this path. Ah, naturally I could never forget your voice!

— It comforts me to hear you say this, yet my comfort is brief, I fear.

— Oh! Do you mean that you no longer love me? I thought that the love of a great god would be eternal, so I have counted on it.

— Alas, if you complain of Apollo's love, it is without cause. Unless distorted, love is hardly the possession of one person, Koronis. No, we must honor Aphrodite's knowledge of things. Love involves two persons, two persons, two sides. The golden bond is a mystery. It is unfathomable.

Both figures were claimed by silence now in the dim and narrow passage between high boulders. Speaking at last, Apollo's voice was solemn and bruised with loneliness.

— My dear Koronis, I fear that you are on the threshold of a great error, one that can only betray our love!

Apollo appeared fully before Koronis now, filling the path as though he had been coming up from the dark ravine while two great boulders on either side enclosed them narrowly on the shadowed path. Only the god was radiant as he gazed fully into the face of the maiden, a face gone pale.

— Oh no, Lord Apollo, you must be mistaken, for my father, the king of the Lapiths, said only this very day that he thought my life was coming along nicely—it is that he is well pleased.

The maidenly eagerness had suddenly drained out of her, stopping her account abruptly. Apollo finished for her, speaking slowly, his tone somber.

— He spoke of Ischys the Strong, I take it, who has succeeded in winning your favor and the favor of your father's kingdom, no less.

The voice of the god was taut and chilly in tone.

— How did you find out? I have scarcely even admitted it to myself. Father does want me to make a fitting marriage, you see, it's only natural.

— His argument would be that the kingdom depends on it, I expect.

Apollo's voice in reply sounded weary. She sought to explain.

— Yes. Always he thinks of the kingdom, being the king. Dear Apollo, I am close to my father. You must realize this.

He continued to regard her steadily, a sadness in his eyes.

— Tell me, Koronis, what is to become of our love? Will you abandon
   it?

   The god's question hung upon the air, heavy as the omphalos in
his temple. The word *abandon* clearly shocked her. He continued.

— A very grave concern assaults me like a deadly arrow: what is to become
   of the child of our love?

   His voice, although tender, held an unquestionable authority,
its source obscure in the deep and unpenetrated rooms of the soul.
Unconsciously, her hand went protectively to the unborn child. She would
hear the lover's voice, her ears receiving the strange text, no matter. He
spoke again.

— Let me be clear. I will never forfeit my son to convenient policies of a
   king or to affairs of state. At all cost I shall shield the child!

   She was outraged that his mind envisioned the workings of her
father's kingdom as a betrayal. Surely, loving her, he would know that there
was no question of her devotion to their child. With warm emotion, she
protested.

— How can you think that I shall not give a mother's love and faithful
   tending to our child, for I shall indeed!

— How do you propose to do this when the fact is that you award the
   interests of the external world namely, this Thessalian kingdom and
   its royal family, first place in your consideration?

   Koronis sat down on a nearby stone and bowed her head, overcome
by the terrible pulls within herself. There was the love of the god and their
child to be born. There was the welfare of the kingdom and her father's will,
and then there was admittedly the pull of her strong attraction to Ischys.
Still, she was not defeated as she appealed to Apollo.

— Far Shooter, as you are lovingly called at your sanctuary on Parnassus,
   would you bring me down with your infallible arrows like some passing
   prey on the mountain?

   The god was struck by the horror of her words, uttered quietly
in great affliction, and he began to pace back and forth within the narrow
space. Anguish filled Apollo as he faced the burden of her spirit. When he
spoke, it was as if he spoke with himself.

— I have long been found to be god of mercy, forgiving homicides who
   seek me out from afar, coming to my altar at Delphi where their refuge
   is certain. Heracles and Orestes were not the least of these unhappy
   fellows.

   Glimpsing hope, she cried out in anguish,

— Oh, do return to your merciful frame of mind, Apollo—for my sake!

— There is something involved that you must understand, Koronis. Indeed, it takes precedence over all other considerations. It is this: to bring to earth the vision and force that *heals* is my present undertaking. To fail this is to forsake the human world in its need. I cannot forsake this even though choosing the mercy that is most true may be at great cost.

Healing . . . it was an idea that seemed to Koronis to be released upon the air for the first time, so newborn it felt . . . a balm soothing to body and soul alike. Gazing at the god now, she smiled slowly, and a serenity came over her. She could have been voicing a lover's vows when she spoke. Apollo bent his head toward her in anticipation, although he was vulnerable.

— O Paean Apollo, you yourself are the great god of healing! Did I not learn this at my mother's knee? She taught me the very ancient refrain that people intone in your sanctuary:

> May Paean never leave us!

— Surely this child to be born—and he will be human as well as godly—will neither equal nor surpass you!

Within the sweeping embrace now of Apollo, textured in love's sweet blossoming and its lingering fragrance, Koronis lost track of time. At last Apollo spoke.

— Our son shall be called Asklepios. The healing legacy that has been mine shall be fully shared with our son, you see. While I shall remain the healer among the gods, the skill and compassion of Asklepios will flow toward human folk. This will happen only when our son walks the earth, provided he is uncompromised. None of this can come to pass, I warn you, unless the child you carry in your womb is fully sheltered from the external world and its many expedient programs.

Troubled Koronis cried out,

— Alas, what is *healing*?

— What indeed? A stream of light, golden as from a steadily burning fire, penetrates the sightless dark of affliction and helplessness. Ah, it moves through the night soundlessly in gentle purpose while one sleeps, rather like a great serpent from Hades' realm. This is healing, which by the hand of the god restores well-being! Still, its mystery is impenetrable.

For a long moment, she envisioned a torch runner shielding the flame he bore from the fire of Apollo's altar to light the fire on an unknown altar. She shook her head from side to side to clear her fantasy. Alas, Apollo, true lover and companion, was about to depart. He spoke in regret.

— The time has come for me to leave you. Alas, I go in sadness, Koronis, knowing your pledge to Ischys.

A heavy silence claimed the two figures. It was broken in time by the voice of the god.

— *O Zeus, is it the Fates who lead the way entirely? Hear me, Father. Am I not your son who must guard the illuminated gateway of human choice however narrow?*

In the moonlight, the two figures were solemn, and Koronis nodded as she took in what the god said. His gaze was not without tenderness as it held her in a reflection that seemed to engage the sight of an eagle flying above Parnassus.

— One thing I leave for you to ever remember, Koronis. It is this: *the healer's birth, having moved safely through the gates of death, shall become golden and lyrical like the song that rises from Apollo's lyre!*

Looking up, she saw that Apollo had departed.

The Death of Koronis

The crow, durable and shining messenger that he was in his nocturnal plumage, guided Apollo and Artemis to the far kingdom of the Lapiths. Arriving at the house of King Phlegyas, the crow took his leave, and the two gods were received into the royal house made festive for the wedding. Making their way among the assembled guests, they found the chamber where Koronis, dressed in beautiful bridal attire, waited with her maidens. Artemis remained outside the chamber. Without hesitation, Apollo entered, with the result that the girls retired with excited giggles, mistaking this radiant one for the bridegroom himself. The two were alone. Koronis raised her face to the god's in astonishment, a look that rapidly was supplanted by joy.

— Oh, can it be you, dear Apollo, come at long last?
— How could I not come? Are you not my bride?

Remembering the source of her happiness brought a smile to her face tinged with bliss. Apollo studied the daughter of King Phlegyas, and something cut him to the quick. The question could not wait.

— I have come for your final decision. Do you remain pledged to mortal man?

Before him, she visibly paled, and her reply was scarcely audible.

— It is true. Oh, it is for the child that is yours!

Her voice became a wail. Wrath arose in the god.

— You would betray me!
— No! The child needs a father, and he must have a place in the world, besides.
— I shall see to our child. Could you doubt that I would? What I cannot do is to entrust him to a mortal father.

His words pierced the air, wounding her, and she answered as one heavy with shock.

— Not even to Ischys the Strong? He is held in high regard by all the people. Apollo, have you forgotten that I also am mortal?

He shook his head slowly.

— I chose to enter the human realm, and of all women, I chose you, Koronis, as my beloved. Did you not give me your heart? How can it be that now you would trade me for a human lover and spouse?

Filled with anguish, the god was incredulous. He raised his voice in order to be heard above the singing of the marriage hymn that had begun beyond the chamber.

— O fellow Olympians, hear me! A child of Apollo belongs to the gods. Save my son!

Motionless and claimed by a silence that seemed vast and beyond probing, Koronis continued to gaze on her true lover. She was unaware of the approach of a third figure until that one stood facing her, causing her to draw in her breath sharply.

— Who are you who comes now between Lord Apollo and myself?

— I am Artemis. Have you forgotten me?

— No, my lady, how could I forget you? I am honored that you attend my wedding . . .

Apollo stepped back to give precedence to his sister, the virgin goddess Artemis, who answered Koronis.

— That is not my purpose. The true bride, the maiden in whom I delight and whom I guard, has gone missing. It is her loss that summons me.

— Ah, but I did not summon you, Lady.

Koronis shook her head, perplexed.

— You are mistaken. There is the hidden one who abides near the living pulse and who undergoes every thought and happening of your existence. She holds the account unedited by the eyes of father and the kingdom, understand. It is this hidden maiden who has summoned me.

— Truly you are known to guard the maiden. Still, who is this maiden?

Dare she ask the Olympian goddess such a question? Artemis lifted her eyes to some far scene removed from the kingdom of Phlegyas and replied.

— She is the one who is ever beside the spring of earth's living waters, for which no substitute exists. This maiden cradles the dance which brings a balm to the work-weary and to goal-ridden humankind, a timeless dance, nor is it of her own making. Within it time is born again and extends its tireless arms like the swaying branches of the laurel tree. Ah, and covered like a babe in the center of the circle dance, contentment is found. Without the hidden maiden, Koronis, life goes dry, brittle, and repetitive. Voices become strident, filled with meaningless insistence, as they spill into the ordinary life of woman.

A puzzlement of another order shrouded the figure of Koronis as she listened to Artemis. Now she drew herself up to her full stature, that of the daughter of the king, as the reality at hand made a powerful claim upon her.

— Lady Artemis, I am grateful for your coming, but I no longer have need of your guarding of the maiden, you see. I am now pledged to marry Ischys the Strong. It is he who will look after my welfare from this day forward.

— No. No, he cannot.

— Alas! What is this that you say?

— Ischys cannot espouse you. You are the bride of Apollo!

— Oh, no! Even now the music of my wedding is under way. Today is the gateway of my whole life to come! A marriage has to be visible or it's not real!

With these last words, her hand flew to her mouth, covering it in horror of what she dared declare. Artemis shook her head slowly, and a look of compassion crossed her face.

— It is I, Artemis, who has the knowledge of the maiden's true gateways, which are largely invisible. The true gateway before which you wait is your espousal to Apollo. This gateway is presently in grave jeopardy, I must tell you.

A look of compassion came over the goddess now before she murmured the words,

— Oh how vulnerable is one who has once passed through this gate!

— That means that I am extremely vulnerable?

— Yes. You are exposed.

— Exposed to what, my lady?

— To the inexorable movement of the path between heaven and earth!

— Alas, fear strikes my heart! Even at this moment, I am summoned to the wedding procession. The bride is called!

Artemis's final words, oddly, were spoken with gentleness now.

— Know this: fear is short-lived while the relationship to Apollo endures, maiden! With my brother Apollo lies the golden life, Koronis. Farewell!

Artemis departed as Apollo stepped forward and took her hands, gazing into her face. Koronis implored him in great distress,

— O Apollo, you alone are my beloved! Save me from this loveless union!

— Are you prepared to leave the house of your father and to come with me, leaving Ischys and the kingdom?

— Oh yes, I am! Lady Artemis has convinced me that divine joy lies outside the kingdom I have known.

— Be quick then. Let us leave by the back gate.

— Where will you take me?

— To Pelion's green realm beyond human spectators. There Chiron's deep chamber can provide a place for our child to be born. Our son shall be the great healer. Chiron himself will nurse the lad.

    Together the two set out for the back gate, but it was necessary to cross the path of the wedding procession, even so. Meeting the procession, they found themselves facing Phlegyas and Ischys, whose faces registered anger and amazement. Koronis murmured to Apollo.

— Oh no! My father and Ischys bar the way! I cannot leave after all!

    Apollo spoke to her with measured words, and his love was great.

— Koronis, trust me. Will you trust the way that is ours, dear one?

— With all my heart, I trust you.

    At that moment, suspended as it seemed in time, Artemis appeared facing her from where she stood at the side of the path, and now she lifted her bow, its arrow poised.

    Nodding somberly, Artemis released the arrow upon the air. Unerring in its path, the arrow pierced the chest of Koronis, and she collapsed upon the earth. At once it was Apollo who knelt tenderly over her. She spoke as she was dying.

— What sorrow descends on the house of my childhood and maidenhood! In loving me, do you also know the abyss of this grief? I believe you do. How I love you, eternal lover, spouse, and slayer! Though you slay me, yet I trust you. My blood is no longer faithful, for it makes a river to nourish the rose garden. Dear Father, farewell! You could not know, neither then nor now. Ischys, farewell, my friend! O child unborn, motherless you shall be and unsuckled by my breasts, yet my love for you is undying!

    Apollo bent close to her ear as he spoke.

— Dearest Koronis, hear me these few last words. Our child, Asklepios, will presently be born from the fire of our love that was known in Chiron's deep cave, but he is begotten from another fire as well, that consuming fire of soul that separates you from life in the familiar kingdom even now. O Koronis, your pain soon passes, and you shall know our marriage in its true delight!

A smile was on her face as she took her last breath. Sorrowfully, the king saw to the bringing forth of a pyre on which her body was now tenderly laid. A flame set the wood afire as the people moved solemnly now in funeral procession. Apollo and Artemis were beside the burning pyre. When the flames began to rise, Apollo moved quickly. He thrust his hands through the flames in order to deliver the child safely to earth. The babe Asklepios uttered his first cry. At the same moment, the cock crowed, piercing the air. Apollo listened intently. Briefly he nodded as if to Zeus and the inscrutable ways of things as he cried aloud,

— *O beginning! O dawn! O cock that knows, all hail!*

PART VI

Demeter and Kore

Demeter and Kore—an Introduction

Since she is mother, Demeter might seem to have no need of introduction as she makes her way through the lengthy modern vestibule of ho-hum. Especially is this the case in the house of psychology where mother has been extensively analyzed and catalogued, with postmortems performed as well. In spite of this fact, this mother of the grain and goddess of the mysteries of Eleusis asks for a fresh look on the part of her observer. Like the context of the gods themselves, this look must partake of the *first time*—that is, of the realm of being that is bountiful and uncontaminated by culture or opinion since it is virginal. Surely this realm, touched as it appears to be by envisioning and yearning, may constitute our slender access to Olympus.

Among the Greek gods, no force of well-being was greater than Demeter. In the seventh century BC *Homeric Hymn to Demeter*, the goddess undergoes a period of grief and loss, and the earth in response falls into famine. Mistress of the natural ground of things, whether it be physical earth that grows the grain or the human psyche, Demeter sustains the process between sowing of the seed and taking of the harvest of the grain. Without her, the loaf that is existence fails. Indeed, she was fondly hailed as Big Loaf.

When the ancient Greek envisioned Demeter, always there came before him a dual presence: the eternal maiden and the ripened queenly woman, as though they were inseparable. Ancient Greek sculptures delineate this dual presence of the feminine in its quiet mystery. The goddess's relationships in love, strangely enough, are catalogued more extensively than those of Aphrodite herself. Demeter's unquestionable bounty is manifested in the phases of the feminine, which she presents—nurturing mother, enduring maiden, solitary wanderer, child nurse, and goddess of the greater mysteries of Eleusis.

The desire for renewal led to the mystery rites at Eleusis, which took place annually in the fall and attracted initiates from far and wide. The marriage of earth with the underworld, becoming for all times the supreme image of human transformation, became the focus of Demeter's rites. Earth knowledge underlay the rites, that is, an affirming of the reality of ordinary life. Such an acknowledgment presented the authentic ground for the transforming movement to take place.

The central focus of the underlying myth of the mystery rites is the loss of the maiden Kore, or Persephone, Demeter's daughter, who is swept away to the underworld by Lord Hades, marking a crucial change in existence itself. Through this unplanned, reluctantly embraced encounter with the hidden realm, the Greek psyche perceived the hope of life's renewal. As for Kore, the eternal maiden, her image evokes a sense of the fresh, unspent treasure of life. Residing in the human psyche, she belongs to the essential beginnings. Arising out of the profound Demeter depths, she comes forth as the bride of life in a union that regularly strides through two realms, earth and underworld. Even so, the latter realm remains undisclosed, hidden we say. Her journey is portrayed as a demanding one, of the kind the human individual is unprepared to engage without the grace bestowed by the initiating rites of Eleusis.

Surely the ineffable gift of Demeter lies in a profound hopefulness both in ordinary existence and in the afterlife. The initiate at Eleusis came to partake of the luminous continuity between the two realms. In this way, he embraced a mystery that is unbroken. Rare in Greek literature was the gift of happiness attributed to a particular god, yet it was reported to be the gift of the rite at Eleusis. "Blessed is one who has beheld the Mysteries," the poet Pindar wrote in the fifth century BC, "for that one knows the end of life and its beginning as given by Zeus."

Kore Meets Hekate

Her shining hair of the hue of unharvested wheat fell freely upon her shoulders while her garment stirred softly. Having climbed the path up from the sea, Kore, daughter of Demeter, turned to wave to her friends the sea nymphs as they returned to their sea abode. Gazing upon the familiar scene in its serenity, she mused on the sheer delight that the circle dance with the nymphs brought her once again.

— Always our dance brings me such joy, and yet is it not a puzzle? The dance claims me, and I become one with the maidens, but then the circle dissolves. Ah, what becomes of the circle itself? Here penetrating the rock face is the ancient cave. I believe I'll step inside where all is dim and cool and rest a bit.

Once inside, she sat upon the natural bench of stone that extended from the cave's wall, allowing her eyes to grow accustomed to the dimness. A movement from the depth of the cavern startled her, and a woman stood before her wearing a white peplos softly belted. Kore noticed that the woman's face was luminous, as if the moon shone upon it. She gasped in astonishment at the same time that the stately figure addressed her.

— Greetings, daughter of Demeter. So you have come.
— It is a winding, rough path from the seashore, and I thought I'd stop at the cave for a rest.

As she gazed at the extraordinary woman, old memory stirred her mind.

— Ah, could you be Goddess Hekate herself?
— I am. From the cave's entrance, I observed you dancing with the sea nymphs below. How indescribable is the ancient circle dance of the maidens!

Her voice grew wistful, trailing off like the aftermath of a wave on the shore. She added a strange observation.

— Indeed, the keeping place of this dance is everlasting.

    Kore was perplexed.

— Its keeping place? Well, I'm glad that you know about our dance.

    Hekate continued.

— As the feet begin the steps, moving in rhythm, each maiden appears to be attuned to a sovereign yet inaudible music, which lifts the vessel of dance much as the sea takes a ship upon its back. In any case, the dance flows among you like a shining stream. Ah so, I see how it must be. This stream is ever full, fresh, and unshaped as it immerses you into life at its source!

    Kore spoke eagerly now.

— Aside from the bond with my mother, the dance is the strongest and loveliest bond that I know. Why, I couldn't bear it if I were left out of the maidens' dance.

    Hekate nodded, sharing Kore's wonder, and grew pensive. After a long pause, she began to speak quietly.

— Ah, the dance of the circle holds within it the strong thread of being itself, that is, before it is parceled out. Nevertheless . . .

    She turned her face to gaze into the depth of the cave, and all was silent for such a long time that Kore believed that the awesome goddess would say no more. Yet she turned her gaze now full upon Kore.

— When a certain time is ripe, you shall be seized out of that circle, Kore!

    Taking in these astonishing words, Kore grew pale, and fear made her voice hoarse.

— Oh no, Lady. You must be mistaken. No one shall tear me away from the circle of the maidens, for then I should no longer be myself!

    Hekate began to pace back and forth on the stone floor of the cave before she could respond.

— The core of the maiden is known to me. Do I not move within Artemis, embodied in the maiden self? I know her well—her hiddenness and her woodland ecstasy beside the murmuring stream in the green shade. When Artemis, the eternal maiden, looks at life, her look penetrates into one's own simple, forgotten places. Tell me, Kore. What is dearest to your maiden heart?

— Why, it is a question I never thought about. What I realize at once, however, is that it is glorious *not to be up-front!* Whether at home or in the world, it doesn't matter so long as I'm not up-front. Besides, as maiden, I am ever at leisure and without weighty obligations, except, of course, for respect toward my elders. I say that dearest to my heart is *being tucked behind.*

Goddess Hekate pondered what Kore confessed to her.

— Tucked behind, you say. True, there is something freeing and exhilarating in that. I believe that a bride also desires this thing that you speak of. Ah, there is more room for a person in the spacious behind—room to play, to dream, to hide.

— Lady Hekate, will you grant that I remain as I am forever—the maiden?

The question clearly startled the goddess. When she replied, her voice was poignant, whether with regret or reassurance, Kore could not tell.

— I perceive that the maiden is your essence and never to be cast aside like an outworn garment. Still, you are Demeter's daughter. More powerful than a maiden's demand upon life is destiny. As for destiny, not only is it conceived by the Fates but it lies in the hand of Earth Goddess. Do not be alarmed, Kore, if the future embraces a mystery. This is my counsel. You see, *you must be sown in the great furrow!* After all, are you not Demeter's precious seed? A lesser destiny were unworthy of you. *O eternal woman, are you not a cycle of deep change?*

— Such words frighten me, Lady Hekate. Tell me truly, shall I lose myself?

— You shall not lose yourself, Kore. Be assured of this, and may it always comfort you to know that I am your invisible companion of the way and shall never be far from you!

Kore bowed in deep honor to Hekate, whose face remained grave in its tenderness, and she went out into the sunlight of Eleusis.

Kore and Lord Hades

Standing on the plain of Eleusis and gazing toward the tranquil blue bay were Demeter and her daughter, whose hair resembled the golden grain that filled the adjoining field. The older of the two goddesses spoke.

— Kore, my daughter, go now and play with your friends as I can see you are longing to do. As usual, I expect that you will find the sea nymphs already on the sea meadow. Wait. I do have a word of warning, knowing how you always are enchanted with the meadow flowers. Should you come upon an unknown flower, do be wary. Indeed, best keep your distance.

Kore laughed at her mother's concern.

— Mother, if the only peril I must look out for is a flower, how safe earth must be for exploring! Well, I am off. Until the return, good-bye!

She hugged Demeter, smiling her confidence before turning and running toward the low meadow. Demeter watched her go, her face in serious reflection for some time. What was it in Kore's promise of "the return" that carried a foreboding, something tinged with gloom for Demeter? She watched as the maiden ran lightly toward the shore where the Nereids awaited her, the sea meadow colorful with wild flowers. How like a young doe she appeared in her mother's eyes, unerringly bent on finding the watering place. Offshore, the island of Salamis lay like a purple tortoise within the azure ring of sea. With a sigh, the goddess turned and made her way to her house on the rise of the small hill. Meanwhile, Kore, reaching the cluster of her friends, the Nereids, greeted them warmly.

— Have you been waiting for me?

They shook their heads in incredulity, smiling.

— Of course. We were just saying, "Will she ever come? Kore is ever ignoring the time of day." Come, let's make our circle!

The invitation brought the laughter of sudden abandon as the maidens made a circle, hands on neighboring shoulders, moving with lively, rhythmic steps, and began the dance. At once the dance claimed them as they described a luminous circle. Now they moved with increased animation, graceful bodies swaying, minds attuned to the imagined music. It hardly mattered whose arm one took, for all identity seemed to dissolve within the dance. It only mattered that the circle was all of a piece, composing the unbroken thread of the everlasting maiden. Marking time skillfully with bare feet, each maiden belonged, for should she lose the bond of the circle, it would be a grave misfortune.

Unseen by the dancing nymphs and Kore, a lone witness watched. His astonished regard took in the enraptured faces, the bodies swaying in their soft, gossamer garments, and abundant hair flowing on lovely shoulders like the water of a shimmering brook. The maidens' laughter and artless cries seized him like a butterfly caught in their net.

He spoke with himself.

— Who would have thought that I should find such a cache of maidens on the sea meadow? Will they dance on forever? The circle makes a fellow dizzy.

Soon they ought to tire of going around, around, and around. Just to watch those delicate feet beating the ground, summoning earth to life once again, I am enchanted! Ah, wait.

One maiden stands out above all the others. She must be Kore, daughter of awesome Demeter. My eyes follow her every moment. What looks of sheer delight her face holds. Ah, desire rises in me and burns like a steady fire. Am I not too long solitary, if the truth is to be known? O to have Kore beside me!

This circle of the maidens is like nothing I have ever known. It closes upon itself like a flower whose petals embrace an unseen magical center. Such ecstasy and strength it possesses. Yet the fact is that so much is going to waste because it is inaccessible. This circle stops creation! One thing is clear: no man penetrates this circle, yet it seduces my male heart. Am I powerless before it? O how I long for the golden joy and sweet delight of Kore, but the dance claims her. Always it is repeating itself. *O Zeus, my brother, where is the change that belongs to the gods, I ask you?*

Again and again the feet of the maidens inscribed the primordial circle upon earth in the ancient dance that is their legacy, the dance that is immune to duty, haste, or ambition. Impenetrable as it appeared to the witnessing god's mind, the circle of the maidens was powerful in its beckoning. Suddenly Kore cried out in excitement, and the dance halted. Bending low over the ground, she spoke.

— Look, friends. What is this at the center of our circle? It looks like a pure white eye!

All the nymphs fell to their knees upon the ground in order to examine the object in question, which turned out to be a dazzling white blossom whose beauty was strangely enticing. They agreed that it was surely a newcomer. Definitely they agreed that the flower had been closed when they made their circle in the cool of the morning, and only after they grew warm with the dance had it opened unobtrusively. Turning their attention full upon Demeter's daughter, the sea nymphs urged her.

— Pick it, Kore! Don't delay, seeing what a splendid gift Earth Goddess has brought us.

It's yours. Pick it for your very own!

With her left hand, Kore had encircled the flower gently, gazing into its face with astonishment as the urgent words hung on the air. At last she breathed a small sigh and spoke in a subdued voice, her eyes never leaving the face of the flower.

— No, it is better if one of you were to take this new blossom, considering that the sea does not give you flowers the way our meadow provides me with flowers.

— But for this very reason, the fact that we are sea dwellers, the new flower of earth is not ours for the taking. Demeter is mistress of the bounty of earth, so, daughter of Demeter, you must pluck the flower. Surely you see this.

Kneeling apart from the other maidens, Kore seemed cloaked in the mist that precedes life-altering action. She mused as she continued to gaze at the white narcissus.

— What a long slender throat, little flower . . . it seems a dim labyrinth plunging downward. How it draws me . . . ah, what was it my mother said to me—something about being wary of the unknown flower? I laughed, of course. The nymphs say you are mine for the taking, flower . . . Now, where have they all gone, leaving me alone? . . . . Mother Demeter calls me her flower. I recall her words:

You, Kore, are the virginity of all things on earth—the beauty, freshness, and immediacy of what is in full supply and, above all, unspent. Such riches of the maiden are inexhaustible. Is it any wonder that I call you the flower of my house? You are like the green shoot earth leads forth to ripen into golden grain. Yet always you remain, *Kore mine, the unharvested one!*

Now earth sends a new flower. Perhaps it will replace me, I wonder . . . Listen! A low voice is speaking in this now solitary place. Nor is it a nymph voice, for it is deep and lordly. Yet I see no one at all.

Although she saw no one, a palpable presence attended the deep voice that began speaking.

— Like an upturned purse, the new flower shakes out every dazzling coin, maiden. Then the flower sheds its bloom and is no more. Listen well, daughter of Demeter.

Some fire of protest rose in Kore.

— What a grim way to look on a thing of beauty! The flower that is from the gods cannot be diminished, surely.

— Oh, but that is wishful fantasy, Kore. Look at the ordinary life of the human individual. Is it not an account of the diminishing of the gods?

She was startled and leaped to her feet to face her invisible companion.

— What are you saying? Must the everlasting bloom wilt and fall as the ordinary earth flower does? What an alarming thought!

She heard her companion make a sharp intake of his breath.

— Actually, this is not the time of questions and of elaborate and consoling telling.

— What is this time that's at hand, invisible one?

Even as she asked, a thread of dread entered her maiden enthusiasm. The voice was hesitant, she thought.

— It is the time of approaching the new, undeclared flower, I'd say.

His words repeated in her mind several times and unaccountably cheered her;

Now she once more bent down beside the white blossom and drank deeply of its fragrance, sighing audibly. There was a smile in the voice, and the companion spoke idly as though time had become strangely bountiful.

— In you, Kore, I see every woman who has lived, for every woman has a maiden heart, you know.

— I didn't know.

— Often I've watched you skipping forth in the meadow to join the nymphs. How my heart would swell within me with desire. The passion for the Kore is sweet in body and soul! Dear, dear Persephone!

The last was murmured with an immense sigh of pleasure as a soft, sensuous wind lifted Kore's garments and blew about her.

— I never saw anyone watching me, no one at all. Who are you? Your deep voice calls forth some full, pleasant stream within me, hitherto unknown. What's your name?

— Do names answer? Do they ever really tell? I think not. Yes, I perceived ageless woman in you, in face and soul alike, picking flowers. The maidens are ever picking flowers, skimming the splendor and radiance of the hour into a basket, forgetful the next hour of what came to their hands. The fragrant air trails you. It records your every passing word and look. Dark paths must be unknown to you, for you are ever ecstatic with what's at hand. Ah, but something has happened, Kore. My nature, long regarded as dark, you have illuminated with a bright flame!

She shook her head numbly in response. None of her simple questions had been answered. She explored cautiously.

— You are a man, this I know.

This brought an appreciative chuckle from the companion. She went on.

— Dwelling in the sacred house of Demeter, I've known neither voice nor touch of a man, you see. I spend my days with the nymphs . . . Ah, I wonder why they have all deserted me?

— Lucky for me to find you alone at last.

There was a boldness in his honesty that at the same time frightened her and pleased her enormously. Shyly she made the invitation.

— Perhaps you would like to draw close to have a look at the unknown flower?

Surely this stranger meant no harm. The invitation may have startled him, for he did not reply at once.

— The fact is that I'm speechless before the true flower that draws me to earth, leaving the dark realm. Until this moment in time, Kore, my days have all been night!

Such a strange and incredible account of himself it was, but it caused in her a strong current of sympathy.

— The sea nymphs will soon return, I think, and if, sir, you would like to linger, you may join us at play in the sunlight.

Once again she bent down and cupped the flower gently in her hand.

— You desire earth's new, undeclared flower greatly. Why, I feel the very
current of your passion. What will you do, Kore?

She seemed to be claimed by a dream as she dropped her face to
the flower, peering down into the enchanting corridor beyond the small
cup of bloom. As she did so, the dazzling face of the flower darkened.
Decisively now, she plucked the blossom and raised it at once to her lips.
In that moment, the ground beneath her shook mightily. At once, a chasm
opened before her. Frightened, she looked up quickly for the engaging
presence. As she held the plucked flower to her bosom, the companion
became visible. He was tall, sleek of form and of dark visage while his eyes
of night shone with passion. In spite of his unquestionable comeliness,
he bore a solemn intensity. Kore's eyes fell now to his hands in which he
held the reins restraining a pair of handsome black steeds that pawed the
ground impatiently. Amazed, she gazed at the golden chariot. Now, laying
down the reins, her companion stepped swiftly down from the chariot and
extended his arms toward her. Faint with disbelief, she drew back. His voice
was quiet.

— Come, my beloved, come away with me! I am Lord Hades. I am
hailed also as Pluto, god of riches, for in me you have no poverty, no
diminishment, my dear. Besides, already I have the blessing of Zeus,
your father.

Words forsook her as her eyes, wide with disbelief, shifted their gaze
from Lord Hades to the yawning chasm on whose thin edge they stood. A
great cry arose in her throat now.

— No! Never can I go with you, lord of the underworld!

Whirling about, she found the path to the lower meadow and fled
like a fleet doe, for the way home to Demeter was blocked by the chasm. Her
bare feet were bruised by the stones, and the rough grasses scratched her.
Ever thundering in her ears was the ground-thumping of horses' hooves in
pursuit. O where was Mother Demeter in this desperate moment? Where was
Father Zeus with his arm of wise protection? Gasping with weariness, she
slowed her pace, and a growing dread weakened her. Alas, the great chariot
drew up alongside. In one swift movement, she felt herself lifted into the
air by a strong arm that drew her inside the chariot. Now she found herself
gazing into the face of the charioteer, his tender gaze dissolving his wrath
at her defection. The chariot whirled about and began a descent so steep
as to cause her to close her eyes and throw her arms about her abductor's
neck, clinging to the steady charioteer for her very life. Behind them trailed

Kore's cries: "O Demeter, Mother! O Zeus, Father! Save me!" Her fear unabated, she rode beside Lord Hades into the dim and ghostly corridors of the Lower Realm. Bending his head tenderly toward her, Hades spoke.

— Persephone, for this is your name here below, it is only a little while longer. I know that it is a fearsome journey, for so was it made from time beyond memory. Look, dear one, you need not fear me, for I have only tender love for you, earth's flower! Besides, it is important that you know that it is my chariot that keeps you safe on this awesome journey. Only stay with the chariot, I warn you. One dare not go alone and unguided here.

Kore refused to be comforted, and instead sought words to express her woe.

— Oh, I want to go home, home to Demeter, my mother!

An anxious look of concern was on Hades' face as he sought to comfort her.

— Stay with me here in my abode, my love, and I promise that all shall be well. Believe me, Kore. Ah, there is a hard truth as well I must speak of. You see, *the way down is not the way back!* That way is blocked for you.

— There exists no way back to my fair earth dwelling? Shall I never return to the circle of the happy maidens? O dark lord, is there for me no return?

Kore's questions, spoken in growing despair, penetrated the misty darkness until Hades' voice, deep and echoing, answered.

— There is no return!

Grief in the presence of failed hope overwhelmed Kore now, and she wept. At once, Hades brought the horses to a halt. Turning, he took his beloved into his arms and comforted her. At last he kissed her with lingering delight, and gazing at her, he watched a slow smile emerge upon her face and a light return to her eyes, erasing the evidence of fear at last.

Demeter Meets Hekate

The Meeting of Two Great Goddesses

Summer had passed, and the days were expectant with harvest when Demeter gazed out over the Thriasian Plain. Her face was anxious as the sun sank into the western sea off Salamis. It was late in the day, and yet her daughter Kore had not returned. As was her custom, Kore had gone to the seashore to take her leisure with her friends, the sea nymphs. But she had failed to return. Suddenly a distant cry pierced the air, soon to be followed by a fainter cry, whether of fear or great surprise, she could not tell. Then the distant words were upon the air: "O save me. O Demeter!" There could be no doubt it was the cry of Kore herself. At once Demeter tore the veil from her head. She replaced her light, delicate garments with sturdy, coarse ones of a darkish hue. Meanwhile, darkness descended over the plain with its fields of grain so that she lit her torch and set out in a swift stride in the direction from which the cry had come. Such was the beginning of the long and anguishing search for beloved Kore. When the fields lay behind her, she sought out the villages to make inquiry about a lost maiden, seeking some clue to her strange disappearance. For nine days and nights, Demeter wandered, and her grief was greater than any passion she had known. Not once in her wandering search did she partake of food or drink, nor did she gain any knowledge of the fate of her daughter.

On the tenth day as she took the footpath in the early morning light, a solitary woman approached, her lovely brow bound with a luminous headband. The woman spoke.

— Greetings, Demeter! My, how pale and gaunt you look. Almost I do not recognize you. What, my friend, has happened to your radiant self?

There was relief in Demeter's face to meet a friend at last.

— Can it be you, Hekate? How fortunate to meet at this moment. Yes, you observe well. There is no trace of beauty or radiance left in me since this terrible thing happened. Kore is not to be found anywhere. Her desperate cry on the meadow reached me, or did I imagine it? Oh, without Kore, the whole world is stripped of delight!

— Alas, that loss is unspeakable . . . I too heard the piercing cry trailing the rush of horses' hooves and chariot wheels. Ah, what is hearing if not recognition and a receiving? Yes, I took in the cry of Kore and tended it until you should come.

Sinking down upon the ground, Demeter wept, and Hekate sought to comfort her.

— I know the dark pathways, my friend, even those of grief and loss, of fear and dread. It's your loss that has summoned me, you see. Do I not abide in the deep recesses and in the hidden caverns rarely explored? The cave of earth's sorrow has summoned me.

Still Demeter's grief overwhelmed her. In time, Hekate stirred, her face brightening momentarily as she spoke.

— Demeter, remember that you are the one with profound knowledge of the threshing floor.

— Why do you speak of this?

— I thought how like a maiden is the fate of the vulnerable seed upon the threshing floor.

Demeter looked as if all hope had departed.

— Are you suggesting that Kore has been taken and threshed like the grain?

— Oh, you must not lose hope for her as the dark cave of earth's sorrow claims you.

— As you speak, Hekate, I am grateful to you. I realize that you know about the grave darkness. In fact, you usually go about only in the night or else in the underworld below. As for me, I am occupied with the fields spread candidly to sun and sky. What can I know of caves?

— This one you have just entered.

Demeter's distress only deepened.

— Alas!

Her goddess companion hastened to reassure her as best she could.

— There are things that do best hidden from the light of day. This I am certain of. The cave can be a fortunate and generous place for hiding what must be sheltered from the day's relentless exposure.

Demeter shook her head slowly.

— But what I give to life grows best in the light of day. Surely you must have observed this in Eleusis' rich fields of grain.

Hekate nodded solemnly.

— At the same time, some things will surely die if held in intense light and subject to wide observation.

— Strange words you speak. I had not considered this.

Hekate's face held tender concern for Demeter as she leaned toward her and responded.

— There are things dear to both of us that thrive only in the night. Seen with eyes of the ordinary day, these things are as nothing. But in the hidden place, this is not the case, for they find their true embodiment. There they are firm-fleshed, and their fresh speech that comes forth goes to the heart of things.

— O Hekate! Even though you are lyrical in what you say, you are biased because the cave is home for you. Only consider this cave of sorrow that has claimed me, though. It is without mercy, having swallowed me into its abysmal depths as surely as Father Kronos swallowed me when I was newborn.

The goddess of the crossroads regarded her in silence. She seemed to have arrived at a turn in the path.

— Sorrow that remains stubbornly on the threshold is not only a plague, but it will isolate you from all others. Speak of this great sorrow to me.

— Will you hear me? Oh, I realize how freely Kore went upon the plain, seeking out the seashore to play and to dance with her friends, the nymphs. She has lived so exposed to the sky and to others. I allowed it, you see. Oh, if only I had hidden her with you, Hekate! After all, she was not just any fertile field!

— As you speak, I realize that you distrust all witnessing eyes, even the gaze of the gods. Would you have hidden Kore from the gods?

— Yes! Zeus, Kore's father, does not suffer Kore's loss as I do. O where can I find her?

Demeter wept.

— Hear me in your grave loss. I was sitting in the cave waiting for the day to spend itself so that I might come forth under the fragrant veil of evening. It was in that narrow interval between ending day and evening's veil that Kore's cry reached me.

— You were hidden away, sheltered and pensive, as you are known to be, while Kore was exposed . . .

— The hearing in my cave exceeds ordinary hearing. I can't explain it.

Demeter was gazing at Hekate intensely as she questioned her.

— Tell me how it was when you heard her.

— I thought, "Destiny is at work here at Eleusis in a mysterious way!"

Hekate's words struck Demeter like a powerful cold wave of the sea.

— There was nothing you could do, action you might take at once?

— Yes. I could tend Kore's cry, much as a nurse tends a child. Tending presented itself as the way. I speak of that sustained attention directed toward the center of what is happening. Faithful attention can preserve a suitable space for what's to come.

Demeter pondered Hekate's explanation in silence. Then she nodded and spoke now as one who muses.

— Kore's cry has become the seed hidden within the dark of earth. How alive and vulnerable is this seed that is Kore! Yet as you speak, I begin to wonder if there is an unseen furrow that shelters her . . .

— There is destiny here, I believe. Neither you nor I nor Zeus himself can interfere with it.

Demeter's face reflected her great sorrow.

— You see, without Kore, I am one-half. Demeter is broken in two before you.

— Heaven forbids such a calamity! Kore, the maiden self, is *timed*—a blossom white as sea foam that pushes up from earth like the narcissus that I saw blooming where Kore and the nymphs danced on the shore.

— You saw such a flower? You perceive Kore as my maiden self, but she is separate, I tell you. She is my daughter who has disappeared.

— And yet the self becomes the maiden of the awesome journey.

— A respectable journey is usually announced and calls for fond farewells.

— As you have surmised, Kore's is no preannounced journey allowing for good wishes and fond farewells.

— Hekate, light your torch and accompany me now as I search for information and clues. I know that the light that emerges out of the dark is the best illumination.

Lighting her torch, Hekate set out on the darkened path with Demeter, who questioned her.

— There is something I need to know. Did you by chance learn who Kore's abductor might be, for surely she has been abducted? O what heartless, greedy thief dared seize the daughter of Demeter?

Hekate shook her head.

— I know nothing of her abductor. Ah, but I can think of someone who might have information—Helios. Indeed, he may well have witnessed the abduction.

— The sun god, of course! Will you accompany me, and we'll go at once to the house of Helios? Certainly he cannot have missed such a major happening on the plain of Eleusis.

— Yes, I'll come with you. Besides, you may need night's protective shawl to approach that dazzling residence.

The two goddesses set out at once for the sky dwelling of Helios. Demeter commented as they climbed the steepest of paths,

— I am at a disadvantage, unable to move at my usual pace. Sorrow is, after all, such an earth-plunging thing. High and noble vision, such as the sun god must possess, can hardly know about sorrow. I prefer not to linger longer than absolutely necessary in Helios's house.

— We shall only stay long enough to ask him the crucial question.

They climbed the steep path in silence for some time, and it was Hekate who at last spoke.

— I sense that what you are passing through is actually human suffering in its profound dimension, a suffering lacking light or affirmation. Within it, a person is shackled liked a victim. In time, your godly grief will take shape, I believe. It is a gift to the human world that you have undergone this suffering.

Demeter shook her head from side to side, as if in perplexity. Speaking after some time, her voice was changed, being drained of distress and almost serene once more.

— Yes, Hekate, you are right, for I too perceive that it is the immense human suffering that I participate in when I rail against the disappearance of Kore—she who is the unrepeatable maiden, who again and again becomes the threshold of new life. Ah wait, do not protest, for I also perceive the unshakable truth: that Kore and I are the two who are *one!* We are not torn the one from the other as I first thought, since that would be an impossibility. Do you see what this means, Hekate? *I, Demeter, am launched on Kore's journey whether I choose to be or not!*

The two figures continued on the arduous path of ascent to the house of Helios, falling silent as they went. Being goddesses familiar with firm earth paths and not equipped with winged sandals, progress was tedious. With relief they at last glimpsed the shining house of the sun god ahead. From the observing sun god, they learn that Lord Hades, brother of great Zeus, came from the underworld in his chariot and abducted Kore to be his cherished wife and queen of the underworld.

Hekate Advises

A woman walked on the Thriasian Plain, making her way in the field where only recently the shafts of wheat stood tall. Following the path that encircled the harvested field, golden in the afternoon sun, she lifted her eyes and gazed seaward toward Eleusis. Having completed her circuit, she turned about and repeated her trek, her eyes searching from left to right. There seemed to be a tension in her hard to contain. Occasionally, she would stop and gaze searchingly toward the distant horizon. Finding no satisfaction there, she left the path and sought the shade of a great old plane tree nearby. When she had sat for some time within the depth of shade, she was surprised by a voice that addressed her.

— Woman, why are you wandering in Demeter's field? The harvest took place three days ago.

Visibly startled, she made an involuntary movement before replying.

— If only I possessed such a rest—rest at the end of a time well spent and golden with satisfaction! But that's not mine. You find me wandering and searching, yet where is there hope of finding something like Demeter's harvest?

The invisible companion seemed to take this in.

— You have a loss, I think.

The woman bowed her head at this sharp assessment and was mute for a time.

— Well, the best has been taken away from me, and that's the truth.

— Alas, what can this grave loss be?

— How can I name it except to say that the happy core of me has disappeared. That's right, disappeared without a trace.

The voice grew thoughtful.

— Ah yes, so. I must tell you that I saw her passing. I saw the happy one as she departed.

    Who was this speaking? What was she talking about?

— What do you mean?

    The companion did not reply at once. When finally she spoke, her voice was reminiscent.

— There was upon the far meadow a wailing. Then I heard a cry to the gods of Olympus. Could it have been you?

— No. I didn't wail nor cry out. I was too frozen in my anguish to do that. Nor did I hear any voice whatsoever on the meadow or in the field.

— First I thought it could be Demeter herself scouting the field among the rows of grain for lost Kore.

— Lady, I am certain that I heard no voice in the grain field nor did I see anyone at all. The field was empty, like my heart.

    As she peered now into the deep shade, she was astonished to see that her companion was visible.

— Ah, now I see your face, and it is luminous, and the large dark eyes that observe me seem oddly familiar. I wonder why you stand there in the deep gloom.

— I am Hekate, woman. It is well that you remember me. What you do not know is that I hear and see what lies in obscurity or what is departed or forgotten. It is mine to keep track of what is lost or has disappeared or is no longer able to be reached.

    The woman's eyes were large with astonishment.

— Ah, so that is how you came to say to me those strange words when I said that my happy side had gone missing. You said, "I saw her passing." You spoke of a part of me as if it were a separate woman.

— The one I glimpsed was a shining maiden, like the Kore. What's more, she has left on a journey. I do recognize the signs of this journey.

— O Lady Hekate, do listen! Can't you see that you are talking about me and what belongs to myself alone? I have no spare person living some separate sort of life. And yet, if only you could know how bereft I am!

— It is your deep distress that I have been addressing, you see. I am not hard of heart, my dear. This happy side you speak of, now become a stranger, is your very own hidden daughter, no less. You have said that she is the core of you. Then why do you cease to own her? She belongs, and yet she has disappeared.

The misery that assailed her seemed to subside, and the fire of her complaints as well.

— Tell me, Lady Hekate, what else I need to know, for you are wise.

— What I know is revealed gradually, never all at once. What happens in the dark occupies my attention when the day-bright consciousness sleeps. What stirs in the dimness of the mind and heart lies close to primary need and desire that is faithful to one's nature. Such stirrings of fundamental desire may come in time to be trimmed of excess and of frivolous experimentation as they encounter the rich source place. In any case, I perceive a long winding journey, which, although it is one's very own, will be blessed with companions.

— What you have described as a journey intrigues me. Still, it is intimidating as well. Where does it start?

— The journey I speak of opens out of your separateness and aloneness. In the wilderness where one misses friends and life's solaces, it may be engaged. Comforting old answers and once-worthy strategies fall by the wayside.

The woman's face fell, and she gasped audibly.

— What you describe must be Hades' dreaded realm!

— So it has been called by many. As for Hades' realm, I myself am contentedly at home there. Is it not the abode of all that has been? At the same time, it is the rich source place. Why else is Lord Hades called god of riches?

Overwhelmed by the incongruity of such a realm, the woman shook her head and sought to turn aside from Hekate's vision of it.

— You spoke of my maiden side, saying that you saw her pass by, for surely my happy side has deserted me. Tell me, could she be claimed by this Hades' place?

— Yes, I believe that she is. When I recall Demeter's own daughter's flight upon the meadow, pursued by the dark lord, I recognize the hidden maiden that is greatly loved, eternally pursued, and whose loss prostrates a person.

— As Kore fled, did she look back?

— Yes, she looked back anxiously. Still she pressed ahead.

— She was brave, I'd say, braver than I should be.

— Braver than you are when you try to survive without her. I warn you that if you learn as many do to live without the hidden maiden, you may feel safe. What you get is a life of somewhat dry repetition and endless taking charge.

Now the woman bristled at this account and protested.

— Well, my mother was wise. She always said that a person must make the best of what she's got.

The goddess paced back and forth beneath the branches of the plane tree before responding.

— Only when one is summoned by the gods should she go on this journey of descent, which is Kore's journey. If no summons comes, then one must follow your mother's advice.

The woman spoke in a low, subdued voice.

— But you saw the maiden self of me departing, you have said. It must be that she is the one who got the summons. As for myself, I didn't see or hear a thing.

Hekate nodded slowly, and her serenity reassured the woman. On the following morning, the woman made her way again to the sun-filled wheat field. Something new was in her gait. Tension had eased, and a faint sense of anticipation was evident. Seeing the old plane tree ahead, she slowed her pace, smiling a little in gratitude toward the tree as she made her way to its canopy of low branches. When she was once more deep within the shaded world of the tree, she called softly, "Lady Hekate, are you there?" The familiar voice answered from some distance away.

— I am here! Never am I far away from Demeter's sacred field.

The woman experienced a strong desire to find at once the stream of her unusual exchange with Hekate.

— I expect you have watched many a plowing then?

— Oh yes, and the sowing and the harvest as well.

The woman took a deep breath before plunging into her story.

— I must tell you something, Goddess. My life has plowed me mercilessly, cutting deep into my ground and casting the soil to one side or the other.

A silence ensued. Was the goddess so unsympathetic? At last she spoke.

— Do you desire to be an unplowed woman, I ask you?

The woman took in her breath sharply, and a wave of anger arose in her, but Hekate was speaking.

— The plowing precedes the yielding of earth. As for the heaps of soil to either side, why, surely they just *shape the furrow*. Without a furrow, one is poorly equipped.

Reminiscence overtook the woman.

— As you speak, an old memory passes before me. I see my father walking behind the ox under the low morning sun as he plows the furrow. The upturned earth is fresh and black. You know, it all feels so surprising.

Her comment held something of wonder in it. Hekate was mindful of Demeter herself, however.

— What an endless procession of earth plowings lies in Demeter's memory! Soon the new plowing must begin. As you must know, there are two familiar plowings that every grain field makes ready for.

The woman nodded, affirming this while Hekate grew pensive as if viewing some unseen ground.

— When earth is encountered as the human ground, one can be forever taken up with the two plowings and the furrow of each that encloses oneself. In the first furrow, a person is planted in the family. Here the seed sprouts and grows, and the vulnerable seedling is shielded. Even so, winds and storms can be rough to withstand. The second furrow, on the other hand, cradles the growth of one's own specific nature and soul bent. This comes about when you have shifted furrows, you see. When first transplanted, you may find yourself wilting, even languishing, for a time.

— How can that be when a person is in her very own element and no longer the family's furrow? It's got to be rewarding, Goddess.

— A true reward is the gift of earth when one has ripened through the seasons. As for being in one's own element, it can be an estranging experience for a time, I've noticed. For one thing, it takes time to learn how to draw from the soil's deep sustenance and how to be in oneself. One is, after all, a newcomer to this furrow of oneself.

The woman's smile was rueful as she spoke.

— Looking back in my life, I can see these two plowings quite clearly now. What a curious thing, though, for when I was in the first furrow, the family, I longed for the second furrow. And when I found myself in the second furrow, what nostalgia I had for the security of the first one!

Hekate shook her head from side to side.

— You are a woman of the times, for you sense yourself as authentic mainly when you are feeling *misplaced*, that is, when you think, "Why am I deposited in the wrong place?"

Both considered this for a while as a strong wind stirred the tree and the branches began to sway, causing them to draw closer to the tree's great trunk as their anchor to earth. Turning to Hekate, the woman addressed her.

— Lady Hekate, whenever you have spoken of Demeter, I have observed that a light illuminates your face—beyond the moonlike radiance that is always there. There is much that you know about Demeter, apparently. Tell me, does some hope for me lie in Demeter?

— Unlike Earth Goddess, she does not awaken the life from every seed that grows. It is the grain—that seed in particular—in which she stirs the life and brings to ripening. It is the ripened grain that embodies the bread of life. Is Demeter not called with affection the Big Loaf?

— Ah, and I honor Lady Demeter greatly. But you have not answered my question, Lady.

— Demeter's mystery holds the essence of hope for the individual and for you in particular, yes. But this hope will yield nothing until you come to invest your faith in the seed—one seed in particular, I'd say. Talking about seeds and germination in general will not accomplish it. Actually, the action required is quite simple.

Hekate contemplated the woman at some length.

— Now you must make preparation for the third plowing, the one known at Eleusis as the plowing of the sacred field of Demeter.

— I have admitted that I have lived and endured through the first two plowings so far. Now I recall that in the rites at Eleusis, Demeter is hailed as "she of the thrice-plowed field!"

— This sacred field is Demeter's alone, actually. I know the third furrow from below, you see. Have I not witnessed the miraculous power that rises to support the third furrow? This furrow is no less than a cradling in the hands of great Demeter.

— Alas, how shall I ever arrive at the third furrow? Nor do I have any notion of how to prepare for it.

— The action, I repeat, is simple. You select well the seed, affirming it as your very own, and you entrust it to the sacred furrow. Then you tend the furrow as circumstance requires.

The woman pondered this procedure, and her expression was earnest, though humble as she asked yet another question.

— Where does the third furrow, the sacred one, lie?

— Do not be embarrassed to ask. It is a necessary question. Why, it lies beyond the opposition of the two familiar furrows, beyond the conflict between family identity and satisfying the individual self. It is the third way.

The woman sighed, whether in sheer relief or in the embrace of satisfaction was unclear.

— And when I have planted the third furrow, how long before I enjoy its gift?

— The gift comes by stages, it appears. One glimpses it as like a rare plant, verdant and coming to flower, which cannot be classified but which brings pleasure. Who can define the gift? It is enough to know that when the fruit ripens, there is a joy, a satisfaction that contains a mystery.

For a time, the two were claimed by silence while the wind, warm and soft now, brought the humming and the slow dancing of the branches of the plane tree.

Pondering Kore's Return

Not far from Demeter's sanctuary at Eleusis, Zeus and Hermes walked side by side. Gazing at the green meadow with pleasure, Zeus spoke.

— How good to see the greening of the earth again. The drought and the famine that followed seemed interminable. I thought that this would be the end of the crisis with Demeter, but the matter of her beloved Kore presents itself again.

Hermes was pensive.

— Is this so surprising? Nothing ever stays the same in Demeter's realm, I've noticed.

— If you are referring to the fact that the seasons are forever in motion, that is true. On the one hand, earth herself moves in a steady rhythm, and one knows roughly what to expect next. On the other hand, she can be temperamental and unpredictable.

Hermes smiled, shaking his head.

— That wasn't what I meant. It is not the seasons that give us reason for concern at the moment. As you know, I recently traveled with Kore as the sole passenger in the chariot as we made our way from the underworld to earth. In transit, my relationship to the maiden broadened considerably.

— Come, Hermes, you are capable of being more specific, I think.

— It is that I was waiting to be certain of having your attention to these matters.

— You have it. Kore is my daughter, after all.

The god of the road leaned against a large boulder and grew reflective.

— I wonder if I can describe it adequately—the scene of the chariot journey through Hades' realm. I was the charioteer when, having left

Hades' house behind, the shining black steeds bore the two of us
steeply upward on the shadowy, winding road through the semidarkness.
Needless to say, we met no other travelers.

— Those are incredible horses that my brother has, I have heard.

— That I can vouch for. The way proved almost effortless until at last we
approached earth's gateway. Then the steeds stopped, shook their heads
in protest, and pawed the ground furiously before the gateway.

— Did they indeed? And Kore herself, how was she on the shadowy
road?

— Hmm, had I not a knowledge of her nature, I should have been even
more perplexed by her than by the steeds. Why, I expected an eagerness
in her in anticipation of her return home to Demeter. Instead, I saw
that she was wide-eyed and pale throughout this passage and would
gaze back repeatedly over her shoulder, as if anxious about what she
had left behind.

— Her gaze was *backward*? Not forward toward home?

— Backward, yes, toward Hades' house. Who is to say what Kore has come
to regard as home?

— That is the important question, of course. Still, she must be grateful
to you for rescuing her from the bondage of the dim realm, and she
surely must have believed that the return to the golden earth and Mother
Demeter would bring her happiness.

— So I thought as well. But listen to these words she spoke in the chariot
as she looked backward: "My home glows in the realm of night like the
moon itself . . . O dear house, your queen belongs to you! How often
your very heartbeat has matched my step upon your floor!" I regarded
her closely, taking in her poignant nostalgia for Hades' house. Then
she murmured so low that I could scarcely catch the words:

> O lord of my heart's passion, king of riches,
> Guard well my throne beside your own, my beloved,
> For I shall surely return to your side!

The prophecy stunned me. Even so, my mind recognized an obvious
truth.

Zeus shook his head slowly.

— She always was an enigma. Has she not told her mother since her return
that her greatest longing is now satisfied, the longing to return to her
mother's side?

Hermes rose to his feet, his face luminous with his realization.

— Zeus, my father, hasn't truth always had two horns? Bull horns at that.

— You remind me of the ancient altars of Crete, my birthplace. The dual horns, each rocklike and authoritative, sat upon the altar stone in a shouting splendor of strength, I remember. Even as a boy, I trembled.

— An awesome duality it presents.

— Yes. Human existence rests upon this duality: the two that stand ever separate and yet rooted in one ground. But we were speaking of my daughter of the two realms.

— Or of the two horns? Well, let me tell you how it was. Kore sat close beside me within the chariot, and we were well jostled about on the journey up to earth. As we went, she began to lose her pallor. Her earlier sadness was replaced by an eagerness, and a brightness shone in her eyes, I observed. Her gaze was only forward on the path now, her head lifted. Why, even a soft smile played at the corners of her lovely mouth.

— Indeed? So she began to realize that she was returning to her true home, that is, to earth and her everlasting mother.

— Well, that is the other horn that you describe, the other truth. Ah, never the twain shall meet.

— Can we know this? The mystery of the unity lies surely with Demeter.

Hermes sighed and was claimed by his musings for a time. At last he spoke almost idly.

— Does Kore herself perceive this mystery, I wonder? After all, she is its chief actor.

— Usually you stride ahead embracing your own conclusion, I know. So what is it?

— Kore herself has no overall viewpoint. She does not view the mystery, I think. It is enough that she partakes of its flesh. Her presence is joyous. At the same time, she resembles the bending, weeping stream that descends, flung like a current of passion. Other times she is the serene queen borne upward into the place of the growing grain of life. There is no question that Kore is at the core of Demeter's mystery, though.

Zeus nodded and was reflective before replying.

— With Demeter's closed hand, she holds this mystery as a golden kernel, while at Eleusis in the dead of night, she is said to open her hand, giving a brief glimpse of the secret. That is the moment of *epopteia*, the open secret!

Demeter and Rhea

It was late afternoon on the Rharian Plain, not far from the sanctuary of Demeter that the two goddesses walked together. Earlier in the day, the treasured reunion of Demeter and Kore had taken place, and there had been incredible joy in Kore's return. Now Mother Rhea and Demeter were enjoying their own smaller reunion. Demeter spoke.

— In the realm of feminine reality, two reunions reverberate through the depths this day. Do you feel this happening, Mother?

— I do indeed. What a journey has claimed Kore, an anguishing one for you, my daughter. Why, it has moved through labyrinthal darkness and despair and has finally come to joy. There is a third reunion to come. You must turn to it now, for it is urgent.

— What is this, Mother?

— The reunion with the gods. After all, you chose to cut yourself off from Olympus in your anger.

— Why should I be in a hurry? After all, only consider how long Olympus delayed in responding to my anguished plea for my daughter's recovery. Had I not turned my face from earth, bringing dire famine, the gods would never have moved in Kore's behalf. True, the human world has suffered. It was unavoidable, but it did move the gods to heed my plea.

— I recognized these hard facts, Demeter, but I am here to ask you, when will your generosity return? The whole earth awaits it.

— I made myself unavailable, shutting myself up in the temple that the people of Eleusis had built for me. It has been for me a cave sojourn, greatly needed.

— A cave, you say?

— Yes. Mother Rhea, you yourself know well about the cave abode.

— Ah, you must be referring to the cave of Mt. Dikti on Crete—that deep labyrinth of earth where I hid the birthing of Zeus.

— Yes. I too had to withdraw into the caring darkness to tend the life of my progeny.

  Rhea frowned, looking thoughtful.

— And yet the gods said to each other, "Demeter, shut up in her temple, only tends her anger!"

— Anger was my intimate companion, true, but so was grief. Yet these were overshadowed by my attention to the treasured well-being of Kore.

— A lonely vigil for you. What you and I know is that the eternal maiden at the core of reality is a luminous thread that weaves invisibly. It is below all sight and knowledge. Other times it dances, as we witness in the circle dance of the maidens which all see and admire. Kore is tender and joyous as she casts herself into the arms of existence, whereas no woman would be so imprudent.

— I am grateful, Mother, to you for holding her essence to the light of day. What I gladly welcome is her light and sure step upon the threshold of what is to come. It is extraordinary and cannot be duplicated.

— What would the life of gods and human individuals be without Kore? You were right to defend her return at all cost. Even so, there is the fact that you have quite upset Olympus. How are you going to relate to the gods, I wonder?

— Kore has returned, and already earth has taken the seed, and the green is returning. What need have I of Olympus?

— It is the Olympians' need of *you* that concerns me.

— The Olympians need me, apart from my caring for the growing grain?

— Most certainly they do. Out of this dire need, Zeus called me, his mother, to come to you and to intercede for the gods.

  Demeter took in Rhea's account thoughtfully. Now she sighed before murmuring a question.

— And if I fail to return to Olympus, what then?

— For one thing you shall deprive me of my honor there. Vicariously, I have enjoyed your seat on Olympus. And have you forgotten that *Ouranus*, Heaven, is my father?

— No, I haven't forgotten, but I sense that something else moves you. What is it?

  Rhea gave an abysmal sigh that alarmed her daughter.

— It is the proximity of a catastrophe. I speak of a divorce that is pending between heaven and earth. I tremble before the possibility of its happening, and so should you, daughter. At first glimpse, the divorce

offers itself as a solution in which things are made simpler, tensions
are resolved, and decisions can be carried out easily.

— I am indebted to you, Mother, for putting all this into words, for you
are lifting before me a changed perspective, namely your own. I can see
what a disaster it will be if earth's representatives only look at things
through earth's perspective while heaven's representatives view the whole
of reality from heaven's high perspective.

— The catastrophe will be felt in the human realm, you see. Hubris
becomes inevitable. The human individual feels superior and right on
the side of heaven alone, or else he feels this way based on the exclusive
interests of earth.

Demeter's face had grown solemn as she contemplated Rhea's
words.

— A middle way is lacking . . . there is no mediation. It is Apollo who
indicates that the authentic way is taken only by taking account of
earth, Olympus, and the Lower Realm. He calls it the right measure.

— There is a light breaking through. I sense it. One cannot wait for truth
to become shining and clear, however.

— Am I, Demeter, the one to act as earth's representative and to reconnect
with Olympus and the gods?

— I see no other way.

— Will I feel compromised if I so act?

— Possibly, but disregard the feeling. It is not worthy of you as a great
goddess. Already you have restored growth to the fields. It is a worthy
beginning.

— Dear Mother Rhea, I give you my word that I shall now return to join
the gods on Olympus!

— So be it! I shall go at once to Olympus as your forerunner to announce
your return.

— Go well, and I shall follow you.

Demeter and Ascalaphus

A big muscular man with fiercely penetrating eyes, he had wandered in the meadow near Demeter's sanctuary at Eleusis for some time. Once again, two priestesses of the goddess stopped to observe the distant figure striding in the meadow. Now the figure turned, as if aware of their attention, and struck out in the direction of the temple. Even from a distance, some powerful current of purpose became tangible and caused the priestesses to shiver. Withdrawing quickly to the shadow of a smaller temple, the women watched the man's approach to the place of Demeter, where he entered with dirt-encrusted sandals. Demeter herself arose from her chair.

— It is rumored that a man has been wandering in the meadow below for some days. Would that be you, stranger?

In the pause before replying, he gazed steadily at the goddess, his eyes examining her with keen curiosity.

— That's me, Lady. I am known as Ascalaphus. Where I come from, nobody tills and cultivates the ground better than I do.

— Ah so? I have respect for the one who cultivates the earth. Actually, you and I are collaborators, I'd say.

He was plainly astonished.

— You don't say? Me and Lady Demeter collaborators!

He slapped his knee soundly and grinned for the first time. She leaned forward earnestly to ask a question.

— And where do you come from, stranger?

— From the realm of Lord Hades. I thought you knew.

She shook her head over so slightly as a veil dropped over her face. He went on.

— She looks like you too. Why, I'd know that face and form anywhere. Look, you needn't veil yourself with me.

— You knew my daughter then in the awesome Lower Realm?

— Sure thing. I know her all right. See her once and there's no forgetting. She's our queen, you see. Prettiest flower a fellow ever saw . . .

Demeter drew herself up to her full height.

— Kore *was* your queen, Ascalaphus. She has returned to earth for all time. Here she reigns with me in the sanctuary on Eleusis' sacred hill.

He lifted his eyes and gazed toward the temple.

— It's sure an awesome place, Lady. I'm gardener for Lord Hades, see? He'd trust me with anything. What I must tell you is that Lord Hades wants her back. He is waiting for her to return home to him. You're not to worry, Lady Demeter, because he's a fine husband for your girl. Besides, she has been happy at his place down below.

Demeter was on her feet and began to stride back and forth, obviously distressed. Now she turned toward Ascalaphus.

— Ah, happiness! What is it? How like a fruit it ripens in the sun and as quickly shrivels and falls! Earth knows this sending forth and the taking back, for earth is she who is alive and strong everlastingly. Rejoice in earth, man of Hades, not the dim Lower Realm!

He heard her with his bushy eyebrows raised.

— I'll keep your advice in mind, Goddess. Still, a bit of happiness as a person goes along never hurt anybody, I'd say.

This elicited a small smile from Demeter.

— Well, Ascalaphus, I see that you are no man's fool. As for me, I long for a full measure of joy for Kore, my daughter.

Now he burst forth with enthusiasm.

— By the Styx, I'm glad we see eye to eye, if you'll pardon the expression, you being divine and all! This means that I can deliver my message at last.

— Your message?

A pallor had come over her face.

— It's about *the seed*, of course.

— What seed?

Even as she whispered the question, she looked solemn now and older.

— Surely you must know that a person can't grow a thing unless there is the seed.

— Do not play for time, royal gardener!

Ascalaphus gazed into the distance for a long moment before speaking.

— Mother of Queen Kore, here is the plain truth, then. My king, Lord Hades, put a seed of the pomegranate into your daughter's hand. Nor did she resist it. What she did at once was she *ate* it! With my own eyes, I saw her do it.

Demeter's eyes were aflame with anger together with some larger inscrutable emotion not to be fathomed. From the two priestesses who had arrived and stood a little distance apart, a soft, strangled cry arose. When Demeter spoke, she might have been addressing herself alone, so low and intimate her voice was.

— It was only yesterday that Kore returned. Did she not return to me alone, for am I not her mother? We are joined again, the maiden and I! Earth herself rejoices, for once again she beholds the full basket. Like the sound of the spring torrent, Kore's laughter rang out as she ran over the meadow toward me where I waited . . .

Demeter's voice trailed off, and Ascalaphus honored the deep emotion of the goddess. Demeter turned and faced the meadow below as a deep cry formed in her, to which she now gave voice.

— O Kore . . . everlasting maiden . . . O daughter of life returned! You are my supreme joy! All unknowingly you drew the god Hades to yourself and shaped the sweet and hidden life of love, even so it was far from me in the realm below. Oh, the alien seed, the seed that seduced you! Long before you took the seed from his hand, the god's chariot bore you swiftly away from me and earth's dwelling. Alas, you partook of the dreaded seed of Hades' dark realm. It has become your flesh!

Grief overtook Demeter as a sweeping tide. Ascalaphus spoke gruffly.

— Kore has returned. Have you already forgotten her homecoming, Lady?

— How could I . . . ? How joyously we embraced. Ah, but when I searched her face, I saw that my daughter who was before was no longer there! Instead, I gazed into the face of a queen. Delicate and lovely she still was, yet oddly she was a sovereign that I did not know.

The goddess gazed unseeingly before her, the stranger seemingly forgotten. A silence claimed them both for a time until, stirring herself, she addressed him.

— Ascalaphus!

— I am still here, Lady Demeter.

It was the voice of one whose patience is tried. Still he inclined his head to take in what Demeter said.

— Tell me, this taking in of the seed, do you know what this means?

— I do, yes, and that's what I'm here to tell you about. The message is this: "Kore belongs to Lord Hades after all!"

— What's this?

— Lord Hades is waiting for Kore's return below. Not all facts are plain, but this one most certainly is.

Solemn and diminished, Demeter drew herself up to her full queenly height as she stared after Ascalaphus's fateful words. As she spoke in a low voice, her splendid authority was clearly manifested.

— For Kore to return to abide by Hades' side is not possible, I tell you! I, Demeter, forbid it!

Turning away from the royal gardener with a swirl of her garment, she lifted her face toward her temple and strode up the path to overtake it, much like one of her worshippers seeking the essential refuge.

The days passed. Quietly Demeter inquired of her chief priestess whether she had seen any sight of "the stranger" or could she confirm his permanent departure from the small plain of Eleusis. The priestess shook her head and replied that she had not seen the large burly stranger again. Demeter took slight encouragement from this report, but she did not relax her watchfulness. When the afternoon was descending toward its close, the goddess took the path down into the green meadow alone. There were certain crucial observations that only an Olympian might make, unpleasant as the task appeared to her. That the god Helios was about to disappear into the western sky over the isle of Salamis was just as well. The help that Helios had been able to give at the time of Kore's disappearance was not volunteered and, sadly, took the form of a passing observation, even though he had witnessed the abduction with his own eye. No, Helios as a witness held no passion for her cause. With such musings, she entered the meadow—a world unto itself and bordered by the sea where on the beach, Kore had been accustomed to play with the sea nymphs. Entering now the dense shade of a plane tree, she came face-to-face with a tall, broad figure standing in shadow.

— Is it you, stranger from the dreaded realm?

He bowed, honoring her before replying.

— It's me, Ascalaphus, all right. Pleased that you haven't forgotten me, Lady Demeter.

The bite of his words caused her to sigh.

— Why have you not returned to the Lower Realm with my ultimatum? Do explain.

— A witness, you see, has to complete his job. What I arrived here with is the firsthand report of the witness.

— What more can you possibly tell me, then?

Ascalaphus leaned back against a tall boulder comfortably and cleared his throat.

— Well, day after day, I have regularly witnessed the married life of my lord and his queen, your daughter. A happy marriage it is, I can report. Soulful looks they would give each other, ones I wasn't meant to see, of course. As I've said all along, nothing gets by me, though.

— Surely she could not forget her home and her life with me!

— True, Queen Kore has had her bouts of homesickness, but what maiden bride wouldn't whose spouse has carried her off to his place in a far country without a proper wedding? Be assured, Lady Demeter, what you're getting is the firsthand report of the witness!

The last he delivered with a lusty ring of triumph in his deep voice. Demeter was not happy as she regarded him with her large dark eyes.

— So you have delivered your message to me, and you have no reason to linger here. One can only conclude that you do not honor my declaration that Kore belongs here on the face of earth with me.

Demeter's words hung on the air that enclosed the two of them, echoing. Ascalaphus swallowed and gazed at the ground before replying in a husky voice.

— Lord Hades is king of a great realm, and he has a right to his wife and queen. He's not one to compromise either!

— How dare you speak to me of Hades' right?

— I must because I'm representing your son-in-law, Goddess. He's the respected king of riches and king of the dead!

Demeter began to pace back and forth, keeping to the circle of shade that the plane tree cast over them. Slowly she was shaking her head from side to side as though assailed by some wordless place. At last she grasped a few words out of the swift current of her thought. Even so, they were petulant.

— I know that the kingdom of the dead is large and famous, but for Kore, I had long hoped that she would be wedded to, well, a *livelier* kingdom! How can I begin to accept so awesome a son-in-law in any case?

— An awesome son-in-law he is, indeed. You've got that right, Lady Demeter.

Was the implication that the great goddess might have in mind a good deal that was not "right"? He plunged on.

— Queen Kore finds Lord Hades dark, handsome, and very splendid, I assure you. Never had he been more splendid that in the moment that he held the seed out toward her!

— Oh, what blasphemy! Since she was a small child, Kore knew well the seed of the golden grain, but never had she known the pomegranate seed nor desired it.

— Well, Lady, I am here to tell you that she could hardly wait to take the seed from the king's hand. Why, I saw the desire in her face. It was the real thing. She held it fondly between her fingers before putting it into her mouth. Then she smiled at its sweetness. I witnessed this, I must tell you.

— And how boldly you speak of the dread deed . . . Alas! Seeing the seed's journey in Kore's hand, *you saw what you might not see,* Ascalaphus!

His emotion overwhelmed him, and he cried aloud,

— But I saw it! I saw it! I alone am witness!

Joining the consternation in the goddess's face, something else was emerging, which caused her to sink down upon a large rock.

— Ascalaphus, I will hear you out. About this seed, was it like one of the many seeds that are cast into the misty furrows of the underworld, whose growth is never to be harvested in the light of day?

— Oh, it was a very special pomegranate seed, I believe, that Lord Hades chose for his lady. Her smile held the evidence, see?

Demeter nodded and was silent for a time. Ascalaphus waited, watching.

— What you witnessed was a sacred happening. In your curiosity and eager witnessing, you trespassed a sacred boundary. It is a fact.

— So where would Lord Hades have found himself the seed if I hadn't been faithfully tending the pomegranate grove, I ask you? Why, I am his indispensable man!

Demeter spoke slowly, fatefully.

— You admit to me, Demeter of the fruitful earth, that you not only witnessed the eating of the underworld's seed but you yourself furnished Lord Hades with the fateful fruit of destiny?

— I did!

— Because of you, man of Hades, the realm of fruitful earth is profoundly altered! You shall never be forgotten. Furthermore, it shall be widely known that I do not forgive you!

Fear came over Ascalaphus now. His voice held bitter scorn.

— What power have you got over me, Demeter?

— Your fate lies in the Lower Realm and is yet to be revealed. Go now!

Turning away, she left the plane tree's shadow and quickened her pace on the path out of the meadow without looking back.

Relieved to be released from the goddess's accusing presence at last, Ascalaphus left the meadow with a swift stride. Shortly the city of Eleusis was behind him as once more he made his way to the Lower Realm on the dim and narrow road. When he had penetrated to the core of Hades' realm but had not yet come near the palace, a great rumbling sound came toward him. Fear struck him, and as he stood still on the path, a huge boulder overtook him, pinning him to the ground. For a long time, Ascalaphus cried out, but no one heard him.

Hermes and Zeus Interview Ascalaphus

It was early morning on Mt. Olympus when the invisible presence of the sun still suffused the sky with shades of deep pink. In his youthful stride, the god Hermes, wearing his full cloak and the broad-brimmed hat of the god of the road, sought out Zeus.

— Good morning, Father.

— Hermes, you are up and about early, I see. Is there some problem I don't know about?

— You know, of course, of the joyful reunion of Demeter and Kore at Eleusis. What I'm here to report is that Demeter has made a major issue of the question of the pomegranate seed that Hades handed over to Kore just before her departure from their underworld palace.

— I am not surprised to hear this. After all, Demeter had hoped against hope that her daughter hadn't touched any food of the Lower Realm. Did you happen to witness their reunion, by the way?

— Like a young fawn, Persephone ran from the chariot I was driving while Demeter leaped like a maenad as she ran to their joyous embrace. The vast hollowness Demeter had been suffering was filled once again, for surely life without the everlasting maiden was existence without its greenness and its flower.

— Ah yes. Joy that disappears inevitably creates the aching emptiness. No wonder Demeter turned away from earth in anger and grief and caused great famine. The famine forced our hand, as she must have hoped it would, and we began negotiations with my brother Hades to permit Kore to return to Demeter.

Hermes nodded to this account.

— And that return is accomplished, I point out.

— You have my greatest gratitude, Hermes, for seeing this through—and the gratitude of the other gods, I assure you. Besides, the earth is already greening once again. Have you noticed?

    Zeus's mind moved forward with some reluctance as registered in his sigh.

— And now, we have this huge issue of Kore's swallowing the seed of the underworld, you say.

    Zeus groaned, shaking his head. Hermes continued.

— Nor will the problem go away if the gods ignore it. Of this I am certain. By Persephone's own admission to her mother, she took the pomegranate seed from Hades and then ate it at once, bonding herself to the underworld, of course. If you could have seen Demeter's face when she heard this! There was the fierce grief and abysmal loss all over again. You can see how it is. No sooner does she get the maiden back home and into her familiar life than she discovers she belongs forever to the underworld. Frankly, my heart ached for Demeter.

— What is painfully clear to me is that she cannot and ought not, I say, endure a second great loss of Kore. It is not just, surely. It is my decision to set about to protect Kore. What are you thinking, Hermes?

— How like the human individual Demeter is, mirroring the dread of the underworld with its nocturnal, misty paths and the stretch of the unknown. As for me, it is my fortune to know the paths of the Lower Realm, as you well know. Nor do I have reason to fear Hades' realm. From all reports, Persephone seems to have had herself a satisfying life down there. Would you not agree?

    Hermes appeared to be enjoying his idle reflections. Zeus nodded, frowning however. He leaned forward, gazing intently at the god of the road as he spoke.

— Let's look at the situation. Kore has partaken of the underworld fruit, that is, of its seed, so that she now belongs to the nocturnal realm a goodly measure of her time. Agreed?

— That is a claim that Hades will not relinquish, rest assured.

— And we must be just with Hades as with Demeter. There's the rub. Tell me once again what happened when you stood in the presence of Hades and his queen?

— Is there some lingering doubt in your mind, I wonder? Well, this is how it was. I had pleaded our case at length for Kore's return to be reunited with her mother, describing Demeter's abysmal grief and her punishment of the growing earth. Hades is a decent fellow, as you know, being your brother and sovereign of one-third of the entire cosmos. He was open to an agreement, although I must say that he smiled grimly at the thought of sharing Kore. He turned to her and said, "Don't despair too much, for it is useless. Go to your mother, my dear." However, get this. He pointedly added that he would continue to be to her the best of husbands. Significant, don't you think? At that moment, she leaned against him and seemed reluctant to act at all. It occurred to me that he was also warning her of a great sadness to come—the separation the two of them were entering upon. After all, he is her lover and her spouse.

Zeus looked pensive. When he spoke, his voice was dry.

— Your account indicates that Kore has up to now taken Hades for granted, the husband who is a permanent installation in her life, one who never required her powers of winning seduction in the first place, a husband, besides, without much upkeep.

Hermes grinned broadly at Zeus's description and continued with some amusement.

— Exactly. After all, it was he who had been aggressive and persistent in bringing about their match. Kore has never known a separation from her spouse since their union. Surely, she is in the habit of taking him for granted, as you point out. If she considered the matter at all, she regards her pleasant existence with the god of riches in the Lower Realm as what the Fates have doled out for her. Now let me be very clear. Not for a moment when I visited did I have an impression that she was anything but happy with Hades, in spite of missing her mother, which is natural, I'd say.

— Your observations, Hermes, throw a new light for me on Kore's journey of descent, I must say . . . Still, you have hardly done justice to the issue of the pomegranate seed. You actually witnessed her eating it, did you?

— All I can say is that I saw that Hades took her hand tenderly for a moment as he gazed down lovingly into her face. The next thing I observed was that she then held that hand closed against her bosom. Recognizing what seemed to be a secret moment between eternal lovers, I honored it by turning aside briefly.

— Wait. Do I understand that in turning aside, you did not see her actually eat the seed?

— True. I did not.

Zeus sighed audibly.

— Besides the three of you, was anyone else present?

— I was waiting for that question. As a matter of fact, the royal gardener had appeared. I signaled to him to stand a little distance away, raising my hand in what I sensed was a delicate moment with the royal couple. The gardener's name is Ascalaphus.

   The realization struck Zeus with a sharp impact.

— Ah, that is the witness!

— Has a witness come forward then?

— Yes. He has journeyed to Eleusis to Demeter's sanctuary in order to give his testimony, as a matter of record. At this very moment, he is waiting for us at the gate of the city. What do you think? Shall we go to meet him now?

   Grimly, Hermes nodded, and he and Zeus set out for Eleusis.

   Looking for all the world like travelers on the Sacred Way between Athens and Eleusis, Zeus and Hermes approached the city gate side by side. From the shadow of the gate, a large dark figure stepped forward and waited. Hermes said in a low voice,

— I recognize the fellow all right. That's the gardener.

   As they drew close, the figure solemnly appraised the travelers, unflinching. Zeus addressed him.

— Would you be Hades' representative here?

— Yes. I am Ascalaphus. I'm no man's fool. Tell me, is it always so bright here?

   He shaded his eyes protectively. It was Hermes who replied.

— Not being accustomed to the light here on earth, I expect you find it unpleasant. There is in addition a certain brightness at the culmination of the Sacred Way of Demeter, I should warn you. We have met before, as you recall. Indeed, we apparently have much in common.

   Hermes grew increasingly relaxed as he spoke, leaning his shoulder against the gatepost. Now Ascalaphus was not a man easily taken in. As for his emotions, they were a plain language on his face.

— I've got nothing in common with you, Lord Hermes. You're one of those gods. I remember that you're the one who came after Kore.

— True. You have made a long and wearying journey. I am familiar with journeys, often enough to the Lower Realm. It occurs to me that you and I share a role in common. We are both messengers.

— We're not on the same side though. You came and took her clean away!

Anger suffused his face. Zeus intervened.

— Ascalaphus, don't distress yourself. You are an esteemed gardener, I understand. I shouldn't have thought that one would be needed in the Lower Realm. Growing plants without the sun must present a problem.

— I'm a night gardener, see? That's my specialty, and darkness is the best time anyway for sprouting seeds. I'd have thought you'd know that. Seeds like the nighttime. That's when the air is moist and soft and all sweet-smelling, and the creatures are moving about quietly. Why, the seeds I deal with would dry out and shrivel up and die if they were left exposed here in Demeter's country. For sure I am at home with my plants in the misty dark.

Zeus and Hermes exchanged somewhat startled glances, and Hermes nodded. Zeus raised the question.

— Isn't it rather difficult to see what you are doing there in the dark?

— It's all done by *feel* anyway, I'd say. There is something else about the night you two probably don't know about: it *sings!* Yep, not always, of course, but I've heard it singing for sure.

— Indeed? Hermes, did you realize that there was song in the underworld? If so, you might have mentioned it. All right, Ascalaphus, we are on an errand of great importance. We want your explanation of your journey here. Your purpose in precise detail, please.

Ascalaphus rubbed his hands together as he made ready for his task, and his eyes glinted with a strange zeal.

— I've come here to Demeter's sanctuary because I'm the witness. That's what I am. There's no disputing it, see? I saw it happen in Hades' own palace before my very eyes. I'm nobody's fool.

Again it seemed useful to reassure him of this fact.

— I am convinced that you are not a fool. Will you begin at the beginning and describe what you witnessed in my brother's house.

For a moment, Ascalaphus grinned with the pleasure of his position.

— It was like this. I just came in from picking a big basketful of pomegranates. Rosy they were, ripened on the tree. I set the basket down inside the courtyard where my lord and his lady liked to take their leisure. I sought them out to tell them about the fruit, knowing it would please them. The next minute, I was standing before them both.

— Was there anything out of the ordinary that you observed?

— As a matter of fact, there was. Queen Kore looked what you call bewildered, and she was leaning upon Lord Hades. The herdsman god here—that would be Lord Hermes—was speaking urgently with the king. He was urging him to send Kore back to earth right away!

Although he longed to improve upon the account, Hermes wisely remained silent.

— And how did you react to this scene?

— Why, I knew she ought not to go! I was sure of it. No, it wasn't right for him to put his wife in the hands of a visiting lord.

Hermes murmured an aside.

— A man who makes up his mind in an instant and who is no more likely to change it than for the sea to boil an egg!

— Ah, that maiden, why, there is nothing like her, I tell you. When Lord Hades brought her home to us, she was all shining and golden like I imagined earth was, and her shape was clear and beautiful. The lord called her his corn maiden. Well, he fairly adored her. Gradually, she looked changed, I'd say.

Hermes showed a certain astonishment.

— Changed? How was she changed?

— When I would come to see them, she became sort of hazy, hard to see clearly, I mean. Still, you could feel her in everything about us, sort of the way a spring spills its waters all about.

Hermes was thoughtful.

— It is curious what you say, for Kore is rather like that. Her delight has always been like a brook making its ecstatic path upon a hillside.

The gardener was full of his subject now.

— I've heard her weep too—tears deeper than Hades' floor.

Zeus commented.

— That would be Demeter, who lives in her heart and weeps. Continue with what took place, will you?

— Well, gazing at her, Lord Hades had a melted kind of look in his eyes, if you know what I mean. I heard him whisper, "Majestic maiden among maidens!" That was just before he cupped his hand over her hand, which was palm side up. That was when it all happened: *he passed over the pomegranate seed to her!*

Zeus laid a restraining hand on Ascalaphus's shoulder.

— Wait! How do you know for certain that it was a pomegranate seed he gave her?

— It was the only fruit at harvest, I tell you. He had a supply of them. Besides, the pomegranate is Hades' own fruit. It has his own secret code, see? Why would he give her anything he was less attached to? He gave her the seed. I am the witness!

— Continue. What happened next?

— At once I was watching the maiden queen wondering what she would do.

Hermes saw that Ascalaphus was enjoying himself overmuch and spoke.

— Wondering is fine, but it is not witnessing, man of Hades. There could have been thousands of seeds of various kinds that Hades had in supply, not to mention those of the basket of pomegranates you brought to the courtyard.

— Yes, but Lord Hades chose one particular seed for his lady. It had to be powerful enough to mate her forever to our kingdom, providing she would eat it. Only the seed of Hades' own fruit—the pomegranate—could do this. This you can't doubt.

Zeus and Hermes turned to each other and nodded solemnly. It was time to hear what Hermes knew, Zeus realized.

— Hermes, how was Kore at this time of taking the seed from Hades?

— I recall the scene vividly. Her mind appeared idle as though she might be in a reverie that began with her spouse's ardent touch, being under the spell of his great dark eyes as well. My own gaze upon her was intense and sent the mute message, *Watch!* If she got the message, she brushed it aside as she might a gnat.

For a moment, Hermes looked at wit's end.

— I feared as much with the maiden. Alas! Hermes, you tried to divert her fateful act. This is clear to me. Well, Ascalaphus, give us the final action.

— Why, Queen Kore lifted her hand, and I saw the seed clearly that she held between her thumb and forefinger. There was a dreamy look on her face. Slowly she placed the seed into her pretty mouth and began to chew it. Lady Persephone ate the pomegranate seed then and there!

From the two Olympians, deep sighs were heard as though some frail hope had been banished. Ascalaphus continued. And now his voice took on great animation.

— *Ha-ha, I says to myself. Ha-ha, sweet queen! Now you belong to us here below forever! Lord Hades has won over the other gods!*

Hermes in a subdued voice made a request.

— Describe the seed itself, can you?

— When I saw it between her fingers plain to view, I knew it was pomegranate, for it was red flesh swimming in its own juice, just like a grape that's been trampled in the harvest of autumn.

The three of them fell silent in the shadow of Eleusis' gate. Zeus stood with bowed head, and in that moment, gazing at him, Hermes saw the leader of the Fates lifting the cloak of awesome destiny. In a deep voice, Zeus spoke.

— Thank you, Ascalaphus. You have borne honest witness to what transpired in the Lower Realm beyond our sight. I can delay no longer but must issue the gods' decree. Attend well, Hermes. The decree is this: for one season out of each year, Kore, daughter of Demeter, will reside in the Lower Realm with Hades, her spouse, where already she is honored as queen. The remaining two seasons she will abide with Demeter on earth. Thus are born the great mysteries of Eleusis. Hermes, the last words must come from you, I believe.

Where conflict and anguish had held forth, a new time appeared to enclose them, peaceful, even satisfying, and Hermes smiled slowly to both Zeus and Ascalaphus before speaking.

— Ah, I perceive that Eleusis is the mediating place from now on between the two realms, earth and underworld. How like the gateway itself it is—a place of beginning the deep journey of descent and the place of the celebrated return to earth!

Demeter and the Woman

In the glowing autumnal light of late afternoon, Demeter walked the boundary of the great field of ripening grain that was like a golden tide on the Thriasian Plain. Descending into a gentle draw, she came upon a woman standing with her back to the grain field, her feet touching its boundary. Neither young nor old, she was handsome in face and form. The goddess observed that her face was turned toward the distant city and reflected a shifting excitement, a play of desire that alternated with boredom, and a certain ready, laughing response to whatever pleasant invitation should come. Demeter greeted her.

— Greetings, woman. Have you come from Athens by foot? What brings you to the boundary of the ripened wheat?

— You mean that this is wheat—what they use to make bread out of? The woman replied.

  Demeter nodded patiently.

— Our family doesn't farm, my father being a prosperous merchant in Athens. You will surely have heard of Mephicles. He is a brilliant speaker at the court of the Areopagus. Well, I am his daughter.

— So why, I ask you, have you come to my wheat field? Is there not bread enough in your father's house?

— I just stumbled upon it, I guess. There's nothing special here that I can see, just a lot of rows of wheat.

  Demeter's eyes widened in disbelief, and her words were incisive.

— Woman, this is not the father world that preserves you as daughter-maiden.

— What do you mean? You don't know me.

— Oh yes. I know you. Or, let me say, the text of your life and outlook is a familiar one to me.

A dreamy look came to the young woman's face. Now she confided.

— As for the daughter part, my father adores me.

The goddess nodded patiently.

— You please him, I imagine. What of your mother?

— She is like all other women in the city—nice but a little dull, if you know what I mean. Say, what's your name?

— I am Demeter.

— Hello there, Demeter. I expect that you like to grow things?

She gestured toward the field as she spoke, much as one who explains things to a backward child. Demeter drew herself up regally.

— I am Lady of the Grain in these parts.

— No versatility? You just grow one thing? For myself, I've got a lot of things going.

Demeter shook her head almost imperceptibly and stared out at the field of golden grain. She turned back to her chatty companion as one who, having stood at the crossroads, chose the path that beckoned.

— Speak to me of your life.

The young woman grinned, pleased to have acquired an audience.

— Well, we are a large family when you count uncles, aunts, and cousins. I do like being in the midst of it. There I feel completely surrounded by those who know me and accept me. At the fig gatherings in late summer, I wear my prettiest embroidered peplos and comb my hair into a silken fold and then stroll in front of my handsome male cousins. Attached or unattached, they give me careful attention. There is nothing like the feeling a woman gets from this. I become someone in particular to admire and to call to. It is like putting a fresh horse to the chariot.

— So let me ask you, is it enough simply to be admired by a passerby?

— It is everything! Before it happens, I am just waiting. I'm not yet alive. When the men regard me and smile, why, then I am *made!* Can you understand this, lady? Already I've forgotten your name.

The goddess sighed before answering.

— I know about it. There is a certain creating of the maiden that comes about when the male world casts its eyes on a woman. Occasionally some young woman will run away from it, though.

Incredulous, the young Athenian gasped.

— Who would run away?

— My own daughter. And do you know that Daphne fled when Apollo, admiring her with his luminous heart and mind, pursued her? Deep within a woman is the sense, you see, that the maiden is in danger.

— I'll always be the maiden. That's how I am. Besides, I love soaking up the men's ideas in their talk and hanging on to them myself. What's this danger to the maiden you mentioned?

— There is danger of losing the treasured ground out of which the maiden arises.

Demeter's response seemed to find no place in a mind that was off skipping happily like a young schoolgirl. The young woman continued.

— At the family gatherings, I like to watch all the aunts, see. They are wives. A wife seems so done and finished. I think I should hate being one—having to do the same things over every day, managing a household, and pleasing a husband, and then there are the children.

She shook her head at each circumstance that occurred to her. Demeter questioned her.

— Have you not noticed, though, that with the wife lies the magic of creating the dwelling place? What should you be without the dwelling place? The wandering maiden is ever in anguish.

— Look, I love to go to different houses, be with a lot of people, and do all sorts of things.

— These things are possible for you because your life is supported. The maiden is ever supported by what is not herself—the parents or others who have been important to her. Tell me, do you feel that you are independent, that you are altogether on your own?

— Oh, I do. Yes, I do.

— Look again. The human maiden does not stand alone. She *leans*.

For the first time, the young woman was silent, and a forlorn look passed her face before her sturdy confidence returned.

— It is as if I have this basket and a light step too, and I go about gathering pretty, pleasant things in it. My father always smiles at me just so.

— I see that you are the ever-gathering maiden. What about your storehouse?

— I have no storehouse. Storing is for past things. You see, I look ahead.

— Do you? I think not, for to look ahead requires having a storehouse for what is harvested.

The woman frowned, annoyed at the direction the exchange had taken.

— You do have strange ideas for a peasant farmer woman.

    She regarded Demeter closely, looking puzzled as she did. It was the goddess who spoke.

— The truth is that I hoped that you might come to recognize me in your own time. Also I waited for the abundant field of wheat to stir a more ancient memory in your soul, woman.

    Demeter rose to her feet, and her stature struck the woman for the first time as that of a queen. Turning, she looked into the face of the woman from Athens and addressed her.

— My major undertaking is tending souls of the human world, for I am Lady Demeter, goddess of Olympus!

    The woman turned pale, and speech failed her for a time. When she spoke at last, her voice was husky and slow.

— Why should I meet you, Goddess? It is said to be bad luck to meet a god you hadn't planned on.

— Obviously you had not "planned on" me. Well, planning hardly matters. No one can plan a god's presence, you see.

— We meet by accident then.

— No. It is up to a goddess whether she comes or remains distant. I have come.

    As Demeter's words began to assume an unarguable truth, the woman's demeanor was changed, and fear was evident as she looked about herself as one seeking a way to escape. She spoke as if to herself.

— I have always known that I am only at home in the city. I don't really like the country.

— Ah, but here you are exposed to your true ground. Having sheltered your birth, earth leads you toward what lies ahead, that is, beyond the maiden. O yes, earth herself awaits you in the field of the waving grain.

— Not me. I'd be bored in the field. I need lots of people, fascinating ideas, and different things happening as they do in the city. In the city, a woman can be almost anything she wants to be.

— Then why are you ever maiden, woman?

— What do you mean? Oh, are you paying me a compliment because I look young and vital?

— No. Maiden is only a part of what earth brings a woman. The maiden is the threshold. Without her, there is no real entrance into the life that unfolds. Still, she is not the whole house. I warn you, you cannot be staying on the doorstep and never crossing over.

— What must I do then?

— Enter the dwelling place which earth is able to shape for you.

    The young woman was beginning to recover from the shock of this encounter, encouraging herself with the thought of her own pluckiness. And she was determined to explain herself.

— I know that I do get bored. More and more things have lost the appeal they once had.

— The maiden that rules your life appears to keep it at a skip, but skipping along is less satisfying than you had thought it to be. Something else looms large and affects you. I speak of the man's mirror held up to the maiden. Gazing into this general mirror, you are shaped by the wishes and demands of fathers, lovers, companions. If you remember nothing else of our conversation, remember this: this maiden created by the mirror is not the everlasting Kore!

    Hearing these words of Demeter, she wasn't sure whether this last was good or bad news. Still, wasn't she an optimist at heart? She must fill the goddess in on pertinent facts.

— People like me this way, though. Funny thing, some of the women envy me but don't seem to want me for a good friend.

    The notion caused her suddenly to feel sad.

— Ah, women know at their core when one of them has rejected the true path of her earth nature. They observe how such a one sets up her own fortifications to defend what she has shaped, whether it be the ongoing child or the extended maiden or the woman of the world. It is a manipulation. It is unnatural. Ah, woman, it insults the great goddesses!

— I am no child, and I am certainly able to discuss politics and ideas one hears in the Agora around the Stoa of Zeus.

    Demeter nodded thoughtfully.

— Yes. What I realize is that you are the woman who is coming. Alas, how much is yet to be distilled from the deep labyrinth of feminine mind! Kore, who is my daughter, bridges two worlds—the one below and the one at hand. You see, she is the guide you must seek at all cost.

    Rather than hope, what the woman seemed to be staring at was the collapse of familiar walls. As she spoke, she glimpsed her predicament.

— You are telling me that I'm in the company of the wrong maiden.

— At last you see the problem. Your maiden-in-residence has no access to the real threshold of what can come. *Only Kore herself can be the Kore!* Honor her.

— I don't know where to start, what to do.

— First, give up the mask of the maiden. It served for a time like an attractive and useful cloak. It is no longer a living place for you.

    The woman felt weak in the knees as though they might give way. Oh, why had she wandered in the fields and stepped over the boundary of Demeter's own sacred field of grain? She turned to the goddess.

— Farewell, Lady Demeter. I shall remember you with an offering.

    Demeter regarded the Athenian woman steadily and smiled, but it was a smile tinged with sadness.

PART VII

The God Pan

Pan—an Introduction

No Greek god received such bad press at the beginning of the Christian era as did Pan. It is a sad fact that he came to be confused with the devil himself, and yet it was to "the great god Pan" that Socrates prayed on the banks of the Ilissus that he should be made pure in his soul and should come to regard wisdom itself as the true wealth. The figure the god evokes is that of a rustic man with horns and legs of a goat, possessing a face that gazes boldly at the human scene, making accommodation to neither accepted manners nor to the current scheme of things. Above all, he is candid and without compromise as he defends life's immediate satisfactions. Truth itself becomes as nature dictates; time and again in myth, Pan appears with the summons of unaccountable life energy.

Among Pan's gifts is the shepherd's song that he plays on his flutelike syrinx, the song that cradles bountiful nature, lending it its poignant voice. In the grotto in the evening, he provides for the dance with the nymphs, a collaboration with feminine nature that brings both order and delight. True, the madness of noontide, feared and attributed to the dark side of Pan, was conscientiously guarded against by the Greeks. Not the least of Pan's gifts is a terse wisdom, such as was given to both Psyche and to Io on their journeys.

As one muses on the god of the pastures, the question arises, how does Pan appear within the contemporary psyche? Ours is a culture now distant from the early Christian age's rejection of the god. What archetypal movement in everyday reality carries the voice of Pan, that voice so possessed with zest and fresh energy? He is the outsider, it seems. His spontaneous responses to a given situation tend to be disregarded, although they are familiar as old knowledge. As his name bears witness, *pan* meaning "all," he is present everywhere and all the time. Pan abides in the ground of natural impulses and unstudied responses. In contrast to the tired worker side of one, he opposes weariness and boredom boldly. His can be a deaf ear to assignment, to duty, to task, while he shows the tendency to play his own tune lustily. He may appear initially to the modern person as comic, as the clown, and as the clever fellow with the bag of tricks. In this manner, he is winsome and his humor welcomed as a relief from an overdemanding life. Still, it should not be forgotten that he is ultimately the reliable shepherd, whose contract lies between the fresh emergence of life and abundant, yet lawful, nature.

Pan seeks existence within a dense, sensuous texture of experience in present time. As a result, there may be disregard of the recognized goals of the individual. Rather, the goals that belong to nature, to whose authority and structures he bows, matter most to him. Jung's illuminating writings on the role of the shadow in the struggles of the psyche bear the inimitable hoofprints of Pan, surely. As Pan picks up his flute of reeds, reminiscent of the beloved nymph Syrinx, he begins to play. One perceives within the rise and fall of the captivating air the solitary pastoral voice as dance is again restored to human existence. Bestowing his riches, the god Pan blesses the human scene.

The Birth of Pan

As the shepherd climbed the rocky slope of Mt. Kyllene, he followed the rough path that the goats had maintained for generations beyond recall. His was the stride of a lithe, young god as he went with a voluminous wool cloak thrown back over his shoulders. The broad three-cornered hat he wore barely managed to conceal the flashing eyes that swept the mountain slope and penetrated the shady vale beyond. Now, sighting water ahead, the sheep and goats scrambled to reach the stream bank in the shady vale and to slake their thirst. The fact that he, Hermes, was herdsman of King Dryops' flocks struck him as no more than a god's necessary digression in the human world, and the thought produced a wry smile. Arriving at the stream bank deeply shaded by willow trees that dipped their branches here and there into the stream, he let his hand rest on the rump of the large ram. At once the ram butted away two ewes from his chosen drinking spot until the shepherd's rod caused him to relinquish his place to Hermes himself. Thirst satisfied, the goats, who had been the first arrivals, were choosing their resting places. Shortly the entire herd would take its siesta.

Hermes sat on the large boulder at the water's edge, the rod loosely held as he gave himself to the dense quiet that had settled over the bank, broken only by the rhythmic plunging of water over stones. At the same time, the shepherd god was watchful. A rustling in the heavy brush on the far bank was followed by a movement which, like a trembling, passed over the green thicket. As he gazed with full attention, the low branches parted, and a maiden emerged. Meeting the intense glance of the shepherd, her eyes registered fear until she calmed herself and quietly waited, drawing on some habitual confidence. Now Hermes was neither shy nor known to squander time needlessly. Besides, it was clear to him that not only was the maiden lovely but that a companion was a welcome sight in his solitary shepherd's life.

— Greetings, maiden!

— Greetings, shepherd. Who would you be? The flocks here are feeding on my father's land.

— Your father's land, you say. Would your father by chance be King Dryops?

    The very idea of the possible connection startled him.

— I am indeed King Dryops' daughter. Stranger, you are a trespasser here, I fear.

    Now this accusation appeared more agreeable than it was troubling to Hermes. Still, he felt a strong desire to ease her concern for the royal rights in the situation. When he spoke, both his voice and his manner took on a relaxed and pleasing manner, such as is known to encourage friendship.

— Actually, I am quite skilled in crossing boundaries, even very significant ones, as a matter of record. Among friends, I am called *guide of the road.*

    She shook her head as if with some regret.

— Still, a person ought to respect all boundary markers. We are taught especially to honor the boundary between a god's sanctuary and ordinary ground. And then, of course, one must respect the boundary between what is one's own and what belongs to one's neighbor. There are stone pillars that clearly mark my father's land. Surely you must have noticed them?

    He nodded, amplifying her description.

— Stone pillars you mean. They are the herms—pillars with the bearded head of Hermes atop them.

    She pressed him more closely.

— Yes. So when you saw the two herms marking the boundary, what did you think, shepherd?

    He looked at her in his leisurely way before smiling in brief reply.

— Studying the head, I found it rather a poor resemblance. But come, maiden, tell me your name and where your home is.

    As his interest focused upon herself in particular, unaccountably she sighed and answered eagerly.

— I am Dryope, and I live here in Arcadia at the foot of Mt. Kyllene, whose hidden paths I delight in. Oh, I do love to ramble on the many paths!

    She concluded with a shy little laugh.

— Ah, you are a rambler. It gives me pleasure to hear this, for you see, I am especially drawn to one who rambles or who has lost her itinerary, for that matter. Dryope, will you cross the creek to this bank? You appear to be very nimble, and there are stepping stones for crossing, I notice. Shepherding is dear to me, but it has its drawbacks, one of them being prolonged solitude. The truth is that your companionship would please me a great deal.

The eyes of the maiden grew large as she soberly considered the shepherd's invitation. Now a slow small smile appeared on her face before she stepped forward and took a small leap to a stone that lifted above the stream. Leaping from stone to stone lightly, she reached the other bank where the handsome shepherd extended his strong arm to assist her. At once she confessed to him, trembling as she did so,

— Never have I crossed the stream to this side before!

— Being the respecter of boundaries, I expect. There is something I meant to mention, a truth actually. Here it is: only afterward is a person aware of having crossed a significant boundary!

She smiled as though this were excellent news, her eyes taking in his beautiful form, the radiant, speaking face, and above all, his voice. A glance assured him that the entire herd was resting peacefully now, and he turned back to Dryope. Of all the routes to take, apparently curiosity seemed to her the most dependable. She questioned him.

— You are a stranger in these parts, shepherd.

— Rarely seen, I'd say, but hardly a stranger. Would you believe that I was born high on this very mountain in Kyllene's deep cave?

— You are from Kyllene? But the mountain is wild and lacks human habitations. What is born on these slopes is wild, surely.

— What I am remains to be seen, or is it that you utter an omen of what is to come, maiden?

She shook her head mutely. Restless, a goat called out. She shivered involuntarily and spoke.

— There is some excitement in the air. Do you feel it?

— Ah, yes. It is expectation, I think. Even now we turn toward what is arriving for the first time!

— There is no one about, shepherd, and no one is expected. Just look around us.

— But do the eyes take account of the whole picture? I think not. Great Zeus is lord of the Fates, and yet not even Zeus dares interfere with the working of the thread in the hands of those ladies, surely.

— The thread of destiny!

  Her murmured words were heavy with misgivings. Dryope, captive of some exquisite excitement in her companion's presence, felt a shadow pass over her spirit, nevertheless, with these words.

  Some hours passed in which their exchange grew in its satisfaction as love began to forge its invisible, luminous pathways. When the sun was low in the western sky, they arose, and smiling, he took her hand into his as they went toward the path that led up the mountain. Before them went the flocks. It was dusk when they reached the deep grotto. Leading his companion off the path, the shepherd drew the maiden to himself while tenderness in its rich text surrounded them. The eyes of Hermes appeared to gaze down a far, shining corridor as he did so. He spoke now in a low voice.

— Dryope, I am Hermes. It is best that you know, you see. You must not
  fear me. Know that I am close to the human individual and am known
  to be especially good in crisis.

  Her hand flew to her mouth as she drew apart, a look of astonishment and disbelief on her face.

— But I thought you were the stranger, the shepherd!
— That too, to be sure. Accept, Dryope, the shepherd who loves you and
  who desires your companionship!

  The passion in his voice shook her as his face held some radiant, yet inscrutable text that summoned her. He was indeed her beloved. Her anxious look faded as a slow smile transformed her face, and she extended both hands to the god. Now he drew her into the shelter of the rock grotto. Within the ancient grotto they remained until the next day dawned, when Dryope returned home, slipping into her own chamber in the royal house of Dryops.

  The seasons passed slowly for Dryope, the beloved of Olympian Hermes. Her pregnancy was a fact not easy in its demands upon her, and her moods alternated between joyous expectation and anguish. Most of the days, she kept to her own chamber or to solitary walks before dusk. The baby grew in her womb but was exceeded in weight by the cloud of the unknown that hovered over her spirit increasingly. Some early mornings she would climb Kyllene's slope to the very grotto of the love that had changed her life, there to sit before the low entrance and recall the tender encounter with her radiant shepherd lover. Simultaneously she was assailed by joy and grief, which like two great rivers had plunged from some unseen height into what had been her familiar, well-managed life. Oh never had she beheld such a face as his when he turned his gaze upon her at the mouth of the grotto! Nor did her maiden heart ever dream of such a companion as this one who called himself Hermes. At that moment, her heart chose him without a doubt. Had she not received his answering embrace unconditionally? Curiously, he had spoken of the act of the Fates, which not even Zeus would interfere with. Alone she remained for some time with her thoughts until there came the first contraction of her womb, and the recognition of it caused her to tremble for the future.

Old in the echoing silence of the past, untroubled by present demands generated in the kingdom of King Dryops, the grotto itself received Dryope into its comforting dimness. Briefly Dryope thought of Crete's deep cave, which the mother goddess Rhea found on her own when she was ready to deliver her child Zeus. And had not Goddess Leto been received into the cave of arched seawater made ready for the birth of Apollo? *But I'm no goddess*, she thought. *I am only Dryope.* She gazed about herself with sudden hope for some small sign of Hermes, but the primordial darkness revealed no companion, none at all. She was alone beyond measure. Tears began to flow down her cheeks, for the grief of abandonment was more formidable than the pains of labor.

The hours passed, and there came a mighty rush within her, and the child was born. At once she reached for her baby, feeling the wondrous warmth and lively movement of her treasure in the dark core of Kyllene. Laughter spilled from her in the sheer joy of the wondrous happening. As she was murmuring fond words to the babe at her bosom, a shaft of pale light penetrated a crack in the ceiling of the grotto, falling upon the baby. In that moment, she beheld her child. A high cry of shock and disbelief came from her as she stared at her son, for he was hairy, there were horns on his head, and he possessed the cloven hooves of a goat! Stricken and trembling, with intermittent sobs, she seized her shawl, wrapped it like a blanket about the baby, and quickly laid him on a bed shaped of dried grasses on the rock floor. With one anguished last look upon the child and a prayer, she turned and left the grotto, fleeing down the mountain to her home once again.

Within the descending dusk, a lone traveler wearing a voluminous woolen cloak stood by the side of the road. A vast stillness appeared to claim him, such as is known at the core of deep waiting. Now he lifted his head as though hearkening to some personal summons, and he nodded. Turning toward the mountain, he was gone.

Kyllene's narrow path was familiar as he strode the steep way in the darkness buffeted by a cold wind. When he came upon the high rock grotto, he stopped. An unmistakable small cry came from the grotto. Throwing back his cloak at once, he plunged into the darkness. All about where the child lay was a muted light, and Hermes knelt at the side of the newborn infant. His was the wisdom of good timing. With wonder, he regarded his son. From the horned head, the wide-spaced dark eyes gazed back at him steadily from a face that appeared human. Still, he saw with astonishment that the small sturdy body terminated in a pair of cloven-hoofed goat feet! In delight, the shepherd god smiled and spoke gently.

— Look here, little one, I am your father. Best take that into account. Ah, there is nothing to fear, little one.

He did not inquire of the child's mother but instead shook his head sadly, envisioning the maiden's flight. The baby was examining his father with a sharp, even critical, eye as he continued to speak.

— Let me tell you how it is. I cross the boundaries easily between Olympus, earth, and the underworld, but you, my son, have crossed two realms within your own being, the realm of the pastoral animals and the realm of the manlike gods! What a marvel you present, an original one I must say.

The baby grinned broadly at this and kicked his legs in a lively manner. Hermes took an animal skin from the folds of his cloak and held it up.

— I happen to have brought along the skin of a large hare, which I shall wrap you in. It will keep you snug and warm, you see. There. How's that?

The babe looked content swaddled in the hare skin, the fur side turned inside against his own skin. Now he laughed in glee, satisfied that having a mountain shepherd for a father brought its advantages. Tucked neatly into the crook of the god's arm, he left the grotto and entered the light of the new day. With long strides, Hermes made his way toward Mt. Olympus, and the rhythm of this effortless travel pleased the baby. A single thought occupied the mind of Hermes: "It is imperative that my goatlike son be introduced immediately to the company of the gods!" After some time, they reached the gates of Olympus. Beside the great gates stood the figures of the three Hours, goddesses of the seasons. Recognition was immediate between Hermes and the goddesses, whom he addressed.

— Greetings, Dike, Eunomia, and Eirene! Judging from your serene countenances, I should say that all is in order.

— Greetings, Hermes, and welcome. As for order, are we not goddesses of order in the natural realm?

— Indeed so.

Hermes looked reflective and drew his brow into a frown. Dike stepped forward, a concerned look on her face.

— Is something out of order?

— Ah, I am afraid so.

Suddenly the god was solemn with regret. He sought to explain.

— In the human world, something of great beauty emerged only to collapse soon after.

Now he threw back the cloak that covered one arm to reveal what he carried.

— Here is the newborn child as proof of my report.

Now the child gazed with lively interest at each of the three lovely female faces that bent over him before he burst into laughter as if a fine joke had just been told. The goddesses were simultaneously amazed and enchanted by the unusual baby. Eunomia asked,

— Ah, Hermes, who would his mother be?

— Dryope, daughter of the Arcadian king Dryops, is the lad's mother. Sadly, she has fled in terror at the sight of her extraordinary child.

Pity struck the Hours, as much, it appeared, for the mother as for her child. One of them addressed the baby.

— Poor little dear! Now you have only Hermes to care for you.

Hermes protested.

— He's not so bad off, actually.

— But he shall surely miss his mother, even so.

— Yes, what you say is true, Eunomia. Still, this child is a god unlike any other we have ever known. Already in his eyes I have read the text of a mind pure and strong as a spring current and as fiercely unarguable as the goat that leads the herd. I believe that he shall come to stand alone in the high pastures, and he will shelter in the mountain grottoes. The nymphs of the mountain will seek out his company, and perhaps they will bind the wound of his abandonment by his mother.

The three goddesses of the gates of Olympus nodded, solemnly receiving the prophetic words of the god of the road. Now they smiled reassuringly upon the youngest god and proceeded to open the great gate. Hermes nodded his thanks, and the two passed through. At once, unaided, the child raised himself into an erect sitting position on his father's arm and peered straight ahead under his hairy eyebrows, his curiosity growing by the moment as they approached the dwelling place of the gods. It happened that the eleven Olympians were lingering at the feast table when the two travelers arrived. When he laid eyes on this luminous scene, the baby threw up his hands and gave an ecstatic cry while the furry hide of the hare fell to the ground. As if in a single movement, the heads of all the gods turned toward the child with murmurs of "Hermes is here!" and "Whose child can this be?" Hermes took the initiative.

— Greetings, fellow Olympians! Will you forgive my tardiness? An extraordinary event has taken place on earth of which I am at the very least the messenger. I have brought you the evidence in this treasured child.

Zeus, who had been quietly assessing the situation, addressed Hermes.

— Where did this happen, Hermes?

— Where nature goes in careless abandon on Mt. Kyllene in Arcadia, my lord.

Zeus's eyes widened with this information.

— Then you know this mountain well, do you not? Mt. Kyllene was the place of your own birth. You have some role, I dare say, in this birth that I presume you are about to explain to us?

— Ah, but how, Father, is one to explain love? The truth is that love overtook me in the presence of the maiden Dryope, daughter of the Arcadian king.

Hermes sighed, more with longing than with regret. Understandably, Zeus sought a fuller account.

— Wait. Were you not the herdsman for King Dryops? Well, you hardly limited yourself to shepherding, it appears.

Zeus bent his head toward the child, and his face took on a tender look. A long moment passed before he spoke, and his voice was as remote from his thunder as ever it could be.

— I assume, then, that this child is your own son, Hermes.

— Yes, Father. Allow me to explain what I am convinced took place in the grotto. When Dryope looked upon the child she bore and observed the horns and the cloven feet, she was terrified. She must have swaddled the child at once, wrapping him in one of her garments warmly, then improvising a bed for him before she fled.

The sadness of the truth assaulted Hermes, and he fell silent. Meanwhile Goddess Demeter rose to her feet and came to face Zeus and Hermes. At the same time, she gazed with affection upon the confident child who continued to regard the gods with an attitude of lively curiosity alternating with patience. Demeter spoke, and her low, rarely heard voice was musical.

— Alas, can it be an easy thing to mother the god world? Hermes, perhaps you expect too much of the human individual.

— I am humbled by your words, Demeter.

Now the rest of the gods arose from the table and gathered around Hermes and the child. Getting a close look at the child, each one revealed a measure of what could only have been delight. As for the child, seated on the throne of his father's arm, he memorized each face, assessing it with his frank and sober intelligence. Now the gods spoke among themselves. Zeus nodded and, clearing his throat, voiced their decision.

— This child of Hermes and Dryope shall henceforth be called *Pan*, for he shall be the god of *all!*

Hermes lowered his face to his son's.

— Did you hear that, lad of mine? You are Pan!

Now Pan, the All child, continued to gaze at the august company, much as one might who is sorting out distant relatives for the first time. Without a doubt, he took the bestowing of the name as an acknowledgment clearly due him. Pan nodded his head slightly, and he grinned.

He came upon her on the stony path at the foot of Kyllene at the spot where the mass of the mountain cast a deep shadow. Her name was being called as from some distance.

— Dryope! Dear Dryope! Where are you?

— I am here beside the great oak tree!

Scarcely had she answered when Hermes himself came to her side. He gazed at her with love, a love mixed with pain.

— Dryope, what have you done?

Slowly she raised her eyes, wide with loss, and looked full into his face.

— The child—the child of our love was not human! Oh, look at me, Hermes. You see that I am only human, a maiden of Arcadia! Seeing him, I was filled with fear, and when I had seen to his comfort as best I could, I fled.

Hermes' spirit was heavy. His shoulders sank perceptibly as if a new weight had descended upon them. Once again he engaged Dryope with a tender look.

— My dear, our child is extraordinary. There is no denying it. But he is no monster, I assure you. He is called Pan. Already I have shown him to the Olympian gods, who not only delighted in him but gave him this auspicious name.

— Pan you say. Why, that is the All . . . It causes me to tremble, this time in awe. Oh, do tell me, Hermes, is he cared for? I've been beside myself with worry.

— There are mountain nymphs who have undertaken his care in a high grotto. Pan feels very much at home, it is reported.

Dryope sighed in vast relief, unburdened of her greatest concern. At the same time, her voice held a note of despair when she spoke, addressing herself.

— How could I bear having a half-goat child within my very own household?

— Ah, but Pan is not so easily categorized, you see. It is a mistake if looking at him one sees only a goat, Dryope. At the same time, can you ask of a god, "What are you?" I think not. The divine substance resists being measured or filed away in a crib for future viewing.

— Oh, what is a mere human parent to do?

— Meet the god in your life and you will benefit from his special qualities. Pan, I believe, is to be the *meeting place!*

— What sort of meeting place do you mean? Much depends on your answer, Hermes.

— Pan is the meeting place of the god world and nature.

— Who can describe the god world, Hermes? No one at all. So what is nature?

— It lies beneath all human conspiracy to create reality, whether the effort is commendable or not. Nature is reality, persistent, indisputable. Even so, for the human individual, it can be a difficult place to encounter at times.

— That explains, doesn't it, why when I first beheld my baby, I was seized by fright. Only fear allowed me to abandon him on a bed of grasses in the grotto, wrapped in my cloak!

Her head was lowered in the grief of her memory. Hermes took her into his arms, comforting her.

— Leave your despair and grief now, Dryope. You did what any woman might have done. What came over you, you see, was the fear of that place of the *intersection*. You thought you fled from a wild creature, judging that your own progeny failed to measure up to the human level. But no, my dear, what you fled from was the epiphany of a god in the natural world, an arrival that has burst upon the world like joyous laughter.

— Your words are strange to my ears. How can I comprehend them?

— Look at it this way: Pan is the delighted descent of the gods to earth's pastures. In order to cope with the rocky, uneven paths, he needs the cloven hooves of a goat to give him a firm footing. Dryope, weep no more. It is not a time for sorrow. It is time for gratitude, I tell you.

Dryope arose to her feet, and assuming her graceful, erect stature, she began to walk now as one in reverie.

— How shortsighted I was to think that one look should decide the entire course of my life! True, it was an eager look desperate to justify pregnancy, labor, and dream. Is it true that I might have the grace of a second chance?

Slowly he nodded.

— An extraordinary birth does not reveal its nature at once, it seems. I believe that what is on its way to you is the gift of the second look, dear Dryope.

A slow smile transformed her face, and her beauty took on a radiance. Dusk had fallen over the shadowy slope behind them as Hermes took fond leave of Dryope.

In the descending dusk, a lone cloaked traveler stood at the side of the road. He was claimed by a vast stillness, such as is found at the core of true waiting. At last he lifted his head as though hearkening to some private summons, and he nodded. Then he was gone, striding off the road toward a mountain path.

Meeting with Io

Although it wears a mask of elemental simplicity, human encounter with the god of nature Pan is far from simple, for a troubling complexity is present in seeking a life that is not only faithful to nature but workable as well. After a very long trek, Io, the cow maiden—her history in tow as the young woman priestess from Argos who is loved by Zeus—reaches the isolated mountain sanctuary known as Dodona. Pausing at the boundary, she gazes toward the sacred oak tree that gives forth the oracle of Zeus, and is surprised when a shepherd approaches her. In this manner began the encounter with the god Pan.

As the sun rose toward its zenith over the Dodona sanctuary of Zeus and Dione, the cow maiden gazed down from the rocky hill. The day's heat was oppressive so that rivulets of sweat furrowed her handsome white hide. Still she remained motionless and lost in thought, not seeking the shelter of a tree. Under the pall of heat, the countryside lay empty of animals and human residents. Exposed upon the rocks, she squinted, scanning the sky to verify that the dazzling orb of the sun stood directly overhead, and she murmured aloud.

— This is the fateful hour of noontide!

She was startled to hear a husky voice in reply.

— Aren't you afraid to be abroad at this time, cow maiden?

Io turned to locate the source of the voice. There stood near her a short somewhat shaggy man with a pointed chin and beard, whose bright, twinkling eyes were regarding her with open curiosity. He wore a rough shepherd's cloak and carried a herdsman's crook. The extraordinary impression he made caused her to gasp audibly.

— Greetings, shepherd. Noontide is the least among my fears, as a matter of fact. And why are you abroad at this hour when every living creature seeks shelter from the heat, or else sleeps?

— Oh well, this is my hour. To be sure it's mine.

This maiden must be a traveler from afar to be ignorant of what is obvious, he reflected.

She was peering more closely at him.

— It is the hour of shepherds, where could your flock be?

— My flock, oh, my flock! She is asking about my flock. Ha-ha!

He was thoroughly amused, obviously. She persisted.

— Well, could you have lost it?

— Ah me, I'm forever losing some sheep or other and having to set out in search. But the goats, no. No goat goes and gets himself lost. He's too smart for that. Actually, I am something of an old goat myself, the Greeks will tell you.

Thinking about goats had visibly cheered him.

— Aren't you Greek as well?

— I am. That I am. But the Greeks have put me out to pasture, you see. They forget about me out here on the distant pasture, and when someone comes upon me suddenlike, why, he panics. They say I'm scary, maiden.

The last observation was delivered with disdain. Io, feeling some sympathy for the shepherd, spoke gently.

— You are a little scary, shepherd. I mean it's rather a matter of not being used to . . . to somebody like you, I'd say.

His voice was somewhat indignant.

— Why, there's nobody like me, nobody at all, maiden! That's a fact.

He turned his keen gaze upon her.

— I'd say that you are a maiden who has seen many far pastures.

— Alas, it is true! But how did you know this?

He smiled broadly now, and his teeth were even and gleaming.

— I could tell right off. Most maidens carry with them the look of what they've been doing and what they are about to do. But not you. In your eyes, I see at once wide pastures in far places.

Io shook her head slowly, perplexed and intimidated by some unseen prospect.

— I didn't know.

The shepherd, drawn to the maiden, sought to comfort her.

— You and I are two of a kind, you see. There's something that ties us together, Io!

With the speaking of her name, she grew pale, and her eyes widened.

— Oh! How can you possibly know my name or even that I am really a maiden and not a heifer?

A silence fell between them as her gaze held and she reflected. She spoke slowly now.

— The fateful hour of noontide is yours you said. I should have known. Why, the hour of noon belongs to the god Pan, and it is dangerous. You are Pan, god of the flocks!

Even as she concluded, she bowed and made the sacred gesture. He nodded in an acknowledgment that seemed oddly tinged with disappointment at being found out.

— You may call me Pan if you like.

Reaching into the depths of his shaggy cloak, he drew out a small instrument made of reeds joined together. Lifting it to his lips almost greedily, he began to play a little tune that sounded very much like a chorus of droning grass creatures. Her eyes were still large as she watched him closely. She was in awe.

— What do other folks call you, may I ask?

— They don't stick around the way you do. Now that's a fact.

For some reason, this caused her to giggle.

— Others are perhaps not foolish like me.

He smiled, accepting her comment as something of banter.

— You do have a thing for pastures, I'll say. Look, Io, you were waiting for Pan in his hour, and you can't deny it.

A certain fear registered on her face

— Alas, noontide is the hour of Pan's madness!

— Whoever passed the notion about refused to meet me but ran away instead!

He looked plainly annoyed.

— Are you suggesting, Lord Pan, that you do not cause madness?

— From the *outside*, my gift might look like madness, but my gift is not an outside thing.

— Is your gift, as you call it, a happening of some sort? Oh, I am ever so tired of happenings on my journey!

— It tickles me when you say my name. It's very nice indeed.

When he smiled, she saw that his wide-spaced eyes were rather like a goat's.

He was continuing.

— About happenings, sweet maiden, since you asked. Pan is nothing without *happenings*, nothing at all. I can tell you've had a hard time of it, but don't run away from happenings. If you do, you'll be living half dead. You'll be all dried up and far away even though your body is right here at hand.

Now happenings were something she knew about.

— The trouble with a happy happening is that it stays on and on in your mind. I am forever looking back at it and wishing that it weren't absent now!

Pan frowned and stroked his small beard.

— You are trying to prop up an old happening, and you really can't. Instead, I'd advise you to get ready for the new happening.

Into Io's eyes rushed some bright stream of excitement.

— Oh! When will the new happening take place?

— At its own right moment. When it's ready, of course. Then the happening will be a *now* thing, and you won't have to wait around.

At this moment, the hidden text that lay deep within her heart stirred like water rising in the well. It was the time for telling.

— Great shepherd, I must tell you what happened in Argos in the far meadow. It was there that I knew my great love, for the cloud lover came to me like Zeus himself! So joyous a happening it was. How can it be dead or else forgotten? Does it belong only to what is past?

— Io, Io, the love of Zeus is not fenced in by past, present, or future, I tell you! It is like the eternal, leaping over every fence, even those of memories and complaints. It is here. It is now. There now, you've heard my pasture knowledge.

Although she took Pan's words in eagerly, she did not understand why it was that love still seemed lost to her. She must not miss what he was saying, though.

— Love when it comes from the gods is hardly a come-and-go happening. Do you know what you've gone and done to this passion from the gods?

She shook her head numbly.

— Why, you've up and decided that it was an *experience*!

— What's wrong with that? It truly was a tremendous experience.

— But don't you see, Io? You might be insulting the happening. A "tremendous experience" is already past and done with and is now hemmed in with sentimental thoughts. Maybe you even drape banners over it and worship it—a mere experience!

A light came into her eyes, and she smiled.

— I am beginning to see how it is. Experience comes and goes. It dies. But this great love that I know is different somehow.

He looked at her, encouraged.

— Still, it is true that this love you have with Zeus is full of happening. When you step into the happening, you meet the one who is waiting for you, and nothing in yourself turns aside. Mysteriously, in that moment, you greet the whole living world!

— You speak as one who knows about love.

He nodded as though encouraging a slow child.

— Now, you best get out of the sun, or else you could faint.

Saying this, he led Io, who was beginning to feel a little dizzy, toward the shade of a spreading oak tree. Its low branches brushed her back and shoulders soothingly. Pan chose a stump to sit on, and she sat on a boulder. She would tell him more about herself, so long had all this knowledge been locked away.

— Before the splendid happening in the far meadow, I was a priestess of Goddess Hera at her great temple at Argos.

— Don't I know?

— How could you know?

— When you ventured to the far meadow all alone, why, I was there. Yes, I observed you walking from the direction of Hera's temple. Why, this maiden has to be the priestess, I thought to myself. It is written all over her.

Io bristled at this description and lifted her chin as she sought an explanation.

— What do you mean, Pan?

He continued as if not interrupted.

— Not one step off the path to the right or to the left, and you looking all shut up like a bean pod. Still, you did remind me a little of Hera as a young queen.

He grinned at his memories, pleased with them, doubtlessly. She burst out, having heard enough.

— Well, little did I imagine!

Pan began to laugh, rocking back and forth with each peal. That she was annoyed was clear as she sat stiffly erect.

— Why are you laughing at me? It is rude to laugh.

— I remembered watching you from behind a tree when I had a strong desire to holler out and startle you just to get you off the path with me for once. Zeus shouldn't get all the luck.

    Again he laughed.

— Then why didn't you holler? Surely you are not one who restrains himself!

— True, true, Io. But something occurred. *I saw the cloud.* That stopped me, you see.

— Wait. You could not have known that a mere cloud over the meadow was anything out of the ordinary.

— Couldn't I? I knew all right. Why, I detected the far footsteps of thunder that you didn't hear, and I said to myself, "Better bow out. That's Zeus coming here, or I'm a used-up goat!"

    As if the thunderbolt had stunned them, the two fell silent. After a while, Io broke the silence.

— To listen to you, a person could believe that only yourself and Zeus bring the important happenings to a woman. But there are others, shepherd. When I was very young and came to the house of Hera, a happening occurred. I had been a favored child made comfortable by my parents, but when the goddess received me into her sanctuary, she taught me to serve the altar. Then, you see, I became no longer child of my parents. There was a happening, I tell you. Never was I the same as I was before.

— Well, I'll be a two-tailed goat! What with all that order and calm and cowlike rhythm that's in Hera's territory, I'd never have guessed that she could produce a happening like that.

— What Lady Hera gave me was as powerful in its way as the fiery love of Zeus!

    Tears filled her eyes, whether of joy or of sorrow was not clear.

— If that is so, cow maiden, all this could account for your spirit being heavy. You are trying to prop up two old happenings—the romance with Zeus and being Hera's priestess!

    She shook her head decisively.

— Not any longer. Now I realize it can't be done. Being a priestess is not like ordinary happenings that come about and then fade away. I am thinking of what you said of underworld love, that it may pass into a new happening. Perhaps it can happen with Hera's priestess too. I do wonder.

— Shall I impart a secret I know?

There was a sly look on Pan's face, his bright eyes upon her. She nodded.

— I myself have a certain power over the new happening, causing it to come about. Consider, Io, where do you think Pan is? Am I only to be found among the sheep and the goats?

— All the tales say that Pan is found in wild and remote places in the moment you least expect to come upon him.

— Yes, but there is more, you see. I am found wherever the human individual dwells deeply under his animal skin! At the core of what pulses, desires, and goes forward to claim its own, there I am found. And when the whole of you dances with joy, I am there.

Folks say that I am wild, bah! What do they know of chaste and ecstatic wildness!

They are so busy thinking that they themselves are *tame* that they lock up the animal. When they do, there's nothing left for me, nothing at all.

Being in the very midst of Pan's secret caused her to feel like a swimmer engulfed by the sea. Her question was feeble.

— People lock up the animal, you say?

— That's right. A person has the beast way down underneath. Sure a person shows himself all decked out in high goals and noble sentiments like one of those speakers before the court of the Areopagus, holding forth on the rock of Athens with not a sign of the animals' being present.

An alarming image filled her mind.

— At the same time, Lord Pan, a good citizen can ill afford to give way to being fierce or greedy, can he?

— Hear me, Io. You can't be wholly alive unless the fierceness is there at the core. But you're wrong about the beast being greedy. Only people are greedy. An animal knows what is *wanted,* that's all. Does he ever ask for heaven and earth? No. Just for a little bit of earth he needs, something that satisfies him.

— It seems that an animal never compromises, though.

— That's right. That's the saving thing about the animal. He will never be other than what he is. That's his truth. It's the animal inside that keeps a person from losing his real self.

A strong breeze had come up and was causing the bending and swaying of the oak branches. Io grew quiet, reflecting on Pan's strange words. She found herself studying the rugged, sturdy god figure whose words had profoundly affected her. She smiled now as she spoke simply.

— I believe that I see that shining beast alive in you, Lord of the
pasture!

> He nodded with a small smile.

— It tramps about freely, be forewarned. Its blood flows with the vibrant
memory of the wild place. And best remember that it is the wild place
alone that *gentles* the beast.

— As the far pastures have gentled you, Pan.

> He read in her eyes some further perception, and he waited for

it.

— I perceive that both exuberance and delight are stored up in you like
water in an underground spring! If only this spring were ever near me,
it might vanquish what threatens me . . .

— Ah well, I was beginning to doubt whether you would ever really see
me, but you have opened your eyes, Io. Never forget this: it is because
of me that you are durable, and maybe even triumphant. However hard
things get, I scramble up to the highest rock on the mountain face so
I can gaze out freely. Pan is on top!

— How I hope I remember this . . . Still, Lord Pan, I glimpse in you a
certain sorrow. One who knows sorrow can hear its echo in the hollow
place of another.

> His face grew somber, his brow furrowed for a time.

— So you have seen that. It is a sorrow that hovers over the locked-up
beast in a person.

> Did you never hear Pan's mournful cry in Argos's far pasture?

> She was on her feet now, and for a long moment, Pan thought that
he glimpsed a future queen as their visit grew to a close. It was the time of
conclusion, and she spoke.

— Do I not go on this journey under the cow's skin? When Pan is in
sorrow, Io is made sad. Wait! It shall not be said that Io the Argive
maiden encountered Pan in far Dodona and failed to honor him. An
offering is needed, an offering which shall be like a mirror of the heart
that gazes upon Pan . . . But what shall it be? I've neither fruit nor grain
to give, no barley cake to be had . . .

> She bent down searching the ground until she found a thin sharp
stone with a knifelike edge. Picking up the stone, she at once bowed her
head low as she began to work the stone over a lock of her thick hair.
Meanwhile, Pan began to play his syrinx, the pipes creating in their hollow
throats a slow, lyrical cry of human longing. The music, poignant and sweet,
caused Io to tremble as she stood with the lock of her hair cut free. When

the music ended, she approached the god presenting him the lock of her hair, bowing as she did so. His sharp black eyes regarded her steadily as he received the offering.

— The offering of the lock of your hair is for me and not for Zeus?

— It is for you, Lord Pan. Was it not you who drew me in the first place to the far meadow above the temple of Argos? It is you, surely, who called forth the sleeping animal within me, stirring the shining delight long before Zeus came upon me in that awesome pasture. Indeed, how could I have taken on the white heifer prepared for me by the gods had not the wild world of Pan already found a place in me?

He nodded gravely.

— Ah, maiden, my eyes have witnessed Hera herself rambling in the tall grasses as a young cow, her hair curling upon her forehead. Nor would she be a great goddess without her invisible cow self, I believe. Never forget, Io, we have a deep kinship, you and I. Go well with my blessing!

He smiled, tucking the lock of her hair into the folds of his cloak where it rested against the syrinx, its voice now silent. Leaving the oak tree, he disappeared over the hilltop.

Daphne and the God Pan

      In north central Greece in age-old Thessaly, there dwelled a nymph who frequented the Vale of Tempe and was daughter of the river god Peneus. Daphne was a delight to behold as she played with her sisters on the wooded bank of the river, whose waters reflected the early morning sunlight like drifting ribbons of gold. She was taller than her companions, her lithe body tanned by the sun, and her long brown hair rippled on her shoulders. As the maidens moved to engage once again in the circle dance, hands on nearest shoulders, their joyous laughter would fill the air. When the dance ended, Daphne went apart, making her way alone along the path of the riverbank and moving with the grace of a shy doe until the green darkness of the woods received her. As she rounded the turn of the path, she came upon a rock cave. At the low entrance, a figure stood waiting who was short in stature and obviously made rugged by an outdoor life. A small pointed beard distinguished his face above the muscular torso and powerful legs while his feet—oh, surely this was an illusion—were cloven much like the feet of a goat! Her eyes were suddenly wide with fright, and her body tensed for flight when, regarding her, the man's eyes softened, and he spoke. His voice was not unpleasant, and surprisingly, it lacked the roughness she expected.

— Greetings, maiden. Would you be a resident of Tempe's vale? What can come bursting out of the early morning in these parts is enough to astonish a fellow, I must say. You mustn't be alarmed on my account. I'll do you no harm.

      This speech caused the tension to drain out of her, and she smiled a slow, shy sort of smile. Finding her voice, however, was another matter. A maiden does not converse with an unknown traveler. Instead, she continued to regard him in silence, although it was evident that he had captured her curiosity. With a small smile and an almost imperceptible nod of acknowledgment, he addressed her in the casual manner that was his.

— Well now, you are wondering who I might be. No need, surely, to keep
you guessing. I happen to be a labor of many lifetimes, of which your
own is a voluptuous pause!

Hearing this most unexpected answer, she gasped audibly but
managed to find her voice.

— Stranger, what you say may be true, but it would be more satisfactory
if I might learn the name you go by. What is your name?

The figure rearranged his rough shepherd's cloak and pursed his
lips as if searching his supply of information before replying.

— Let me see. Which one? I have many names, as it happens.

At the moment, he resembled some absent-minded person who
had misplaced something important in a drawer somewhere.

— Maiden of Tempe, a name is rarely as reliable as it sounds. Once
assigned, it tends to flounder about grasping for who the person happens
to be, before at last it comes to cling like dried sap on a tree. Mostly a
name misses the mark.

He shook his head in regret. Although astonished by the traveler's
words, Daphne was not only intelligent but tended to be persistent when
pursuing what engaged her attention. As the sun appeared suddenly over
the treetops, a flash of recognition struck her.

— I only know, traveler, that my own name has never failed me. Besides,
I realized that you are familiar to me after all. Would you be the goat
god Pan himself?

His eyes widened as though caught off guard.

— Since your curiosity persists, let me tell you my names. Well, I am called
Fruitful One. Folks address me as leader of the herds, shepherd, and
All Feeder. Does this surprise you? I have even been called Deliverer
and occasionally god of oracle, although I mostly am glad to hand that
one over to Apollo.

Hearing these titles, she bowed her head in honor to him,
looking uncertain and a little pale. His voice and his look were reassuring,
however.

— And you, nymph, do I even try to pin down who you are? Why, I dare
not. Who you may be lies hidden, I am sure. It is a thing unrevealed, its
likeness spun out in the dance of life. Still, I do recognize you, I do.

— But you have never seen me before this meeting!

In spite of her protest, he went on relentlessly.

— Why, I recognize you in any case. Before me is dancer, huntress, song
of the dawn, muse of the hidden waters, moon that illuminates the

human night, healing laughter, and companion of the consoling shade, and she who gives love in the solitary places!

— Oh, do stop, Lord Pan! Let me tell you who I am. I am simply known as Daphne.

— It is just as well. In fact, it hardly matters. Actually, it is a fitting name because, looking into your eyes, already I perceive the long gray leaves of the laurel . . .

His last statement caused him to grow pensive, and he raised his eyes as if gazing on a long unseen path. A long pause sheltered them. It was Daphne who broke the silence.

— This is the country of my father, the river Peneus. Do you often come to this cave, I wonder? My father rules the region and supplies folk hereabouts with food and shelter, you see.

— I honor Peneus. Still, greater than Peneus is Earth Goddess, she who is known for her rich abundance. She shelters me here in the rock cavern, as a matter of fact. The great treasure is earth's, after all. There's no doubt about it. Daphne, let me tell you that it is a bounty that must not be compromised.

— But what of the cities of men? Are they not bountiful? I have heard that they are marvelous to see and very fine besides to dwell in.

Pan frowned considering this. He stroked his beard before answering.

— At first they seem that way. It turns out differently if a person remains in the city. No self-respecting shepherd would do such a thing, of course. Ah, I observe how dreamy and bright your eyes have become thinking about the city. But I must warn you, Daphne, shy maiden—

— It is true that I am shy by nature, but what is there to fear in the city, I ask you?

— The power of its huge body and mind in which the single person dries up like dew under the hot sun. If you're not watchful, the city can claim you. Then your only comfort is in knowing that you behave like everybody else in the city. After that, you'll begin wearing the substitute cloak all the time.

Daphne's hands flew to her cheeks as he spoke these dire words.

— The substitute cloak? What is that?

— Designed to fit everybody, it's what the city has created. Wearing it, you're guaranteed to *match*, see?

— Match who, Lord Pan?

— Everybody in the city, of course. Wearing this cloak, you'll lose the natural cloak that Earth Goddess favored you with, for sure. Call it the cloak of your own wildness, if you like. Without it, your laughter and your dancing step will cease.

Sitting down on a boulder at hand, Daphne cupped her chin in her right hand, sobered by what she had heard, and she pondered. Both were silent. Now she questioned the god of the pastures.

— Is this why you are found in the high pastures and in the grotto and along the solitary stream? Is it that you are guarding the wild territory?

He nodded, pleased at her deduction.

— You perceive me well, Daphne. But I must warn you to guard the treasure of the maiden. Is it true that you dance before feasting on the riverbank?

She nodded. He continued to speak.

— In the city of men, one must work before eating, not dance. Of course, I'm not the only guardian of the wild place. There is Artemis. Often I get a glimpse of her striding on the unpathed mountain slope, the hind and the hounds at her side, her bow carried lightly while the steps she makes are silent.

Welcoming the shift in their exchange, Daphne responded eagerly.

— Oh, Lady Artemis loves the depths of woods. There she looks for the hidden spring that always flows regardless of the season. We honor her as everlasting maiden!

Pan was regarding her thoughtfully.

— Ah, the resemblance is strong, yes. Daphne, you are very like her except that you are dark whereas she, like her brother, is fair. It is not simply the visual beauty of the maiden that you share with Artemis. Rather, it is the beauty of the maiden who always escapes capture.

— Saying such things, why do you look sad, even regretful?

— Because I shall never win the goddess nor yourself, for that matter.

Now it is like a woman to filter the words of a man eagerly to strain out the compliment to herself, however meager, and Daphne's voice was warm with pleasure.

— Comparing me to Artemis herself, you do me honor. Actually, I have longed to join the company of Artemis. All her maidens must remain ever virgin, it is said. She keeps them from being surprised by men who are naturally attracted to the maidens.

Pan's anger flared suddenly.

— What a waste! Why must she claim many a lovely maiden for her company alone? It can cause a man to panic, it can.

— Oh, Lord Pan, you yourself are the one who causes folks to fall into panic. It is well-known, in fact. A panic especially feared may fall upon one at noontide.

Pan's voice proceeded now out of a grumble.

— Well, I am hardly immune to what I cause. We can have no influence over Artemis, it is certain. It is you I wish to contemplate, maiden of Tempe's vale.

A slow, leisurely smile came to her face as she gazed into the silent depth of woods beyond them, and now she turned back to Pan in his contemplation. After a while, he spoke aloud.

— Being virgin belongs to the dawn. It will burn off when it meets the searing light of the world. Perhaps this is why Artemis seeks out the leafy woods to shelter the maidens from the sun's bold rays. Ah, what is it that perplexes the maiden? She cannot see herself unless she can find a mirror. There it is. The mirror is Artemis herself. Who is the maiden now seen? She is glimpsed as a little ahead on the path with her light, dancing step. Always she is waiting, although she is unaware of it. Like the arrival of spring, she is green, silent, and full of promise. Shy alike of the world and of men, the maiden possesses a beauty more hidden than dazzling to behold. She is the violet growing in the oak's deep shade. Ah, yes, Daphne, I have joined the nymphs in dance and song in the grotto, so I am near the maidens. The maiden is a measure of unspent being, chaste upon the lap of endless possibility! Always she draws me, I tell you, and always I long to woo her over the boundary. But the radiant territory does not let her go. Gazing at the maiden, I observe that always she abides, for she seeks no goal, no achievement. Neither plan nor strategy does she have. She is the newly ripened fruit ready for plucking, and yet she escapes every harvesting and . . . alas, Daphne, river nymph, the sun is over the shoulder of the mountain, and I must leave you. Farewell!

The Love of Syrinx

The wooded glen lay wet and sparkling with dew while a fragrant breeze played over his brow and his locks as he wandered happily on the wooded path. Where the path rounded to reveal the bank of the river Ladon, Pan came upon a lovely maiden. In her lap lay a chain of white starflowers, the asterion, that she was weaving. Looking up quickly, she observed a roughly attired herdsman whose energy seemed to fill the glen, and her eyes widened with apprehension. Pan remained at a little distance and smiled encouragingly.

— There is no cause to fear, maiden, when a shepherd wishes to break his solitude in such an inviting place. As a matter of fact, I am known to be good company!

His smile was lazy, and he sat down on a nearby boulder with decided confidence. Frowning, some faint recognition registered in her mind as she replied.

— Why, you are Goat Man! Many tales carry your fame, yet I have never before encountered you here on the riverbank. Naturally you have startled me.

The least he could do was to acknowledge the fact or else apologize, but he did not.

— Well now, I do hope the tales have done me credit.

He showed no doubt whatsoever while the maiden blushed and lowered her gaze.

— Hm, you do not answer. More important, do tell me your name, maiden. Could you be daughter of the river god Ladon?

— Yes, I am. My name is Syrinx, and my home is beside these waters.

She gestured proudly toward the river.

— Syrinx, Syrinx . . . it's a name that keeps speaking like dry reeds in the wind, I'd say.

If you like, you can call me Pan. Most folks do, you see, and I should delight in hearing it from your lips. It is lonely to go about where one's name is not spoken, and especially if the person one meets is a woman so like a starflower herself.

Loneliness was apparently a saga unknown to her, but she was quick to respond, even so.

— Pan . . . Pan . . . That's a name of the god of pastures, the one the herdsmen all worship in the hollow grottoes.

— You have worshipped Pan, have you?

— Indeed so. One dare not overlook one of our great Arcadian gods.

Besides, Pan is rather charming in his own way. Why, he is so . . . so fresh!

Finding the word for what she seemed to have in mind caused her to giggle. From him, her words evoked an immediate defense, however.

— *Fresh?* And why wouldn't he be fresh? There is nothing to wear out or to go stale in him. That's for sure. Look, nymph, in Pan lies the new beginning, I tell you.

— It is the way of a god, I suppose. Tell me, herdsman, why have you chosen to live in the remote pasture?

— It is hardly a choice. Why, the pasture is in me. I belong to it. That is simply the way things are.

She shook her head slowly from side to side.

— There are rough places in the far pastures.

— There are rough places in me, maiden.

That something still protested in her was clearly evident.

— But sharp stones can cause a person to lose her footing!

He regarded her closely as he replied.

— Then she best learn to pay attention, I would advise.

— What of the unguarded cliff that may loom up suddenly before oneself?

Surely the lovely maiden was turning out to be cautious indeed. He sighed before replying.

— The eyes are not sufficient protection, nor is the mind's habitual expectation, I tell you. There is something you best know. In the far pastures, it only works well when the *feet* are wise.

Her eyes fell at once to Goat Man's feet, which she stared at for some time with wide eyes. Incredible though it seemed, the feet resembled those of a goat.

— Oh, now I understand. Goat Man, you are one who thinks with his feet!

Pan laughed heartily at this observation before stepping to her side.

— Come, maiden, let's stroll along this peaceful riverbank to where the plane tree spreads its broad branches over the waters. It is the hour of the day for taking the sweet loaf of leisure.

Together they began their stroll, and the low chorus of bees and the wind in the grasses filled the air. The hours passed as for some time they walked the river path, and their companionship grew in the vast silence that sheltered the path. Now Pan turned to her.

— You are quiet, Syrinx. Tell me about your life here.

— Books are written by men, and they bind all that happens with words. Goat Man, my ways have no words to bind them up, you see.

He grinned in fond appreciation.

— Good! That means that your ways are free and unfettered and never mere repetition. Why, I am certain that they are a treasure to be desired!

His words puzzled her.

— A treasure? I don't understand. A treasure is something people search for because they don't possess it. But I live in my ways, surely, so they cannot be a treasure.

Her logic caused him to begin to hum a little tune before he spoke again.

— My dear maiden, your ways are shining. I must tell you that they beckon me, much as the river calls to one of its far pools. Hear me, Syrinx. Your unrepeatable ways are the treasure I greatly long for!

— Is it that you desire these waters that are my element and my home, the waters of the river god who is my father?

Her summary of the situation caused him to stop and shake his head as he gazed into her face.

— Syrinx, it is rather your very own waters that draw me. Unless I partake of these waters, how am I ever to be refreshed, I ask you?

— Goat Man, who refer to yourself as Pan, there are other springs that will surprise you in this river glen, I ought to tell you. They are very beautiful. I tell you.

— No other source can bring me what already I perceive in you! Look at me, if you will.

She did, shyly.

— Good. I am the traveler come upon a deep, echoing cave into which I gaze enthralled. But I cannot cross its threshold unless I am welcomed. You must see this, surely.

Apprehension passed through her as she noted the failing light of day.

— Ah, the sun is no longer on our shoulders, and we pass into shadow!

In that moment, Pan slipped his arm about her and drew her to himself, speaking in a low voice as he did so.

— Without Pan's love, dear Syrinx, a maiden will waste away and fail to find the path to woman!

A sense of alarm seized her, soon followed by an inscrutable dread that caused her to cry out to her goddess.

— Alas, O Earth Goddess, tell me if these words are true!

Pan sought now to calm her fears and to see her serene once again.

— Beloved Syrinx, you are the one alone whom my heart yearns for. Oh, do not ask me to let you go. Don't leave me devastated, I beg you. Until this moment, you showed no eagerness to part with my good company, none at all.

For a little time, a serene look returned to her face, and she responded to his plea out of some invisible quiet.

— Ah yes, it is true. Your company has pleased my heart in some mysterious way. It caused the dance to arise in my limbs . . . Still, I must confess something. I am one of Hera's virgin maidens who may not be taken by a man's love. I am vulnerable like the deer before the hunter's raised bow, alas! But remember this, Pan, you shall find in me the invincible walled city!

With a small choking cry, she tore herself free from Pan's impassioned embrace and fled down the riverbank, which she knew so well, casting behind herself a look of profound regret. Pan followed at once in pursuit, calling to her. Fleet runner that she was, she moved ahead with her shining tresses lifted in swift flight until, at a sharp bend in the path, he lost sight of her. Rounding the bend of the descending path, he found himself stopped at the river's edge. Before him stood the nymph, who smiled slowly at him with a fondness that was indelibly mixed with sadness.

— O Syrinx, my beloved, I have found you!

He stepped forward, his arms outstretched, and took her once more into his embrace, and in that moment, Pan was consumed in the ecstasy of love. Even as he gazed into her face, she began to change. To his disbelief, he saw that what he held in his arms was a bunch of tall slender reeds, their roots hidden by the water at the river's edge. His cry, deep and filled with anguish, penetrated the river glen.

— Syrinx, O incomparable maiden! How could you abandon me, who am the god Pan?

Darkness cloaked the riverbank where Pan stood, and still he remained motionless, his face somber and unbelieving as he continued to stare at the river reeds that he held against himself. Day came, but it was deprived of the promise Goat Man regularly greeted in the day. Through the blazing heat of noontide, he would not part with the strange evidence of his lost treasure, but remained holding the reeds tenderly. As night once again settled over the riverbank, the voice of Pan cried aloud, poignant in its grief.

— O Syrinx, Syrinx! From me you would have known true delight, for Pan's joy is ever at hand waiting to burst upon the day and its hour! It is not a thing saved up or filed away in what folks call the future. Never, never, my dear one, am I known to betray the present time for some ghostly day to come. Pan is faithful always to the time at hand. I tell you a secret. Pan guards the deep place where you dwell happily. There. Now you know.

He paused to attend to the bending, sighing, and crisp murmuring of the reeds, inclining his ear. The first light of dawn broke over the Arcadian glen, and as it did, a sweet satisfaction began to grow in Pan, grieved though he was. Again and again the lyrical voice of the reeds played over him, speaking to his great heart. The sun had risen now from the night arms of the dark oaks of the wooded bank when Pan spoke.

— Ah, the reeds are speaking at last. There is a languorous sigh that shakes my beloved Syrinx as she replies through the thin-voiced reeds. What is it that you are whispering to me? Ah the words come, *"Pan has not lost . . . Pan has not lost . . . Pan has not lost!"* Now I see how it is! O dear Syrinx, you shall be my new voice, but there is something to be done first. Pan's hour is now, as you know. Love itself is no longer love when postponed or abandoned!

Now Pan set to work. Passion once more streamed through the whole of his form like the river itself, and it was partnered by delight. He took his shepherd's knife from under his rough cloak and began to cut each of the hollow reeds, reeds still warm with his long embrace. As he worked, he murmured, "Come away now, my strange but lovely bride!" When he had cut the reeds each at a different length, he bound the seven together with a leather thong. At last he put the odd instrument to his lips and, for the first time, gave it Pan's living breath. Astonishing were the sounds from the pipes that rose on the air creating the new music that penetrated the glen like a single voice hollowed out from the core of love. A small smile, intimate and sustained, was in the god's sad eyes as he made music. Pausing, he bade farewell to the abode of Syrinx.

— O Syrinx, now you shall be always near me, inside my cloak speaking and sighing, singing and longing!

Taking the instrument in his left hand, he turned and left the river glen.

Echo and Pan

On the sunny crest of a hill in the high pasture, the god Pan rested his arm on a large boulder as he gazed at the stream bank in the green glade below. A lightly clad nymph was sunning herself there. The sight of the lovely nymph pleased him, and grinning broadly, he made a series of leaps over the rough mountain side to the stream bank. Supporting her head on one arm, the oread was in reverie so that his approach startled her. At once Pan sought to reassure her.

— Ah, nymph, don't let me disturb you. Could you be one of the maidens who follow queenly Hera?

She was studying the rustic shepherd's countenance, gasping at the intelligence of his eyes that appeared to take thorough account of everything at hand including herself. And could those be horns on his head? Wary, she replied.

— Yes. Great Hera of Arcadia and of ancient Argos is my goddess . . . Could you be the one they call Goat Man? That one is said to rule these mountains and is known to emerge from the hidden places. Ah, what is it about you? How *sudden* you are!

— Just so. You and I are alike then. Are we not both drawn to the mountain grotto? We have a great deal in common. That's without a doubt.

A doubt crossed her face.

— In common, you say. But being in common has to do with my life with the nymphs. Wherever Hera leads, you see, we follow. She teaches us things.

Pan was frowning now with a slight shaking of his shaggy head.

— You say that you learn by *following*?

He exclaimed the word as if it might be a beast that bites.

— Well, yes, how else can a person learn? Hera tells her maidens something important to know, and each of us turns and repeats it aloud to her companions. One may repeat it only once, but sometimes one repeats it a great deal.

Pan inclined his head toward the nymph, as much observing the play of excitement in her face as the content of what she was telling him. Now he straightened himself briefly and sighed as he questioned her closely.

— Tell me, what sort of Hera things are you in the habit of repeating? It is important that a good fellow know, you see. Besides, I never realized that Hera needed help in getting her point across.

She smiled indulgently at his ignorance.

— Why, when we nymphs are parting with our goddess at dusk, she will say to us, "Maidens, beware of the lover who lurks in the shadow of trees and stones, I say! Flee!"

At once, Pan's face was flushed with anger.

— Why should you repeat a thing like that, I ask you?

— When an alarming thing is told and one repeats it, it is tamed somehow so that it is far less frightening. Surely it is a misfortune to be left entirely alone with an alarming piece of news.

Pan regarded her quietly, and his look was somewhat troubled.

— Echo, maiden, hear me.

She was astonished when he spoke her name. He continued, and it was not possible for the goat god to be less than honest.

— You have no cause for alarm with me. Even so, I admit that I am said to be a great lover in the hidden place of the pasture.

— Alas!

The nymph Echo sprang to her feet and seized her cloak that lay on the ground. Pan put his hand gently upon her arm.

— Don't run away, lovely nymph!

Now he led her toward a large boulder and smiled an invitation to sit beside him.

— There is still much you must tell me. Tell me, if you will, about repeating. It seems you do a rather great deal of it.

Echo nodded in agreement.

— By day and by night as well, I repeat. I say what others say, and I do what others do.

Now the god was aghast. Again he asked a piercing question.

— Whatever for?

— What for? . . . What for? . . .

She said it like a refrain.

— Oh, don't you see how it is, Goat Man? Most things tend to flutter, bending this way and that. It is repeating that decides for things. It makes them firm. Oh, and something else. It pleases folk to hear themselves echoed. Everyone comes to expect it of me, you see.

Her voice descended in what might be regret. In Pan, there was a growing restlessness.

— Echo, how can you simply comply with what folks expect? Why echo everybody and anybody?

— Because, Goat Man, I am a refrain. *I am what comes afterward!* I never have to begin anything, nothing at all. Instead, when things settle into their places, I pay tribute to them by repeating them, calling out to others to draw their attention.

— Is such echoing done by the mouth alone? Or do you engage in acts as well?

— Both by mouth and by action.

Pan grew pensive, but he did not look happy.

— You say that you are one who begins afterward, that you are a refrain. You enter when a thing has already happened. Echo, hear me. For me that is already *too late.*

She gazed at him with some sympathy, it seemed.

— To echo is less trouble, to tell the truth . . .

The god became visibly changed as a passion arose in him; and his eyes, in a sweeping glance, took in the green glade and the high pasture crowning the mountain as well. His voice was deep with emotion as he spoke.

— Echo, dear nymph, what is it to be ever echoing, except to be after the fact? You miss the true happening, casting yourself on what has passed, what has spent itself. And then, O misfortune, you are filled with words and acts that are borrowed! Why cast yourself on what has lost its own voice, I ask you?

The nymph also was aroused now, disturbed by Goat Man's response.

— Oh, oh! I am a voice too . . . voice too . . . voice too!

Pan drew a little apart and mused, his brow furrowed.

— Am I not in the presence of the echo itself? Something draws me to the nymph and seduces me irrevocably. After all, the echo gives itself as an outward thing before becoming the enchanting voice of the nymph that is able to prolong what would die too quickly. O dear Echo, maiden, you are the hollow vessel that holds the words spoken and the acts done so that they endure for a little time. Without you, there are essential things that die too quickly.

Pan turned to Echo where she rested on the boulder. Regarding her for a long moment, he smiled with affection.

— Would you accept some advice, maiden? Before repeating what you hear, it is best to winnow out what may prolong misery. And then, of course, you would be a loss to Hera and certainly to myself were you tempted to become a mere gossip.

Echo looked perplexed by these words of advice, and it was a perplexity tinged with annoyance.

— But you don't understand how it is. I prolong each thing as it is said. There isn't time to notice what the thing is like. What you suggest is impossible.

She grinned, and her look was mischievous before adding,

— How I do love the sound of my voice repeating!

Pan shook his head from side to side, his busy eyebrows knitted.

— Am I not the father of impulse? Still, I hear you, Echo. As for me, when a thing lacks the real sap of life, it is empty, and I keep my distance.

— You make things complicated, I think, and a rather great deal of trouble.

Pan smiled a little sadly, but not without tenderness, and the silence that settled over them was like moisture dripping in the far grotto. It was Echo who broke the spell.

— Goat Man, tell me, am I beautiful?

— You enchant me, lovely Echo. As for your beauty, it appears to stand near you but still a little apart. Does that surprise you?

She rose to her feet and took a few steps into the deeper shade as she spoke, her voice forlorn.

— There is a strange presence that would rob me of my rightful beauty . . . beauty . . . beauty.

— Ah, I would speak of that strange presence, for it is not a thief. Rather it holds a gift for you, nymph. This stranger that you sense is the hollow rock grotto. Echo, it is the true dwelling place which earth has provided you. It is a place unrepeated, and I can lead you to it. Do you hear me? This grotto, mind you, is unrepeated. Therefore, it can belong to you as your very own.

His words had not removed the fear she felt, and her voice rose in protest.

— Oh, in such a place I shall be too lonely!

— Not lonely, yet alone. One is alone in earth's grotto shaped by one's nature and destiny, but not lonely. Let me explain: I, Pan, shall come to you, bearing my love!

— Such words are strange to me, and I am afraid.

— Echo, my words seem strange because they are meant for your ears alone, words which are repeatable.

— Tell me, then, what lies inside the grotto you speak of.

— This grotto contains all that is ancient, all that is real, all that shelters the human spirit. At the same time, you shall find there what is your very own.

— To reach this grotto, I've no idea how to get there . . . how to . . . how to.

— I shall be at your side. I, Pan, am your companion, and I love you!

— You call yourself Pan, but Pan is a god. The thought makes me tremble.

— Echo, would you like to know the *way of beginning*? With me it will be shown to you.

— O shepherd Pan, I am all endings . . . endings . . . endings!

— When you know our love in the grotto, this will change. Of this, I am sure.

Echo covered her ears with her hands to shut out these alarming words, for she was afraid. Seeing her reaction, he spoke to comfort her.

— The words I speak to you are for you alone. I know they seem strange. That could be because you find them unrepeatable.

— Unrepeatable! Unrepeatable!

— Echo, delay no longer. Come away with me at once. I am Pan himself, Goat Man as well. I sense in you the longing for the deep grotto. Let me lead you there. Remember, it is this grotto that can shelter the life that's your very own.

— Very own . . . very own . . . Alas, Goat Man, no!

Echo became agitated and began to pace back and forth near where Pan sat on the boulder. His eyes followed her with an affection that was alternately joyous and somber. Now she stopped a little way off and slowly turned to face him. When she spoke, her voice took on a new intensity as of that of a woman beginning her heart's confession.

— You see, already I am in love, for I love the beautiful youth Narcissus! Ah, the day has no delight if I fail to get a glimpse of him. Sometimes I hide behind the rock in order to feast my eyes and heart upon him when he lingers by the pool in this glade.

Sorrow weighed down the god, and his voice was bitter with disappointment when he spoke.

— So you love another. I have lost. Tell me, does Narcissus love you?

Echo shook her head sadly and made no reply. Pan spoke with strong emotion that gradually became scorn.

— That youth only wants to see his own image repeated in the world. He is in love with himself alone. He cannot love another. Gladly will he take your echoes, but yourself he will throw away, I warn you!

Echo had mastered her fears and now spoke decisively.

— What you say, Goat Man, doesn't matter . . . doesn't matter. Noontide approaches, and I must leave. Farewell, shepherd Pan!

Turning about, she ran swiftly down the glade toward the water's edge, the spot frequented by Narcissus. For a long while, Pan remained at the meeting spot, a forlorn figure grappling with the sadness of love's loss. The hours passed, and the sun sank low over the mountain. Something nudged his elbow, and he saw that the ram of the flock had come seeking him, nudging him with his nose. A bit of the god's misery fell away. He arose and laid his hand tenderly on the ram's head. Now the two of them made their way back to where the herd sheltered under the overhanging rock.

PART VIIII

Hermes

Hermes—An Introduction

A keen intelligence coupled with a lively capacity for scheming and trickery burst forth in the treasured sixth-century BC portrayal of the child god in the *Homeric Hymn to Hermes*. By wearing huge sandals that he devised to confuse his footprints, young Hermes managed to steal fifty head of Apollo's excellent cattle, a crime that Apollo took to Zeus to be judged. One is greatly amused and yet uneasy with such a trickster and what he is capable of. In the Olympian settlement, Apollo got his cows back minus one while Hermes made him a gift of the original lyre he had created. It is the lyre that was said to fill Apollo with sweet longing and came to partner him in song and dance. There would appear to be no finer trickster than the Olympian god Hermes, who also is messenger of Zeus.

Remarkably as the myths unfold, Hermes becomes messenger of the gods, *Angelos*, mediating the Olympian perspective to the human world. In this distinctive role, neither deceit nor trickery are seen. Instead, such a darker role is manifested in Hermes not only as god of exchange, being clearly noted in the marketplace, but also in his remarkable schemes of rescuing divine-human progeny. At the same time, it proves to be the case that the carrying out of the will of heaven rests upon certain acts that remain hidden or else incapable of being observed by the senses. In this sense, *Angelos* can be accompanied by the trickster.

Hermes might well be described as the *god of the middle*. (It is to be noted that in the case of the hero, Athena assumes this place.) Repeatedly in myths, he appears at the side of the individual in a struggle between opposing forces. Walled into a predicament, the one in crisis is shown a safe passage by Hermes. He rescues young Dionysos from the royal house of madness, and finding Odysseus approaching a dark fate in the house of Circe, he comes to the rescue with the magic of the moly plant. There was no predicament so dire, so deserving of despair but that Hermes as

Hodios, god of the road, was able to find a workable path out of it. Ever comfortably at large in the dark, he illuminated the way ahead through the light of his staff.

It is in myths of extraordinary rescues that the god Hermes comes to be most fully embodied. Haunting these accounts is a poignant sense of what has been lost or abandoned, a perception that accompanies the god. In the rescue, timing is everything, it seems, calling forth as it must a response that is as rhythmic and immediate as the heartbeat. An intimate resonance with the individual who is seized by his predicament comes upon Hermes. He must act at once, engaging his winged step, for no time can be lost. Hovering over the well-known rescue myths—the rescue of young Dionysos; of Apollo's abandoned son, Ion; of the youth Phrixos from the altar of sacrifice; of the infant god Pan; and others—is the heavy specter of loss. At once with Hermes' arrival, hope is restored. His staff illuminates a path that works, leading to safety as it is engaged. In this way, Hermes goes astride the awesome opposites of extreme loss and of finding, for the benefit of human existence.

Hermes Creates the Lyre

Emerging from his birth cave, Hermes set out to explore the wilds of Arcadia that lay all about his mountain abode. He had been happily claimed by a grove of oak trees as he tramped energetically along when suddenly on the path before him, there appeared an odd creature indeed. The creature was round, slow-moving, and carried a noticeable hump on its back. At once, young Hermes fell to his knees for a closer look, at the very least pleased to have company in the dusky light of the grove. Spilling out at once were his spontaneous words of hospitality.

— Why, hello there. Welcome to our path! Who would you be? Will you tell me about yourself? I am new to things in these hills, you see.

Startled at the meeting, the creature drew back a little and turned its eyes fully upon Hermes, not replying for rather a long pause. At last it began to speak in a small voice that sounded as if it came from a place far inside. In any case, the greeting was in Greek.

— *Kalimera*, sir. I am old. I can't say how old. You don't count things when you're old. You just know that you are important.

His gaze upon his small companion was filled with lively curiosity, causing the creature to blink repeatedly.

— Why do you move along so slowly? Are you just getting used to things maybe? Right now, what are you looking at?

This time, the creature replied promptly.

— I'm looking at the ground, of course. What else ought a person to look at? Except for the seasons, nothing changes. The ground is the ground. To make sure of it, though, I take very small steps. Yes, and most of the time, I simply tuck under.

— What is there to tuck under?

— Why, I tuck under my shell, naturally. What else am I to rely on? Which reminds me, shouldn't you be at home under your covers?

— If only I had a shell to go about with and to tuck under . . .

Hermes' voice trailed off in the mist of longing. It was with some scorn that the creature spoke now.

— But I am the tortoise, and you are not!

Young Hermes received this announcement with some excitement.

— So that's what you are—the tortoise!

His burst of enthusiasm caused the tortoise to tuck under her shell at once. He asked himself, *Where has she disappeared, I wonder?* He raised his voice calling out.

— Tortoise, tell me, are you an inside thing or an outside thing? One has to decide, I think.

Without reappearing, she answered from some distance.

— Mostly I'm an inside thing, yet sometimes I'm outside as well. Inside is safer, though.

— Safer? What are you afraid of?

— The world, all of it. Still, something is different here on the path . . .

— What is it?

Her eyes grew bright, and she blinked them excitedly.

— Something new is beginning that hasn't happened to me before. I sense it.

— All of which could be very good news, you know.

He smiled down at her. She sighed.

— I've never met anything like you before.

At times, her voice had been muffled by the distance of some far inside place, and Hermes had had to strain to make out her strange words. Now speaking, he revealed his impatience, for again she had gone into her shell.

— Come back out, please, for I need a companion I can talk with. Otherwise, I shall be going on down the path alone.

As he waited and watched, Tortoise gradually began to emerge from her shell, her eyes gazing about warily. This action caused Hermes to jump up and down in his delight. She questioned him in alarm.

— Whatever is beginning to happen?

— Don't you see? It's that I'm happy to get a good look at you at last. Why, you are beautiful, Tortoise Maiden!

She was dumbfounded. With her bright eyes, she searched his face.

— No one has ever called me that before. You say that I am beautiful? I do know that I'm beginning to like you rather much.

He laughed, smiling full upon her.

— "Beginning to"? You are always saying, "I am beginning to." Why is that?

— Do you really want to know?

— Certainly.

— Well, dwelling in my vaulted shell, I am *before* beginnings . . . all of them. My shell may look to you like a small hump, but inside my place is a deep cave that goes into the dark on and on. As I said, I am very old. I am at the roots—a living stone among the stones!

— Tortoise Maiden, sister of the stone, you do say odd things. But why do you say "I am beginning to" if the fact is that you are before the beginnings?

— Ah, clever boy, you noticed that. Well, the truth is that you came along, and that caused a strange stirring in me. "This boy brings a beginning," I thought. Somehow the notion pleased me.

Hermes shook his head from side to side considering these remarks, finding them denser than the shade of the oak trees.

— Tell me, what are you beginning, Tortoise Maiden?

She drew back, visibly startled by the question as it was put.

— My mind, you see, is best for *behind* things and has nothing at all for things that are yet ahead.

Hermes drew himself up handsomely, his natural confidence beaming.

— Allow me to see ahead for you then!

He lifted his face and grew quiet with his eyes closed, while she observed him with an expectancy not known before. He murmured words so low that she had to draw closer to catch them.

— Ah, ah yes . . . what a sight I am seeing!

Although impatience had hitherto been unknown to her, Tortoise cried aloud,

— Do say what it is you see without your eyes!

— Why, I see a great festival with people gathering in the street. They are wearing green garlands on their heads, and they appear joyful. Yes, and then there is the music . . . the voice of the flute pierces the air while the flute player strides down the street and is gone. Now the music is altered, I think. Listen, Tortoise Maiden!

She cocked her ear as best she could as he continued.

— The music grows more delicate . . . it is gentle, while the flute's voice is not. It is like a wild creature that has been tamed. What is the source of this new voice? Oh, now I see.

— What do you see? Tell me at once. Impatience is new to me, but it could upset my digestion.

— All things seem to have their order. What I see is yourself in the midst of the festival. You are round, ample, and bejeweled. Wait. You are being carried on the arm of the bard! What's this? Why, the voice of the new music comes out of you and none other!

    Tortoise Maiden, you are my music!

    Do you hear me?

— Music coming out of *me?* But I've never sung a note, not ever.

    Hermes grinned at this confession reassuringly.

— That's not a problem, not if you stay close to me.

— Didn't you say that the music you heard floated on the air like something delicate? Well, I'm a creature of small slow steps that hug only the ground. Besides, I'd never take to floating.

— Just wait. You shall see what is possible.

    Her look was puzzled, but now a wistfulness crept into her voice.

— I've never been to a festival, not ever.

    His generous smile warmed her heart now.

— You are going to love it. Again I see you in what is to come. You are dancing and singing tales of the gods! Believe me, Tortoise Maiden, you are alive again!

    An ominous note reached Tortoise Maiden and was reflected in her solemn voice, which soon was filled with anguish.

— Alive? Again, you say? Alas, I was afraid when I first met you on this path. Something awesome seemed about to happen. I could not guess what it was. Now I too see it . . . Oh! This ordinary tortoise among tortoises shall surely die! And it's all because you have created a *beginning* for me!

    The voice of Hermes was thoughtful when he spoke and seemed older. It was not without tenderness, however.

— Ah, and what if you are to die by my hand? Tortoise Maiden, know that you are dear to me. It is my hand that holds you and shelters your deep life. With Hermes, there is no abandonment. I bring rescue, the rescue of what is about to fall into oblivion.

— Alas, what is rescue?

— Tortoise Maiden, listen to me. If you die by my hand, it is that I shall create you anew in the lyre! In the seven-stringed lyre, you are going to live forever. You'll be everlasting like a god. And know this, when anyone touches you, you will begin to vibrate with heavenly sounds!

Tortoise Maiden was looking put out, and her frown deepened.

— But I don't know any heavenly sounds. How is a person to make them?

Hermes laughed with affection at his companion.

— It is that I shall give you a new voice, a voice unrivaled in its beauty. As for your natural, much beloved shell, it is your immortal part even now. Well, it shall become the house of the heavenly music. And be assured that for all time to come, the lyre shall bear the life of yourself, maiden of earth!

Tortoise Maiden bravely extended her slender neck as she gazed at him, her eyes thoughtful now as she blinked once, twice, and once again before settling into a smile as she replied.

— So be it, child of the gods.

Meeting Calliope

Now Hermes continued on his way, happily taking in the wondrous landscape on the peak of Mt. Olympus and reveling in his solitary adventure when near the Pierian Spring, he came upon a lovely lady. With her deep-set dark eyes, she observed his approach thoughtfully.

— Lad, where are you headed, striding along so jauntily?
— Why, I'm just out for a ramble. Who knows what a person like me will stumble on?

Hearing these words, the lady caught her breath. Her voice was subdued as she replied.

— On Olympus, one does not stumble about. Are you aware that Olympus is the dwelling place of the gods?
— I do hope that there are a good many cows around as well.

She considered this, frowning in perplexity.

— So it is that you have some business with cows?
— Who, me? Cows? Cows are too slow for me. I like to run long distances and feel the wind in my face. Lovely lady, would you happen to be a cowherd?
— I would not, no.
— Well, that's good.

The lad smiled, looking relieved. She continued to be puzzled and pressed him.

— Yet you come seeking cows. Apollo is known to have a fine herd of them.
— Is that so?

His face was a mask of innocence. Nor did he deny her his opinion.

— Well, shepherding animals is hardly a good pastime for a person with my talents.

— Sshh. You but tempt the Fates. This is, after all, Olympus, home of the gods. Anything said here, where all is immortal, becomes true for all time.

For the first time, his face registered a wave of awe before his striking assurance returned, radiating about him.

— To think that I got to the right place all on my own . . . You seem to know all about Olympus. Who would you be, lady?

— I am Calliope, firstborn of the nine Muses.

— Greetings, Lady Calliope! My name is Hermes. I am in luck, for no sooner was I born than I thought I'd like to meet a singer of tales. You are one of those, aren't you?

— I am. It is the long, enduring tales that draw me, you see, for I am the epic Muse.

— What is this spring that is beside us here? It sings loudly, I'd say.

— It is Pieria. By this very spring were my sisters and I born. It is old in memory.

— Who is your mother?

— Mnemosyne herself!

— That's Memory! I'll wager that you never forget a thing.

His words hung on the air and repeated themselves in his ear, coming to have a dire implication for his hidden project with cows. Here was an intelligent resident of the place, the head Muse, no less, the last person that he desired to be witness of his undertaking. And what a witness Calliope was going to make if he didn't pursue his plan cleverly! She was replying now.

— The remembering of the Muses is not what you think it to be. Every happening has its bold shell, which is what people notice and appear to recall. Not so with the Muses. Our eyes fall upon the hidden core of what happens in experience, and we extract the living narrative, much the way that the spindle holds the thread. Like the flowing waters of the Pierian Spring, the tale we sing is ever flowing, ever continuing. Always we sing of the essence of experience and give it immortal breath.

Hermes thought about this and sighed.

— Actually, that's what I'm after—immortal breath.

— Looking upon your bright and mischievous face, young Hermes, I begin to wonder what your tales will be, for there will be many. Ah, I see it now.

— What do you see?

A worried thought passed his mind, *I hope it isn't the cows I'm going to steal!* Calliope replied.

— You shall be the one who always finds the way that leads to the favorable outcome. As for your very own ways, they tend to remain well hidden.

Hermes bowed to Calliope, adjusted the cloak upon his shoulders, bade a polite farewell and departed. The Muse remained on the bank of the stream gazing after the lively young god.

Nephele and the Golden Ram

Far from the royal house of Thebes, the modest house that stood on the low hillside was home to Nephele and her children. Had she not been queen before her husband, Athamas, took his new wife? Shaded by a great old oak tree, the cottage was approached through the doorway, which the grape arbor framed. At the entrance, a statue of Hermes Propylaia stood, its tray receiving offerings of grapes. Nephele stood now beside the arbor, a small bunch of grapes in her hand, and her lovely face was troubled as yet another time, those parting words of Athamas returned to her:

— You have been a good wife and mother, Nephele, but the great city of
　　Thebes summons me to take as wife the daughter of its royal house,
　　Ino. In such a world as ours, I have no choice, you understand. Know
　　that I shall provide for you. It is fitting now that distance lies between
　　us. You understand, I am sure. And so, farewell, Nephele!

At the time, she could find no voice to make reply, and at once the gray cloak of shock and grief had descended upon her. Even so, she was thankful for the consolation that lay in their two children who lived with her in the cottage—Phrixos, the elder, and Helle, his sister.

Life had been overhung by a black cloud ever since the Theban delegation had returned from Delphi where Apollo had been consulted with the somber question, "What can the city of Thebes do to end the famine that has taken over the land?" The oracle that the returning delegation delivered into the hands of King Athamas seemed unbelievable. The harsh truth of it assaulted Nephele each time she thought of it. Did Apollo really speak those words? No, surely not. Besides, had not the man who worked the vineyard quietly brought her a puzzling report? He had been on the lower hidden path when he observed the Theban delegation returning from Delphi, watching them as they entered the woods that precede the descending road to the city. Exactly here within this secluded corridor of the road, he was amazed to see Queen Ino herself appear dressed in a dark cloak, a solitary figure who stepped out from the deep shade of the trees. As he watched in astonishment, the queen stepped onto the roadway to signal the delegation to stop. At some length, she spoke to the delegates, whose faces registered what might have been shock or fear. A heated discussion arose among the delegates with obvious dissension occurring in the exchange. A few shouted exclamations reached the ears of the vineyard worker: "But the thunderbolt of Zeus!" At once, Nephele knew that these words were an echo of the queen's threat. There was no longer any doubt in her mind that what Ino sought was the alteration of the oracle itself! Indeed, it was on the following day that what was called the oracle of Apollo was read aloud before all the people of Thebes, severely altered though it was. The words proclaimed were to haunt her day and night:

— *Famine has laid bare the land of Thebes. The return of the earth to bearing seed will only be possible when Phrixos, eldest son of King Athamas, is sacrificed on the altar!*

Not only Nephele but also many of the Thebans grieved to hear these words. Sadly but in compliance with what he believed to be the will of Apollo, Athamas ordered the preparations for the sacrifice of his firstborn son, a sacrifice to take place with fitting ritual the following day at dawn. Little did he suspect that Ino, his wife, had rewritten the oracle to accommodate her own interests, namely opening the way for her own son sired by Athamas to be king in the future. Before the sun had set, Phrixos was led up the sacred hill to the altar mound laid high with wood, where he was bound firmly with ropes. This sad task accomplished, the people one by one departed leaving him alone. Abandoned and fated to die, Phrixos endured the long sleepless night and dreaded the breaking day.

As the sun went down on Phrixos's last day in the kingdom of Thebes, his mother, Nephele, wearing a light gray cloak, continued to stand motionless beneath the great oak tree near her cottage, and her face bore the evidence of her sorrow. Briefly she lifted her gaze to the softly swaying branches as if in yet another entreaty for the life of her son. Quietly she murmured praise of Zeus, at the same time imploring the help of faithful Hermes. If only this were Zeus's own holy oak at Dodona, which gave forth a saving wisdom, but instead it was her long familiar tree in the yard, which appeared altogether unaffected by the crisis. O how could any living thing be indifferent to Phrixos's undeserved fate? She lowered her eyes as an abysmal sigh escaped her while in the same moment she prayed aloud,

— O Hermes, God of the way, hear me and come!

She was aware now of a small rhythmic sound on the road, which she took to be the light, energetic footsteps of some youthful traveler passing by. Dusk, for the first time a dreaded arrival, was cloaking the hillside. As she looked out, she saw that a traveler came into view, and her name was being called. A soft, involuntary cry came from her lips. Again the call of her name was borne lightly on the air.

— Nephele!

She strained her eyes to take account of the traveler and stepped away from the darkness of the tree at the moment that the figure rounded the path to face her. The striking figure wore a broad-brimmed traveler's hat and a voluminous cloak while in his hand he carried a shepherd's staff. Now he smiled slowly, stopping a few feet away to await her recognition.

— Oh, oh! Can it truly be you, Lord Hermes?

In contrast to the dire circumstances, his voice was relaxed, reminiscent of other times, it seemed.

— No swooning, please, as lovely women are known to do at my arrival. I say this because there is not time for it. In fact, there is no time to spare.

In spite of her somber state, she smiled.

— Welcome! O how glad I am that you have come in answer to my calling. One prays, but one doesn't expect a *happening*, surely not at once.

— Are you saying, Nephele, that you prayed to me in all earnestness and yet expected no happening?

— Oh, you must not misunderstand me, Argophontes. It is a fact that we humans tend to be frail. We can only hope, you see.

— I assure you that hope is not frailty. It is your best strength, as a matter of fact, especially if combined with a steady eye on the next step to be taken.

Her eyes were examining his appearance in detail.

— Tell me, why do you come in a shepherd's garb? There is no problem at hand with the flocks. Why the staff in your hand?

He regarded her question, considering it for a time.

— I am before the light. I must penetrate the night where my staff is surely needed. Be patient, for the answer to your question will appear shortly, but first I must prepare you. Shall we sit on the boulder under the oak tree, well out of view? It is dangerous to encourage witnesses in the kingdom of Thebes, I've observed. Besides, I'm known to prefer the audience of the single attentive individual.

    He smiled encouragingly with these last words, and the two of them withdrew to the protective darkness of the oak tree, sitting on the boulder. She turned to the god, gratitude in her face.

— O Hermes, your very company has ended the shaking of my limbs in fear and dread.

    He nodded in acknowledgment, but his face was grave now.

— What has summoned me is the approach of a terrible action destined to blacken Thebes and bring you unimaginable loss.

— You know then about the sacrifice of Phrixos!

— Yes, I do, but keep your voice low. It is not sufficient to be unobserved. We must also not be overheard.

    She murmured in a voice so low that he bent to catch her words,

— O Hermes, lord of the way, it is you who is the true god of rescue!

— Yes, I admit to that.

    He smiled ruefully. Her whispering voice took on excitement now.

— An immense gratitude overwhelms me. Surely Phrixos will be saved from a terrible fate, and I shall have my son in my house as he was before!

    Hermes shook his head slowly as if with some regret.

— No, Nephele. There is a turning, you see. Things will not be as they were before. This I must tell you.

— Do you mean that you aren't able to save Phrixos after all?

— That isn't what I meant. His life shall not be extinguished on Thebes' altar. This you can count on. However, what I shall not save him from is his own destiny.

    At the word, her cheeks paled.

— How grateful I am that you will save him, but alas, what destiny can this be?

— There is a sacrifice you shall know that cannot be bypassed, Nephele, for Phrixos will go into permanent exile.

— Oh, how soon will this come about?

— Within this very hour. Tell me, what is dearest to your heart?

— There is the sustained desire that puts me in anguish even now. It is that Phrixos stay alive and that he be well!

— So be it.

    Moving quickly now, Hermes arose, and turning toward the woods beyond the oak tree, he gave a low whistle. At once there was a crackling in the brush as of something making its way toward them. Now the low branches parted, and a huge ram stood before them. What was even more exceptional than his size was the radiance that enveloped him, for his thick fleece was golden. Sheer astonishment overtook Nephele, who was speechless as she gazed on the animal. Hermes nodded to the ram before turning to reassure his companion.

— You need not fear him. After all, he is the *ram of the gods*.

— But a pastoral animal. I don't understand. In the midst of our crisis, the gods have sent a *sheep*?

— Exactly. Look closely upon the deliverer!

— How can he possibly save Phrixos?

— There's no time for further pondering and calculations of what's to come. You must act at once. Do you understand, Nephele? Already the night is advancing. Up to this point, I have shepherded the ram of the gods. Now much depends on you, for it is you, mother of Phrixos, who must lead him to the altar where your son lies bound. Allow the ram to stand by while you unbind Phrixos.

Nephele regarded the great ram with worry now and protested.

— Alas, Lord Hermes, I am no shepherdess, and I've really no skill with animals. O yes, I am accustomed to acting alone, but I am frightened.

Although capable of swift and effective action, Hermes also excelled in patience, and it was with gentle patience that he led Nephele now.

— See this rope that I've looped about his neck? Take firm hold of the end of it and begin to lead him. That's good. Do you see how he responds to your touch? He is a gentle fellow. Only trust the extraordinary gift from the gods in this desperate hour. And, Nephele, make haste, I say!

At once she began to lead the great ram forward at a lively pace while Hermes accompanied them as far as the edge of the road. Turning now, she addressed him.

— See this? It is the knife that I have carried hidden in my garments. Always I was hoping for a chance to cut my son's bonds. Now it is to happen! When I have freed Phrixos, what must I do next?

— See that Phrixos mounts the back of the ram at once and, finding that his sister has made her way to the altar, lift Helle to the back of the ram beside her brother. Make your fond farewells quickly, then tap the ram's rump, and you will see that he will lift off the ground and, with his great strides, will carry the children to safety far from Thebes. Soon the ram of the gods will put distance between Phrixos and the deadly plot of Queen Ino. Farewell, dear Nephele, and take heart!

Making the sacred gesture, she bade farewell with a heart of gratitude as she increased her pace to a slow run toward the altar, the ram keeping to her side as his golden radiance illuminated the path.

Making her way toward the woods that collared the hill's summit, Nephele reached the circle of trees shrouded in darkness while the ram of the gods trotted at her side in cheerful confidence. At once she tied her companion to a tree, and going forward toward the altar in the clearing, she came to where Phrixos lay bound atop the large pile of wood. Nephele dropped to her knees beside him. She laid her hand over his mouth in caution as his lips formed the surprised exclamation, "Mother!" Observing his bonds, she brushed aside tears lest they fall on him. The vivid image of Hermes dispelled her fear, and a new strength made its way through her. Furiously she cut the strong ropes that bound him, releasing first his arms and afterward his legs. Phrixos sprang to his feet, at the same time shaking his legs to free the numbness. It was then that his eyes fell on the ram a little distance from them, sniffling at his short tether. To repress his astonished reaction, she laid a finger to her lips. A whispered exchange engaged them, initiated by Phrixos.

— Mother, how did you come by this creature that emanates a fair golden light? A ram, no less.

— The ram is to be your rescuer. This very night, the god of the road, Hermes, visited me at our house. I tell you the truth. He came shepherding the great ram of the gods!

For the first time since his ordeal had begun, hope arose in Phrixos, burning with a steady flame.

— All praise to the gods! How is the rescue to be accomplished, I ask? Of course, it must include Helle as well. Even though she is presently untouched by the Theban plot, in my absence, she'll be in grave danger.

Even as Phrixos's question hung upon the air, a voice from nearby reached them, yet no one was seen. The voice was palpably close at hand when it addressed them.

— Hear me, Phrixos. The *how* of the great journey about to be launched cannot be known in advance. It is enough that you know that the ram's back is your means of escape. Trust it, by all means. Once seated on the animal, hold on for dear life as he lifts you and Helle away from the bitter ground of Thebes forever!

Even as he heard these saving instructions, Phrixos felt the inexorable movement of a destiny that deprived him of choice, claiming him. His face was pale with the anguish of separation as he spoke.

— Alas, what of the fact that I have loved my home, my mother, my father, and this kingdom? How can I give these up for all time?

The invisible figure could be heard to utter a deep sigh before he replied.

— It is a hard truth, for the land of Thebes bears no seed. Such is its malady. And have you not suffered from its condition? I am Hermes, god of rescue and of the road ahead. I must warn you that your rescue will not immediately bring you ease or solace.

Briefly the figure of Hermes stood beside them, visible and luminous, and Phrixos noted that the god's face held undeniable compassion. In a low voice taut with unshed tears, he replied.

— Lord Hermes, my gratitude for your deliverance exceeds all bounds! Tell me, will the ram of the gods take us to a far city then?

— He will carry you over the Aegean Sea to a far country. There your life can flourish, that is, on one condition.

— Alas, a far country you say . . . and what is this condition?

— That you shall never forget the Golden Fleece, no, not as long as you live. I speak of the fleece of the ram of the gods. Regard it with the highest honor. You must keep it safe. You must secure its well-being because it carried the incomparable light of the gods on earth. First the ram will carry you over deep waters and all manner of terrain. At the same time, he is known to travel swiftly and silently upon the invisible pathways known to me. Come, don't delay. Get onto the ram's back now!

During this low exchange, Helle had come, and she stood at a little distance back from the altar looking on the strange scene. Phrixos sprang lightly upon the ram's back as Nephele, who led Helle forward by the hand, lifted her daughter to the ample golden back as well. As Phrixos encircled his young sister with his left arm, the ram of the gods turned his head to regard his passengers with his great dark eyes before uttering a gentle bleating in acknowledgment. The two children bent low to embrace their mother in tender farewell. Even as they did so, their tears no longer restrained, the predawn silence was torn by distant voices on the lower path of the hill. Nephele spoke quickly, a brief return of fear registered.

— O my children, go at once. Go swiftly! Know that my heart's love shall always be with you. I pray to the gods to give you a good life. Farewell!

At once Phrixos pressed both heels into the ram's furry sides. As he lifted the single rope rein, the splendid animal appeared to lift up into the air and began to make huge strides eastward toward the sea, departing the ancient kingdom of Thebes. Nephele remained watching until the three figures were lost forever from view, and she was alternately filled with deep gratitude for the rescue and profound grief for the lifelong parting.

Hermes Rescues Ion

In the predawn hours, an agile figure wearing a voluminous cloak made his way among the Long Rocks on the steep slope of the Acropolis of Athens. On his head, he wore the traveler's broad-brimmed hat, and he carried in his hand a staff that appeared to emit a thin trail of light from its end. Reaching the legendary spot, alone among the rocks, he bent down to enter the cave. Memories streamed upon him of the little girl priestess of Athena, carrying the sacred basket into the depths of this very cave in the Panathenaia festival. Today held one such ritual. Indeed, he was counting on the goddess's attention being occupied elsewhere, not on what he was about. Within the cave, there was no evidence of dawn as the darkness received him. Nevertheless, his keen eyes at once spied the low ledge on which safely perched was the winnowing-fan cradle. Gazing down for some moments upon the child, he sighed. How extraordinary this baby was, a tide of delight and far-off satisfaction filling the observer. Hermes spoke to the child, who regarded him unblinkingly, and his voice was low.

— Ah, it's true, *you're it!* You are in luck that I recognized you, little one. I happen to be close to Mnemosyne, who is a great goddess, always remembering what is worth remembering. Human folks tend to forget what is best to remember, while they develop a great facility in remembering the trivial things that pass. So you smile at that. A good sign, I believe. You seem to like it here in your cave chamber, even though it looks like you are forever left in the dark. I am all for hunting out some possible light for you, I must tell you.

  The baby's eyes repeatedly checked out the cave's entrance, expectantly. Seeing this, a look of compassion crossed the god's face.

— Your mother has taken good care of you. I see this from your well-fed look, your fine garments, and blanket that she sewed for you, and amazingly, she has pinned exquisite ornaments on you as well. Listen to me. Don't close your eyes. You are about to take a journey, and I am coming along with you to keep you secret and safe. Those are my priorities. Baby Ion, here on the Acropolis, you are *disowned*, I tell you. This is the grave problem. I have come to rescue you, see? Ah, lad, don't howl. You could upset your rescuer, and you only have one of those. That's better. Could that be the beginning of a smile?

Hermes laughed as he took up small Ion into the crook of his left arm. He made sure that the finely woven blanket was wrapped about him and that the distinguishing ornaments were in place. Opening his woolen cloak, he tucked the babe into its sheltering folds, holding him close to his heartbeat. A look of alarm was on the infant's face, however, and leaning toward him, the tall companion whispered.

— Don't knock it. It's a good cloak and an excellent bed to be in. Nobody else has ever complained of traveling inside it!

Hearing this, the child stifled his cry.

Swiftly now and with long-schooled stealth, Hermes left the cave and descended the sacred hill in the last moments before the dawn of the new day. As they left the Acropolis behind, Ion gave a great mournful cry into the city's silence, a cry that haunted Hermes.

— Ah, little lad, I think you realize the tragedy of being owned and disowned, and you miss your mother. Let me tell you something. You greatly desire to be owned by those who love you. That's natural. Yet it is the devil to be owned! You are going to live as one who is not owned, for your ancestry is hidden still. And so it must be.

Ion straightened out his small body and cried lustily at these words. Following the path steadily westward, Hermes continued in a low voice.

— Don't worry. Creusa, your mother, will never forget you. She will hold you in her heart. This journey is not to escape your mother, I can tell you. It is to escape the enemy. By the way, if you continue howling, I fear that you will alert the enemy. You look puzzled at all this. Who the enemy is cannot be named precisely. It has so many faces, the enemy does, some of them looking benevolent enough to be your granddaddy, for that matter, who is king of Athens. We need to put distance between you and the enemy. This is clear. Besides, it is the choice of the gods. You're wide-awake and listening quietly now, I see. Ah, I believe that you have decided to trust me. Good. I am Hermes, god of the road.

Through the rugged mountains, climbing and descending steep and narrow paths more often frequented by sheep and goats, Hermes made his

way steadily toward Delphi. Often he spoke to the abandoned child, for
comfort and reassurance were among the gifts of the god of the road.

— Do you know why I wear this big cloak? I see I have your attention,
even if it is rather critical. Well, it's what a Greek shepherd wears in
order to weather the elements. A shepherd has to be with his flock
around the clock. No time off. Why, he can rescue a lamb that's fallen
into a gulch or he can carry inside the cloak a kid that has hurt itself.
I am a shepherd, see? As a matter of fact, I think of you as the little
kid I am rescuing. Now you are grinning—great! You've made my day.
I think you are coming to appreciate my cloak, actually. A shepherd is
a lonely sort of fellow. That's why he is such a reliable companion . . .
Ion, you'll be lonely in your life, I must warn you. Don't let loneliness
make you feel sorry for yourself. Actually, it is what saves you from
being an *anybody*. *You get to know who you are if you are lonely enough.* You are
no sheep, lost with the flock.

Baby Ion looked as if he was considering the words of his shepherd
and guide. The lonely part did not sound particularly pleasant to him.
As they rounded the path, Hermes stopped to gaze toward Mt. Helikon
searching for a sign of a Muse, for he knew that the nine Muses were at
home on Helikon where at the spring Hippocrene they gathered regularly
to refresh themselves. Interrupting his musing, Hermes spoke.

— There is something else about the shepherd. He knows all the paths,
and he knows where and when to take shelter from devouring animals.
That road off to the right leads to the city of Thebes, the place
that was founded by Cadmus when he was guided by a white heifer.
Cadmus was on a long journey just like us. Thebes has seen dragons,
boy, and it has seen loves even of the gods, with Aphrodite's necklace
sheltered there. It has known great births and battling warriors. The
ground of Thebes swallowed up the seer Amphiaraus in his chariot.
Would you believe that the city had seven gates? Still, we aren't going
to Thebes, lad.

Baby Ion frowned as if taking in the fact that Thebes was a rough
place and hardly a desirable destination. Even so, the look on Hermes' face
was definitely nostalgic.

Dusk lay gray and heavy over the sanctuary of Apollo on the lower
slope of Mt. Parnassus as Hermes and Baby Ion arrived at remote Delphi.
The fear of hostile pursuit lay far behind them while above them the two
dark peaks of the Phaedriades were watchful in the enveloping silence. Below
them, olive trees descended to the gulf, while in their midst, the temple of

Athena stood as guardian of the sanctuary of the oracle of Apollo. For some time, Hermes stood gazing upon the holy site. The baby stirred and began to make cooing sounds. The god smiled at this as though it were adequate commentary. Suddenly, however, Ion thrust both legs out, lifting and dropping them forcefully.

— Come now, lad. What's this you are saying? Am I at your command then? I do believe that you are ready for this place. Let me tell you how it is. This is the message the gods have for you: *Delphi is your new home, for you shall dwell in Apollo's sanctuary.*

Night was falling all about them as they made their way to the plateau where the temple stood, its stone columns ghostly in their unbending majesty. Standing before the temple in its solitude, Hermes removed Ion from his cloak and held him up in his arms to look upon the temple. Ion made a cry that was a high musical sound.

— That says it all right. My, but you are wide-awake, lad, although I expected that you would be. A few final remarks and I shall leave you, but never fear, you shall shortly be in good hands. Notice that there are several steps leading up to the temple. Listen well. The way of approach to the presence of Apollo is a step at a time. Do you understand? No one leaps there because he's clever. No one goes through the air to reach the god's wisdom. The ascent involves the human step, one at a time. It is the earth path that the god requires, and it is gradual. The truth of the matter is that, like all things in Apollo's realm, the way is *measured!* I shall make your bed here on the first step . . . . There! When Pythia, the priestess, comes at first light to the temple, greet her with your wondrous smile, lad. And as a last thought between us, know this: *it can take a lifetime to find one's true ancestry, but it will come to you, never despair!* Now, farewell, son of Creusa. I leave you in your new dwelling place under Apollo's watchful care. Sleep now, lad.

Hermes turned and departed, making his way down to the waters of the gulf. A veil of quiet fell over Ion tucked under his blanket on the temple step, a quiet that seemed human in its solicitude.

Odysseus and Hermes

A male voice of quiet authority spoke from lower down the path on which he was walking.

— Greetings, Odysseus! The times have been rare indeed in your eventful life, I must say, when you have observed that *the gate has two sides.*

— What's this? What gate are you speaking of?

The words of the speaker startled the seasoned hero.

— I speak of the only gate that concerns a man. How can it be named?

This strange reply caused Odysseus to stare into the deep shade of the wooded passage ahead, and he was able to perceive dimly the image of a slender agile figure. A candlelike glow gleamed from the end of the rod he carried, which was much like a shepherd's staff. As was characteristic of the Trojan hero, recognition came swiftly.

— Lord Hermes! Why, can it be you?

— Greetings, man of Ithaca. Or do you yet belong? The ordeal of the return is arduous, even for a warrior of your reputation.

The god's words fell upon him sharply, piercing what thin armor he still had. And yet, something in them seemed to offer a longed-for missing loaf. The pain of things at home on Ithaca's isle persisted, even so. Odysseus sought to explain.

— It was the suitors alone who were responsible for the dire predicament.

A small smile altered his troubled look as he continued, nevertheless.

— My lord, I owe my return, escaping the captivity of Circe, to you. Had you not picked the moly plant and given it to me, I should have ended up as one of her pigs. How grateful I am to you for my escape!

The god looked thoughtful.

— Circe's bounty can confuse a man to his detriment, I realized, and your predicament summoned me. Ah, but I must tell you what I perceive at this moment, Odysseus. It is the circle of return, and it draws me irrevocably. I am accustomed to listening for the place of beginning to utter its pristine voice of delight as it reaches toward life. Such listening is indispensable. Time passes, and the human individual comes midway on the circle path. Several voices are heard at once, intense, taut, often filled with distress, voices of one held in crisis, in the midst of the battle, in abandonment or extreme loss. Such was Achilles' own voice when I reached him where he lay dying on the field of Troy. Oh, the middle place stretches endlessly, it seems. Was I not haunted by Penelope's voice as sadly she sang at her loom during the years of awaiting your return?

Odysseus was uneasy. Was not the god unrelenting as he pressed him?

— But you spoke of return, a circle traversed to the starting place, one presumes. Will it receive me, this return? I must know, you see.

— Always you have been an impatient man, Odysseus, man of ingenious action.

Hermes smiled, softening his judgment as he continued.

— I believe that you called Penelope herself hard-hearted when the patient process of authentic recognition was upon her?

Reminded of this, Odysseus blushed in embarrassment, lowering his face. Hermes continued.

— Held in the vise of battle or crisis or loss, the human individual lets forth a great cry. Still, this marks only half of the circle's path in life. Next comes the voyage of recovery, of return to the familiar, the unfinished. There is a remembering that is called for. How many years was your voyage home from Troy?

— Nearly ten years. Actually, my journey of return has been almost as long as the war itself on the fields of Troy.

The thought settled him into gloom. Hermes shook his head slowly in incredulity, or could it have been in part pity for the man?

— Nor was it all voyage, since it included some extended stopovers, I believe.

Odysseus nodded curtly with a deep frown on his face. He did not find the god's account altogether pleasing. Hermes continued to regard him as he remained silent for a time. Odysseus raised his face at last and spoke with a steady voice, something of his familiar confidence revived.

— Lord Hermes, you see that I have arrived home in Ithaca at last. It was no small accomplishment, considering the fury of the sea, which was not the least of my combatants. Without question, I am home again! Is the circle of return not completed then?

The god pondered the question, considering the hero's account of things as though it might be new information. He replied gravely.

— The return is under way. I am able to assure you of this. It has entered the final segment of the path. After your joyous reunion with Penelope, tell me, has Mnemosyne come to you bringing old memory, I wonder?

— Memory? How strange that you should ask because the fact is that the past has recently unrolled before me as though it were present time. Didn't you say earlier that the essential gate has two sides? Well, I was in some manner taken to the far side of this gate, it seems. I was like one who goes down the path into Hades' realm below.

— What a privilege.

— Memory was stirred. Indeed, it was like a great dream that enveloped me. Had you not just now inquired about memory, it surely would have faded.

— Did you encounter anyone you knew in the land of the dead?

— As a spectator, I saw Agamemnon. The king of Mycenae had located Achilles and was speaking to him at length, praising him and recounting his death, telling him of the seventeen days that the Achaians mourned for him. Agamemnon described the funeral and the creating of the noble tomb with its fine gifts. Then it was, Lord Hermes, that I glimpsed your arrival, leading a group of men on the path into the underworld as you held forward your staff. In amazement, I saw that they were my enemies—the suitors!

Odysseus's voice was cut off suddenly by tears, and he did not continue. The silence that ensued was a comfort. It was Hermes who spoke at last.

— From your dream, I perceive that Achilles is meeting his death, and it is a death of lasting acknowledgment.

Odysseus was plainly astonished.

— Why do you speak as though this is happening in present time? A great loss indeed, Achilles' death is already an old fact. It is history.

— If you believe this, then you have not been listening to Goddess Mnemosyne. After all, she has the power to bring the past to life again, to give it flesh before one. It is your life that is addressed now, man of Ithaca. Consider what you have witnessed:

The warrior passes, who is greatly honored.

I go now. May the return yet be accomplished, Odysseus. Farewell!

PART IX

Hera

Hera Pondered—An Introduction

Once one has nodded to the fact that Hera is the queen of heaven and wife of the lord of the gods, there has been a tendency to assume that she is adequately acknowledged, yet this hardly proves to be the case. Hera not only presents a wealth and complexity of response but also her nature is rich in its attributes. Wreathed with the asterion, the starflower, she was hailed as Hera, "the Flowering." Always it is the maiden that is at the core of her mystery. In her lower sanctuary at Argos, she was worshipped as *Parthenos*, the virgin, for the wife had not yet emerged. On the island of Samos, where her worship was very early, it is Hera the maiden who flees to the lygos thicket to hide herself when it is announced that Zeus has arrived seeking her for his bride. Even when the marriage with Zeus is consummated at Hera's house on the high hill at Argos and she becomes his wife, the *Parthenos* remains as the maiden who in the annual rite arises anew from the sacred spring Kanathos. Indeed, the pomegranate she holds in her hand in the great statue by Polycleitus was an indication of Hera honored as the underworld Persephone. It is her title of *Teleia*, given to Hera of the mountain top, that proclaims "the completed one, the fully realized," for now she is wife at the culmination of the sacred marriage.

Our gaze falls upon the goddess Hera in her ancient sanctuary at Argos, where she was especially disclosed in her bounty. Here is *she who loves her house*, the Greeks pointed out, placing a finger upon a primary force that belongs to an earth goddess and is essential to human existence in its feminine aspect. Her passion is for the very act of dwelling, of claiming one's own abiding place. This compelling force accompanied Hera's desire for uniting man and woman in marriage and blessing the birth of children. Surely Hera's house is not to be perceived as an external house or a physical address. By nature, the state of dwelling is invisible; the abiding passion for the act of dwelling pervades her more difficult and complex attitudes toward human behavior as well. Because she greatly loved her house, the first temples built in Greece were dedicated to Hera. Even at Olympia, where Zeus came in time to be supreme, Hera preceded Zeus in a long established worship.

What is it to dwell, to engage this fundamental action of an animal, a human being, or a god? It is to be contained, to be sheltered within a given place; and when the place is claimed as one's own, there approaches the relatively serene action of dwelling. When fully engaged, the act of dwelling gives rise to the sense of belonging, carrying with it a quiet, intimate satisfaction. In addition to safety, a continuity is provided. Having claimed one's place, one is at home. Closer than a spouse is this claim. At the center is not the exterior place but a state of being.

When the strong hero appears, however, an opposite movement occurs, one that appears to be an enemy of such dwelling. The heroic spirit responds to a higher, often elusive summons. With this response, the tranquil condition of dwelling is sacrificed, for a journey compels the hero, causing a significant movement. As Karl Kerenyi wrote, one who journeys is at home when he is under way, for he is at home on the road or on the sea. When the individual abiding in the Hera perspective encounters such heroic movement, what happens is opposition, rebuke, and antagonism. This could account in considerable part for Hera's opposition to Heracles in his undertakings. Hera is upholding her end of things, and her action is less personal in its text than it first appears.

In the course of life, there are many kinds of shelters offered by the culture, and one usually tries out several of these. Among them are a course of study or training, a job, a career, a partnership, a marriage, parenting, a religious or philosophical path, an adventure. One of these choices may come to take precedence over all others, requiring the greater portion of one's concentration and energy. For Zeus, his union with Hera was an ongoing shelter, and he submitted annually to the mystery of its renewal. To accomplish his Olympian marriage, Zeus had to go to Hera's house, as the ancient rites indicate, since to Hera alone was attributed not only the well-being of marriage but a providing of its true and satisfying dwelling place.

Now the marriage of the supreme masculine and the eternal feminine brought a paradise of delight, according to its description in the *Iliad*. The three-hundred-year honeymoon of Zeus and Hera confirms this, surely. Nevertheless, the union of the two Olympians was not always easy and at times was tempestuous. Greek commentary from early to late antiquity attributed this turbulence to Hera's jealousy and outrage as she faced the many loves of Zeus, which excluded her. The question arises as to how just the resulting image of Hera is that received such wide acknowledgment. More to the point, has there been an obscuring of what was envisioned as the supreme feminine? Hera was consistent, indeed tireless, in her view of her existence as *wife*, which she regards as an ongoing aspect of the great feminine. Hera's perspective on the archetype of wife is enlightening, even for the modern individual. She holds wife to be one—only, permitting neither substitutes nor additions. She must have experienced love as engaging the delights that Aphrodite brings, only to become a fast-bonded devotion between the luminous, inimitable masculine and the abiding and queenly feminine. As she who dwells, Hera insists on love's unarguable place, a place not to be challenged or given to general competition. When her beloved Zeus forsakes this dwelling place, however briefly, Hera is in anguish.

And what of Zeus himself? In the vital and ever-narrative movement of the god, he reminds us of the hero's destiny of being ever on the way, in movement. The inherent nature of spirit is manifested. From Hesiod's cosmology is drawn the fact that heaven and earth are inexorably drawn together to become lovers and partners. Time and again, Zeus manifests his passion toward the human realm, and as a result, there emerges into human experience the progeny that is of the two realms. At the same time, his action defies the continuity of dwelling in his Olympian marriage that Hera insists upon. There appears to be an uncompromised autonomy that belongs to each of these great gods and what they create in human existence. The Greek resolution in the face of these opposing forces is instructive: each is honored, given a throne.

In the context of Hera and the hero, there arises an image that is difficult to accommodate, and yet the image may provide an important window through which to view the myths at hand. The image is taskmistress. Within its many variations—taskmaster, taskmistress, boss, commander, foreman, etc., we sense the trail of a dark shadow that hovers over the work at hand. The presence of the taskmistress challenges one beyond present achievement and is rarely welcome. In relationship to Heracles, Hera in her role as taskmistress is at the core of his work. At the same time, it removes her from the image of the heartless, almost demonic punisher. Instead, she becomes partner of the hero in facing the task.

There is one among the Twelve Labors of Heracles in which Hera played a role, and it is the second labor, the slaying of the Hydra. Heracles arrived with his nephew, Iolaus, at the great swamp of Lerna where some of the most abundant springs of Greece poured forth. Within the swamp lived the monstrous Hydra with her nine heads. He came alone to face the creature and set himself to what seemed the impossible task of decapitating the circling heads with his faithful club. At once he found that he must extricate himself from the powerful tentacles that the Hydra coiled tightly about him, which threatened to choke him. When he had succeeded in decapitating a couple of heads, an enormous crab appeared, facing him in a way that brought terror. The crab had arrived to defend the Hydra, no less, and it was sent by Hera herself. Now it was two monsters against one human individual. He succeeded in slaying the crab before he called to Iolaus to help him in the crisis. The two managed to decapitate the eight mortal heads of Hydra and to bury the ninth one, which alone was immortal.

Hera's sponsoring of the crab against the slaying of the Hydra would seem to deny any idea of partnership with the hero's undertaking. Yet we must not grow faint in our search for elucidation. Surely this is no malevolent trick on Hera's part. Such would hardly be worthy of the Olympian queen goddess. Her action in the second labor may be regarded as an act of *limitation*. Measure is ever at issue for the ancient Greeks, Apollo being the decisive voice of the wisdom of measure. Heracles is severely limited by the participation of the crab against him in the task. He experiences his human vulnerability, his frailty. In the moments of the terrible encounter in the Lernean swamp, whatever high unassailable identity he knew, as son of Zeus endowed with Olympian strength, falls away from him. It is as if he sheds a wrongly claimed cloak in the midst of that ordeal. Similarly, in the twentieth century, Jung warned against the grave danger to the psyche of identifying with an archetype in its godlike power. Yes, the crab saves Heracles. At once he seeks help from his young assistant. Because of Hera's enigmatic gift of the crab, Heracles is restored to human measure.

Before Hieros Gamos

A woman of striking countenance walked along the bank of the Imbrasos River that coursed the flat sea plain. She moved in an indefinable grace that stirred in the observer a radiant ancient memory. Pausing, she stood very still gazing at the temple on the low rise, its Doric columns golden in the light of the setting sun. Her brow was furrowed as though something perplexed her. Observing the steadily flowing river, she began to speak.

— O Imbrasos, river that saw my birth here on far Samos in the midst of the Aegean Sea, Hera seeks you out! No one doubts, least of all you, that I am *Parthenos*—everlasting maiden—and thus I would remain. Entering the temple at dawn on this very day, a dread crept into my belly, I must tell you, for I saw the object at last that my priestesses had been hovering over for days, preparing it with excited whisperings. It was the bed!

The river, full of deep murmuring sound, spoke to the goddess.

— Ah, the marriage bed, then? It would be strewn with mounds of fragrant flowers of early summer and the withies, for this is the season of the *hieros gamos*, as you know. What is disturbing you, Lady?

— Alas, a little distance still from the holy object, I stood very still, and my heart sank as my eyes took in the bed, and its intent assaulted me like some small thunderbolt. In that moment, I knew that I could not lie there! Do you in your loud murmuring hear me, Imbrasos? I said that I cannot lie in the bed prepared for me!

— The bed is within your house, Hera. Always you are at home in your house, for is it not said, Hera is *she who dwells*?

When she responded, her voice was slow and musing.

— Yes, I do love my house and therefore the temple. Naturally I enjoy the comings and goings of my maiden priestesses, who keep a good house for the most part. You see, I am only truly contained when I am found within my house. There I am gathered in and near the pulse of life.

— As the full harvest is gathered in, Lady?

— Even so.

    The river's deep voice probed further.

— So, what is it like to be uncontained?

— Fragmented, a person presents a piece of herself here, a piece there, without ever presenting the whole of what she is. One isn't all there. Usually she is responding only to the outer practical demands of a situation.

    Now the river's voice was musing, nor was the god of the river inclined to edit his musings.

— Surely you yourself, Hera, have been known to be uncontained on occasion.

    She sighed an abysmal sigh as he went on.

— For example, from some reports, when Heracles was severely challenged by his Twelve Labors, you were said to add difficulties to his difficulties. Some accused you of being malicious. As for myself, I am keeping an open mind.

    Hera groaned aloud as her hands flew to her cheeks.

— Alas, my critics view me through their limited lens! Let me tell you the truth instead. I have not an easy role to bear with splendid Heracles, son of Zeus. I am for him taskmistress! It has not been easy for him to endure the taskmistress. Still, without her, the genius of the hero would not have been fully called forth, I tell you.

— Hmm, taskmistress you say. Well, you do get a kind of obscure thanks in the fact that *Hera* is the root of his name.

— Ah, so you noticed that, did you?

    Her companion returned to the matter of her house.

— So, what is it like being contained within Hera's house?

— I am neither fragmented nor dispersed, for I am gathered in. My house centers me, and I am one only. As a result, the response that another gets from me is from a bountiful and serene place. When I am held within my dwelling place, what one receives is from a natural, undiminished place such as earth herself is known to provide.

— I must say that it is good news that your house keeps you in excellent condition, Hera. Now, there is a different matter before you, having to do with the bed of love. What will you do with this matter?

— I cannot say. I only know that I am frightened somehow.

— If you remove the bed, what will Zeus do? Will he still come?

— Zeus!

What was it that startled him in her voice, for she had cried out the single name with a passion tinged with alarm, surely?

— Yes, Lord of Olympus. He is said at this season to set his sight on far Samos Island, for he desires you for his bride.

— Zeus is the Olympian who sets forth again and again, always straight in his purpose. How like his very own thunderbolt he is! What can he know of what it is to *dwell*? Dwelling belongs instead to my knowledge. When he arrives, his step eloquent upon the threshold, then is my dwelling place altered! I know this, and I am fearful.

— This alteration of which you speak has long been regarded by the Greeks as a thing dearly longed for. As a matter of record, Zeus goes with his purposeful stride toward the place that draws him inexorably, for he is never frivolously attracted, I think. Hera, *Zeus is drawn to the very place where he does not dwell!* Indeed, he lacks the formula for dwelling.

— It is strange what you say, and I admit the truth of it. Yet why should I concern myself with truths that reside in Zeus?

— Alas, would you deceive yourself? The answer already abides in your heart: *you love Zeus.* That is reason enough. Why are you opposing him?

— Because I am Hera, supreme goddess of Samos. Look upon me, Imbrasos. I am everlasting *Parthenos*—she who cannot be taken by any man, mortal or immortal!

— No one here on Samos questions these facts, I assure you. Can it be that you are trembling the way a maiden does on the threshold of her marriage? I expect that even a great goddess trembles. Ah, yes, I am beginning to see how it is. Surely you tremble, maiden Hera, because who can withstand the coming of Zeus?

— At last you begin to understand how it is, dear river god. Again and again it arises within me—an enormous no, and it passes through my entire being. Yes, it is cold to the core, and yet it has a certain passion of its own. This no that is mine is Hera's defense. It is like the wall that protects the city, unassailable and stern. Without the no, what shelter do I possess? Do not take it from me, Imbrasos, I beg you!

After a silence broken only by the river's thundering over rocks, the voice of the river god came.

— I do not seek to change you. How could I? It is the sacred marriage to come that will do that. Yet it is evident that this marriage will not come about without the deep protest of your no. The way of the no is gloomy and narrow, a dark passage at best. Ah, Hera, do not allow it to keep you out of the light too long. As your friend, this is my counsel.

Light footsteps were approaching, and Hera looked up to see that her chief priestess was coming toward her on the riverbank. At once, the priestess addressed her excitedly.

— My lady, here you are. We have been searching for you. Surely you realize what festive day is upon us. You cannot have forgotten? Why, it is the day of your wedding—a joyous day! Soon the bridegroom will arrive, and he will seek you out at once.

— For a long time, you have been my trusted priestess, Parthenia. Now listen to what I say. The bridegroom comes, seeking me in my dwelling place, but consider that my dwelling place is vast. It is not limited to the temple, which alone cannot contain me. The whole of the dwelling place knows my step intimately.

The priestess gazed in some perplexity upon the goddess before responding.

— Knowing this well, we have created anew your special dwelling place on the mountain—Hera's house. Small as it is, how happily it will shelter the holy union. All is in readiness, my lady. You are not to worry.

— Come, my daughter, not even Hera's house can contain me where I truly dwell! Oh, who can put limits upon me, circumscribing my being into a narrow channel designed to be predictable and final? Know me, priestess, and know that this is not possible. Always I exceed where the holy rite places me. Always I am greater than what you perceive in your goddess.

— How can being wife of Zeus himself be too narrow for you? Alas, what are we to do?

Her voice rose in a wail, and making the sacred gesture, she turned and ran down the riverbank to tell the other priestesses. Alone again, Hera became thoughtful.

— Something moves, not as an object which the eyes or the senses perceive. It is an inexorable movement such as the moment when the Fates have finished their counsels. Ah, it moves toward me. There can be no mistaking now. It is the moment of destiny for eternal *Parthenos!* O maiden Hera, what shall you do?

Hera's voice rang out over the riverbank so that even Imbrasos suspended his murmuring and slowed the current's descent to the sea. After a little while, the goddess's voice was low, even secretive, as she murmured to herself.

— Now I perceive a way . . . It is that I shall flee! Come, feet, be swift and light as the movement of the woodland doe and carry Hera away to a hidden place as in a great wind. My sandaled feet meet air and ground alternately in a rhythmic pounding, as if to awaken Earth Goddess anew. Well, there is distance now between me and the temple as I turn toward the tall thicket of shrubs and sea grasses. Ah, this hidden wilderness receives me into its verdant, dense realm. Now I can go more slowly, for I am out of view of the temple and safe—safe even from my dear priestess. The thicket is dark and a tangle of branches, but it is the place I seek for hiding. Here the wild lygos grows profusely. See how it blooms, sending out its blue, white, and rosy candles. On all sides, the branches lay hold of me in their wild weaving. Why, the whole green world reaches out to claim me! What has happened? I can move not another step but am seized and gripped. It is the withies that grow here in the hidden place. They are binding me as with many leather thongs! Behold Hera, the maiden made prisoner in the lygos!

Hidden in the Lygos

The tall stranger walked restlessly up and down the path before the great temple of Hera, and his comely face with its lively intelligence held an enigmatic look as he would stop to gaze at the splendid temple. An hour had passed since he observed the priestess entering the temple, her arms laden with fragrant green branches. He watched now as she emerged from the columned entrance, her arms empty, and he stepped forward, clearing his throat.

— A moment please, priestess. May I ask what have you done with that load of fragrant branches I saw you carry into the temple earlier? Surely one does not lay a fire in Hera's temple.

The eyes of the priestess assessed the extraordinary stranger, widening with a pleasant response, which spilled over her first words until, disciplining it severely, she addressed him as a somewhat backward student of Samian tradition.

— Ah, so you are a stranger recently arrived on Samos Isle . . . Well, to be sure, we never build a fire within the goddess's temple. Look at the great altar behind the temple and you will see that the fires have already burned there, sending the smoke of sacrifice skyward. The heap of ash grows high.

She gestured in the direction of the very old altar. He nodded and pressed her with a small smile.

— And are you about to reveal the purpose then of the wild boughs? I should have thought that roses or perhaps lilies might be more likely to please your goddess. Surely Hera has no taste for wildness!

— I see that you do not know our goddess well, for you are mistaken. Why, she prefers the wild lygos tree to all else! Here on Samos, we know her desires well.

What was it that he read in her look when she revealed this about her goddess? Although tinged with awe, her emotion betrayed a sudden upsurge of worry, he perceived.

— To say that you Samians know Hera quite thoroughly is saying a great deal, I believe. Well, I must confess that I know nothing of the lygos.

— I should think not. It grows only here on the flat banks of the river Imbrasos, putting forth its white and blue and pink blossoms in high summer. Look toward the river below us.

Together they turned their heads and gazed down on the shining river's narrow stream. The dark-eyed gaze of the stranger lingered thoughtfully upon the river's verdant bank before he commented.

— A dense thicket of black green as far as the eye can follow, one sees. Nothing in particular can be distinguished, it appears. Surely a person can easily get lost within that thicket, or maybe hide out indefinitely and never be found again, priestess!

— Indeed!

She gasped audibly as she spoke, lowering her eyes to the ground, and the stranger observed her keenly, his face solemn. Quietly he laid the question down.

— No one happens to be concealed there, I trust?

She did not answer but shook her head slowly from side to side. Did this indicate "No" or, possibly, "I cannot speak"? One does not dare guess in the presence of Hera's high priestess. As if turning the page of their exchange to a new chapter, she spoke calmly and with dignity now.

— Today is the day that we call *hieros gamos*.

At once a wave of pleasure claimed him, slow-moving and laden with small delights that entered every nook and crevice, and his smile was of one who gazed upon a future scene.

— Yes, I know. But the preparations present some mystery I am unable to comprehend. Tell me, priestess, is Hera, the bride, ready?

Hearing this question, the priestess shook her head. She appeared mystified and at the same time tense with some worry. Should she tell him or not? Her companion's very presence proved persuasive.

— No, Lady Hera is not ready. First she must be *found*, you see.

Shock registered on the face of the lordly stranger.

— Your goddess is *lost*?

— Lost she cannot be. It is that she has disappeared. Hera has hidden herself!

Would she regret having divulged this intimate knowledge she possessed? He was voicing his obvious astonishment. Truly he took a genuine interest in Samos's life.

— That's incredible! To think that Hera has run off! I thought that she would barely be able to contain her eagerness for this marriage!

— Oh no, she is not eager in the least, even though the bridegroom is to be Zeus himself. Did you know that, I wonder?

With a very large sigh, he nodded. She continued.

— Fled from the temple, she did, and left us. She has been gone for some time. Sure as the new moon is dark, she will have fled into the lygos thicket. She seeks the wild place. Often she would say, "I must go to the withies." That's what we call the lygos branches. This is the way it is with Hera: always she hides from us!

Now the lordly stranger took in this shocking revelation as best he could. After a long painful pause, he asked the question in a low voice,

— She is known to adore Zeus, though. Will she even hide from him?

The priestess nodded without hesitation.

— Oh yes indeed. She even hides from great Zeus, her beloved. It is what she is wont to do. She must answer the call of the river and lose herself in the dense green darkness of the lygos as she goes all alone.

— Then there is nothing for it but for Zeus to pursue her in the thicket, surely!

It occurred to her that here was a man used to getting things done. Still, she must shake her head in protest.

— Stranger, it is strictly forbidden for a man to enter the lygos thicket.

— What if the man is Zeus himself?

She shook her head firmly.

— He is male as well.

Now the stranger could hardly argue this fact. He groaned instead. That he looked defeated was an observation that puzzled her. She would attempt to explain further.

— Sheltered by the lygos, a woman returns to her chaste and virginal self. It cannot be otherwise. That is why no man may enter here.

— Are you certain that this goddess of yours is Hera herself and not that maid of the wilds Artemis?

— Ah, it is a mystery, for the more one comes to know the goddess, the more she presents many aspects. Great Hera is hardly destined to bear a single face to mortals, or to Zeus, for that matter.

A small smile returned to the face of the stranger, and he relaxed once again.

— I do well to remember that. Tell me, priestess, do you place the lygos boughs within Hera's temple in hopes of bringing her back, back to where she belongs?

— For us who know the goddess, the meaning of this custom speaks plainly. The lygos has been sheltering the goddess rather like a wild mother, keeping her chaste. In this way, the lygos prepares the bride. Bringing the boughs into Hera's temple, we line the sacred marriage bed with them. When I perform this rite, something within me cries out, "O Lady Hera, we've found your hiding place in the lygos and bear in our hands some of its boughs. May these boughs continue to preserve your wildness and your bloom!"

The words of the priestess caused the stranger to shake his head slowly.

— Hera's choice is a strange one to my ears, while the gift of her priestesses to her marriage is even stranger.

— *Strange* and *stranger*—are not these very words the ones that attract the protection of great Zeus himself, for he is called god of strangers? Stranger, look to Zeus for your hospitality on our fair island!

With a slight bow and a smile, she departed, and he watched her go thoughtfully. Yet his thoughts continued to be filled with Hera herself. He murmured aloud.

— Already I am delivered to the hearth fire of dear Hera, I believe. And when will she receive me? I must wait. Ah, waiting does not come easy for Zeus.

With the sound in their ears of the rhythmic breaking of the waves on the beach flat, the priestesses stood within the tiny clearing that was roofed by branches bearing hundreds of candlelike blossoms. Their shelter was the dark maze of the ancient lygos thicket. Against the largest tree leaned the most sacred wooden image of Hera. On closer scrutiny, it was plain to see that the goddess was bound from shoulders to feet by the strong withies, the entangling boughs of the lygos. It was said that far away in distant Sparta, the great Artemis had her holy image similarly bound.

Yet a new time had descended upon the sanctuary, and the priestesses sensed it now as a bright sense of expectation passed through them. The chief priestess trembled as she leaned toward Hera's ear and spoke aloud.

— You were bound, dear Goddess, and you could arouse no one. It was for your safety and ours. Ah, but the hour has come. It is the hour of your unbinding, for the day of your wedding is dawning!

Having said these words, she was joined by the priestesses in cutting the goddess free of her bonds. They hoisted her upon their shoulders and, departing the lygos thicket, carried her with solemn grace in the direction of the temple, the green withies dangling from her form like garlands. The first stop on the way was at the spring, where they performed the rite of purification. Later, the great procession of all the people would take place through the streets when Hera, present in the sacred image they now carried, would be carried to her bridal bath. As she rises once again from her bath, the people will hail her as Parthenia, the virginal one who awaits her divine bridegroom. Only then will Hera be ready for great Zeus.

The Cuckoo Scepter

She stood on the low hill gazing at the Bay of Argolis, her radiant beauty distinguished by a sovereign brow. As Zeus observed her at a little distance, he took note that on the golden scepter, which she held rather carelessly, there perched a cuckoo, its beady eyes surveying the immediate vicinity, its only commentary a periodic fluttering of wings. Clearly, this was Goddess Hera's own bird, and it had no intention of taking flight. Slowly he made his approach. It was the bird that he addressed aloud.

— Good morning, bird. So you are the bold creature that dares lay your eggs in some other bird's nest instead of within your own! And what does it matter to you that the other birds are not forewarned of your plan?

Only the bird heard the words of Zeus, blinking twice solemnly. Hera was aware of his approach and looked up, smiling as she greeted him with some surprise.

— Greetings, Zeus! And what brings you to the green plain of Argolis, I ask?

Zeus looked thoughtful before he replied, as though considering the question he had not yet asked himself.

— Greetings, Hera. I thought I'd like to look in on you within your own kingdom, that is to say, this *queendom*. Besides, it is rumored that spring in these parts is unparalleled in the whole of Greece.

This acknowledgment pleased her, although when Zeus himself spoke of spring's possibilities, she had best be wary. Her response was nevertheless immediate and spontaneous.

— Oh yes, spring is my season. How it fills my eyes with new delight and swells my heart! However much my travels take me about, come springtime, I must be at home in Argos. But then, you know this.

She gazed at him now with tender, intimate regard, which had the effect of bringing a certain fire to his eyes, a fire known to be supplied by the god Eros.

— Ah, Hera, you are the vision of spring itself, which fills my heart. You are all the shining river nymphs and dancing nymphs of Pan put together in one womanly form, I tell you!

Hera blushed, and even her brow seemed no longer sovereign but more like a maiden's. Zeus continued, his voice now taking on a sense of wonder.

— It is said that you renew your virgin being around this time every year. We are told that it comes about through your bathing in a certain spring.

— Ah, Kanathos has extraordinary waters, yet what takes place is a mystery. I do not speak of it. Who dares tell my secret? I shall not take you to Kanathos, Zeus.

Zeus replied, his eyes brimming with laughter.

— That's quite all right, you know, for I have no need of it.

— Indeed!

— Come now. Have I offended you when I only meant to state the facts? Actually, what first captured my attention on my arrival was your little bird.

— My cuckoo? Isn't she dear? Ah, she is so faithful to me. She is never out of my sight.

The words struck him like a blow.

— By Olympus, do you regard that as a virtue? Why, my eagle is ever making a point of being out of my sight!

Hera was disconcerted and fled to the defense of her bird.

— Faithfulness, Zeus, is surely a virtue. I were not queen goddess in this region if I did not require it.

Zeus supported his head with his right hand and sighed audibly.

— Hera, my love, what is faithfulness?

Although with many subjects, speech might fail her, with this one of faithfulness, she could speak at length without a pause. Her eyes were bright as she replied.

— It's knowing to whom one belongs and honoring that bond with constancy. Why, in faithfulness, uncertainties fall away, there is no wandering, no frightful interruption . . .

To Zeus's ears, she seemed to be reading from a strange text. He spoke quietly.

— My dear, I shouldn't have thought so.

    The sovereign brow frowned, and her temper flared.

— You dare to oppose me in Argos? Or can it be that faithfulness is foreign to your nature?

— Two questions at once, both of them spearing me sharply! Shall we invite your bird, the faithful cuckoo, to join us in this spot where a dilemma claims us?

— Yes. You know that I adore my cuckoo.

— Let me see. Have you observed her habit in springtime, by the way?

    Hera looked puzzled.

— What do you refer to?

— I speak of the time when she must lay her eggs. There is apparently no difficulty about the laying itself, and she carries through with this nobly. At the same time, she insists that the eggs be laid in *some other bird's nest*. This is what is unique with her. Perhaps she but thinks to have the mothering task shared. What is clear, however, is the fact that she is no longer faithful to her own nest.

    Hera looked startled for a moment before, smiling indulgently, she passed her hand before her face as if to shoo away a fly.

— Can it be? Oh well, she really is quite charming, don't you think?

— If charm is the main thing at issue, yes, I agree. But faithfulness?

    The look on her face was that of a maiden whose idyll on the bank of a stream had been interrupted.

— O Zeus, don't be tiresome!

— I've been described in many ways by a woman who admires me, but never as *tiresome*. Yet those you describe as faithful are somewhat likely to be tiresome, it appears to me. Ah, look who comes.

— Why, it is Hermes. Greetings, Hermes, and welcome to ancient Argos!

    The three gods greeted each other warmly, and Hera indicated a third boulder as Hermes' seat in the shade of the old oak. As the god of the road took his seat with a satisfied sigh, his eyes fell upon the cuckoo, who was frowning upon his arrival and ruffling her wings energetically now. Hermes raised his eyebrows at the bird, giving her a nod of acknowledgment. "Keeping score, are you?" he asked Hera's bird companion with a grin. In response, the bird closed her eyes as if to begin napping. Hermes spoke thoughtfully as he continued to regard the cuckoo.

— She has long been your companion, Hera, has she not? Of all birds, she is a curious choice, is she not?

    Hera frowned.

— Why do you say this, Hermes?

— Well, you see, she possesses this broad outlook on the dwelling place. You yourself, above all the Olympians, place great value on your very own dwelling place here in Argos. Always this bird, on the contrary, must be making some new investment in some other bird's nest, taking over the place with her eggs, I mean. Yes, cuckoo, distant one, the exotic nest is the one that regularly summons you.

Zeus heard Hermes out although his eyes were on Hera's face, watching her response. He spoke briefly now.

— Hera finds the bird altogether charming, she has told me.

Hermes took this in with astonishment.

— Ah then, you are of two minds, Hera. On the one hand, you find this wide sharing of love's bounty to be charming while, on the other hand, when it comes to the matter of a spouse, you find it abhorrent. Well, I do find that a person who accommodates each of two minds tends to be better company and more sound than one who is ruled by one mind alone. What do you say, Zeus?

Zeus's face was suffused with pleasant relief like one who, lost in a wilderness, comes suddenly upon an inviting footpath. A slow smile accompanied his response.

— Thank you, my friend, for this observation. It illuminates the place where I find myself abandoned somehow.

A look of alarm followed by concern occupied Hera, who was speechless for a time. Turning tenderly to Zeus, she spoke.

— Dear, dear Zeus, it grieves me to hear you speak of your abandonment! Springtime is the tip of the bud, of the not yet to be, and here in Argos, we have been breathlessly awaiting your arrival. Oh, you have come, the bridegroom I have been waiting for, and your coming prepares the way of the new maiden! When she comes to be, you shall take her happily as your bride. Of this I am certain in my heart.

Both Zeus and Hermes threw back their heads and laughed with joyous relief. Zeus took Hera's hand tenderly, but now she arose to her feet and made ready to depart. Zeus only held her hand more firmly.

— Let me go, Zeus.

— Why should I, after your words spelling out our love?

— Because we are in the time of the not yet. Even so, the bud swells on plant and tree.

— Linger with me, my love.

For a long moment, Hera was helpless to oppose the lord of the gods. Now the queen goddess of Argos smiled at him and withdrew her hand, leaving her message with her beloved.

— The time is at hand for my ritual bath. I go at once to the spring Kanathos for the transforming bath! Farewell, Zeus. Farewell, Hermes.

Reluctantly, he let her go. Now Hermes and Zeus departed, striding across the plain side by side.

The Shepherds and Hera's House

(Scene: House of Hera, Mt. Akraia above Argos)

The two shepherds led the flocks up the steep, rocky path of Mt. Akraia and reached the summit as dusk settled over the plain of Argos. A chilly rain began, and the rising wind howled around the stones. With a gesture, the older shepherd indicated that they make their way to the overhanging rock for shelter. With gentle calls to the sheep and the authoritative guidance of the rod, they gathered the flock into the cavernous rock shelter, stationing themselves at the entrance. Only a few yards away stood the tiny treasured house. As they gazed toward it, recognition came slowly, and each made the sacred gesture. It was the older shepherd who spoke.

— Hera's house it is, and wouldn't this be the time of the holy marriage?

— It's May. It could be . . . . Boy, We're packed in here all right. I'd give anything for a little room in this damp, dark place.

— Consider we're lucky to be out of that cold wind on the peak. Besides, it could be some sort of privilege to bed down this close to Hera's house. Has that occurred to you?

His younger companion shrugged his shoulders. Curiosity was his primary emotion of the moment.

— Has anybody ever witnessed this holy marriage—I mean, has anyone been close enough to verify that it happens?

The older shepherd didn't welcome this young skepticism, as his reply showed.

— When it comes to a most holy thing, witnessing isn't called for.

Curiosity is, however, not a thing set comfortably aside; the young shepherd threw aside his heavy cloak as he pressed the issue.

— In a little while, how about we go to the place and peek in the window?

The older shepherd's *no* was explosive.

— I was just asking. Who gets here first, I wonder, or do the two gods come together arm in arm? I mean, how's it all arranged?

— Ioannis, you don't know? Hera is here first. After all, it is her house. Long, long ago, folks found out that Hera longed for a house of her own, a place where she might abide peacefully and happily, on and on. And so, she got her house. If anyone—even a great god—desired her companionship, he had to come to her house, see?

— Wait a minute, didn't she have a splendid temple? Why would she want this tiny house in an inaccessible spot, and why make such a deal of it?

— Well, the fact is that the *hieros gamos* only takes place in an inaccessible, far place. It can't happen close to other folks. It can't even be close to other gods, it appears.

— Really? It's the most private thing I've ever heard of.

Now the older shepherd nodded, smiling his agreement.

— Private—it's all for the two of them. You're finally making sense.

His companion looked regretful.

— Every wedding I've been to gathered in a lot of folks, friendlylike. This *hieros gamos* doesn't sound, well, friendly.

— The marriage of Hera and Zeus isn't like that. It's different, and it's the best. That's why it has to be sheltered properly. Otherwise, it follows the course of any other good wedding.

Slowly, curiosity in Ioannis was giving way to something else less familiar, yet compelling.

— This wedding's different, you say.

— Of course it is.

— Say, Hera may already be waiting alone in her house over there. The place looks silent and sort of waiting. How can she be sure that her bridegroom will come?

— Well, there's much that a fellow can't understand about this happening. No, I don't believe that she can be *sure*. I've heard one of her priestesses say that it takes time and a fair amount of doing in order for Hera to be altogether ready to be the bride. Unless she really has herself ready to be the bride, the bridegroom—Zeus himself—doesn't get summoned.

— What the priestess says confuses me even more. Why, Hera is a great goddess. I can't imagine her needing a lot of preparations to get her in shape, even for marriage.

The old shepherd sighed.

— Ioannis, the happenings of the gods are not the sort that are finished and perfect and packaged away for reuse. Hasn't this occurred to you? The more mysterious and important the happening is, the more likely it is that it must be in the making, coming together moment by moment.

Ioannis, perplexed, shook his head as he took this in.

— Tell me, what do you suppose that Zeus is doing during this getting-ready process of Hera's?

— I've wondered that as well. He must be on hold. That is, he must be waiting as he pays attention to all favorable signs. I don't think that Zeus would dare to come to Hera's house until he was reasonably sure that she would welcome him over her threshold—him and no one else.

— What is this sacred marriage like anyway? Have you any notion?

— It is a beginning, a happening that creates a world. Some folks say that it must be an experience, but I think they're wrong. If a person could witness the marriage in that little house, I believe that the dazzling light would fairly blind us. It causes a fellow to wonder if there is love that is too luminous to live. Still, the old stories describe a cycle in the holy marriage, one that shifts from light and ecstasy to darkness and struggle before it circles back to the satisfying place. It could be like a cycle that breathes in and out.

Silence settled over the shepherds now, their ruminations having shaken them both alike. After a long pause, Ioannis recovered and, smiling, asked a bold question.

— I wonder if Hera, once she has achieved the setting that works for this high marriage, will desire to take other lovers who come along. After all, she is said to have her Aphrodite side, even borrowing Aphrodite's girdle to wear.

Clearly the question alarmed the old shepherd, who gazed toward the house of Hera and made the sacred gesture before replying.

— No, absolutely not. One thing about her is her utter faithfulness to Zeus. It's not about duty, I think. It's about the mystery—the *hieros gamos*. You can never improve upon it or ask for variations of it. Oh, Hera truly desires to dwell in the house of her holy marriage, and Aphrodite gave her the radiant strength to delight in it. Not a single Greek doubts this.

— One more question: what causes Hera to pick this remote spot for her dwelling place, her waiting place?

— I asked her priestess this question, and she said, "The maiden arises anew in Hera—she who is fresh and not spent, who stands on the unseen threshold, waiting and smiling." The maiden is Hera's summons. She dare not go to the little mountain house until the summons comes, and when she goes, she is light-footed and prepared to be dwelling anew. If the maiden fails to dwell in Hera's house, the bridegroom does not appear . . . . Well, my young friend, it is time for us to bed down and sleep. For some time, the sheep have been sleeping. Ioannis, if we were to stay awake the entire night, we couldn't witness the *hieros gamos*. That's because it remains invisible!

Hera Wanders

Where clouds embrace a high mountain peak, there might be found a solitary small stone house, reminiscent of the nuptial chamber of Hera and Zeus. One such site was Mt. Kithairon in central Greece where the festival of the Great Daidala took place every sixty lunar years. Every seven years, however, the city of Plataia celebrated the Little Daidala in which the wooden statues of fourteen nymphs of Hera were borne through the streets. In the cart drawn by cows, the statue of the splendid bride, carved of dark oak wood, rode, and she was known as "the false Hera." The entire stately procession moved up the mountain toward the altar and its bridal chamber. According to Plutarch's telling of the myth of this ancient rite, Hera had been in extended withdrawal from her spouse, Zeus. What is enacted within the festival is Zeus's own stratagem to win Hera back. Becoming curious, Hera is drawn to the outskirts of the festival to observe. When she sees that Zeus is about to take a splendid bride as replacement of herself, she rushes upon the scene, displaces "the false Hera," and regally takes her place again at Zeus's side as his bride. On the peak of Kithairon, the procession arrives at the altar, also called the nuptial chamber, and makes sacrifice to the gods. The rite ends with the burning of all the wooden Daidala.

On Kithairon in Boeotia, Greece, the queen goddess of Olympus made her way alone on the mountain path. For some time, she had wandered far from her beloved Zeus or any other companion. Heavily veiled she was, and a dark mood cloaked her spirit. Even so, she was not deterred from seeking a solitary destination high on the mountain, the region of the stone nuptial chamber that the people of Plataia visit in their rite of the Great Daidala. Hera was given to a solitary musing.

— I can scarcely remember when I was not wandering. And to think that I am she who knows the art of dwelling. Do not people say of me, "Hera loves her house"? My heart is heavy, and loneliness assaults me fiercely. Although I am guardian of marriage, look how changed I am! Where has the wife Hera gone? Oh, where is Zeus, who often comforted me and certainly brought me delight, lingering as he was wont to do at my hearth? Alas, I have become Chera, the solitary woman, a woman stripped of her beloved! O Fates, hear me. Why have you singled me out in this way, for always I have perceived life as *duo*? If only I had Artemis's taste for such solitude, but I do not. My heart is a half only, Zeus has the other half . . . . Someone is ascending to this spot on the rocky ledge. A woman comes.

The woman was astonished coming upon the veiled figure, and she murmured to herself.

— Why, here is a lone woman. From afar, I saw a dark cloud shaped like a woman perched on the brow of the mountain here and thought I'd investigate. It seemed a curious thing since everywhere else the day is bright and cloudless. What I find is no cloud at all but a veiled woman. Greetings to you, stranger.

— Greetings, woman. Do tell me who you are, for your face seems familiar.

— I am priestess of Goddess Hera.

— Indeed!

— I think you best take the path with me, for there is grave danger here on the ledge. Besides, any moment we expect the great event. Everyone in these parts is in high excitement.

— And what event would this be? Tell me at once.

Hera's face was anxious as she asked, laying a hand urgently on the priestess's arm.

— The announcement has been made that Lord Zeus will presently marry again, and so naturally, the sacred preparations are under way.

Hera leaped to her feet in alarm.

— What is this you say? Why, it is an outrage! You pronounce such a blasphemy without grief?

— Lady, do you mean that you do not share our joy?

— It is that he is married to Hera everlastingly! Zeus belongs to her as day is bound to night. Not even Zeus can think to dissolve this union made by the gods! Only give thought to Hera herself, will you? Has she not been ever faithful to him and to him alone?

Puzzled, the priestess continued to regard the stranger solemnly. She replied at once, however.

— That we cannot affirm, my lady. You see, Goddess Hera has disappeared altogether. She has hidden herself where even Zeus cannot find her.

The face of the goddess held a look of sudden hopefulness.

— Do you mean to say that he has been searching for her? Zeus has been looking for Hera?

— O yes, he has indeed. Without her, he is sad, you see, rather like an abandoned leaf in winter.

Hera sighed aloud.

— Apparently he does not endure this state for long. From what you have told me, the slightest breath of Aphrodite has carried this leaf to another woman!

The priestess shook her head slowly, somewhat appalled at the stranger's judgment of the great god.

— Perhaps it is only a rumor that he is preparing his new marriage. Time will tell . . . . Stranger, you are removing your veil. Although you have a face of majestic beauty, I see upon it a storm of passion, anger, and grief, surely!

Hera arose to her feet and spoke quietly.

— Priestess of Hera, it is the shadow face of Goddess Hera.

— I must go, for I shall be needed. I am the priestess who is to ride in the chariot beside the sacred bride herself! I must get ready quickly.

Raising her voice, Hera called after her as she left,

— Only remember, priestess, do not betray your goddess!

Alone again, Hera made her way down the mountain slope until she found a suitable lookout spot and seated herself on a boulder. Here she would watch the procession, although the thought of its carrying a new bride for Zeus was unbearable.

The celebrants had led the way, and now a cart drawn by white oxen moved slowly forward. Within the cart, she saw the fourteen wooden idols with their lovely maiden faces, the Daidala. She recognized them at once as the fourteen nymphs of the goddess. Each was lovingly carved and distinct from the others. Next came the flute players, their music sprightly, penetrating the air as it cast a shimmering cloak of sound over the countryside and silenced every nonbridal thought. The vivid spectacle held Hera's attention so that for a little time, the remembered serenity of the sacred marriage came over her, and then she roused herself. After all, a dread event was about to take place—the marriage of Zeus to a new partner! Two maidens dressed in flowing white moved in stately gait as each balanced upon her head a bronze basin of holy water. A pair of white heifers, perfectly matched, came into view so that for a moment, she thought she beheld her beloved priestess Io once again. The heifers were drawing the chariot that reflected the sun brilliantly from its golden sides. Hera began to speak in quiet reflection.

— Who can the charioteer be? I know this rite well, and I am certain that some alteration is being made. What a lordly, magnificent figure he is. Oh, oh! It is Zeus himself! Is he alone? I do hope that he is alone . . . . The celebrants are obscuring my view . . . . Now I see . . . O agony of agonies! He has a bride beside him! How sweet was mere rumor conveyed by the priestess compared to this bare fact! Let me have a better look at this bride. In honesty, I admit there is no lack of beauty or of splendor. Why, she could be *me*! Oh, Zeus is taking another bride, a new wife!

Hera covered her eyes in painful disbelief, but only for a moment, for she could not bear to have this fate of hers unwitnessed.

— How absolutely still she sits, strangely so. Well, she won't be lively enough for Zeus. Of that I am convinced. See how admiring he is of her, his head bent toward her as he smiles his dazzling smile. How each of those smiles does pierce my heart! Alas, I can bear no more!

Hera leaped to her feet, tore the veil from her head, and rushed down the steep mountain path, striding now like the wind. Her face held her passion, and grief brushed by a tide of anger as, reaching the procession, she ran up to the golden chariot driven by Zeus and pulled the heifers to a dead halt. In the same moment, she leaped lightly into the chariot, her blazing look of injured love apparent in the face she now lifted to Zeus. If Zeus was astonished, he showed no indication of it. As she gazed at him, his look was eloquent. Although he did not speak, his message was clear.

— *Where have you been, Hera? I've been looking for you.*

Nor did she speak. Instead, she went swiftly to the side of the very still bride, turning her about to face herself, the queen of Olympus. Robed in exquisite bridal garments was the maiden, rich layer upon layer concealing her youthful body. Although the voluminous veil was heavy over her lovely face, the large brown eyes stared forth unblinkingly. Without another thought, Hera ripped off veil and bridal garments as well while the bride uttered not a single word. In response to her fury, had she not heard a gasp? Whether it was Zeus's or that of the bride, she did not know. Now Hera took hold of the slim body, thinking to remove her from the chariot to the ground. Astonishment was in Zeus's face, and her arms fell to her side, for in taking hold of the slim body with both hands, she had laid hold of *wood*! Now the celebrants heard the odd cry of one who has been divinely fooled. Relief now flooded through her, even so. Immensely quieted now, she finished tearing apart the Daidala, the wooden idol. Immediately afterward, Hera smiled, first at Zeus and then toward the priestess and the celebrants before taking the seat of the bride. Zeus's smile indicated that he was greatly pleased with the outcome and indeed looked forward to the renewed marriage. Bending his head now toward Hera, he spoke in a low voice.

— It's good to have you back, Hera, my dear.

With this, Zeus tapped the heifers with the whip and raised the reins, and the procession wound its way up Mt. Kithairon for the rite of the sacred marriage. On the peak, they reached the goddess's altar in the shape of the square stone house of the sacred marriage. Upon the altar, the brushwood was set afire and received the offering of the seven Daidala, the wooden idols. A great sigh went forth from the people as the supreme Daidala, the life-sized image of Hera, was consumed in the flames.

Serenely waiting, Zeus and Hera prepared for the rite of the sacred marriage.

Hera and the Trojan Women

This dialogue is based on an episode in book 5 of Virgil's *Aeneid* in which the Trojan women, separated from their men who are engaged in elaborate funeral games, grieve for the death of old Anchises. Wearied from seven years of wandering on the seas following the flight from burning Troy, the women are discontent. They greatly desire to settle on this friendly shore of Sicily that has given them hospitality. Resonating with this desire of the women, Hera herself has sent the goddess Iris to persuade them to secretly torch their own Trojan ships. This accomplished, the endless sea voyage will be at an end. True to the Roman tendency to view feminine emotion with alarm, Virgil regards Juno-Hera's action as demonic rather than sympathetic. The following conversation seeks to explore the crisis from Hera's point of view, however.

Two Trojan women walked in silence along the Sicilian shore, and they were old friends. Even before the Trojan War, they had known each other as playmates. The taller woman spoke at last.

— It's the pull of the sea for them, the plunging adventure into the unknown, which never gives more than temporary anchoring places. Why, our men know nothing else, do they?

Her quieter companion nodded and sighed before framing the question.

— Angela, what are we to do?

— We women, you mean.

— Yes. We have grown uneasy, and it is not simply because the men are away doing the funeral games for dear old Anchises. I am sure of it.

— Really, Heracleia? Haven't you heard many women complaining that their men have left them out of the whole festive celebration?

— Oh yes, I've heard the talk, but that is not what is really troubling us.

— So, tell me what you think.

— I've been needing to tell someone, Angela. You see, last night a goddess came to me in a dream. Such an unexpected thing indeed. It was Hera, queen of Olympus herself, she who supported the Greeks against us in the awful war.

    Angela's eyes were wide with amazement.

— You mean to say that Goddess Hera visited you? Hmm, she could probably tell that you are more open-minded than the rest of us.

    Angela grinned at the thought.

— Such a visitation was uncanny. Under the curtain of sleep, I saw majestic Hera, and her countenance was sad, for she stood among the fallen stones of a ruined house. At first I thought it must be a house fallen in Troy, yet something pricked my memory. Why, yes, it was rather Hera's own sacred house on the mountain above her famous temple at Argos in Greece. Angela, the sadness of her face was profound.

— Hera's own house is in ruin, you think?

— Yes. Appalling, but it must be true. Then Hera turned toward me, and she spoke these words:

    Where, oh where is my dwelling place? I, Hera, desire to dwell!

    I was overcome, and I woke up.

    The two friends fell silent, pondering the words of the goddess. Staring at Heracleia as if her face held some unknown landscape, Angela spoke.

— Weren't you named for the goddess herself, Heracleia? The thought just occurred to me.

— Yes. But what has this fact to do with the visitation?

— Well, we can't say, but it bears reminding at the very least . . . . So Hera has lost her house. You know, that makes her homeless. Like us.

    A spark of insight brightened the smaller woman's face, and her words tumbled out fast.

— Angela, Angela! Hera is showing us what's wrong with us Trojan women! Don't you see? She has laid a finger on our passion, naming it. This is what it amounts to, I believe. Each of us longs for her place to dwell, the place that belongs to herself!

— I believe you're right. The fact is that I am sick and tired of traveling the seas and housekeeping on a small ship. The men don't understand. Settling down and living in one place isn't *heroic* enough for our menfolk!

    The jab of sarcasm was not lost on her friend, although Heracleia followed her own train of thought.

— Still, the fact is that the goddess came to me, a Trojan woman. Have I failed to mourn the lost home? Have we Trojan women grown passive, even indifferent to settling and building the city that will shelter us?
— Hera is nudging you and all of us women. There's no doubt about it.
— My task then is before me. The goddess's sanctuary is near, the place where the Romans honor Juno. I shall go there at once and press my question.
— What will you ask?
— I shall be very simple. I shall ask Lady Hera: how can we Trojan women find the path that leads us home?

A shining look was on Heracleia's face as she spoke, one that partook of purpose. Already her voice revealed her absence as briefly she bade Angela good-bye and set out for the sanctuary on the hill.

Meanwhile, Angela continued to walk the stony beach where a fury of waves rose in gleaming foam to crash against the rocks. Lost in thought, she strode along a considerable distance before looking up with surprise to observe that she had reached the cove where the empty Trojan ships were at anchor. She stood very still now, breathing hard as the years of the hard sea voyage stretched before her in memory. Had not the voyage brought them at last to hospitable, desirable Sicily? She sighed, thinking of it. Her thought fell into place now.
— We women have had enough of this journey on the seas! It is time to choose our place, to build our houses and the protective city walls. It's time to settle, I say! Sicily is a good land. Why must Aeneas and the men keep pushing toward Latium?

The sound of the breaking waves and the rough rocking of the ships at anchor drew her attention for a time. At last she burst forth.
— I am a person of action. When I see the right thing to be done, I don't pussyfoot around! No, I put my shoulder to the wheel. Besides, I'm capable of organizing the women to act. Ah . . . the solution is right here before me: *burn the ships!* I go at once to recruit the women to act! For the time being, it is prudent to avoid Heracleia.

Heracleia climbed the steep path of the hill overlooking the harbor and reached the sanctuary of Juno, whom she knew as Goddess Hera. Upon the altar of the wife of great Zeus, she laid her offering of seedcakes and sang an ode of praise to the goddess, and her voice was sweet with inarticulate longing. A calm descended upon her, but it was brief, for there came through the air a barrage of sound much like a fierce wind that knocks over all things in its path. Her heart beat rapidly with trepidation, and she cried aloud,

— O Lady Hera, can it be that you are angry?

Over the rough sounds of a veritable tempest came the voice.

— I, Hera, am full of anger, woman!

— Oh, please declare the cause of your anger, for I am helpless before it!

She waited as the tempest blew fiercely. At last the voice returned.

— I tell you, daughter, that the men of Troy have ignored me, angering me beyond measure.

— Alas, how can such a thing be?

— They insist upon a journey that is endless. What of my gifts to life, I ask? They are ignored entirely. I am forgotten, abandoned, torn from my dwelling place! Do you wonder that I am in a fury?

Not in her wildest imagination would she have guessed at such a situation. Heracleia realized that she must somehow find once again the lost connection.

— Lady Hera, will you speak of your gifts? You see, as a Trojan, I would give them the honor they deserve.

The voice fell silent. Presently, the tempest died down, the wind subsiding into a gentle breeze. Still Heracleia waited before the altar of Hera. At last the voice came, and she knew it to be the voice of the goddess.

— Heracleia, it pleases me that you bear my name.

— I am happy to know this.

— You ask me to speak of my gifts. Mine is the *gift of dwelling!* To dwell is to abide in the place you acknowledge as belonging to yourself.

The words began to fall in place in Heracleia's mind, and her voice was tinged with excitement as she replied.

— Ah yes, you came to me in a dream, Lady Hera. You stood mourning the ruin of your house!

The goddess murmured to herself.

— The human individual is slow to learn.

Hera stepped forward, and Heracleia sensed the lively presence of the goddess as she spoke.

— The most appealing choice of the moment is not necessarily the true dwelling place, I tell you. The true dwelling place houses oneself forever. It is the true fit, you see.

The woman shook her head in incredulity.

— How is this possible?

— One's true house must be built upon earth's rock. There is no other suitable foundation.

— Earth?

— Yes. Earth is mother. She is the foundation. She holds the beginnings. Were Demeter present, she would add that earth holds the crucial return to life as well.

Heracleia continued to frown in some perplexity.

— Lady Hera, Troy was a great city that stood strong, upheld by earth. We Trojans know that we must indeed build our city with its walls and its houses on solid ground.

It was the goddess's turn to be assailed by perplexity. Her voice was breathless and low as she asked the question.

— Then what has happened to this knowledge of the Trojans? Are they not about to take to the sea again, leaving Sicily? Oh, my fury rises to assail these sea wanderers!

Hearing these fateful words of Hera, the woman grew pale. A long tense pause held the two figures. At last, lifting her eyes, a look of horror came to her face, and she cried out.

— Alas, can it be? There is a great fire over the water! Our ships are all aflame!

Hera gazed at the conflagration, and solemnly she nodded.

PART X

The Invisible Loves

Through some blurring of vision, the modern era has come to look upon *myth* as a fraudulent account of things, forgetful of the fact that myth has always been a container of persistent, unarguable human truths. In the light of this, no true myth is far-fetched, for within our experience of it lies a penetrating recognition. A growing familiarity assails the mind as a myth addresses us, stirring memory like a ghostly companion. Still, we are modern individuals, and the compelling questions presses: Did this really happen? Is myth true?

Our limitation in finding the answers lies partly in not being clear as to what reality amounts to. Does reality amount to what is observed by the five senses, then to be deposited into a file known as "history"? Ah, but loving, longing, feeling misery, and all conditions of thought and feeling have their reality in us as well, never mind that they are not found in the observable world. Myth goes astride both realms in its account of experience—the observable and the nonobservable, the external flow of events and an invisible, more interior life. Because of its human breadth, myth might well be regarded as the historian of the human spirit, tracking the path of the psyche as it goes.

In the Greek myths, which these dialogues address, the invisible loves involve the loves of the gods themselves whether they be the Olympians, Dionysos and Pan, or other immortals. Falling in love is a way into life, and the gods proved adept at it. At the moment that the engaging other one stands in beauty while a sense of inscrutable invitation haunts present time, the lover is awakened and summoned into life. The fire of Eros, god of the golden bonding, blazes up. Meanwhile, Himeros and Peitho, as Yearning and Persuasion, the lovely companioning goddesses of Aphrodite, hover in readiness. As for the lover himself, his will appears to dwindle as he is drawn into a covenant with life that is to bind him, like it or not. Such is the covenant shaped by the wounding arrows of Eros, who, although the initiator, does not provide the embodied condition that is love. For this development, one awaits Aphrodite's presence.

She comes. Her garments flow as they shape a pathway, for her presence is rather like a tree that spreads its verdant branches in summer; she comes with the *whispering voice*, a long-honored attribute of Aphrodite. Without law or bulwarks, indeed without animus, she rules.

Only observe her *sidelong gaze*, which the ancients recognized, for it is indifferent to strategic plotting. In her gaze she greets what companions her nature as longing finds its match. She has little inclination toward methods that categorize, sort, and file candidates to that bounty that is called love. That same bountiful nature despises what is stingy or elitist in human circles, for she is Pandemos, goddess of all the people. Ah, Aphrodite comes, and what is it that fills the air? First, one notes the sweet fragrance, but there is something else—the *fair wind*, for was she not hailed as goddess of the fair wind? Surely no true life journey makes it through without her fair wind. The blissful experience that characterizes eros love partakes of her company. As daughter of goddess Dione (according to her birth myth in the region of ancient Dodona), Aphrodite enjoys a deep earth heritage, which may be observed in her capacity for sustained attention and ongoing devotion. Even so, in the city of Thebes, she was honored as "she who turns the heart to love and she who turns the heart away."

And what of Himeros, who brings desire and yearning and is Aphrodite's companion? Awakened by Eros's arrow, she often enough takes refuge in the body, and yet she is not of the body. She appears to be closer kin to the deep human reservoir of timeless images. In the course of one's life, Himeros sleeps and tosses about in her slumber a rather great deal. A wish as a sign of her presence may wash up to consciousness, stark in its concreteness, before subsiding in a moan like a wave of the sea. Somewhere lies the knowledge that the yearning experienced is a more ample presence than a wish can begin to contain.

The Greeks observed that Himeros often mingled with other goddesses, namely with the Graces and the Hours and with Persuasion (Peitho) and Eros, all in the company of Aphrodite. How strange it is that in our times, Himeros often is found in the company of boredom, weariness, and emptiness since to experience desire and yearning is regarded as being deprived! Even though fulfillment is yet to come, Himeros is neither bored nor deprived. It is anticipation that lies in her nature and makes the qualitative difference. A radiant image lies before the gaze of Himeros, one that holds satisfaction. Desire is a powerful affirming of this invisible image as it murmurs, "Oh yes!" Without this spontaneous affirming of what may yet come, Desire is asleep, and one feels more dead than alive.

At the same time, Desire calls for its fulfillment in life as it embraces the possibility that this may not materialize. A movement is perceived that is beyond mere affirming, for in the next step, Himeros enters a state of anticipation. Due to the presence of Peitho, one is fully persuaded. What was mere possibility has stepped forward on the threshold, it seems, and requires earnest support in order to move into life. Aligned with Himeros and Peitho in this heightened state of anticipation, one steps into life anew.

Considering Aphrodite's role in entering upon a new and zestful beginning, it is not surprising that her altars were visited on the approaches to sanctuaries of other gods. Within such a happening, which myth may present as the love of the god, the life of the deep imagination is stirred as numinous archetypes are evoked. Initiates in procession from Athens to Eleusis for the annual mystery rites stopped en route at Aphrodite's altar to make their offerings. Travelers to the sanctuary of Asklepios at Epidauros no sooner entered the gate of the sanctuary than they engaged in honoring the altar of the goddess. These facts suggest that the experiences at Eleusis and at the healing sanctuary, unique as they were and inexorably tied to human meaning, involve the mystery of Aphrodite's gift to life.

Although there are myths of their pursuit by would-be lovers, three goddesses—Athena, Artemis, and Hestia—remain by choice virginal. Again and again, the archetype of virginal being appears in the context of significant beginnings, whether of the city's life or the individual's. Behind every bride in myth, the image is evoked of a bountiful, desirable, yet unspent source awaiting at the threshold of what is to come. Being itself as eternal maiden awaits one.

The dialogues presented here are especially focused on love encounters of Apollo and Zeus. What is it to be chosen by Apollo Far Shooter, as Daphne and Koronis were? It is perhaps to encounter the ever-departing footsteps of a majestic beauty of form and substance cloaking the world of experience, a spouse oracular in his wisdom and close to the Muses. Sad for his human spouse is the fact that Apollo cannot be owned. Alas, it is unworkable for Koronis to think of the god as "my husband." As for Hephaestus, the limping craftsman god, he proves less elusive and less beguiling than handsome Apollo, while he proves to be far more workable as the husband-in-residence on the isle of Lemnos. On the other hand, such accountability may lie in the very nature of the god of work. As for his beloved wife, Aphrodite, time and again she finds life espoused to work overly challenging, with the result that her romantic fantasy turns to the god of war, Ares.

Not only was Zeus the highest god for the Greeks but he was also the great lover. Although on Mt. Olympus in the company of the gods he is the faithful husband of Hera, on earth, the odyssey of his loves seems unending. In the Roman Age, the god came to be perceived as proving his sovereign power through his wanton enjoyment of women as sexual partners. There is a different perception of Zeus's loves that easily eludes us, however. It is that Zeus revealed a divine passion for entering human existence, intersecting human experience in a way that for a brief time brought the joyous union of heaven and earth. So it was that when Zeus entered the underground chamber where King Acrisius kept his daughter Danae captive, the darkness was penetrated by golden light. Love flowered, and Danae knew the first sign of her freedom and her worth. Not only Danae but other spouses of Zeus were impregnated, and their progeny came to play significant roles in times of crisis.

As was said earlier, falling in love is a way into life, and the gods were adept at it. When the engaging other one is perceived waiting within a shadowy gateway through which a slender golden light streams, then is the lover summoned. The fire of the god of the golden bond blazes up while Desire and Persuasion, both lovely companioning goddesses, hover at Aphrodite's elbow. And the lover, his will retired, is born into a covenant with life that binds him.

Such a vulnerable one was luminous Apollo, whose loves sadly lacked durability in the world. The beloved nymph Daphne fled everlastingly into nature as a tree while Koronis was brought down into death by Artemis's unarguable arrow. In contrast is Danae, daughter of the king of Argos, to whom Zeus's love brought the goldenness that caused her to break out of years of darkness and to find herself and love's offspring deposited on a new shore. As for the beloved of the gods, it is interesting to observe that it is not always the chaste young maiden who is chosen, for often the beloved in the case of Zeus or else Dionysos was a married woman. In such cases there occurs the *love of the second time*. With winning force, Zeus claimed Queen Alcmene of Thebes in the absence of her husband, King Amphytryon, and they parented the hero Heracles. It was in the regal serenity of the swan that Zeus claimed Queen Leda of Sparta when she wandered on the riverbank. In one of the best loved tales, Dionysos claims as his bride Ariadne when she was abandoned by Theseus on the island of Naxos.

PART XI

Aphrodite

Aphrodite Is Born

The account of Aphrodite's birth on land to the oracular goddess Dione may be as early as the ninth century BC and is found in Hesiod's *Theogony*. When Zeus sought out the distant sanctuary of Dodona in northwestern Greece, Dione held the oracle there that manifested through the quaking leaves of the sacred oak tree. She was served by priestesses, and even the abode of the goddess was connected to the roots of the sacred tree. Zeus took lovely Dione to be his wife, and together they came to share the celebrated oracle of Dodona.

Dione had been for many months the wife of Olympian Zeus when the pains of labor came upon her. She moved as one under a great burden as slowly she made her way to the cool, shaded circle of the mighty oak tree. Calling her devoted priestesses to her side, she instructed them to take the thong and sound the bronze cauldrons, one after the other, where they encircled the tree. As for herself, she went to the center of the circle where she might lean against the beloved tree. Into the vast silence of the mountain sanctuary, the solemn voices of the bronze cauldrons now penetrated, sustained in deep sonorous tones that created a protected place for the great birth to come. When the tones had diminished to a gentle humming, Dione spoke.

— My time has come. It cannot be delayed. The fruit of Dione and Zeus has ripened. Ah, the day welcomes the arrival, I believe. Was it not the speaking tree that counseled me to take Zeus's love "so that the magical goddess may be born?"

A particularly strong contraction stopped her speaking, and she gasped, at the same time indicating that the priestesses withdraw, leaving her alone. When she spoke again, she addressed the unborn child urgently.

— Oh, do wait, child of mine, for the oracle is speaking. Nor is it Zeus who speaks. It is earth's voice.

The womb itself ceased its ardent labor, attentive as the oracle spoke.

— *Out of the depths running full and sighing on a thousand shores*
She comes, buoyant and luminous like foam of the sea
Daughter of Dione, Aphrodite of the whispering voice.
From her step the flowers bloom
Within her hand the fruit grows sweet
A golden world is set on earth
Whose wonder bears the face of love.

Dione pressed the oracle now.

— Do tell me, will my daughter forever bring gifts of joy and delight to mortals and gods alike?

There was a sigh upon the air as the voice replied.

— *A goddess she shall be of great delight to all, yet after her trails at times a path of sorrow. Adored and dreaded alike shall she be.*

Whether it was the strength of a mighty contraction or the pain of the oracle's ambiguous truth that seized Dione it was not known, but she gave a great cry. In that moment, Aphrodite was born. At once she appeared as a ripened woman, fair and full-bosomed. Dione smiled upon her astonishing beauty, and her pleasure was not far from awe. Newborn Aphrodite gazed fondly into the face of Dione and spoke.

— My dear mother, how I have longed for this day of my birth, and how grateful I am to you for its arrival! You and I, we *know*, don't we?

With this enigmatic comment, she laughed happily. Both looked up with surprise as three figures, radiant and smiling, approached the oak tree. There was no doubt that they were the Hours, and Dione and her daughter acknowledged the goddesses, each bowing graciously. Over their arms they carried fine, gossamer garments with which they at once set about dressing Aphrodite. On her head they placed a garland of worked gold, and her ears they adorned with flowers of copper and gold. About Aphrodite's lovely neck, they fastened a necklace of gold fillets, which they had made for her. Fully dressed and adorned by the Hours, Aphrodite took leave of her mother. How could she explain what called her in this hour?

— Ah, Mother, the serene bowl of deeply interior Dodona has begotten me, and it shall always be dear to me, but the sea summons me strongly. I must embrace the sea in order to make my journey to the human world that awaits me. I am overdue, you see.

Dione murmured aloud,

— It shall be said, Aphrodite is she who arrives from the sea, and you shall first come ashore at the isle of Cythera. Ah, my daughter, it will ever be Dodona that knows that you are daughter of wise Earth—Earth that is beloved by the gods, Earth that is the oldest ground in the human soul.

Aphrodite and the Lemnian Woman

Her soft, voluminous garment blowing about her, the veil lifted from her face, the goddess set her graceful sandaled feet upon the damp sand of the seashore and began her stroll at dusk. She was lovely to behold, had there been an observer, but the narrow strip of beach below the sharp rocks was forsaken. Thundering, the sea arose in waves that broke at her feet trailing the sense of an immense sigh. She gazed down into the sea foam, white as milk and dancing with a life of its own, and an ancient memory stirred within her. The pause lengthened as she gazed upward to the volcanic hills of Lemnos where, deep in the grotto, her spouse spent his days inside the cavern partnering the fire that shaped his creations. Always he worked, it seemed. With his lame feet, strolling on the beach held no invitation. She looked up to see a woman approaching.

— Woman of Lemnos, what brings you to the lone seashore at this hour?

— Greetings, lady. You ask what brings me here. I'll be frank with you. It is disappointment—love gone all wrong! Of all the things I know, none is as unreliable as love. It's a fact. We women know all about it.

These words were a rough assault on the goddess's reverie, and she recoiled visibly.

— What's this you say? Why, love is not unreliable, nor is it disappointing, not ever. What may indeed prove unreliable is one's lover, but not love itself. Of this I am certain.

The woman sighed with some impatience.

— Same thing, isn't it?

Clearly the woman of Lemnos thought herself better informed than her companion.

The goddess shook her head.

— It is not at all the same thing. What happens is rather on this order. Two persons are carried by the great stream on a buoyant and splendid voyage not of their making. This is love, and the stream that upholds it is everlasting, I tell you.

The woman had a small amused smile as though indulging her companion.

— You're pretty dreamy, aren't you? Why, I could tell you a volume about love and lovers, if you want to know. Sounds like you could do with some practical data, if you don't mind my saying so.

The goddess's eyes blazed momentarily.

— Well, I do mind!

As she turned to gaze into the face of the woman, she now took on a height, a beauty, and a radiance that was astonishing. The woman's hands flew to her cheek, and she cried aloud, at the same instant making the sacred gesture.

— Oh! Oh, you are Aphrodite herself!

— Lemnos is my home where I dwell with my husband Hephaestus. You seem bewildered, woman. I do believe that this meeting is fortuitous for you. Tell me, what grieves you? These happenings you call love, I fear, are attached to a string of ever-haphazard human assessments.

The words of the goddess were disconcerting. Yet the woman nodded and began bravely.

— He left me some time ago, my lover did. Oh, it wasn't fair, not in the least! We loved each other, and besides, we were well suited. Everyone said so. I never see him now, but his face haunts me every single day. You see, Lady, I grieve for my lover.

Aphrodite fell silent in the ensuing pause. Her voice was somewhat tender as she spoke now.

— Ah, I see how it is, for I know love's deep grief well. What I perceive is that you grieve for a particular man. It is not for the lover himself that you grieve!

Amazement and anger tumbled together in the woman's reaction.

— How can you say I don't grieve for my lover?

— It is difficult to imagine, I believe, but the lover is *invisible*.

This time, she heard them—the words *The lover*. The goddess continued.

— Always one longs to give the lover a face and a body, a living voice, in short. When the lively capacity to love and be loved is paralyzed by the attachment to one person who fails to respond to you any more, how bitter the disappointment is! It is that love's vessel is no longer at hand.

— My lady, you being an Olympian goddess can't be expected to understand how it is with us ordinary folks. Nobody I know wants an invisible lover for a partner, I can tell you. Why, you could never pin him down or come to a reliable agreement. Just think of it. You would have yourself a lover you couldn't even be embraced by! It's unthinkable. Besides, it's thoroughly impractical to even consider. The facts are that I was not loved properly, and I now am miserable!

Aphrodite had strolled ahead slowly, and the woman hastened to keep abreast. Both fell silent for a while, watching as a stronger tide of the Aegean began to assail the shore with crashing waves and retreating foam. Dusk settled heavily over the island. It was the goddess who broke the silence.

— When I am near the sea, I feel that I am again born anew. Until this takes place, I go often enough unobserved, a mere practitioner of desire and passion, but not for long, fortunately. The primordial depths catch me up—like a sea creature—and bear me ashore and into life! Perhaps you perceive me more clearly now, woman. Again and again I must return to meet the sea. Where else is there such a mysterious reservoir on earth, I ask you?

When the woman looked up from the sand at her feet, the extraordinary companion had departed, and she murmured to herself.

— How strange this meeting was, like nothing I've ever known . . . I know that love is a happening, yet what is this different look she cast on it? A kind of glimpse, I think. In that glimpse, she sees love as an appealing face in a dim mirror. Can love be a vision as well as a happening, I wonder? Strange, there is something I begin to see . . . it is very shining, and it is beautiful. Now if only I can find him again and make sure he's real . . .

Some time passed for the woman of Lemnos. Since the unusual encounter on the seashore at dusk, she found herself changed in part. What was it? Well, no longer did she take satisfaction in reviewing her lover's heartless departure, however painful. Of course, a woman has the right to take note of the injustices she has suffered. There's that. The fact was that love, which was the main issue of her life, no longer declared itself loudly with wailing. Occasionally she found herself recalling the goddess's words about the invisible lover. Each time, she shook her head over the incongruity of the very idea.

As she descended to the seashore, the dusk was thickening over her island home. Some distance away, standing upon a large boulder and gazing out to sea, was a woman whose graceful form caught her attention.

She drew in her breath sharply with recognition before moving confidently toward the boulder. It was indeed Aphrodite who lifted her face and greeted her.

— So it is you, woman of love's sorrow . . . Have you come looking for me?

— Greetings, Lady Aphrodite. Yes, although I didn't realize that I came looking for you. But I have been eager to tell you something. It is this: love seems somewhat changed to me now. What I mean to say is that it's no longer so unreliable as it was when we first spoke. Even so, for the life of me, I cannot fathom how this is so.

— Indeed?

Aphrodite's eyebrows were raised in some surprise, which may have been blended with amusement. If this woman of Lemnos were in charge of the goddess's reputation, its prospects were undoubtedly poor. The woman spoke with new energy.

— You know, I believe that you might have had some effect on me. I wonder if I may ask your advice? How can I furnish my life with more pleasure and, well, fulfillment of desire? At present there's not much of either one. Everyone knows that you, Lady Aphrodite, are goddess of pleasure and desire!

Aphrodite gasped audibly as though she had stumbled upon some monstrous creature blocking her path.

— So is this what you seek—a great quantity of pleasure?

The woman grinned.

— Naturally. That's what everybody wants. The trouble with pleasures, though, is that they expire too fast. Now I expect you will know the kind that have a longer life, so to speak.

The goddess stepped down abruptly from the boulder and whirled about. Her words were sharp with anger when she spoke.

— Woman, know this: *I am neither a market nor a warehouse!*

The Lemnian woman was alarmed now.

— Oh, I never intended to offend you! I apologize, Lady, I just want to use you as a wonderful resource, you see.

Aphrodite spoke solemnly.

— I am Aphrodite. Understand this, woman. I cannot be used!

At once, Aphrodite turned her face aside, and an overwhelming sense of loss swept over the woman. Words failed her. Only the pounding of the waves seemed unchanged. When she spoke, her voice seemed older, its urgent demand gone, and her face was thoughtful.

— All hail Goddess Aphrodite! I shall honor you.

The moments passed, and still Aphrodite was turned away. The woman waited. Once she murmured to herself, *Apostrophia! She who turns away!* Darkness cloaked the narrow beach where only the shining of the sea in its heaving, rhythmic roll was visible in the light of a new moon. At last the goddess turned toward the woman, regarding her. When she spoke, her words seemed to come from an impenetrable distance.

— Always I have company. Do you happen to know my faithful companions, I wonder? The three are Himeros, or Desire; Peitho, who is Persuasion; and Eros. Like three deep springs, they bring to love the fresh life.

— Lady, each time I have come across you, you have been solitary. I saw no companions whatsoever.

— Alas, human perception is slow and frightfully narrow in what it takes account of! Indeed, in order to be considered real, a thing must have a body with arms and legs to fling about. So it is believed!

Aphrodite spoke scornfully before arising and beginning to walk back and forth, studying the sand at her feet. She continued.

— Because you have come to me desperate in your need, I am drawn to you, woman. Let me tell you how it is with pleasure. Pleasure is a satisfaction measured out for a brief time before it expires. If you would collect pleasures, you must always be checking your supply, like one who counts the coins in her purse. Each coin is fast spent. Surely you see this, and now you know that I am not goddess of pleasure!

The woman was astonished, and a look of incredulity remained on her face. When she spoke, the words came painfully.

— Lady Aphrodite, if you are not goddess of pleasure, what are you? Nothing is more pleasant and altogether wonderful than being in love!

— Ah, that is true. You see, I am simply *goddess of love*. I thought you knew this.

— I guess you might say I had the cart before the horse, Lady.

— Indeed. But do not be without hope, for I assure you that one who has the delight of love has joy, which is no ordinary pleasure soon to expire. No. This joy possesses a luminous text that illuminates the love brought about through the invisible lover.

— Oh, it's him again, the one you can't get a good look at!

Although her voice was complaining, the goddess laughed indulgently.

— There is something more that we have not touched upon, and without it, love is not the true gift of the gods.

— Tell me, what can it be?

Although she wanted to hear about it, she was beginning to feel tired of love's complexity. The goddess continued.

— It may seem a difficult truth to take in. You see, authentic love in its luminous text is everlasting!

— You are telling me that when I've got this love, it can never wear out or grow stale? Now that is hard to believe.

— Hear me out, woman. Love, which is my gift, is everlasting. It is one's access to it that can falter or disappear. You are human after all. The joy of this love, so rich in its unfolding text, bears only a passing resemblance to pleasure, it turns out. When a person confuses the pleasure at hand with this shining, speaking joy, she finds herself presently plunged into despair.

In the moist darkness of the beach, the woman sat hunched upon the boulder now as she listened to Aphrodite. The woman's eyes shone with tears, and her heart was full. The goddess, smiling now, spoke.

— May the Graces who guard the wondrous order that satisfies go with you!

Aeneas Meets the Radiant Stranger

The smoldering city with its fallen walls and collapsed great gate lay behind him. Standing within a small grove of trees, he gazed back at the scene he had fled as a great emotion washed over him. A little way off, his old father sat upon the ground resting. What other lifeline had he except his attachment to his beloved father? What a relief to have succeeded in rescuing him out of the burning city. A sound of someone approaching on the path alerted his senses. Rounding the path and coming into full view was a woman, her white garment tucked up to accommodate her graceful stride. With growing astonishment, he observed both the leisurely movement and her face of unusual loveliness. An early memory stirred within him. She stopped at a little distance and addressed him.

— Greetings, young man, I see that you are a traveler come from afar. Alas, you are covered with soot and ashes!
— Fair lady, I have just managed to crawl through the fire as Troy burned—Troy, my beautiful dear city!

Grief arose in him and stopped his voice. Her voice brought comfort, strangely.

— Ah, but the Fates have been kind, have they not? You have managed to get out alive, young man. What is your name, may I ask?
— I am called Aeneas.
— Aeneas . . . *Aeneas?* Why, you are Anchises' son! Can this be true? Tell me at once, were you alone in your desperate flight through the flaming fortress? I must know.
— I did not flee my city alone, and yes, I am Anchises' son. How could I leave my father behind? He's an old man, and infirm besides. I lifted him upon my shoulders and carried him on the circuitous escape route.

With a cool, intense scrutiny, he regarded the radiant woman. Caution informed his attitude, for one who is in flight may be in danger.

— How do you know my father's name or the fact that he has a son, you
   being a stranger?

There was a quick intake of breath on her part, and she stared
into the distance, frowning. When at last she spoke, her voice was low as
if coming from some distant memory.

— Ah, how could I forget the face of youthful Anchises? Why, you are
   the mirror image of him.

He shook his head as one not easily taken in.

— Lady, you are too young to have known my father as a young man. Do
   not try to deceive me.

— There is a memory in us that is timeless. Why else is Mnemosyne
   honored as an everlasting goddess by the Greeks?

Aeneas fell silent in a long pause, and a guarded look settled over
his handsome face. It was the look of one too old in loss and too young
in manly vigor to be ensnared again by life. As he continued to regard her,
boldness seeped from him to be replaced by distant, dim memory. His
words were murmured as in reflection while his voice held wonder.

— How like Aphrodite you are! And to think that she is the goddess who
   is said to have been my *mother!*

The improbability of the notion caused him to grin in what might
have been amusement.

— Ah, what a lineage you possess then. Actually it is like a fine but
   invisible cloak you wear, I'd say. May I advise you? One cannot succeed
   in disguising one's true ancestry indefinitely, Aeneas.

He reacted, visibly bristling.

— I disguise nothing, lady! I am an honest man.

— And a prickly one, I'd say.

She smiled as she made the comment and continued.

— Now, allow me to brush the ashes and soot from you. The memories of
   Troy's war I cannot remove so easily . . . . There, is that better? I happen
   to know your father's story, and it is singular among the tales of men
   and heroes. Here in this stopping place between your lost world of
   Troy and the future, shall we consider that story?

While she spoke, she poured water from a nearby spring over his
face and limbs, washing away the residue of ash, and he submitted rather
like one in a daze, only nodding to her gratefully. This ritual completed,
she took a seat on a boulder and began her account. Briefly he scanned her
from head to foot while at the same time he experienced a certain balm in

the presence of this extraordinary stranger, whose loveliness affected him greatly. The musical sound of her voice seemed strangely familiar.

— It was in a distant mountain pasture that Goddess Aphrodite came upon a shepherd's hut far from the city of Troy, for the goddess is known to wander without a plan, you see. On either side of the entrance to the small hut made of branches, the cattle slept, for darkness had fallen and the time descended when the pastoral world took its rest. The radiant goddess in her flowing garment regarded the low, rough entrance to the hut briefly before ducking her head. O yes, she crossed the threshold, for such a step has the nature of destiny. Slowly she approached the rough pallet where the shepherd lay sleeping. Now the shepherd was none other than Anchises. As the goddess stood regarding him, desire and admiration rose within her and contended for possession. And then, although one cannot account for how it happened, a hidden fire descended and consumed both shepherd and goddess alike on the spot!

The stranger's face had closed as if forbidden to speak further. Still her words had astonished him. Clearly what came over him was alarm.

— Lady, why did the gods not rescue my father from such a catastrophe? He is a good man and honors the gods, after all.

— Aeneas, this was no catastrophe. It is of the fire of Eros that I speak, so unlike other sorts of fire. Is it not a fire that one gives eager hospitality to? No one will deny the satisfaction it brings. Why, it is indescribable.

— Only speak plainly. My father fell *in love*, you mean.

His storyteller considered this.

— Oh yes, at least that.

She passed her hand in front of her face briefly as though silently rejecting such a summary of the event. She continued.

— And what followed was that you were conceived and in time brought to birth by Aphrodite.

Although he had heard the tale before, her telling of it stirred old memory in him. At the same time, it was not an account easily believed. He pressed her.

— A rough shepherd's hut sheltered such a love? Aphrodite is said to bring a heavenly love. This love my father knew was obviously a thing of earth. Yet Aphrodite is called Ourania, Heavenly One.

For a moment, she regarded him with something of pity for his failure to grasp how things were.

— It was a heavenly love, yes, of the sort that one never recovers from.

— Are you saying, lady, that Troy was not the first great fire my beloved and long-suffering father has endured?

— Exactly. Troy was, after all, the second fire for Anchises. But do not undervalue the fire that Aphrodite brought with her, for that love was a splendid, a golden thing.

— I can believe that. Yet how overwhelming for Anchises it must have been! Ah, but this second fire—Troy's burning by the Achaeans—has struck my father as an old man, one no longer able to walk alone. Only observe the consequences of this fire—it destroys us both! Oh, if only the first fire could have made him proof against all other fires that assault human folk!

His cry stood between them now with its implied criticism of Aphrodite. Meanwhile, the woman, who appeared to have a close relationship to the goddess although an enigmatic one, became agitated. She arose and began to pace back and forth, the translucent folds of her peplos in rapid movement.

— Aeneas, you demand too much of the fire which belongs to love alone!

She sat down again, the troubled look fading as she grew pensive. He questioned her, his voice tinged with skepticism.

— How can I forget that Aphrodite's love is widely reputed to be *un*dependable?

Her cheeks were flushed with emotion, and he shook his head slowly.

— I wish that I could trust it as you do. Such love is undependable, I say. If it were otherwise, why did my mother leave me and abandon my father too?

— Refugee of splendid Troy, it is not Aphrodite's fire, I tell you, that is undependable. What is undependable lies with the human individuals who receive the fire. Failing to tend her fire and give it a fitting hearth, they allow it to go unsheltered. There lies the problem. Pleasure alone cannot claim love indefinitely, although it may make a gallant attempt. Unfortunately, pleasure proves to be an inadequate shelter. Alas, before one knows it, love has gone missing.

— A hearth, you say, is needed. The problem lies with the hearth. Well, this is something practical that I can understand. Is such a hearth feasible? What ordinary hearth can a man devise that will contain Aphrodite's fire, I ask you?

Now Aeneas was a man who gazed relentlessly at hard facts, for he was one who got things done. He doubted that the woman before him had a capacity for the practical.

— How to contain Aphrodite's fire? Why, there have been many worthy hearths.

She made as if to continue but closed her lovely mouth as a veil of dream appeared to cloak her. Her voice when it came was more distant now.

— Recall the great tales you have been taught, for each bears witness to a hearth of sorts. Oh, I know that it is difficult for you to perceive these, for they are not visible structures of stone at the center of a house.

— Describe a few of these, lady, if you will. I am a patient man.

She smiled at his view of himself and, with a slight nod, continued.

— When Zeus visited Danae in the bronze chamber that imprisoned her, he brought the splendor of love. In that moment, a hearth came to be, one that Danae tended. In time it was this hearth that brought about her freedom and, with it, the flowering of woman.

— Why, that is incredible. No one mentioned the hearth before in telling that tale. What else?

— There was Apollo aglow with love's fire when he pursued lovely Daphne. She refused the god as you must know. Yet love's hearth did not fail to appear.

— How could it, since she refused him and became a laurel tree?

— Oh, the hearth is there all right—everlastingly. And it is Apollo who especially tends it, it appears.

Aeneas found it urgent that he remind the stranger of a fact.

— These are the loves of gods you speak of. The experience of mortal man is different, you know.

— What of the poets—Homer, Hesiod, Pindar, and the rest? When love's heavenly fire came upon the poet in the encounter with the Muse, why, then the ongoing hearth was created. No poet in his right mind questions this hearth, Aeneas.

At once he thought of the goddess who was recognized as the faithful guardian of the hearth and spoke of her.

— Even so, I doubt that Hestia, goddess of the hearth, would acknowledge the existence of these hearths you speak of.

Already his sturdy skepticism took on a gentler aspect.

— Besides, inspiration is hardly the same as the love that Aphrodite saddles a man with, my lady.

At once she threw up her hands to ward off such reasoning as if it might pollute her excellent dish in the making.

— The distinction hardly matters. Let me tell you, when poetry overtakes a person, the first fire—Aphrodite's—is present. Yet, Aeneas, it is in the second fire that this disaster is unlike love's fire, which you have been defending so nobly. There is disaster for the city and its people, yes. This you know well. But do you know yet the thrust of the fire within your destiny and that of Anchises? At this very moment, this is at issue.

These words sent a wave of sorrow through him, and he shuddered. Deep emotion was in his voice as he responded.

— I have lost my beloved home and the familiar hearth that received me all my life. It is an abysmal loss and a sorrow I cannot hope to console! Look at me. What do you see beneath the ashes you removed so tenderly? Despair hovers there, I tell you. You see a man at the end of his tether!

For a moment he thought he glimpsed pity, but it was not compassion that was uppermost in his companion. Still, her voice was gentle as she replied.

— Beneath the ashes, I glimpse a path of light. It is rather like what a torch illuminates. Aeneas, there is another hearth to come. It will be one of your making. I am certain of it. The fire of love creates a world apart, private, excluding the familiar world often enough, and nothing is more significant for oneself. The second fire, on the other hand, may make a *bridge* between the realm of ecstatic love and the world as you know it. This is how the burning of Troy can be your good fortune instead of your disaster. Only time will tell—and your acts, naturally. Oh, the second fire must not find you too young or too insistent upon immediate pleasure.

He shook his head slowly from side to side, incredulity on his face as she continued.

— The second fire is as sweeping as the first was for Anchises' life. O yes. The burning of Troy closed the familiar, desirable world while the fire of heavenly love had earlier opened a world not known before.

How could she so swiftly pass over their disaster? He cried out in protest,

— A world of great magnitude has fallen with Troy!

— Yes, I do not deny it. Ah, I am beginning to see you more clearly now.

— Tell me what you see, lady.

— I see a man making his way through grave sorrow and loss, carrying his ancestry as he goes!

He nodded as he felt the dark curtain of sadness.

— Hear me, Aeneas. You are not deprived of your gifts. Your vital strength of mind and body burn brightly. Let me ask you, have you forgotten your deep connection to Aphrodite?

The question was too much. Almost it made him bitter. He groaned aloud.

Oh, Aphrodite is far, far from me!

— No, you are mistaken. It is that what you now experience is the mourning Aphrodite, she who lost her beloved Adonis. But Aphrodite's joyous aspect is a sturdy thing, I remind you. She is known to rise again out of ashes, and when she does, she brings delight and joy. You shall see.

— Wait, what are you saying? The *love's* fire can occur in the wake of the fire that ruins a person?

— It is possible. Yes, I do perceive a steady fire ahead. It is for certain the fire of Aphrodite. Strangely, it appears to hinge on having lost a world. Ah, this fire will not be the lightning flash, ecstatic and overflowing, which lovers know, a fire often quickly expended. No, what I perceive is a steady burning. Only do not lose hope, Aeneas. A new land opens to you because of it. Farewell!

Aeneas remained staring after the departing figure until she descended a path that was out of sight. Slowly he smiled.

Penelope and the Voice of Aphrodite

On the island of Ithaca, Queen Penelope found herself in her private chamber where she spent so many solitary hours, often working at her loom on the robe she was making for elderly Laertes, her father-in-law. Staring into space, she often found herself reliving those joyous years with Odysseus, her husband, a custom usually reserved for evening, before sleep claimed her. Yet today, as the dusk fell like a soft curtain over the fields, she found herself considering the crowd of visitors who each day, uninvited, filled the open rooms of her house. Old friends and townsmen, they were, not easily denied hospitality, even when some of them pressed their suit for her hand. She mused.

— But do they have to take over our house, ever feasting at the table and spending long hours of leisure here? Certain ones, when I enter the room, turn the long gaze of admiration on me. Ah, it is not without desire, I observe. Almost the gaze could bring me pleasure, but then comes the sharp realization that it is to Odysseus, dead or alive, that I belong! Nor is it the rites of marriage that cause me to cling to him like hardened resin to the pine tree. There is this bond. I was not born with it, but it descended on me when I was yet a maiden and has never released me, even through twenty years of war and my husband's failed return to Ithaca. For certain, it was Aphrodite herself who devised this everlasting bond, a thing she does in secret behind all eyes, the tie unarguable and golden that shapes the lasting belonging! *O Lady Aphrodite, when you come with this magic of belonging, the power to choose is fast asleep!* Ah, but what is left to me now? The suitors take over the house, each presenting himself as a most excellent successor to the lord Odysseus—a man who cannot be replaced. Well, I shall keep to my chamber.

From the doorway, a voice penetrated the stillness of the room with a question. Its arrival was like that of a small fishing boat plowing through a rough sea. At once she realized that it was not Thalia, her old serving woman, but a voice that was unfamiliar, the voice of a woman.

— What is this you do in the solitary hours, Lady Penelope?

— I grieve for the loss of the man I love.

— Alas, I perceive your great sorrow. Is he noble then?

— Yes. Odysseus is noble and, at the same time, ordinary.

— Good. Then your love is of the earth and not thriving on ideals of perfection. Curiously, the love that Aphrodite brings thrives on delight, and yet at times it is nourished by sorrow.

— Sorrow? How can this be?

— It is in love's loss, you see, that the luminous quality of the gods leaves a golden trail, a trail that nothing in life compares to.

— But surely Aphrodite is known to bring joy and delight to those who love.

— Yes, indeed. Still, when her beautiful young lover Adonis dies, she is inconsolable in her grief. Why else do the people of Thebes worship the mourning Aphrodite?

Penelope's hands flew to her cheeks as if to restrain the painful assault to memory. The voice of the companion took on gentleness as it continued.

— Tell me more about these solitary hours you spend each day.

— I weave upon the loom.

— What is the cloth there that you are making?

— It is the funeral robe for my father-in-law when he shall be in need of it. In death, Laertes deserves to be well-provisioned, you see.

The voice fell silent taking this in.

— So you know exactly what it is that you make?

— Of course. Is that so surprising?

The voice did not answer at once as if there might be a mulling over of the question. Again the voice was speaking.

— To know with such assurance exactly what the cloth is that one weaves troubles me, Penelope. In such a case, all is conclusion already, both heart and mind having apparently finished with it. No matter that there is still considerable work for the hands to execute. What is a woman's work, I ask you, with heart and mind already spent? One is left with a cloth to be viewed, probably admired, and subsequently put to use. No more than this.

Penelope looked like one who has been struck as she drew in her breath sharply.

— To hear you talk, you could be one of the Fates, who are all about the thread, the cloth, and time! Alas, the gods know that I am denied the robing of my dead husband, if he *is* dead, that is. My father-in-law is an old man, and he will soon require the death robe.

A pause ensued, and a long shadow fell across the room. The voice that spoke now seemed more vibrant, even musical.

— Penelope, there is a duality in what you do, you see.

Again Penelope gazed about the room, hoping to find the source of the voice.

— A duality you say. So you perceive this. It is two things I do, yes, each seeming to contradict the other. Yet on the loom, these two become a working pattern.

— Ah yes. The suitors all talk of Penelope's duplicity. And so, where did you learn this art, which they regard as deceit?

Penelope regarded the question with surprise and looked at a loss until suddenly a slow smile touched her lips, and she spoke in a low voice.

— My suitors do not truly see me, and this is a fact. You might as well know, you being a woman. This thing I do has two faces, I admit, yet my mind and heart are one. How can this amount to deceit? You ask where I learned the skill. What can I say? I do believe that I learned it from Aphrodite!

Her eyes dropped to the loom, and she was amazed at her own words. When she lifted her eyes, momentarily she glimpsed her companion. A radiant woman stood a little distance from her, so that involuntarily she made the sacred gesture. The figure was speaking.

— You must understand that what Aphrodite brings is true. It is circumstances that may deceive. After all, the golden bond is the handiwork of a god. How can it not be true?

— Oh, it is true indeed! For that reason, my love of Odysseus is alive and unready for any funeral robe whatsoever!

Her voice had rung out triumphantly, and in that moment, her former queenliness seemed to cloak her once more.

— An honest report then. Tell me, what is the meaning of this daily unraveling of your progress with the weaving?

    Penelope's face again was shadowed with sorrow.

— O the waiting, the intolerable waiting! Don't you see how it is? For twenty years I have been *one who waits*. If when I am dead, an inscription is put on my tomb, let it be: *She who waits.* You have questioned closely my work at the loom, indeed quite alarming me. It is the working of the threads and watching the design emerge that have eased the waiting.

— Ah yes, the waiting. What do you know about this waiting that engages you?

— Well, our old nurse regarded me thoughtfully one day and said: "Waiting is a passive, boring thing that we women are used to. When you're maiden, you wait to attract a suitable mate and again must wait for a proposal of marriage. Through a tedious pregnancy, one waits for the child to be born. And how often does a wife not wait for her husband to make the decision that affects them both? I tell you, if we women had more clout, my lady, we'd do a whole lot less waiting!"

    Penelope smiled wryly, remembering, before concluding,

— Surely there is substance in what she says.

— Penelope, don't you recognize the goddess's handiwork, I ask you? Smiling and of good hope, Aphrodite brings a different kind of waiting. It emerges out of the heart's remembering. It is a rhythmic thing having its own pulse. Such waiting is greatly to be desired, don't you see? Waiting and sustaining are the very ground of love!

    The words of the companion echoed and repeated in her ear.

— How long can I endure this waiting, even so? It wearies me mostly.

— That is the wrong waiting, I think, the one that serves emotional demands and ordinary impatience. Of course it is natural, but it is not the goddess's gift. Aphrodite's waiting draws on an old knowledge that sustains one. It is an earth knowledge such as great Rhea knew. Embodied by memory, it gazes at the scroll of life that is largely hidden yet sustaining. Such knowledge that Aphrodite has is held a little apart and tended, although sometimes in pain. It is the knowledge in which the very pulse of love is felt as it evokes a sustained attunement, its rhythm entering all that you do. Penelope, observing you in your solitude at your loom, I see that you have learned to wait.

— It seems a small learning and one forced upon me at that.

— Pay attention. Aphrodite forces nothing upon a person ever. What she does is to stir luminous desire in present time, the desire for what is beloved, and her presence is greatly persuasive, of course. Besides, have you not observed how she brings the Graces with her—the goddesses who cause all manner of things to work favorably?

— Ah, she is awesome! What will come from this kind of waiting then?

— Why, without the wise waiting, your life becomes only a conspiracy to carry on. Such waiting is marked by the order and rhythm of earth, and within its hidden folds, a slow, rhythmic dance begins.

— But there is no music, none that I can respond to. How can I dance without music?

When the companion spoke, the voice had the authority of immovable stone.

— Sure as Ithaca is your home and Odysseus's kingdom, you do hear the music. At times it is slow and solemn as a funeral dirge, yet it carries love's uninterrupted voice. Ah, and there soon returns the joyous, even sprightly, music, and one is lifted into the dance.

— Can it be? In the dance, my feet shall no longer be heavy, and going through the familiar routine will lose its tedium perhaps.

Penelope began to muse, and her face held something near eagerness. She went on.

— Within the cloth I weave, I no longer see mere passive waiting. I begin to imagine the dance you speak of, however incredible it sounds. Something is different now. I am no longer in despair.

— You were less of a woman before the long work at the loom, I think. Now Aphrodite holds in her hand the waiting. It is in the waiting that your true strength flowers.

Penelope's hands for some time had lain on her lap, the loom shrouded in stillness beside her. She remained in silence for some time. At last she murmured aloud.

— No. You are mistaken. My strength has not flowered, for I feel only diminished in Odysseus's absence. I suffer, body and mind!

The voice that responded seemed closer now.

— It is that you wait in the bud. In the bud, the desired future is already present like unborn flesh. As for your body, it holds the dream of the flowering and is impatient with the bud. Only remember, the bud swells with life and a certain shaping. It is hardly empty!

The last statement was made in scorn, surely. When Penelope responded, her voice was a whisper.

— Yes, but . . . will the flower ever open again in my lifetime?

— A foolish question, to try to get ahead of the rhythmic order of things! It is the destiny of the bud to flower, you see. Already it embodies love, although in a hidden fashion. It swells with expectancy and your passion, I think. Only know that the flower will open to its ecstatic circle, enfleshed, unmatched in beauty, and yes, completeness.

The words repeated themselves in her ear. "Who is my companion?" she asked, but there was no reply. Nor did the voice speak again that day.

Aphrodite Loves Ares

Dusk spread over the northern Aegean island of Lemnos as a woman, framed by the high stone doorway of her house, gazed toward the peak of the volcanic mountain. Had there been an observer, such a one would have marveled at the scene, for the woman was unusually lovely to behold. An attitude of quiet grace accompanied by a sense of ease was evident, creating a context in which she appeared independent of familiar authority and custom. Was she not a queen? Even to a keen observer, however, there remained something undeclared—a mystery overflowing stern boundaries much as a spring current does. Content to neither enter nor exit, Aphrodite remained in the doorway. When would her husband, Hephaestus, creator of beautiful works, appear, returning from a long day at the forge in the mountain cavern? She speculated idly. As yet, there was no sign of him on the path. Even so, she was not given to worry. As she observed the path below, her eyes widened suddenly as she saw that a stranger approached, and his lively, bold stride stirred her strangely. Certainly it contrasted with the patient, lame gait of her husband. As the stranger drew near, she saw that he wore gleaming armor and a helmet, while what looked to be a legendary sword hung at his side. A warrior, perhaps? Now the handsome figure looked up to meet her gaze, causing her to gasp in astonishment.

— Why, Ares, is it really you? How rare indeed for an Olympian to call on us! Do come in.

Smiling, he regarded her as the two stood together in the stone doorway.

— Aphrodite, I have found you!

— At home on Lemnos, yes.

With this dignified response, she invited him into her house, aware that his admiring glance was hardly deficient in boldness.

— Thank you for inviting me into your house. If you don't mind, I'll remove my helmet and leave my sword with it. There!

— You must explain why you have come in full armor to the house of Hephaestus and myself. Surely no battle is anticipated?

    Ares blinked, and his voice was not without passion.

— Ah, let me look at you, Aphrodite. Although dressed like a Greek lady, I find you exactly as I've always dreamed of you!

    She smiled a little shyly and looked puzzled.

— You say that you have dreamed of me . . .

— Indeed. Always I see you with flesh shining and radiant as though you might just have emerged from the sea and stepped onto an island! That is the island I've been searching for, Aphrodite.

— You speak eloquently. Even now my memory returns to the time I was carried on a wave of the sea. How solitary I was, rather like an abandoned woman, and yet the sea foam carried me as if I were under an invisible sail. Ah, then I glimpsed an island shore before me, and I stepped out of the sea onto that shore. In that moment, I felt earth's presence beneath me, and earth's joy coursed through me! This is how it was when I came ashore on lovely Cythera for the first time.

— For the first time, you say. You are preeminently goddess of first times, are you not? Of this, I'm convinced, Kytheria. Besides, there is your reputation.

    Whether the last was an afterthought was not clear, but the comment caused her to frown. Her voice was cool now as she rearranged the cover on the comfortable guest chair.

— I expect that you shall believe what you like, Ares.

    Ares was silently assessing the relative merits of the chair and the couch nearby, and removing his armor, he chose to stretch out on the couch, his strong, lean body now visibly at ease. Aphrodite's eyes registered surprise as she remained silent, frowning slightly.

— I do not mean to displease you in any way.

— It is that the couch has been accustomed to receiving Hephaestus, the lord of this house.

    The god of war grinned in what might have been a challenge. She went on swiftly now.

— The couch knows every inclination of his supple body. It occurs to me, Ares, that you will probably find the couch, well, a *misfit*.

    Ares was enjoying himself now and grew expansive.

— Not at all. Don't give it a thought. Actually, I am feeling unusually comfortable. But I've no desire that my presence startle you. You will surely find me not at all like my lucky brother.

— I had quite forgotten that you and Hephaestus are brothers, for you are so unalike!

Sitting down opposite him, she shook her head in disbelief. Now he prodded her, obviously pleased with the turn of the conversation.

— Tell me what these differences are that seem to impress you. I'll be pleased to be informed.

— Unlike my dear husband, you are always bold. Why, always you go forward swinging your sword in challenge!

Ares, who had been leaning on his elbow as he regarded her closely, burst out laughing at this description of himself.

— Come, I don't always swing the sword. Sometimes I simply wear it at my side, my lovely goddess.

She passed her right hand in front of her face as if to discourage a fly.

— To me it is all the same. It was awful when I went on the battlefield of Troy to rescue Aeneas, for I was wounded in the hand and couldn't bear to stay. You lent me your chariot and horses to carry me away from the battle and back to Olympus. Thank you again for rescuing me, Ares.

— Don't mention it. I expect that you must have noticed that my horses are also bold. Boldness seems to be my most familiar attribute.

For a moment, a dream passed over her face, and her voice was low when she spoke.

— Such boldness draws me strangely. Sometimes I see you as a lion soundlessly tracking his prey upon the mountain, muscles taut, all in readiness for the pounce!

Ares leaned toward her, greatly pleased at her description.

— I can hardly deny that I am a lion of a warrior.

Did this please her?

— Is it that you are warning me, Ares?

— When I'm with you, there is a languor, most pleasant actually, that courses through me. It renders me quite unfit for battle. Aphrodite, with you I shall never do battle!

She savored his words before some truth seemed to shake her.

— Yet you are always the warrior. Admit it. To be sure, war is your bread and olive oil!

— Come. Would you doubt the confession of the true lover?

— The warrior who loves does not lose his passion for conflict, I
   imagine.

He had hardly imagined that Aphrodite could indulge herself in
such wariness, and he regarded her for a long pause.

— Look, love of my heart, you do discern me well, I admit. So now I
   must press the urgent question. It is this: what better match could there
   be than war and love? You and I are eternally partnered, I tell you. We
   are the real guts of the cosmos. Actually the human world has long
   perceived us as the mighty opposites that rule life. You can't deny it,
   my dear.

— Ah, such a match—which you dare to call inevitable—causes a trembling
   within me. I begin to see that you are different from the other gods.
   Why, *Ares's mind is all body.*

Her words struck him like a well-aimed arrow. Had his face
momentarily lost its ruddy confidence? He murmured to himself,

— She could be flattering me, but I cannot tell. Again she is speaking . . .

— Nor am I known to flatter anyone. If you love me, you will recognize
   in me what is indestructible truth. This is how it is. When my full gaze
   is upon my companion, both mind and heart are known to fill with
   praise. This happens when I behold that one's beauty. Beauty is a shining
   thing and, alas, may even be hidden. Yet I am like one who pans for
   gold out of dirt and rock. Inexorably I am drawn toward beauty that
   arises in present time. This I praise with all my heart. As for flattery, I
   shun it. How could I engage in what is false to love?

Ares shook his head, frowning in considerable perplexity at her
explanation.

— Few, I would say, manage to see with your eyes, Aphrodite. You said
   that my mind is "all body." So what do you say of Hephaestus? What
   about his body?

Ares felt confident that he was about to guarantee his own distinctive
gifts when he asked the question. Aphrodite replied at once.

— Unlike your body, Ares, Hephaestus's body is all *dreaming mind,* it seems.
   Always he is dreaming new shapes, forms that will be embodied over
   his fire.

Now the god's voice was dry as he pressed her.

— I was simply asking about his body, which is famous for not being
   beautiful, if you will pardon my candor.

Aphrodite rose to her feet and began to walk slowly back and forth across the chamber, her garment flowing like a shining stream over her lithe form. She was as one alone with her thoughts. Turning, she gazed at Ares as she spoke.

— There is only one source of beauty that I am aware of. It lies in the companion who holds the heart's full regard. You would hear the truth from me then? I tell you that Hephaestus possesses the most beautiful Hephaestus body imaginable! And to think that one is looking on a dreaming mind!

— Few of us Olympians view things with your eyes, Aphrodite.

He shook his head as if pondering some mystery he was not likely to make progress with. She gave him her astonishing smile now, which was like a long tale slowly to be told.

— Tell me, Ares, am I the judge of a beauty contest or am I goddess of love?

— The latter, of course. As a matter of record, I am here to test the truth of that singular capacity.

She blushed. Then laughing, she scolded him lightly.

— You are handsome indeed, Ares, but don't be tiresome!

— No one ever accuses me of being boring. Even if my boldness puts you off somewhat, remember that you also find yourself without a defense against me.

The two gods sat now, silently regarding each other. With a small sigh of resignation, she spoke.

— Unlike Hephaestus, you only seem to materialize in the moment of action.

— Like a pounce, you mean? It is the pounce that makes a lion particularly alive, I must point out.

— But one who possesses the light of mind reflects, does he not? Hephaestus has spoken of this to me, you see.

— You speak of the god of no pounce.

— How jealous you seem of your brother, Ares. After all, he is the great creative god, the god of work.

— So what is it that he says? You have me curious now.

— Why, he says that reflection is *living twice*. And something else, even more puzzling. He says that the second time, one comes to possess life more spaciously, even with greater delight. Always I have been goddess of the first time, so I know little of what he means.

Ares was on his feet now as passion seized him, and his words came like flames. Yet they were pleasing to her ears.

— Aphrodite, O Aphrodite my love! We only live in present time, and you yourself are the one who brings radiant bounty with you when you consent to be there. Don't resist me and my burning love! Whatever you do, you must not let Hephaestus teach you how to live *backward*.

Aphrodite appeared to be unprepared for such a passionate confession from Ares, long her friend. When she could reply, her voice was low and almost tentative.

— Oh, do not worry, my friend. I shall never live backward. True, the present time is where I live, and to the present hour, I'll bring my bounty . . . that is, if I choose to come.

— O Kytheria, stay in this moment we now possess, I beg you. Speak no more of other loves. Do you hear me? I am wearied to hear of them. Look at me, the bold warrior god who loves you with a love to exceed all others you have known. Stay with me, Aphrodite, my beloved!

A blush stole over her cheeks, and she lowered her eyes to the stone floor. Even so, she could not prevent the sigh of desire that escaped her lips as slowly she walked toward enchanted Ares. She looked like one who rambles in a meadow.

So it happened that on far Lemnos, Aphrodite led Ares to the bedchamber in the house she shared with her husband, Hephaestus. There within the high marriage bed, the two gods reclined, and in a time fragrant and generous as a long summer, they knew their love. Much later, gazing upward, they marveled at the bed's ceiling, which was the newest creation of Hephaestus. Thin as a veil and intricately woven was a netting of bronze, over which the light of the single oil lamp played. Even as they admired the ingenious creation, the handsome net descended toward where they lay. Almost at once, the weighty bronze veil covered them completely. Aphrodite was first to cry out, and her outburst was followed by an agonizing groan from Ares.

— Alas, we are the fish caught by Hephaestus in his great net!

Their feverish struggle to free themselves began. In time, they were exhausted and yet could not extricate themselves, so binding was the net in spite of its appearance of delicacy. Alas, voices were heard, first at a distance, growing louder as they were accompanied by firm footsteps. The Olympian gods entered the bedchamber now led by Hephaestus himself, for he was not one easily cuckolded. As Hephaestus witnessed the lovers' scene before him, although they had drawn well apart, his face revealed all manner of emotion—outrage at the cuckoldry of Ares, anger at Aphrodite's infidelity, which alternated with relief at the possibility that she would now be restored to him, and gratitude for the presence of the other gods whose sympathy largely lay with himself. Once released from the net, scowling Ares snatched up his armor and sword, dragging them behind him as he departed. Meanwhile, Aphrodite had restored her missing garment and, unperturbed, was gazing into her mirror as she rearranged her hair. With a solemn nod, the Olympians took their leave, Hephaestus walking them to the outside gate.

Remaining in the chamber with Aphrodite, however, was Hermes.

When she had completed the restoration of her appearance, he spoke.

— Greetings, Aphrodite. I am afraid that our visit has fallen at an inconvenient time.

She looked at him sharply before the anger faded. After all, was not Hermes among her closest friends? She nodded simply, denying nothing. He took the initiative.

— The end of such a love comes swiftly. Ah, but the recovery takes longer, it seems.

— Hermes, you do understand. Alas, the fragile vase one values shatters unexpectedly. Oh, how can it ever be mended?

— Your distress is heavy to bear. Tell me of this love, if you so desire.

She regarded the god of the road intently before shifting her gaze to stare out the window toward the sea. At last she seemed to have reached a decision.

— Yes, I will speak about Ares. His arrival at our house, and it was in the absence of Hephaestus, was totally unexpected. After all, the island of Lemnos is scarcely on anyone's route. It became clear that he had come to see me alone. Something about the god of war captured me at once, although I resisted it.

— And what would that be?

— It is that he is so *unwoman!*

The description brought an amused expression to Hermes' mobile face as she continued with a certain excitement in her voice.

— That boldness, how can I describe it? With burning eyes fixed on some invisible goal, he charges ahead fearlessly. Why, nothing distracts the man. He is ever engaged. I suppose that must be what it is like to be in battle.

Hermes pressed her with a question.

— And were the two of you engaged in battle, dare I ask?

Aphrodite gave Hermes her sidelong look and a slow smile before replying.

— Hermes, I am not easily won.

— Indeed not.

He smiled his dazzling smile. She continued to describe her lover.

— There is a kind of indifference in him as though he hardly cares where he steps. This must be due to his fearlessness, I suppose.

— Well, there certainly is that about the fellow. You didn't find this off-putting then?

— At first I was angered by his manner and his, well, presumption. Yet in time, it fairly vanquished me!

— Wait, Aphrodite. You have spoken of his boldness and of his ability to conquer. I should say that neither of these is "unwoman," as you put it. When it comes to the way of love, both aspects belong to *you*, as a matter of fact. And you are certainly woman. I point this out because the two of you are known to express boldness and the skill of conquest. I can see that you and Ares have long had quite a bit in common.

— How can you say this? Only look at how different we are!

How could Hermes reach such an outrageous conclusion?

— Naturally your realms of action are very different. When you have entered the situation between a man and a woman, doesn't something of boldness and a mad plunge take place? All familiar scenes of one's life are at once curtained off lest they lay claims upon one. *Ares has entered!* so it appears to a reasonable observer like myself. Yes, I'm inclined to say that Ares is usually present in the onset of love. I, for one, have always found the god a bit mad.

The color flared in the goddess's cheeks, and she looked a little peeved.

— O Hermes, how could you? You ignore the wonder and sweetness of love altogether and make it sound like a declaration of war!

Hermes looked the picture of pastoral tranquility now as he stroked his staff and readjusted his voluminous cloak.

— Well, I expect that I was affected by Hephaestus's stormy countenance when he left this bedchamber a short while ago. Still, is there not a kind of inevitable battlefield when two worlds come together as two persons? Each world is prepared to defend its right.

— Come now. You are being imaginative, although I suspect that you are defending Hephaestus's side. Have you forgotten that I am daughter of Dione, the oracular Earth Goddess? In her wisdom is the knowledge of true human need, you see. Love is not a strategy. It is a thing emerging from earth. It spreads its roots in the deep places and causes life to be crowned with green, new growth followed by the fragrant blossoming! Why, it is no battlefield. Besides, I remind you that Ares and I were long friends before love visited us.

— Ah, Aphrodite, only consider how it goes. When Eros's arrows fall, two people who were friends become utter strangers, each being an envoy of a far, unknown country. Only as strangers are we plunged into the small god's enchantment, you see, not as friends. Oh yes, it is over strangers that love spreads its net and takes two people captive.

Aphrodite pondered these strange words of her good friend Hermes. Now regarding him, she smiled a small smile as she spoke.

— There is a certain truth in what you have said. It is as strangers that one comes to love. My memory is stirred now. Together with Himeros, Desire, my dependable friend, I once came upon such a truth. She said that one only desires what one is not, and one only comes to love what one has never before known. Yes, it is invisible and abiding desire that draws a person toward a far island shore. Ah, Hermes, this far, strange shore ever draws us. It is the land of one's innocence . . .

— You say this because the lover stands whole in himself. Nothing is bent or exhausted or groveling. He recovers that innocent wholeness he knew as a child, I think.

Hermes watched as Aphrodite, who stood at the window observing the rise of the moon, drew her cloak about her lovely shoulders to keep out the chill of the evening. He also rose to his feet, preparing to depart. Now Aphrodite turned back to him and spoke earnestly.

— Let us not speak further of this love I have known with Ares. Ares has gone, and the love Hephaestus and I have receives me again. Ah, it is a source of wonder as well. You say that Ares leaves his boldness with me, boldness that accompanied love's onset. What is my gift to Ares then?

Her question hung on the air between the two gods. Hermes responded with his question.

— As Dione's daughter, what does your earth wisdom ask from you as
   love's gift?

     Aphrodite fell silent, pondering. At last she spoke simply.

— It asks that love's gift be the recovery of one's innocent self!

     Hermes was smiling as he took heart from her words.

— So be it. Was this then the sum total of what you bestowed on Ares?

— One thing more. Perhaps I have sabotaged for a time his capacity to
   do battle!

     This brought laughter from the god of the road, due in part to
the subtle look of triumph on her face. As often was the case, he had the
last word.

— Only remember how sheepishly he dragged his armor behind him when
   he departed this house. I should say that for a time, you have gentled
   the battle god. Farewell, Aphrodite, my friend!

Aphrodite and Hephaestus

       High above the seashore on Lemnos, the god of work entered the courtyard of his house, where lying in the shade of a large plane tree he found his lovely wife. Sitting down on the couch, he regarded her with affection.

— I left the forge early, as you see. Bored are you, my dear?

— The fact is that there are very few distractions that draw me, Hephaestus.

       He smiled slowly, his eyebrows raised.

— Of all our companions on Olympus, I should have said that you are surely the most vulnerable to distraction. No one holds a candle to you, Aphrodite.

— O Hephaestus, there you are with your fierce focus, always watching the thing taking shape over the fire of the forge. I would never dream of competing with you! Why, you have never been distracted, I am sure. Since you went missing on Olympus, all the gods are smiting their brows and bemoaning the fact that they have lost their creator.

— Indeed? Do you have evidence for this conclusion?

       This was the best news he had heard.

— I am good at discerning longing, you see. And besides, the gods cannot imagine you hidden in your grotto creating beautiful works at your forge while all about you stands the harshness of unforgiving rock.

— And are you disturbed as well that my work seems to be cradled in the harsh, unforgiving rock as you put it?

— Well, yes. How can I not be? Only consider that nowhere in the grotto is there the color and softness of fabric! There is not even a couch!

       This fact caused her to shudder. As for Hephaestus, he threw back his head and laughed heartily, amused by his image of the forge refurbished and furnished by Aphrodite. He took her hand as she continued, for he might as well hear her out.

— No, hear me, Hephaestus. The couch brings a person *ease*, and without ease, one has not the Graces in the work.

These words sobered him, and the regal force of the creator god came over him.

— What is this you say? You are serious after all. Always I must have the presence of the Graces. Otherwise, the evolving form loses its essential dance, the work dries up, and beauty collapses into a mere formula that's generally extolled!

Hephaestus had risen to his feet and now stood a little apart from the couch. He studied Aphrodite's face before pressing the question,

— My dear, is it ease that is the Graces' true gift, do you suppose?

— I only know that ease belongs to their mystery. Why don't you ask Eurynome about this? As mother of the Graces, she will be able to answer you. You and Eurynome, not to mention her sea nymph companion Thetis, have enjoyed a long friendship, after all.

— Actually, I have a nine-year debt to their excellent hospitality in the sea grotto . . .

— There it is again—another grotto that has claimed you—the sea grotto. You do have a weakness for the cavernous darkness and the severity of rocks, Hephaestus!

She sighed, shaking her head. The god gazed at her at some length and considered her words.

— Dear Aphrodite, can you possibly understand that, without the dim, primordial passages that lie ever underground, my work would not be possible? My forge requires this kind of shelter. Ah, the hospitality that receives me there is indescribable! Even the fire takes on fierce energy as though it had taken on the content of my mind's dream! There is something else. Once I am within the forge, the work brooks no distractions.

At ease upon the couch beneath the plane tree, she fell into musing once again.

— Tell me, Hephaestus, do you think of me as mostly given to distraction?

— Hmm. It does appear to me that distraction is your way of going about things. Yes. At the same time, I would add that you possess a considerable art with it.

— Only consider what I am like when I am with my faithful companions Desire and Eros. Why, I never neglect what I am about. Not for a moment do I lose track of where the luminous path of delight leads out of the gray routine, skirting as it goes the dusty rooms where all is dry repetition. No, my dear spouse, never am I distracted where it matters!

His eyes widened with astonishment, and after a moment, he murmured, "Never distracted!" A perception was forming, and he nodded.

— You know, I find what you say baffling. Maybe you are not distracted after all. Well, it certainly is a fact that you regularly distract me! I must admit that the grotto's forge offers me shelter from your power to distract. Actually, I hadn't meant to tell you.

From the goddess's face, it appeared she had just received bad news and was looking appalled.

— Do you mean that you require protection from me, your wife?

— Let me make myself clear. I do not at all *desire* protection, yet I need it. Without my work at the forge, I fear that life with you could overwhelm me.

He smiled at her slowly, reassuring her of his true affection while at the same time allowing for the digestion of his words.

— You—an Olympian god—require protection?

— I a god, yes.

Aphrodite now grew pensive, and her usual ease seemed gradually to be returning.

— You know, I just thought of something. It may simply be the case that you and I are well matched, you see. Has that occurred to you?

— It has indeed. As a matter of fact, I have never doubted it. During the nine years spent in the sea grotto with the nymphs, I came to realize two important truths. One of these is that work is my treasure. I believe that you know this. The other is more difficult to describe. I came to see that my work requires the coming together of what does not match. Actually, I have come to think of it as the *match of the unmatchables!*

A groan escaped the goddess. Quickly he went on to explain.

— Don't you see how it is? I simply had to bargain with Zeus in order to get you for my wife and beloved.

— Why, Hephaestus, what is this that you are saying? That you and I don't match? Alas, this is bad news!

— No, my dear, it is hardly bad news. Think about it, as many onlookers of our marriage may already have done. Why, you are very beautiful while as for myself, I am lame and walk awkwardly among the handsome perfection of the other gods!

A look of dejection passed over his face, and he fell silent. Her eyes as she regarded him steadily took on a grave tenderness. Strongly desiring that she understand, he continued,

— This condition of mine at first seemed to me an alarming destiny, but in time, I found it more hopeful than it looked.

— How is it hopeful? You must tell me.

— The match of such opposites as yourself and myself is never finished but is ever in the making, I think, summoning afresh the indispensable ingredients: First there is desire, desire that sees for the first time since what it gazes upon is unrepeatable. Next is what can best be called the blossoming, for this is when our love takes on its incredible beauty of fragrance and form in present time. And the third thing is the exquisite and shining union of love and work.

He smiled in delight. From the goddess a deep sigh of satisfaction came, and the two fell silent as overhead the branches began to bend in a slow dance under the hand of a soft wind. When she spoke, her voice was low.

— How true is this account of things! Still, isn't it necessary for Desire to decide whether or not she will be the bride of work? Hephaestus, what I find intimidating is work's agenda, you see. It does tire me just to think of it.

He regarded her with tenderness and spoke quietly in his deep voice.

— As god of work, I also have a say in this contract. It is my experience that Desire can be a rather demanding mistress, driving the work without mercy at times. Still, in the absence of Desire, the work of the forge deteriorates into mere repetitive acts of image and skill.

She pondered these words, her eyes blinking with their lively accounting as she responded.

— Always Desire and Persuasion are my companions, as you know, yet I am more than desire. Otherwise, I would not be goddess of love. Again and again you enter the life of my heart, Hephaestus. Ah, but then you depart. What am I left with but the echo of your departing footsteps, followed soon by the distant hammering as some unseen piece of raw metal is shaped under your hand?

For a long moment, she looked, however lovely, like an abandoned woman. The god looked anxious as he spoke.

— Come now, I am not the one who comes and goes. It is rather you, Aphrodite, you yourself, let me point out. Still, I must admit that this trait belongs to your enchanting and unpredictable nature. As for the work, it requires everything of me at times. Indeed, in work I possess an invisible master who holds me under contract.

— Contract you say. But contract is a thing of *law*. It has no affinity with desire or with love itself. What a foreign thing is a contract! At the same time, love is more binding than a contract can ever hope to be. Ah, Hephaestus, love is everlasting!

— And that is unarguable. Nothing is more powerful than its bonds. I know this. Still, in the human realm, there is great difficulty, and it worries me.

— What are you thinking of, then?

— I am thinking of those who greatly desire to receive love. They pound on the gates, and they find them locked. Love gives them no access. It is not a comfortable fact.

She fell silent pondering his words. When she spoke, he found the path of her thoughts surprising.

— If I were to meet one of these locked-out persons, I should at once ask, "Did you forget my garden?"

He smiled a teasing sort of smile.

— In other words, you would use your immeasurable power to distract the person from what's at issue.

— No, Hephaestus. How could you misunderstand me? Don't you see? My garden is intimately connected to love's realm. Only think of my sanctuaries whose approach is through the garden. Why, it is not pleasant distraction, no mere decorative passage. What contains me is the garden, or am I not spread out and thriving in the natural soil of human existence? How different is Aphrodite's garden from some forceful agenda two persons are inclined to settle for! One who walks through my garden passes through what by nature is moist and green and blossoming. It is a passing through what is endearing and fragrant in human possibility. Surely you see this. I assure you that those I favor have their initiation in my garden.

A leisurely narrative moved in the regard he gave her. Together they watched the swaying branches and the arrival of two doves. When he spoke, his voice was almost idle.

— I quite delight in your talk of love, you know, love itself being known for that sudden surge of delight to which nothing compares. Besides, the bounty of it is beyond compare. But there is something I long to know: is this great love *faithful?*

The question caused her to sit up abruptly.

— Faithful? I'm not sure I understand the meaning of that term. When the bonds of love are present, one has no need to ask for more, surely.

— I am not so certain of this. When love comes with its singular joy, one desires that it continue in one's life, that it be accessible and, well, in place—rather the way your garden is.

— That is true. Even so, there is something that every one who loves must get used to. It is that love thrives only in present time. Ah, what an incredibly bountiful present is love!

For a long moment, she looked regretful knowing that she had not fully answered his concern. Continuing to regard her, he shook his head slowly.

Hermes Comes

Days passed, and the house of Hephaestus and Aphrodite, serene within the high, shallow bowl of the mountains, witnessed the rhythmic order that at times manifested itself in the household. The guest who had just arrived and who could count on receiving generous hospitality was none other than their fellow Olympian Hermes. The three stood in the courtyard in the plane tree's shade as Hermes removed his three-cornered traveler's hat and Aphrodite took his voluminous cloak in a graceful movement as she spoke.

— The pomegranate-colored couch is especially for you, Hermes. Do be at ease here while the maidens bring out bread, olives, cheese, and wine for our repast.

Murmuring his thanks, smiling and inimitable Hermes stretched out on the couch.

Nor was any one of the gods more handsome than Hermes although the responses he evoked were usually to his other outstanding qualities. Not the least of these was a kind of inspired meddling in the latest predicament. Hephaestus in particular felt a great warmth toward the god of the road, for it had been Hermes who had advised him to return home to Olympus after his long sea grotto sojourn, ever bolstering his confidence of a good reception. The three gods munched on the olives, tossing the seeds in the bushes, and, after pouring a libation to all the gods, sipped their wine. After studying his brother's face quietly, Hephaestus, who was never roundabout in his approach, offered a comment.

— I say, Hermes, I am aware that you are always well informed, since you apparently live with your ear to the ground of all three realms. Nevertheless, I must call to your attention a singular fact about my second fall from Olympus when I landed here on the isle of Lemnos.

— Oh? Is there something I don't know?

Hephaestus laughed.

— I doubt that there is anything that gets by you. Nevertheless, what I wish is to express the obvious. It is this—that I have neither desire nor intention of relocation on Mt. Olympus. On Lemnos I am completely happy, as you may observe. Just thought I'd mention this in case you have come on some errand of the gods.

— Hephaestus ended by raising his eyebrows in question. Hermes' reply was smooth.

— Actually, it gladdens my heart to see you so content, brother, and I hasten to assure you that I am on no official errand of any sort. You both being dear to me, I had the desire to look in on you. It's that simple. Still, I'll bear in mind your declaration. So what is new?

Relieved of a certain burden of old memories stirred up, Hephaestus gave Hermes a broad smile now. It was Aphrodite who responded to Hermes' question.

— It is the *match of the unmatchables*, as Hephaestus calls it, that is occupying us. For myself, I find such a match a most unsavory prospect while he finds it quite a lovely arrangement! Do tell us what you think of it, Hermes.

— Hmm, I take it that this match is your own that he is describing. Right?

She nodded, but he saw that there was some distress in her face.

— So by "unmatchables," some play between total opposites is perceived, I imagine. Is that correct, Hephaestus?

— Right on.

Aphrodite grew impatient with the tedious logic of it all and spoke in an animated manner to Hephaestus.

— We are male and female, dear husband. Is such opposition so perplexing to you?

Hephaestus's smile was tinged with amusement.

— It is most decidedly, since you ask, yet gender is not the opposition that's been occupying my thoughts.

— What then?

Hephaestus took his time in replying, regarding his beloved wife steadily after a brief look at Hermes that exchanged an unspoken comment.

— Well, I am the god of work, as the Greek world regards me. And you, my lovely Aphrodite—why, you are the god of love. No one would argue these facts. There is between love and work a great opposition as each assumes its shape in life. Still, I am convinced that without love, the work grows feeble, scatterbrained, and tedious.

Hermes nodded his agreement and spoke.

— Just when I expected to entertain myself in this extraordinary household thought to be contentment itself, I learn that I am faced with this profound opposition! Forgive me if my sigh is muttering, *O poor me!* Can it be justified? Wait, Aphrodite, be patient with me while I sort it all out.

The goddess smiled fondly at the god of the road, who continued.

— While work leans earnestly toward the future, scanning the horizon as it does so, love settles altogether into present time, as if it were its house and extensive grounds. It fairly ignores the fact that a future exists that can make demands upon a person. O yes, without a doubt, love is abundantly decked out in present time.

With the look of the housewife who just misplaced her key to her cupboard of fine linen, Aphrodite questioned Hermes.

— Oh, are you suggesting that love is blind after all? Of all heresies aired in the marketplace, that one is the most devastating, surely!

— My brother would never insult love, my dear, and certainly not in this household. Nor is he ever caught putting his foot into his mouth.

Hermes raised his eyebrows in commentary before continuing.

— I should rather say that love is indifferent toward time that is not abundantly present. What's more, love carries within it the immediacy of its full blossoming, its realization, while work clearly does not. Always work must embrace slow, even agonizing beginnings. Love is its own conclusion since it has nowhere else to go or more to accomplish in order to be fully itself. As for work, it seems ever unconcluded! Is this not true, Hephaestus?

— It is true. Work is like a lion, splendid in its strength and its roar, that no sooner has felled one prey than it has appetite for the next. Work has the passion to begin again, to continue, not to simply sit back and admire the achievement.

Aphrodite was looking even more distraught if that were possible.

— How can you say such things? Hephaestus, are you discouraged that you compare your works of art to the prowling of a beast? To the bare appeasement of appetite? What of beauty itself? Doesn't beauty draw you always into each shaping, the giving of the exquisite form? Men and gods alike praise your works for their immediate and yet lasting beauty, and, dear spouse, I speak of *concluded* works!

Hephaestus smiled slowly and sighed with satisfaction. Hermes spoke.

— Indeed, Hephaestus, you have many concluded works of great beauty and excellence. Aphrodite is correct in this. It is not easy to put one's finger on something that is in the habit of concealing its face, you see. Such is the case with work. In the passion of its engagement, it hides its face within the longing toward what is yet to come. Work remains—in spite of what it has already created—a spirit that moves on. There is in the great craftsman, I'd say, a spirit that cannot be housed, for it is ever yearning and ever dreaming.

Aphrodite gazed now at Hephaestus and smiled as one who rambles on some hidden path. When she spoke, her words were washed with a fresh stream of energy.

— As for me, I could not bear a single hour that failed to unfold its own fulfillment, its dream, its finished work!

Astonished to hear in words what he already knew about her, Hephaestus threw back his head and burst into laughter. Now he added his own assessment.

— As for myself, I could not bear an hour of work which failed to unfold the vision of what lies always and inevitably ahead. One catches the far glimpse of what is yet to be given shape and substance over the fire. Do you know when I am most uneasy, even miserable? It is when the pause of a finished work extends before me for a long time.

You see, I fear that I am surfeited with illusion, the illusion of having completed work . . .

The three gods arose in the gathering dusk and made their way on the path to the stone house. Nor was the mountain silent, for it emitted some volcanic muttering out of its core.

It was Aphrodite who offered final words.

— Ah, how strange is work compared to love! Is it not ever panting after the handsome completion, sweating as Hephaestus does over the fire of the forge? And yet, when it overtakes the completion, it complains bitterly! How out of sorts work can be . . .

Dusk had descended upon the courtyard where they conversed. The three rose to their feet and moved toward the house where the lamps had just been lighted.

PART XII

Myths of Zeus

Zeus—An Introduction

The divine pursuit of the beloved is a major theme of Greek myth. As a luminous thread, it weaves through the fabric of legendary engagements such as the labors of Heracles, the heroic deeds of Theseus and Perseus, the Trojan War and the recovery of Helen, and many others.

As a result, the urgent question arises: how is one to regard the many loves of Zeus as the Olympian who gives the final shaping to the will of the gods? In answer to the question, considerable commentary has occurred over the centuries, a good deal of it offhand, some of it humorous as well. In short, Zeus in his power and privilege is perceived as engaging in unrestrained physical passion and possession of his unsuspecting lovers. What he leaves behind in a vast record of unfaithfulness to his wife, Hera, and to his other mates as well is of no small consequence.

Such a view of the lord of the gods at the very least goes astray as a picture of the great Olympian. This is not the same Zeus, majestic and with extraordinary human understanding, whom the Greeks so widely honored in Phidias's statue of the enthroned god at ancient Olympia. To perceive Zeus as a rapist suggests either one greatly deprived who must fulfill his compelling need, or else it points to a figure who is altogether self-serving in his bold exercise of power. In any case, neither image reflects the *imago dei* that is embedded in the human psyche. The fact that Zeus supremely embodies the divine in the Greek perception of reality compels us toward a larger conception of the god's loves.

At the very least, the acts of Zeus carry indefinable spirit. Is he not partnered by the eagle of sovereign winged presence, the farseeing one? In search of elucidation, our attention is called to some of the god's love encounters, whether his beloved is woman, goddess, or nymph. Into several of these encounters, Zeus carries the bountiful fullness of nature within a particular form. As bull, for example, he draws Europa to himself. As swan, he wins Leda. As eagle, he leads away Ganymede; while as the cloud, he approaches Io. Nature manifests its force, its tangible order, and its ways like a language that cannot be translated. On the other hand, to glimpse evidence of the luminous spirit brought to earth by Zeus, one has only to consider the progeny of his love relationships. There are the births of gods: Artemis and Apollo born to Leto; Aphrodite to Dione at Dodona; Dionysos to dying Semele; also Athena, Hermes, the Muses, Hephaestus, the Graces, and the Hours. It is through the acts of his human children, however, that Zeus's spirit especially shapes consciousness. Among these are Heracles, Helen, Perseus, the immortal twin Pollux, and Minos.

Dione and Zeus

Within the serene green bowl of the Pindus Mountains of northwestern Greece, two priestesses approached the sanctuary of the goddess. The taller woman turned to her companion and spoke.

— Ah, there is the sound of small vibrating wings near my ear. It is like the warm, sweet pulse of a small cosmos not yet known. A curious thing . . .

She turned, and at that movement, a small hummingbird lifted from the nearby flower, the luminous green of the small body brilliant on the summer air. Her companion observed it as well and commented.

— I wonder what the little bird portends here in Dodona's remote sanctuary. Could it be an *angelos*, do you suppose? Don't you wonder what a messenger from the gods would be like?

The first priestess considered this.

— An important arrival could be about to happen, you know. My ear still sings with the pulsing of those small wings.

— Just imagine what if some extraordinary traveler were to approach right here where the two of us are alone ready to tend to Goddess Dione's altar. Listen.

The two fell silent as they sat now within the circle of the sacred ancient oak tree. A tiny breeze had arisen unexpectedly in the lingering heat of the afternoon. As a gentle movement stirred the oak leaves overhead, the priestesses closed their eyes as if attending to their murmured text. The first priestess broke the silence now.

— The oracle speaks, saying that the traveler who comes will be unusual. This one will leave a mark upon Dodona, one that Dione both greatly longs for and dreads!

— Oh, can it be? A bold hero is coming, or else some god, I fear!

— The oracle does not name the one who comes.

— The oracle belongs to our goddess, for she is wise. Does it say when this man traveler will arrive?

— No, it does not, but I too sense that it is a man who comes. It must be soon. Let's make double offerings for Dione to reassure her. What do you say?

At once the two priestesses began to prepare the fruits and small acorn meal cakes for the altar. The last rays of the setting sun departed as dusk descended over the small valley. Standing before the altar, the two women began to sing an ode of praise to Dione, goddess of the oracle.

It was early morning in the remote valley of Dodona, and the sun-filled air was golden while dew still sparkled on the leaves. As for the priestesses, a tension was palpable. A vague apprehension assailed them, due in part to an excitement in the air that did not declare itself. The sky was cloudless from horizon to horizon, and yet there came the rumbling of distant thunder. Quite soundlessly, a chariot approached the sanctuary unobserved by the priestesses, and as it drew up, a kingly figure wearing armor and a goatskin aegis leaped lightly to the ground and strode toward the sanctuary. Reaching the circle of the sacred oak tree of the oracle, the figure slowed his pace and gazed on the great oak. Wonder filled his voice as he murmured aloud.

— So this is Dodona's palm of earth, this shaded circle of oak trees far from the cities of men? It is said that the voice of the oracle enters the human world here. Yet apparently the divine wisdom is not poured first into a woman, filling her throat with a chanting ecstasy. No, it is not at all like Pythia's receiving Apollo's oracle at Delphi. Hmm.

He turned at the sound of footsteps and beheld a stately woman, who was neither maidenly nor tall. Queenly, he thought, and something about her—a grace that was sovereign—filled him with unexpected happiness as she came near and lifted her lovely face in greeting. As she did so, he noticed that she wore a light peplos fastened at the waist with a slender girdle of silver while on her head she wore a garland of summer flowers. She was speaking.

— You are expected, traveler from afar!

A simple acknowledgment that startled him. Had her voice held a suggestion of resignation? She regarded him with dark, thoughtful eyes. The traveler nodded, acknowledging her words.

— Actually, lady, you astonish me. How could you possibly know of my coming? Ah yes, of course. The ancient oracle you possess here must have told you.

— Indeed, it was through my oracle that I came to expect the arrival of Zeus himself. What is knowing? Is it not a thing much like glass through which light passes finding no obstruction, none whatsoever? It is knowledge that astonishes us, is it not? How it passes through many walls, walls of sound much like the beating of wings or else the trembling of oak leaves!

A certain satisfaction shone in his eyes as he responded to her.

— You are a seer, no less. I am convinced of it. I remind you also that knowing penetrates soft walls of flesh.

He paused, quietly regarding her, causing color to arise in her cheeks. He continued.

— Where there are hard walls of old belief, they may not stand against it. What is certain is that I find myself in the presence of the goddess herself. True? At the moment, I'm not sure that I am ready . . .

The admission caused him some embarrassment, it appeared. Astonished, she responded at once.

— Not ready, you? Can Zeus be found at a loss?

Most certainly she had recognized him. Regretfully, he considered how attractive anonymity had looked to him.

— I am not so confident nor so unwise, for that matter, as to overlook the fact that I have entered the territory of a great goddess.

She took in her breath sharply as though the idea startled her.

— From Zeus, the Olympian, I never expected such acknowledgment!

— How can that be? In the company of an Olympian, do you doubt your power?

— Perhaps I do . . .

She gave him a sidelong glance with a flutter of the eyelids as though such shuttering might protect her from his penetrating gaze. Now he gave her a slow smile, relaxing comfortably like one who found himself at home.

— I must tell you, Dione, that I have longed for some time to seek you out in your dwelling place, but something did not allow it.

— How strange. Surely you have great power. You are known to carry authority and strength of action for the whole of Greece. Besides, I have been told that you have many temples with altars bountifully laid.

He nodded briefly, and a look of indescribable longing came to his face.

— Yet here at Dodona, I've no power. Surely you see this.

— And why should you need power here in Dodona's remote sanctuary?

The very notion caused her to shudder involuntarily before she hastened on.

— As our guest, you shall receive the finest hospitality that we can give. Dodona has long sheltered me and my priestesses who serve the oracle in the sacred grove. Indeed, I shall speak to them at once to look after your comfort.

Now Zeus smiled his most disarming smile, which illuminated the spot where the two of them spoke together. Even so, in the midst of her pleasurable reaction, she felt a slight sense of alarm. In this manner, Zeus and Dione were to pass many enjoyable hours together. Instead of the ambrosia to which he was accustomed, the priestesses served the lord of the gods cakes made of acorn meal kneaded with wild honey while they filled his cup many times with sweet mead. And the day, extraordinary in its bounty, passed.

The second day, its air crisp and fragrant with wild flowers blooming, found Dione and Zeus setting out on the steep path of the sheep, which climbed the hill into the shaded depth of a woods that hid a rippling spring. The two fell easily into step together, and their talk lost its guardedness. The languid, pleasant hours passed, and they laughed.

Zeus turned to her now.

— Dione, tell me, how old is your oracle here in Dodona's tranquil bowl so distant from cities of men?

— The oracle itself is beyond time, beyond history.

— Then your priestesses do not guard a recorded history?

— No. Here in Dodona nothing is written down. The speech of the oracle is *heard* only, you see.

— Ah, that explains what I have sensed here. There is a cleansing that cannot be described. What it amounts to is that speech here is altogether true. It is a virginal thing, for it lies close to one's being and manifests in present time. Am I right?

Dione's eyes widened, and she gasped audibly.

— In two days with us, you have seen this, Zeus? I am astonished. It is a mystery, but the word arises afresh here. There are those who desire to collect and preserve the spoken words of the oracle. I feel that words had best not become a separate life to be lived. However tempting words may be, life must have earth's gift, the living body!

— And I, Zeus, have need of earth's gift. Love is known to awaken earth, I believe. For one thing, it opens one's eyes to a new realm, for that is what I now see before me.

    He spoke with wonder, causing her to regard him with surprise. She went on to explain.

— This new realm you perceive, it is Dodona's word as I know it. Dodona's word is not separated from the feminine presence. You find it in living act and gesture. Ah yes, one is not the same after receiving Dodona's word!

— Is every stranger who comes here changed as I seem to be?

— Oh, no, certainly not. What is crucial is the hearing. Dodona with its vast silence, its mountain walls of enclosure, and its solitude provides the true possibility of hearing. One can't hear, you understand, unless the possibility of hearing is ripened.

— The possibility of hearing, you say. Hmm, would this be some earth thing?

— Yes. The traveler who comes to my sanctuary has his ears tuned for the summons of the bronze cauldrons' deep sustained tones. Always they summon one to attend to the divine voice.

— Tell me about the these cauldrons, Goddess. We lack such extraordinary equipment on Olympus, I confess.

    She smiled at the thought and continued.

— The bronze cauldrons circle the most sacred oak tree from which the oracle comes. When the question is given and the reply is being awaited, the cauldrons enter the splendid but inscrutable commentary, you see. At the same time, their vibrating body of sound binds and protects the circle of the oracle's abode, excluding any outside influence.

— Remarkable, truly remarkable. With these faithful cauldrons, Goddess, not a single supplicant will miss hearing the significant reply, surely.

    Dione shook her head slowly, frowning slightly.

— The cauldrons perform a faithful service, but hearing the oracle in its fullness is not easily arrived at, it seems. The hearer gets the gist, so to speak, and often leaves at once content with this alone.

    Zeus nodded.

— Being in a hurry and going off with the gist of things is the way of human folk.

He spoke gently, attempting to comfort her. She smiled a little sadly.

— Alas, I must remain present, sustaining the supplicant! How easy it is to forget earth's rhythmic mode—the saving and incubating of the seed, the coming of the vital green growth, the time of the fragrant blossoming, and the season of the fruiting. As with the oracle itself, all must lie in the furrow, spring into life, and come to fruit in good time.

Dione's voice trailed off, like a hound dog exhausted after the hunt. Zeus arose from the stone where he had been sitting and stood at Dione's side, his radiant smile addressing her alone.

— Dione, you are earth maiden indeed! How mysterious is Dodona's oracle . . . I could never have imagined it so. In this very moment, it is your *word*, my dear, that is upon me. It confounds all my senses. Why, it brings me a delight that is akin to a child's play. Yet you yourself are not what I have known a word to be, for I find you lush and full, gentle and beautiful. I do believe that, as word, you are all *body*! In my ear is a sound like honey dripping slowly from the comb. Come now. Give me your hand! Let us go into the spring!

Delight was in Dione's face now as oracles were tucked away for attention at a future time. She rose to her feet in response to irresistible Zeus and gave him her hand while together they ran down the embankment to the shining spring. Dropping their outer garments, they jumped into the cooling waters, and their musical laughter filled the morning air.

The third day of Zeus's visit at Dodona found the two gods taking their ease under the oak trees. Here time was bountiful, the hours plump and gentle in their presentation, so that time appeared to lose its transitory quality. Taking note of the fact, Zeus sighed.

— Dear Dione, under your tranquil influence the days pass like a rare idyll that can't be described.

— Ah, a rare and rich season is upon us since your coming, Zeus. So why are you anxious? Why the frown and abstracted look?

— With you I would speak plainly. The fact is that I have not accomplished the purpose for which I set out for Dodona in the first place.

— Purpose? You came to Dodona with a plan not yet revealed? These are foreign notions to our realm, I tell you.

Zeus looked incredulous.

— Come. I fail to understand you.

Dione rose to her feet and began to speak in a newly animated manner with an energy that caused a faint quaking in the bond of love that enclosed them.

— When you arrived at Dodona, you approached me wearing your armor. Before your coming, I had long observed you male Olympians. I noticed how you form a plan, a purpose that goes forth much like an armed warrior to battle. Why, for me, such a purpose would surely enslave the day and its hours!

Zeus shook his head slowly as he attempted to take in this unusual perspective. He answered her simply.

— Well, how can I deny this?

— But don't you see what happens, Zeus? The day ends up trampled. It is used up. Oh, it grieves me to think of the loss! You see, the day belongs to earth. Therefore, I say that it is mine!

Zeus regarded her with grave concern.

— Believe me, I have no desire to distress you. Speak to me of this day that you call yours, Dione.

— Earth's day is the best we have. It is the measure given mortals or immortals alike. I tell you that life, *zoe*, lives only in present time, although its time is not mortal. Yes, day is from the hand of Earth Goddess, one of whose names I bear. O what are past and future compared to the day, shining and unspent, warm and breathing like flesh?!

Nor is it a package to take possession of. It must be lived!

Zeus was visibly moved as the imagery of Dione's day passed before his mind.

— Frankly, what you describe takes on a life of its own, dear. I am accustomed to regarding the day much like the road stretching before one, a road to receive the clamoring hooves of horses and chariot wheels engaged in one's pursuits. No more.

Dione lowered her eyes, and her voice softened as if she had become keenly aware of the delight of Zeus's companionship.

— Already you are beginning to perceive the day that is Dodona's, I do believe: a time deeply layered with hours, soft-fleshed and pulsing with *zoe*. Trust it, Zeus, for it moves inexorably in its own true season.

— Were it not seductive as well, I would have thought it invisible.

He murmured to himself now.

— *Day!* Its very dawn has been wooing me for some time. Now I realize this. Over and over again it bids me to come and capture it . . . And now I know that it is to capture her, Dione herself! I have hastened to Dodona, driven by my purpose. Dione, hear me. My way is different from yours. Surely in your earth knowing, you perceive this. The question is, will you allow me my purpose?

Hearing these passionate words, Dione stepped toward him, and Zeus caught her, encircling her waist with his arm. Breathless, she asked the question.

— What then is your purpose?

— To have you for my wife, Dione, my beloved. Love renders me bold and does not flinch at the purpose that would bind us both together! I swear to you by the River Styx that this love is in its true season and will do no injury to the day!

Dione turned a solemn, tender face to Zeus as she regarded him fully in the silence. At last she smiled. It was as if a hidden text informed her. She spoke.

— Wait here. I go to consult the holy oak alone.

For some time, Dione remained within the sacred circle of the bronze cauldrons while Zeus waited outside. At last she motioned to him to enter the circle, at the same moment placing a finger upon her lips for silence. Hand in hand, they stood together beneath the great oracular oak tree. Now a small stirring among the branches broke the stillness, setting the leaves into a soft murmuring. When the murmuring ceased, Zeus turned to her.

— What does the oracle say?

Almost he did not recognize her voice when she spoke from the oracle place, and he lowered his head so that his gaze fell upon the roots of the tree.

— The oracle says,

—This day's fruit shall be plucked, that as earth receives the lightening so Dione shall receive great Zeus. In a matter of time, a magical goddess will be born on earth!—

Hearing this, Zeus stepped forward and took willing Dione into his embrace, and time was lyrical. Joy spread over the circle of the oracular oak tree, and Zeus took Dione to be his wife.

Marking their union, Dione spoke to her beloved.

— For you I have a gift.

— Have I not received your love? I have your gift, Dione.

— Yet I have a greater gift for you, I must tell you.

— Dione!

Had he guessed already, she wondered. Astonishment was on his face.

— Perhaps you have guessed. It is my oracle that I now present to you, Zeus. Henceforth, it shall be known as the oracle of Zeus at Dodona.

Zeus threw back his head and laughed joyously.

— You are granting me access to the wisdom of earth herself?

— Yes, to none other.

— Dione, we shall share the oracle. It will be known as the oracle of Dione and Zeus.

— The divine voice is one and one only, surely.

He regarded her thoughtfully. At last he nodded.

— Then the oracle of Dodona is one voice. Yet beneath the oracle the ever-renewing source of Dodona's wisdom flows like an underground spring. Yours, Dione, is the wisdom of earth!

(Note: To continue the narrative of the ancient Dodona myth, see the dialogue "Aphrodite Is Born," which is found in the Aphrodite section.)

The Love of Semele

Having reached a large meadow outside the city of Thebes, the handsome stranger sought the shade of an oak tree as he gazed toward the powerful city walls and its gates. Nor was he alone, for a young woman whom he had observed descending the winding footpath from the city now stood before him. Momentarily she was alarmed to face a stranger on her solitary ramble. He smiled reassuringly and spoke, his fine and lyrical voice distinctive, although for the life of her, she could not identify his city of origin.

— Daughter of Thebes, I've no wish to startle you. Having traveled from afar, I am happy to reach your great city—Thebes of the seven gates.

She had recovered her usual poise now.

— Greetings, stranger. Ah yes, among the cities of Greece, Thebes enjoys fame for its seven gates.

— The fame of Thebes is also due to the high reputation of some of its inhabitants, surely. Tell me, are there really so many ways of approach? I admit that seven gates are able to confuse the wayfarer. I wonder, can a man be sure he has gone through the right gate? And is he obliged to depart by the same gate that he originally entered, or can it be that he is free to choose a different one?

The lovely young Theban woman was thoroughly perplexed by the stranger's words at first, but her confidence returned.

— We Thebans are not troubled by such questions as you raise. Living as we do within our illustrious strong walls proves to be quite satisfactory, you see.

— Hm, satisfactory you say. *Satisfactory* is not the most valued criterion known to a person, surely. You Thebans have a fabled king who is highly honored, I believe, Cadmus.

The stranger was not as poorly informed as she first judged him to be, a fact that caused her to respond eagerly.

— Indeed. Actually, I am daughter of Cadmus. My name is Semele.

His eyes lingered upon her thoughtfully, and she observed that the deep eyes held some shining text. The effect upon her was so powerful that she trembled. With a small nod, he spoke gently, smiling.

— Greetings, Semele, daughter of Cadmus! Your father once slew the dragon that possessed this mountain hideaway and then sowed the dragon's teeth, only to deal with their hostile progeny before founding the city. Is this true?

— It is true. My father is very brave. And where, traveler, do you come from?

— From the north. From Mt. Olympus.

The very thought of the fabled mountain excited her now.

— Why, the gods themselves are said to live on Olympus!

Pacing back and forth now with his arms folded, he appeared to be a man lost in his thoughts. He shook his shoulders involuntarily as though to free them of some burden, she noticed. His response was brief and simple.

— Yes, Semele. There are those who call me Zeus. I thought you best know.

She appeared to give this piece of information a hasty accommodation before responding as she had been taught.

— Traveler from afar, certainly you shall find fitting hospitality among us!

Now the stranger from Olympus bent his head in acknowledgment, but his smile was enigmatic. As for the Theban young woman, a fire that was strangely pleasing stirred within her.

Time passed in the meadow on the Theban plain like a bountiful season, and Semele frequently found herself in the excellent company of the traveler from Olympus. At each meeting, his presence evoked within her bosom a pleasing fire steeped in delight. A shining tale emerged that sang in mind and heart as Semele came to know Aphrodite's sweet bounty. And the Olympian came to love the Theban maiden with the result that she became the beloved of great Zeus himself. As the season passed, she discovered that she was with child, and the two lovers rejoiced with this knowledge. One day as she sat beneath the great oak tree within the meadow, she heard the familiar footsteps approaching and looked up to greet her beloved. Now it had not been easy to accustom herself to his auspicious name, and yet she cried out with delight.

— O Zeus, you have come! Do sit beside me.

Gazing tenderly into her face, Zeus sat down beside her as he took her hands into his.

— Semele, in this hidden spot of ours, we have love's cosmos, surely.
— How can there be a cosmos with only two people in it?

    He laughed easily.

— That exactly describes the cosmos that Aphrodite creates. Only make an ode of thanks to her, I say. You see, if there were a third person, it would crowd us.

    A look of worry settled over her face.

— I am afraid I must tell you something. A third person has come, you see. Oh, I didn't see her face, but her voice has taken up residence for days now.
— A frown replaced what had been his look of contentment. His voice was taut as he questioned her.
— A voice you say? What voice, Semele?
— The voice of Hera!
— Do you mean to say that the great goddess has come to visit a woman of Thebes?
— Yes. It is she who is the queenly wife of great god Zeus. I do wish I could catch a glimpse of her, for she is said to be beautiful.

    His face was solemn now, as though to lift his thoughts was like lifting great stones.

— You have heard her speaking then. What is it she says to you?
— Well, I'm somewhat embarrassed to tell you. It is all because I call you Zeus, you see, while the fact is that he who is Lord Zeus himself is her husband!

    A low, sustained groan came from Zeus before he pressed her gravely.

— Semele, what did she say?

    She forsook her reticence, and he saw that her youthful passion took possession in earnest.

— O Zeus of mine, Lady Hera says that my lover must be holding out on me! Those were her words. What she says is true, I realize, because you never describe your life to me and what you do! And yet, I could never complain of our love, for it leaves me desiring nothing more! Oh, I am conflicted!
— Yet you have come to believe that I am "holding out" on you, as the voice put it? Is this the case, Semele?

— What else am I to believe? Lady Hera went on to say, "A wife has the right to know everything about her husband."

Rising swiftly to his feet, Zeus turned toward the far northeastern horizon, and his face was somber, his mind veiled. A heavy silence ensued, broken at last by a deep sigh. Turning, he looked once more into Semele's face, and his voice was gentle as he questioned her.

— You are convinced that there is something I possess that you must share somehow. I see this. As you know, I would grant you the favor that you desire so ardently. Only tell me then what you desire that is mine.

He waited, his unblinking eyes upon her. Held within Zeus's gaze in that moment, she sighed happily and answered him.

— I go with Lady Hera's counsel, dear one. I say to you, "Show me your thunder!"

Zeus let out a loud cry as he seized his shield, holding it before his body as if prepared to do battle. At the same moment, Semele leaped to her feet facing him, her eyes wide with fear. His words rang out on the air.

— The thunderbolt, no! Semele, you don't want to draw near it, I tell you.

— Alas, Zeus, your shield has come between us! Am I become your enemy?

— Not you, no. You could never be my enemy, my dear. It is that I would protect you.

— How am I threatened?

— By the desire to share the thunderbolt's power. I fear that you see yourself as lady of thunder!

Semele wrung her hands at these words, and her shoulders sank as though she were oppressed by some obscure loneliness.

— Am I not your wife, and am I not soon to bear our child? I simply want to share all that is yours!

— Both are excellent reasons for me to protect you.

There was some comfort in those words. She grew wistful as she mused.

— But the thunderbolt is legendary in its power. Besides, is it not a dazzling thing to behold?

He shook his head, his face plain with worry as he heard her.

— Look. The thunderbolt is no mere spectacle, Semele. If you must know, it contains the primordial fire of heaven.

Semele clapped her hands as if pleased with this information.

— What a wonderful source it is then! Surely, one's ordinary torch goes dead and useless without the heavenly fire!

    When he spoke in reply, it was to address some intangible measure, it seemed.

— A small measure of fire to illuminate what one is about is good, of course. Such is the lamp or the torch. But Semele, how different this is from the thunderbolt.

    The eyes raised to meet his troubled gaze were pensive now. Almost idly she asked the question.

— Tell me, what is thunder? Oh, I know that it rumbles and that it mates with the lightning. It is powerful indeed.

    Momentarily he lifted his gaze, scanning the sky before answering.

— When heaven is no longer tranquil, the clouds darken and writhe in the sky. Heaven frowns upon earth fiercely as it becomes the invading warrior. Presently the immediate horizon is filled with sword-flashing strokes that illuminate the sky.

— You are describing what a big storm is like, which is a familiar thing in our Theban mountains.

— Hear me, Semele. The thunderbolt of the gods is no mere storm upon the mountain. It is *the naked thrust of spirit!* A mortal would be foolhardy to stand willingly in its path!

— Still, one so longs to witness such a dramatic manifestation of the gods. Ah, it excites me to think that the thunderbolt belongs to my very own husband!

    A blissful look was upon her face. As for Zeus, his gaze was lifted toward distant Olympus, his face troubled. He spoke in a voice now whose deep quiet was arresting.

— Hear me, dear Semele. There is a certain frenzy, a madness among men who are desperately seeking their rightful access to the thunder. Their timetable for accomplishing this feat is also frantic. Do not fall into this madness, I warn you. A person ends up trying to wear his sizable piece of thunder, or he may seek to exhibit it in his house, or else fill his words with captive thunder. Again he flaunts it in the position he holds in the world.

— Can't a person incorporate the thunder in his life?

— No, it is not possible. Heaven is ever in movement, coming to be and passing into yet a different phase. Thunder is the living breath of spirit, and no one captures it. No human person can possess it. It is delusion to imagine that one can, I tell you.

Semele persisted in explaining herself.

— I am a curious human being. I do know myself well. How I just love to delve into things! O Zeus, please do not vacillate. After all, you promised me a favor.

Bring now your fabled thunderbolt for me alone to witness!

The somber eyes of Zeus searched the far horizon for a long moment. Now with deliberation, he went apart a little distance. As she watched, he raised his strong right arm skillfully into position behind himself and took aim toward the sky above Mt. Helikon. In an instant, he released the thunderbolt. At the same moment, Semele leaped forward so that she might fully engage its mystery and its shining power. Alas, in that moment, the fire of the thunderbolt engulfed her. In great anguish, Zeus cried aloud,

— O Fates, why have you done this? O Atropos, you with the shears in your hands, why have you cut the thread of life of my beloved Semele, ending her young life, I ask you?

Rain came down upon them like a wet veil now, and the daughter of Cadmus lay dying on the ground. At once, Zeus took hold of his beloved wife and, from her womb, delivered the unborn child as she died. Swiftly he took the babe and sewed him into his own thigh. For a long time, he remained beside fallen Semele, and Zeus's sorrow was great. Time passed, and at last he spoke, his voice once again tranquil.

— *O thunder babe, son of Semele and Zeus, you shall yet come safely to birth! O Dionysos! O Insewn! Your birth to earth will bring the magic of play and life's deep joy!*

Mnemosyne and Zeus

Mt. Helikon's high green slope was her frequent haunt, the dense woods welcoming her as she sought out the spring that emerged from the earth to plunge joyously over the rocks. Sitting upon one of the adjacent stones, she smiled as the music of the spring filled her awareness. Time was languid and without accounting. Now she lifted her head, listening as the sound of some swift movement on the path from the north alerted her. Approaching was a lordly figure possessing a certain majesty and pleasing to the eyes as well. Her eyes were bright, whether with puzzlement or expectancy was not clear as the figure entered the small clearing by the mouth of the spring and stood regarding her at yet a little distance. Her eyes widened now in recognition, and she spoke.

— Greetings! Why, can it be you, Zeus? What an unexpected meeting this is.

Not waiting for an invitation, Zeus made himself comfortable on the rock facing the lovely goddess.

— Actually, I am used to such a response as yours, Mnemosyne. Even so, being consistently unexpected is disappointing, I admit.

Did she look slightly embarrassed by this admission? Quickly she went on to explain.

— How could I expect you, I ask? I am, as you know, a Titan. It is widely known that you have turned your back on the Titans. True, we are the older gods and less impressive than you Olympians.

— Justifiably I quarreled with your brothers, Goddess, for they slew my infant son, Dionysos. I've no quarrel, let me assure you, with you and your sisters. Instead, I must confess that I miss you elder goddesses.

The goddess was startled by this admission. At the same time, something remained wary in her response.

— Is there some special need you have of us then?

Zeus's voice became meditative in reply.

— There is a radiance that resides in you always, it appears. How can I describe it? It is a trail of golden light known to illuminate the long corridor of thoughts and deeds in the lives of gods and humankind. As I gaze on you even now, I perceive in those deep, shining eyes one tale after another. Indeed, your glance itself is ever some fine telling. How you draw me with a strange force, Mnemosyne! What is your secret?

— Secret? What secret do you speak of, Zeus?

Rising now, he smiled down on her and extended his hand.

— Come, let us walk in the grove. Shall we?

As she arose and they set out on the wooded path, Zeus addressed her question.

— You have this way, inscrutable as it is, of holding the life of the knowing past within a shimmering present time. This is your secret alone.

She shook her head as if finding his response puzzling.

— Come, Zeus, you speak of memory. Can it be that memory has become especially desirable for you?

— Ah, it is the richest treasure of all. And you, Mnemosyne, hold that beloved treasure!

He turned swiftly, facing her, and spoke with an intimacy and a passion she had never known before.

— For you the whole cosmos is a golden tale, one you knew before I was ever delivered from Rhea's womb. O give yourself to me, Mnemosyne, ageless goddess!

— What a delight it is to walk on Helikon cloaked in these fiery words of Eros's treasure! Even as we walk, Zeus, I see before me the many women you have loved. Actually, your brides make quite a procession, you realize.

Mnemosyne gazed into the distance, looking thoughtful. Zeus, frowning, murmured to himself,

— Ah, what does this new time bring me? Obviously, keen memory has its drawbacks.

Now the goddess of memory was, above all things, clear-sighted, and what she said now revealed as much.

— Zeus, I should have little interest in being one among many loves of the lord of the gods, I believe. Do remember that there are those who relish the immediate experience only, however. They are spoken of as those who live in the moment. Why not court one of these?

— What's this? Mnemosyne, are you sending me away empty-handed?

Never could she have imagined that the god's voice could hold such profound regret. She looked at him quickly, and not without compassion. Yet she did not forsake her position.

— Can't you see how it is for me? I've no desire to embrace a piece of present time which with a single blow strikes away the living past and the yet-veiled future! Such a love were like a decapitated head that rolls on the ground.

This declaration made him think of a reigning queen as she draws her cloak about herself. His voice was incredulous as he spoke. Nor was pleading beyond Zeus.

— Know me, Mnemosyne. I would never, never seek from you such an aborted love!

— What have I for you then?

— It is you, my dear, who must answer that question.

A silence fell between them, deep-textured and keenly listening. It was Mnemosyne who spoke at last.

— In my hand *I hold the single scroll. The scroll cradles life, and it knows!*

Hearing these words, Zeus gazed at the goddess, his look zestful and shining like a great wave of the sea crashing on shore.

— What an incredible scroll you possess, but it is the scroll keeper herself whom I desire! After all, you are the radiant source, that shining lap of mind that has access to this life-cradling scroll. Your beauty is beyond description, Mnemosyne, for you yourself are that visionary one we know as everlasting Memory.

The heart of Mnemosyne received this tribute from the lord of the gods happily before becoming again reflective.

— You speak as if all of the store of Memory were pleasant. It isn't, you know.

He smiled ruefully.

— I realize that fact. However, the capacity that holds the past in a vital, luminous frame as a thing of quiet order and clear form—why, this is beautiful. In all this, I perceive your ongoing radiance, Mnemosyne, holding it dear to my heart. Besides, the shining scroll that is your treasure is unsurpassed. This is a fact not to be disputed.

As a deep satisfaction welled up within herself and washed over her abundantly, she laughed now, much like a nymph of the wooded glen who has just completed the circle dance.

— Speak no more of the past, Zeus, however valued you find it. You see, I have a strange feeling that it is rather *present time* that is beginning to assume sturdy shape and a substance all its own that captures me! In this very hour on the mountain path, time itself begins to grow large. How indolent it has become and yet how ample! Sun-drenched it is and sweet like the figs of late summer . . . Alas, I do believe that I sense a change in myself, for I find myself forsaking the long gaze at what lies behind!

The two gods stood very close while looks of tenderness passed between them, each look cognizant of an ancient, remembered trail that received the two figures now. Zeus spoke in a low voice.

— Speak on, my dear. What you describe becomes the song I've been longing to hear. You speak of the birth of a new time, a beginning. Ah, what of this hour alone that holds us? Love requires its own hour in present time. It will settle for nothing less, nothing borrowed, nothing temporary, for it requires the full sum that it can spend lavishly!

— O Zeus, I fear that you may be all expediency itself, pressed by immediate need! My lover must be not only immortal but ongoing in the world's time, for my spouse is everlasting!

— Do I not qualify to espouse you? My dear Mnemosyne, what is it you fear from me as your lover?

— I fear to deliver my mind and soul, the body of me into a single hour! It is simply said, you see. You ask for, well, a *nesting*. I, Mnemosyne, am no goose sitting upon the nest from now on, her head tucked under her wing, closing out the greater world! Oh, what is to become of me?

Now Zeus, whose mind was ever lived with the possible and the hoped-for, seemed to be quietly regarding the solution.

— Mnemosyne, why not let the past—and the future, for that matter—take care of themselves for a while? Let their burden fall from you. Are you not drawn to me as I am to you? Stay with me, dear goddess!

Turning aside, she murmured,

— How can I resist great and glorious Zeus? Already I sense a yielding in myself. Am I a fragile wall against which the great tide plunges?

Slowly she lifted her face to Zeus, and at the same moment, she extended both hands and smiled. As he inclined his head toward her, she spoke.

— The unbroken tale, ancient in its trail, moves forward even now! Ah, it becomes ours, dear Zeus!

— Ah, love is the unspeakable treasure, as I thought it to be. When one tries to capture it, however, it is soon lost. Why, what approaches is the abundant telling of our tale, one that will never run dull or dry!

The two saw that in the shade of an enormous oak tree, a dark entrance opened among the rocks. Stopping before the entrance to the cave, Zeus indicated that the goddess wait while he examined the interior. Shortly he emerged again and, taking Mnemosyne by the hand, led her gently into the deep cavern. Here for nine days and nine nights, the cave sheltered the lovemaking of Zeus and Mnemosyne. Indeed, the unrolling of the mysterious scroll trailed the luminous path between heaven and earth.

In the depths of Mt. Helikon's cave, the nine days of lovemaking came to an end, and Mnemosyne spoke. She who could give herself generously to present time was, nevertheless, aware of the luminous trail into the future.

— When the time is fulfilled, I shall bear on nine days in succession our nine daughters, Zeus. I thought I should prepare you for this singular event.

— This is astonishing news, dear Mnemosyne.

With his searching glance, he gazed down the corridor of the immediate future.

— You see, I've had limited experience of daughters, I'm afraid. Speak to me of these daughters, my dear. What will they be like?

— Each of them has a voice that summons the human individual, and each voice is altogether distinctive in itself. Oh yes, and they are known for feet lively and graceful in their stepping.

— You speak of them as if they already were in full existence. Dancers, you indicate, and perhaps poets or singers . . .

— Yes, but more than that, each daughter shall bring the sustained music and the rhythmic step of the In Between.

— Could you be referring to the region between heaven and earth, I wonder?

— Yes. Paths exist that connect the two realms, but they remain exceedingly difficult to find, you see. Such is the experience of human individuals.

Now Zeus nodded thoughtfully.

— I am beginning to see how it is. Each of our daughters shall be an *intermediary*, for she will lead the traveler on the best path.

Intermediary . . . she repeated the word, listening to its sound.

— It is a word that leaves the necessary knowledge still obscured.

Zeus sighed audibly.

— Do tell me what you know, Mnemosyne. For example, how shall I tell these girls apart? As their father, surely I need to know.

— They shall be called the Muses. First is Calliope of the lovely voice, whose ear is inclined to epic deeds among human individuals. Clio will celebrate the past, for hers is the love of what is behind the present situation. Erato will be devoted to love poetry as she plays her lyre, as she is imbued with Aphrodite's knowledge of the golden bond. Euterpe will engage in the lively music of the flute, delighting in what is ecstatic. She is attuned to Dionysos, you see. As for Melpomene, she possesses a tenderness to the depth of sorrow, as the mask of tragedy she holds suggests. Polyhymnia, holding the veil, will compose many sacred songs as she stands before the mystery. As for Thalia . . .

— But Thalia is one of the Graces, surely.

— Our daughter Thalia shall be new upon the earth, Zeus. She will be our lighthearted daughter, I assure you. Her very name indicates a cheerful disposition. You will recognize her for her preference in wearing the sock of the comic actor. Last of all is Urania, named for her love of the sky. Only look for the daughter who gazes at the night sky with its orderly procession of stars.

Zeus had responded to each daughter's portrayal with a slow shaking of his head as though incredulous in the face of such births.

— Surely the Greek earth will be altered! Already, I begin to imagine them. Our nine daughters, the Muses, will form an extraordinary procession on this very mountain, a procession of radiant women. Greece shall be created a second time, I believe!

Mnemosyne smiled with lingering tenderness at Zeus before adding a final comment.

— One thing more is essential to know. Coming to the side of the individual she favors, the Muse becomes the shepherd, for she will guide that person safely on the path of the In Between!

Their words ended, the two gods took a tender and reluctant leave of each other and parted.

Leda and the Swan

The sand of the riverbank was hot to her tender feet as she abandoned her sandals and ran toward the shining waters to plunge in. At once, the familiar forms of life in the royal house drained out of her, much as if memory had sprung a leak in the bottom of a jar. Laughing aloud, she cried, "Eurotas, dear river, you have torn away my world as if it were a mere dream!" Actually, the notion frightened her as much as it brought a surge of relief. Laughing once again, she struck out swimming into the rosy-hued waters of the setting sun. A bracing solitude filled her with its amplitude. After her swim, she climbed the bank panting and collapsed upon the warm sand, and her loose, thin garment clung to her body like a silky new skin while her long golden hair lay like river moss on her back. A little distance apart, a pair of deer drank from the river and attracted her attention so that she did not notice a soft approach. A man stood near her, casting a lengthening shadow on the sand. Startled, she knew as if by instinct that it was not Tyndareus, her husband, for he had never found the hidden place of her play. A strong foreboding caused her pulse to race as she sprang to her feet. The tall stranger spoke gently.

— Come, there is no cause for alarm, river nymph.

His reassurance had little effect, however, on the trembling that had overtaken her. Now she dug her bare toes into the sand and hugged her body as a wave of modesty not unmixed with annoyance arose in her.

— I see that you are a stranger to Lacedaemonia. Are you a traveler then?

He considered her words with the look of a man observing a girl at play.

— I have known the treacherous crossings of seas and mountains.

— Have you arrived with some important message for our city from a far place?

— Ah, the message. You believe that under my cloak I may bear some neat, well-groomed truth in a small scroll, perhaps. But no, what I bear is not for Sparta, if you must know.

Glancing down a little anxiously at her thinly cloaked body, she was glad to see that her garment was drying out now so that it blew about her in careless folds. The handsome deep-voiced stranger perplexed her.

— If you are not sent as emissary to our city, for what cause have you come? Sparta is not on the travel route to other great cities.

He smiled, considering her question at some leisure as though it might require something that was missing to work out the answer. In the fading light of the day, she still perceived his face clearly. Like stone, it was all definition and seemed indifferent to time and human anxiety. Raising her face, she gazed into eyes that were striking in their address. Such was their power that all concerns for manners and hospitality fled from her awareness. Oddly she felt at peace. Nor were the stranger's eyes like the commanding eyes of Tyndareus, stern in their purpose. The stranger's look laid no obligation, no future to be served, but rather indicated a rejoicing in the time and the territory at hand. A small thought now inserted itself: *he enjoys my company!* She must not neglect the path of conversation, however.

— My lord, what is your world like?

— I should say that you have stepped upon its soil.

— What a strange thing to say, yet only if I weigh it.

He laughed, amused. She rushed on.

— My lord, I sense that something you bring is not yet delivered. Surely you bear some message . . .

— Since you insist, I must fit myself to Sparta's messenger, I suppose. There is this problem however. From my viewpoint, the word is always something of a loss. Only consider that if you were to stand near lightning, then words would seem both tardy and cool to you, I believe. Again, the message rather amounts to the task of bottling up Eurotas into a water jar one can store on the shelf.

— Alas, no one would be fool enough to attempt to put our river into a jar!

As for lightning, no one has stood near it and lived. That is a fact. Tell me, is there then no message at all?

— None for the kingdom. Nevertheless, lovely nymph, I do have a word, and it is for you alone.

That his gaze held some order of admiration that she had never known before, she could hardly deny, and unquestionably it held passion's fire. Her words stumbled forth, even so.

— Stranger, I must tell you something. It is that I am not a nymph of the river, for Eurotas is not my father. In fact, I am no nymph at all, if you must know.

Strangely she was blushing as she experienced a curious fall of her spirit in the confession. As he responded, an authority original and enigmatic permeated his words.

— Not a nymph? Can you hold back the power of the place that makes an immortal nymph of Sparta's queen? I think not.

Her voice, at first tense with disbelief, subsided into a wail.

— Oh, oh! So you do know who I am!

This seemed the worst possible turn in what had been their extraordinarily pleasant meeting, for a new, shining realm had risen between them strangely here on the riverbank, to be sure. A fear crept from her throat to her belly with the thought, *He knows who I am!* Reading the disappointment in her eyes, the stranger stepped toward her and, reaching out, took both her trembling hands in his own. His voice was quiet and untroubled.

— There is no need to worry, Leda, for I shall shelter you.

— Shelter me? But how can you?

Already there was a glimpse of hope. He smiled slowly.

— You'll see. Shall I tell you my past, the relevant part? For a long time I've observed you as you came to the riverbank, and each time, I saw how the queen of Sparta was like a garment left behind. Is this not true?

She gasped audibly. How did he know? she wondered, shaking her head as she responded.

— How could you have witnessed a thing so well hidden, that took place only in my heart's play?

— Ah, I shall keep your secret in deep confidence, never fear. I do treasure the hidden life of woman, you see. As a matter of record, it is my stronghold, sturdy as the stone citadel we see there on the mountain top. Only that hidden life perceives me as I am.

— Riddles, you speak in riddles, my lord. As for myself, I am left with the facts. This hidden life you speak of divides me. Surely you see this. Can you understand how it is, I wonder? Am I not wife of Tyndareus, king of Sparta? It is inevitable then that I am Sparta's queen. Yet here on the bank of Eurotas, I am neither woman!

The low voice in which he asked the question was tender with expectancy.

— Who are you here now, Leda?

— I am the maiden of the wilds!

Some ecstasy that surely belongs only to the special arrival filled the stranger whose voice was like the leap of the satyr.

— *Parthenos!* O lovely maiden returned to earth!

She murmured to herself.

— Toward whom does my heart move so strangely, so irrevocably stirred? . . . Stranger, who are you?

His eyes rested thoughtfully upon her face, yet a fire burned in them as he remained silent.

— You do not answer . . . Extraordinary thoughts haunt me and the remembering of old myths. Alas, I am divided into two halves, and neither half satisfies!

— Come. It shall no longer be true.

He spoke idly, asking a question of her.

— Do you, Leda, honor Goddess Hera, I wonder?

— Indeed so. Is she not spouse of great Zeus? If only you knew my city, you would know the temple of Argive Hera that rests high upon the hill over Sparta. It was there that, when the river flooded, Goddess Hera raised her hands and saved the people.

— Then she has shown compassion here. It is well. Tell me, what is her ancient idol like in the temple, and how is it honored?

— How curious that you come asking questions about Hera. Why, the ancient wooden image is greatly honored for we address her as *Aphrodite Hera.*

He smiled at this as if immensely pleased.

— What a happy union, I say, is that of the queen and love's magic!

The exuberance in the stranger reminded her of a sudden waterfall.

— Again your words puzzle me, my lord. Is this always true when you speak? Naturally it is a happy fact when Hera and Aphrodite are joined.

— And do all Spartans pay homage to this sacred image?

— O yes. We dare not do otherwise. My mother, wishing me to have a blessed marriage, took the marriage offering to Aphrodite Hera in the temple on the eve of my wedding to Tyndareus.

The memory of this event loosed a flood of affection for her mother and for her own vulnerable maiden self. He interrupted her musings.

— So, you women of Sparta have seen the face of Aphrodite in Hera. I always knew that it was there. Tell me, have you guarded it well—this tender presence in such an untender kingdom?

— True, a harshness lies in Sparta. Is she not the consummate warrior city? Stranger, allow me to tell you about the sacred offering to Hera on the eve of one's marriage. When the animal is slain, the gall must be wholly cut out and discarded before presenting the sacrifice to Hera. This is to prevent bitterness entering the marriage.

— Well, well, it seems the Spartans enter marriage with their eyes wisely open. Tell me, does this cutting away of the bloody gall work? Or is it Hera herself who sees to the sweetness of the marriage?

      She shook her head in perplexity, it seemed, and he smiled ruefully.

— I see. Perhaps it is Aphrodite who is not quite reliable in holding up her end of things.

— Oh, stranger, we must not judge the gods. The night has closed in upon us, and I must return home. Otherwise they will be uneasy and will search for me. Only give me the message you say you have for me now.

— Must you go? I did promise you my word, didn't I? The word haunts my senses, my thought, and particularly my heart in this time of finding you.

— Only say it.

— Agape . . . *Eros Agape!*

— The beautiful love that is the friendship of equals! It is to be found?

      Her voice was hushed, and her face flushed with surprise.

— I speak of the love-friendship that is not a bond servant but finds its sovereign place. O Leda, hear me. Little time is left of this day's measure. I love you, my maiden queen! O beloved *Parthenos,* you are earth's vision of what is to come bringing the harvest and, no small fruit, my contentment!

      With these words, he took her swiftly into his arms, and they knew the golden embrace that was timeless while a radiant realm spread itself about them. At last Leda drew apart from the extraordinary stranger and, she who was queen of Sparta, like a lost twin returned, spoke.

— O heaven! O earth, my mother! I am lost!

— No, Leda, not lost. You are only *found!*

— It is that now I am hopelessly divided. Goddess Hera has not rescued me, and Aphrodite comes only to afflict me.

— Be calm, dear Leda, and hear me. The division you speak of is a fact.
Even though it may be difficult, *only the house divided can stand now.*

— How can I, a woman, live divided?

— By finding the true bridge that works between the gods and the human
world. Then, although at the core you find that you are indeed twins,
you shall come to live peacefully united.

— And who are you who brings me this golden love from which a beautiful,
enigmatic text flows?

— I am the stranger who is the swan upon Eurotas's waters!

The dark of night descended cloaking the riverbank so that the
stranger was no longer clearly visible although his presence remained.
Suddenly a very large creature appeared, white and startling as a full moon.
Observing the majestic creature, Leda was amazed, and her pulse raced as
the creature descended the riverbank toward the river's gentle current. At
the water's edge, the great bird spread its enormous wings while at the same
time extending its neck toward the sky, much as one might do when raising
a cup of praise in libation to Zeus. As the bird entered the waters and deftly
pushed off, its body lightly skimming the shining surface, Leda murmured
in awe, "Why, it is the swan!" She found herself running into the river on
the trail of the swan, pacing her strokes so as to follow at a little distance.
For some time the two figures continued in the shining waters under the
sky of night. A palpable sweetness filled her being as she swam in the swan's
wake of combed waters. In this manner, Eurotas, as though it were their
common source, bore them along. Time was lost track of. Now the moon
climbed the sky and provided a silvery trail on the river.

The tranquil pursuit of the great swan could go on forever, Leda
thought, and she strongly wished that it might. Had her heart not responded,
brimming over with delight, in the encounter with the stranger? Yet following
the swan, oddly, seemed to be all of a piece with the stranger. Oh, the swan
was beginning to circle about. He was making his way directly toward her.
Coming close now, he fixed upon her his shining eyes, black as Hades; and
with an audible gasp, she realized that she was gazing into the eyes of the
stranger himself! Before she could act in any way, the great white wings
spread over her now, and she found herself enclosed in what seemed to
be heaven's canopy of summer at noonday, flooding her with light. The
warmth of a great bosom received her, its pulse rhythmic. Powerful arms
of the swan—or were they legs?—lifted her toward himself. Ah, within
this tranquil realm, all was light and deep-feathered down, and she was

altogether sheltered. Hadn't he promised to shelter her? Only now did she acknowledge that she lay in the manly embrace of the stranger after all. Now Leda cried aloud, and her voice was full of joy.

— O swan! O stranger! Surely it is a god who visits me!

    The voice of the stranger was close to her ear.

— Dear Leda, inexorable is the way, I tell you. It is time that you know. *I Zeus am your lover!*

— Dear Zeus . . . , if only I had known. Ah, but now I have known the sheltering wings of the Olympian himself!

— Our love is the bridge so that your world and yourself are no longer painfully divided.

— O beloved Zeus, do not ever abandon me. The loss would be unbearable.

— The chamber that guards our love is within you, Leda. As for losing me through my inevitable departures, you must remember that one who has known me under the swan wings will never lose me!

    A bliss, spacious and satisfying, held the two figures now, and they fell silent.

    Some time passed, and Leda asked a question.

— As for the future here at Sparta, my own native ground, what will come about?

— A child of great beauty and appeal will be born. Already she is conceived, a daughter who will be as famous as the heroes of Greece. May you have delight in her.

— O joy! Let us call her Helen, and someday she herself will be queen of Sparta!

The Revolt against Zeus

It was after midday on Mt. Olympus when the gods gathered in the sacred grove. Present were Poseidon, Hephaestus, Athena, and Hera; and the four of them wore sober, troubled expressions. Poseidon took the initiative and addressed the group.

— It is one concern alone, one of unimaginable consequences, that draws us together, friends.

Hephaestus responded at once.

— Each of the four of us has been worried, Poseidon. I suggest that you put a shape to this issue that has us so distressed.

Poseidon reflected.

— Would that Apollo were here and could be our spokesman, but he refuses to have anything to do with a counteraction, I think.

Athena came to Apollo's defense.

— Ah, his relationship to Zeus is, after all, a delicate one. He cannot think to upset the source of the oracle. By that, I mean the mind of Zeus.

Poseidon continued, smiling at Athena.

— Our deed calls for unprecedented boldness. One wonders that you, Athena, are able to put at risk Zeus's good opinion of you.

Hephaestus spoke in honest admiration of Athena.

— It is not that Athena holds Zeus's good opinion of herself lightly. It is rather that she has summoned courage for what needs to be done. Do state what is at issue for us, Poseidon.

— Very well, fellow Olympians. We have before us the problem that Zeus the triumphant presents. That is to say, having vanquished the Titans, he was emboldened to lead us in the war against the giants. As you know, confronting each giant, monstrous in size and muscular strength, was agonizing. Still, we were victorious, were we not?

Athena reflected on the barbarous encounter:

— The toughest among them was the giant Alcyoneus, I believe. How Heracles did struggle to deal him a fatal blow, but the blows delivered upon the nine-acre giant affected him no more than an April shower.

Poseidon reminded her,

— Still, Alcyoneus was slain.

— Oh yes, but only after I made my way to Heracles' side and urged him to drag Alcyoneus well away from the soil that was his native land. When Heracles did this, the giant at once weakened greatly and was terrified. Then it was that Heracles dealt him the mortal blow.

— We gods emerged victorious then from the Gigantomachy. True, Athena, it required human collaboration to accomplish this. Well, these two vast victories over the Titans and then over the giants have taken a certain toll on Zeus. Do we all agree?

Each nodded to Poseidon's summary, stirring uncomfortably even so. Now Poseidon had no choice but to address the change in Zeus.

— There is a change in Zeus. Triumph is a strong wine, after all. Could it turn his mind, I ask myself? One finds almost inaccessible that finely attuned power of listening we have known in him. He is quick to anger and can become vindictive at the slightest provocation. Where are those judgments reflecting majesty and justice that we have known in the past? I tell you that unless some change is brought about, he is not fit to be lord of the gods!

Athena and Hephaestus gasped audibly, but Hera nodded vigorously.

— Hear, hear, my friends. I've been silent until now, but I must tell you that I was the first to notice the germ of conceit in Zeus, and it seemed to grow like a wild vine. How helpless I felt! Why, he has become impossible to live with amicably!

With this confession, Hera's face showed great distress, and she drew down her veil. Poseidon sought to comfort her.

— There, there, Hera. As his wife, it's worst of all for you, I expect.

Athena was reflective.

— I wonder how we might turn the tide of things . . .

Poseidon smiled at her.

— Turning tides is my specialty, Athena.

— Oh no, Poseidon. Surely you are not offering to inundate Olympus with one of your tidal waves? Heaven forbid!

— Don't distress yourself. I am not about to inundate the Acropolis of your Athens. I was simply reviewing my talents in the light of the problem.

Hera laid her hand on Athena's arm.

— Surely you do see that Zeus must be stopped or else made to take account of himself.

Athena's eyes shone brightly now as an inspiration came to her, and she nodded decisively.

— The key to the remedy presents itself, doesn't it? It is *limitation!*

Zeus has simply overstepped the limits. Can it be that in the process of banishing the Titans, sending them back to Tartarus, he may have absorbed something from the Titans, something excessive, defying all intelligent measure?

Hephaestus agreed, as if Athena had just expressed his quiet mind.

— The right measure lies in Apollo's wisdom. Certainly the solution to our problem lies here. Would that he were here to counsel us.

Athena regarded Hephaestus.

— Aren't you being much too modest, Hephaestus? What Apollo perceives when he says, "Nothing in excess," you also know. For are you not the craftsman of excellent works, fitting together parts with delicate precision and balance?

Hera interrupted.

— What are you thinking of, Athena? Have you already some scheme in that lively mind of yours?

— A plan has not taken shape, no, but I am strongly convinced that in Hephaestus we shall have wise assistance.

Poseidon pressed Athena.

— You've not been engaged in some idle reflection, I think. And now you are turning us toward Hephaestus here. What's on that mind of yours?

Hephaestus intervened.

— Athena, dear, tell me. What would you have of me? There is nothing that I would deny you for long, I think.

At once, Hera recognized the display of true devotion.

— Ah, for you, he will do anything, Athena, for old loves burn brightest.

Athena's cheeks grew rosy with the direction the conversation had taken. The words tumbled from her.

— It is not for me that you must do this thing, Hephaestus. Your action is awaited by all the gods and the human realm as well!

Poseidon, whose patience was limited at best, spoke urgently.

— Athena, get on with it! Otherwise you are going to spoil Hephaestus's passion for the action.

The others turned now to Athena, and their eyes widened with concern as they noted her drawn look. She drew herself up to her full stature and spoke quietly.

— Not one of us would wish for less than the victory of the gods. What is troubling, however, is what has followed in the trail of great victory. A confident impetuosity has invaded some of Zeus's acts. It is an appalling thing. So, it comes to this, friends: Zeus must be restrained!

There were gasps, clearly of shock, with these words coming from Athena. Was not she the most beloved daughter of Zeus? Hera's voice was like a mournful refrain.

— O yes. Athena is right. He must be restrained. Still, I can't imagine how it can be done.

Hephaestus had been quietly studying Athena, and he was sensitive to what he recognized as anguish in her. He spoke.

— Athena, I do believe that you have in mind some mode of restraint. Where do I come into the picture, by the way?

She lifted her face earnestly to Hephaestus and spoke with eagerness. It was as if the two of them might have been alone.

— O Hephaestus, you are unsurpassed in devising the thing that works in the situation at hand! Some device is needed at once to restrain Zeus, you see. Perhaps a thing of metal fired in your cavernous forge on Lemnos?

— Wait a minute, Athena. You and Hera are stepping onto very treacherous ground, I fear. Such an action on our parts easily assumes the countenance of rebellion. A limit to be imposed by us on the lord of the gods? I'm leaving at once for my forge to think this over. You must give me a little time. When I give the sign, let us gather for a second meeting here at this spot.

As dusk descended, blurring their sharply individual contours, the four gods took leave of each other.

At the end of the following day when the setting sun had left the sacred grove in shadow, Hephaestus returned to the spot where the three gods awaited him. They looked up expectantly when without a word, Hephaestus quietly deposited on the ground a shining heap of metal chain.

The two goddesses shivered at the sight, and Athena visibly paled as she raised a sober face to Hephaestus and commented.

— So it has come to this—a heavy chain!

Hephaestus saw that she was badly shaken, yet he met her with a steady, resolute face and responded.

— Yes, I am afraid so. Neither cleverness nor deceit could I use against great Zeus. At the very least, we owe him directness and candor as we proceed.

A cry went up from Hera.

— O but Zeus in chains—it is unspeakable!

Now always Hephaestus knew the luminous trail of the new shaping in which the enduring forms find embodiment, a solitary journey he took time and again. He knew the moment of rest, of quiet, joyous regard of what was a completed work. Yet he was removed from human life where it dealt with the impact of his work. He sought to explain to the goddesses.

— You laid on me the task of forming our counteraction. Always in working in metal, the craftsman must faithfully follow a single purposeful path. What one shapes in the fire cannot be many things at once, you understand. Nor can one alter one's intention midway. Oh, am I the only one among the Olympians who has to regularly undergo the ordeal of the narrow choice? Surely the gate of authentic choice admits the single one, often enough pinning his arms to the side as he struggles through the small opening. In our undertaking, I am the pinned-down one, you see.

Athena's face was contemplative, and both gratitude and compassion for Hephaestus shone there.

— Friends, hear Hephaestus. He is the craftsman, the one who shapes the hero's path through the ways of earth's matter.

Poseidon nodded to her words and paid tribute to Hephaestus as well.

— I well recall when you made that earlier awesome choice in order to remedy things. Remember when you were compelled to take up the ax and strike the head of Zeus in order for Athena to be born?

— How could I forget such a decisive moment, the loneliest I ever knew? Still, it had Zeus's full approval. There's the difference. To bind Zeus in chains is a more chilling action, surely. Nor can we know the outcome.

Poseidon was impatient now for action.

— It's clear to us that Zeus needs to be restrained. He must be restored to the measured mind for which he is known. No more delay, friends. Dusk is already upon us. Here's the plan, then. When the night has advanced so that Zeus is deep in sleep, we three shall leave the grove in stealth, carrying the great bronze chain. The chain must be well stretched out, so as not to cause clanging of metal on metal. As for you, Hera, you are to await us in the bedchamber where Zeus sleeps. However, you must remain wide-awake. We shall await your signal of a brief flashing of the lamp before entering the chamber. Can you do this, Hera?

— It's not an easy thing you ask of me. I am to be the one who gives the permission to bind my lord and husband?

— Obviously none of the rest of us can be on hand in Zeus's bedchamber late at night without suspicion.

Hera sighed and nodded.

— Of course, it can be none other than myself. You can count on me . . . . Oh, Athena, if only you were in my place! How do you manage to have the courage to accompany heroes in going about perilous deeds?

Athena smiled thoughtfully. The plan settled among them, Poseidon spoke idly now.

— Hmm, I hear the sound of the distant sea, the waters rising in a kind of opening before making a thundering slap on some shore . . . . Rest a few hours, friends, but do not fall asleep. The crucial hour lies ahead of us within the depth of night.

Evening cloaked the heights of Mt. Olympus, spreading a palpable serenity over the homes of the gods. Hermes, having arrived at the house of Zeus, was partaking of the latter's hospitality. Nevertheless, periodically he looked toward the courtyard as if to check on some growing agenda there. Now he spoke.

— Zeus, already night is upon us and it is late for guests, I realize, yet one of the goddesses insists upon seeing you.

— So this is the meaning of your glances toward the courtyard? Who is she who comes here at such an hour?

— It is gentle Thetis, the sea nymph. I warn you there is an unusual urgency in her whole demeanor.

— Thetis wishes to see me? Perhaps evening is to her like the sea's dim atmosphere. My curiosity is stirred. Do show her in, Hermes. And leave us in privacy, if you will.

As Hermes strode out to the courtyard, Zeus mused, *She is the most famous of Nereus's daughters and known for her beauty and her aloofness.* He looked up to observe that a deep golden glow filled the corridor through which Thetis now made her way. He greeted her warmly.

— Lady Thetis, welcome! And to what do I owe the pleasure of this nocturnal visit? Is there a problem at the bottom of the sea?

Her expression remained serious, if not grave, as she replied.

— If you please, Lord Zeus, were there a problem in the sea, it would be beyond your domain.

— Hmm, well spoken. Your shy manner can deceive one. What accounts for the urgency of your visit then?

— I have come to confess that I heard what no ear should hear nor any mind conceive.

Zeus frowned, his eyes regarding her closely.

— What's this you speak of?

— There is a conspiracy against you as lord of Olympus and of mankind, no less!

— Come, come, dear nymph, do not be so distressed. Why, anyone can have a bad dream . . . Have I not triumphed over the Titans and, more recently, led the gods to victory over the giants, slaying them?

— No one doubts these victories, Lord Zeus. Even so, had it not been for Heracles' help, it would have been problematical in the war with the giants. Now trouble brews from a most unexpected quarter. This I have learned.

Zeus arose from his chair, and simultaneously his voice was edged with anger.

— Who are these undeclared enemies? Declare them at once, Thetis.

— Who they are, I cannot say, or I dare not utter their sacred names. But, Zeus, beware! Do not sleep this night, I warn you!

— And what have I to fear?

— The *great chain!* The chain approaches that will bind you. Oh, you are at the mercy of the hands of the gods. I can say no more.

Zeus murmured to himself,

— The gods themselves would perpetrate an evil deed? Would they chain me, their lord?

He strode restlessly back and forth. Now he addressed her calmly.

— Thetis, your concern for me moves me profoundly. Someday I hope to show you my deep gratitude. Tell me, can you give me any help? You have your special gifts, being from the realm of the sea where your role is a queenly one.

— First I had to come to inform you of the trouble brewing. But I am here for yet a further cause. I know someone who can bring you the needed protection, I believe. It is Briareus.

— The hundred-handed immortal you mean? Excellent! If Briareus is on my side, he'll make a great guard.

— Since you approve of him, I go at once to bring him here.

With these words, she turned and departed swiftly, trailing the golden veil of light, which, like a silken curtain, fell about her. Anxious and given to a stream of painful and dark thoughts, Zeus remained seated in his bedchamber. Nor was there any danger of sleep overtaking the lord of the gods. Some time passed, and he heard the quick footsteps of the sea nymph followed by a companion with a clumping, heavy gait. At the door of Zeus's chamber, Thetis turned and spoke.

— Briareus, remain here outside of Zeus's door and allow no one to enter. Do you understand? Not even Lady Hera is to be admitted. Most important, you are not to harm anyone who comes. Take heed.

The huge hundred-handed one spoke in a resentful voice.

— Not harm 'em? You've tricked me. That's what you've done! You are taking away my right to act! As guard of great Zeus, I'll deal out what punishment fits somebody tryin' to do in the top god! That's treason, ya know.

— It may look like treason to you, Briareus.

— And it don't look like that to Zeus? Thetis, I don't take no nonsense off nobody!

— Be still now. We dare not awaken the household. It is not for you or for me to judge this action against Zeus. You are here only to keep Zeus safe.

— And that's what I'm going to do in the way I see fit. Why else have I got these hundred hands if not for dealin' with things as they ought to be?

Now Thetis spoke slowly and with emphasis, lest there be any doubt about the instructions.

— No, Briareus, not in the way you see fit. Your instructions are from me alone. You are to protect Zeus, but you must not inflict any injury on any other god. Do you understand?

— Yeah, I'm not stupid.

— Good. We understand each other then.

The long night passed, one sleepless for Zeus, who remained alone in his bedchamber. Why had Hera not come as was her custom? Wait . . .

had there been some struggle outside the chamber's great bronze doors that were being guarded by Briareus? Briefly he had registered the sound of metal clanging against metal, he thought. Already the sun god had mounted his chariot and had ascended the sky for an hour before Zeus, wearing the chlamys and carrying his scepter, emerged from the bedchamber. Taking in the scene at once at the doorway, he saw that Briareus had gone, while lying upon the threshold was a large shining coil of metal waist-high. The sight of the great chain wrenched from the lord of the gods a cry.

— Who has laid this great chain on my threshold?

Now the four gods who had secretly conspired to bind Zeus had been waiting for him to appear. They came forward, each greeting Zeus with sober countenance but not without the customary respect. Zeus regarded each god thoughtfully in an assessment not unlike that of a warrior in crisis. Slowly he acknowledged each one.

— Poseidon . . . Athena . . . Hephaestus . . . and you, Hera dear. Such an early visit is unprecedented and takes me by surprise. Tell me, what do you know of this great chain lying here at my door? Surely its power lies in some hostile suggestion!

Even as he put the question, he gestured for them to sit down together under the portico, and he himself took a seat alongside them. Poseidon was first to reply.

— Be assured, Zeus, we are here to address the chain, but it will require time.

Hephaestus's terse comment startled Zeus.

— Neither the chain nor what makes it necessary is forged in a day.

— Must you answer me in riddles, god of the forge? Well, I can likely surmise the situation on my own. I would guess that my new night guard, Briareus of the hundred hands, must have frightened the chain bearers so badly that they dropped the chain here and fled. I dare say he is even now pursuing the culprits down the slopes of Olympus!

His theory caused him to chuckle. The four visiting gods exchanged looks before Poseidon spoke.

— Brother, I seriously doubt it.

— What are you saying? Have you some direct knowledge of these nocturnal charades?

Before Poseidon could answer, it was Athena who, gazing at Zeus earnestly as she recalled their long devoted relationship, spoke.

— Zeus, my father, the events of the night were of a different order than you perceive them.

— You were witness to what happened, Athena? You astonish me.

— Yes, I was witness. I am witness and actor as well.

— Do explain yourself. I am at a loss, you see.

　　The face of Zeus reflected sober concern now.

— The great chain, I must tell you, is our doing, the action of the four of us here. O Zeus, this action rises out of our desperate need to restrain you!

　　Her face distraught, she gazed down at the stone floor of the courtyard. Even so, she was keenly aware of Zeus's scrutiny of her as he took in her account of things. One at a time, he stared at each god, incredulity on his face. It was Hephaestus who came to Athena's assistance.

— What Athena has said is a fact. Zeus, none of us denies it. In order to carry forward our urgent purpose, it was I who forged the chain. We meant to bind you—no less, no more.

— You would bind *me*? But why? Would you make me a common prisoner? You would bind the lord of Olympus?

　　His voice was dry and strange. Hera's voice became a pleading refrain.

— O Zeus, Zeus! You have ceased to listen to us! Don't you care about us?

　　Poseidon sought to answer his brother.

— There's no way to make you a common prisoner, Zeus. Our perception of things is not so flawed as that. You see, it is that you have ceased to be Zeus Philios, companion of gods and mortals alike. Instead, you have become Zeus the triumphant. And I might add, well on the way of being a tyrant as well. Well, that's the short of it.

— It takes a tyrant to know one, surely.

　　Grim and dry was Zeus's voice as he commented. Poseidon was honest.

— It is a fact that I've had my own moments.

　　Zeus turned to the other three solemn gods to ask the question.

— What are the plans of the four of you for the great chain? I had best know.

　　Hephaestus, whose candor and excellent perception gave shape to matter, including the dwelling places of the gods, spoke frankly.

— Obviously our plan has been foiled. What happened was that the huge guard with the hundred hands took the chain out of our hands, depriving us of our means to carry out binding you. I lay the truth before you, Zeus.

In succession, Zeus registered astonishment, outrage, thoughtfulness and loneliness. Athena took account of this, wondering still whether her father would come to remorse. Now he was speaking.

— So that is what I heard in the night. The chain struck the threshold depositing itself in a great serpentine coil. I must thank Briareus for his excellent protection. Seeing that I was saved from your perfidy, why have you gods not removed the chain since it holds evidence of your guilt?

Athena replied at once.

— Don't you see how it is for us? It is time for our purpose to be made clear. We are without shame, for we are clear in what we are about. Is it not to serve here on Olympus the deathless and luminous perception of limitation, of the good measure? Would that Apollo were at hand to explain.

Admiring her clear response greatly, Hephaestus sought to mediate the situation.

— You must see now that we are not your enemies, Zeus. We are companions, rather. Our guilt would be a sobering matter indeed if we were engaged in a power struggle with you. This can be no battle of wills, no greed on our part to gain some larger portion of authority among the gods. Against you, Zeus, we bear no personal grudge that we desire to see you shamed. No. But truly we are responsible for the great chain that binds, imposing its unarguable limits!

Athena added a thought, quick as the owl's dive when it seizes its prey.

— Let the chain lie as a reminder, I say!

Zeus pressed her.

— Reminder of what, Athena?

— Of the limit ever to be placed upon the exercise of power.

— Whence comes this limit of which you speak?

— Ah, who can say from whence it comes? Yet I believe that we recognize it. Surely limitation lies deep in the Olympian soul. It is present at the core of justice. Within the wise spirit it resides. Even in measured desire, is not its presence known? Limitation must abhor excess in all its forms, yet most of all, it registers pain when the delicate balance is not only missing but its very contours are no longer remembered!

Her three companions nodded to her words, and the face of Zeus underwent visible change. Once again the lively, inscrutable intelligence appeared and became luminous before them. The lord of the gods spoke simply now.

— True, in the conflicts that occupied me, this vision you describe, long dear to me, became obscured.

He rose to his feet and stood before his companions now, and he smiled as he regarded his four companions.

— It returns. The vision of the beautiful form of all things returns! Ah yes, it is higher than Zeus, and it seeks the Greek soul for shelter. O my Olympian friends, take the great chain away now, for what you so greatly treasure is recovered . . . . Whose voice do I hear at my ear? I do believe that is Sophia, she who carries wisdom. What does she say? Strange words . . ."Measure is best, as Apollo has said, for even the lord of the gods is subject to it!"

PART XIII

Journey of the Argonauts

The Hero—an Introduction

The Greek hero is not so much a legendary or historic person as he is a resident of the human spirit. Certainly he is not the same as the winner of a competition, for competition plays a very small role in the emergence of the hero. Although not picked out as the best of the bunch, he nevertheless presents the basic qualities called for in meeting the predicament in question. How is the hero to be recognized then? He is one who is summoned, and this powerful summons appears to be an interior phenomenon. In the myths, the hero finds himself encountering a luminous, possibly ghostly, presence well ahead of his decision to undertake the task. Often enough this presence is revealed as Athena, who is well-known for her assistance of heroes. As if mirroring it in her famous shield, the goddess brings to the encounter a vision that is dual in nature: she perceives the disturbing life predicament, and at the same time, she envisions the task or work that offers the remedy. With such a vision she came to guide Perseus in approaching life-numbing Medusa, and again she appeared at Theseus's side in Crete's Labyrinth to counsel the hero's approach to the Minotaur. As for the hero himself, he is less a bearer of a brilliant plan than one who simply acts to rescue the human spirit from being diminished, even devoured. It appears that his saving action lies in responding to crisis at once, being illuminated by the vision of a better human condition while given to a great deal of persistence in seeing through the needed action. The popular expectation that the hero exhibit a highly skilled performance and extraordinary strength is mostly a romantic notion aside from the core of the heroic spirit.

It is a fact of psyche, one confirmed in myth, that the heroic consciousness proceeds in a partnership. Although given as the Greeks were to a good store of common sense, the hero finds his perilous task in the company of the elusive goddess Nike, Victory. Nike proves to be a most welcome interior partner. She is not one of the Sirens seducing the hero away from life and the world, but instead she seems to function as a guide restoring the balance to life in present time. Such a restoration is hailed as victory. In Greek sculpture, Nike appears as a winged woman figure poised on the corners of certain temples. It is not surprising to find that the Athenians envisioned Athena as an embodiment of this victorious spirit, even building her a temple on the Acropolis dedicated to *Athena Nike*. In this context, the hero appears to embrace the optimism of the Greek spirit as a sound manifestation of the human condition.

Introduction to the Argonauts

Of all the images that have captured the human soul in its deep longing, none appears to be more wondrous than the Golden Fleece, astonishing in its earthy simplicity. Albert Camus wrote that all paradises may indeed be lost paradises. Similarly, it appears to be the nature of the Golden Fleece to be lost. Its absence is still able to distress the modern person and to urge him toward a quest, much as it did Jason and the Argonauts. Ancient memory is stirred, bursting into present time with its luminous account of a fundamental struggle for a golden and enduring meaning in existence. Undergirding this struggle is less a structure of specialized knowledge and technical expertise than the vision of the Fleece as it arises afresh from the human spirit. In the myth's account, it is Hermes, god of the road, who in the depth of night arrives leading the ram of the gods to the rescue of young Phrixos, who is bound on the altar of sacrifice. Safely arrived at Colchis on the back of the ram, Phrixos sacrifices the animal to Zeus, at the same time preserving the extraordinary fleece.

When the Fleece has gone missing, its loss stretches into indefinite time, leaving a compelling trail in memory. In the epic as told by Apollonios of Rhodes in the *Argonautica*, this loss awakens the heroic spirit. The young man Jason, called out of his idyllic life with Chiron and the centaurs on Mt. Pelion, soon sets forth in the company of fifty heroes aboard the *Argo* on the perilous quest of recovering the Fleece. Through the Clashing Rocks and Scylla and Charybdis's terrifying passage, they pursue their journey and are at the mercy of what strange ports hold for them, yet always the legendary fleece draws them onward. Nor are they deterred by the knowledge that, where the Fleece lies, it is guarded by a great serpent. Wild bulls must be encountered and yoked to the plow, the ground itself plowed, and its terrifying harvest of armed men dealt with before Jason with Medea's help approaches the serpent. Ever sustaining the heroes is the vision of recovering the Fleece, the gods' gift to earth.

Not intended as a comprehensive account of the tale of the Golden Fleece, what follows is a selection of dialogues that focuses on several episodes of the epic contemplated during a two-year seminar study of the *Argonautica*.

Jason Meets Hera

Mt. Pelion, that wild and lush green world over which the centaurs roamed—already he missed it sorely. This was a solitary trek, and Jason was a very young man, albeit a brave and knowledgeable one, having spent his childhood at the knee of the wise centaur Chiron. Dense woods enclosed him, while just ahead was an opening, and the distant sound of water cascading alerted him to the fact that he was approaching a river. It was springtime, and the river would be running full, not an optimistic prospect for making the necessary crossing. He smiled grimly. He reached the riverbank just as the sun set. To his astonishment, an old woman leaned against a boulder gazing down at the swift current below. As he observed her, he saw that there was something extraordinary and not unfamiliar about her, yet for the life of him, he could not identify it. Now he went forward addressing her.

— Greetings, lady. How is it that the end of the day finds you on this remote riverbank? Ah, I see in your face how weary you are. Can it be that you have been abandoned here through some misfortune?

— Alas, what a splendid young man I see! And my old eyes assure me that you are strongly built. You ask if I have been abandoned. Only ask yourself, motherless boy.

The lady's speech was perplexing. For a moment, her question had unnerved Jason. How could she know that he had been raised since infancy without a mother? He looked at the woman more closely now, this time without the mind's careless categorizing. This was no ordinary old woman. Her eyes held his with some seeming authority as she continued.

— The river at flood is formidable, but crossing it is an enormous task no matter what its season happens to be. So it is with the great crossing-over.

— Lady, from your speech I perceive that you are wiser than most. Would you be a seer in these parts?

Again he found her not inclined toward answers, for she sat silently regarding the tumbling current below the riverbank. There seemed no point in asking whether she wanted to get across the raging stream or not. Instead, he grew pensive and found himself in conversation with himself.

— *As I gaze upon this lady, whom I thought to be old, I now see a more erect woman with a barely contained energy of an unusual sort. Wait . . . I seem to recognize someone long forgotten, someone dear to my heart, but I do not know who that might be. Mother is the word that assails me and brings a shine of tears to my eyes. But she is not my mother, of course. There is something here, something amazing. It is like a star in the night, distant, bedazzling, and regal. For a minute, I thought, "The lady is a queen!"*

— Are you traveling far, my lad?

— Far, yes, to another world in fact. I go to Thessaly's ancient port city, Iolchis.

— Does your father know that you are making this singular journey alone? And your mother, can she know?

— Alas, lady. Have you not already pronounced me "motherless one?" I have no parents, for I was abandoned in my infancy, being brought to the great centaur Chiron, who raised me on Pelion's wild and beautiful mountain.

— A worthy job he did in raising you, I see. Ah, only look now. The river is rising. You best delay no longer.

— I must begin the difficult crossing at once! Oh, but I cannot leave you behind here on the bank alone.

— I fully intend to cross myself.

Jason regarded her intently, frowning and not without exasperation although he was assured that she meant what she said. Swiftly he reached a decision. He knelt, one knee to the ground, as he spoke.

— If you must indeed cross as well, lady, then mount my shoulders at once, and I shall carry you over the wild current!

Nimbly the lady climbed upon his shoulders, straddling his neck. Slowly he rose to his feet and began the descent of the steep riverbank, and as the dusk settled over the river ravine, he stepped into the swift waters. Fighting for his balance against the force of the current and the weight of the woman, Jason slowly made his way through the waters, sweating profusely and breathing hard in the struggle. One misstep and his companion would fall into the current and be borne away. Not only was the drag of the waters enormous upon his body but sharp stones also threatened time and again to upset his footing. There—the far bank was only one huge step away. With a gigantic exertion and a loud groan, gripping the woman tightly, he managed to make the step safely. She cried out as he did so. Carefully he set her down on her feet on the dry land, and his voice was that of a man as he spoke, nor did he look at her, for his eyes gazed at the path ahead.

— O extraordinary woman, we have made the crossing! Now we enter the land of my unknown father while Pelion, that dear haunt and guardian of my childhood, is forever lost to me!

Briefly Jason wept as a man might under such circumstances. Only then did he turn to the lady, this time in utter amazement, for a change had come over her. Age had dropped from her, and she had grown in stature. He saw that she was not only beautiful but also queenly in all respects. When she spoke, her voice no longer trembled or sought comfort and assistance. Hers was a face and a voice that appeared to be sustained by an unseen world. Why had he guessed her to be a seer? Clearly a goddess was at his side. She was observing him, and now she spoke.

— Jason, Jason, *I am Hera!* Never mind embarrassment, for recognition of the gods requires time, not to mention trial and error in abundance.

— Goddess Hera, all hail!

He at once made the sacred gesture.

— Alas, it never once occurred to me that you might be a goddess. Why should you, a great goddess, honor me in this way?

— The whys of the Olympians and the whys of mortals never match, so why trouble your mind with such? Not knowing my identity except that of a stranger, you risked your life in fording the river, carrying me across. For this I am grateful and am prepared to bless your way ahead and assist you in time of crisis.

— Lady Hera, I who always was regarded as an unfortunate lad am now among the most fortunate, I vow!

— I came as a stranger, but did not a measure of recognition begin in you?

— Yes. Ah, so! I beheld a starlike radiance in the dark, and out of this came one word—*mother!*

— The mother whom you abandoned has returned, you see.

— It was *she* who abandoned *me!*

— Yes, that came first, but did you not return the abandonment fourfold?

Jason's head seemed to be spinning, for his mind was thoroughly muddled. He might not argue with a great goddess, this was clear. He sighed instead and looked to her to continue speaking.

— Among the many tales the Greeks tell regularly, few honor me as mother, I'd say. Oddly, the human individuals I am most involved with are not my natural children, and yet they may acquire me as mother. I believe that this is your destiny, Jason.

— Wait, Lady, are you departing now?

— I am, but not without this admonition. When on the great journey that lies ahead you come upon dire trial or misfortune, you must call upon me, for I Hera am your protector.

The goddess faded away in the darkness, and Jason was alone.

The Beam of Dodona

The *Argo* had been for some time under construction. Surely no more skilled and devoted shipbuilder could be found than Argos himself, who stood at the side of the emerging vessel shaking his head. Jason observed Argos, frowning. Another impasse in their undertaking? Would the *Argo* ever be completed and ready for her launching? Jason moved to the builder's side.

— Don't lose hope, Argos. After all, the gods themselves have decreed the journey to recover the Golden Fleece. Still haven't found a good-enough beam for the keel of her, is that the problem?

— Right. We've searched. Haven't found a source for a beam that measures up.

— Man, we can't give up. Why, the *Argo* is almost completed. I shall come again tomorrow at day's end to see what you have found.

With these words and a sympathetic smile, Jason took his leave.

It was dusk of the following day, and Argos and Jason stood quietly side by side gazing at the dark skeletal form of the *Argo* on the lonely shore. Neither seemed inclined to speak. Unmistakably there came the sound of soft footfalls. They both turned, straining in the dim light to see who might be approaching. The figure was tall and moved in a graceful, lively stride. Recognition came now to Jason, and he trembled. He ran forward and made the sacred gesture.

— Goddess Athena! Can it really be you, coming like an owl in the night?

— Greetings, Jason. Greetings, Argos.

Jason bent toward the goddess, puzzled.

— What is this shadowy darkness on your shoulder, what burden?

— Ah, I expected to unburden myself unseen beside the *Argo*, actually. What I bear on my shoulder does have its weight, I must say.

A moonless darkness had settled over the seashore. Still, Jason perceived the object in question now, and he cried aloud,

— Argos, come, help me lift this beam that the goddess is carrying!

At once Argos had come forward, honoring the goddess before he moved toward the great beam. The two men bent to receive the great timber on their own shoulders, relieving the extraordinary goddess. Now they moved to the side of the *Argo* where they lowered the beam carefully to the ground. Having accomplished this task, Jason turned to thank the goddess, but she was no longer present. Meanwhile, Argos with his deft fingers was examining every inch of the wood and murmuring with inarticulate delight. Jason caught the words,

— It's of oak . . . must have been cut from a very large old tree . . . nothing like this in Thessaly!

— Where could it have come from then?

— North and far west, I'd say, nearer to the Ionian Sea. It's my guess that it may have come from the Pindus Mountains where the ways are steep, impassable. Or it might come from a valley below those rugged mountains. Jason, it's our beam—a miracle!

A look of sustained wonder was on Argos's face. Jason sighed as a deep gratitude swept over him. For some time they knelt on the ground examining the fine beam minutely, the two of them hushed except for an occasional exclamation of sheer joy. Afterward, the two men went their separate ways into the dense darkness. A wind had risen by now so that the waves a little distance away were rising and crashing against the shore. For the first time, the sense of the great voyage ahead came over him, stirring him profoundly. Jason realized that the beam Athena had brought had the needed strength, but it was more than the comfort of this fact that spread itself over mind and spirit. He began to feel his own strength, much like that of a seasoned bull. He was smiling at the thought when he heard his name called through the silent night.

— Jason . . . Jason . . . Jason, where are you?

He shook himself and replied, at the same moment moving farther away from the sea.

— Here I am!

Then he saw her. She stood out of the wind in the shelter of a great rock awaiting him.

— Lady Athena! You departed from the *Argo* so suddenly, just when I would have spoken with you.

— I have been waiting for you, as you see.

— What an amazing gift you have brought to the *Argo!* At last we have a great oak beam to lay for the ship's keel. What gratitude I bring you, Goddess.

Even in the darkness, there was a shining about her. She nodded, acknowledging his appreciation as she informed him,

— If you were to search the whole of Greece, you would not find such a beam as this one I have brought.

— Tell me, where did you cut this oak timber then?

— At Dodona.

Jason gasped audibly with this revelation. She went on.

— Yes, I cut it from the sacred oak of Zeus, no less, the oak that stands in the distant sanctuary of his oracle.

With Athena's words, a certain dread touched him. When he spoke, his voice was hoarse.

— Lady Athena, what is the meaning of this act of yours?

— Why, Jason, you need not be anxious. You see, Zeus has allowed it. Otherwise I should not have taken the cutting.

Jason pressed her, however.

— But what is the meaning of this?

— First, the beam is not a charm. The perils of the true voyage cannot be charmed away. No, the beam of Dodona is much more.

Jason seemed to be musing now, the sense of dread departed.

— Do I understand that this beam comes from the oracular tree of Zeus and Dione?

— Ah yes. Therein lies the strength of your vessel and the perseverance of the journey itself.

Jason fell silent. The question seemed inconceivable, but at last he asked it.

— Goddess, is it possible that this beam has some of Zeus's wisdom?

— It cannot be otherwise. What I have cut with my own hand for the journey of the Golden Fleece is the speaking beam of the god's oracle.

— The beam that we shall lay as our keel has a *voice?*

Such a fact was incredible. Jason desperately needed reassurance.

— Indeed, it does. Jason, you must take care to attend to the voice of the keel, distinguishing it from all familiar, ordinary voices making their appeal. Remember this meeting of ours when you launch the *Argo,* will you? Until we meet again, farewell!

With a lingering look of what might have been compassion, Athena smiled at the hero and departed.

Jason Loves the Lemnian Queen

Here on the eastern Aegean shore where the *Argo* lay anchored, the wind had grown calm as Jason gazed up toward the port village, taking stock of the industry of the islanders. Could the incredible rumor be true that here on Lemnos lived only women, women who, in brief, had killed their husbands on account of their bringing home captive wives to replace them altogether? Occupied with such thoughts, he reached for the extraordinary mantle, which had been Athena's gift to him as leader of the expedition. He could not touch it without a sense of awe and admiration consuming him. Putting it on with care, he saw that the great silken mantle hung from his strong shoulders to his knees. The mantle was splendid with legendary scenes woven by the hand of the goddess, reminiscent of Athena's own sacred peplos woven by the women of Athens. Now he raised his hand to indicate his departure to his comrades of the *Argo* and strode up the path away from the beach toward the village, a solitary and splendid figure.

Her eyes had followed every movement of his approach from the moment he stepped off the Thessalian ship, and she arose to stand at the gate of the courtyard, a stately figure, to welcome the ship's captain. Although a young woman, she spoke with dignity. Indeed she might be the queen, he thought.

— Welcome, traveler, to the isle of Lemnos! I am Hypsipyle.
— Greetings, Queen Hypsipyle. I am Jason. My comrades and I are on the journey of the *Argo*, presently anchored on the beach below.
— We observed your arrival.

She led him to a shaded spot and gestured toward a chair while she sat down in the chair facing his. Seating himself, Jason extended his right arm on the arm of the chair. Plainly visible on his silken sleeve was a scene of two gleaming chariots in a race to the death. Hypsipyle leaned forward, her eyes wide with some dark emotion as she gazed upon the scene. He waited for her to speak.

— What a beautiful and extraordinary mantle you wear, leader of the sea-journeying heroes. But what can this event be that your right arm presents boldly before my eyes in startling color?

— Does it startle you then, my lady? I do believe that it does. Why, it is a tale I was taught at the knees of Chiron the centaur on Mt. Pelion. It is the account of a hero's deed forever etched in Greek memory. Goddess Athena herself wove the silken threads you see here. Ah, does it distress you?

— Indeed. Alas!

She had endowed the two words with some deep, echoing emotion. Even so, she quickly added that the mantle was of singular splendor, unlike anything she had ever seen before.

— It was a gift of Lady Athena at the start of the *Argo's* journey, as a matter of record. I must say that it is my great treasure. Even so, it is not a garment easy to wear.

Jason sighed softly.

— Tell me what this tale in the mantle is about, will you, Captain?

— The mantle contains several tales, actually. Do you have some special interest in this one?

— With your right arm you extended this one toward me. It is not wise to ignore what the Fates have spread before one.

— Well said, Hypsipyle. A queen is not made in a day, I must say. My admiration compels me to say this.

He smiled slowly, regarding her. Was it a blush that arose on her cheeks? He continued.

— Regard the scene closely then. It is a contest between chariots, you see. The charioteer who has drawn out ahead on the race course is none other than that hero of the south of Greece, Pelops. The chariot that is gaining on him is driven by Myrtilos, who is hoping to outwit Pelops.

Her eyes grew large with excitement. Now she asked with alarm,

— Alas, who is the fierce older man in the pursuing chariot who is watching Pelops and ready to hurl his spear?

— That is the powerful king. He is the lovely maiden's father, I am afraid.

— What is the maiden's name?

— Hippodamia.

Hypsipyle considered the situation, a restraining hand upon the king's chariot on Jason's sleeve

— I begin to see how it is. Her father, loving her, wants to keep her from all suitors. I presume that this Pelops is a suitor.

— He is. He hopes to win Hippodamia as his bride, nor would he be an unworthy bridegroom, a man prepared for kingship himself.

— But the father does not want such an outcome. Only look how he aims his spear. How cruel to think of slaying this worthy young man! And Hippodamia herself, surely she is drawn to this fine hero. What is it about the old king?

Her question hung heavy upon the air between them. She spoke slowly.

— Ah yes. I think he believes that the old ways and the familiar arrangements are best and that, where power has always resided, it ought to continue to be supreme. It doesn't matter to him that Hippodamia thinks otherwise, does it?

Jason was stirred as if by a niggling sense of injustice, and his response was almost rough, his voice steely.

— Of course it matters, Hypsipyle! And apparently it matters to the gods, for only look at what happens. It isn't all portrayed here on the sleeve, of course.

— Only look! The king's chariot has lost a wheel, disabling his chariot, no doubt!

— You are perceptive, Queen. Do you also perceive that deceit and trickery are at work against the king?

She did not reply, but a look of horror was on her face as Jason pronounced the outcome.

— King Oinomaos falls to his death with the crash of the chariot.

— Nemesis, alas!

Jason and the lovely young queen stared at each other, and Jason wondered at the power the tale held for her. He spoke quietly as one who muses.

— The old king must die. He has come to care only for his power and destroys what opposes him. Unless the king dies, the people have no life worth living. But look. The new hero king comes!

She was frowning in perplexity still. Soberly, she asked the question.

— How can it be?

Jason regarded her intently for a long moment, and then he smiled, all the tension gone from his voice now as he replied.

— He comes because the maiden lies eternal in the way of things . . .

— Pelops became Hippodamia's husband, did he?

— He did.

— Did he become king as well of the south of Greece?

— He did.

— Captain of the quest for the Golden Fleece, it is not easy when the old regime goes. There is upheaval, abandonment, and anguish! Such consequences we women have known on Lemnos. And worst of all, the voices of little children are silenced.

— There is no future worth living until the tyrannical old rule is dead, nevertheless. No dialogue was possible with King Oinomaos, you see.

— No dialogue . . . no dialogue!

She had uttered the words twice like a poignant refrain, and Jason could not doubt that the woman before him made her way through a grim personal text as well as the tale of her land. There were tears in her eyes. Sensing the presence of some unspeakable sorrow, he dared not reply.

When she finally broke the silence between them, she lifted her gaze to address him now more directly.

— Sometimes the repressive, cruel ruler is not just one man but many, and the many have overwhelming power. There is no escape, no grasping for the hem of a life that works. Can you understand? Without it . . . without it . . .

— Without what, Hypsipyle? You speak in riddles.

— *Without the raising of treacherous hands against the oppressor's hand.*

He blinked quickly and asked her the question that gave her no quarter.

— You speak of your history then, the history of Lemnos?

She nodded slowly, her head lowered as one who honors a grave. The pause was tense and long.

— Hypsipyle, grieve no more for the past, for what has been. One must pay one's debt to sorrow, true, but to permit sorrow to be greedy were unwise.

They both fell silent. Each of them separately was startled by the fact that the companionship had become oddly comfortable. It was the Lemnian queen who broke the silence.

— Now I have observed that on the front of your luminous mantle is a cave scene. Why, the Cyclopes, those one-eyed ones, are hard at work fashioning what must be the thunderbolt of Zeus! An awesome thing! How is one ever to withstand Zeus's bolt? Surely the women of Lemnos have been struck deep within the bosom!

— No one can stand to look upon the thundering face of Zeus. But do look again at the mantle. Only look at the silken scene below this one. What do you see?

— The hero Pelops pulling up at the finish line.

— Exactly. *The hero has come. Often the hero turns out to be many,* Hypsipyle. Do you hear me?

      Jason pressed on, for now he must prepare the way for the Argonauts.

— What else do you see?

— The woman—Hippodamia, I think. Whatever can she do in this tale of heroes?

— Everything. What I mean is that she will bring Pelops the bounty of earth, bring it to his home and bed. Do you hear, Hypsipyle? Can you receive this tale which Athena herself has woven within my mantle? It is we the Argonauts who come ready to bring you what indeed may signal for the Lemnian women a satisfying gift of life, for slumbering in the tale of the goddess is the very body of life!

— Ah yes! Yes, Jason, come, stay here on Lemnos with us, you and your company! How can we ignore what the Fates have spread before us, I ask you?

      Jason smiled and took Hypsipyle's hand. Then, bidding her a brief farewell, he set out to return to the ship to bring the news of the queen's generous welcome of the *Argo*'s crew to the island.

Phineus and the Harpies

Each morning, the seer made a gruel from the grain and boiled it over the fire, and this was his only real sustenance for the day. After the early meal, it was Phineus's custom to sit in the courtyard where in the course of the day, friends would stop in to visit, bringing food for his table. The truth of the matter was that few morsels of this food were ever consumed. Thin and gaunt the body of the aging seer had become, and hunger seemed ever to assault him, the reason being that the Harpies appeared regularly, swooping down over his table and snatching up all the food for themselves. Behind them they left desolation, and their defecation fouled the entire courtyard. One day, following a particularly devastating assault by the demonic bird women, Phineus straightened his old shoulders, rose to his full height, and turned to face the lingering large Harpy before him. Something of his old authority was in his voice as he spoke.

— You, Harpy, stay, I say! I have something to say to you.

The great feathered creature turned her woman gaze full upon the seer with a stony stare. Only the nervous flapping of dark wings revealed her uneasiness in being addressed for the first time. She replied.

— Food all gone. Why stay?

— Because you must answer my question. Why do you do this to me over and over again, devouring all that nurtures me? What's this great punishment that befalls me daily?

— Steal what we need, Harpies do. We are nature. Not like seers. You punish nature!

Now Phineus was shocked by these words.

— I am a punisher? That is a lie. Do you know why I am respected by people? It is because I have wisdom.

— You wise? That's a laugh. If you were wise, you'd grab what you need.

— Hear me, bird woman. Grabbing is not my way. After all, I am civilized. All you Harpies ever do is grab, I must say.

— We get what we need, and we get what we want. Being civilized makes you no more than a decoration folks count on.

Phineus sighed audibly. Still, something in him could not give up on the Harpy.

— Look. All this grabbing from folks' supply causes you to be despised, you know.

— You don't understand snatching, and you never will. A seer sits around holding his chin and gazing on things. He'll go to ruin that way.

— A man is a fool who never deliberates, never waits for the long pause that takes in the seed and awaits the sprouting. Have you ever deliberated, ever pondered before you go into action?

All the time they were speaking, the Harpy continued to gulp down the remaining food of Phineus's meal with considerable satisfaction. Now she looked up briefly.

— No, but I know how to *dive in*. That's something you don't know about.

— Well, no, I won't deny what you say. My point is that that is all you do—you dive in and you devour.

Harpy could only look pleased with this description of herself.

— Haven't you heard all that praise that goes around about initiative and having confidence? We Harpies have got both.

Now the spirit within the seer sank even lower, and he stared at the ground before him. The Harpy raised her eyebrows.

— You look done for, finished. Are you?

Anger flared on Phineus's cheeks briefly.

— How can you ask such a question when you snatchers are robbing me of every morsel of my food!

Harpy took this in soberly and nodded as if it might be an interesting problem.

— Your reactions are too slow. Have you thought of that?

Phineus groaned aloud.

— I have, and the thought depresses me.

A cagey look gleamed in her eyes.

— I could teach you a thing or two, when it comes down to it.

— Really? I don't think so. Harpy, what's your price, by the way?

— Are you ready for it? Here it is: give up being a seer. Everybody knows you're blind anyway. Ask a blind man to see for you? That's a riot!

Phineus was on his feet facing her, much like a lion leaping out of the bush onto the path. His voice was ageless when he spoke.

— I shall never give up being a seer! How could I, for it is the gods who have willed it!

— OK, OK. Let's not get touchy. Oh well, I could still teach you something.

— What then?

— Grabbing. If you'd been listening properly, you'd recognize my gift. Trouble with you, Phineus, is that you don't know how to grab what you want, never mind what you need.

— It's a desperate act, and it's indecent because the grabber grows stronger only as the provider grows weaker. I'll have none of it!

Harpy looked disappointed in him. She spoke, reminding him,

— You have to admit that it's useful, though.

The strength of the seer clearly was returning to him. He raised his voice now.

— All you Harpies do is grab and run! Are there no boundaries of ownership and of right action to be acknowledged? Every time you swoop down upon the scene, you act as if you are entitled ones! Well, you are not.

A thought trickled down now into the mind of Harpy, causing her to begin to smile.

— Say, seer, haven't you heard? Mighty Zeus himself has decided that we are useful to him. That's right. Needn't look amazed. Calls us his *hounds*, he does, hounds of his purpose!

With this triumphant declaration, Harpy began to walk back and forth, a very smug look on her face. Phineus replied.

— Doesn't Zeus give wisdom to Apollo himself at Delphi? He would never punish a faithful seer, the state that has determined the course of my life. Of course, he sharpens the blade that has dulled, I suspect. Wisdom's thrust must be sharp to penetrate the world, after all.

— You admit it then.

— You accuse me unfairly, Harpy. Zeus brings the blessing, even when it is long in coming.

Harpy flapped her wings extravagantly, made a deafening cry to her sisters who waited for her at a little distance, and took off into the sky without a backward glance. Phineus sensed the Harpies' departure and uttered an abysmal sigh. Soon reflection with its cooling balm came over him once again, and he spoke to himself in a low voice.

— What has this long harassment by the Harpies brought me? Ah, over time it has hollowed out a place I had not known before. My heart's desire is hollowed out, empty and waiting, just as my body's appetite is an empty cup waiting to be filled. The heroes of the Golden Fleece have come, and they have recognized the hollow place in me and have honored it. A blessing comes to me at last! What is this work of the Harpies but a dark work of nature? What if against this darkness, the vital shape of what I am yet to become is illuminated? . . .

Time passed, and the visit on Phineus's isle of the amazing group of men known as the Argonauts had raised the seer's spirits immeasurably. When the heroes of the *Argo* observed his dire predicament with the Harpies, had they not put their heads together and come up with a solution? For this reason, those zestful young men, the sons of Boreas, had kept watch over the table of Phineus. When the Harpies swooped down and attacked, it was with a loud cry of rebuke that Zetes and Calais put their hands to the sword and set out in swift pursuit of the startled bird women. Nor would they fall back until they managed to take vengeance upon the snatchers.

Jason was walking alone at the water's edge when he overtook the sons of Boreas, Zetes and Calais, moving rapidly down the beach, their swords gleaming at their sides.

— Zetes, Calais! Are you off on a maneuver already?

Smiling, Zetes responded.

— Time for action against the Harpies, who just fled. Calais and I aren't fellows to stay passive, pondering like some philosopher!

The dig hurt, and momentarily Jason drew back as if recoiling from the blow. He managed to speak quietly, encouraging their mission, however.

— The great bird women have been cruel and relentless in taking away Phineus's food supply. The old seer is blind and miserable. Of course we must come to his defense. I am clear about this.

Zetes, strategist that he was, reminded him,

— Do you also understand that there can be no further delay in acting?

Jason nodded, but added,

— We must act, but act wisely. Are you two willing to undertake this pursuit of the Harpies single-handedly? I know that you are strong, worthy sons of your father.

The armed brothers both spoke at once.

— Just the two of us, yes. We're on our way. Justice must be dealt out.

Jason frowned, regarding them intently.

— It is for the gods to deal out justice, remember. That you are willing to serve the process, however, stirs my deep gratitude. Now, what is the plan?

— We're going to seize the Harpies. This is our vow. We are the liberators.

— What shall you do with them?

— Slay them. Such creatures of evil intent who torture the fount of human wisdom must die!

— Ah, but will the Harpies die? Such power as they possess may prove to be immortal. Zetes, Calais, none of us on the *Argo* can undertake this task as well as yourselves. You have the support of the rest of us. Go now, and may your quest succeed. Only take this warning: you could well meet one of the gods on the way. Pay close attention and do not fail to give such a one due honor.

The three embraced, and the sons of Boreas went forward at a keen pace, running, keeping watch on the Harpies, who, having made a long pause on the far stretch of beach to look for tasty morsels, now took to the air again.

Grueling hours of pursuit of the Harpies followed, crossing stretches of sea and uninhabited islands. Coming over a mountain summit, Zetes and Calais found themselves within hand's grasp of the startled Harpies, who cried aloud in terror. Confident and filled with the zest that was their bounty, the sons of Boreas reached out and, with gleeful laughter, as of those who triumph, laid hold of the two besieged Harpies. Nothing could describe the taste of victory. However, even as they grasped the terrified bird women, a voice was heard from the sky itself. Incredibly, their names were being called!

— Zetes! Calais! Stop at once!

Trembling, the two Argonauts fell back, dropping their arms helplessly as before them on the path appeared a radiant figure, a goddess, who was regarding them sternly. She spoke.

— Sons of Boreas, what it is that you do? Whatever it is, consider again.

They recognized the messenger of the Olympian gods and made the sacred gesture at once.

— Goddess Iris, it is that we are attempting to right a terrible wrong, the wrong that the Harpies have done against wise and blind Phineus.

They have regularly stripped him of all his food. The poor man is perishing.

— That is true, but what it is that you propose to do, I ask you?

— Why, we shall slay these dreadful bird women, wipe them off the face of earth for all time! This is our heroic task.

There was a considerable pause during which the goddess directed her gaze into the distance and was silent. Now she spoke.

— At best it is an exalted undertaking, one that bestows upon yourselves a cloak of fame. But you shall not be successful, I warn you.

— What's this you say?

The brothers stared at each other in disbelief. Iris continued.

— Justice belongs to the gods. Besides, the Harpies cannot be slain like ordinary mortals. Your swords are hardly sufficient to accomplish such a deed.

The men's faces paled hearing these words, and they turned to stare at each other. Zetes spoke to the goddess.

— Is this evil to be perpetuated then? Do you imply that the gods will permit the Harpies to continue?

— Sit down, heroes of the *Argo's* journey. Now we shall speak outside the terrible wind of crisis. Let me tell you how it is. You Argonauts, one and all, have seen the dark face of the Harpies. You have witnessed their indifference to human feeling, to suffering even. What they have revealed of themselves is only their insatiable appetite.

— These are the facts, spoken in truth, Goddess. Surely you are not going to tell us that the Harpies have a *good* side as well?

Iris arose to her feet now and paced slowly before them.

— You must divest yourself of this garment your mind clings to. I refer to a righteous simplicity. Do it at once. The whole of reality as it affects the human world cannot be framed into black and white forces, dark and light deeds. Well, it is true that I come to reveal what the gods have to say in the matter.

As she spoke, the faces of the men recorded surprise, outrage, and other more ragged emotions. Calais reassured the goddess.

— Speak on, Goddess Iris. We will hear what the gods say.

Regarding each man separately with something akin to pity in her face, she spoke.

— What I must tell you is that the Harpies have yet another face than the one each has presented so far to Phineus. This face marks them as the guarding hounds of Zeus!

The men leaped to their feet in amazement and excitedly addressed each other.

— It is incomprehensible! But we dare not offend Zeus . . .

— What are we to do now, Zetes? And what is to be the fate of poor Phineus? I am at a loss!

Turning again to the zestful ones, Iris spoke final words.

— The Olympian gods have heard your plea for the seer, and here is what I am to tell you. Namely, that the gods shall henceforth put distance between the Harpies and Phineus. Never again shall the bird women come near him! As for you two defenders, put away your swords and return to your comrades.

Zetes and Calais made the sacred gesture, and their gratitude flowed toward the messenger goddess. Sheathing their swords, they turned back to rejoin the other Argonauts.

Jason and the Voice in the Night

In spite of the gentle rocking of the *Argo* that lay at anchor in the bay, Jason could not sleep. For the first time, he had met dreaded monarch Aietes at his handsome palace in the city of Kolchis, and naturally he had explained that he and the Argonauts had come in quest of the Golden Fleece. After all, the ram of the gods had been given to a prince of Greece, to Phrixos, as his means of rescue from being cruelly sacrificed. Surely since Phrixos is dead, the Fleece rightfully should be returned to mainland Greece. Even as Jason went over the facts, the sense of the awesome task to come lay heavy on his mind. How swiftly had clever Aietes devised the ordeal. He is a tricky king to deal with . . . And what a task—the job of yoking wild, fire-breathing bulls to the plow! At the first hearing, he had been numb with shock. Reviewing it step by step in his mind since that moment, he saw that here was a hero's task that suggested the impossible. True, he could say with all honesty that the journey of the *Argo* had received the favor of the gods, most especially the attention and guidance of Athena. He must invoke the help of the Olympians, but it would be foolish to expect one of the gods to perform this outrageous task *for* him! Wasn't Athena always known to step back once her man was shaped for action? As he mused, the Argonauts who lay nearby slept soundly into the shuttered hours of the night. Finally, with a low sigh, he arose and made his way quietly to the *Argo*'s helm, laying his hand upon it firmly as he gazed out on the moonlit waters. How long he stood there, attentive, motionless, he did not know. The breeze had been soft, the vast silence comforting when he was startled by a distant howling that came from far out to sea. Its volume grew and was borne upon a rough wind that now struck the *Argo* and would have knocked him to the deck had he not grabbed the helm fiercely with both hands. At the same time, a voice spoke quietly at his elbow, although no one was to be seen.

— Alas, it is true. You are the helmsman now, and the fate of the *Argo*'s journey lies altogether in your hands, Jason!

— These are honest words though they lack comfort.

Jason had muttered this to himself.

— What? Is comfort the first request of the hero? I shouldn't think so. Yet bold action when engaged in a dire situation can be rash and, well, unimaginative. You are in error if you proceed with impressive boldness, I believe.

Jason was quick to attempt his defense.

— It is my assigned task that is rash and bold. Companion of the night, I am not flaunting my boldness. Surely to approach two huge brazen-footed bulls which are snorting fire and to try to put a *yoke* upon them asks for the impossible. I am not accustomed to foolhardiness, I assure you.

As Jason spoke rather disdainfully, a realization, small and belated, came to him: his companion had the voice of woman! The earlier fury of the wind had obscured the fact, but now the wind had gentled. She replied.

— Jason, you must consider these great bulls who are presently your foes. I agree that one dare not stand in their path when they charge.

— Hmm, do you think I might step aside swiftly, maybe cleverly, like an ancient Minoan bull dancer then? Lady, whom I believe to be a goddess, will you instruct me how this might be accomplished?

— Cleverness is not your strength with the beasts. Only listen. *Consider the bull! The bull is life! The bull is destiny!*

Jason dropped his head, awed by his companion's words. When he spoke, there was pain and perplexity in his voice.

— How is one to approach, then, the bulls?

— The great bull must be brought to your side. He must cease to be the foe.

— Alas, this is no simple act you prescribe! How does a person go about it, again I ask?

— Already you have been given what is needed. I refer to the *yoke*, of course.

Jason grew thoughtful, pondering her words.

— Ah, reduce his power to act, you are suggesting. Bind him, no less. I begin to see.

— Not bind him, for then he loses his innate freedom, which must be preserved, even honored. You are to put him *under the yoke*. When you see that the two bull heads are in place beneath the wooden bar, in that moment, the power of the great bull is captured for your plowing. You will observe that the bull power is undiminished but, rather like the spring current of a great river, flows powerfully into the channel you have provided. I speak of earth's furrow.

Jason was aware that a small current of spirit was reemerging in himself. At the same time, the way in which the goddess spoke of the yoke mystified him. He pressed her to linger on it.

— The yoke—it is a mysterious thing, I'd say. Why, from what you say, I see that it is able to ensnare the animals, to tame the wildness.

— It is no mere effective tool in your hand, however. Do not misjudge it. In the years to come, I counsel you never to underestimate the good yoke. It tends to be hidden from one's observation, I warn you. Rarely does the yoke seem dazzling or beautiful in itself, even though one has the pale knowledge that it is useful. Unfortunately, no one is likely to praise the yoke under which one's very life flows steadily, unimpeded. Of course the yoke has its price which you must pay. When you come to look hard at the yoke, I warn you, it is easy to be critical, to feel oneself a victim, scorning the yoke's power over your very life. How foolish a person can become in the presence of such a benefactor!

As for Jason, the sense of tomorrow's severe ordeal of yoking the wild bulls descended upon him once again. There was nothing for it but to address what lay at hand.

— The truth of the matter is that tomorrow will soon be upon me, and I must make use of the yoke that the king provides me. Yes, I shall remember your good words—that the yoke must be greeted as my benefactor. Once yoked, the fiery bulls can plow the land. Already as my eyes gaze ahead, I perceive that Aietes' plan for our destruction may yet evoke the peaceful order of the plow! O companion of the night, this cannot come about, I think, without your assistance. Do not abandon me, Lady!

— Nor shall I. Have no fear, Jason. There is other assistance under way as well, which you shall have knowledge of shortly. And now I must leave you. The wind has gentled, you see. One thing more, Jason, never doubt the power of the good yoke!

His invisible companion departed, and as she left, Jason thought he could discern the soft rustle of her garments with each step. An old image from a childhood story hovered over his mind in which he saw shining Athena standing in a field with a plowman and his oxen while in her hand the goddess held the ox yoke.

Jason and the Dioscuri Reflect

Jason and his Spartan comrades Castor and Pollux sat at leisure just above the harbor where the *Argo* was at anchor. King Aietes' terrible ordeal was behind Jason. Even so, an abiding sense of incredulity hung over him. Silence set upon the three of them. Jason sighed aloud and shook his head from side to side. The Dioscuri regarded him closely, and it was Castor, the more assertive twin, who spoke.

— Tell us, Jason, why in the name of Olympus did you leave your spear behind, stuck in the ground alongside your bronze helmet, while you went forward to meet the raging bulls carrying only your shield? When I saw you do this, I thought this is the end of Jason, and disaster for our entire journey! Why, you were foolhardy, man.

— Perhaps. That did occur to me briefly, but I saw that this was the only way to proceed—trusting Medea and her goddess.

— What do you mean? Did she forbid you to carry the spear then?

— No. She gave me something far superior to ordinary armor—the magical ointment with which I covered myself and which she assured me would give me great strength and protection against the bulls' fire for one day.

Castor scowled and kicked up dust with his sandal, obviously skeptical.

— You still would have been smart to carry along your spear, man! Why, you went forward looking like a naive boy!

— If I clung to my faithful spear that I was used to, how could I go with the new hidden armor? I simply couldn't have it both ways. The choice wasn't easy since I couldn't see the way ahead. What I chose was a way generated out of night and, I must admit, out of Aphrodite's golden passion.

— You are mad, man! But at least you came through it all safe and sound.

      Castor gave Jason a reluctant smile. Pollux, the quieter brother, spoke.

— What you did, Jason, took courage, and besides, you honored the wisdom of a woman who alone seems to know the hidden life of this kingdom. This extraordinary priestess of Hekate, daughter of hostile King Aietes, what is to become of her now? Have you thought that her father could destroy her for assisting you, Jason?

      Jason trembled visibly.

— I realize this. Besides, I love the maiden, and I have given her my word that she shall be my bride. Without a doubt, Aphrodite's hand is prominent in what has happened. Still, it is Medea who is the greater captive of the goddess.

— How was it that you decided, among all the Argonauts who are qualified, to pick Castor and myself to assist you with the yoking? I was truly honored.

— Ah, that is easier to answer than all the other questions. You two, whom folks call the Dioscuri, make excellent middlemen. You are known to make yourselves available in crisis, especially in a storm at sea.

— Clearly this was no storm at sea.

— I realize that, Castor. At the same time, my ordeal was to face the bulls—the fury of raging nature. You both know the secret of calming nature. So I said to myself, "The sons of Tyndareus may well be able to tame the bulls." Of course, you required the yoke.

      Pollux was sizing up Jason, and now he shook his head as he began to speak.

— That is one of those explanations one gives himself because it sounds plausible, but, Jason, there is something else behind your bringing in Castor and me. I sense it definitely.

      The words of the son of Zeus delivered Jason a jolt, so that he sat very still. His face was somber, yet reflective, as he nodded briefly and spoke.

— Here in the country that guards the Golden Fleece, things appear differently than I have ever encountered them before in my life. Medea, for instance. She is something of an enigma to me, although a pleasing one, I admit. The feminine nature of things, so alien to our voyage, finds a way to penetrate us. You see this, do you? Wherever we go these days, a goddess hovers, it seems. She is protecting us from a dark and ruthless king, if the truth is to be known. Somehow, in the midst of all this, I half-perceived a working way. It involves the mortal twin and the immortal one, see?

This confession excited Castor, who had been looking bored.

— You mean that we are the way, Pollux and myself?

— Yes. When one gets this close to the Fleece itself, one needs to be down-to-earth and ordinary and without pretensions. One wants the Fleece and is determined to make the necessary journey to recover this treasure. And, of course, one wants to stay alive. That's the mortal side.

Castor looked pleased for the first time.

— All right. What else can there be?

— Why, the immortal side. It has to be there, partnering the undertaking, holding the vision, protecting it in a time of extreme vulnerability.

Pollux had been thoughtful, and he spoke now rather like an echo.

— What you are implying, Jason, is that your wise choice had little to do with us your friends, the twin sons of the king of Sparta, beyond getting our brief assistance. At the same time, your choice does have to do with engaging the twins who are always with us, although rarely in balance—the mortal one and the immortal one. I speak of the invisible ones, you understand. One is limited and bound to earth while the other is connected to Olympus, the everlasting. The hands of each of these twins must lift the yoke that binds the bulls to the plow. Is this right?

— Yes, Pollux, I think so, providing that you realize that what must be yoked is the furious energy of the bulls when it comes charging us.

— How does one recognize this?

— It is full of earth's consuming, scorching fires. In the human bosom, one of these rages as envy of another's destiny while another flames up as insatiable desire. Ambition, cold-faced and hard, thrusts into life with its bull horns and lays its victims to either side indifferently. Oh, many fires assail our existence, my friends.

Castor was pacing restlessly. Now he stopped in front of Jason to direct his question.

— Come now, Jason. Pollux and I held the yoke, and you managed the yoking. The deed is done, isn't it? It's action that matters, action that makes the score. I wonder what old Aietes thought at the moment that we triumphed and the yoke was in place, the famous king sitting out there in all his dazzling armor, wearing his golden four-crested helmet. Only think of what a contrast you were—stripped to the waist, holding only the shield in front of yourself as you awaited the charge, and then how you bounced the beasts off that shield without giving an inch!

The three of them laughed in great relief while the twins slapped Jason on the back. Castor and Pollux took their leave now. Lingering near the *Argo*, Jason watched the sun go down as he reflected on the events that followed the extraordinary yoking. Reactions of elation, of dread, of trembling were still present, yet he felt the satisfying sense of a task completed. In his mind, he followed again the bull-driven plow down the great furrow, sweating and sowing the serpent teeth as it made its arduous way. Again he saw with terror how fighting warriors sprouted up from the furrow and opposed him. Then he remembered the great stone and the strange power that somehow emerged in him to hurl it. When he arose to return to the ship, he murmured to himself,

— Old forgotten serpent teeth that our journey here managed to bring to light. Still keen in their bite were the teeth I sowed in the furrow, and fighting men sprang up in deadly conflict. Because of Medea's wise counsel, I kept my distance. She told me to take up the great stone, and I did. I hurled it into their midst, and they turned against each other . . . It was the stone that turned the tide!

Medea and Hera Meet

Alone in her chamber, Medea paced back and forth as her mind replayed the extraordinary success of Jason's task of yoking and driving the bulls to the plow, carving out the fresh, long furrow in Ares's field. For a certainty, it would not have succeeded without her help, using Hekate's ointment. Again and again the spirit in her soared with drunken pleasure at the thought, and with the image of the *Argo*'s captain, her heart's passion rose like a strong tide. Stopping her pacing, she stared at the closed doorway where surely she heard a step at the threshold. She waited, but there was no knock, no call. She became aware of the sudden departure of her high and pleasant confidence as a change came over her and a vast apprehension descended over her spirit. At this very moment of panic, she heard a voice nearby, startling her.

— Medea! Daughter of Aietes, time is short, very short I tell you—too short indeed to be caught up in Jason's success on the meadow! Nor is there time for Aphrodite's sweet musings . . .

Medea, pale now, spoke half to herself.

— The voice is a stranger's, and yet there is something familiar about it . . . Lady, you speak with authority. Are you a queen come to our shores?

— Indeed. I am Hera.

— A goddess? Goddess Hera, all hail!

The figure, a radiant and queenly presence whose look was intent upon Medea, nodded in acknowledgment.

— Hear me, maiden. I have for some time watched over Jason's perilous voyage. He delights my heart, you see. The time is critical and this kingdom no longer safe, I tell you. Your father's anger rages, and besides, he recognizes your hand in the bull-yoking-plowing feat. Your very life is in jeopardy!

A look of incredulity was on the maiden's face as she shook her head slowly.

— Ah, Lady, I have long been assured that Father is extremely fond of me and of my sister likewise.

— Have you not clearly chosen Jason and his interests as dearer than your father and the kingdom? The tie with your father is broken, and your life is in jeopardy.

Pallor altered her face, and her eyes widened in fear at the words of the goddess. Trembling, she answered.

— Alas, what have I done! I have betrayed the life that has been dear to me. But I love Jason . . . My lady, you who are known to be so long faithful to Zeus, your lover, surely you can comprehend my love. How could I refuse to help the man I love?

— For this new love, I am not here to rebuke you. Not even do I judge you for forsaking your father and the kingdom.

— Forsaking Father? I shall honor both loves. This is my intention, and it is only reasonable.

— Look, Medea. Your reasoning is flawed. It is not possible to follow your father's way and Jason's simultaneously. Jason and Aietes remain in extreme opposition, far, far beyond compromise. The Fleece of Zeus has parted them like the falling of a sword that makes them enemies. Tell me at once without further delay, do you plan to help Jason face the dragon so that he can steal the Fleece at last?

— Yes. That I shall surely do!

The goddess walked back and forth, a frown on her brow as she considered the situation. Turning to Medea who watched her, she sighed and spoke quietly.

— Now Aietes regards himself as owner and ruler of the Fleece, ever since Phrixos sacrificed the golden ram to Zeus and hung the treasure upon the great oak in the sacred grove of this kingdom.

— That is so. Power is great with Father, as you know, and few ever have dared to challenge it. It never occurred to me before, but he is himself rather like your Zeus!

At these words, Hera drew in her breath sharply.

— No one is like Zeus, and least of all is your father, Aietes! Many try to imitate the lord of the gods but fail miserably. Aietes takes power to himself for his own benefit while Zeus shepherds all the race of mortals. Hear me, Medea, if you attempt to hold both your father and Jason close to your core, you shall be split apart. You must make a choice now. Other women can well retain love of father and spouse, but not you in your situation. Oh, I know that it will be exceedingly painful for you, my dear.

— Will the gods help me, my lady? Already you have counseled and companioned me. For this I am deeply grateful.

— There is another who takes your destiny to heart. That is Aphrodite. Without Aphrodite, who delights and lightens the heart, leaving father and companioning Jason will be impossible.

— So I must choose. This is what you are telling me.

The pallor left her face, and a new rosiness came to her cheeks while a slow smile played at her lips. Her voice when she spoke was no longer that of the distraught girl but the voice of woman.

— I go now to join Jason, departing forever my home! Lady Hera, I shall always be in debt to you for showing me the way to my true marriage!

Taking the Fleece

The Kolchian maiden Medea neither dawdled nor did she make haste to reach the creature's lair in the huge oak tree. Instead, she steadily advanced, penetrating the sacred grove that was uninhabited by a single human being. At a little distance behind her, Jason followed in grave dread. Aware of their entering its territory, the serpent, sleeplessly guarding the Fleece, hissed. Its unearthly voice filled the countryside with strange echoes. Still, Medea did not pause but quietly went forward until she stood in the very presence of the huge serpent. The undulating coils lay all about him and struck terror in Jason's spirit. As Medea cast her eyes upon the serpent, she was without fear or demand as her large eyes held its gaze. As the text of the *Argonautica* reads, "In sweet tones she called on Sleep, supreme among the gods."

— O Hypnos, do come and close the eyes of this weary guardian of the great Fleece. Bring him the all-pillowing rest! Lady Hekate, my faithful goddess, come with your torch and indicate the path for us through the impenetrable dark!

She spoke quietly to the serpent now, drizzling a magical potion over his head. At once, the air was filled with an overpowering fragrance. She continued to speak.

— Never before in Aietes' kingdom have you ever rested in peace, great serpent. Do you not long for the return of that peace that nature bestowed upon you long ago? Breathe deeply of my fragrance as I summon that peace. Ah, you find it enticing, satisfying . . . Always in my land you have served the ruling power. Did this not render the Fleece of the gods impotent? Sleepless, fiercely guarding you have been, but through the art that Hekate has disclosed to me, you shall be free, I tell you. Your eyes have closed. Ah, may you sleep in peace now . . . Come, Jason, do you see there upon the great branch of the tree a golden dawn, radiant and splendid? Like a forbidden fruit of immense delight it is! Ah, the Fleece shall be ours!

As Medea observed the guardian serpent closely, her serene confidence never failing, Jason was tense like one ready to leap when the signal to action comes. Deep slumber overtook the fearsome creature now, and Medea whispered the word "Now!"

At Medea's signal, Jason climbed into the old tree's high branches, which bent deeply with his weight. Now independent of his movement, the tree registered a mighty tremor as if remembering a long turbulence of spirit. Instinctively, his right hand went to the weapon on his hip as he regarded the sleeping serpent, resting there for a tense moment. To slay or else to spare the serpent? The fateful choice of the hero descended on him with an incredible weight. Remembering the serene countenance of Medea, however, he chose to spare the fierce guardian. Now he extended both arms gently toward the glowing bed of the serpent and gathered to himself the entire Golden Fleece. Holding it against his bosom, he felt a current of life at once sheltering and radiant, for surely the Fleece was the great gift of the gods. And Jason dropped his chin into the ram's wool in deep tribute before raising his face to Medea with a triumphant smile.

Jason and the Desert Goddesses

Laden with excellent gifts, the Argonauts boarded the *Argo* and departed the land of the benevolent Phaiakians. For a time, the sea appeared mildly disposed so that their voyage was serene. But a change came over the waters. Fierce winds assaulted them causing huge waves, and for nine days, the sea raged under a fierce tempest. Would their treasured cargo, the Golden Fleece itself, ever make it safely home to Thessaly? Worry was on every face as the men struggled to keep the *Argo* afloat. At the end of the ninth day, a huge wind seized them and drove them high upon a desolate beach on a far Libyan shore. Springing from the *Argo*, they gazed at the uninhabited shore with horror, as, under the gloomy sky and against a far ridge of dark hills, a vast landscape stretched before them with no sign of herds, of men, tracks, or oases. A brooding silence descended over the Argonauts as they viewed the desolation. Ankaios, the steersman, addressed his comrades,

— This is ruin for us! Even if a good wind should blow, there's no way we can sail from this shore. Look at how shallow the water is and how it's full of treacherous shoals!

Not one man disagreed with the outlook. Words rang out in misery instead.

— After all our toil in getting the Fleece, Zeus will not fulfill our day of returning!

Every man wept, and his spirit became as desolate as the Libyan Desert itself. Each took his mantle then and, choosing a solitary spot at a little distance from his comrades, covered his head to await certain death.

Jason sat motionless, gazing at his comrades in despair. High on the beach, the *Argo* herself was cloaked in solemn abandonment, and her plight brought sharp grief to his heart. He thought of Athena and how distant the beloved goddess seemed now, she who had lifted them out of crisis when they were faced by the Crashing Rocks. With a deep sigh, he now covered his head. A brief time passed under the dark mantle before he heard the sound of soft steps approaching. Still he remained motionless. Now he sensed the touch of an unseen hand that was gently lifting the mantle from his head. Fully exposed now, he found himself face-to-face with three tall women cloaked in goatskins. Speechless, Jason gasped in astonishment as he took in the large intelligent eyes that were studying him, and the figures spoke.

— We are guardians of Libya. Sheepherding goddesses we are. Even so, observe that our voices are human.

At once Jason made the sacred gesture, dropping his eyes. Belatedly he rose to his feet. He spoke now, although his voice was hoarse.

— And we are the Argonauts, who have won back the Golden Fleece that was lost to the Greeks. But the gods fell silent. They have abandoned us on this desolate shore, as you see.

— Why suspect the gods' voices to be at fault when the crisis lies rather in your hearing? Hear us, Jason. We are shepherdesses.

Jason found himself staring at their rough garments.

— Why, you are covered from head to foot with the hides of goats!

The goddesses' reply struck the leader of the expedition as an enigma.

— Remember this fact and honor the goat, we counsel you. The goat forever guards what nature knows.

Jason shook himself and began to feel alive again as he replied.

— I perceive such knowledge in you, Goddesses, for you are gentle in nature and of a mind not easily distracted—stubborn, as we say, like a goat. Surely you must have a history of enduring under difficult and trying conditions, surviving on this desert land as you do.

His companions smiled for the first time.

— So you see this? It is well. Then you are ready to receive our message, for it is indeed urgent. Here is our message:

Enough of this self-pity! Arouse the Argonauts at once. As soon as sea goddess Amphitrite unyokes the swift chariot of Poseidon, you must set yourselves to offer full recompense to your mother for all the long pains she suffered while carrying you in her belly. Only then shall you return home to Achaia!

Jason strode back and forth before the three goddesses, torn between incredulity and perplexity on the one hand and gratitude to the shepherdesses on the other.

— This sounds strange to my ears. Surely being carried in my mother's belly is a long-forgotten event. How can remembering it help us in our crisis?

— Ah, Jason, is it that you are waiting for some straightforward scheme of cause and effect to rescue you, one that calls forth the heroes' skill and cleverness? This is not to be.

Now Jason was not one to be led down a strange and circuitous path for long. He pressed his advisers.

— Then I implore you to tell me how to set about paying back my mother for bearing me!

The tall immortal women turned aside to speak quietly together. Now they turned back to Jason.

— You must recollect the womb, that is, recollect what being carried in the womb taught you. You have not always been the hero with well-honed will and driving purpose. Before you became a hero, you were life, full and innocent of all contracts as you were serenely sheltered and safely carried.

— Wait, Goddesses. The manner in which I was carried in the belly of my mother constitutes some important knowledge? The simple facts are that my mother was pregnant with me and there was apparently nothing unusual in my birth.

The three stately figures shook their heads somberly as they gazed at him.

— No? Ah, what a pity that recollection is closed to you, hero. It is the mind that is mother that you must recollect, that mind that companions the womb. When life brings a fateful pause upon a man, one like abandonment on the Libyan Desert, then it is the mother knowledge that holds the secret of life that emerges.

A look of helplessness showed briefly on Jason's face, followed by a movement that indicated a growing exasperation.

— Great guardian ladies of Libya, I fail to comprehend! What you say makes no sense to me, I am afraid.

The three figures exchanged looks of grave concern. Tallest of the three, the middle one, was spokesman now.

— The great Mother has many faces. Most of these go unacknowledged since in general people have greater regard for their self-reliance if the image of Mother is left out. Unlike many of the assets we prize, Mother cannot be achieved. Nor like a foreign princess can she be won.

Jason sighed aloud and sank down upon a boulder.

— Speak to me, if you will, about the many faces of Mother. I expect I should be forewarned.

— Always she precedes you, for she is first. She is there before you became a glimpse in her mind or a seed in her belly. She is like earth, the ground, the source that gives you flesh, embodies you in life. As the old tales taught us, first there was earth, and then heaven came into being and mated with earth.

Jason was on his feet again, a new energy rising in him. He strode back and forth as he spoke.

— It is strange, but as you were speaking, something in me was altered. Could it be the hero? A tension passes out of me. What I sense is something close to calmness. I realize that I, Jason, am *derivative* somehow. Also I see that once again I am to be derived from Mother here on this desolate land. Strangely, an invisible womb encloses me. Can it be that I am about to move out of the unmade into a new making? The notion astonishes me.

The goatskin-clad goddesses heard these words with satisfaction. Jason returned to practical considerations.

— Now you must instruct me. How am I to recompense my mother, how to carry her, as you indicate?

— Coming out from under the death mantles, all the Argonauts must now undertake to be protector of Mother. Indeed, as you journey inland, all of you must become as Mother, for with every step you take over our parched soil, you shall carry her, you shall bear her full weight. You yourselves are to be the pregnant ones. Mother will be borne aloft and thus tended and honored. As you go, sing her gratitude. In this way you shall be saved from desolation and the death that threatens you. Go well, Jason!

When Jason raised his eyes, he saw that the benevolent shepherd goddesses had departed. It was Peleus who approached him now, so that at once Jason shared all the words of the goddesses. Peleus nodded and responded.

— Jason, you know what they are talking about, surely. The *Argo* is our mother! She has faithfully carried us in her belly, sheltering our long journey to win back the Fleece!

Jason nodded gravely. Now he responded, and his energy seemed that of a man who, contrary to the facts, had been both feasted and well rested. His voice overflowed with excitement as he spoke.

— Let's call all the men out from under their mantles now! We'll lift the *Argo* upon all our shoulders and carry her inland on this new journey.

We'll find a navigable body of water that will take us then out to sea. I am sure of it! These goddesses knew what they were talking about, Peleus.

Before they could act, they sat for a long pause in silence while they gazed toward the *Argo* in gratitude. And they remembered her sacred keel.

PART XIV

Perseus

Perseus Meets Athena

Perseus, exile of the royal house of Argos, sought shelter from the fierce wind that had blown relentlessly for two days since his encounter with the old crones, the Graeae. Within the rock grotto, he began at once to make supper of bread and cheese, for he was ravenously hungry as well as exhausted. Sighing with the primitive satisfaction of being fed, he gazed out of the mouth of the grotto to the sea below the steep cliff and was surprised to the see the flash of a white garment in the fading dusk. *A traveler in this desolate spot at this hour?* He waited, musing on his own wanderings when someone approached on the cliff's narrow path. A tall woman of lively step stopped a few feet from the grotto entrance. Recognition came with astonishment.

— Why, can it be you, Goddess Athena? You found this spot at the end of the world?

There was a slight smile on the luminous face as the woman replied.

— Greetings, Perseus. The end of the world? It is possible that such an end is a beginning.

Perseus shook his head, puzzled by the response as he made the invitation with a gesture of welcome.

— Come into the grotto out of the wind, Lady Athena.

Athena entered, and the voice that had seemed somewhat remote now took on a close-at-hand companionable quality.

— So far, as I have observed, you have made your way without faltering, son of Zeus. Tell me, when will you reach the Gorgon sisters?

Perseus sighed.

— Each day I hope that that meeting will not be before tomorrow.

Grimace was in his voice, and she nodded in understanding.

— Indeed you have reason to dread such an encounter.

Now the goddess manifested her knowledge of the prudent action, for did not one come to discover her as goddess of the next step?

— The dread that lays hold of you is to be expected, Perseus. The Gorgons are old in their power and can easily take charge of a person. In their presence, one can come to believe that they know best.

Perseus listened, and the face of the son of Danae was solemn.

— What do you advise then?

— I have come to protect you, and not much time remains for action. Pick up my shield, will you?

At once he picked up the great bronze shield, so beloved by the Athenians, and laid it between them on the grotto's stone floor. He gazed at her anxiously.

— I hope that there is not a sudden need for it at hand?

Athena sought to reassure the hero.

— Listen well, son of Danae. You have looked upon the world in a way that has been fresh-faced and welcoming for the most part, as you have shown your passion for life. This is the way of *the first look*. One is not fully alive if he is indifferent or else careless with the first look. Ah, but engaging the first look makes one exceedingly vulnerable. Why else do the afflictions of childhood and youth mark one so deeply? Were you not gravely afflicted when your grandfather, King Acrisius, put you and your mother into a rudderless boat and pushed you out to sea? What a dark day that was.

Perseus' face registered the familiar bitter memory.

— The grim tale you tell, Lady Athena, has been my life, but what has it to do with going to meet Medusa, the Gorgon?

— Precisely everything. Exposed to life in the course of the first look, one can become captive of a misfortune experienced. One becomes paralyzed. Such a paralyzing occurs when Medusa's look falls upon oneself.

Every thought and act of one's life appears to circle around the earlier dark happening and is deformed by it. One is Medusa's victim.

— If I am under Medusa's power, as you suggest that I am, why of all people am I chosen to challenge her in her dwelling place?

— Do not underestimate the gods, Perseus. You are well chosen, believe me. There is hope. Look again upon my shield, for it holds your answer. It reveals the way beyond the first look.

— How can that be?

— It is my shield that holds in reserve a response to the second look that is to come.

Perplexity was in Perseus' attentive gaze at the shield.

— I can see that its splendid shining surface is like a mirror, rather like gazing into a different world. Hmm. What do you know? Your entire figure, Goddess, is reflected in the bronze as you stand against the high stone wall of the grotto.

— You observe well. The shield, when you keep your eyes trained upon it, is able to contain the coming crucial encounter as it happens. It will bring about the second look with its sustained light. Even so, this glimpse will seem less bright and less clear than the intellect had hoped for.

Perseus Slays Medusa

His stride revealed an unusual energy, and his face held the decisiveness, keen as it was comely, of the hero moving toward his task as he approached the far wilderness. On his head, he wore the odd Cap of Hades, for so it was called by the generous nymphs who had given it to him in the land of the Hyperboreans. "It will render you invisible to all observers except for the gods, Perseus," they had explained. In his left hand, he carried the treasure of Athens—Athena's own shield, lent to him by the goddess. He had just been joined by two tall companions. They were none other than the gods Athena and Hermes. Perseus spoke candidly.

— What a godforsaken land we have come to!

Athena looked puzzled.

— How can it be godforsaken when Hermes and I are here on the path?

— A slip of the tongue, Goddess. Actually, I can't tell you how glad I am for the company of both of you Olympians. Athena, you have spoken to me about madness, saying that I must act to save the human world from madness.

— This is the only way. For some time, I have considered the remedy, you see. When the hero Heracles went mad and would have slain Amphitryon of Thebes, what I did was to throw a stone at him. The stone brought him to himself, and thereafter it was revered as the Sober Stone.

— If you've got an extra one of those, do throw it at the mad Gorgon. Will you?

Athena regarded Perseus closely, shaking her head slightly.

— No. With Medusa, it will not work.

— Are you saying that she must die then?

The two gods exchanged glances, but it was Athena who, sighing, answered.

— She must die. When you come upon Medusa, the only mortal one of the Gorgons, hold my bronze shield out like a mirror to catch her image. Remember that you under no circumstances must look upon the Gorgon. Instead, gazing at her mirrored image, you must cut the head clean from the neck.

Had Athena not given him these instructions before? Hearing them in the land of the Gorgons struck him with a chill and dread, however. Hermes was assessing the hero, seeking to determine his ability to stick to the plan. He spoke as if they had been in the middle of a conversation.

— There is a contagion in madness, you see. The opinions of the mad are invasive and toxic indeed. How easily one is tempted to believe that only others are mad while oneself is quite immune to the possession.

Perseus was confident.

— Count on me to keep my eyes on the great shield of Athena, Lord Hermes.

— Good. Now here is my sickle, which I am lending you as well. You are going to need it.

— Oh, what a beauty it is. Is it new?

— Actually it is quite old. This is fortunate since it possesses a long memory of harvesting as well as cutting away any excess that obstructs the way. The time calls for this harvest sickle.

— But it is not the season of harvest. The sickle perplexes me.

— To use the deadly sickle at will is perilous, but the time is ripe for the deed. I must warn you that only a narrow slot in time opens for this deed. Let me show you how to grasp it. It is unlike the sword, for you must not cut away from yourself but toward yourself.

— Why, I could die before Medusa meets her death!

— Not if you attend to the way of the sickle. The harvest must fall at your feet.

Athena added a last admonition.

— Pull the Cap of Hades well down upon your brow, and you will be invisible to the Gorgon sisters. It is your needed protection. Hermes, have you not often worn this cap yourself?

— When the crucial act needed to remain hidden, yes, I have worn Hades' cap.

Perseus found Hermes' account of the cap somewhat disconcerting. He protested.

— There is something else involved, surely. Doesn't my action have to show forth to everyone in order to make a difference? Why else risk being a hero?

Hermes smiled, appearing for the moment somewhat amused before responding.

— Oh yes, no worry there. Your deed will make a major difference. In fact, it is worth a great deal. Go to it now, Perseus!

Athena added a reminder for her peace of mind.

— And do not forget that you serve the gods in this undertaking.

— With the gods' sickle in hand, I go now toward a strange harvest. Perceiving the meaning of this task of mine will come in time, I suspect.

Alone now, Perseus set out on the path that penetrated the dense wilderness. At times he made his way through mist and fog, and he became anxious that the sun might go down before he reached the place of the Gorgon sisters. For certain, he needed light to accomplish his task. Now the sounds of voices—shrill, raucous, and sometimes plaintive—reached his ears. He stopped to listen. Yes, the voices were feminine, yet he could not discern their words. When the voices ceased, Perseus moved forward into the gloom and came upon the Gorgon sisters huddled upon the ground, their monstrous presence shadowy. He recognized the youngest, who sat a little apart, her head bowed and swaying in a circular movement. At once he held the bronze shield so as to catch her full reflection upon it. Slowly he raised his right arm holding the legendary sickle, at the same time bending from the waist and spreading his legs wide as a man ready to harvest the grain. He raised his voice now in a deep, full cry that filled the air and echoed from the rocks as his eyes stayed focused upon the shield.

— Medusa, I have come! I am Perseus, son of Zeus and Danae. The gods Athena and Hermes have sent me to perform this deed. Hear me. It will cure the madness that plagues you!

With these words, he brought the adamantine sickle down in a mighty thrust that severed Medusa's head clean from the neck. Eyes still focused upon the mirrored scene in the shield, he took the head and placed it within the leather pouch, which he wore on his back, and turned and fled down the path. Their realm violated, an enormous howl of rage and anguish arose from the two remaining sisters, and they set out in pursuit of the Argive hero. But Perseus remained invisible to their eyes since he was wearing the Cap of Hades. After some time, they lost all signs of him, and Perseus moved on to find Athena and to present her with the serpent-coiled head of Medusa.

Athena appeared at the side of the dead body of Medusa, and she was alone.

Over her arm she carried the sacred goatskin of Amalthea, nurse of infant Zeus. Now, she laid a tender hand upon either shoulder of the beheaded Gorgon and spoke.

— It is the awesome hour of birth. How difficult is the passage between the consuming darkness and the hour of beginning!

With these enigmatic words, the goddess raised the goatskin Aegis over the body of Medusa. In that moment, as if summoned, an armed warrior was born from the gaping neck womb, leaping to the ground. Athena addressed him.

— Chrysaor, welcome to earth! You shall prove valiant in conflict. Go on your way with my good will.

No sooner did Chrysaor depart with energetic stride on the path that led out of the home of the Gorgons than the body of Medusa heaved a second time, and there leaped forth from the neck womb a shining white horse. Incredibly, he was winged and powerful. Athena nodded, satisfied in her expectation as she addressed the beautiful horse.

— Ah, son of Poseidon and Medusa, it shall not be sufficient for you to roam on earth. No. Rising upon your wings, you shall ascend between the human realm and the gods, coming and going at will. O winged Pegasus, for you I shall create the beautiful bridle in time. At hand, the task is completed, separating out from madness two shining births to life.

Athena continued to stand beside fallen Medusa. As she contemplated the strange and difficult passage she had witnessed, she took from her flowing peplos two vials. With care she filled one vial with blood from one side of the bloody neck while the other she filled with blood from the other artery. She spoke quietly, although no hearer was present.

— Here I hold in my right hand the vial of Medusa's blood, and it shall forever have the power to heal. I shall put it into the hand of Asklepios, for is he not the god who heals? As for the vial of my left hand, its blood also shall endure but shall carry the power to destroy. This vial

I shall entrust to the king of Athens. O House of Erechtheus, receive this gift but use it with grave forbearance. This is my counsel.

Remaining in this dreaded place, Athena's face was solemn as she continued to regard Medusa in death. At last she spoke, and her voice was tender.

— Medusa, your anguish is overcome. Most important, the madness is ended. Still, your difficult ordeal shall be honored, for your head shall find its abiding place at the center of the goatskin Aegis. There it shall rest for all time. Looking upon your face, the Greeks shall not forget the dark struggle. *Alas, that life's frenzy and human wisdom eat from the same bowl!*

With these ambiguous words, the goddess fell silent. When she spoke, it was in afterthought.

— It is the Aegis worn upon my bosom that will summon the Greeks, for through me they will seek the reconciling balance which alone brings peace.

A woman paced back and forth before the temple of Athena. She had watched the slow-moving procession of warriors, hoplites, horse-drawn chariots, and people on foot, making its way up the steep Sacred Way. In the midst of the procession, there was the boat wagon bearing like a white sail the new peplos for Athena. With loving hands, the garment was lifted and carried into Athena's very old temple as her annual gift. The peplos, exquisite in its handiwork, was of the hue of golden crocus and was woven with scenes of the lives of gods, heroes, and memorable individuals. Slowly the woman entered the temple and made her way toward the holy wooden image of the goddess. Burning in her like the flame of the altar lamp was her desire to speak with Athena. In a low voice she began to speak.

— How beautiful you are, Goddess Athena, in your splendid new robe! In the dusk the peplos glows like a fallen sun within your house.

A slight movement upon the disk of the shield of Athena, resting against the goddess, drew the woman's attention.

— What's this? Why, the sacred snake is circling the shield, pausing to raise his head and to stare into its dusky mirror!

The woman was astonished when Athena's voice was heard, preceded by a distinct sigh.

— The snake knows that only lately, the deep sorrow of woman was mirrored there.

— What woman was this?

— The human soul's unworkable dwelling place: she is called Medusa.

Momentarily visible through her wooden image, the face of Athena held sadness. Instinctively, the woman's glance went to the Aegis that covered the goddess's bosom.

— Ah, it is Medusa's head that hangs there. I recognize the wild, dark eyes that regard me. O Medusa, something terrible has happened to you, I believe. Do you still suffer the consuming madness?

Her voice held the pain of one who suffers for her friend. In this moment, a young woman stood at her side, and she was beautiful. It was Medusa herself, and she addressed the woman.

— You behold the hideous head upon the sacred Aegis. Yes, it is mine. It was a fate I could not escape.

Facing the woman, her eyes solemn in their sorrow, she described that fate.

— The Argive hero, Perseus, that son of Zeus, beheaded me!

— Oh, sad, sad loss, my friend!

Medusa reassured her, surprisingly.

— Do not grieve for me. You see, the madness is gone.

— Do you mean to say that this human affliction shall never occur again?

— Ah, only Athena can answer that question, woman.

Although she remained invisible, Goddess Athena herself spoke to the two women.

— Hear me. So long as you remain under the Aegis, madness shall not overtake you.

The woman pressed the goddess.

— Why is it, Lady Athena, that you chose to hang the dead head of Medusa at the center of the sacred Aegis? At best, it is a gruesome ornament.

— It belongs here now, and it is not an ornament. The Gorgon's head communicates a truth that is dual, one not easily told. On the one hand, it reminds everyone who looks upon it that there is a grave limitation in the nature of things.

— You speak of some boundary an individual cannot exceed?

— Yes. The dead Medusa head of madness is a *no* that the gods have spoken.

The maiden Medusa spoke now, her voice anxious.

— The *no* of the gods causes me to tremble afresh! Is there no more palatable truth to be told? Is there something that can yet illuminate my dark passage?

Attentive to the cry of a Greek in distress, Athena answered,

— There is the other powerful truth as well, I assure you. It is deeply sewn now into the goatskin and shall remain there. Worn on my breast, the head of Medusa proclaims a safe and satisfying passage for the passions that otherwise can overwhelm human existence. The perspective of the gods is reaffirmed, you see. Oh yes. There is a luminous continuity that unites what has been, is, and shall be. This continuity is the meaning of existence. Even so, the path the person follows passes through a dark struggle.

The woman shook her head from side to side in perplexity.

— Listening to you, Goddess, it seems that the dead Medusa backed by the Aegis marks a kind of gateway through which we can pass safely. Without it, we fall into all sorts of excess and crazy action.

Athena nodded slowly.

— There is a certain sacrifice. It is necessary. Apollo holds the wisdom of this when he says at Pytho on Parnassus, "Nothing in excess!"

The voice fell silent, and the woman found herself again solitary. Now she sang an ode to Athena, and her voice shed its complaint as well as the urgent need of her mind, above all else, to accommodate the demands of human reason.

Medusa and the Woman

An Athenian woman climbed the Acropolis in Athens and made her way to the ancient temple of Athena. Entering the shelter of the columns, she paused to recover her breath and to wipe her forehead, aware of the summer day's heat. When she had entered the dim interior, she found herself alone as she approached the holy image of Athena. Her attention was upon the breast of the goddess, which was amply covered by the great goatskin aegis. From the center of the Aegis protruded a shaggy head wreathed in serpents with a wild-eyed broad face staring forth. The woman trembled under the impact of the grim encounter. As for Medusa on the Aegis, she held the observer's gaze and would not let her go. In that moment, the woman became aware of her own duality, for she was the captive observer and, at the same time, the responding woman. After an interval of time, it was the observer that seemed to expire. Left in her place was the woman alone. Aware of a hidden floor where some kinship lay, the woman spoke aloud.

— Alas, sad, sad head of woman, you afflict me! Your great dark eyes regard me steadily. They say, "What do you know of suffering?" Yet you are all unspokenness. Your eyes accuse me, and the writhing serpents intimidate me. If I remain here, patient and listening, I wonder if you might speak to me . . . or is speech also fallen into your abyss of silence?

From the head of Medusa came a soft, low groan. The woman felt a faint stirring of eagerness.

— You are alive then?

A low whispering made its way through a far corridor.

— Was that the whispering among the boughs of the sacred olive tree, I wonder? Surely, Medusa, Goddess Athena has not taken your voice from you.

At last the whispered words became discernible.

— My voice climbs, climbs upward.

— From where does it come?

— From the abyss, the black abyss!

— Oh, do leave that place for it can't be healthy for a person, surely!

There was a lengthy pause. The rasping voice when it came sounded resentful.

— Why have you summoned me?

— I can't say except that, looking on your face, I perceive a prisoner.

— Ah, you recognize me, do you? Yes, I have long been a prisoner.

— Look. I don't believe you to be evil, Medusa.

— What am I?

— Why, misunderstood . . . yes, long misunderstood and rejected as well.

A sigh arose from the Gorgon head.

— Ah, your words are a balm poured over me!

— Strangely I feel some shift occurring, and it is welcome. Medusa, we shall speak as woman to woman now.

Small sounds not unlike sobs emerged from the region of Athena's breast. The woman pressed the captive now.

— Tell me about your fate, Medusa.

— It won't take long. It is this: *to love and be damned!*

This declaration caused the woman to cry aloud as if struck by a blow.

— Wait. True love is known to be a blessing, surely.

— No! Love is my curse! It overtook me—a heady thing that fed and filled me and took away my taste for every ordinary and familiar thing I knew. Like an ecstasy it was, and it took me over. With glee I cried, "All the world is mine!" And it was.

The woman's eyes grew large with astonishment.

— What man was your lover then?

— You don't know? My lover was not a man. What woman would pick a man when there was a splendid god about?

Her voice held scorn. Now she confessed.

— Poseidon himself was my lover, woman.

— The great god of the everlasting waters?

— The same. He moved with the arched grace of galloping stallions, their mouths foaming like sea waves, I tell you! How could I resist him, I ask you, for you look like a reasonable woman?

— Oh, but how mighty is the sea, Medusa, and besides, Poseidon is brother of Zeus. Awe would have been more prudent than passionate desire, I do believe.

— An ardent lover is too busy for awe, I tell you. I had beauty, and I had my lover, period. It was a golden world that I entered. How his image haunts me, for Poseidon is kingly! Again I see his strong bronze shoulders as he strides beside the sea, his dark locks whirled about by the wind. The dark eyes flash under the heavy brows as they regard me. Ah, the memory of his laugh breaking free, spilling over us joyfully like a buoyant wave on the seashore!

Medusa's face changed, softening with grief. The woman regarded her wonderingly.

— Was Lord Poseidon drawn to you because he found you beautiful then?

— No, no. That's the wrong order. Of this I am certain. I wasn't beautiful, you see, but Poseidon came and he beheld what hadn't been there before. Then I became beautiful!

— What a strange tale. Did the beauty remain—even when the god had departed?

— Yes, indeed. The beauty remained so long as the love lasted.

Her last words were spoken in a faltering voice, ending with a sob. After a deep sigh she spoke again.

— What happened was that Athena came to the temple and dropped this dark fate upon me, punishing me.

— Was it Athena's doing? We Greeks believe that it is the Fates who deal out one's lot.

For a long moment Medusa looked confused. She stared into the past as she spoke.

— I witnessed Athena's wrath for violating her temple. There's no question that this dark fate that swept me up was the goddess's doing. Why, the golden world that I thought was mine cracked and heaved and fell apart!

— And Poseidon did not rescue you . . . .

Medusa's reply was spoken with a deep groan.

— No.

— You speak of your good fortune and a woman's happiness. So, why are you so dreary about it?

— Why? You ask me why? If you don't know the answer, woman, then you too can fall into love's black place, I tell you.

With some alarm the woman realized that she was being warned.

— Tell me what happened to you.

— Well, as the excited cry kept ringing inside me, "The world is mine!" I drew my lover to me inside Athena's temple. After all, why not show the goddess what a divine gift looks like up close? So my lover and I made love before the holy image of Athena.

Astonishment overtook the woman, and was quickly followed by horror.

— You made love before Virgin Athena?

— We did. What, after all, is more worthy of adoration and praise than love?

— You thought you were *instructing* Athena?

— Yes. Now Goddess Aphrodite knows all about the realm of love's great pleasure, but what does Athena know? She adores harnessing the ox to the plow, making pots, weaving cloth, and leading warriors into battle. All work and no play she is! Woman, I tell you that there is not one ounce of ecstasy in any of Athena's gifts.

Medusa shook her head from side to side in amazement.

The woman had received the whole of this explanation incredulously.

— So you had in mind to share this love of yours with the goddess?

— *Share* it? Ha, no woman would ever share her lover. It's true that I failed to bring an offering to Athena, but as for my love, it was for me alone. Can you understand this? A woman is hardly in love if she finds she can give some of the love away.

— You make a woman in love sound really quite desperate.

— Love makes a woman that way. She narrows down the choices.

— Some further happening took place that landed you in your present predicament, I believe. Did your making love call Athena to the scene?

— It did, all right. Woman, I was totally unprepared for her anger. Why, she took it as an outrage that we had made love in her temple before her sacred image.

— O Medusa, surely you were more bold than wise!

— Why, Athena herself is bold in deed, you must admit. Well, her wrath fell upon me. It undid me. Lifting my face to her bright eyes, I saw that she would not forgive me.

— Alas, what a fate to suffer! When did you know that you were changed?

— When I looked into my mirror, I saw the Gorgon face, and it froze me! Why, where had all my beauty gone? Only my large dark eyes stared from the face. The thick, curly locks writhing about my head became snakes, and when I spoke, a bitter litany issued from my voice. Grief and anger alike seized me, and a vast gloom enveloped me. From that time, I've been flung about in a dizzy cycle of love's fragments, its disappointments, its aching need.

— Oh how you have suffered, Medusa, I can hardly imagine!

A silence fell over the two figures, and as it extended itself, it became like a welcoming room whose dim interior was penetrated now by a small steady stream of light. It was Medusa, her voice calm now, who spoke.

— Strangely, I came to see something else in Athena's eyes.

— Oh, what was it?

— For a long strangely sustained moment, I glimpsed in Athena's eyes my life stretched out. Why, it was like a cloth being worked on the loom, a cloth I saw that she fancied somehow. I couldn't see it up close, you understand. In that long moment, I was fully persuaded of this fact, however:

Athena has seen the whole of my life's cloth, and she treasures it!

— For certain, the women of Athens honor Athena as goddess of the whole cloth that's finely worked. When you perceived the cloth, what then?

— In that same moment, I knew that I had lost my way!

A look of profound sympathy was in the gaze of the woman now.

— Medusa, Medusa, hear me. Athena is known for her mercy.

— Woman, you don't understand. Remorse is unknown to me, and I cannot ask to be pardoned.

— Whatever you do, do not betray the treasured cloth!

With these words flung into the echoing silence of the temple, the woman turned from the Aegis and departed.

PART XV

Heracles

Heracles and the Hydra

Dusk was settling over the countryside, and Lerna's wide marsh was just visible in the midst of the green plain as the two drew up in the chariot. Iolaus laid down the reins and sighed audibly. It had been a tedious, hot journey southward from Tyrins. Both men gazed at Lerna with her abundant springs pouring forth from the earth, filling the air with the sound of rushing waters. They had reached the northern boundary of the great marsh of Lerna, dark and brooding, a vast spread of watery waste that greeted every traveler who came here. Heracles took up his lion's cloak, the club, and bow and quiver as well. Leaving the chariot, the two struck out on foot, following close to the great marsh's edge. Uppermost in their minds was the fact that the second labor imposed by King Eurystheus lay before them. Slaying the lion of Nemea, as the hero looked back on it, seemed child's play compared to what lay before them in the marsh. He smiled grimly as he spoke.

— A shallow but a deadly place for sure, Iolaus.
— There's no denying it. Look, there's a thousand watery eyes gleaming out of what might be huge patches of green scales! You know, that could be your monster right there. Let's hope you're not planning on spending any time here. Well, are you?

Asking the question, he shivered.

— At this northern edge of the marsh, no. I suggest we skirt it, moving along its western boundary while there is still a little light. I need to track the marsh closely. Watch out, our steps can be treacherous. Listen, will you, for any movement within these dark waters.

They stopped and listened in the vast silence. Iolaus made his report.

— Nothing I can hear . . . The place must be alive with snakes, and what is quieter than a snake, I ask you? By the way, there is a tale that says there's a nine-headed monster living in this marsh, and it is known to devour cattle and sheep and crops. You don't believe this, do you, Heracles?

— That would be the Hydra, and she is female. Look, I am not into believing or disbelieving, Iolaus. I am into checking out the facts.

   Iolaus's reply to this held a mournful tone.

— You do go after dreadful things all right and never let up until you've done them in. Not me. I'm out for the adventure, to watch how things go.

— The observer, that's what you are then.

— That's right. I certainly don't intend to get any closer to this foul marsh.

— I could envy you, my friend, being the observer, that is. Say, do you suppose she hangs around the spot where the great springs pour forth?

— Do I suppose *who* hangs around?

— Hydra, of course.

— So you really believe that scary story?

— Someone has to check it out. The darkness has moved in swiftly, and there's no moon. Bad luck for us. Let's stay close to that rhythmic sucking and slurping of the waters. And for the love of Athena, watch out! Make sure each step you take is on solid ground.

— You're the one walking between me and that green hole of Hades, so you're the one to watch your step. What an awful thing it would be to lose shining Heracles to this grim place . . . By the way, where are we spending the night?

— There is not a soul living this close to the marsh to offer hospitality, I am afraid. Sorry about that, Iolaus.

— You might have thought of that before taking this route to Lerna!

— Don't worry. Aren't you the one who is out for adventure? Soon let's hope we find a spot to bed down for the rest of the night.

— A nice *dry* spot is what I'd like. I like my bed dry, see?

   Heracles laughed now.

— You know, it is good to have your company . . . . Now count ten steps due west . . . . Ah, here. This seems a good-enough spot to stretch out for a few hours. Good night.

— Wait a minute. What time is breakfast?

— Let me tell you that we must be off before light breaks, or the birds can announce our approach.

— I can see now that you are planning for us to sneak up on Hydra on an empty stomach!

    The hero smiled into the dense darkness.

— On the way, you can munch on bread and olives I brought along.

    It was only a matter of minutes before both men fell asleep.

Dawn on the Marsh of Lerna

    The land was still under the cloak of darkness when, awakening out of his dreamless sleep on the hard ground, Heracles raised himself on an elbow. On the eastern horizon, one could discern a thin line of light. Although wrapped in his lion pelt, he shivered in the bone-chilling air of the marsh. Now, getting to his feet, he called to Iolaus, and shortly the two men were once again silently edging their way around the marsh. From time to time they stopped to listen intently for movements in the marsh waters. Heracles spoke.

— Understandably, a person chooses to be the spectator of what happens, Iolaus. But you know, the Fates may determine otherwise.

— This is heavy talk before breakfast, I must say. Say, are you possibly telling me that you want my help if you meet Hydra?

— Something like that, but only if things get desperate. Have some olives and cheese.

    He offered the opened bag, grinning. Iolaus helped himself generously. Heracles continued.

— Here's the plan. First I'll go it alone, for this is my way, you see. Only when I begin to feel the weight of the task altogether on my shoulders is true strength summoned out of my core. This doesn't happen if from the beginning the task at hand is divided up among my comrades and me.

— What's this you're saying?

— That the son of Zeus is not a committee!

— Well, whoever said you were? I've watched how you go at things.

— Something else keeps returning to my mind. Iolaus, I am not sure that it is good to be led by the sense of adventure or the lure of exotic encounters.

— Look who's talking! When have you ever stood back from an adventure, I'd like to know?

— I know how it looks. True, the sense of adventure is not absent. Still, I have come to understand that I must not be *led* by it. It isn't the primary thing I am about.

Iolaus gazed at Heracles in astonishment, much as if he was seeing him for the first time.

— What is it that leads you toward one of these tasks then? I mean, what is it that really eggs you on?

— I thought that perhaps you knew. The answer is, Goddess Athena! It is what her owl eyes perceive that I serve. The path is laid out for me. It is not of my devising.

— Wait a minute. Aren't you forgetting something? It is Tyrins' king, Eurystheus, who has ordered you to perform the Twelve Labors.

— Of course. Yet it is only Athena who truly summons me. This I know. It is she who wants the Hydra slain, for she can never abide for long any devourer in the human situation.

— What you're telling me is that not even the son of Zeus goes it all alone. The goddess comes along . . .

The hero smiled slowly, pondering Iolaus's words.

— Well, yes. That is my good fortune. Even so, the summons that stirs in me addresses the solitary one. It cannot be otherwise.

They had half-circled the great marsh of Lerna when the sound of thundering waters reached them, for nowhere in the whole of Greece did the waters emerge out of the earth with such great force as the springs of Lerna. Poseidon himself had called them forth in a time when severe drought parched the region, and he did it for the sake of the maiden Amymone. Before them the great stone basins and channels received the outflow before overflowing the plain below, hollowing out the vast and treacherous marsh. Within this marsh lived the legendary Hydra with the nine monstrous heads. The outpouring deafened their ears, and they drank deeply of the pure, cool water. Straightening up, Heracles pointed silently to the rocky ridge above the source of the spring. Swiftly in the predawn dimness, they climbed to the ridge where the lair of Hydra surely lay. Heracles paid tribute to the spring as they went.

— I had to know the taste of the fabled water at the source, and what a source!

— How can that wonderful water turn into those foul marsh waters, I ask you? It's hard to believe.

— Shh. Quiet. Listen!

Ahead and to the right, a small cave could be seen having an entrance no more than three feet high. As they paused listening, they heard thrashing movements within followed by low, guttural sounds. Intermittently came strange moaning cries. They remained very still, Iolaus's eyes large with an emotion half fear and half anticipation. Heracles took charge in a whispered exchange.

— She is there all right. We have found her lair. Stay back, Iolaus.

— Look, you aren't planning to go into the cave, I hope. She is not my idea of hospitality.

Heracles took up the fine bow, which had been the gift of the god Apollo, and fitted an arrow to the bowstring as he edged nearer to the rocky lair.

— One thing more, Iolaus. Be an observer so long as you can!

With these enigmatic words, the hero moved stealthily toward the low cave. Kneeling before the entrance on one knee, he cried in a loud voice,

— Hydra, I am come! I'm son of Zeus and Alcmene. Come out of your lair and face Heracles!

Angry shrieks issued from the cave at once. Now at the opening, one head, beastly and wild-eyed, appeared upon an enormous serpentine neck, and Heracles, catlike, jumped back. Seeing an easy prey, Hydra opened her mouth hungrily, the jaws gaping, but she did not emerge. Heracles called out over the clamor of the hissings and raging shrieks.

— Hydra, powerful devourer, the gods have decreed that you must die! When the gods have decided, they will brook no delay, I tell you!

Two heads glared out from the rocky entrance, and now three, but still the creature did not leave her lair. Raising his bow, he shot a fiery arrow into one long neck and followed with a second arrow that lodged in the second neck. Seized with rage, Hydra slithered forth from the cave, and astonishment dealt Heracles a powerful blow as eight monstrous heads, raised tall as men, stood forth from eight erect necks. He comforted himself with the knowledge that the eight heads were mortal. But what of the ninth, which was said to be immortal . . . where was it hidden? He called to Iolaus now.

— It's good, Iolaus! Hand me my club.

— Here, take it. What's good? She is a terror to behold!

— Take my bow and quiver and the lionskin as well and stand clear, all right? This is it, my friend. This is our main chance.

Taking the club into his right hand, he lowered his head, eyes ever watchful of the encircling necks and their ghastly heads, the ravenous mouths. Slowly, relentlessly, he approached. A neck and head shot out to grab him, but he brought down a mighty blow to the head with his club, flattening it. Another neck shot out swiftly, more rageful than the first, the head screaming its fury. It met the same fate delivered by the club. Now an enormous tentacle reached out and took him by the waist into its vise, drawing him inexorably against Hydra's body. With arms free, however, he managed to club at the remaining heads with all his strength, pounding each one flat. To his horror, Heracles observed that with the death of each head, two new ones grew in its place upon the neck stem. Nor was Hydra without other resources. A huge crab, obviously her friend, arrived and bit him upon the foot before he managed to club it to death. Meanwhile, the eight destroyed heads had multiplied to sixteen, while the immortal head still lay in the center of the Hydra. Heracles felt a tide of despair rising in himself. Then an idea came to him, and he called to Iolaus.

— Light the torch quick, and bring it to me now! It's our only chance, Iolaus!

At once Iolaus went to the chariot to fetch the torch, murmuring to himself as he went, "O ye gods of Olympus, what am I doing here? I was only meant to drive the hero's chariot." Running to Heracles' side now with the torch in hand, he observed the hero panting hard as within the unearthly grip of Hydra, he wielded the club at the sixteen heads, one after the other. It was necessary to lean toward his face in order to catch his words, so faint they seemed.

— When I have flattened each head, you are to hold the torch to the neck stem. First we'll begin with the head on this tentacle that grips me without mercy . . . . There! The grip gives way. Iolaus, I am free! I can breathe again!

Adroitly moving from one flattened head to the next, Iolaus cauterized each serpent neck as if reviving some primitive, forgotten skill. One by one, neck by neck, the fire from his torch destroyed the regenerative power of the water monster. Now he commented.

— We'll not be seeing any more of this poisoner of the great waters. That's for sure.

Heracles was pale with exhaustion and barely able to speak the final instructions.

— We're finished, Iolaus. Let's get out of here. What I've witnessed in this place has struck me to the core!

Even as they turned away from Hydra in her destruction, the hero felt a familiar presence over his left shoulder. A voice addressed him, which he recognized as that of Athena herself.

— Well done, Heracles! It has been a life-and-death struggle against Hydra and against the grave sickness of the waters, and you showed courage!

— Oh, the stagnation that is worse than death! I'll never forget the horror of it. Once in Hydra's presence, I sensed the death of hope itself heavy upon the air . . . Well, now my task is completed.

Slowly Athena shook her head, and compassion was in her face as she responded.

— No. You are mistaken. It is not yet the end.

If the goddess had struck him with her hand, the blow could not have been greater.

— Not the end, Lady Athena?

— At present, you find yourself within the grateful pause, I should say. You see, there is the matter of the ninth head. I speak of the central one which was protected by the circle of heads. This single head remains.

— But that is surely the immortal head, as common knowledge has it. How am I expected to kill a thing that is immortal? That surely is not humanly possible.

— There is a way open to you. Even now before the sun rises, since this is not a deed of the day, you must take your sword, son of Zeus, and cut away the ever alive head of darkness. Once in hand, take it and plant it in the earth on the path that all travelers take who come to Lerna. Only act at once.

As she gazed at him, she saw that hope had again found a narrow path as a light shone in his eyes. He spoke breathlessly.

— I am on my way, Goddess. Will you remain close by a little longer? That is my hope.

Reaching the chariot where his helpful friend waited, he asked Iolaus to wait for him a little while, for he had a final task to perform alone. Taking his sword, he returned to the remains of Hydra. Seeing him approach, the ninth and only surviving head fixed a deadly stare upon him. Under the malignant force of its gaze, he felt his strength ebbing away. It was with great effort that he succeeded in averting the gaze, staring only at the point where the head met the neck. Taking aim at this single point, he struck with his sword decisively, and the ninth head fell to the ground, leaving Hydra altogether lifeless. He picked up the head by the hair, and turning his back on the rocky ridge, he descended to the travelers' road. Beside the road he dug with his sword a shallow grave and laid the immortal head therein, covering it quickly. Now he laid a boulder atop the small grave before leaving it.

In this way did Heracles act under the guidance of Athena and complete what came to be called for all time the Second Labor.

The Oracle's Counsel

Time had passed since the slaying of the Hydra of Lerna's great spring, and Heracles felt a satisfaction in having completed the second task of the labors laid upon him by King Eurystheus. And yet all was not well, for was he not saddled with the painful aftereffects, the multiple bites sustained from the deadly encounter with Hydra? Miserable with the festering wounds on his body, he journeyed northward, crossing the serene bay and making his way to Delphi under the craggy Phaedriades. He would consult the oracle. Nor did consulting the oracle amount to seeking an expert medical opinion, no. When Apollo spoke, one awaited the eagle-eyed perspective of the mind of Zeus himself.

Arriving in the early morning at the temple with its golden-hued columns, Heracles pressed his demand to be taken at once to the priestess, but was informed that he would have to wait out a whole day, this being the sixth day of the month. Pythia only received the oracle on the seventh day, the day holy to Apollo. When the seventh day dawned, the hero from Thebes was found early at the temple awaiting the moment that Pythia would receive him. The rays of the sun had not yet reached the summit of the rocky cliffs when word was brought that Pythia would receive him now. Leaving his friend Iolaus to wait under one of the laurel trees, he approached the door of the oracle chamber. Iolaus wondered how long it would take for the god to answer the question. Only an hour ago, Heracles had rehearsed his question aloud. The words of the solemn question repeated in his mind even now:

I slew the Hydra of the bountiful spring of Lerna, and she had nine heads. In the struggle I sustained deep bites from Hydra that refuse to heal. How can I be cured, O Pythia?

The question brought back the memory of the awful engagement beside the Lernean marsh and the howling, bloody struggle of it. Iolaus shivered involuntarily. Looking up now, he discerned a movement at the

low door to the adyton, and Heracles came forth. He stood stock-still on
the stone threshold as he gazed toward the part of the temple where the
cult image of Apollo was sheltered within the walls of stone. Swiftly Iolaus
went to Heracles' side and pressed his question eagerly.

— Heracles, have you got the cure?

Heracles' face was solemn. As for his mind, it seemed that it was
still behind in Pythia's small chamber.

— No, not yet. Let's go down to the spring Kastalia. There I'll tell you the
exact words the oracle spoke to me.

Together they set out, not speaking further until they reached the
cool, sequestered glen beside the swift-flowing spring. Here they sat down.
Heracles still appeared withdrawn, for it wasn't every day that one received
the voice of the god. Iolaus was more generous than usual in his quiet
waiting. At last Heracles spoke.

— Here are the words of the god as Pythia delivered them to me:

Do you desire to be cured then? Go eastward to a river where you
may find growing on the banks an herb that resembles the Hydra. Take the
herb and make an ointment of it which you must apply to the bites. Then
you shall be cured.

Now you know, Iolaus, as much as I know.

Iolaus sprang to his feet and began to pace back and forth, his habit
when a strong reaction seized him. He stopped in front of his friend.

— There are two huge problems looming for us. First, how are we to
locate this small special herb on some bank of a nameless river? And
the second problem is, how can any tiny plant look like monstrous
Hydra, I ask you?

— I grant you there are problems, but there is no other way. The oracle
has spoken, I tell you.

Heracles again fell silent and continued in what seemed an unusual
frame of mind for the hero. At last he returned to Iolaus.

— Pythia is right, you know. In a way it's the same reply she gave to famous
Telephos when after the Trojan War he consulted her for his incurable
wound. What she said was, "Seek out your wounder, and when that
one becomes the physician, you shall be cured!" There's nothing for it,
Iolaus, we must seek Hydra's many faces again, however dreadful they
were. I haven't finished with her yet.

— Wait a minute. Pythia said for you to look for this unknown herb—not
the marsh monster herself. She's dead now anyway, thanks to you.

— You are overlooking something, I believe. I had overlooked it as well. Only remember what our last act was at Lerna. We buried Hydra's last head—the immortal one, that is—into the earth beside the road travelers use. Hydra, although vanquished, still breathes her life into the ground, you see.

— Heracles, look. Reality has always been your thing, not fanciful thinking. You can't believe that Hydra herself is alive and growing in some little herb beside a river that we don't know the name of, can you?

— I don't know what to think, but I do trust the oracle. What's very real are these festering bites on my legs and feet as proof that I am not finished with Hydra. There is nothing unreal about *them*, my friend.

The sympathy in Iolaus's face was real.

— Yeah, they're bad all right. A bite gets inside a person, and look how many she gave you, each one flaring up like fire. Well, whatever you need to do to get cured, I'm with you.

— I am grateful, Iolaus.

Together they set out traveling eastward through the rugged mountains and small valleys, yet their pace was slow due to Heracles' painful condition. After two days, they had reached a wooded glen at nightfall when the sound they had been hoping for greeted them. Not far away, a small river spilled into its narrow fall over rocks with a steady, rhythmic voice. At once, weary and yet hopeful, they bedded down for the night under the trees. Still, sleep did not come. Gazing upward into the dark ceiling of overhead branches, Iolaus spoke.

— This place is scary. Do you feel it? It's not at all like Delphi where a fellow can't go too wrong, what with wise Pythia being on hand and the fragrant temple and folks honoring Apollo all around with offerings and gifts.

— Scary you say . . . I'd have called it something else, yet you're not far off the mark. It's like the feeling that rose in me during my first labor. I had entered Nemea's holy grove to Zeus only to come face-to-face with the ferocious Nemean lion.

— That killer? What was the first thing you did?

— We took account of each other solemnly in an awful moment. The lion read his fate, it seemed, and I engaged my own. As you know, when I left Nemea, I had slain the animal. Now I possess his fine skin as a memorial, you might say.

— Are you saying that this place is as dangerous as Nemea was?

— It partakes of something besides fear. I feel it. *I am summoned!* Do you understand? And it has to do with these cursed bites deep into my core. O, ye gods of Olympus, Hydra has assaulted me with some dark primordial life that belongs to her! I'm only mortal, after all. A man, if he does well, looks straight ahead in the direction he has set himself, only permitting a few wary glances to either side as he goes. As for Hydra, she gazes equally in every direction as she moves. It is as if she possesses an unbroken circle of sight steeped in an enormous and ruthless appetite. As she goes, her cry proclaims that life is to be devoured and all excess embraced.

— But what on earth do you have to fear from Hydra?

— Obstruction of the hero path. Treachery and, well, paralysis, you see.

— You talk about her as if she were alive still. Have you forgotten that we cut off all nine of her heads, Heracles? Those terrible eyes are closed forever. Surely you can't be worrying that an herb is going to do you in.

— The ninth head is everlasting, remember, unlike the other eight. True, we buried the bloody thing in the earth. Apollo has said that there is hope for me in this herb, nevertheless . . . A metamorphosis could it be? Only the gods understand the mystery of metamorphosis. That I would not forget. It seems that I am to be cured, first, by finding Hydra's likeness growing out of the earth and, second, by smearing its substance on my wounds. What has wounded me is to be the cure, strange as that sounds.

— Just listen to me, for I'm the one holding fast to common sense. If you start smearing this Hydra ointment onto your body, you aren't going to be the same. Hydra is grim stuff, grim as Medusa. Even Perseus knew better than to take a close look at Medusa.

Heracles smiled at his friend, and the moment of humor punctured the cloud of gloom.

— What you say tempts me to reconsider, actually. Yet I cannot. How can the human individual make demands and set requirements on a change a great god may be bringing about? There is one thing I am certain of. I know that the path of the hero will remain mine through it all!

— Is that so? Now that does reassure me.

Iolaus yawned extensively, and the two bid each other good night and fell asleep.

Athena Advises

In the deep black of night on the riverbank, Heracles' restlessness assaulted him, and sleep eluded him. Toward morning, however, he slept at last, and most fortunately, a dream came to him. In his dream, the goddess Athena entered his familiar bedchamber and stood before him in a faint light. She appeared to be shining and dressed in the fine peplos woven by Athenian women with scenes of gods, heroes, and maidens spread splendidly upon it. Her hair fell freely from her unhelmeted head, yet her left hand rested upon her shield. She addressed him in a low voice.

— Man of Thebes, do you suffer yet from the Hydra's treacherous mouth?

— Ah, it is you, Goddess! Welcome! Yes, I suffer from Hydra.

— Your affliction saddens me. Besides her many heads, Hydra is known for her many powerful tentacles that can seize a person within her terrible stranglehold. Holding fast a mortal, she then takes her enormous bites. This I know.

— Are you not aware that I have slain the Hydra, my lady, with Iolaus's help?

— Well done, indeed.

She smiled before a pondering occupied her. Again she spoke.

— Ah, but you have not finished. There are the festering wounds, I observe. I tell you that there is only one way to win. As goddess of victory, I perceive this clearly and would counsel you.

If such is possible for a sleeping man, Heracles was wide-awake in the presence of Athena.

— What must I do? How act? Don't hold back, Goddess, but tell me what it is that I need to know.

— Always you have been drawn to action. This time, however, it is essential that you seek to *know* instead. A knowing is required that enters not only thought but every practical sense you possess, every arousal of desire toward the world, and every faint and subtle stirring of spirit within you, as well.

— Alas, where is my clue to how to go about such a thing?!

— You will find the immediate clue in your pain and distress, hero. When Hydra's tentacles encircled your waist and drew you to her, what did you most fear?

Alcmene's son paled visibly as he relived the dreaded encounter.

— Why, I feared the end of the hero that I am. I feared the loss of the strength and zest that I have possessed and which have made me accountable!

— Accountable, you say. This zest of yours—is it not first for your own pleasure or satisfaction? Or to serve self-esteem?

— Well, when you put it that way, you put me on the spot, you know. Of course the hero has to satisfy himself and his standards for accomplishment. How else is he to remain the hero, I ask you?

— Yet it was you who spoke first of being accountable. I only puzzled over what you meant by this.

— Why, Lady Athena, have I not been accountable for eliminating what is monstrous, or else what is either mad in its destructiveness or given to horrible excess? As for Hydra, the second labor given me, you should have seen her when she emerged from the depths of Lerna's spring. She was all excess and monstrous appetite!

Athena was quiet and pensive. When she spoke, he found her words startling.

— Her excess is different from your own, of course, yours being a subject of praise by the Greeks.

— My excess, Goddess?

— Well, is it not the case that you are altogether the hero?

Heracles felt a trembling in his limbs as these words repeated themselves in his head. Athena continued to speak.

— Each bite afflicts the hero, for does Hydra not infect you with her all-around sight, one alien to your own? This sight is primitive, and it is destructive when it captures the individual in its stranglehold. It leaves one in this predicament: one is everywhere and nowhere at the same time. No path or considered purpose is possible, and the spirit falls into paralysis as a result.

— O Athena, you have rendered my dilemma even worse than I could have imagined!

— Patience, man of Thebes. There is not a cause for despair. Actually, there is a way open to you, a way of rescue. Already you have engaged its first step, for did you not bury Hydra's immortal head under the earth? She has lain in the furrow, Heracles. Consider that. Now you must prepare yourself to recognize the Hydra that grows anew out of the earth. As herb, she has undergone metamorphosis. This herb now becomes your medicine, as Apollo already has told you. The profoundly altered, yet renewed, Hydra must be taken in. She becomes the healer of the afflicted hero!

Heracles would have pressed the goddess urgently to instruct him how to proceed. However, when he turned his face again toward her, he saw that she had departed.

The two travelers who had recently visited the oracle of Delphi sat on the riverbank in front of the shelter of branches they had quickly devised. Heracles, stretching his legs out, regarded his wounds from the struggle with Hydra. For several days they had remained here gathering the Hydra herb, pounding it into an ointment and applying it generously to the festering bites. Iolaus summed up the project.

— They look a hundred percent better, don't they? Besides, I haven't heard one groan of pain from you in days now.

— They are healing, Iolaus, *healing*. It's amazing. And yet these bites have altered me. Look at my right foot. I know it will never be the same foot of the hero.

— What are you talking about? You're almost cured!

— Something that Athena said when she visited my dream leads me to realize this—this alteration. It's as if Athena said that you can't be clean and pure after what's happened to you. You'll be somewhat altered, see?

Iolaus did not like being encouraged to see some remote possibility.

— So how are you changed, man? Greece depends on you as her greatest hero, remember.

— Perhaps it has to do with Hydra's sight. She has eyes looking in every direction. For her there is no back side of things, nothing out of view. A hero's sight is straight ahead, naturally. A hero has an enormous back side, if the truth is to be known, a side he can't begin to see into. Athena spoke of a primordial sight in connection with that female monster. These bites, Iolaus, have leaked into my flesh some of this primordial sight, I imagine.

— What is going to change in your right foot? That's what's worth knowing.

— My step will be changed some way. How, I can't say, except that there will be a memory and a knowing that I have never known before—old remembering, Iolaus, very very old, like Earth Goddess's memory.

— It sounds a little spooky to me, my friend. Not sure I can help you out on all these labors ahead of you if Hydra is going to haunt you.

Heracles grinned at his loyal ally and gave him an affectionate shake of the shoulder. The two of them laughed and set about making plans to depart the river bank on the following day.

Heracles Captures the Stag of Artemis

In the south of Greece lay the wild and verdant region of Cerynea. Among its remote hills, the goddess Artemis was wont to wander with her companion, a beautiful stag whose horns, exquisite as a rare sculpture, were golden. Legendary in travelers' tales, he came to be known as the Cerynean Stag.

Wherever Theban-born Heracles would go, people were astonished at his amazing strength and skill. As fate would have it, he came to serve a difficult taskmaster, Eurystheus, king of Mycenae and overlord of Tyrins, who, though small in both stature and courage, designed the Twelve Labors for the hero. Already Heracles had successfully accomplished two labors assigned by Eurystheus. As he entered the king's palace, all eyes followed him, admiring his lordly presence. An outside observer would have perceived how the manner of the king changed with his arrival as he began to speak in a loud, commanding voice.

— Heracles, I've heard that you managed to slay the Hydra of Lerna's spring. Don't expect praise from me, for you won't get it. After all, it was a straightforward job.

A wry smile marked Heracles' face briefly before he spoke quietly as one who mused.

— What an incredible devourer Hydra was! Why, she presented nine heads in a terrifying circle, each of them fixing its eye upon me. When I managed to amputate one head, it was at no small risk to myself and my companion, but there was not a moment to enjoy our triumph since another vicious head grew rapidly in its place. In the midst of the struggle, I came face-to-face with a terrifying truth:

When you come upon evil of unending vitality, it is human folly to think of dispatching it!

Still, we managed to dispatch Hydra somehow.

Eurystheus yawned at length. Heracles' voice took on a decisive strength.

— Eurystheus, the task you assigned me is completed. As a final act, we even buried the one head of the monster that turned out to be the immortal one.

In his familiar voice, delivered as if in the midst of a heated argument, the king attacked.

— Well, a real hero would have done it all alone. As it was, you had Iolaus's help.

Heracles groaned within himself. Not having a need to defend himself in any case, he spoke.

— What I have come for is to receive your assignment of the third labor. I should not risk my life for these ordeals, actually, were it not that the oracle of Delphi, bringing me out of exile, decreed that I serve you as taskmaster.

— Ready, are you, for what I have for you? All right. You should find this a pleasant change after the Hydra.

The king giggled and looked for a moment like a child holding a trick he was about to play.

Heracles bent forward, frowning in the intensity of his gaze, his patience sorely tried. Eurystheus burst forth in a loud voice,

— Bring me the deer of Artemis! And no helpers this time.

— That elusive beast? Who can find him?

— That's your problem, I would point out.

The hero lifted his gaze and stared out the window to the wooded mountain slope and became meditative.

— The goddess's stag is said to possess magnificent antlers of pure gold!

This notion excited the king greatly.

— I can hardly wait!

— Hold it, Eurystheus. What is it that you have in mind? I shall never slay nor do harm to the beast that companions Artemis, I must tell you. Only a fool would do such a thing.

— Don't be jumping to conclusions. You were ever a hasty one.

Heracles bit his tongue at the truth of the statement, but he persisted.

— So if I am not to harm the creature, what then?

    The king's voice grew dreamy.

— How lovely it would be to salvage all that gold! What good do golden antlers do the forest or the goddess herself, for that matter?

— Do not forget that Artemis herself values her stag immeasurably, for he and often the hound as well accompany her in the wilds. Assuming that I succeed in coming upon the stag, what do you propose that I do, Eurystheus?

— Why, capture him, I say, and bring him here to me. That's all that is required of you.

    Again the king's eyes glinted with a certain lust, perhaps for the gold. The hero fell silent as he stared down a long and lonely corridor of what might be hopeless wandering and search. Nor was he ready to encounter Lady Artemis in this act of theft.

    He had lost count of the days as he cut his way through the dense forest of Cerynea with its steep hills and sudden plunging ravines raging with spring torrents. Certainly he saw many deer. Often a small herd of them, sensing his approach, fled swiftly. Still he had not observed the solitary one, the great stag known to keep his own company when he was not at Artemis's side. There was an odd reluctance in himself this morning, a kind of foot-dragging inertia when it came to pushing on, searching farther depths of forest. Why not permit himself to linger within this dark cluster of trees and brush that had sheltered him for the night? And so, he remained. It occurred to him that he waited as one who expects a guest.

    On his knees he found an excellent lookout spot from which he now observed the arrival of morning shafts of sunlight. Always he kept his eye focused on the narrow barely perceptible path just beyond the trees. A little time had passed when he detected a slight movement below at the place where the path began its upward ascent toward his shelter. His listening being acute, he discerned the lightest of footfalls. Shortly, a radiance flooded the ascending path, and he was astonished to see two figures approaching. Not a man to procrastinate, Heracles arose to his feet and stepped forward on the path at the same time that he recognized the taller of the figures.

— Greetings, Lady Artemis! I am Heracles of Thebes and especially happy to welcome you.

    Momentarily she looked puzzled and possibly wary as well.

— Greetings, Heracles. Your fame is known to many. Man of exile, you appear to have wandered far. What brings you to my territory in particular, I ask?

The presence of the goddess in her beauty affected him greatly as his gaze shifted to the marvelous beast at her side. A pause ensued before he was able to reply.

— What an extraordinary beast companions you, one with golden horns, I perceive. The stag keeps his silence, I expect.

— Silence? Not necessarily. His language is that of the wilds. It is an ancient and primordial tongue that goes untranslated in the human world.

— It must be, then, that you yourself communicate in that language.

Artemis considered this and nodded briefly as she lay down her bow and quiver beneath the tree.

His attention remained upon the stag that dropped his head to graze a patch of grass.

— Many have sought a glimpse of your splendid stag, yet rarely has he been sighted. Walking at your side, he must visit extraordinary country, and he seems to go free of fear.

— Oh, but he is not always at my side, hero. Since you mention it, I should say that fear is a keen knowledge he possesses. Without it, he would be deficient in the wilds.

— You speak as if fear were a kind of asset. For one on a hero's assignment, it is definitely a weakness.

Artemis gazed at Heracles, her eyes bright, her temper possibly short.

— I've no patience with either man or animal who is without fear.

— Goddess, I would not challenge you, to be sure. As for the keen knowledge you say fear consists of, tell me what it is your stag fears.

— He is vulnerable to the hunter, and he realizes this. After all, he is the prize, and the hunt is determined to seize the prize however it can be managed.

Saying these words as if explaining to an inattentive child, Artemis gazed at Heracles during the long pause that followed. If ever Heracles doubted his quest, it was in this moment. When at last he spoke again, his voice was thoughtful as he sought her understanding.

— Lady Artemis, you yourself are called huntress throughout Greece. As reality decrees, a man must try his strength and know-how against nature if he is to survive and prove his worth.

Even as he spoke, the virginal goddess seemed to have turned aside, reaching for the bow she had stood against the tree trunk and putting the quiver over her shoulder now.

— Please, Lady Artemis, don't leave. Speak to me first of your stag's extraordinary antlers. Surely there is both strength and majesty there.

— Ah yes, the horns. In the beautiful antlers lies an authority that is very old and well tried, and it may not be taken away. If I failed to honor the great horns, how could I be his trusted companion?

— Strange, but suddenly I feel my own head as bereft and insignificant since I lack such horns.

She nodded as if she agreed with his assessment.

— Listen well, Heracles. A person best not argue with the great horns. They are fierce, you see. They are the structure of unalterable nature made visible.

Heracles frowned, his perplexity evident.

— Yet you are one of the Olympian gods. You partake of a far greater authority than that of your beloved stag, surely.

— Authority is not a loaf of bread to deliver a slice here and a slice there until the loaf is consumed. No. It is in the depths of nature that my own virginal being and the stag's authority meet. In those depths we are united, you see. Remember this, man of Thebes.

For a long moment, Heracles appeared like one washed over by the strong wave of Artemis's words; in a low voice, he asked,

— What are you saying to me?

— More than once you have been gored by the horns of nature's stag, I believe.

— Lady of the wilds, you have mixed me up with somebody else.

— I think not.

Heracles was recovering his own sense of himself, it seemed.

— Look at me. Have I grievous wounds in my body to validate your account?

— Deep and lasting is the wounding that your own nature has inflicted on your life. Can you deny those times of overpowering anger and savage rebellion against the boundaries, times you were led into dark action?

Heracles bowed his head and studied the ground for some time. When he made reply, his voice was somewhat changed.

— I do not deny those terrible acts that were my undoing. They are utterly repugnant to me now. What I wish to understand, however, is how could what happened be caused by the horns of the stag?

— Like the stag, your nature is beautiful. Oh no, I do not flatter you. You
    see, what is repugnant and destructive is *excess!*

Regarding him for the first time with tenderness, Artemis smiled.
Heracles also smiled, but he made the sacred gesture as he did so. Now he
laughed as if suddenly free of a burden.

— Goddess, I thought that the radiance you gave to the path as I watched
    you arrive was something unusual and, well, pretty to look at. Little did
    I guess what an illumination I was in for! Golden horns indeed . . .

— There will be times when the treasured stag will companion you briefly,
    for he is a lens between worlds. Of course, he shall always be mine.

The latter she had said significantly as if she knew already what
the third labor consisted of.

— What if I have difficulty trusting the beast of my nature that formerly
    led me into rage and dark actions?

— Only go with the stag companionably at your side, the two of you in
    balance, neither winning. You are not the beast. A certain shepherding
    is required, of course. And, Heracles, if ever again you allow excess to
    rule you, you shall be destroyed. Remember. And so, farewell, hero.

Holding the golden bow, she laid a hand on the shoulder of the stag,
and Heracles watched as the two departed together over the mountain.

The Capture

Heracles remained in the Cerynean woods for many months until he
came to know every feeding or resting place of deer that inhabited the rugged
country. In his mind he mapped the sites of the watering spots, making it
his custom to frequent them early mornings and again at dusk. Always he
looked on from a cover of brush lest he frighten the animals away. Still,
the stag of Artemis did not appear. The seasons came and passed. Twice he
sighted the stag, but always he was at a considerable distance. Making his
way to the spot in swift pursuit, he would discover that the stag was not to
be found.

When a year had gone by since his encounter with Artemis and
her companion stag, the hero decided to change an essential aspect of the
hunt: he would hunt only at night when the moon alone was the source of
light. That night the moon was full when, throwing the lionskin over his
shoulder and taking up bow and quiver, he strode forth into a silent but
silvery world. He murmured to himself,

— Something tells me that I have stepped into Artemis's world.

Keeping to the deep shadow of the brush, he moved stealthily as he made his way down the steep ravine. On the path of descent, he suddenly rounded a curve in the path and came upon the great stag.

At once he thought,

— How simple it would be to let fly one arrow meant only to graze the handsome flesh, causing the beast to falter long enough for the capture. But I dare not incur the wrath of Artemis. What is left to me but the fair chase? Sensing the slight movement of the hunter, the stag of the golden horns leaped over a high wall of brush and fled. Heracles pursued him. Twice he called out to the stag,

— I won't harm you!

Panting and exhausted after a long flight, the stag reached the bank of a swift flowing river, the River Ladon, and he stopped. In a moment Heracles was at his side, laying both hands firmly upon the beast. Taking the lionskin, he bound one front leg to its rear partner before gently hoisting the stag to his back. With the passion of his whole being, he spoke now, and his voice was quiet.

— Ah, stag of Lady Artemis, at last I have succeeded in capturing you! Nor shall I forget the words of the goddess: "You and the stag shall go as companions. Only shepherd him wisely!" Well, my friend, that is what I intend to do. It is far to Mycenae, and I shall carry you there to show to the king, for this is my task. Ah, do not fear what shall happen afterward, for I promise to return you to your abode in Cerynea. Yes, you shall be unharmed, and I shall set you free!

And Heracles kept his word.

The Augean Stables

     Eurystheus, king of Mycenae, regarded his cousin whose splendid, strong body alone brought him wide admiration, quite apart from the singular feats he had to his credit. Envy was ever pestering a fellow, even a king. No normal Greek should be as strong as Heracles and have accomplished such extraordinary acts. There was something indecent about it all. What angered Eurystheus most was the way people talked about Heracles as being Greece's unsurpassed hero. He can move any obstacle, they say. Well, we'll just see about that. Standing before the king, Heracles observed him, while his keen-eyed assessment held neither humility nor fear. Only wariness prevailed. Eurystheus spoke.

— The king of Elis is the man with the greatest herds in the whole of Greece. You have heard of him, have you?

— Yes, indeed. King Augeas's herds have become legends. The large bulls he owns set him apart, it seems.

     Eurystheus was fast tiring of discussing anything meriting praise that lay outside his own kingdom. Now he spoke irritably.

— There is certainly a problem with all those animals. Why, the land all about Augeas's herds is filled up with manure. The stench fouls the air for miles on all sides. Nothing grows on the contaminated land, of course.

     Eurystheus was most eloquent and most pleasantly occupied when he was describing the negative impact of another's action. This observation was not new to Heracles. It was time for the king to get to the point. Why had he called him in except to assign the fifth task for him to accomplish?

— Eurystheus, are you suggesting that I negotiate with Augeas to reduce his large herds?

— Send you to *negotiate?*

He was speaking in scornful laughter.

— You with your high idea of yourself should be so lucky! No. My instructions to you are: travel to Augeas's vast stables and corrals and remove all the accumulated manure, scraping down to solid ground. This is your fifth task, and you've only one day to accomplish the whole of it.

Hearing these words was sobering, and sweat broke out on the hero's brow. At once he protested.

— Accomplish this vast clean up in the space of a single day? You are mad, O King!

Eurystheus was clearly enjoying himself.

— I must say, cousin, that I'm not half as mad as yourself in the stories told about you. The fourth task of capturing the Erymanthian wild boar and hauling him here to the palace on your shoulder was an idle pastime compared to cleaning these stables. It is said that you like nothing better than a challenge. Well, the Augean stables are that. And if the job occupies you more than one day, you have failed! You do have your reputation to keep shining, I expect.

Again Eurystheus burst into derisive laughter. Heracles saw that he must handle his predicament with some caution, and his voice was calm and efficient as he spoke.

— Such an undertaking brings up the vital question: by what means is it to be accomplished? Do you, O King, foresee how I must proceed?

— There's no foreseeing this and foreseeing that!

His voice was mocking. Now in a loud voice, he hurled forth the single word and signaled to his servant.

— Baskets, I say! You there, fetch a supply of baskets and give them to the man. Heracles, you will have to clean out the whole vast plain of King Augeas in baskets. Now get on your way!

When Heracles reached the region of Elis, he at once sought out the vast pastures and stables of King Augeas. On his shoulders, he carried a number of large empty baskets, which he now deposited on the ground with a sigh of relief. Throwing the lion pelt over his shoulders, he stared out over a vast sea of shining cattle manure and was assailed by the terrible stench. At the same time, his spirit sank with the weight of being one man faced with an impossible clean up job. Precious minutes were spent as he sought to summon some strategy to his mind or, at the very least, to find confidence before the overwhelming task. He became aware of a breeze now, light and unbelievably fresh. Why, it carried a fragrance as if from a place not polluted by the herds. Looking up, he saw that a figure approached with an energetic stride, one who wore a finely woven peplos. He recognized her with pleasure.

— Goddess Athena, can it be that you have found this godforsaken place? All hail!

— Greetings, Heracles. If the place were godforsaken, how do you account for my being here?

She smiled with affection, and continued.

— I must say that, watching your approach, it was difficult to sort you out from the load of baskets . . .

— Baskets? Can they address the work of cleaning up Augeas's mess?

The Theban looked rather embarrassed.

— I only brought them along to please Eurystheus. Alas, I recognize that cleaning up so much muck is enough to do a man in! Actually, I have not yet decided how best to proceed. If I were allowed a week to tackle it, there might be a ray of hope, but I'm limited to one day to accomplish the whole of it.

Athena went aside into the deep shade of an oak tree as two men approached Heracles. The elder of them carried himself in a regal manner, his self-confidence in abundance, and the young man could well be his son and heir. As for the Theban hero, he himself was never short on confidence and innate authority. The royal figure spoke.

— I am Augeas, king of Elis and owner of all the land and the herds that lie about us. This is my son, Phyleus. And who would you be, man of baskets and wearing a lion's skin?

— Greetings, King Augeas and Prince Phyleus. I am Heracles, a certain doer of far-flung deeds.

He was assessing the king with his keen eye as he spoke. Now he added pointedly, gesturing broadly to left and right,

— Actually, I have come to offer my services in cleaning out your corrals.

Augeas cleared his throat elaborately, then replied.

— The manure has gotten ahead of us. Impossible not to happen when one is richer in herds than any other man in the whole of Greece, of course. Well, I can use a strong man, which you appear to be. Can you stick with a job, see it through properly, I wonder?

— I can indeed.

— What wage do you expect, seeing that you are not from these parts?

Heracles dropped his chin into his hand, considering. A look reminiscent of Hermes himself passed over his face before he looked up and replied.

— If I succeed in cleaning the stables free of manure in a single day, then I shall require a tenth of your herds as wage.

The king's eyes widened in astonishment.

— A *tenth?* You think well of yourself indeed. To clean up this plain in one day is a fantasy, lion-pelted man. Look, if you can succeed in doing it, I swear that I'll give you one-tenth of my herds.

Heracles' eyes took the measure of both the king and his son now, for Phyleus had nodded, affirming the oath.

— Then it is settled. And could you supply me with a horse and wagon for hauling away the manure?

The owners agreed, and Heracles walked the boundaries of the fields as he established the territory of his task. The trek in itself was arduous even though he had not yet lifted a single shovel. Returning to the large oak tree, he stepped into the shade in search of a relaxing pause before the task began.

In the dense shade, with a hand resting upon the dark trunk, stood the goddess. Heracles greeted her in pleasant surprise.

— Goddess Athena, you have not left me to my own devices, I see. The sight of you gladdens my heart.

— As for my heart, it never would allow me to abandon the man who faces a gigantic task.

— How like music to my ears are your words. The facts of the matter are that I am in a grim predicament.

— Indeed. Looking over the predicament, you must admit that your prospects of succeeding are dim, Heracles.

What? Athena herself is introducing a gloomy outlook.

— Are you saying that there is no hope for me here in Elis?

— Only your prospects are dim. But you must not confuse such prospects with absence of *hope*. Hope is of a different order, and you dare not go forward without it.

— What's this you are saying, Goddess?

Heracles was puzzled. Besides, even a goddess might have to be persuaded into lucid communication. Athena mused.

— Ah, hope is the unending life illuminated by what sings in oneself. Actually, it proves elusive when one tries to tie it down in words.

Impatience tinged with worry was evident in Heracles.

— Time is short, and the task must be undertaken. Still, tell me what I need to know about hope since you say I dare not be without it.

— You must be a realist and acknowledge both faces of reality, as hope does. Hope arises out of a context of something dreaded, and it goes ahead of one bearing a torch. There is a slender trail that is illuminated.

— But, Goddess, if you know me, you must realize that optimism goes with me. Otherwise, hero deeds would be impossible.

— Ah yes, your optimism can be a healthy asset, at least part of the time. It can preserve the feeling of being on top of the situation while it generates a plan or a strategy. Hope has none of this, being simple and without strategy. Within it is the pulsing animal sense of life. When hope is present, time expands and unfolds a vital narrative. Oh, without hope, one is not fully human. Already I believe that it haunts you, man of Thebes. Guard hope well. It's the best thing you've got . . . . Time passes. What shall you do?

At once Heracles began setting out the baskets with ample space between them. He took shovel in hand now.

— I'm starting the shoveling of manure now into the baskets, which I'll load onto the wagon and dump into the deep ravine.

Athena laid her hand upon his right arm, and her look of concern stopped him.

— Surely what you propose is against hope, Heracles. So many baskets, the countless loads!

— Lady Athena, you are goddess of work. Advise me.

— Give up the baskets plan altogether.

— You leave me at a loss. What under the sun am I to do?

— For the moment be silent. Now listen well. What do you hear?

— Nothing at all, that is, nothing except the fast running of the two rivers, the Alpheus and the Peneus.

— Now you know.

A small smile lighted Athena's eyes with this conclusion. A flash of insight illuminated the face of Heracles at the same moment. He cried aloud, his voice excited,

— The rivers, of course! You're a genius, Goddess. Quick, help me to alter their channels. I'll make one channel to the barnyard, diverting both rivers so as to deliver their swift running waters to sweep away the manure. Next I'll prepare a second channel on the other side of the barnyard to carry off the laden waters, leaving the huge area fresh again. Thanks to the rivers, Augeas's stables will be clean once again.

Working with boundless energy and against the pressure of the hours, Heracles dug out first one channel and then the second one, opening the dikes he had improvised. At once the foul fields received the force of the clear waters, and the heavy accumulation of manure was taken away by the abundant waters of Alpheus and Peneus within a single day.

Encounter with the Amazon Queen

In her chamber that looked out upon the ever-flowing river Thermodon, Hippolyte stood admiring her fine girdle that she had just put on, her flowing white garment lying on the chair beside her. With spontaneous affection, she ran her hands over the exquisite handiwork and the finely wrought golden clasp. The thought welled up within her pleasurably that the girdle was hers and hers alone. Slowly she put on the overgarment that concealed her treasure as Periandra, her faithful assistant, entered the chamber.

— Hippolyte, do come at once. A stranger has arrived by ship from Greece, and he asks to speak to our queen. A forceful man, he is, I'd say.

— Oh? Describe the stranger.

— Well, his manner has more urgency about it than it does grace. That's for sure. The question is, shall we give him our customary hospitality?

— He lacks grace you say, not the best of recommendations for him to be received on the plain of Thermodon.

— Oh, I didn't mean that he was lacking in grace. It's that he's got a directness in his manner like an arrow shot from the bow.

 Periandra appeared to stare at some invisible image with wonder.

— His physique is astonishing, so powerful, I mean, and when he moves, it makes one think of a cat of the wilds. Did I say that his great cloak is a lion's pelt? When I remarked upon it, he spoke offhandedly, saying, "I was hardly more than a lad when I brought down the Thespian lion."

 Hippolyte, who had been brushing her hair, set down the brush carefully.

— Would this stranger be from the region of Mt. Helikon then?

— He comes from Thebes and is of the royal house of Amphitryon. Nor is he unattractive, Hippolyte.

Periandra grinned broadly as she added the last. Hippolyte shook her head and spoke decisively.

— In any case I must see him, even if he were not as distinguished a traveler as you describe. Engage two other women of the house, and the three of you go to the ship, invite him to be our guest, and escort him here, will you? I shall await him in the courtyard.

As the traveler from Thebes entered the courtyard, Hippolyte arose from her chair under the grape arbor to receive him, her gray eyes quietly regarding his approach. Gazing steadily at the tall stately Amazon queen, Heracles did not end his brisk stride until he stood a few feet before her, a boldness that caused Hippolyte's eyes to widen. For a brief moment, the hero was at a loss. Now his voice came, deep and echoing through the hollow space of the arbor.

— Greetings, Queen Hippolyte. I am Heracles of the city of Thebes. I must say that it is good to find Zeus *Xenios* honored here with his gift of hospitality.

— We Amazons are not a backward people. After all, we are long neighbors of the Greeks. Even your exploits have some fame here on Thermodon's plain, I must say. Do sit down.

She proceeded to do so, and he sat down as well, his eyes following her every movement. Hippolyte turned to her companion.

— Periandra, will you draw cool water for our Theban's refreshment?

— Thank you. My sea journey has been a long and somewhat tempestuous one. May your kindness extend toward my mission as well.

He spoke pointedly as though he had already explained his arrival. She replied quickly, a faint look of worry passing her face.

— That, Heracles, will naturally depend upon what your mission is.

— All of which will be discussed in time. For the present, will you allow me to linger awhile, enjoying your hospitality?

— You will find that we Amazons are a gracious people. Our hospitality is extended to you warmly . . . that is, assuming your mission, as you call it, is in no way hostile to our interests.

Briefly some amusement showed in his face as he replied dryly.

— A queen is not made in a day, I see, but like the grapes overarching us, it appears to be a condition long shaped and well-ripened.

She smiled as a lovely warmth spread over her marble-chiseled features.

— It is best that you understand the limits of our generosity, for our generosity is no mere artifice.

— Yes, I perceive that to be the case. What's more, I value your candor. Now I can assure you that my project is not hostile to your personal interests or well-being or to the welfare of the Amazons.

For the first time since his arrival in port, Hippolyte was able to relax. Periandra brought in a jug of water from the spring and filled two silver cups. Meanwhile, the balmy afternoon passed in congenial talk. Heracles responded to her warm interest in his travels with accounts of many places and encounters, even describing a few of his heroic exploits, taking care to edit them in such a way as to be palatable to the beautiful queen. He spoke of his completed ordeals as much like routine tasks left behind. When he turned and invited her to speak of herself, Hippolyte was disconcerted and replied briefly and a little absently. Only later after they had dined and she had bade him good night did she speak with Periandra.

— You said from the start that he is as direct as an arrow. Oh, how true that is. Nothing goes by the man, and he observes even the smallest details.

— O Hippolyte, do you mean that the Theban tried to seduce you?

The very notion filled her with high excitement.

— No, Periandra. There was no seduction. Heracles leaves that at least for tomorrow!

Now both women laughed gaily. Hippolyte could not yet lay her observations to rest, even so.

— He possesses both grace and manners, I notice. Yet there is some enormous energy in him that could possibly trample both.

With these words, she slipped off her filmy chiton, dropping it to the floor. Unclasping her girdle, she slipped into reverie as was her nocturnal custom. One hand played over the remarkable details of the girdle, probing their hidden text. After all it was only during the night hours that she went free of the girdle's embrace. *Without you, my lovely girdle,* she thought, *I should not be Hippolyte.* With the glad thought, she quickly fell asleep.

In the cool of early morning, Heracles watched as Hippolyte and the other Amazon women carried offerings of barley and honey cakes to Artemis at the altar for the virgin goddess. Unquestionably, she of the golden bow was highly honored in the land. As for Heracles, he paced the ground before the guest quarters again as he had already done numerous times that morning. Yet the sun indicated high noon when Periandra appeared to fetch him to dine with them. Tossing the lion's pelt over one shoulder, he followed her, sweating visibly with the labor of reducing his stride to Periandra's gentle pace. Hippolyte rose to greet him.

— Please join us, Heracles. Our fare is simple, but we enjoy a happy digestion.

— A veritable feast, I'd say! Thank you.

As they sat down to the stone table, a fragrance arose, for the surface had been been wiped with stalks of mint. Spread before the two women and Heracles were platters of olives dripping with brine, white goat cheese, chunks of bread, a pitcher of warm goat milk, and a pitcher of wine. At the nearby spring, a melon cooled. When they had dined, they rested on couches until the cool of the day returned. At one point, Heracles began to speak of his travels.

— It appears to me that each land has its particular scourge or else its particular treasure that draws one.

Hippolyte reassured him.

— In our land you will find no monstrous beast devouring life.

— What a pity. I should have welcomed the chance to slay such a beast.

— What we must fear is rather the invasion of hostile men. Hence, we tend to be wary and sensitive in assessing travelers who come to our shores. Undoubtedly, you have observed this.

How indeed could a man in his position have missed it?

— Such an assessment is only prudent, I'd say. Tell me. Do many travelers come here?

— No, not many, for we are off many of the more traveled sea routes. Still, an invasion is our great fear, especially since we are a country of women. At the same time, we are strong and fearless in our defense.

He stirred with some discomfort.

— The Amazons' reputation in warfare is well-known.

— Let us not speak of warfare, which is a tedious necessity at best and not close to the heart of a woman.

— The heart of a woman, you say. Now that is an unknown land to me!

He smiled slowly, regarding her.

— Tell me of this province, for surely you have generous access to it.

Hippolyte fell silent for some time. At last she spoke, beginning like one uncertain of the way.

— The heart of a woman is a land learned slowly with gentle, unbroken
   attention. Time is nothing here, while power to vanquish or to dominate
   it is hostile to its welfare.
— Are you saying that in this territory of woman, the skills of the hero
   are meaningless?

     He gripped his chair now with both hands. She answered him
simply.

— That is true.

     Astonishment was followed by a strange sense of loss. But only
for a moment, for now he laid back his head and gave a great shout of
laughter, causing Periandra at the far end of the courtyard to jump in alarm.
Hippolyte called to her.

— Periandra, our Theban guest finds us amusing.
— Queen, it is the laughter of a *man*.
— Yes on both accounts, ladies. I apologize for my outbreak of humor.
   No offense intended.

     Heracles realized that the interlude of unguarded dialogue had been
brief, and he was determined to restore it if he could. His gaze, sensuous
and intense, settled upon her face.

— There is knowledge that you alone can give me, Hippolyte, I believe.
   Nor am I yet a fit pupil. A man has his destiny . . . and he has his
   limitations.
— You are son of Zeus and of Alcmene, as is well-known. Your destiny
   is that of the hero. Isn't this true?

     He groaned as he answered her.

— Yes, that is my destiny, I am afraid. As a consequence, my knowledge
   of the feminine realm is rather slim.

     Periandra called across the courtyard in reply.

— Heracles, it happens that men are ever more plainly read than women
   are!
— Thank you, Periandra. It is a piece I had best remember in Amazon
   land.

     With her usual soft-spoken candor, Hippolyte spoke.

— We are also more inherently peaceful except, of course, in matters of
   love.
— A curious exception. To be frank, what I am counting on is your
   peaceable outlook and, well, your generosity, Queen.

In the leisurely whiling away of the hours, the accustomed directness of the hero was compromised, however. Realizing this, Hippolyte's anxiety grew. At last she turned to him.

— You are known to be all directness of purpose and strong action, yet oddly directness falls to me in this moment. I ask you, Heracles, what do you want of us? What do you demand of me?

— So you would force my hand. Never has reluctance together with the heavy hand of caution held me back as it does now, strangely. I lean forward, the eager charioteer, but the horses pull backward rearing against my purpose!

— Again I ask you, what is this purpose?

Periandra put in her two drachmas.

— I'll bet the horses are right!

Heracles dropped his voice, speaking quietly.

— May I speak to you alone in this matter, Hippolyte? Frankly, I have not the strength for two women.

He ended with a deep sigh. Periandra was on her feet ready to leave now.

— Before I go, let me say that the rumor is told that you had fifty women in one night at Thespia!

— A clear exaggeration, Periandra. It was only forty-nine, for the fiftieth proved reluctant, and I should not care to force a woman.

Laughing and slapping her knee, Periandra departed. A quiet, pregnant with the fragrance of the arbor and languid with the afternoon heat, cloaked the two figures. Heracles' gaze was upon Hippolyte all the while. Before him was the queen—stately, beautiful, possessor of an enigmatic authority that did not rule by weapon yet manifested in the gentle, unyielding gaze of the gray eyes that met his. Without thinking, he took a step toward her. The words burst from him.

— By Zeus, I could love you ardently forever, Hippolyte!

She smiled slowly, and a little blush stole into her cheeks.

— But have you the *time*, Heracles?

— Don't spar with me, I beg you.

The queen spoke in what seemed to him her invisible solitary dwelling place.

— Every land has its treasure you said. What is it you seek from us?

— King Eurystheus of Mycenae, who is my taskmaster, has placed this ninth task upon me. What I seek only you can give—you personally, Hippolyte. Only give it and none of your people need know.

— Surely you understand that I alone cannot give away what belongs to all Amazons in common.

— It does not belong to all in common. Of this, I am certain. Hippolyte, it belongs to you alone. Only you can grant it to me.

She shook her head, murmuring to herself,

— A personal treasure?

At once he answered her.

— Personal but legendary, yes. I have come for your *girdle!*

Had he physically struck her, the shock would not have been greater. Her face turned pale as her hand flew to her throat as though to shield the breath itself as she stared at the hero. Before his eyes he saw the queen dissolve and a frail maiden took her place. At once an energy leaped up in him, his eyes shining as the hero's greed for triumph possessed him once again. Her voice was low, but its innate dignity was there.

— *How dare you!*

Heracles was on his feet although he would not touch her. His voice alone was left to lay bare his passion.

— I do dare, for boldness is my daily bread!

— That boldness has no credential here, none whatsoever. I care not how much the whole of Greece extols it!

Her voice rose with authority once again, and a fire burned in her eyes. Seeing this alteration, Heracles relaxed somewhat, becoming amicable once again.

— Come, dear Amazon. Only consider that I have come peaceably to ask of you a mere garment that graces your handsome body, a girdle that can be replaced. As for me, my well-being, even my life, depend upon the successful completion of my mission . . . Hippolyte, surely there is friendship between us.

Was the last, uttered softly and with hesitancy, a question grown frail in a mere afternoon? Her reply was adamant.

— You are fast betraying that friendship.

— It is not for my personal bounty that I ask the girdle from you.

— Alas, it is even more abhorrent that you ask for someone else's interest!

— Hippolyte, Hippolyte, listen to me. I would never seek your girdle as my prize! Frankly, I much more desire the girdle's *mistress.* Mind and sense declare her to be the true treasure.

— You are wasting your time on the plain of Thermodon. I shall never give myself to you, Heracles . . . . Wait. Tell me, how had you planned to take my girdle? Already my mind runs to appalling scenes.

— Stop your anxious mind. Have I not requested that you remove the girdle and give it to me as a gift of friendship? Never will I take it from you so long as you live. This I swear.

Hippolyte uttered a great sigh.

— So you are relieved?

She was silent, but a new light came into her eyes. She spoke quickly.

— Heracles, you must wait here. I shall return within an hour.

— An hour? Should it take so long?

— Impatient man of Thebes, you must wait!

Heracles nodded, smiling a little with what may have been tolerance. Turning, Hippolyte walked to the far end of the courtyard and went through the outer gate.

Hera Counsels Hippolyte

Reaching the sacred grove, Hippolyte entered the deep shelter of many trees and continued her rapid pace until she reached the sanctuary of Hera. Standing before the altar table, she took from the folds of her peplos the honey cake and placed it there as her eyes lifted and rested on the sacred wooden image. When she spoke, her lips did not move.

— Lady Hera, it is Hippolyte, queen of the Amazons of Thermodon's plain. I come seeking you for refuge and for counsel, for it is a desperate hour.

The voice of the goddess spoke in reply.

— Ah, Hippolyte, what misfortune threatens?

— A strong man comes to our shores from Thebes, and he is demanding my fabled girdle!

— Indeed? Does he then come professing love and offering you marriage?

— Alas, he does not. Clearly he comes only for the girdle as a prize to take away. Well, it is true that as an afterthought he speaks of desire for me. Still, sharing his life with a woman is an alien thing to this hero who wanders from one hearth to another. I am sure of it.

— And what is your desire?

— My desire? Why, to have him gone and never see him again! . . . Yet, strangely, when this powerful hero is present, I am drawn to him. He caused my pulse to race, and my voice when I spoke trembled.

— What you describe is hardly different from the desire that Aphrodite brings. Some call it love, Hippolyte. Tell me then, what shall you do about his demand for your girdle?

— Why, I shall refuse him altogether. As for Aphrodite's realm, it has no fitting place here. O how can I explain the girdle? It appears to bind my body intimately, yet it binds much more . . . In the years that I have worn it, the thread of my very self and the threads of the girdle have become interwoven, you see. No longer am I able to separate one from the other. O Goddess Hera, you who know the mystery of everlasting union of lovers, I tell you this: *who takes my girdle takes me, and nothing remains behind!*

— Ah, so you know this. It is my knowledge that you draw from, you see. Most certainly the girdle, like a shining cup, holds your very being in its bounty. Let me tell you more. There is one way alone that the girdle can be given happily, it appears . . .

— If there is a way, do tell me without delay, for time grows short.

— Listen closely. Three requirements must be met, and then the girdle can be bestowed on another without harm to yourself. First, only the virginal one may give the girdle since it is the gift of love's first season. It is attached to a profound beginning. Never forget this.

— I am myself such a virgin, for I have known no man.

— Shall I describe the second requirement? It is more difficult. The girdle must be offered freely, not on demand. This means that only the wearer can give it in her own time and in her own protected place.

— Oh, I am convinced that this is true! What is the third requirement?

— Why the girdle itself must be given with a love that echoes the everlasting union. This union can be recognized by its deep sustaining chord, vibrant and full like the voice of the sea.

— But everlasting union, you say. Why, it sounds inhuman, Lady Hera. It can only be a thing of the gods.

— Would you love tentatively, thinking to guarantee greater safety and perhaps a way out? If you do, you shall lose yourself, Hippolyte. I tell you that the love which engages the everlasting union circles back upon a woman to bring her great bounty, a bounty which I know. Only in this way must your girdle be given. To contrive another way were a grave mistake.

Hippolyte, who had sunk down upon the stone floor before the image, remained in stunned silence. At last she spoke, but her voice seemed drained of energy.

— How deeply you perceive the soul. I would bow to your knowledge.

— The question remains of how you shall go about it. What shall you
do with strong Heracles? Only a son of Zeus makes such a demand
on you.

    Strangely, Hippolyte began to sense the return of her energy. Had
it begun with the shift of attention to Heracles?

— What a curious thing that the man bears your name, Goddess!

— It is widely complained that I have made his tasks more difficult. But I
ask, can the ripening into a full-fledged son of Zeus be an easy labor?
I think not. Therefore it requires myself as taskmistress. So have you
decided how to answer the hero?

— As for Heracles, I cannot grant him my girdle!

    Her words rang out into the deep silence of the sanctuary.

— To whom will you then give your beautiful girdle?

— Only to you, Goddess Hera, as each woman is wont to do on the eve
of her marriage. Still, my marriage is a far-off event, if at all. That is
why I desire to give you my girdle for safekeeping.

    Hera seemed unprepared for this.

— Indeed? Dear woman, what will you be without the fabled girdle, I ask
you?

— One of many, undistinguished.

— What you have said is that only when wearing it are you fully yourself,
though.

— True. O Lady, there is an inviolable territory that is untouched, having
great beauty and delight. There life is most desirable. One only glimpses
the splendor which the girdle mirrors to oneself, actually.

— This means that without it, your true identity is forfeited. You are
lost.

    Hera fell silent. When at last she spoke again, Hippolyte thought
she beheld the queen of Olympus.

— This must not happen. Here is my counsel: *keep the girdle.* Heracles must
not have this inmost woman thing that he has not yet won!

— And if I refuse him, what might he do?

— What does he say?

— He swears that he will never steal the girdle from me so long as I live.

— By the Styx, I do not like the sound of this oath. Guard yourself well.
Remember!

— At our meeting, I shall leave my bravest guards outside the door.

— There is yet a better path: allow Heracles a glimpse of the Olympian queen—that is, allow my image to illuminate your being. When you see that he is greatly affected, then tell him that you refuse to part with your girdle. Ah, this lion-pelted man will stand in the presence of a force he has not known before, I think.

Hippolyte was puzzled, and frowned as she inquired.

— What force do you speak of?

— Are you yet unaware of it? It is mine, and yet it is your heritage as well. It can alter his purpose.

— Lady Hera, I am only mortal. There is no way I can bear your shining queenship.

— You shall see that it is possible. Now take these words that I'll whisper in your ear for Heracles, will you?

Receiving the whispered words and reassured by Goddess Hera, Hippolyte left the sanctuary.

The Final Encounter

She had watched her queen as she set out for the sacred grove with an uncertain stride, her countenance troubled, and Periandra was afraid. Not one to mull over a decision, she decided at once to take precautions. At once she summoned several Amazon archers to assume a hidden position and to guard the house, and she began her own anxious watch. At last she caught sight of Hippolyte returning down the path and watched as she stepped over the stone threshold into the house where the Greek hero awaited her. Heracles rose to his feet, his face tense with expectation as he spoke quietly.

— You have returned. And you are empty-handed?

— As you see me, O Heracles of far Thebes!

Lifting her eyes, she regarded him solemnly before moving past him with a confident, slow grace not unlike that of Hera. Astonished, his eyes followed her. Now she turned toward him, standing beside the courtyard chair that might have been a golden throne guarded by griffins. Heracles blinked. When he spoke, his voice was deep and filled with emotion.

— It is that I must await your answer, Queen.

She grew pensive as one who removes herself suddenly from the clamor of the road on which a heavy chariot descends.

— Strange . . . but I am unprepared for the sadness that falls upon me, for ours is a friendship surely. Heracles, know this: my fabled girdle belongs to me. It defines me. Oh, you shall not have it! . . . . Well, it is best that you make ready your departure, I think.

A flash of anger crossed the hero's face, and his hand tightened on his club. He responded in a low voice as if addressing himself.

— Few have ever defied me. Yet there is a woman who opposes me, a woman of extraordinary grace—the queen of the Amazons without a weapon!

Hippolyte arose and walked past him once more, and although her gait was stately, her eyes were downcast. As she reached the door of the house, Heracles sprinted toward her, coming up from behind and encircling her waist with his strong arm, drawing her back against himself. A small cry escaped her. His voice spoke quietly near her ear and was husky.

— Will you leave me with nothing at all?

Strangely, the arm of the hero did not seem hostile. The thought suggested itself to her: *although unyielding, it is almost a welcome presence.* At once she rebuked the thought, however. No reply to his question was possible. Suddenly the unnatural stillness was shattered, and the blissful moment fell into pieces. The parched air of summer sang with many arrows that were shot over Heracles' head. The Amazon archers had announced their stern presence! They had come to defend their queen, who was held within the arm of the stranger. As the hero emerged from the shelter of trees, a half circle of drawn bows faced him. The keen warrior mind of Heracles was not sleeping, for at once he lifted up Hippolyte, holding her in front of himself as a living shield, his back to the empty courtyard. The archers held their arrows but did not lower their bows. Heracles spoke quietly into Hippolyte's ear.

— Your girdle, Hippolyte! It is a simple offering to make to avoid senseless deaths. Quick, my dear. Seize your last chance. Only act!

— No, never! O Heracles, you swore that you would not take it from me.

— So long as you live, yes. I am a man of my word. Look, you must send your archers home. They will obey only you.

— You are mistaken. My archers will never leave so long as you hold me captive.

It was in that fateful moment that Heracles turned aside and gave a shrill whistle into the air.

From the Greek ship, Heracles' men, now armed, appeared as two Amazon archers, having slipped to the far side, let fly their arrows. The extreme tension exploded, and a battle ensued. With his club, Heracles, still holding the queen with one arm, held off Amazons who sought to free her. Then a dreaded moment came when the hand from Hades' realm fell upon him, and Hippolyte slumped in his arm, for she was wounded. A bitter cry burst from Heracles that joined the anguished cry of the Amazon women. "Flee!" was the queen's last command to her people. Heracles laid her gently upon the ground, for he saw that she was mortally wounded. Only Periandra remained. Bending over the prostate form, Heracles' face held the sorrow of infinite regret. He murmured words out of the abyss.

— Too late!

With her remaining breath, Hippolyte answered him.

— Heracles . . . , hear me. I have a message for you from the queen of the gods, she who opposes hero deeds that call a man a god for his brutish strength . . . Hera says,

O Heracles, son of Zeus, you shall surely lose this labor's dearest treasure, for what is it to gain Hippolyte's girdle and lose the queen herself?

. . . Alas, Hermes comes with his staff . . . He smiles!

With these words, Hippolyte died. From a myrtle near at hand, Heracles reached out and plucked a branch, and closing the fingers of her hand around it, he placed the hand tenderly on her bosom. Moving heavily like one visibly aged, he arose and without a word made his way to the Greek ship, which shortly set sail.

For many hours, Heracles stood gazing silently out upon the heaving sea of night. When the night was well advanced, one of his men came to his side and presented him a strange bundle wrapped in a bloody cloth. From the end of the bundle, there gleamed the golden buckle, for it was the treasured girdle. In that moment, a great emotion held the hero as he gazed wordlessly down at his burden. He would not touch the naked girdle but held it against himself, still wrapped in her garment, as he turned and faced the dark sea.

Heracles Steals the Tripod

In the quiet bay below towering Mt. Parnassus, he anchored his ship and began the steep ascent, casting his gaze toward the mountain plateau where the temple of Apollo stood golden and still in the early morning sunlight. It was as if he walked a flat plain, so swift and effortless was his stride on the path. The gaze that fell upon the high plateau was far from peaceful, for he was a man intense with purpose. Reaching the sacred olive grove that skirted the lower slope, he paused to admire the gnarled trees in their silvery canopy that sheltered the fragrant silence. The winding path through the grove brought him to the small plateau of his goddess, and entering the temple of Athena Pronaia, he laid a barley cake and a round fruit on the altar table before the sacred image. The words he spoke as he made the sacred gesture were drowned out by the call of passing birds. Nor did he linger but resumed his ascent of the mountain. He was a man in a hurry.

Even so, he had not gone far until he was compelled to stop, training his gaze on the majestic temple that affected him beyond what he was prepared for. In its Doric splendor, it seemed a thing of soaring spirit, sustained longing, and human labor. He shuddered involuntarily as he observed the overhanging cliffs, the stern brow that was the Phaedriades and which caused him to slow his pace. His energy flagged, for he was an ill man. Certainly his hope seemed a fragile thing before the sternness of the gods of this place. In the long pause, a lone eagle crossing the sky dipped a wing that cast a long shadow over the Sacred Way he walked.

In time he reached the temple itself exposed on a great palm of rock. In the shadow of one of the columns, a woman stood observing his approach with a slight frown. He saw that she was slight in stature, her face unmarked by age, a face cleansed of emotion and indeed quite unreadable.

While still a little distance away, he stopped and addressed her.

— Greetings, lady. I am a traveler just arrived here at Pytho. If I'm not mistaken, you appear to have some knowledge of this sanctuary of the sort that gives one confidence.

She responded with a startled movement.

— Confidence is not fitting here, I warn you, man of Thebes!

His face reflected pleasant surprise.

— Ah, is it that you know who I am? Do you mean to say that I am expected?

The woman nodded slowly, regarding him steadily as though trying to decipher a difficult text. Nothing in her response indicated either excitement or pleasure, he was sorry to note.

— You are Heracles . . . and you are of considerable fame.

He smiled broadly with satisfaction.

— Yes, I am Heracles. And you? Could you be the priestess, I wonder, the one named for this awesome place of the great serpent, Python, of ancient lore?

For the first time, her face softened before the traveler.

— I am Pythia, yes. My parents named me Xenoclea . . . Does my name startle you?

— Xenoclea, meaning "hospitality celebrated," right? Your name affects me as this entire place does, I must say.

For the first time, she bent toward him earnestly as she spoke and was less guarded.

— For every Greek, hospitality toward the stranger is a sacred duty. None offends against it without incurring Zeus's anger.

Heracles was visibly disturbed. The last thing he was prepared to discuss was hospitality with its obligations. His innate authority asserted itself now.

— I know all about that, Pythia, and it is not what I came to hear. May we go to the chamber of the oracle now? My question for Apollo presses me sorely, you see.

A priest of Apollo came forward and requested that Heracles wait while he prepared the priestess in the holy chamber, promising to summon him when all was ready. Heracles had no choice but to wait, but unable to calm his sense of urgency, he paced back and forth in front of the temple for what seemed an unduly long time until the priest returned and, gesturing to the traveler in silence, led him down narrow stone steps into the dark interior of the temple itself. The adyton was the small holy chamber where he came to stand alone facing the ancient tripod on which Pythia herself sat. Her head was garlanded with laurel branches while in her right hand she held a fresh bough of laurel, its pungent fragrance filling the small space and enveloping the omphalos, the navel of the earth, as well as the image of Apollo. Pythia made no sign of acknowledgment of her acquaintance with the questioner, a fact that initially had the effect of annoying him. Her face appeared to be rapt in some interior drama that illuminated it with a certain radiance. At least this fact did not escape him and stirred a certain wonder in him. Now the priest gestured to him to present the question, and turning away, he departed, leaving Heracles alone with the priestess. For a long moment, he was, for the first time in his life, at a loss for speech. Pythia stirred, and he began.

— Priestess of great Apollo, who knows the mind of Zeus, hear me. I stand before you as one who is guilty of a crime against hospitality! For I slew a friend who was guest in my house.

There, he said it. What had been the inevitable flow of events resulting in misfortune, leaving himself as much victim as his guest, was now boldly stripped from him to stand forth in its stark truth! He found that he was trembling as he continued.

— Already I have undergone at Amyclae the purification rites for homicide. Nevertheless, I am left with a terrible sickness, while ghastly dreams fill my nights. That is why I come to ask the question:

O Apollo, how may I be cured?

A cloak of dense silence descended over the two figures in the dim chamber. The laurel bough began to tremble in the hand of Pythia. Still she made neither sign nor gesture, nor was a word uttered. Waiting, he thought he heard small humming sounds, then soft moaning which came surely from the rapt body of Pythia. Distant thunder rumbled. He began to reflect, *Have I neglected any honor due Apollo?* He thought not. Pythia raised her eyes and was gazing at Heracles in an unflinching manner as she began to speak in a voice that seemed to come from afar and echoed in the small chamber.

— Heracles, man of Thebes, there is no oracle to give you!

The shock of her words struck him like a deep arrow that lodged in his breast. Despair arose in him, but it was at once overtaken by a tide of anger.

— Do you withhold the oracle from me? So be it. I shall establish my own oracle!

At once he stepped forward toward Pythia and seized the tripod with both hands, tipping it so as to unseat the priestess. Now he hoisted the surprisingly heavy sacred seat upon his shoulders and strode out of the chamber, leaving Pythia pale and stricken upon the stone floor. Furious was the determined will that fueled him with new energy as he strode out of the sanctuary. Reaching the path of descent, he found a shortcut through the sacred grove. Only when upon this steep hidden way did he stop to readjust the weight of the tripod on his shoulder. He proceeded now with a fresh sense of exhilarated confidence as he leaned into the sharp curve of the path.

Emerging from the blind curve, he saw that the way ahead was blocked by a tall figure standing in the tree's shadow. He drew in his breath sharply as he found himself face-to-face with the god himself.

— All hail, Lord Apollo! . . . I would never have expected to meet you treading the path of the answer, like one of us.

He smiled a little foolishly; his voice had not sounded manly to his ears. Apollo answered him.

— This is my territory after all, man of Thebes. When you enter a god's ground, you are well advised to expect to meet the god himself.

— Belatedly, I see this. It is that I was hardly prepared for such a meeting, Lord Apollo.

Apollo spoke as if in reflection.

— Pytho is the ground of the question, and the question must shape itself well ahead of the answer.

As the god spoke, his luminous eyes settled upon the shoulder of the hero where the stolen holy object rested. Frowning, he spoke into the tense pause with a strong voice, his eyes flashing now.

— What are you doing with the holy tripod, Heracles? *It is mine!*

The god stepped toward the hero, laying his right hand firmly on the tripod. Heracles' voice was small, almost petulant.

— What happened was that Pythia refused me the oracle!

— That is her privilege.

— What kind of priestess is this who can't perform every time?

— A discerning priestess, I should say.

— Am I not a hero of great renown, having performed the labors that King Eurystheus placed upon me? Twelve years I served these tasks without faltering. Had I turned aside like Pythia, all should have been lost surely!

The face of the god had softened with something not unlike compassion, as he recognized the truth of the hero's account of himself. His voice was no longer severe as he spoke.

— The Twelve Labors you did exceedingly well, Heracles. There is no question of this. They were performed with Athena's help, I would point out. Still, approaching my oracle is action of a very different order.

Even as Heracles welcomed the god's appreciation with relief, he felt a certain helplessness before the mystery of the oracle. When he spoke, every thread of defense fell abandoned.

— It is that I am ill, Lord Apollo, and my dreams haunt me to distraction. I am not myself. I seek your help!

— You seek my help by stealing my tripod? It is the wrong way!

— I had this impulse, you see, to find out what makes the oracle work.

The god's voice held disbelief.

— By removing the holy seat of Pythia? The tripod is the bridge between heaven and earth, surely. Without the bridge, what hope is there for a person? Oh, one must never dishonor the bridge.

Heracles nodded as he became thoughtful.

— There is *dynamis* in that seat.

— True. The tripod connects Pythia to Earth Goddess, who first held the oracle here on Parnassus, revealing her wisdom through dreams.

Heracles was gazing on the tripod as the god spoke, and there was a covetous look in his eyes.

— My lord, I was just thinking, if you'll just grant me your blessing, I can sit on the tripod myself.

Apollo's brow darkened.

— Do you realize that this is the brew of madness? Were you not purified of the madness that caused you to slay your guest, Iphitus?

— Yes, the purification rites were given me by Deiphobos, son of Hippolytus at Amyclae. Only look at me closely, my lord. If I seem mad to you, it is only that things have become urgent with me. What you perceive in me is the passion to know the answer. This is what has compelled my sudden action.

Momentarily the god grew reflective.

— Ah yes, it is when great need is wed to the desire to know that Apollo is summoned indeed.

— You have put your finger on my condition.

— Actually, it is the human condition. But you see, Heracles, there is a problem. It is this: you are hardly ready for my oracle.

— How can this be?

— Why, you stole the holy tripod, a deed that indicates you altogether intend to make your own answers, howbeit under my name! It is hubris of the worst sort. Am I not the giver of the luminous response, bringing it forth out of the mind of Zeus like a babe that is born to a woman?

— Still, my lord, what man does not have to search out his own answer, born out of the past, his life, and a fragile future?

Apollo stared at the hero for some time before turning his face back toward the high temple plateau, contemplating it. At last he spoke, his back still turned away.

— My quarrel with you, hero, is not merely with your substitution for the answer.

— What else?

— You have overlooked the realm of the question, which is a labor in time.

— I overlooked the question? Surely not. It was Pythia herself who rejected my question, sending me away empty-handed.

— Take your hands off the tripod and hear me, will you? Neither tripod nor its priestess can give you what is needed until you have undergone the arduous path of the question.

Sweat made rivulets down the hero's cheeks, and his mouth was grim.

— Alas, it all is a riddle to me!

Apollo nodded as if he had at last answered wisely.

— The way to the oracle is a winding path. It can never be swiftly overtaken. It is a common belief that the distance between a thought and its conclusion is short and direct, but I tell you that the distance between what is lived and its wise resolution is long, hero. This long and intricate path is the way. Oh, it tries the individual sorely, but it will come to reveal the awaited question, you see.

— I have lived already many years, have experienced and accomplished much. Certainly I am no beginner, my lord, no young hoplite pursuing the chariot around the race course!

— All this I freely acknowledge, but sometimes the years beget the question and sometimes they do not. How fortunate are you, Heracles?

— How can I answer Apollo's question? I cannot. Besides, I sense that I am in over my head. Only consider my history, for I have come to Pytho twice in my lifetime seeking your oracle. I admit that both times I was faced with grave consequences arising from my rash actions. Standing before the priestess the first time, I was utterly distraught from having slain my children in a fit of madness. The oracle directed me to serve the king of Tyrins, and I did, performing the labors for twelve long years. Well, that frightened king who often hid inside a jar was able to place inhuman demands on me.

— Indeed. Such a man you had to serve, who brought down the tyrant's fist on each of the Twelve Labors! For the hero there seems to be no justice.

Heracles found himself regarding Apollo with new eyes and a softened look.

— Those are comforting words, Far Shooter, and I shall treasure them. Now I must face the fact that I slew both friend and guest, Iphitus!

— Man of Thebes, there is a pause that exists between great passion and the shaping of the act, an attentive pause holding your future life in its hands. Why have you trampled this pause? It could have saved you an enormous amount of trouble.

Heracles shook his head.

— This is late advice, you understand. Besides, you know that I am a man of bold and swift action. Well, the purification rites have been undergone. It is my sickness that remains and torments me.

— According to the nature of one's spirit, guilt can have a great serpentine tail that takes the form of sickness . . .

— The truth is that I am hounded by my misery in the night as well as by day, pursued as relentlessly by the Furies, it seems, as Orestes ever was. On the other hand, I've never met a Fury face-to-face.

— One can be pursued relentlessly by the Fates without seeing them.

    . . . . Heracles, I believe that the season of the question is upon you. You show all the symptoms. What happened with Iphitus may be the husk that yet will yield the seed.

When it had happened, Heracles could not say, but the holy tripod now lay in the hand of Apollo alone. He sighed audibly, and his voice was quiet as he spoke.

— How shall I know if I have the right question?

— The path you take must be free of the answers which you've long depended on. Find this path, for I perceive in you the desire for such a grace of space for yourself. Remember this. The path of the essential question is uncluttered with answers.

The god's gaze fell upon the hero's lionskin cloak.

— Nor does it work to run down the question like the hunter's prey—all appetite, passion, innocence, and fright.

— I've no notion of how to proceed, Lord Apollo.

— Acknowledge the many voices that cry out to you. One takes the form of desire, another, of railing against things. Other voices are entombed and have no speech unless you count night's dreams and the interior thrashings.

— Lord of Pytho's fierce gorge with its uncanny springs, tell me, which voice will hold the question I seek?

— Listen well. Honor the many voices in such a way that they become as one voice. Recall how wolves circle the fire at a little distance. Ah, the fire is the flame at the core of you. Pay attention to it. The many voices must gather to evoke the single voice out of the fire!

Dusk was beginning to cloak the olive grove where they spoke, and they both turned silent. Only the sound of the soft wind in the branches was heard while a bird nearby called out and was answered by a bird call from deep within the grove. Heracles inquired now of his companion,

— How shall I tell the difference between the watchful wolf, which could devour me, and the fire that warms my being? I am wondering how I shall recognize the single question when all those different voices will have dissolved.

— You will know it when it comes. It is like a long missing brother. The question is not an abstract thing, not an elegant and handsome presence. It is your closest kin. It dwells near the essential fire of existence.

Heracles took this in, nodding slowly. Now he smiled.

— The great Sphinx stands in stone before your temple, and she is no more enigmatic than your counsel. I wonder if I am able to follow the path you describe . . .

— Remember that action on this path is not dazzling. It is no spectacle that draws admiring observers. On this path one comes to shepherd the question, you see.

— The strangest labor yet for me! Now tell me, will Pythia receive me when I follow the path you describe?

— I believe that she will. Why don't you turn back soon and return to the priestess? You are wondering if you have arrived at the question.

When the tripod is returned to its place and you approach the seat of the oracle, the authentic question will take shape within you.

— Lord Apollo, may the tripod be forever yours!

— Now that you perceive this, return the tripod to the holy chamber where it belongs.

    The god's face grew somber now as if lost in an interior vision. His voice sounded more distant as he spoke.

— Ah me. There will come a whole race of people who will steal the sacred tripod, for they think to generate the answer themselves!

    Hearing these words, a force arose in Heracles like the bull's when released from his tether, and it filled him.

— But blood rises in my veins once more, my lord. What of human confidence—is it not the most excellent thing a man possesses?

— When stripped of hubris and not teetering on the boundary line that separates Olympus' summit from the human world, yes. Ah, but time grows short. Go now and consult Pythia while my voice is yet with her. May the Graces go with you, Heracles!

    The god smiled now at the hero, and a radiance shone in his face. Heracles made the sacred sign and sang a paean to Apollo before turning about and climbing once more toward the sanctuary.

Index

D

E

Z